D0811210

RASERO

THE PEGASUS PRIZE FOR LITERATURE

RASERO

A Novel by

FRANCISCO REBOLLEDO

Translated by

HELEN R. LANE

Weidenfeld and Nicolson
LONDON

First published in Great Britain in 1995
by Weidenfeld & Nicolson

The Orion Publishing Group Ltd
Orion House
5 Upper Saint Martin's Lane
London WC2H 9EA

Originally published in 1993 by Editorial Joaquín Mortiz, S.A. de C.V.,
Grupo Editorial Planeta, Mexico City

A catalogue reference for this book is available from
the British Library

ISBN 0 297 81617 9

Printed in Great Britain by Clays Ltd, St Ives plc

Publisher's Note

The Pegasus Prize for Literature, sponsored by Mobil Corporation, recognizes distinguished works of fiction from countries whose literature merits wider exposure in the rest of the world. *Rasero,* winner of the 1994 Latin American competition, is by the Mexican writer Francisco Rebolledo. Published originally in Mexico in 1993, it is Mr. Rebolledo's first novel.

The Latin American competition—for the first regional award in Pegasus Prize history—attracted 427 entries from seven countries: Argentina, Brazil, Chile, Colombia, Ecuador, Mexico, and Peru. An independent jury of distinguished literary figures chose *Rasero* from fourteen semifinalists selected in separate national competitions. Chaired by the Colombian poet and literary critic María Mercedes Carranza, the jury included Affonso Romano de Sant'Anna, a Brazilian novelist and poet; Dario Jaramillo, a Colombian novelist; and Gregory Rabassa and Margaret Sayers, both award-winning translators of Latin American fiction in the United States.

A chemistry instructor who dreamed of becoming Cervantes, Mr. Rebolledo left the classroom at age thirty-eight to pursue his literary goals without distraction. The result was *Rasero*—a heady mix of politics, passion, philosophy, science, and art. Set in eighteenth-century Europe, it is the story of a young Spanish émigré to Paris. Hungry for wisdom, Fausto Rasero tries to reconcile the promises of the Enlightenment with the chilling prophecies he finds in his clairvoyant visions of events such as the Holocaust, the dropping of the atom bomb, and the Vietnam War—visions induced, strangely enough, upon the hero's sexual climax. Through Rasero, we incidentally encounter Madame Pompadour, Diderot, Voltaire, Mozart, and a host of colorful secondary characters. But Rasero's love for a beautiful young widow is the light that ultimately guides him to maturity and the wisdom he seeks for so long.

Rasero was translated from the Spanish by Helen R. Lane, a gifted translator from the Romance languages. Ms. Lane's translations include Augusto R. Bastos' *I, the Supreme* and Juan Goytisolo's *Landscapes After the Battle,* as well as *The Three Marias: New Portuguese Letters,* by Maria Isabel Barreno, Maria Louisa Horta, and Maria Velho da Costa. Ms. Lane collaborated in the translation of André Breton's *Manifestoes of Surrealism.* Among the prizes she has received are the Gulbenkian Foundation Translation Prize, the National Book Award for translation, and the PEN Translation Prize. She is also the recipient of the Gregory Kolovakos Lifetime Achievement Translation Award.

We wish to express our appreciation to Mobil Corporation, which established the Pegasus Prize for Literature and provides for the translation into English of the works that the award honors.

For Marcela, my Mariana

And the dragon stood before the woman
which was ready to be delivered,
for to devour her child as soon as
it was born.

—Revelation 12:4

Selfishness and its faithful spouse, Stupidity, will be your gods.
And they will be loved and respected as never
a god was adored on earth.

—Fausto H. Rasero, *Why I Despise You*

Contents

Acknowledgments

To Cecilio Balthazar, Angel Miquel, Diana Leyva, Marcela Krafft, and Tristán Rebolledo, for their understanding, affection, enthusiasm . . . and patience.

To my daughter, Bernarda Isabel, who came into the world along with *Rasero,* bringing us enormous happiness.

To Raúl Busteros and Edén Ferrer, for the invaluable help they offered me in support of this work.

To Aurora Díez-Canedo Flores, for her meticulous final revision of the text in Spanish.

To Joaquín Díez-Canedo Flores, for the great encouragement he has given me, and above all, for having confidence in my work.

Exceeding a mere debt of gratitude, I owe immeasurable thanks to my beloved friend Jacqueline Fortson, who revised and corrected the original manuscript, bestowing on it her enormous affection and intelligence—I confess I don't know which is greater. It was she, moreover, who took on the responsibility of choosing the typography and the format of the original edition.

To my dear and admirable uncle, Adolfo Sanchez Vazquez, who has given me all his support and enthusiasm to launch and promote my published work.

To Federico Alvarez, Javier Guerrero, and Federico Patán, who brought their great talent to the task of presenting the novel in Spanish.

And to my new, and already old and dear, friend Manelick de la Parra, an ardent and impassioned reader of my *Rasero.*

For this edition in English,

To Mobil Corporation, for creating this prize, to which in the final analysis this translation is owed.

To Rodolfo Miller, the president of Mobil México, for all the kindnesses and courtesies he has extended me since the Pegasus Prize occasioned our meeting.

To José Luis Durán and Susana Torre-Garza, for their tokens of friendship, abundant to the point of embarrassing me.

To Mónica Samper, an unforgettable bearer of good news.

To my colleague Michael Morgan, the former director of the Pegasus Prize, who is a member of my generation and a sharer of my concerns.

And to my cherished friend Helen Lane, the patient translator of *Rasero,* who at times contrived to make me like my novel better in English than in Spanish.

F. REBOLLEDO

Jiutepec, Morelos, autumn, 1995

Rasero

I
Diderot

Paris, December, 1749

In the little house in the rue St-Victor, Diderot was gathering his strength in order to forget the terrible nights he had lived through in the fortified tower of Vincennes. It was hard for him. The smell and the rats lingered in his memory—above all, the smell. He had not managed to rid his senses of it, for it was so pungent and disagreeable, an odor of urine and burned turds, of garlic and cooking oil, of scorched lime and rancid fish, that it had invaded not only his sense of smell but really all his senses. It was in his sense of touch: his hands, washed a thousand times since leaving prison, were still damp and sticky from absorbing that repugnant mixture, which seemed to have entered his bloodstream and traveled through it until it arrived at his pituitary, saturating it with the smell of Vincennes. His sight also played him false, for he thought he saw on every object, whether table, plate, or book, a sort of sticky sweat: tiny dewy drops, greenish yellow like pus. He knew that that substance was the condensate of the smell, that if he touched any object, the viscous essence would stick to his hands, make its way through his blood, and reach his sense of smell. At times, he saw his own body sweating and felt like a slug dragging itself along and carrying the loathsome odor with it. On such occasions, he filled the tub with lukewarm water and submerged himself, barely leaving his head above water. Only in this way could he rally and gain a few moments' respite from the smell that tormented him. In the warm water up to the tip of his chin, he thought of how Marat, many years later, would avail himself of the very same recourse, and he wondered whether Marat—that hothead Jacobin he never did get to meet—felt as hounded by the smell.

He was in the bedroom, watching the winter darkness come over the Paris sky, when Lizette entered with word that his good friend Jean d'Alembert had arrived. He had her show him in, since he couldn't bring himself to get out of the water. He observed the mathematician step into the room, humble, taciturn, without a wig, his thin chestnut brown hair tied back in a queue. He was dressed in black, like a village schoolmaster. Nothing about him hid his years as an orphan; the hospice showed through every pore of his skin. His deep gray eyes bespoke enormous intelligence but also permanent melancholy, as though he were always on the point of dissolving into tears, into a fit of weeping that, by being soft and gentle, had to be so much sadder, more heartfelt.

D'Alembert took off his tricorn and greeted him. As he did so, Diderot realized with disgust that his friend was also permeated with the smell: his clothing of black fabric bore a thin yellowish haze like the breath of a visionary. A fallen angel, covered with the dust of heaven, he thought, or rather, of hell—and remembered the divine Dante telling of the torments of the world below. He invited d'Alembert to sit down, indicating a chair by the door, agreeably far from the bathtub. He could not master the impulse to get away from the stench emanating from his friend, and he ducked his head underwater for some time, until it occurred to him that it was worse to drown than to endure the terrible smell. D'Alembert was not astonished to see Denis plunge beneath the water. He had learned to know him and understand him. He professed an enormous liking for him and no less an admiration. How could there be behind that ruddy face, with its fat cheeks and its peaceful and kindly eyes—the face of a pleasant baker from Champagne—such a powerful intelligence, such a demoniacal one, so to speak? His friend went underwater, d'Alembert thought, to help cool down his brain—that imposing machine that for twenty-four hours a day never stopped, always thinking, imagining, mapping out heaven only knew what ambitious projects. That broad forehead that Diderot carried with a certain vanity was always crowned with tiny drops of sweat, the result, no doubt, of the intense heat emitted by the dynamic activity taking place within. He almost expected that steam would come out of the bathtub when his friend lowered his head into it, as though it were a slab of metal just out of the furnace.

"Forgive me, Jean dear"—his sparse wet hair was plastered down over his skull, giving it the appearance of a Byzantine helmet—"I've had a string of bad luck with my body. It's sciatica, I think. Oh, my friend! How quickly we age."

"Enough of that! You don't fool me, Denis. You're still holding together. It's just that you've been sitting too long. The same thing used to happen to me, until Abbot Bernis taught me to write standing up. You can't imagine the difference! Since then my body has weighed on me so little that I sometimes forget it exists. It's a marvelous sensation."

"Didn't Abbot Bernis tell you about varicose veins? Working standing up relieves the strain on your back, but it's torture on your legs. And mine are weak. Maybe the solution is to work lying down, like the Moors. They say Avicenna wrote all his works recumbent on fluffy cushions."

"Yes, as a beautiful odalisque masturbated him. I've heard about that. But don't get your hopes up. Antoinette would never let you work in such a way. Incidentally, where is Antoinette?"

"In some church or other, no doubt, praying. The intensity that faith can reach in someone weak is incredible, Jean. A long time ago, when we first met, Antoinette had become as much an agnostic as I am."

"No, don't exaggerate."

"It's true. And now it turns out that, after the loss of those three children, her religiosity erupts all over again, livelier than ever. She doesn't talk to me about it, but I can feel it: she's more comfortable inside a church, speaking of heaven only knows what with a wooden image than she is with me. Very likely, and quite against her will, she considers me responsible for her misfortune. As though it weren't mine as well! This is something I'd like the two of us to discuss dispassionately some day, my dear friend: Why does faith in God increase in direct proportion to the misfortunes we blame upon him? I once asked Voltaire the same question, and he answered with subtle irony: 'Instead of asking me, why not put that question to the dog of a beggar? Because it's well known that the worse a master treats those poor little creatures, the more attached they are to him.' "

"That's a clever answer."

"Yes, like all his others. But we must get back to our own business. The first volume of the *Encyclopédie* is due out next year. How's that introduction of yours coming along?"

"Slowly, very slowly, like a windmill when there's only a faint breeze blowing. I've tried to take the approach you suggested, of not writing until I've thought the whole thing through thoroughly, until I've discovered all the possible traps where inanity might be hiding in wait. But it's hard, believe me, very hard. At times, my mind engages in its own mean tricks. It leads me to think that by the sheer fact that I'm writing to explain a subject or an idea, I must betray it by including something else along with the original idea, something that disfigures it, that makes it come out different from the way I conceived it in my mind. On being put down on paper, the idea seems to be stained by the very ink I'm writing with, and wanting to clean it up, I begin to load it down with analogies, adjectives, logorrhea, until I find that the syntax, far from making it clear, hides it almost completely. And worse still, when I'm forced to polish it, I contaminate it with another idea without at first realizing it—another idea that in most cases, believe me, is diametrically opposed to the original. Then my pen runs frantically after it, trying to catch up and eliminate it. But often all I accomplish—and I realize it when I read the paragraph I've just written—is to make a rigorous and even dazzling presentation of the parasitical idea, which has succeeded without the least effort in usurping the place of my original insight. Perhaps all this sounds muddled to you, but it's not easy to explain."

"No, Jean, I understand very well. This certainly happens to me too." (The smell was now beginning to go away. Except for the tub, perhaps talking, immersing himself in a conversation in which each neuron of his brain had to be alert so he might choose exactly the right word to fit the idea in his head, the way a ring fits a finger, was the only way to banish the smell and the rats from his senses. Wrapped up in the dialogue, he did not cease to notice the accursed smell; rather, he did not allow himself time to pay close attention to it, to take a whiff of it in its full force. It was for that reason that after he got out of Vincennes, he had become, if that is possible, even more loquacious, more vehement. His ideas, flowing headlong across every nerve of his body, inhibited memories and reduced the power of that odor.) "You can't imagine the complications in translating that stupid English dictionary! The Saxons, my friend, definitely do not think the way we do. I don't know whether that's due to their language or whether, on the contrary, their language results from their way of thinking. The fact is that they embellish their arguments with a sort of (how shall I put it?) spirituality—very pagan, by the way, but in no way rational, or so it would seem. The impression is that the old Druid sorcerers have been reincarnated in their minds. Everything written by an Englishman has something immanent, teleological, in a word religious, about it. Take Newton, for example. After conducting an impeccable analysis of motion in which his prodigious intellect succeeds in ordering and presenting nature bare, unsullied, clear, and in perfect equilibrium, as only Euclid did before, after that titanic labor, he tells you of an absolute and indispensable God who has suddenly turned up—or not so suddenly, because if you think about it a little you realize that he's always been there, crouching like a lynx in wait for its prey. So the upshot is that this whole splendid system his reason has established is sustained by an omnipresent God, a God who, if you follow Newton closely, is after all the cause, the reason, and the effect of movement and is in himself inaccessible and unrecognizable. You can take my word for it that that God is identical to Aristotle's unmoved mover."

"Yes, I've sometimes thought so."

"But that's terrible. Why the *Principia* then? Why those axioms? Why those beautiful demonstrations of the movement of the planets? Why explain gravitation if in the final analysis everything is supported by God? And we've been hearing about God for a long time, my friend. Sometimes I feel that Newton was a sort of mystic with inappropriate skills. Having the skill of a craftsman who is looking for God and can find no better means of representing him than in an assemblage put together with his own hands, as a painter would represent him by creating his portrait. The *Principia,* if you fathom the original intention of its author, ends up a mechanical portrait of God."

"I think you're exaggerating again, Denis."

"Not a bit! If anything, I'm understating the case. Doesn't Newton bring in God in postulating an absolute time or an infinite space?"

"But even dispensing with God, the system functions perfectly, and that's what counts."

"You see! You're French. You've just spoken like a real Latin! In the final accounting, what matters to you is what's real, what can be understood and transformed. Think of Descartes, for example. He does exactly the opposite of Newton. When you begin to study his work, you may think that you're dealing with an ardent believer, who is much more concerned with God than even the Englishman is. But if you get inside his ideas, you'll see that God is of very little interest to Descartes. Remember his system. What does he do? In the first place, he offers the existence of God as an incontrovertible axiom. And then, after that, he penetrates, in a manner of speaking, into the real, into thought, matter, whatever you like. In that way, he develops his argument and arrives at conclusions that don't depend in the slightest on that God so beautifully adorned and solemn whom he describes to us in the beginning. By affirming the existence of God, Descartes makes a concession to his era—and perhaps to his conscience, because whether he was an atheist or not doesn't change one iota what I'm telling you—so as to be able to work in peace on his ideas, which, rest assured, have nothing to do with God. For Latins, God is a superior being we have imposed on ourselves at sword's point—or by being roasted over green wood—whom we must respect and fear, for in some way or other he is a sort of arbiter or supreme adjudicator of our relations. That is why we keep him safe and sound in our churches. Ask any Frenchman, or Italian, or Spaniard, where God is. Any of them, or the overwhelming majority, will answer that he's in the churches. Because, in the final analysis, that is where he ought to be, duly cloaked in incense, adorned, and adored. Outside the houses of worship we are only ourselves, wretched mortals—and if there are priests there, they are something like home distributors of God, when necessity requires that. When someone is about to die, for example, and cannot make his way to the nearest church, the priest brings God to him at his house and absolves him, lifting from him the enormous weight of dying without having drawn up the requisite balance and settlement of accounts with the Creator—and also relieving the members of his family of the burden of a few louis. On the other hand, ask an Englishman, a German, where God is. Either will doubtless answer, God is within me, God is everywhere. And they spend their whole lives and write complete works searching for him. Fortunately for us, we have found him long since."

D'Alembert listened in awe to his friend's peroration. Of all his qualities, the one he most admired and, why not admit it, envied, was the delightful ability to let his mind range far afield, to leap from the height of one idea to another, as a bee flits from flower to flower. Diderot was interested in everything; nothing was safe from being dissected to bits by his implacable intellect. As though he had carefully saved each one of the sharp-edged knives his father had made, his mind always had what it needed to cut, divide, slice to pieces any idea, separating it into tiny fragments, perhaps of the size of Leucippus' atoms, and then to put all the pieces together again, according to different patterns, reincorporating them in another entity that to all appearances had nothing to do with the original. He himself was not like that, he did not have that instinct for the whole that his friend had. He was far from being a "pantophile," as Voltaire called Diderot. He was too well disciplined. He could not force his mind to stray. He needed method, reason, logic. Perhaps it was for that reason that he was a sublime mathematician. From a very early age, in the warm arms of Madame Rousseau, who rather than his mother was his only fixed point in the world, the only shelter he had available from the cold loneliness that had permeated his body from the very day that his frivolous, real, absent mother, a housemaid in the service of Madame Tencin, had abandoned him as a newborn babe on the stairs of Saint-Jean-le-Ronde, from that very early age—he reflected—he had taken a liking to order, loved perfect balance: he permanently situated his mind in the world of logic, where every syllogism must fit every other perfectly, where nothing is left to chance, where everything is deduced and deducible, where there are no gaps save ignorance, where one can analyze something down to the infinitely small in order to find the reason for it, its fluxion, as Newton would say, so that, freed of its mysteries, exposed, its enormous simplicity your doing, it can be reproduced, it can be worked out to infinity without losing its quality, even though it is little more than a curve traced on paper. What else is mathematics if not that?

"So then, Jean, since we've located God and have him sheltered in a safe place, we can focus our attention on the things of this world. Despite what you've told me about your private war with the pen, syntax, and ideas, you must write the introduction to the *Encyclopédie*. There is simply no one who can do it better."

"And why not you, Denis? It would be more suitable. You've worked on this much more than I have."

"Please. Forgive me for cutting you off, Jean. But we've been over this point often enough. Why not me? Look, my boy, because I'm Denis Diderot, the son of a knife maker in Langres. A perfect unknown, or almost a perfect unknown, since there are now a few people who are beginning to be aware of me. And do you know how they think of me? As the lowlife who at Vincennes"—all he did was say that accursed name and the odor reappeared—"received deserved punishment for having written obscenities (that was what they've called them) and insults against God and his Most Holy Mother the Roman Catholic apostolic church." He heaved a great sigh. The odor, stronger than ever, began to make him sick to his stomach. The bath water had got cold, and his body, racked by rheumatism, felt it. "Have Voltaire write it? That man, my friend, is too well known. Besides, in spite of all the admiration we may profess for him, you have to admit he's as treacherous and vain as an Indonesian peacock. If he wrote the introduction, you may be sure he'd find a way to say that the *Encyclopédie* is a collective work in which many men are participating but to get across that in reality he is the only author. Admit it, Jean, that man is incapable of sharing anything with anybody . . . unless it's the profits made through speculation with the savings of Parisians, and his take is always the lion's share. Montesquieu? I spent six months writing him the most fawning and flattering letters I've come up with in my entire life. And do you know what his answer was? Well, Baron Montesquieu, the author of the *Persian Letters,* the investigator of the Roman Empire, the man who worked for fifteen years putting Locke's ideas into French in his *Spirit of the Laws,* the great Montesquieu, though I came close to kissing his ass in my letters, has committed himself to at best a single article! And do you know on what subject? On 'aesthetics and good taste.' Montesquieu offers us that, and you want him to write the introduction! The only one you haven't mentioned is Buffon. I'm sure he'd tailor his introduction to the tastes of the Countess d'Egmont and the menageric of pompous dandies who go to her soirees. Someday, when I really feel a grudge against you, I'm going to hand you something he's written, for you to edit. You'll find out what torture is. And that's if you manage to do the job, if the syrup in his texts doesn't glue your hand to the page or the odor of rose water clinging to his words doesn't make you throw up."

"You're unkind, Denis."

"No, my friend, it's Buffon who's unkind. I believe he's doing very little kindness to science by popularizing it in that foppish style of his—although, it must be granted, he knows what he's talking about. But from there to writing the introduction, never. Please tell the maidservant to bring a pailful of hot water; my body's beginning to go numb."

As his friend headed for the kitchen, he immersed himself again. He indeed felt very ill. That confounded project was beginning to stink as much as the prison of Vincennes. He sensed intuitively, and he knew his intuition never failed, that he was going to end up taking it on all by himself. D'Alembert, despite a great show of enthusiasm, is going to get bored after a while, he thought. Or worse still, he's going to get scared. Because he's not up to bearing the torture of Vincennes or the Bastille. He'll never risk losing the freedom he's gained since his early years as an orphan, and he won't move so much as an inch from the comfortable protection of his charming Julie-Jeanne . . .

"So you see, Jean dear, there is no one as well suited as you for writing that introduction. Look. First of all, in spite of everything you've told me, you write very well; second, you're the most respected man of learning in the country, an Academician at the age of twenty-five, famous since you were twenty; and third, your reputation as a mathematician protects you from the inquisitors and the other fathers of the church. They can't see in you, as they can so easily in me, an enemy of God and of the worship of him, for a very simple reason: they don't have the slightest idea what mathematics is, and their faith is not sufficiently great to impose on them the penance of studying it. They treat you the way the vassals of King Midas treated him when they saw his idiotic attire. So it's settled. Go on scuffling with your ideas and polishing your syntax, but don't fail to write that introduction. And be quick about it; the booksellers are putting a great deal of pressure on me. They've told me they think they can sign up more than two thousand subscribers and charge them ten pistolas for the entire work, the robbers."

The bells of Notre Dame were ringing for five-o'clock mass. The room suddenly grew dark, though this did not seem to disturb them.

"Rasero should be along soon. I told him to come at five," d'Alembert said.

"Rasero?"

"Yes. The young Spaniard I told you about."

"The Andalusian?"

"In person. I took the liberty of inviting him to your place this afternoon. I want you to meet him. He's a queer bird."

"Voltaire is more attracted to queer fellows than I."

"I don't mean that. He's very intelligent. At least I think so. In no conversation that I've had with him—and you know I always talk about mathematics or things of that sort—has he failed to follow me to the last detail. On top of that, I must admit that he backed me into a corner several times. He's very quick-witted, despite his appearance of sluggishness."

"What's he like?" At that moment they heard a knock at the door.

"The best thing is to get to know him yourself."

Diderot saw, barely illuminated in the last afternoon light, a man of medium build dressed impeccably in dark blue, with neither wig nor hair, who greeted his friend d'Alembert extremely politely.

"Denis, I'd like you to meet Señor Fausto Rasero."

"How do you do, my dear sir. I trust you'll excuse me for receiving you in this place and in this state, but my body is worn-out."

"There's nothing to worry about at all in how you're receiving me, Monsieur Diderot," Rasero said in his peculiar accent. "You don't know how eager I've been to meet you. Denis Diderot, the hero of the tower of Vincennes!"

On hearing these words, Diderot felt that the odor was once more starting to envelop the world. It was everywhere and mercilessly assailed his sense of smell. Even the water in the tub had taken on that yellowish odor. The room, like a painting done in a single color, had become tinted by the stench. He was about to go underwater again, but on lowering his head, he noticed something strange and lifted it at once. Apparently everything was still the same, purulent and foul smelling: the tub, the sheets, the walls, the door, Jean . . . but not Rasero! His blue attire, his pale skin, his shiny bald pate did not give off the least little whiff of the repellent smell. Rasero was the only object in the bedroom that retained its color: he did not smell, or to be more precise, he did indeed, though the odor was a pleasant one, unbelievably pleasant to Diderot's nose. He gave off a fresh, woodsy fragrance. He smelled the way a forest smells at dawn; he smelled of everything that the accursed castle of Vincennes cannot smell of . . . he smelled of freedom.

Diderot was in ecstasy. His eyes lingered on the face of the Andalusian. A peculiar face, incidentally: his eyebrows, very fine, arched above eyes of normal size, though set very far apart and almost without vitreous surface, filled almost completely by their enormous black irises. The rest of his features were harmonious without being handsome: the nose small and fine-drawn, the mouth with delicate lips and strong, regular teeth, the jaw ending in a point, diminishing the strength of his face but on the other hand giving it a certain charm. Furthermore, not a single wrinkle furrowed his face; it was perfectly smooth, enough to make any lady of the nobility die of envy. A beauty spot applied to his left cheek was the one concession to the fashion of the times. He was not wearing powders, paints, or rouges.

The bad smell having departed, Diderot suddenly felt very good, better than he had felt for a long time—as when he had strolled at dusk through the gardens of the Palais Royal with Antoinette long, long before the hell of Vincennes, when his marriage was still a dream and he knew that he was young and full of vigor, capable of meeting the world and conquering it, or as when he began to hatch in his mind that project he was not to abandon for the rest of his life, even in his worst crises brought on by the foul smell and by revulsion . . . He wanted to take advantage of this new situation, to treasure each instant he was living through without the burden of the foul smell; he wanted to drink wine, to talk about a thousand things. He wanted, in short, to open his sense of smell, and all his senses, to the sweet fragrance that was invading his body.

"Gentlemen," he said, "why don't we go on into the dining room? My body has had enough water. If I stay here where I am, I'm going to end up looking like a raisin—like, incidentally, Monsieur Rasero, those which are so delicious in your country. What is their name again?"

"Muscats."

"That's right, muscats. Go on into the dining room, please." His hands, wrinkled from the water, smoothed his hair. "Jean, ask Lizette to open a bottle of wine, and pour yourselves some. I'll be with you in a moment."

The apartment was a modest one. The pieces of secondhand furniture seemed too large for the small room. A few undistinguished engravings adorned the walls. Nonetheless, the place had its charm, owing, doubtless, to the books by which it was literally occupied. They were everywhere: in two old bookshelves on the wall, stacked in double and even triple rows; on the table, one atop the other in columns three feet high. They were even on the floor, where the piles formed a miniature labyrinth through which it was not easy to thread a path. Rasero noticed that, irrespective of the apparent chaos, the books were systematically arranged. He could see that each heap corresponded to a single subject matter, without there being a single book in it that fell outside the field. In front of him, on the table, was a column of old books on chemistry. He could read the names of the authors on the spines—names that brought back memories of ten years before, when he used to listen rapt to the disquisitions of

Dr. Antonio Ulloa, his teacher and friend, the discoverer of platinum, the greatest chemist in Spain. Ulloa talked to him—and there came to him their illustrious names—of Calinicus, the Syrian alchemist, the inventor of Greek fire, which contains a certain proportion of petroleum as the inflammable element, saltpeter as the provider of the spark to set it alight, and quicklime as the contributor of heat when in reaction with water . . . of Livadius, the author of the first textbook on modern chemistry, which at that moment was within Rasero's sight (a small, very old book, for which his beloved teacher would have given his meager fortune) . . . of Mayow, the English chemist who studied the phenomenon of respiration in a new way and demonstrated that only a part of the air is used either in breathing or in combustion, leading to an experiment that later on would bring fame to Lavoisier, who at that moment—Rasero did not know this—was only six years old . . . of the great Moorish savant Rhazes, who first made plaster of Paris, able to heal broken bones by holding them together, and the discoverer, to boot, of antimony, contrary to the lies and imaginings—as Ulloa called them—of Westerners, who attribute that discovery to an Irish monk . . . of Becher, the German adventurer, who inspired Dr. Stahl and his theory of phlogiston . . . of Maimonides, the great Spanish physician, the enemy, from days as remote as the thirteenth century, of fanaticism and fraudulent tricks, and hence an implacable critic of astrology but an enthusiastic defender of astronomy . . . of Kunckel, the German who succeeded in isolating phosphorus, a discovery that—Ulloa used to say—can also rightly be attributed to Brand, another German who was the contemporary of Kunckel, one of whose books, incidentally, was also on Diderot's table . . . of Aubert, a French chemist able—the only thing that Ulloa knew about him—to give a book a title like *De metallorum ortu et causis contra Chemistas brevis et dilucida et Progymnasmata in Joannis Fernelli librum de abditis rerum naturallum causis,* a work that he now had before his eyes, in the house of the pantophile Diderot. There were also here van Helmont, Beguin, Aldrovandi, Avicenna, Paracelsus, Boyle, Boerhaave, Toscanelli, Lefèvre, Pott, and Cristóbal Acosta, the African author of the *Treatise on the Drugs and Medicines of the East Indies,* a very old book of which Ulloa prided himself on being the possessor of the only copy in existence. My beloved teacher would not be very happy to see this additional impression, Rasero thought.

"Are you interested in chemistry, Monsieur Rasero?" Jean d'Alembert asked.

"I believe so. To tell the truth, I know little about this science, just what Dr. Antonio Ulloa, my former teacher, managed to drum through my thick skull. A wonderful person, incidentally. He was the one who convinced me of the possibilities of this science provided that—a point he strongly emphasized—it sever itself from alchemy, not the mother but rather the stepmother of chemistry, which has caused many centuries and many fine minds to be wasted in the search for something as useless as gold. Because, just imagine, if by sheer chance the alchemists had been right, if they had found that magic operation capable of transforming base metals into gold, what would have been gained? Very little, in my opinion; the world would soon have had an excess of this metal and as a consequence its price would have plummeted. In the rage to turn lead into gold, after a few years it would have been lead that was valuable, since it would have become scarce and, as we must concede, it is much more useful than the yellow metal. Hence, according to Ulloa, the alchemists were mistaken from start to finish. Nonetheless, and perhaps unwittingly, they made significant discoveries that constitute the origin and the basis of chemistry, a truly modern science. Ulloa spoke to me of more than two hundred substances, including metals, minerals, alcoholic spirits and acids, salts, and gases, discovered or prepared by alchemists—substances much more useful than gold, with an endless number of applications in our daily life. That is the path that must be followed, and I believe that it is now being followed: as time goes by, there are fewer and fewer who seek the golden road. Perhaps Newton was the last of the learned greats to believe in alchemy. And as you see, he did not succeed in making a single contribution, however minor, to this field. There is no comparison with what he did in physics, and this notwithstanding that, as his biographers relate, for each hour of his life that he devoted to physics, he devoted five to alchemy."

"Yes, I've heard something of the sort."

"To Ulloa, who is a fanatic about chemistry, the key to transforming substances lies in their composition, either by breaking them down or by putting them together to form new compounds. The principles of life, of foodstuffs, of health are contained in them. When we attain a thorough knowledge of their properties and the mastery to transform them at will, the possibilities that will open up will be almost infinite. Our lives, our world will change radically."

"For the better or for the worse?" asked Diderot, who had just sat down at the table and poured himself a glass of wine.

"A good question, Monsieur Diderot. I have often asked myself the same thing, and I always find on either side arguments no better than those on the other . . ."

How can you tell them of what you have seen so often in that world you visit each time you reach orgasm? In that world—and this you know very well—chemistry and a host of other sciences have an established presence. You have been able to see countless objects that do not exist in your own time—such as those little glass bubbles that give off a yellow light far more powerful than any candle, or those crude metal carriages that move about swiftly on inflated rubber wheels without the aid of a draft animal, or those strange liquids of a thousand different colors that people drink all the time, fizzy like champagne, but with a flavor that you take to be at once sweetish and acid. And I say, "you take," because in fact you haven't had the slightest contact with that world except for its visual character: every time you try to touch an object, your hand passes through it as though through a phantom. Nor can you smell it or taste it. You glimpse that strange world during the fleeting instant of orgasm, in the same way a spectator sees a play at a theater.

". . . though I believe that, for good or for ill, that is where we're headed. It isn't in man's nature to forgo the use of what he discovers. We need only take a look at history: we have willingly brought into our cultural heritage, or our arsenal, depending on the case, every invention, however terrible it may appear to be. Perhaps Pythagoras and his disciples were not so wrong in pledging not to share with the world what their intellects might discover."

"Perhaps it would have been better that way. But the fact is that that hasn't happened. Our future is doomed to gorge itself on whatever stupidity we invent," Diderot said with a smile.

"That, indeed, is how it seems. And all of you, on the information I have, are accomplices in this process, for what else, if not that, does putting together an encyclopedia such as the one you all have in mind achieve? Because, according to what I've been able to gather from Jean, your project is much more ambitious than Gua de Malves'."

"That coward! He wanted to do a French translation of a dictionary for English physicians. That's all his poor brain could think of."

"But that way he was safe from the tower of Vincennes," d'Alembert rejoined.

Diderot was pleased to perceive that hearing that odious name did not affect his sense of smell.

"Yes, my friend. Propagating unbiased knowledge, shorn of lies and superstitions—furnishing the tools, so to speak, to render our ignorance and perhaps our existence less painful—seems to be a crime. But we mustn't stop on that account. History, as Monsieur Rasero was saying, also offers us magnificent examples in this regard. Didn't Giordano Bruno die at the stake for upholding a truth that today, two centuries later, seems to us so obvious that we teach it as a commonplace to schoolchildren? Didn't they make the great Galileo recant and imprison him in a tower for daring to see what has been waiting in the sky for millions of years for a sharp eye to discover? We men are very stupid: is there any doubt about that? We cruelly punish not ignorance but what defies it. The knowledge we acquire, for which so many men have given their freedom, their honor, and even their lives, is the greatest obstacle to our attaining new knowledge, because the new knowledge may contradict the old and even refute it, because the new knowledge can demonstrate that our learning is not all that learned. And knowledge that is surpassed by later knowledge, my friends, is nothing other than ignorance, and no one likes to be ignorant. And so we sharpen our claws against anyone who dares question our knowledge. This is a cruel process but an inevitable one. I can imagine the adversity that the primitive man who discovered how a stone is more effective than bare fists in fighting an animal must have faced. They doubtless killed him with his own invention . . . By the way, speaking of primitive mankind, tell me, Jean, whom are you thinking of to write about religious matters?"

When they had put him in charge of the project, the damned book marketers had imposed as a condition that religion be included among the subjects of the *Encyclopédie:* theology, the history of the church, and other such swill. He understood that it was a requirement he could not get around. There wasn't the slightest possibility of seeing the work published if he left such subjects out. The trick would be to include them without making them seem important. Or better yet, to include them but accompanied not by an apologia but rather by a pitiless and corrosive critique that might escape the inquisitors and censorship. It was going to be very difficult to obtain such writing.

"I think that Abbot Mallet is ideal. He's a firm believer, it's true, but not a single hair on his head is that of a fanatic. In addition, he's fairly well removed from the various cliques at the Sorbonne and shows no interest in having a closer association with them. In the view of that bunch of cretins, Mallet is no more than a village priest. I've read some of his writings, and it seems to me that they reflect an archaic Catholicism, much closer to the parables of the Gospels that to the theorizing of the scholastics. This strikes me as ideal. Even those confounded Jesuits will find it hard to refute Christ's own words. They won't find firm ground from which to attack us."

"You don't know them, Jean. It suits their purpose, those wretches can prove to you that Saint Paul was a Jansenist or the Savior himself a Lutheran. And it suits their purpose to destroy us, you can be sure of that; what happened to me at Vincennes was only a warning. But still I think you're right; Abbot Mallet is someone to my liking too. At least he's a firm believer, a species that's dying out, especially among priests. Do you know what he told me the other day? That he respects me because I'm a firm agnostic—that he can have a satisfying exchange with a freethinker like me because, even though I have no religious faith, I don't make fun of it. Mockery is what he can't tolerate. 'Wouldn't it annoy you if I poked fun at your atheism?' he asked me in all seriousness. 'Certainly!' I answered him. I swear I don't know how I kept from exploding with laughter. Yes indeed, he's a good man; I'm sure he'll do a fine job. But we must be prepared: our excellent Mallet isn't the picture of rude good health, let's say, and in no time at all he may be rushing off into the arms of his beloved Father. Duclos has thought that Yvon can be useful to us, and I agree. Although he's a bit cynical, he knows the history of the church better than anybody else. What do you think?"

"It seems like a good idea to me. But remember too that Abbot Preste is very enthusiastic about the project. I think we ought to include him."

"If you have any dealings with him, count me out. I can't bear that man. And what do you think, Monsieur Rasero?"

" 'Sancho, we've met up with the church,' our Quixote once said. It's a very difficult question. I confess that I know the three abbots you've mentioned . . ."

How not remember Yvon and those interminable arguments about the existence or nonexistence of the aforementioned God, during which, consumed by desire, you contemplated the neck of Inés, his marvelous niece, with whom you finally went to bed, and a great deal farther than that, to an enormous crowded city in the middle of the ocean? There were very tall buildings, many of them twenty stories high or more. The streets were not paved with stones but were as smooth as the floor of a house. Great numbers of vehicles without draft animals were going back and forth upon them. People were walking hurriedly alongside them, headed in both directions. They were in very odd attire: the men were not wearing wigs, and the women's legs were bare up to the knee. You were surprised to see that many of the people were black. You were wrapped up in the observation of that extraordinary scene when you saw in front of you an enormous vehicle with a great metal box in the back. It was approaching at breakneck speed. You realized that you didn't have time to get out of its way. Fear paralyzed you and, still worse, made you forget that you were in the middle of a dream. You thought with resignation about how fleeting life is and how final death is, when the vehicle drove clean through you. Only then did you realize where you were and remember with relief that no object of that world could touch you, much less do you harm.

". . . and the three of them seem to me to suit the project. They're neither Jansenists nor Jesuits, nor do they belong, as far as I know, to any of the sects that are all the rage. The more neutral the *Encyclopédie* is in this respect, the likelier it will be to see print, though all this is like walking on a razor's edge. I'm also willing to recommend Abbot Prades to you. He has an exceptionally keen mind and is well connected at court. I'm sure he could be very useful to you."

"Prades, of course! Why didn't I think of him?" Diderot said. "I'm going to write to Voltaire to help me persuade him; Abbot Prades won't refuse Voltaire any favor he might do him."

The more Diderot came to see of his young visitor, the more surprised he was. Who is this bald young man who's been able to banish the odor of Vincennes and who speaks with such wisdom and accuracy about anything and everything? Why did he leave his homeland? What is there about his person that radiates something partly ironic and partly obscene? What makes his gaze give the impression of a perpetual search for something? . . . Why do I notice all this, if he is less expressive than a camel? . . . He took a large swallow of his drink. It was a harsh, dry wine, which left its mark as it went down his throat; it heated his body, lubricated his mind, and whetted his desire. A red wine aged for three years, made especially for him by a peasant in Melun.

"A splendid wine," Rasero said, as though he had read his mind. "It's rough, reminding me of the ones they make in Navarre. They're not subtle, but they're noble and not at all treacherous. They've never given me a hangover."

"That's what matters most to me in a wine. And besides, it's cheap enough. If you like, I can have some sent to you."

"I'd be grateful for that. I'm starting to get tired of the burgundy that your dear Julie-Jeanne so generously sent as a gift. I hope you won't tell her that, Jean."

"Your secret's safe, Fausto. The truth is, I too like this rough wine better than my ladylove's delicate burgundy," d'Alembert answered with a smile.

At that moment, Antoinette arrived. She was a smallish woman, with a frail build and delicate and well-proportioned facial features. Her big eyes, set off by thin, sharply defined eyebrows, were the center of interest in her face, whose paleness made them seem even darker and deeper; they told of sadness and resignation. She was wearing very simple clothing, and her head was covered with a kerchief. She greeted d'Alembert cordially, and discreetly accepted a resounding kiss from her husband.

"Antoinette, I'd like you to meet Señor Fausto Rasero."

With consummate courtesy, Rasero barely brushed the back of the woman's hand with his lips and placed himself at her service. Antoinette felt that peculiar tingling that runs down the back and ends between the legs, a sensation she was well acquainted with, though she had not felt it for a long time. Surprised and smiling, she looked at the young man capable of awakening her desire in this way. Rasero noticed it, and his thought turned to where a love affair with this pretty, sad woman would lead him. But he at once pushed the idea from his mind, for he was convinced that Diderot would never forgive him and nothing interested him more than maintaining that friendship which was just beginning.

"Antoinette, why not make us some bacon and eggs? Forgive me, friends, for offering such meager fare, but ever since I got out of that accursed castle"—now, he thought with satisfaction, that horror had become a very distant memory—"my finances are not as sound as I might like."

"Please, Monsieur Diderot, do we look like courtiers? I, for my part, am still able to enjoy bacon, fortunately."

They ate quickly and in a silence they broke only to ask to be handed salt or bread. They were in a hurry to finish—the men to continue their conversation, and the woman so she could withdraw to her room and get away from the desire which that man aroused in her. As soon as they finished eating, Antoinette excused herself, bade her husband's friends good night, and went straight to her bedroom. In the dark, she threw herself on the bed but couldn't clear her mind of the Andalusian's round head and inexpressive face. Beyond self-control, she did what she had not done since her teens. It had happened back then that Diderot, taking advantage of a moment's distraction on her mother's part, had kissed her and stroked her body. She had stood stupefied, her eyes glazed, trembling with desire. That night, when everyone was asleep, in silence, alert to the breathing of her sister who was sleeping next to her, she had gently and deftly manipulated her private parts as she held in mind Denis and his kisses, until finally, accompanied by almost no exterior motion, a hot spasm shook her body. Only then, rapturously relaxed, could she sleep like one of the blessed. That was how she lay now, rigid and in silence, as though her sister were lying next to her, as she manipulated the most intimate part of her body with the same facility and her mind tried to imagine a kiss from the bald young man.

Diderot opened another bottle. He was a little tipsy and in high good humor. He was conscious that the magic respite his sense of smell, and his entire body, had gained owed to the presence of Rasero. So he offered his visitors more wine. He didn't want them to leave; he was afraid that once he was by himself that odious yellowish sensation would invade him again. He began to speak of the economic situation of the country, for which he predicted a black future. Rasero had mentioned the physiocrats with approbation a while before. Up to a point, Diderot agreed with him; he could speak well of Quesnay, whom he regarded as an honest man well versed in his field; he had even considered him as a possible collaborator for the *Encyclopédie.* In the fervor brought on by the wine, however, he launched into a caustic speech that didn't spare the physiocrats, nor the mercantilists, nor the absolutists, nor any of those "cretins who think that the human being is a piece of merchandise that can be used and then thrown away like an empty wine bottle." He went on, "What those ignorant learned fools never think of is educating the people, though education, my friend, is the only remedy against this monstrous world we are so laboriously building . . ."

D'Alembert was also in good spirits. He enjoyed the banter of Fausto and Denis. He sat silent and listened attentively to what they had to say. At the same time, his brain was retaining each term, each phrase; it was filing away what was important and setting aside for future reflection the points he found of particular interest. Besides, he was happy with Diderot's decision making him the author of the Preliminary Discourse—that was what he planned to call it—of the *Encyclopédie.* In fact, he was quite far along with it and, whatever he had told his friend, he was satisfied with his work. He had discovered that his early aptitude for philosophy had not completely atrophied. And it was more than that: in the text that he was working on, sentences could be found that went far beyond his natural field of mathematics. Stimulated by the wine, he was even considering writing an unequivocally philosophical article. Descartes . . . why not? After all was said, d'Alembert too was a mathematician and a philosopher . . . and French.

Once the bottle was empty, the three fell silent. They sensed that the moment had come to part. That terrified Diderot, who was not inclined to relinquish so easily his recently acquired well-being.

"Monsieur Rasero," he said as he opened another bottle, "I don't want it to look as if I'm prying, but I'd very much like to know what winds have carried you to Paris."

"The winds of the future, I believe. I left the Court of Madrid in 1740, when I was sixteen. I must confess that I have some fine friendships rooted there—above all, that of Dr. Antonio Ulloa, whom I've already mentioned to you, and the illustrious don Julián de Hermosillo, the founder of the Academia Real de la Historia, who took a liking to me, perhaps in response to the love of reading that has driven me from a very early age. Thanks to him, I gained admittance to the great Biblioteca Real in Madrid, which at that time was headed by don Agustín Montano y Luyando, a man of most unpleasant temperament, but also of undeniable learning. I spent delightful afternoons in that library, devouring every book I could get my hands on. And I believe it was there, under the effect of all those kinds of reading, that I began to fall in love with France, or more particularly, with its capital. I came to realize that it was Paris' destiny to be the axis of the world in this mad century, and I developed a passion to come and live here. I took advantage of my father's relationships—

he knew don José Campillo well, the prime minister of Spain—and I managed to secure a post as secretary to the ambassador of Madrid to the court at Versailles . . ."

You didn't want to tell them how happy it made your father to be shut of you. In your father's eyes, you were a useless idler, lacking what it took to ride a horse with poise at a gallop or bring a falcon down by shotgun. A bald, pale, taciturn boy, who spent hours at a time closeted in libraries reading heaven only knew what stupid things till his horrid insect's eyes turned red. A scion of the purest Oquendo stock, with nothing of the Rasero lineage about him except for the name. As sullen and lazy as his damned mother, like her someone who took pleasure in throwing up to the older man, don Enrique de Rasero, his drunken binges and his orgies and who looked upon him with contempt—as if the boy's confounded noble lineage gave him the right to treat his father like a ruffian. When he, damn it, was nobler than any Oquendo—when there ran through his veins the blood of don Ignacio the Lame, the conqueror of the Moors in Toledo, given a noble title by King Alfonso VI in person no less, of don Iñigo López de Mendoza, who reconquered Andalusia in the way the Cid had won Valencia back, and of so many other illustrious men (as he said to himself when he couldn't name a single one of them). In short, the hateful kid was going off to Paris with those French fairies who don't know how to do anything but powder their faces and feel up one another's behinds.

". . . but I arrived in Versailles just in time for another war, the War of the Spanish Succession, since Charles VI of Austria had just died. Those were dreadful times. Instead of being in Paris, strolling its streets, meeting intellectually exciting people, I found myself imprisoned at Versailles, surrounded by a bunch of cynics and scoundrels devoted body and soul to licking the arse of the sovereign and his current favorite. Gossip, underhanded schemes, and slander that wouldn't have been out of place in the most wretched brothel were the daily fare. And I encountered even that only when I had a little spare time, for I spent uninterrupted hours, day after day till I got a cramp in my hand, writing letters on top of letters that the ambassador sent to the four corners of the earth . . ."

"Young Rasero, please write . . ." The ambassador, an old man with crude manners, adopted the latest fashion in dress: laces and embroidery appeared everywhere on his coral pink coat. His wig, swept high in the way young men favored, never fit his head snugly and let a patch of the thick shock of black hair he was so ashamed of show at the back. It was his habit to change his attire every day, though he didn't step into the bathtub more than four times a year. The musk and orange water with which he drenched himself mingled with the odor of rancid tripe that his skin gave off, so that there emanated from him a fetid smell comparable to the one that keeps your new friend submerged in water or in torment when he is out of it. "To His Excellency, the honorable don José Campillo, count of Valparaíso, marquis of, etc., etc. Your most illustrious and distinguished Lordship and Prime Minister: As a function of my post and in accordance with your pertinent instructions, I beg, by your leave, to call your attention to the present report on the events which have happened from October last to date regarding that subject which is of such concern to us and which, as I well know, has caused Their Highnesses, our sovereigns, don Felipe and his beloved spouse, may the Lord long keep her in good health and enjoying abundant happiness, doña Isabel Farnese, many a sleepless night, this being none other that the unfortunate matter of the Austrian succession, in which, as we are well aware, doña María Teresa, having recourse to a very personal interpretation most cleverly presented in the Pragmatic Sanction, signed by our Sovereign, His Highness don . . ."

". . . and that was a torment. Whole pages whose contents could be stated in a single paragraph. The ambassador turned his aversion to action into a wearisome diligence with regard to letter writing."

"It's a deplorable propensity of bureaucrats," d'Alembert said.

"Remember that once upon a time they were paid by the piece, their salary calculated according to how many folios they'd written."

"Well, unfortunately, in Spain, things haven't changed. I spent five years stuck in that hell," Rasero continued. "Every so often I managed to escape and come to Paris. Believe me, it was like a breath of fresh air."

"But I've heard," Diderot interrupted, "that the social life at Versailles is really something to see."

"Don't believe that. I can't imagine anything more pathetic than the social evenings they held when the younger of the Neslé sisters was the favorite. A very ugly woman and more puritanical than a nun, she played her role of official mistress with such a complete lack of charm that she might have been the royal gravedigger. The atmosphere at court was gloomier than a village cemetery, believe me. Our beloved king has never known how to be happy—as though the weight of the crown is too heavy for him to bear. I've observed him many times presiding over some official ceremony or in the salon of the Neslé sisters, and his demeanor has always been the same: timid, withdrawn, as though his role as king were too much for him. And it's not that he's lacking in intelligence—far from it. Rather, he's the victim of his melancholy, his indecisiveness. You should have seen him when Cardinal Fleury died. He was the very picture of despair. In a letter he sent to his uncle, the king of Spain, he acknowledged that the old cardinal had been like a father to him and that when he lost him, he was left not only an orphan for the second time but also a ruler without a guiding light. And I would go still farther: he lost the one person he really trusted, someone who relieved him of the enormous burden of making decisions, who always had the last word—something, sirs, that our sovereign is incapable of uttering. The king's unhappiness pervaded the palace. It made the enjoyable social event a rarity indeed . . ."

How not remember that famous evening when the king organized a masked ball to celebrate the dauphin's marriage to the infanta of Spain? It was a splendid party. Lavishly lighted, the palace shone like a diamond: heaven only knows how many candles and tapers were burned that night. The gentlemen, dressed in amusing disguises, formed happy little groups, where they cut to pieces the celebrity of the moment, and, slipped between one bit of gossip and another, financial information was passed on at firsthand. The ladies showed off splendid dresses, from which their breasts of a thousand shapes and sizes jutted out, some of them uplifted in virtue of the young tissues but others constrained to their prominence by the cruel corsets and tight bodices that literally encased the women's waists and pushed their pink flesh upward. You were not in disguise; you merely hid your face with a hooded cloak. As you drank champagne, you watched the dancers and chose, as a leopard would amid a herd of gazelles, the one who would share your bed that night. You wondered where amorous games with that dark-haired young woman with small breasts but ample hips, the one whom you had decided on, would lead you, when a woman entering the salon made a deep impression on you. She was pretty without being extraordinarily beautiful; nonetheless, the charm and self-assurance that she radiated were delightful. Behind her mask, her great irises of an antique blue hinted of very beautiful eyes. Her smile cast a bright light on anyone who looked at her; her perfectly aligned teeth, as white as ivory, gleamed invitingly beneath very red lips that promised pleasant words and sweet kisses. Her skin, very pale, made you think that this woman was going to die young; an air of fragility enveloped her. She was accompanied by a mature woman, who you presumed was her mother. The two of them seemed abashed by the hostile gaze of the women and the lustful stares of the men. You gathered from her comportment that she was not a noblewoman, that she was one of those young commoners in whom the king showed more and more interest, to the horror and loathing of the ladies of the court. The two of them stood petrified at the threshold, unable to make up their minds to enter. You took advantage of this to approach them. "Madam, miss, allow me to introduce myself. I am don Fausto de Rasero y Oquendo, the attaché of the ambassador of Madrid to Versailles." The matronly woman gave you a friendly smile, though she made no effort to hide the scorn in her eyes. She was looking for someone more important for her daughter. The latter, on the other hand, answered you with good humor: "Sir, you shouldn't have revealed your identity. We are at a masquerade ball. Please forgive us for not introducing ourselves, but we won't do so until the time comes to take off our masks."

"I apologize for my error, mademoiselle. In all truth, your presence has flustered me."

"Flustered a diplomat? Please, Monsieur Rasero!" She smiled once again. Really, she couldn't think of anything else to do—she who was noted among her friends for her self-control, for her innate capacity to handle any situation with grace and charm, especially any involving men, she who was capable of making three men at a time restless and of filling them with ardent desire as she smiled calmly and took stock of each of them, in order to chose the best one (though she was soon disappointed: the one she chose was never the one her instinct and that old fortuneteller had promised her, and she was soon ready to rid herself of him and begin looking for another). Now, on the contrary, the presence of this man whose face she couldn't even see had greatly discomfited her. The desire that she so easily aroused, though she herself was never set afire, inflamed her body with such violence that she could barely remain standing. She suddenly found herself driven by an uncontrollable yearning for the body of that hooded Spaniard. To her relief, her gaze met that of an old friend, and she seized upon her as a shipwreck victim would upon a piece of floating timber. You did not let go of your quarry. You greeted her friend and were delighted to discover that your mysterious lady had hastened to her to get away from her mother. As soon as there was no one else around her, she turned back to you. "Sir, is your office far from here? I've always been curious to see a diplomat's office."

I've caught her, you thought. Then, with a bottle of champagne in your hand, you took her to your quarters. You barely spoke. It was just rush to the bedroom and get undressed. Taking off her mask, she told you her name: Jeanne-Antoinette Poisson, Madame d'Etoile. The name mattered little to you: the only thing on your mind was to embrace her. You made love madly. You kissed each other, bit, and sucked, as though your lives depended on it. After you finally penetrated her, when from inside you you felt the discharge coming, you were in an appalling place, a place unlike any you'd seen before. It was a field surrounded by an iron fence. Men dressed in green with rifles on their shoulders entered, transported on top of the sort of vehicles without draft animals that you had seen many times, although these were cruder and heavier: they had no windows, and instead of wheels, a sort of broad chain driven by circular gears made them move across the ground. The men, their heads encased in green iron helmets, were smiling, holding between their lips tiny cigars wrapped in white paper similar in some respects to what people in the New World enjoyed. The real horror was below them, where many persons seemed to be cheering those dressed in green. If they could be called persons. Almost all of them were naked. Some were wearing loose trousers, very old and threadbare, with broad black and white stripes. They were incredibly pale. Their heads were shaved, with fuzz growing on their skulls, and they were emaciated, with a thinness surpassing anything human. It was possible to count their bones, there was so little flesh on them. They were nothing but living skeletons. Some of them were so weak they couldn't even get to their feet to applaud those dressed in green; the best they could do was to turn in their direction a horrible grimace intended to be a smile. There were women and children among them, their heads also shaved and with the faces of skulls. You came out of that frightful place when Jeanne-Antoinette nudged you gently to one side. She was a wonderful woman. She smiled contentedly and looked at you tenderly. "Ah, Monsieur Rasero! I've never been to bed with a Spaniard before. I have to say I've been losing out on something." You were wrapped up in looking at her. The cheeks of her dead-white face had taken on a faint flush. Her smile could melt the most rigid spirit's resistance to her charms. The perfect oval of her face and her bright half-closed eyes were in violent contrast with what you had just seen in that field. It was like having life and death staring at you out of two masks. Life, fresh and smiling, was at your side, and you saw it each time you opened your eyes. The other face, death, was in your head, and all you needed to do was close your eyes to see those horrible faces with their sunken eyes and withered flesh. You began to fondle your companion anew. You told yourself you wanted to try it again to see if you went somewhere else, to a more pleasant place that could blot out the frightful images swarming in your mind. But, deep down, you wanted to return to the same inferno: a morbid sensation attracted you to it. Jeanne-Antoinette was all worked up; perhaps she too traveled elsewhere. You made love again, and you returned to that inferno. The men in green had climbed down from the vehicles and were now surrounded by the people in rags. They pulled at the sleeves of the men's uniforms, implored them, took the words out of one another's mouths. They all wanted to speak to the men in green. You saw tears in their eyes, despair and helplessness as well. The soldiers—because you presumed that that was what the men in green were—were surprised and a little frightened. They tried to answer everyone, but that turned out to be impossible. Finally, an elderly man climbed out of a small vehicle, one that did have wheels. He too was dressed in green, though he was not wearing a helmet; in its place he was wearing one of those strange hats in the form of a dish that you had seen on other occasions. He appeared to be the leader, for at a shout from him the soldiers freed themselves from the grip of the starving men, lined up in front of him, and saluted him respectfully. Accompanied by his aides, he walked to a brick building standing in the middle of the yard. They went inside, and you went with them. It had a large room, with bare whitewashed walls; only a red-and-white flag and a large pencil portrait of a man with an angry expression and a ridiculous mustache above his lips were hanging on them. In one corner, in the back, the leader, his men, and you saw a huge pile of clothing, almost all of it black and very worn. Alongside was a smaller heap, of objects you took to be eyeglass frames, all of them made of gold. There was also a mound of little pieces of gold, many of them shaped like teeth. You all walked down a narrow corridor leading to another room. This one was smaller than the first, and its walls were not whitewashed; the fired bricks here were exposed. In the middle of the room were five or six large rectangular tables lined up in the same direction, with small spaces between. The place must have had an unpleasant smell, for on entering it a lot of the men made a face of disgust and held a handkerchief to their mouth. On one of the tables you saw a corpse. It was naked and plainly as thin as those that the soldiers had left outside. On drawing closer, you realized what lay in store for it; in the wall at the back of the room there were five openings with iron doors; each had a coating of soot at the top. These were ovens, like those bakers use. But here they were not used for making bread but were the equipment for incinerating corpses. You saw a shadow of horror pass across the leader's face. You saw the cadaver again, just a little bit deader than those that were outside, and you did not want to see any more. What accursed sin am I expiating that makes me see these horrors? you wondered. What does what I see mean? Is it only my imagination? And if it is, what causes my mind to conjure up such monsters? Or has what I see already happened, or is it going to happen some day? That last thought made you shiver. You were unable to compose your mind. The questions you asked yourself mingled with the horrible images swarming in your head and with the words of Jeanne-Antoinette about heaven only knew what things. "It would be so nice if you came visit me. During the summer we open the castle and receive our circle. Everyone's very accomplished. People it's possible to talk to about anything, for hours on end, without wearying of the conversation. I'd like ever so much for you to meet them."

"Don't worry. I'll be there. I'm sure someone of your refinement rubs elbows with people of quality. Besides, I have to admit that I'm keen to meet interesting folks—those one can talk to about something besides the weather and the tastes of our sovereign. But, at the moment, the sensible thing is to get back to the ball." You were hoping that the ambassador hadn't yet arrived; you were in no mood to sustain his reproaches. Jeanne-Antoinette dressed quickly. Her costume as Diana the huntress really suited her. She felt to you like someone very close, as though a long time had passed since you saw her come through the doorway of Hercules Hall. She was happy and didn't stop chattering. On the way back, you weren't surprised to hear that this delightful woman was a friend of Abbot Bernis, of

Montesquieu, of d'Alembert, and of Voltaire. You realized that you had made a very valuable friendship, even if the price you had to pay for it was high. The picture you retained in your mind of the bony corpse didn't let you forget that for an instant. When you arrived at the Great Gallery, the ball had reached its height. You observed that, despite the effort of the grandly liveried doormen, many low types, coarse fellows, and loose women had stolen in and were greedily vying for the dainty tidbits, fruits, sweets, and drinks arranged in a spread worthy of Pantagruel. A group of courtiers was forming a circle with the objective of keeping that rabble away from the infanta María Teresa, who was gaily dancing with a good-looking young man whose mask concealed his identity. As she danced, the infanta tried to guess who her partner was. "The attaché of the Swedish ambassador," he told her—or perhaps the Count of Kunitz himself, the Austrian ambassador and future prime minister. Thus he shuffled names as his partner, following the measure of the minuet, shook her head and smiled. How far the poor infanta was from guessing that she was dancing with a Spanish commoner, the palace cook! The following day, when this became known, the courtiers had enough gossip to season their conversations for at least a month—the time the infanta kept to her rooms, waiting for the flaming red that embarrassment had lent to her cheeks to disappear and—why not?—perhaps desire as well. Fortunately, the ambassador had not yet arrived. Madame Poisson, Jeanne-Antoinette's mother, approached them the moment they were inside the Great Gallery and studied her daughter with a faint show of annoyance. She was a mature woman in whom the marks of great beauty were still visible. Still, she did not have her daughter's grace; her manners were common and uninhibited. The mass of makeup covering her face could not hide the dark circles under her eyes. This woman, you thought, is very ill. You were about to fetch yourself a little something to eat when the music stopped and a murmur arose from among the courtiers. They all, men of the noblest lineage, joined together in a compact body easily distinguishable from the rest of the company despite all the variety in it. Heading for the door of the Bull's-Eye Salon, they formed a semicircular barricade. When two footmen, dressed in white-and-gold uniforms, solemnly opened the great door, eight men entered the salon costumed as yew trees, the trunk covering their legs and body and branches suspended from their shoulders and head. The costumes were identical and produced a very amusing sight as they came forward, for the trees bowed with each step. By the laughter and flattering exclamations of the courtiers, you guessed that one of the yew trees was the Beloved Sovereign. Surely the clever trick of disguises exactly alike was an idea of his, you thought. A brilliant idea, according to his toadies, which he no doubt thought up during one of those soporific sessions of the Cabinet of State. People began to shout, "The king!" "The king!" in chorus, until one of the yew trees bent its arm—or branch—and removed a piece of the trunk that was serving as a hood. Louis XV, with his haughty eyes, wore a satisfied smile as he listened to the jocular remarks of his courtiers. At times, a strange expression came over his face, not unlike that of a lad surprised in the act of playing an ingenious prank. Diana the huntress, the surpassingly beautiful pagan goddess, planted herself in front of the monarch and made a deep curtsy. The king took her arm to help her to her feet and did not let go for the remainder of the evening. A murmur made its way among the courtiers like the waters of a river. "Who is that newcomer?" the Duchess of Angoulême asked the Duke of Richelieu.

"She's a bourgeoise," he answered her. "She's married to a Monsieur Charles-Guillaume Le Normant, the nephew of the lord and master of Tournehem. She receives a generous pension and has a magnificent castle in Etoile. It's said that the philosophes often visit her."

"How dreadful! I hope this is simply another of our sovereign's whims."

It was not a whim; it was much more than that. Three days later, at the ball of the city council of Paris, Louis and Jeanne-Antoinette met again; they spent the entire night together and silently disappeared when day broke. Madame Poisson finally saw becoming a reality what she had dared dream for her daughter for fifteen years, something her good friend, Madame Lebon, had predicted: "This girl will one day be the king's mistress . . ." Given the title of the Marquise de Pompadour and firmly ensconced at Versailles, Jeanne-Antoinette was never to lose her fondness for the fine arts and for good minds. She found ways to amuse the king, rule the court, and protect her friends. At the same time, she effectively defended herself, and with extraordinary shrewdness, against the intrigues and lies of her many enemies at court. Thanks to her, and to the friendship she offered you that day, which did not fade for a single moment, you have been able to meet many people whose acquaintanceship has amply satisfied your childhood longing to establish yourself in this country. Among them, you met this lonely man who is now listening to you, absorbed in thought, retaining each word in his head as he smiles at you with his thick lips and his melancholy gaze.

". . . and I had to remain in that boring court for five years." Rasero continued as he poured himself more wine, "The death of my father, though it is sad to say such a thing, meant my liberation. I inherited his estate, which brings me a comfortable income. Finally I was able to leave Versailles and settle in Paris. I have to say, though, that I made very good friends at court—above all, the Marquise de Pompadour, a wonderful lady! I met her shortly before leaving Versailles, and since then we've formed a profound friendship . . ."

"She's a great woman," d'Alembert interrupted. "What I don't understand is how she can tolerate that atmosphere around her. They harass her from the moment she opens her eyes in the morning till she goes to bed at night."

"They also flatter her all day long," Diderot put in. "Remember that, my friend. Although I agree with you: I believe she's a very unusual woman. It's because of her that the government of this country doesn't end up falling completely apart. Our beloved monarch grows more inept by the day, and his ministers couldn't be more obtuse and corrupt. A storm is about to break over France, my friends, and not even the charms and the cleverness of our dear marquise will be able to prevent it. But, please go on, Monsieur Rasero."

"There's little to add. I left the court in June of '45, after the battle of Fontenoy."

"Were you at the battle?"

"Yes, I was invited to join the sovereign's retinue. It turned out to be an interesting experience. It was the first time, and I believe the last, that we defeated the English fair and square. I must confide that wars have never interested me. They're a lamentable spectacle; those who profit from them always survive, and those who have no interest whatsoever in their result die. Even so, I'm forced to concede that the battle of Fontenoy had a certain charm: a hundred thousand men doing everything possible to kill one another with the permission of their marshals. They say—I did not see it with my own eyes—that the Count of Anterroches and Lord Hay each out of courtesy offered to allow the other to begin the attack. Be that as it may, our troops fought very well, considering that the enemy forces outnumbered them by more than twenty thousand men. What is beyond question is that we owe that famous victory to Marshal Maurice de Saxe. What a stoic man! Suffering from a fatal case of dropsy, his body worn out, unable to mount a horse, he went from place to place at the front in a sort of wicker cradle drawn by two Percherons. It was really a singular sight. This giant bassinet, carrying a man near death, came and went between the ranks of combatants as though an enormous baby were directing the massacre. He wouldn't go off to rest until the enemy began to retreat. He was in that cradle for more than two days, and not one complaint, not even one curse, was heard out of him, only meticulously detailed, precise orders. Speak of noble blood! Moreover, as I imagine you all know, Count Maurice de Saxe is a bastard, the illegitimate son of King Augustus II of Poland. Yet many people now think that he really is not his son, for the daring he showed as a soldier does not square with the lack of will and cowardice of his supposed sire. But putative son or not, he was the real hero of that battle, and we all thought so. When they moved him in his grotesque bassinet so that he could appear in front of the king, a murmur of admiration went up as he passed by—which, incidentally, didn't please the king at all. Poor Louis had planned his arrival on the field the way an actor prepares his stage entrance. After all, it had been many years since a king of France was present at a victory on the battleground. He was dressed in a supreme marshal's imposing uniform and tried in vain to command his face into the severe and arrogant expression of war leaders. But when he saw Marshal Maurice arrive in such a sorry state, whatever countenance he had managed with such effort to affect vanished as though by a spell and turned into a facial drama of compassion, admiration, and envy, all at the same time. Never, his gaze acknowledged, was he going to possess the valor, or even more estimable than the valor, the tenacity, of that man—that iron will capable of prevailing over his bodily infirmities to devote himself completely to the one task of fighting, of organizing and firing up his troops, so that the battle, the slaughter, would go his way."

"However that may be," Diderot said, "that was the day the king reached the high point of his life. Since then everything has been downhill."

Yes, the king was at the apogee of his life, and you believed you were too. Inheriting your father's estate had freed you from the post you detested; you would finally abandon that dolt of an ambassador and all that clique of arse kissers. You were eager for the festivities to end so you might return to Versailles to pick up your belongings and move to that pretty town house in the rue St-Jacques you had bought. Happiness had settled over the battlefield. The soldiers were laughing and embracing, the king was looking at them with satisfaction, and Maurice de Saxe, lying in his bassinet, was weeping like a baby. Afterward, they went to Tourney to celebrate. The wine flowed like water. In the taverns of the city, songs and anthems reverberated in eight languages, as though it were Babel during a holiday. Pretty Flemish girls were flirting with the soldiers and generously helping them squander their money. You celebrated with two plump servant girls, as happy as hummingbirds. You hardly understood a word of what they were saying to you, nor did it matter to you; their bodies, intertwined with yours, were eloquent enough. You spent the entire night and part of the next day at that revel of laughter, wine, food, sex, and visions. Curiously, you journeyed several times to a place very much like the one where you were. There were soldiers there also, some of them in green uniforms and others in coffee-colored ones, who were laughing and drinking straight from the bottle as they lewdly caressed laughing, drunken women whom they were holding on their laps. Like all of you, they too were celebrating a victory.

"I believe so too," Rasero said. "Although since I left the court, I have learned little about what is going on at it. To tell the truth, I've learned little about what's going on anywhere. I've been deeply absorbed in my studies."

Since you left Versailles you have hardly left your town house, except to seek amorous adventures that might sometimes take you to those strange places. You have been involved in a twofold effort: to know the thought of your era and to decipher those visions. You have made very little progress, especially with regard to the latter attempt. When you think you have understood a vision, that you've uncoded the message you presume is welling up from the depths of your consciousness, another vision comes along that in some way negates the formula you have devised for interpreting the earlier one. After, for example, you had convinced yourself that those vehicles without draft animals that you have seen so many times represent a mental propensity toward the pursuit of perfect motion, without the slightest expenditure of energy—an idea that has preoccupied you since reading Pascal, Leibniz, and so many others—after, that is, you arrived at the happy conclusion that the images of those contrivances were nothing but the symbol of perpetual motion, you suddenly saw, as you were frolicking with a whore from Montmartre, one of those vehicles brought to a stop with a cloud of steam pouring out of the front part of it. From inside the carriage a man emerged, greatly dismayed, who went over to the front extremity, raised a sort of lid, and peered inside. You could see a mechanism made of iron with wheels, belts, and gears, very like the mechanism of a church clock. The jet of steam was coming out through the little circular mouth of a strange flat object, which you presumed was a boiler. On seeing the mechanism, you thought of Savery and Newcomen and their curious devices capable of using steam to power movement, and you realized to your regret that those vehicles moved owing to such a contraption—that the iron mechanism and the heat of the steam took the place of a draft horse, that they were not a symbol of anything. You realized that the same must be true of those crude artifacts you had seen flying like birds. Surely they too moved by means of a machine. They were not figments indicative of your mind's proclivities but simple objects propelled by a natural force. And that realization terrified you, for it again forced you to reckon with the idea you were avoiding like a leper: that your visions are not fantasies or the product of your imagination, that they are real events taking place in the future. Somehow, according to this grim idea, when you make love, you connect with the future, as though you are entering through a doorway that leads to a shortcut across many years. Fortunately, you soon succeeded in putting the unsettling thought out of your head—especially given that you have visions so absurd and fantastic it does not bear supposing that they concern something real. Like the time that, just after you settled in Paris, you saw, while in the arms of Madame de Saissac, an immense light and in a matter of mere seconds thousands and thousands of Asians burned to a crisp. That, it reassured you to think, couldn't have been anything but a nightmare.

"Monsieur Rasero, why don't you take a little time off and work with us?" Diderot asked. "I'm sure you'd be a marvelous collaborator on the *Encyclopédie*. I haven't read anything you've written, but I need only listen to you to know you'd acquit yourself very well."

"I thank you very much, Denis, but I'm afraid that's impossible. I consider your invitation a great honor. But I've promised myself not to write a single paragraph until I think some things through. And, as I can see, that's going to take a good while. What I'd gladly do, though, if you all like the idea, is read and comment on everything you're willing to show me. I know that what I could contribute isn't much, but even so, I doubt that an additional opinion would hurt."

"Certainly not, sir. Your advice would no doubt be very valuable to us. It's a pity you can't cooperate by means of your pen, but that's plainly out of the question. We must bow to the demands of that inner, mental struggle you say you're waging."

What can it be that's tormenting this man, that's preventing him from even writing? Diderot wondered. This doesn't go with the image I've formed of him. Whatever's troubling him must be far out of the ordinary. He was tempted to ask more questions, to dig around a little concerning this enigmatic thinking-through that his new friend had mentioned. But he restrained himself; his good sense told him that it was better to leave things as they were. There would be more than enough time to know this young man better. He heard the crowing of an early-rising rooster and poured himself the last glass of wine in the bottle. He realized sadly that the moment for farewells had arrived and wondered whether the odor would assail him as soon as the Malagan had gone off. He hurriedly drained his glass to get the moment of saying good-night to his friends over with as quickly as possible. He embraced them effusively and accompanied them, despite their protests—for the early morning was very cold—to the street door. He saw them walk off down the stone pavement. His friend Jean, very tall and a little hunchbacked, was walking along in great strides, clinging to Fausto's forearm, as the latter, standing straight and tall, proceeded with short, quick steps. He went back inside. The candle, burned almost all the way down, was gently guttering, bringing the shadows of objects to life. The odor had returned. His eyes told him so before his sense of smell: the place was tinted a yellowish green. He wasn't up to getting into another bath. Full of the smell and of sadness, with big tears running down his cheeks, he headed for the bedroom. He undressed hurriedly, throwing his clothes into the farthest corner, for they were so impregnated with the stench that they almost stuck to his hands. He got into bed. Antoinette was awake. She hadn't managed to sleep like one of the blessed after masturbating, and had tried four times in all. The buzz of voices in the dining room and Rasero's face in her mind had kept her from falling asleep. When she felt Denis alongside her, she embraced him and clung to him as tightly as she had pressed her first son to her breast, but despite everything, her child hadn't absorbed enough heat to go on living. Lying in each other's arms, without saying a word, they caressed each other frantically, and made love to each other fully, completely. Antoinette could sleep at last, and Denis, forgetting the stench, dreamed that he was walking on the snowy steppes of holy Russia.

II

Damiens

On the Way to Ferney, April, 1761

The carriage, drawn by four horses of good height, unhurriedly traversed the gentle valleys of Champagne. Upon the coach box, the driver and his boy drank to each other's health with the wine they had just bought in Nogent. Their big swallows reddened their faces and whetted their tongues, which reviewed in more and more piquant detail the shapes, and in particular the big breasts, almost leaping out of the low-cut cleavage, of the plump tavernkeeper's wife who had sold them the wine. The horses, not feeling themselves spurred on by the driver, also trotted happily along. Every so often, they looked toward the river, and the sight of cool running water made their palates, already tortured by the harness bits, drier still.

Inside the coach, traveling alone, seated in the back alongside the window, drinking a sweet port and nibbling on a fried chicken leg without being really hungry, was Fausto Rasero. The jolting from the road, which the soft seats upholstered in velvet did not fully dampen, produced in his back and neck a swaying motion that invited him to fall asleep. He remembered that it had been a long time since he had traveled anywhere, that he had clung to Paris like moss to a rock, that in almost twenty years he had not journeyed farther than Fontainebleau, when the Marquise de Pompadour invited him to those interminable hunting parties. And those were journeys on roads so smooth and in vehicles so comfortable and swift that he scarcely was aware of the pleasure of riding across the countryside; it merely meant going just a little farther than to Versailles. Long journeys, real journeys, lay far in the past—as when he had traveled all the way across Andalusia on his way to Madrid. Up until then, he had never been outside Málaga; the immense sea and the range of mountains that eventually plunged into the sea were the only landscape he had ever seen . . .

When the crude carriage climbed to the top of the mountain range, the little boy Fausto literally felt that he was in the process of being born again, that he was emerging from an enormous egg to see a vast world on the other side of the mountains. He contemplated with fascination the region of Antequera, where his father possessed great stretches of vineyards. The wealth of the Rasero family, the one whose blazon was a live-oak branch, came from those vineyards—although in reality they had belonged to the Oquendos, his mother's family. His father's family had squandered its fortune long since, by following two paths as diametrically opposed as heaven and hell: the heirs of don Ignacio the Lame threw away the family's fortunes both on pious works and on orgies. As though they had come from two seeds no more alike than an egg and a chestnut, half of the Raseros were fanatics to the point of heresy—like his great-granduncle, don Hermenegildo de Rasero y Cuesta, the parish priest of Antequera and bishop of Málaga, who, owing to his extraordinary religious fervor, was in the habit of imposing extremely severe penances on his faithful flock. Doña Fernanda de Bazán, the grandniece of the illustrious admiral don Alvaro de Bazán, the marquis de Santa Cruz and the fearsome organizer of the invincible Armada, was ordered, for example, to do penance for a confessed prurience by burning herself with a firebrand "in the place where desire itches" until the itching had subsided and purer thoughts had taken its place. Perhaps doña Fernanda's desire was greater than her confessor had calculated or her skin too delicate, but what happened is that the hapless woman perished from the burns she inflicted upon herself. There were those who affirmed that the death of her illustrious uncle, which occurred shortly thereafter, was due to the sadness brought about in him by this lamentable incident. Later on, don Hermenegildo had the unfortunate idea of suspecting of heresy the venerable statue of Saint Francis of Assisi in one of the chapels of the cathedral of Málaga. There was no way of convincing him that the statue was merely a representation of the Tuscan anchorite. He was certain that it was the Evil One who had taken possession of that piece of wood. That was the reason, don Hermenegildo explained, for the lascivious gaze the wooden statue directed toward any lady who entered the cathedral—reaching the extreme of ogling, without the slightest discretion and with its eyes flaming with lust, the image of the Most Holy Virgin, dauntlessly cradling her Divine Son in her arms, that was located directly opposite that of Saint Francis. Unable to tolerate such irreverence any longer, one Sunday, after midday mass, don Hermenegildo burned the diabolical image in the churchyard after having first brought to bear on it all sorts of exorcisms. The scandal was of such proportions that it reached the ears of the cardinal of Spain and even those of Pope Gregory XII. But in reality it had never occurred to don Hermenegildo that he was burning a statue at all: the Saint Francis had been carved in Florence a century before, and once it had been gilded and decorated, miraculous properties began to be attributed to it. It was brought to Spain by the emperor Charles V after the sacking of Rome in 1527, and his son, the fervent Philip II, held it in special veneration, to the point that it was only with the greatest reluctance that he parted with it in donating it to the cathedral in Málaga. Despite everything, don Hermenegildo succeeded in weathering the storm, but shortly thereafter he committed another of his characteristic outrages—the last one, incidentally, since he lost his mind soon after. From the pulpit of the cathedral of Málaga, no less, he urinated on the believers attending mass, because he considered them impious, people of little faith. They say that his effluvium came from this surprising tap with unheard-of force and in torrential quantities. Not even the most agile little acolytes were able to escape the wrathful liquid. The faithful, on their knees, prayed with a fervor surpassing any they had felt before, receiving with resignation the urine-redolent downpour that, undoubtedly, the Lord was sending them through the intermediary of that most holy man. After that epic deed, don Hermenegildo ended his days confined to a Carthusian monastery near Benajarafe. It is said that after that no one ever understood what he said, for he spoke in an unfamiliar tongue, with soft sounds, in which neither the *r*s nor the *j*s were pronounced, nor any other strong consonants—as though he were giving forth from his throat a single sustained note by way of vowel sounds and dividing it up into words by gently clacking his tongue. *Tlalocan* was the word he uttered most often. "Tlalocan," he would repeat until he was exhausted.

On the other hand, his great-grandfather, don Carlos de Rasero y

Cuesta, was a Rasero of the opposite stripe: his binges and amorous escapades became legendary. It seems that the same forcefulness that his brother demonstrated in urinating showed itself in him in the ejaculation of sperm. It was even said that the entire population of Alora was descended from this potent gentleman, who boasted of having taken his pleasure with more women than the sultan of Baghdad. The story goes that doña Elvira de Pantoja, a Sevillian more beautiful than Helen, wiser than Minerva, and more of a harlot than Messalina, was the cause of don Carlos' downfall. She was just past sixteen when he met her; at the time he was already close to sixty, though he had not lost the least bit of his vigor: he was still able to down an entire barrel of joy-juice, eat a whole leg of lamb, and service four she-bodies till they begged for mercy, then to sleep like a log, but not before going on to masturbate several times. When don Carlos saw the girl for the first time, he felt the itch of desire that's the privilege of celibate youth. The girl became aware of this immediately and beamed a smile at him capable of making the statue of David walk. It was no trick at all for don Carlos to win the girl: although his epic exploits had greatly diminished his fortune, it was still enormous, regardless of the excesses. Doña Elvira, fully conscious of the inclinations and of the wealth of her suitor, was not at all shy about accepting his wooing. Ironies of life: the storm began just as he thought that he had reached port; after intense bargaining, which resulted in the imposition of a heavy price—he was obliged to sacrifice his possessions in Korea in addition to a hefty pile of precious coins—the girl finally agreed to grant him her favors. She came to Don Carlos lubricious and a virgin—the girl's mother had given her pledge on the latter question and, more important, had promised to return the possessions of don Carlos that pertained to the agreement if it turned out that the girl's hymen was not intact—in the charming little house in Torremolinos that he had bought from a bankrupt pawnbroker and reserved for his most refined pleasures. Standing naked before him, the girl could not have been more beautiful, as though Phidias himself had modeled her contours. Her breasts, ample and set wide apart, with perfect rosy nipples, neither great nor small (neither the breasts nor their buttons), had the smoothness of porcelain from the Orient. Her green eyes, at once impish and ingenuous, awakened in don Carlos the most contrary feelings, ranging from what a saint might feel before the image of the Mother of God, to those of a faun before a little gathering of nymphs. Such perfect beauty intoxicated and frightened the poor man so much that he stood there contemplating her, as mute and motionless as a Tancred, for a long time. When he finally pulled himself out of his immobility and prepared to do what he knew so well how to, his hands, instead of caressing her, joined together, palm to palm; his mouth, instead of kissing and nibbling, began to pray; his proud phallus, always ready to stand up and fight, shrank until it was very small, endeavoring, in its embarrassment, to hide itself in his crotch; and his eyes, dazzled by such beauty, closed as they began to shed great tears. So this is the macho from Antequera, the girl thought scornfully. Perceiving herself adored like a goddess, she grasped the extent of her power and realized that she could marry into a great fortune. She brought her body closer to the old man while he prayed on his knees; she brushed the soft hair of her pubis across his face; she wound herself about the Malagan like a snake, holding him tightly and twining her long legs around his waist; she kissed his ears and nibbled his neck as she sank her fingernails into his back. She caressed and licked every millimeter of his body, giving special attention to his impotent but once-powerful cock. Yet it was useless—and she knew it very well. Don Carlos was incapable of responding, or to be more precise, he responded by weeping harder and harder. "My virgin!" he began to say to her in his strong Malagan accent. "My virgin!" he repeated as he sobbed like a Mary Magdalene. "You little shit! You son of a bitch! You fairy!" she answered him in her refined Sevillian accent. The exchange of epithets went on for some time, until don Carlos ejaculated without having worked himself up to a fever pitch. The woman pushed him away contemptuously, as she slathered the sticky fluid on her long thighs. "Get away from me, child, and come back when you're a man," she said to him with a smile. Lying on the rug curled up in a ball, don Carlos could not stop looking at her and weeping. "My virgin, my virgin!" he gently murmured. This scene was repeated for twenty years, until don Carlos finally left this sad world. He was never able to have a real climax with his beloved, and she never ceased to be his "virgin," the only woman in his life capable of giving him so much pleasure and so much pain at the same time . . . and to run through his fortune. His "virgin" ceased to be one shortly after their first encounters, when between her rebuffs of him, her scornful remarks, and her manipulations, she gradually excited herself and, on attaining no satisfaction whatever from don Carlos' prayers, was obliged to seek out someone to extinguish the fire that had begun to burn within her. Juanillo Cabrera, a servant of don Carlos', turned out to be an excellent fireman. A healthy lad, vigorous and not very bright, he generously gave the Sevillian what a worshipful regard kept his master from giving her. Juanillo was the first bead of a rosary of lovers that doña Elvira had had, a rosary long enough to circle the globe. Not even the gates of the walls of Paris had opened as many times as that woman's legs. Malicious backbiters said that if doña Elvira had hoarded—the way she had hoarded the old man's wealth—all the semen that her womb received, it would have filled a lake the size of the Dead Sea. Even so, to don Carlos the girl was his "virgin" until the last day of his life—and the last coin in his pocket. They say that after that disastrous first time don Carlos went mad and lived shut away in Torremolinos, like his brother in Benajarafe, anxiously awaiting for Tuesdays to come round, the day his beloved had agreed to visit him.

But the boy wasn't thinking of any of this as he crossed the Guadalquivir valley. From the window of the carriage he contemplated, fascinated, the vineyards, the olive groves, and the irrigation ditches of old Andalusia, the pretty little towns, gleaming with whitewash, that smelled of jasmine and of olive oil hot in the pan. They stopped at the entrance to Lucena to give the horses a rest. Angustias, his nurse, was thrilled to catch sight of a couple of gypsies playing the guitar beneath the shade of a live-oak tree, as others around him shook split-cane stalks that gave off the sound of a crowd of people clapping; they were about to have a round of merrymaking. In a little while, several gypsy girls joined them and began to dance smoothly to the rhythm of lively *bulerías.* When the woman and the boy approached the group, the men looked at them with mistrust. "You're a fine pair, you two!": a boy, obviously a young gentleman, dressed in black garments made of fine cloth, as bald as a hard-boiled egg, with eyes set wide apart, black and very bright, and accompanied by a tall, pretty gypsy woman, with long hair as black as pitch and full breasts that could feed a regiment. The girls looked at them in a more friendly way, and on seeing that the two of them were watching them, began to dance even faster and make more provocative movements.

"Que tu parmito mi arma, que tu parmito . . . ," an old man sang in a harsh voice. He was sitting upon the root of the tree, graver than a policeman on duty, his back very straight, his eyes staring at nothing in particular, and accompanying himself by softly clapping his hands.

He looked like a Bedouin from the desert reciting verses from the Koran at eventide as he looks toward Mecca. It was a joyous song and at the same time a lament. Fausto had heard it sung many times by Angustias, his beloved Angustias. But she sang it faster, accentuating the rhythm more, though her beat was less steady.

"Que quítate del sol que te vas a poner que tu carita morena . . . ," his nurse sang melodiously as she pushed the rocking chair back and forth with her foot and stroked the bald head of the child, who, dozing in her lap, sucked her enormous breast. When he was lying like that, listening to the woman singing somewhere faraway, feeling the sweet warm liquid trickling down to his belly, the child was completely happy. One time Rasero confessed to his friend Voltaire, "I've never been as happy as when I was a small child and spent hours at a time in the lap of my pretty nurse listening to her marvelous gypsy songs."

"Well, I can't say the same," his friend answered. "My childhood in that damned Collège de Saint-Louis was an inferno. Given the slightest opportunity, those revolting Jesuits mercilessly sodomized you. And you should have seen how our cries of pain excited them. The bastards . . . they left an ineradicable mark on me. Because of them, I've never been happy, nor will I ever be able to be."

How much these words of the philosopher surprised you, and how far you were from really knowing him. You could not believe that this thin, nervous man, with those impressive eyes that came near to piercing straight through whatever they saw, with that prodigious intelligence that enabled him to write a work like *La Henriade* at the age of twenty-eight and have French society in his pocket—to have the most cultivated and refined society in Europe at his feet when he was not yet forty—that this amazing Frenchman who understood Newton, who boldly ventured to explain the abstract and involuted arguments of the learned Englishman to d'Alembert himself no less, who dared to contradict and leave in an awkward position (although this of course happened much later) the divine Maupertuis and his famous principle, you could not believe, as I was saying, that Voltaire was incapable of happiness because certain perverted monks had forever embittered an existence such as his. But on seeing his face, drawn and sad, on seeing his skinny, sickly, shrunken body sitting all hunched over in an uncomfortable armchair in Madame de Saissac's salon as he held a glass of cognac with both hands, looking absently at the reddish liquid, thinking of heaven only knew what, there was no doubt about it: Voltaire was the most unhappy creature on earth. "But, my dear, that happened many years ago," the Marquise de Pompadour said to him sympathetically. "The reasonable thing to do is to forget it."

"Forget it, madam?" Voltaire retorted, pleased that the conversation was centered on him. "Forget those frightful afternoons, when those damned priests locked us up like despicable ruffians, accusing us of having filched from the pantry a few pieces of chocolate that they themselves had hidden away? They forced us to pull down our underpants, baring our backsides for a brutal whipping with nettles . . ."

"How dreadful!" the marquise interrupted, genuinely indignant.

"And that wasn't the worst of it. After receiving lash upon lash, we wept our hearts out, our buttocks swollen and purple like those odd monkeys from Africa. Seeing us in such a sorry plight—though you may not believe it, madam—excited those filthy swine to the point of frenzy. They looked at us, their eyes blazing with desire, and began to kiss our bleeding asses until, with fevered lust, they shamelessly offered us up according to the rites of Sodom. That, my dear, is something that cannot be forgotten . . ." You listened to him, moved and incensed, as did the rest of those present. Only the Duke de Richelieu appeared not to be particularly impressed by the story. He was standing behind the philosopher and made no effort to hide a mocking smile as he listened to him tell of his misfortunes. As on so many other occasions, the cynicism of that man made you angry. A pimp and ambitious, that fellow was totally lacking in virtue—unless low blows, rapine, and the ability to think up underhanded intrigues, at which the duke was a past master, are counted virtues. His plump, flabby body slipped like a shadow in and out of the corners of Versailles. He never missed an evening gathering at which he discerned a chance to spread his poison. He knew all the members of the court and despised them all; at the same time, he was hated and feared by everyone. Even the Beloved Sovereign felt uncomfortable in his presence, for the ugly little duke had inherited from his great-grandfather the ability to discover any and every secret. He knew—and no one understood how—all about even the most obscure episodes in the king's intimate life. And he had learned very well how to take advantage of the power in that: he was placed in command of whole armies although he knew nothing about the martial arts—save for sacking and plundering, which he carried out with awesome thoroughness throughout Flanders, where his passage was compared to that of a Horseman of the Apocalypse. Now he was mocking Voltaire, as he did all the philosophes. His ancestry, though widely doubted, gave him such a feeling of superiority that he never considered it necessary to read a book or listen well to a concert to feel himself wiser and cleverer than the most eminent of the plebeian philosophes. His big double chin trembled beneath his lips, which laughed sarcastically as they looked at you. Though Voltaire was unable to see him, he was somehow aware of the duke's mockery; perhaps he saw the reflection of it in your eyes. At any event, he aimed the dart: "Dear Fausto, to endure being raped in this way in a man's tender years leaves a definite mark on his life: either he ends up as I am, perpetually sad, with the sensation of having been stained with an indelible ink, incapable of savoring the pleasure and the carnal enjoyment that are what loving a person means." As he spoke those words, Madame Du Châtelet gave him an offended look.

"I beg your pardon, my dear, but it's true. You know very well that I love you as I have never loved anyone else, but my love can't help bearing with it the bitterness of the poison of the priests at Saint-Louis. Either such a man ends up like me, as I was saying, Monsieur Rasero, or on the contrary, he acquires a rare taste for those perverted habits, and with the passage of years turns into a lustful, arrogant, cynical being . . . and an obese one. There is not the slightest doubt of it." Now the terms were reversed: everyone present smiled, except the Duke de Richelieu, whose face took on an expression of wrath. The self-congratulatory look the philosopher gave you left you with no doubt that he saw his antagonist's face reflected in your pupils.

At that time you had just met Voltaire. Little by little, in the course of those pleasant evenings in the quarters of the Marquise de Pompadour, or at the performances of the philosopher's works for the theater that that diligent lady organized in the pretty little theater improvised beneath the Grand Staircase of Versailles, you gradually made out the way the tortuous mind of that extraordinary human being worked. Hence you were scarcely surprised to hear him say, "I'm the happiest man in the world. There has never been, nor will there ever be, a man happier than I am," after the enormous success his play *La Princesse de Navarre* attained, when he became the pampered darling of the court at Versailles. He was appointed royal historiographer, enjoying a fat pension, and was knighted. Nothing could have made this man, who had said so much, who had written so much, against the nobility and its "decadent mores," happier than to know that he was now a knight. Deeply moved, he that day embraced the obese Duke de Richelieu, the "most likable and keen-minded man in all of France," according to what he said to anyone who cared to listen to him. As puffed up as a toad, Voltaire in his vanity found no better way to thank the king for so many favors than to write a series of vulgar little verses dedicated to the Beloved Sovereign and his favorite—ornate verses, of the worst sort, for which in the end he paid the price of exile, since in his eagerness to please the favorite, he in a number of them showed Her Royal Highness in a most unflattering light. And the queen, despite being ugly, wizened, and living in seclusion, was the queen of France and could not be and should not have been treated with disdain.

Darkness was beginning to fall when they reached Troyes. The city, unlike Paris, still had a marked rural flavor. The houses on the outskirts had very well cared for vegetable gardens, and poultry, pigs, and even cows wandered as they pleased over the rough cobblestones. As they approached the center of the city, the street paving became smoother, and larger and better-constructed houses could be seen. The main square, in front of the great Gothic cathedral, was the heart of the town. For more than five centuries, merchants from all over Europe had gathered there for the annual fair. At its best moments, the fair at Troyes was the most important one in Champagne, overshadowing, in magnificence and splendor, those of Provins, Lagny, and Bar-sur-Aube, its eternal rivals. Stretching and shaking his legs, numb after the long journey, Rasero walked over to the main facade of the cathedral. It was an imposing building, built in the middle of the thirteenth century, when the work of master masons reached perfection. The statues carved on either side of the great portico were rigidly upright and elongated, as were all the works of Gothic art. Nonetheless, their outlines hinted at soft curves; moreover, the faces of the figures they represented dared to smile. Timid, almost imperceptible smiles, to be sure, yet giving evidence of a distinct difference from the austere, sober faces of those carved a century before in the Church of Saint-Denis, in the capital of France. Those smiling faces and their slightly curvilinear shapes presaged a happy, stable era, in which courtesy first, and later on, sensuality, came to form part of the daily life of the great noblemen, who began to break away from their cruel hunting parties and their tournaments, to have hours at a time in calm evening gatherings around the hearth, listening to the love poems of the divine Ruteboeuf, the novels of courtly life of Philippe Rein, or a little later, the unforgettable stories of Christine de Pisan, the first woman in history to make her living from her writing.

That cathedral was built in an enlightened era, when Italian, Venetian, Spanish, and Portuguese merchants came to the fair year after year to offer goods that, barely a century before, existed only in the imagination of the inhabitants of Troyes: the lightest of silk fabrics, so soft and thin that a dress made of them could pass clean through a lady's tiny finger ring; exquisite fragrant spices brought from the far end of the world, which softened and gave an appetizing flavor to meat, although—it is only fair to admit—a little while after a meal they set people's bellies on fire; saffron from Asia, tiny bright red stamens that colored, seasoned, and gave a special aroma to any dish, turning it into food fit for the gods; jewels of a thousand shapes, colors, and sizes that great lords avidly sought for adorning their chests, the hilts of their swords, and the necks of their ladyloves; precious books made of the best parchment, in which each little vignette, framed in pure gold paint, was a work of art in itself, books for which the learned doctors of the Sorbonne were able to offer great sums of money . . . It was the era in which Europe began to rediscover, to rescue, by way of the beautiful Arabic manuscripts of Córdoba and Toledo, the great culture of the ancient Greeks and Romans. Aristotle was revivified and with him logical and orderly thought; Ptolemy came to life again to put in order the starry heavens; the ingenious signs invented by the Arabs facilitated to an infinite degree the art of making calculations, a laborious task almost impossible to carry out up until then, because the system of Roman numbers was so cumbersome. In that square, culture was exchanged by the medium of lengths of cloth from Arras and wines from Burgundy, or by the medium of gold coins, which from that time began to become plentiful and widespread.

As Rasero contemplated the church, he was reminded of the reading he had done on that extraordinary Gothic Renaissance. Many names, buried a long time in some chink of his memory, emerged, free to gambol amid the handsome sculptures he had before him. They played with the grapevines, the apples, and the laurel leaves skillfully carved in stone. Two professors from Paris, Ousmari de

Bène and David Dunant, leafed smilingly through their *Leçons de philosophie naturelle* and cupped their mouths with their hands to jeer at the stern bishops at the Council of 1218 who had condemned them. A number of Dominicans, fat and happy, danced about exuberantly, still very far from turning into stubborn inquisitors. At the head of them, with a great bald spot in the middle of his head, the Italian Thomas Aquinas was reciting, in an almost singsong voice, his *Summas,* which were meeting with the full approval of Albertus Magnus. The others were holding in their hands the *mirrors, treasuries, bestiaries,* and other encyclopedias that reminded Rasero of that sharp-witted and inquisitive spirit which, five centuries later, would inspire his beloved Diderot and d'Alembert. Inside the church he saw Adam de La Halle directing musicians and actors at the same time. They were performing an allegorical *auto sacramental,* perhaps too festive to be religious. At the far end of the cathedral, he could see Jean de Chelles, measuring with his arms the rose window, enormous and radiant, an art form that was his invention. There, seated in the choir, three famous personages were having a heated dispute, engaging in the art of debate, a recent discovery. Guillaume de Lorris, the author of the *Roman de la rose,* a veritable summa of courtesy, was explaining in fluent terms the importance of clarity and balance in written texts. Jean Renard, for his part, was insisting that truth was the axis round which any literary work should rotate. He was striking with his palm copies of his *Escuffe* and his *Guillerme de Dôle* that he was holding in his other hand, as though those thick tomes were irrefutable proofs of what he was saying. The third man, silent and taciturn, seemed not to be taking part in the disputation, showing by his aloofness his disdain for both clarity and truth. He was gently stroking the spine of his *Aucassin,* much less preoccupied with clarity and much less faithful to the truth than the works of the other two participating in the debate, but at the same time much tenderer and more human. The first novel ever written—Rasero remembered—in which peasants and people belonging to the new middle class are the central characters, thereby anticipating by several centuries the immortal Cervantes.

From the main altar he saw Saint Louis descending, mounted on a huge white horse. He was wearing eighty kilos of armor; his hair was short, and he had no beard: it was the only way his helmet would fit him. His gray, nostalgic eyes seemed to peer out of the gates of Byzantium. When he halted in the middle of the church, all those present gathered around him to do him homage and honor, for this starving Capetian was the symbol, the guide, the pivot around which all that period revolved, when the Gothic shone as never before and the *langue d'oui* spread from its native Ile de France to every corner of the kingdom. Alongside the king, master Joinville was painting a fleur-de-lis on the monarch's helmet so that, once he was wearing it, everyone would know that it was Louis, king of the Franks and ruler of Paris. With a certain surprise, Rasero suddenly understood the origin of heraldry: coats of arms were, in that world of illiterates, the only way of recognizing a person hidden behind the paraphernalia of war. The forearm whose hand is holding up a club made of live oak—the coat of arms of the Raseros—must have been painted on the helmet of don Ignacio the Lame, his illustrious ancestor, shortly after the memorable battle of Toledo, in which he, armed with a club, put to flight, all by himself, eight terrifying Moors who had ambushed King Alphonse VI. When, no longer absorbed in thought, Rasero raised his eyes, he found that all the people there had disappeared, with the exception of the horseman and his mount. The man put on his helmet, which showed, incidentally, not a fleur-de-lis but the forearm with the cudgel made of live oak. The horseman raised his visor, and on seeing that new face, pitted with smallpox, missing a number of teeth, with round eyes, set far apart and very dark, Rasero realized that don Ignacio, the heroic founder of his dynasty, was before him. The black horse was rearing. His rider was controlling him with his left hand as he raised a club in his right. He gazed into the eyes of his descendant for a moment, gave a fleeting obscene smile and said in a very loud voice, "Faith and duty call!" as he turned his horse around. He gave the animal's croup a smart blow with the wooden club and headed at a full gallop toward the main altar, where he disappeared.

When Rasero left the church, night had already fallen. The coachman, who had waited for him patiently inside the carriage, informed him that supper was ready and his room made up at the inn on the square, directly alongside the cathedral. It was roomy and comfortable, not at all luxurious, but very clean and pleasant. From the white walls hung gleaming copper saucepans, and above the hearth was a crossed pair of old sabers. As he took a taste of a strong red wine that reminded him of the one that his friend Diderot had been so fond of, Rasero wondered whether he had done the right thing in undertaking this journey. Why, after more than ten years, had he accepted

Voltaire's perennial invitation to visit him? He did not find personal dealings with that man particularly pleasant. He enjoyed much more the correspondence that they had kept up for so long. And the truth was that in his letters Voltaire's talent showed itself in its chemically pure form, so to speak; it was nearly free—save for the frequent references to his health—of all the tiresome attitudes he assumed when he was there in person, free of his endless complaints when he was in a bad mood, and free of, what was worse still, the displays of insufferable self-complacency and arrogance, which are more annoying and ungrateful in an intellectual than in others, to which he was given when he was feeling euphoric, or even less appealingly, when he was "badly wounded by the muses," as he used to put it. Rasero did not feel the slightest curiosity to see what ten years had done to the philosopher's appearance. He would be just as skinny, as sickly and feeble, making no effort to hide his more than sixty years—unless he happened to be in one of his moments of diabolical lucidity: then his eyes would gleam like sapphires, his whole body would grow tense, rigid, like a feline lying in wait, and he would speak vehemently, with the veins in his neck standing out. At such times nobody would think of him as being more than thirty; such was the power of his intellect. Rasero had no desire to see what he looked like, and even less desire to argue with him. He was frightened by the idea of finding himself face-to-face with Voltaire, not saying a word, nodding his head as he listened to Voltaire's eternal philippic against Frederick, learning one by one of the base acts committed against him by the despot when he had lodged him in Potsdam, of the animosity of the learned men, the musicians, and the painters who surrounded the monarch. The philosopher would recount to him in detail how those idiots delighted in humiliating him, mocking his ideas, ridiculing his writings, how they brought up in front of Frederick, over and over, the painful subject of that bastard Desfontaines, as though the king was not perfectly aware that that pervert had Thieriot, the eternal and beloved friend of Voltaire, in his power and had made him swallow all those vicious lies. He would hear how the philosopher was unable to explain to the monarch the origin itself of that calumny, or tell him in precise terms what his friend's weakness was. But it was all owed—and this he could tell him, Rasero, but never the king—to his beloved Thieriot's being a homosexual. An accursed ephebe had made him utterly lose his head and his last penny as well; he dragged him through the vilest mud—yet, despite knowing very well that the odious lad made that swine Richelieu, that pervert Choiseul, and worse still, three or four noble ladies of the court writhe with pleasure, he was unable to leave his side and wept like a village lass when the youngster scorned him. It was this whole dizzying turn of events that had led his beloved Thieriot to commit such infamy. But how to explain all this to Frederick? How to shut up those dolts once and for all? "The king," he will say to you, staring you straight in the eye, like someone revealing a frightful secret, "the king, my friend, is a homosexual. We all know it; he knows that we all know it, but how to tell him all that? Officially, nobody knows anything. Officially, he is more of a real man and more virile than that great-grandfather of yours. A Prussian soldier can't be a whore. How to tell him then? There's no way. Simply tolerate, everlastingly tolerate, that inferno, my friend . . ." And so on and on, listening hour after hour, continually nodding his head, continually saying nothing. Because when Voltaire fell into one of those trances, it was impossible to contradict him—or you could do so if you were ready to take a dressing-down still more violent, more terrible, more larded with epithets, and what's worse, directed not at Frederick and his courtiers at Potsdam but at you, the unfortunate creature who dared contradict him, at you, at your mother, and at all those who formed your negligible circle.

Why were you going to Ferney then? Perhaps because you were tired of Paris, fed up with the intrigues in the Parlement, disgusted by what they did to Diderot, disappointed by d'Alembert's desertion, saddened by La Pompadour's illness, sick of the monarch's ways, indignant at the cowardice and baseness of so many of the philosophes, weary of hearing talk of wars in the snows of Canada, in the backwoods of Louisiana, or now in the jungles of Bengal, feeling queasy after so much reading, so many articles for the *Encyclopédie* (where the mechanism that makes a loom function is described in detail, down to the last screw), frightened, very frightened, by those damnable visions, and sad, above all sad . . .

You have been unable to shake off that sadness ever since the ill-starred day—four years ago—when you met up with that unfortunate wretch. You were drinking in a tavern in the avenue Paris, in the town of Versailles, when he came over to your table. He was a mature, good-looking man. His teeth attracted your attention: he wasn't missing a single one; they were gleaming white and perfectly regular. His mouth was so handsome that you forced yourself to prolong the conversation in order to contemplate it as the man spoke to you. In the beginning, you didn't pay much attention to what he was saying, for the teeth held you spellbound, but little by little, the trembling of his hands and his voice, and the vehemence with which he spoke, forced you to pay attention.

"Monsieur d'Argenson says that it's necessary to give him a warning at least, a reminder of his duties toward France. And to me it seems only right . . ."

The man was surprised at himself: Why am I speaking to this stranger in this way? he thought. He's doubtless a noble, probably a courtier . . . By speaking to him like that, he risked that the bald man would inform on him, and then he wouldn't be able to do what he had been planning for such a long time—through many sleepless nights, weighing each detail, praying to the Virgin until he lost his voice, as he waited for a sign, however small it might be, that she approved of the deed he had contrived, so he could know what he intended to do was only right and fitting. Finally, after he had asked her for so long, the Virgin gave him her leave, making him aware of it in a way that was unmistakable: she let gentle tears run down her wooden face. He saw the tears, wet his fingers in them, and brought them to his mouth. He then experienced the most extraordinary taste that had ever reached his palate. It was a mixture of honey, nectar, dew, and mother's milk. By her tears, the Virgin endorsed his undertaking, and he realized that, from that moment, there was not anyone or anything that would stop him. He carefully worked out his plan down to the last detail; the choice of a weapon cost him several more sleepless nights, until one night an inspired dream inclined him toward a paper knife. He woke at daybreak weeping with joy as he wondered why he had been so stupid, why the thought of such a weapon, able to inflict a wound but not to kill, had not occurred to him. An angel had to appear in your dream, you ass, he said to himself, for you to see what has always been right in front of your eyes—because, in fact, the paper knife had always been there, across from his bed, on a little table that held a big Bible, some of the pages of which were still uncut. And now, when he had only a few minutes left to carry out his plan, he abandoned the palace, went off to a tavern for wine, and began to tell the whole story to a perfect stranger. Can he be a man sent by the Lord to put me to the test? he wondered. He did not know about that, but what he was certain of was that that man was not going to betray him.

"A monarch cannot abandon his people and leave them adrift," Rasero heard him say, "much less fall into the hands of those scheming priests. Those damned Jesuits! They're destroying France . . ."

Give or take a few words, Rasero had often heard such talk from the mouths of the magistrates of the Parlement—though this man didn't look in the least like a member of the Parlement. Doubtless he was a poor, good, ordinary man.

"But heaven has already given the order to draw the line. God has tired of this, and soon, very soon, he'll send a warning to our Detested Sovereign." That was the first time Rasero had heard this epithet attached to Louis by a man of the people. "And I, dear sir, yes I, little Damiens, am going to be that instrument. The Virgin, in her inexhaustible grace, has decided on me as the Absalom that our beloved kingdom cries out for."

"Do you want to kill the king of France?" Rasero asked, making no effort to conceal his stupefaction.

"God keep me from committing such a terrible deed. I shall not harm our king, merely give him a warning, that's certain. I shall simply pass on to him the message of our Savior and his Most Holy Mother."

"And how are you going to warn him?"

"You'll soon find out, sir, you'll soon find out . . ."

The man downed the last of his drink; his hands ceased to tremble, and his face grew flushed. He said no more, politely paid the bill, and left the tavern with a firm step.

Damiens went back to the palace. He had been at Versailles since ten o'clock that morning and was pleased to see that no one noticed his presence; it was enough to be dressed decently to be able to wander around the immense edifice without anyone's bothering him. As he walked along the sumptuous corridors, he wondered anxiously if the king might not have come in while he was in the tavern. Why had he been so stupid as to leave the palace? Three years turning that plan over in his mind, and now he'd perhaps ruined it forever. What good would it have done him to have returned from Artois and run the risk of being arrested for the absurd robbery he'd committed in that Paris bookstore, to have spent the last sou of his pay on that fine outfit of blue velvet he bought in order to move about Versailles unchallenged, if at the precise moment of putting his plan into action he had had no better sense than to go off to a tavern in the avenue Paris to drink wine with a stranger—and as if that weren't enough, to confess his plans to him? "Fear," he remembered his father's saying, "debases a person's reason and paralyzes his senses." Yes, it was fear that had taken him away from the palace, that had made his throat dry and conducted him to that tavern to relieve it. Perhaps his faith was not as great as he had envisioned. The certainty that the Virgin would intercede for him, sparing him punishment, or at least making it gentle and bearable, seemed to have abandoned him when he left the door of the Bull's-Eye Salon of the palace to flee to the tavern. He began to feel he was no longer capable of carrying out his plan, of doing what the Virgin had ordained. Dejected, his eyes brimming with tears, he headed down the stairs leading to the main door of the palace. Just at that moment, when he believed himself crippled by fear, the sound of voices brought him out of his paralysis. "Here he comes! Here he comes!" he heard, as an army of footmen, guards, doorkeepers, and functionaries milled about on the esplanade.

The pounding of the horses' hooves on the smooth pavement announced the arrival of the sovereign's carriage. Without taking time to reflect, Damiens slipped in among the crowd. Nobody noticed him: they assumed him to be yet another of the many beggars abounding wherever the king went. Louis got out of the calash. He was bundled up tightly, his face pale and his nose reddened by the cold. Leaning on the arm of a doorkeeper, he made for the entrance to the palace. The crowd drew aside respectfully to let their sovereign through, bowing to him as he passed. Among them was Damiens, who as he bowed stroked with his right hand the horn handle of his weapon. As the king went by, Damiens violently pushed through the guards in front of him, gave a feline leap, grabbed Louis' shoulder with his left hand, and pulled him toward him. Once he had pulled him very close, he plunged the knife into his side—gently at first, but on feeling that something was in the way of the knife's tip, harder, until he was sure that it had pierced through to the flesh. Only then did he remove it, pulling it out slantwise to make the wound a little larger. Everything happened in an instant, no one taking notice until the king was heard crying out, raising his bloody hand, "Help me, I'm wounded. It's that cur there! Arrest him, but don't kill him." Damiens, with the weapon in his hand, was standing stock-still, wondering, perhaps, if he had been able to do what he had done.

Exactly as Damiens had hoped, the wound was a slight one; the heavy garments the monarch was wearing on that freezing day of January kept the knife from doing grave harm. The tip barely scratched his flesh. Still, the small wound was enough to sink the Marquise de Pompadour into a state of deadly anxiety; counseled by those surrounding her, she began to ready her baggage to leave the court, after the example—she had feared nothing so much as something like that—of Madame de Châteauroux, who had had to leave the monarch's life once and for all so that he could die free of sin after making confession, that time, thirteen years before, when he suffered an attack of that terrible illness in Metz—an illness that was expected to be fatal, except by death itself. And all because the king's confessor and the Jesuit clique spread the rumor that Louis was badly wounded, just to drive the detested concubine from the palace. Just when the Marquise de Pompadour was on the verge of leaving, she received contradictory information about the monarch's condition, and her natural attunement to things, which had never betrayed her, advised her to stay. She herself also participated in the battle of rumors, making everyone believe she had finally left. She thereby confused a fair portion of her adversaries. And so she waited in anguish for hour upon hour, until the king, having come round to the awareness that his wound was not by any means a mortal one, dismissed his confessor, packed his sins away for confession on a timelier occasion, and sent for his eternal lady friend.

Few concrete details came out concerning the attack. The regicide—who was Robert François Damiens, born in 1715, the son of farmers, and a footman by occupation—turned out to be a poor fanatic inflamed by the constant diatribes he had heard at his patrons' home against the king, his ministers, and the court. Although it was suspected that the members of the Parlement of Paris—which was engaged in a long-standing struggle with Versailles and with the archbishop of Paris, who had even gone so far as to threaten them with excommunication—had had a hand in the affair, there was no way to prove that. The unfortunate Damiens, locked up in the dungeons of the provost of Versailles, with his feet mangled by torture, had the fortitude not to implicate anyone else. The courage that in his youth had earned him the name of Robert the Devil did not abandon him—not even when he suffered the cruelest tortures. He took all the blame upon himself and endured alone the frightful punishment that awaited him. He firmly held to what he had declared in the beginning and even put the affirmation to the monarch in writing: he had attacked Louis because it was necessary to give him a warning from providence. The people of France needed the king not to be distracted from looking after them. He had never wanted to kill him, had only wanted to give him a warning. The king's agents were also unable to learn the identity of the mysterious gentleman with whom Damiens had spoken in a tavern in Versailles shortly before the attempt on the king's life and who, they were certain, was the key to the conspiracy. You were grateful for the cold of that winter that required you to cover your head with the bright red wool cap Voltaire had given you as a present, for without it, your bald pate made you more conspicuous than a beggar at a court ball. In the beginning, when you learned of the terrible tortures they were subjecting that poor man to so that they might discover your identity—which the unfortunate fellow didn't even know—you wanted to present yourself and make a declaration. But you thought better of it; no one was going to spare Damiens from meeting the same fate as Ravaillac, and if you spoke up, the only thing you'd achieve was to find yourself tangled in a very bothersome business: they'd bring to light your friendship with the philosophes and your dalliance with the wife of the Marshal de Montmorency, a woman who happened to be—Paris is the size of a handkerchief, there's no doubt about it—one of Damiens' employers. The band of Jesuits would see in a Spanish emigrant the perfect figure to place at the head of a conspiracy against the monarch that those who wore the red toga might have instigated. Better to leave things as they were. You avoided become involved in the civil war that different groups of the nobility were waging and that, as you saw with greater and greater clarity, would end up being the cause of the collapse of the thousand-year French reign.

After the attack on Louis, in the course of a veritable marathon of abject and servile oratory, the members of the Parlement rushed to show their devotion to the monarch and their respect for him. What's more, overcome by collective panic, they implored His Majesty to be appointed the ones to judge the infamous regicide. The travesty of a trial was lightning-swift and one-sided: they declared the accused guilty of a crime of lese majesty and handed down the death sentence that the law prescribed in such cases. They did not allow him the possibility of appealing or of asking for clemency; the sentence was to be carried out the day after the verdict was announced. The magistrates thus got rid of that bothersome fellow who had dared to raise his hand against their king convinced that he was fighting for the cause of those who were now condemning him to death.

A strange feeling, a mixture of guilt and pity, made you go to the Place de Grève that morning. There was a large crowd: the good people of Paris did not want to miss out on the spectacle. The fishwives and other merchant women from the markets arrived at the square wreathed in smiles and bundled up in coarse woolen shawls. They were carrying their wares in large baskets, and many of them had also brought their children, who were capering about in the crowd. The men—officials, apprentices of a thousand trades with their broad ill-shaved faces, almost all of them pitted from smallpox—smiled cheerfully. Some of them blew in their cupped palms as they hopped up and down to drive away the cold; others took the edge off it with big swallows of rough brandy. There was a festive atmosphere, shared in by many bourgeois and nobles, though for the nobles, from the windows and the balconies of the buildings that overlooked the square. You were not especially surprised on learning, there in the square, that ladies of noble lineage had rented, for good solid louis, the best situated balconies, directly in front of the spot where the scaffold had been erected.

Peddlers were offering the public roasted chestnuts, hot boiled potatoes, salted fish, milk sweetmeats, and even rag dolls—dressed in cherry-colored garments, each of them with its tiny wig—representing the king. Other dolls, dressed in black-and-white garments and with a great mane of coffee-colored locks made of wool, represented the regicide. A roll of drums heralded the arrival of the criminal. He arrived standing in a manure cart drawn by two oxen. A long rosary hung from his hands, which were bound together at the wrists. At his side, a priest dressed in black was praying with his eyes half closed. The crowd suddenly fell silent and parted to allow the detachment of soldiers preceding the two-wheeled cart to pass through. On the scaffold, unnoticed as he climbed up on it, the executioner was waiting, along with his assistants. The man was big and strong. Defying the cold that had settled over the square, he was wearing a black leather vest without a shirt underneath, thus showing off his powerful arms. Beneath the scaffold a pyre had been built. The soldiers formed a semicircular barricade around it, measuring some forty paces. It was there that the final part of the execution would take place. Four uncastrated Percherons pawed the ground nervously, breathing out clouds of steam through their nostrils as, violently shaking their heads, they tried to free themselves from the halters tied to the timbers of the scaffolding. Finally the cart with the condemned man arrived at the foot of the scaffold. Two soldiers lifted him out bodily, and carried him to the scaffold, for the unfortunate man could not walk, since his feet, cruelly thrust into ankle boots of rough leather, had been smashed to pieces during the torture to which they had been subjected. When Damiens reached the top, he knelt, raised his eyes to heaven, commended his soul to his Creator—perhaps still placing his hopes in the promise to alleviate his torment that the Virgin had made him with her syrupy tears—and offered a devoted kiss to the crucifix the priest placed before his face. Meanwhile the executioner, aware of the enormous responsibility he bore and having taken it to heart, was carefully making a last survey to ensure that everything was in order: he stirred the iron ladles in each of the three cauldrons heating over burning coals to make sure that the liquids inside them had come to a good boil; he ordered one of his aides, a redheaded boy who had no ears, to blow on the coals under the one in the middle, for the thick substance it contained was not bubbling sufficiently; he carefully inspected once more the crude table that held the instruments for his work—an ax, several butcher knives of different sizes, some rusty iron chains, and two blacksmith's tongs. He was pleased to find that everything was as it should be but still passed his expert fingertips along the edge of the ax and the knives to make certain that they were well honed. By eye, he compared the heights of the stool and of the butcher's block that were in the middle of the scaffold, and he was reassured to see that they were properly adjusted for the function they were meant to serve. He took a look at the horses and the pyre of dry wood piled up beneath the scaffold. He did not want the least detail to disturb his work, because, after all, the execution of a criminal guilty of the crime of lese majesty is something that doesn't happen every day. In fact, it hadn't happened for 147 years, since the madman Ravaillac had put an end to the incredible life of Henry IV. And now, a century and a half later, the execution was going to be repeated, step by step, as enshrined by tradition. But in this case he, Pierre Brachet, a useless man in his wife's eyes, who couldn't even kill a hen with compassion, was the one who was going to perform the solemn task. Hence it was more than a week since he had had a drink, he hadn't even touched a prostitute, and he had been praying to God for everything he hadn't prayed to him for even once before in his whole life, asking him for the self-control and firm pulse that would let him discharge his historic task with dignity.

When the priest had finished praying for the soul of the condemned man, two guards carried the criminal over to the stool in the center of the scaffolding and held him on his feet, in front of the little stool, for him to hear the ritual pardoning of the executioner. Damiens forgave him with a nod of his head. Once the ceremony of the pardon was over, two of the executioner's assistants roughly but solemnly removed his shirt, his trousers, and his high shoes, leaving him dressed only in skimpy white underwear that reached down to the middle of his thighs. They immediately sat him down on the stool and tied him to a post by a chain wound around his waist. Another assistant brought the butcher's block over to the criminal's knees and put the man's right hand on top of it. The rite was about to begin. A drum roll silenced the crowd. Then the royal crier, standing in the middle of the scaffold, unrolled a parchment, and reading in a very loud voice, gave notice to all those present of the monstrous crime that the ruffian Robert Damiens had committed against the sacred person of the sovereign and of the just punishment that the Parlement of Paris had prescribed for him. Once his declamation was over, the drums rolled once again as the executioner gazed at the crowd, as nervous and grave as an actor making his debut at the Opéra. Finally, with a well-aimed blow of the ax, he lopped off the hand that had attacked the monarch. The hand falling to the platform of the scaffold seemed to be directing the clamor that came from the crowd. The redheaded assistant poured boiling sulphur over the bloody stump. Damiens gave an emotionless shout from deep within that first shocked and then excited the spectators. Pierre, the executioner, asked for the tongs that had been heated red-hot and placed the end of them on Damiens' chest; he skillfully ripped off a good chunk of flesh as his assistants carefully poured melted wax and lead into the wound. Damiens, perhaps self-hypnotized, did not even moan. The Virgin, when all was said and done, had fulfilled her promise: the pain, the martyrdom, his body itself no longer existed. They were something very far away; his soul had already passed through heaven's gates. The executioner went on with his work with the tongs until not a millimeter of skin had been spared. The body of the condemned man, smeared with blood, sulphur, lead, and wax, called to mind the Greek statues made of bronze just after they were removed from the sea. The silence of the victim communicated itself to the crowd. With their eyes wide open, people didn't believe what they were seeing: pieces of flesh the size of an apple were torn out of the body of that man, the wounds bared his skeleton, bathed in melted lead, and yet he remained dauntless, his mind far away from that torture. There were any number of women and several old men who knelt and began to pray, convinced that that man was a saint. The executioner, disconcerted but determined not to lose his composure, scrutinized Damiens' body and concluded that it had been punished enough. He ordered him to be untied and pulled at the regicide's shoulder four or five times with the tongs, there where the post had protected him. Afterward, each of his wrists and ankles was shackled, and he was carried down to the esplanade. Halters removed, two of the Percherons were placed on each side of the criminal. Four chains fastened to the victim's limbs were tied to the harnesses of a horse apiece, as at the same time the pyre was lit. When the executioner was certain that everything was in place and tied securely, he ordered the horses to be led off at a trot. Suspended in the air with his limbs outstretched, Damiens looked, for a moment, like a Christ falling from heaven. The horses were whipped to make them pull harder, each of them toward a different cardinal point of the compass, but only the man's left arm and right leg were torn off; the other two limbs would not part from his body. No matter how hard the animals were whipped in the rump, they did not succeed in completely quartering the wretched man. Disconcerted, the executioner had to use an enormous butcher knife to cut his trunk loose, as he wondered whether more or less the same thing had happened to the hapless Ravaillac. When he amputated Damiens' right arm, he discovered to his horror that the unfortunate man was still alive and was even able to utter the word *mother*. "Mother," he heard him say, "Mother!" Pierre could not bear this. Deeply perturbed, he violated the protocol set by tradition and himself carried what was left of Damiens and threw it on the pyre. "Mother, I thank you!" was the last thing he heard him say. The thick cloud of smoke with the acrid smell of burned flesh rose high in the air, holding the gaze of an ecstatic crowd, which, in a fevered trance, began to scream and applaud in what amounted to a convulsion. It was without question, as Damiens himself had said when he heard his sentence, a "day very hard to bear."

You were standing near the scaffold; you almost didn't move during the two hours and some minutes that that horror lasted. You contemplated with fascination Damiens' indifferent face; you saw for the last time, shortly before he was flung upon the pyre, his beautiful white teeth that gleamed even more brightly for being the one part of his body that had escaped torture. The crowd began to disperse; in people's faces you thought you saw a strange mixture of amazement, pleasure, and fear. Almost no one spoke, or people did so very quietly, as though they wished to show respect for the ashes of the victim. In the windows and on the balconies that surrounded the square, you saw tears, grimaces of disgust, and sensual smiles. Your own face, however, was more inexpressive than ever—if that is possible—and your brain forced itself in vain to grasp an idea you could not put into words. You wished d'Alembert were with you; he was perhaps the only one who could help put an end to your confusion. His penetrating analytical mind would have guided you step by step until you reached the thread to pull upon in order to undo the tangle. You would then have been able to explain to yourself how such an atrocity could occur at the height of the eighteenth century, in that era when reason, stability, and good taste appeared to have prevailed, when Gabriel spent hours at a time contemplating empty spaces and then filled them with materials as rough as stone and mortar but succeeded in erecting perfect buildings of magnificently balanced proportions, ethereal ones, it might be said, whose contours followed those which had come from the hand of Michelangelo two centuries before, lines that master himself had laid down merely as an extension of the ones the Greek geometers had traced more than two millennia earlier. In an era when one had only to sit down to listen to a concert to become aware of the domain of sounds—marvelously given forth by instruments made with such exquisite craftsmanship and affection that they in effect captured within their wood and metal the sighs, the panting, and the songs of the sirens who had not succeeded in driving Odysseus mad—that once released in space combined in a celestial harmony with an abrupt, cruel, and precise rhythm, only finally to break out into delightful melodies, incubated in the souls of the musicians of the eighteenth century, the greatest who had ever existed. In an era when the keenest intelligences forced themselves to the limit of the superhuman in order to understand the laws that rule nature, to translate the brute signs that are the key to life and death, to establish, in monumental works, the principles of human conduct, and to propose, in other works no less extensive, how we must relate to one another in order to arrive at the establishment of a just, educated, and prosperous society. In that era when everything was claiming to be modern and to have come a long way from its primitive stages, the preserve of ignorant and savage men—in that proud and haughty century, a man was quartered in a public square before a crowd of gratified witnesses, because he dared to do what came to scarcely more than pricking the skin of a monarch who had traded his duties toward his people for the delights of the flesh. But d'Alembert wasn't there to help you. The last time you had news of him, a couple of months before, you learned that he was hidden away in some town in Normandy, frightened by his own work, incapable of continuing a task that had already been subjected to three condemnations, and to harassment by the authorities any number of times. There was finally happening what Diderot, with his gentle calf's eyes, had suggested to you the day you met him: "Jean will abandon the *Encyclopédie.* In the long run, his orphan's caution will prove more powerful that his fits of philosophic enthusiasm."

The supper was delicious. He had been served a thick onion soup, with sharp grated cheese and thick slices of fried bread on top. The main dish—beef cooked in spices—was in no way inferior to the famous dishes of the *maître de la cuisine* at Versailles. The meal was accompanied by a bottle of red wine from Burgundy, at least five years old, and very white bread, fresh out of the oven, light as a feather despite the enormous size of the loaf, "bread of the kind that can be found only in the provinces," Rasero thought. The good food and good wine relaxed him little by little until, despite his mind's insistence on remembering, his sadness finally fled, yielding its place to a warm sensuality. The serving maid brought him the desserts: several kinds of fresh fruit and little pastries filled with cream and wild blackberry jelly. Rasero looked at her as she served them: she was a very young woman—she couldn't have been more than seventeen—short in stature but well proportioned; her flesh generously filled a pink skin that looked as smooth and fresh as that of the apples in the basket she had placed on the table.

"What's your name, my pretty girl?"

"Annette, sir," the girl answered with a flirtatious smile that bared a double row of little gleaming white teeth. A pair of dimples formed in her cheeks, perhaps a bit too red for the taste of a courtier. This young woman is going to live to be at least a hundred, Rasero thought.

"Would you like coffee, and brandy or a liqueur?"

"What kind of liqueurs do you have?"

"We have mint, cherry, and almond . . . I recommend the almond; it's really good: I made it myself."

"Then I'll have coffee and almond liqueur, Annette."

"It will take just a moment, sir."

Her buttocks, round and sturdy, swayed gracefully as she headed, with quick little steps, to the kitchen. It would be a fine thing to make love to that girl, Rasero said to himself, and began to think about proposing that she spend the night with him for a few louis. He had made up his mind to do that, when he saw with dejection that it was not she who brought the coffee but a corpulent grown man. He was wearing trousers and a brown cloth vest, a very clean white shirt, and below his paunch, a white apron spattered with wine stains.

"I hope you've found everything to your liking, Monsieur Rasero," the heavyset man said with a smile. His face might have been handsome, but the marks of a severe case of smallpox, his ill-shaved beard, and the loss of his incisors made it irredeemably ugly.

"Altogether, it was a truly exquisite meal."

"So you really liked it then?" the man said, very pleased, as he sat down at the table without invitation and poured himself a glass of the almond liqueur. "Ah sir, my wife is a jewel. She has a gift for cooking; there is no little dish, however simple it may seem, that doesn't turn into food for the gods when it's prepared by her hands. That's why I fell in love with her, I swear it, sir!—and I'm still in love with her after twenty years of eating her marvelous dishes! I can't understand why the Lord has been so generous with me—even though, to tell the truth, I'm not a wicked man, just a bit of a tippler and talkative, that's all." At that, he let out an earsplitting peal of laughter, as though he'd heard the funniest joke in his whole life. "And that young one, my Annette, inherited her mother's hands. The supper you've just eaten was prepared by her, all by herself, believe me. And what do you think of this liqueur? Try it, sir . . . To your good health! Don't tell me that it doesn't seem as if the angels themselves made it." He burst into laughter again.

The sweet liquid that was evaporating on Rasero's palate, impregnating it with the subtle taste of almonds, testified to the words of that burly, good-humored man.

"It is indeed delicious," Rasero said.

"Ah sir. If I were given to boasting, I'd tell you how many important people, of the most noble lineage, have eaten at my inn. And do you know what? All of them, absolutely all of them, have come back again. Nobody has yet tasted my Christine's dishes and not come back for more. The great Voltaire, do you know him?"—he did not wait for an answer—"has eaten at my inn more than twenty times; whenever he journeyed to or from Paris he'd stop here, no matter what time of the day or night it was. Once, shortly before he went off to Prussia, he turned up at the inn at four in the morning and made my Christine get up to make him crêpes with mushrooms, his favorite dish. Haven't you tasted them? Oh no, of course not; ah, you poor man, Rasero! You poor man who haven't tasted the crêpes with mushrooms that my wife makes. But you'll be back, like all the others, and then I'll have her make you some, I promise you, sir."

"I hope so," the Malagan replied very seriously. The man looked him in the eye, barely smiling; then suddenly he again broke into hearty laughter.

"Ah, Monsieur Rasero! You're a very likable man; it's certain you'll come back."

He said this roguishly, holding out his arms; then he effusively embraced his guest, who was rising to his feet, and insisted on accompanying him to his room, which was on an upper floor of the inn.

"Are you going to read? I can bring you another candle," he said to him on the way upstairs.

"No, thank you, I've enough light with this," Rasero answered, gesturing with his head toward the small candlestick with a candle burned halfway down that he was holding in his hand. The man went into the bedroom first and inspected every detail and even tested the air with his nose, several times raising his face and dilating his nostrils with a mistrustful expression.

"Everything is in order," he finally said with satisfaction. "Have a good night's rest, Monsieur Rasero." His great peals of laughter accompanied him down the stairs. He's a happy man, Rasero thought with a certain envy.

It was a very hot night, and so he decided not to wear his nightshirt but to go to bed in his underwear. Before doing so, he took out of his baggage his bedtime reading, the biblical Book of Revelation. Many years before, he had acquired the habit of rereading it before going to sleep; in fact it was in the summer of '45—a year of terrible visions—that he began what was to become that nightly ritual . . .

You had recently settled in Paris, very happy at having finally left the court and its horde of schemers. You celebrated the event in your town house, drinking plenty of bubbling wine from Champagne, eating crawfish, and frolicking about with your tireless friend, Claudia de Saissac, a warm and generous woman with few equals—with long limbs, large eyes, and an enormous mouth, able to down pleasure whole, in a single gulp. The two of you made love as though your lives depended on it; you pinched each other, bit each other, and went about your licentious coupling with the vigor that can come only from knowing that you are young and eternal. You had, naturally, a number of visions, although you didn't pay them very much attention; the champagne in your head and the avid mouth of Madame de Saissac on your body distracted you from them. What's more, you were tired of those images that had lately been repeating themselves monotonously: soldiers dressed in green, covered with dust, with heavy rifles slung over their shoulders, marching through cities in ruins; the clumsy iron vehicles, advancing slowly and implacably, grinding to pieces any debris that appeared in their path . . . nothing but war and its consequences, as though those phantoms that visited you during orgasm had nothing better with which to be concerned. As dawn broke, the two of you made love for the last time of that night; you thought you couldn't come again, your back hurt, and you felt drier than a grape lying forgotten in the desert sun. But the skillful contortions of your friend, along with the work her tongue did on your ear, managed eventually to make you explode. It was an intense and prolonged orgasm, a fruit ripened by excitement and weariness, that plunged you into a terrifying vision: what you had seen fleetingly just a few days before, those unclear images of Asians being burned to cinders in seconds, repeated itself, but now you had more time to look at the horror. It was a big city alongside the sea; enormous iron ships appeared at the end of streets with people—all of them Asians—hurrying up and down in both directions. Suddenly, the light . . . a light of a greater intensity than any you had seen in your life. It was like peering into the heart of the sun, a blue-white light that reminded you of the one inside the ovens at Sèvres when they reach a heat sufficient to harden the porcelain. But here the light was immense; it covered everything. In an instant—which to you seemed eternal—the terrible intense glow melted every object in its reach. The buildings, the vehicles, and the iron posts along the streets were softened in seconds, as though they were made of wax, and the scorched debris mounted upward with prodigious speed, forming a giant whirlwind. The people—you managed to see only some of them—were incinerated instantly, each in a minuscule flash, like one of the little balls of phosphorus your teacher Ulloa smilingly watched explode in the air when he removed them from the flask of oil that contained them. The light disappeared at once; a dense darkness took its place. That was due to the dust, the earth, the debris, the remains of human beings that overhead, very high up, had formed a great cloud hiding the sun. Madame de Saissac smiled in satisfaction seeing you with your closed eyelids aslant with pleasure. You moved over to one side, embraced her, and pretended to be asleep; your head was full of light and little balls of exploding phosphorus. After a time, your friend, taking care not to awaken you, got out of bed and dressed; she wrote a note, left it on the night table, and went out of the bedroom. As soon as you were alone, you leaped out of bed and began to pace back and forth the length of the room. You were not prepared to face up to the vision you had just experienced, you did not want to think about it, nor were you interested in understanding its meaning. You felt genuine terror at the thought of considering it thoroughly; your one fervent wish was to forget it. You looked around the room in the hope that your eyes might draw your mind to something else, you took a generous swallow of wine, and you even tried to whistle a little tune that was popular in those days. It was useless; the light had nested in your brain like a grub in a fruit, and there was no way to banish from your memory the images of those bodies being burned to ashes. You next tried to read, and picked up the first book at hand, Montesquieu's *Persian Letters.* You opened it at random and tried to concentrate on what lay on the page. But the delightful, sensual descriptions of a harem in Baghdad, with its good-looking women whose hair was as black as pitch and whose eyes were as green as olives, who barely hid their nakedness beneath diaphanous silks and sighed with melancholy as they thought of that handsome young man who had looked through the narrow jalousies of the palace and passionately wished that he was clever enough to fool the odious black eunuchs watching over them, did not go far toward occupying your mind or removing from it the accursed light that obsessed you. You put that book down and picked up another one; it was a bulky old Bible, the only keepsake of your mother you still had. You also opened this one at random: "And the fourth angel poured out his vial upon the sun; and power was given unto him to scorch men with fire. And men were scorched with great heat . . . ," you read in surprise. It was the Book of Revelation. You couldn't help being struck by the remarkable coincidence between what you had just seen and what the apostle described. That occupied your thoughts and therefore relaxed you. You decided to read Revelation from the beginning. You had done so before, but so long ago that you had practically forgotten it. The Bible and religious subjects, although they once mattered to you, had not held your interest for a long time now. Why waste my time, you often said to yourself, studying something that doesn't exist, or if by some chance it does exist, isn't going to affect in the least either me or the world I live in? Now, on the other hand, from the moment you began to read the introduction, you were fascinated, and not because the terrifying vision that you had just experienced had aroused in you a sudden religious fervor—far from it. What powerfully attached you to the text by Christ's youngest disciple, what sparked in you enormous feeling for him, was his use of a simple verb: *to see.* "And I turned to see the voice that spake with me. And being turned, I saw seven golden candlesticks . . ." The Book of Revelation is the description of a vision, or perhaps of several. Saint John, like you, saw something that was not in his world; he saw and recounted what he saw, that was all. He was very different from the other prophets, who did not speak through their own mouth, did not see through their own eyes, did not write with their own hand: they were mere intermediaries of the divine will. Could it be that John had his tremendous visions while mounted on the rump of that beautiful Jewish woman? you wondered, smiling. In any event, you realized that reading the apostle calmed you, consoled you. You read Revelation slowly, without trying to understand or interpret the images that came to your mind, letting them pass through your imagination as what they were: visions no less real for being impossible. "Even so, come, Lord Jesus. The grace of our Lord Jesus Christ be with you all. Amen." You read and fell fast asleep. Your mind was finally exquisitely empty, and your body, at peace, began to regain the strength that your dear friend, with her love play, had robbed you of . . .

From that time on, Rasero fell into the habit of using the Book of Revelation as a sort of sedative. Reading it had the same effect on him that boiling-hot poppy tea had on his beloved friend, the Marquise de Pompadour: she drank it before going to bed, and without it she was unable to get to sleep. As he had so many other times, Rasero opened the book—although it was not part of his mother's Bible now. A short time after acquiring his inclination to read it over and over, the realization came to him that the whole Bible was very heavy, and therefore unnecessarily burdensome to take to bed with him. Why, after all, force his arms to support more than a thousand pages of thick parchment when he was interested in at most forty of them? He decided then to produce a manuscript. For that he used some folios of Angoulême paper that his friend d'Alembert had given him as a gift, perhaps with the hidden intention of spurring him to write. He spent several afternoons transcribing the biblical verses of the apostle in the careful calligraphy that Fray Silvestre, his first instructor, had taught him. Without knowing why, he decided to leave blank the space that remained when he came to the end of a chapter, so that he used up a great deal more paper than he'd have had to. Nonetheless, when he finished his work, he still had left more than half the folios he had tenderly cut to measure one foot by a quarter of a foot.

He was on the point of taking the manuscript to be bound—he had already secured a handsome scarlet-dyed calfskin to serve as the cover—when to his elation he discovered what was behind his impulse to leave so much space blank. That night, as he was coming out of the Opéra, after seeing the performance of an unbearable drama by Rameau, he invited the painter François Boucher and a pair of pretty actresses to his house. The artist brought Rasero up to date on the gossip and intrigues at court; they drank heartily to the health of the recently appointed academician François Voltaire—"François *de* Voltaire," the painter corrected him in an ironic tone of voice. Amid laughter and with obscene gesticulation, Boucher told his friend how Madame de Pompadour was seeing her beauty, her health, and her charms further undermined with each passing day, though not her influence upon the king, whose friend and confidante she was becoming with the passage of time, rather than his mistress. "And his procuress," one of the actresses added in a fit of laughter. The bacchanalia lasted until dawn, when, naked, drunk, and overcome by sleep, they lay like rag dolls, some on the bed, others on the carpet.

A sharp headache awakened Rasero. When he opened his eyes, he from the floor saw his friend comfortably settled in an armchair. He looked fresh and happy. He was resting his legs on a footstool and was holding on his right thigh some blank sheets of Angoulême paper on which he appeared to be drawing something. Not without great effort, Rasero got to his feet to see what the painter was doing. Across from them, the two young women were sound asleep on the bed. They were naked, and the early morning cold had impelled them to cuddle in each other's arms as though they were a pair of lovers. Boucher's skillful hand was swiftly tracing on the paper the young women's contours. For drawing, he was using a bit of charcoal he had taken from the hearth. Little by little, the two bodies took shape on the paper. The thighs, the buttocks, the breasts took on volume when the artist's little finger rubbed the charcoal dust on the sheet of paper; the tangled tresses, those of one of them blonde and those of the other with a reddish cast, emerged fluidly from the piece of charcoal, as though they were rolled up inside it. He made a very beautiful sketch; the image of the two women with their bodies intertwined in sleep was at once gentle and erotic, peaceful and joyous. It pleased Rasero very much, and he told the artist so. With satisfaction, Boucher signed the sketch and gave it to his friend. "A souvenir of this mad night," he told him. When he went over to put the unused sheets of paper back on the writing desk, he spied the manuscript of Revelation. "So you're interested in the divine now, my friend?" Boucher asked, making no effort to hide a mocking smile.

"The divine? Not at all. I'm interested in visions," Rasero answered a little diffidently.

As he leafed through the manuscript, Boucher remembered the solemn, cavernous voice of Brother Caussin as he read them the verses of Saint John in the Collège de Reims. The youngsters were overcome with terror on hearing the awesome descriptions of the punishments that awaited those unfortunates who had never learned to live in harmony with the teachings of the Lamb, of the implacable judgment that hung over the head of each sinner who had not repented in time. On reading the biblical passages and noticing the large blank spaces between the chapters, an idea crossed the painter's mind. "Monsieur Rasero, something has occurred to me. Please let me take the manuscript with me; I'll return it in a month." Rasero couldn't come up with a reason to say no; a certain reticence kept him from telling his friend that he needed that text in order to go to sleep at night. He resigned himself to lugging about his mother's old Bible for thirty days more and lent the manuscript to Boucher, wondering why the devil he wanted it.

When the month was out, Boucher returned the manuscript to his friend on the dot. He sent it, wrapped in a length of cotton cloth, by courier, who also brought a letter addressed to Rasero:

Dear friend,

I am unable to understand—and, naturally, I have no business trying to do so anyway—what reasons led you to transcribe on that satin-finished Angoulême paper the work of the youngest of the apostles. What I was able to understand as soon as I began to leaf through it is that my mind has treasured an uncommon memory of it since childhood's tenderest years, and I could not resist the temptation to pay tribute to that memory. I am a painter and have never been anything else, and it is as such that I wanted to pay my tribute. Betraying your trust but placing my hopes in your understanding, I dared illustrate, in the blank spaces I found, certain scenes from Revelation. I am sorry to have done so without your consent. I have often wondered whether perhaps you left those spaces blank for a deliberate purpose. If that was the case, may the earth swallow me up as I await your forgiveness, for without question I have ruined your work. But, even so, I would be lying to you if I said that I regret what I have done. Ah, my friend, I enjoyed making these illustrations enormously. Who knows what hidden ferment suddenly exploded inside me when I read the saint's passages and when my hand reached to create on paper his hallucinating visions, but it made me experience a delightful and frenetic month. In short, the manuscript is yours, and I now return it to you, either utterly ruined or enriched. With all my soul I hope the latter is the case. Yours,

François Boucher

Rasero anxiously undid the wrapping of the manuscript. He saw twenty-two splendid illustrations in sepia aquatint. Traces at once light and vigorous re-created the fantastic visions: the celestial court with its four creatures around the Lord; featherlight angels sounding the terrible trumpets; spirited chargers ridden by the lords of disaster; monsters with ten crowned heads and long dragon's tails; Constantinople, the eternal whore, beautiful, imperious and perverted; fire pouring out of a gigantic chalice which consumes the entire human race; the Divine Mother, cruelly slit in two and abandoned in the desert, helplessly contemplating the Evil One as he devours the fruit of her womb; rivers of blood flooding a third of everything that exists; clouds of giant locusts swallowing the verdure in their path; pagan priestesses of Syria, worshipers of Astarte, fornicating with Baal and his army of devils. And finally, the light: the serene light of the just, blessing until the end of time those who by their acts have freed themselves of all evil.

Rasero spent a long time in rapt contemplation of the manuscript. He was happy; he never suspected that that naïve diversion of his would become a work of art. By the same courier, he sent the painter a case of bordeaux wine, aged since the days of the Regency, which had been given to him by the wife of the Marshal de Montmorency. Along with it, he sent a very simple letter:

> Dear Boucher,
> Your inspired impertinence has enriched my manuscript to the heights of the sublime. Yours,
> Fausto Rasero

That same day he took the work to be bound in the workshop of the printer who rented the bottom floor of his town house. On the smooth sheet of parchment to be used as the title page, he ordered printed in gold letters

THE BOOK OF REVELATION
By Saint John
Illustrated by François Boucher

This was the book he reread that night in Troyes and that accompanied him on his bedside table until the last day of his life . . .

The light of the candle lasted only a little while; he barely had had time to read a couple of chapters of Revelation when the room was plunged into darkness. The heat kept him from falling asleep. He could hear in his gut the path traversed by the magnificent supper he had consumed. Lacking the energy to think, he distracted himself by looking out the window at a tiny star in the constellation of Orion. Sleep gradually overcame him, and he fell fast asleep before he knew it. As he closed his eyes, the image of the star lingered in his mind.

His nose was dreaming of the aroma of muscats at his old mansion in Málaga, when he felt a body next to his. Unlike the heat of the night, that of this body did not bother him; on the contrary, it seemed altogether pleasant. Still asleep, he turned toward it and slowly caressed the soft forms. His hands unhurriedly ran over the shoulders, arms, breast, belly, thighs, and legs of that delectable body that smelled of peaches. The woman clasped him to her and held him tight. They lay there a long time caressing each other, until Rasero finally awoke from his sleep. He opened his eyes and could see in the semidarkness the face of the girl, who was keeping her eyes shut and biting her lower lip. To be on top of her was a real delight; her body, ample and youthful, seemed like a cloud of cotton. The girl opened her legs and began to knock against Rasero's privates very hard with hers. It was not easy to penetrate her: her vagina was very tight and narrow. "Perhaps she's still a virgin," he thought. He had to use all his strength, and with a brutal thrust of his haunch he was finally able to nestle inside her. The girl, on feeling herself full, moaned very softly and speeded up the motions of her buttocks. Rasero could hardly restrain her violent movements; several times he was on the point of being pushed out of her by her frantic heaves. He tried to calm her by kissing her neck as he said in her ear in a very low voice, "Gently, darling, gently . . ."

Finally, they managed to match each other's rhythm and coupled for a long time, like a single being rocking itself in time to its desire. When Rasero reached orgasm, he opened his eyes and still saw only semidarkness. But it was a different darkness. He was in a vast enclosed space filled with people occupying theater seats—something like the Opéra, although this enclosed space was larger and had no boxes nor oil lamps nor decorations on the sides. Dark-colored curtains covered the walls. The faces of the people were dimly lit by the bright beam of light coming from the stage—or from where the stage should have been, because in place of it there was a large wall on which Rasero saw two gigantic human figures, those of a man and a woman, moving inside a room. It was a hallucinating image: the two beings, flat against the wall, as though it were a mural but one that moved. They came and went in the room; now they sat down, now they stood up and embraced and kissed. All of a sudden, the woman drew away, and seating herself in an armchair, began to weep bitterly. The audience, for its part, gave the images its full attention. Rasero had never seen anything like it, either in his world or in his visions. The figures moved like shadows on the wall, although they were luminous colored shadows, sharp and clear down to the last detail. "Ah, Monsieur Rasero, this has been marvelous," he heard Annette say. "Ever since I saw you come into the inn, I knew it would be marvelous." Rasero experienced a very curious sensation as he looked at the woman's body, faintly illuminated by the moon's glow. Her full contours seemed rounder to him than ever; he delightedly contemplated the volume of that flesh. In amazement, he felt her breasts, her back, her belly. He had never been as aware as he was now of the depth of things, of that third dimension that prevents our being like shadows created on a wall.

"Monsieur Rasero, I should like to ask you for something."

"Whatever you like, my girl. I can't refuse you anything now."

"I've always wanted to live in Paris. Take me with you. I know how to cook very well, I'll keep house, you'll never lack for anything. Please."

"But what would your parents say, Annette?"

"They'll consent. They too want me to go to Paris. I have no future in this town; they know that very well. They don't want me to spend my life waiting on people passing through. In Paris, I'll be able to learn many things. I may even marry a rich man."

"You aren't even there yet, and already you're thinking of abandoning me."

"I beg your pardon, Monsieur Rasero. If you wish, I'll stay at your side my whole life long. I know that you're a very good man."

"Well, we'll see."

"No. Please say yes," the girl pleaded as she held him close.

Rasero couldn't decide; the young woman's request had taken him by surprise. He hadn't lived with anyone since his arrival in Paris. Only old Amelia came three times a week to clean his house. He never ate there; he had fallen into the habit of lunching in a tavern across from his town house and always dined either in some café or at the house of friends. Could he get used to Annette's plump presence in his house? On the other hand, he had to admit, he was tempted by the idea of being well taken care of in his home and of eating every day the delicious dishes that—he was certain of it—the girl was to prepare for him. Moreover, she was a charming young woman, and really deserved someone's help. He had to agree that it wasn't right for her to have to spend her life waiting on ill-mannered louts. He could educate her, teach her how and what to read, bring out her best points. He could make of her a very attractive, refined woman; it would not be hard for her to find a good husband. Not without a smile, Rasero thought that at one and the same moment he was being offered a cook, a lover, a companion, and a friend. It was too much, more than enough to overcome his natural unsociability, his long-standing instinct for living the life of a solitary man.

"Very well, Annette, I'll take you with me. But it will be after I return from Ferney, within three or four weeks. You must be ready by the time I come back, agreed?"

"Thank you, Monsieur Rasero. You won't regret it, I swear to you," the happy girl said as she embraced and kissed him until she was exhausted.

They made love twice more, and each time Rasero saw once again that strange public hall full of people watching the colored shadows gliding along on the wall.

The next day, as he was traveling in his carriage, Rasero tried to make sense of the vision he had had three times the night before. He leafed through a little memorandum book bound in black leather. For many years now, he had noted down in it the visions that came to him. In fact, he had sorted them according to an odd taxonomy: "War" was the title of the thickest packet of annotated pages. In them he had described, in a succinct, almost cryptic style, a great number of visions that he took to be related to military engagement. One could read, for example, "January 20, 1741. Columns of soldiers parade down a broad avenue. To the rear, vehicles without draft animals advance, dragging behind them what appear to be cannons"; "March 30, 1742. A large cellar full of people, almost all of them women, children, and the aged. They are clinging to one another in terror. A man is vomiting against a wall. A strange war: everyone is participating in it"; "January 20, 1743. Immense expanses covered with snow. Defeated soldiers sleep and die there"; "March 17, 1744. A four-story building cracks apart like an egg. Clouds of fire light up the night"; "June 15, 1751. An iron device spits out live flames. The fire burns a shack; Asian men come out of it. Outside, they are met with a rain of bullets"; "May 11, 1757. Men, apparently Arabs, fire from the windows of a building at soldiers in the street who take refuge behind a large vehicle." The descriptions filled any number of pages. He had so many of this sort, often so much alike, that in many cases he simply noted, "July 15, 1743. Like July 2, 1743," or else he noted down no description at all, only the date on which he had had the vision.

The second group had "Landscapes" as its title, and in it he recorded visions of strange places, in the same style: "May 17, 1742. Enormous city. Very high buildings. The streets have very smooth paving. Many people are walking on either side of it. In the middle, vehicles without draft animals move along in both directions"; "August 10, 1752. A street in full daylight. A great many shop windows displaying very odd merchandise. People peer into them from outside, fascinated"; "November 15, 1753. A street. Night. It is brightly lit by an infinite number of little glass ampules of various sizes that give off a yellow light, though some give off a red light"; "April 12, 1758. Field. A broad, flat expanse. A vehicle without draft animals driven from on top by a man; the rear wheels are very large. It drags along behind it several blades that plow the soil." As in the previous case, many visions were repeated and some were noted only by date.

The third group was named "Devices" and included a long list of vehicles and apparatuses of all sorts of shapes and sizes: "February 19, 1741. Vehicle without draft animals. It appears to be made of iron. Black. Glass windows, with four wheels of dark material. It moves swiftly; it gives off a bluish smoke through a little tube in the rear"; "March 4, 1742. Iron ship. Gray color. Very large—some hundred paces long—and has no sails. Two enormous chimneys in the middle. On either side, on deck, rows of gray tubes that appear to be large cannons"; "July 8, 1742. A device that flies! I saw it suspended in the air. Gray in color, four wings, the two front ones very large, the rear ones small. At its tip it has a sort of dart; I believe that that is what propels it"; "December 10, 1743. A vehicle with two wheels, very thin, that look like hoops. A man seated in the middle of it causes it to go forward by moving his legs. Curious device"; "April 14, 1745. Two-wheeled vehicle. It resembles the others, but is wider and cruder, and the man who is driving it does not move his legs. Very fast"; "June 1, 1750. Iron ship. Red and black. It is at a dock; they are unloading large wooden crates from it with an iron hook tied to a rope that, passing over the top of a tower, also of iron, winds around a roller at ground level"; "June 22, 1754. Blue-colored vehicle. Two wheels in front, four in back (two together on either side). A wooden pen in the rear. It is transporting two cows"; "February 20, 1756. I saw a flying machine take off from the ground. Very large, colored white with blue stripes. A row of skylights on each side; in the front two larger windows. The front wings, enormous, each have two darts. It rests on several wheels; it moves forward along a very smooth road, and when it reaches a very high speed, one section of the front wings breaks apart and the machine takes flight! I believe it transports people inside"; "September 15, 1758. Small red vehicle. Four wheels, no roof. Two persons inside. The one on the left has his hands on a hoop; he appears to be driving it. Very swift"; "October 8, 1760. Gigantic tube ending in a point flies up into the sky giving off great puffs of smoke and fire through the bottom part."

The fourth group was called "Curiosities," and in it were listed the visions that didn't fit within the other groups. For example, "September 8, 1741. Clothing. The men, wide, loose trousers. Shirts without lace ruffles or jabots. Some of them are wearing a short, tight-fitting coat, without tails. Their ties are very narrow and long, and have a knot at the neck; they do not wear bow ties. The women, light dresses, without a corselet and without a décolleté neckline. Very short, they scarcely reach below the knee. They look cool and comfortable"; "August 13, 1750. A couple making love!"; "December 20, 1752. A vast enclosed space, very brightly lit. Large pieces of furniture resembling bookcases are lined up, forming aisles. They are filled with colored cardboard boxes and glass bottles. People walk along them, take the objects from the shelves, and deposit them in a sort of little wire basket that glides along on four little wheels"; "October 20, 1753. The Hall of Mirrors at Versailles! With few pieces of furniture. Many people, in their strange attire, are going through it"; "April 17, 1754. A street market. Almost identical to ours, except for certain strange merchandise and people's attire"; "May 2, 1755. A large enclosed space. Behind very long iron tables men and women dressed in blue. Small objects move along the table, apparently on a moving belt. Men inspect them and, in certain cases, manipulate them with pointed iron devices"; "February 28, 1758. An iron tower. Very high, perhaps three hundred paces or more. In the middle and at the top it has ledges from which many people are looking out. It appears to be in Paris." Here Rasero noted, taking advantage of a brief halt along the way: "April 9, 1761. A large concert hall. Without balconies, chandeliers, or decorations. The audience looks, spellbound, toward a large wall that rises there where the stage ought to be. On it, or rather, created on it, enormous human figures (a man and a woman), like colored shadows, move from one side to the other as they talk." He reread it slowly and had to admit that, although it might appear absurd, the description was completely accurate.

The fifth and last group had "Horrors" as its title. The list began, "December 13, 1730. The first . . ." It referred to the first vision that he had had in his life. He did not see any need to describe it; he would never forget it. Now, thirty years later, it was still fresh and clear in his mind, down to the last detail . . .

When it happened to him, he was seven years old and a strange child. Motherless since the very day he was born, and sneered at by his father, he grew up under the care of his nursemaid, Angustias, a gypsy woman with broad hips and full breasts. On the same day that Rasero came into the world, she had given birth to a stillborn baby boy, so that her master's child was able to drink the nourishing milk her breasts had stored up. Angustias was a happy, good woman, who, as can be imagined, loved little Fausto as though he were her own son. She spent long hours rocking him in her lap, singing gypsy *tanguillos* to him, and she was eager to satisfy the slightest whim that the child might have.

Angustias was the only person in the old mansion in the calle Miaja who was convinced that Faustito was not mentally retarded. His father had given up on him when the child reached the age of two and hadn't made the slightest effort to speak. An Oquendo, don Enrique said to himself, as bald as a buzzard and as stupid as an ass. If that man—an idler, a carouser, and a braggart—had the ability to give anyone affection, he obviously did not lavish it on his son. And seeing him grow up, thin, frail, and withdrawn, merely increased his scorn for him. He had dreamed of having a strong, clever, mischievous boy, such as he knew that he himself had been, and not that pale, sickly weakling with a head like a hard-boiled egg that his son was. It wasn't worth the trouble to stay in Málaga to take care of him, since he was being looked after very well by that gypsy woman with cow's udders who never, incidentally, was willing to grant him her favors, even though he knew she was unstinting with them toward the wretched household servants. So don Enrique went off to Madrid, to the court, to enjoy the immense income he had inherited from his wife's dowry. That witch was good for something, he said to himself, though, except for her money, she was about as charming as the plague. He rarely came back to Málaga, and when he did, he was accompanied by a band of ne'er-do-wells from the court; they spent two or three weeks drinking joy-juice, dancing and singing, accompanied by a group of gypsies, going into the mountains to hunt or to the sea to fish for flounder. He almost never saw his son: "Is he still mute?" he asked Angustias. Without waiting for the answer, he turned to Fray Silvestre. "I pity you, my good man. What the devil are you going to teach this boy!" he went on to the placid old Franciscan tosspot he had hired to educate his heir.

Rasero never loved his father. Perhaps his aversion began on the very day of his birth, which, strange though it may seem, he remembered perfectly. He had only to close his eyes to see his father's face that day as he leaned over to look inside his offspring's cradle: ill shaved, his eyes bloodshot, and his breath reeking of wine. "An Oquendo," was his verdict as he looked at him with revulsion. "And what about her—is it certain that she is really dead?"

"As dead as Queen Isabella the Catholic, sir," the midwife answered him.

"Well, thank goodness for that," he said, lost in thought . . .

"Go with God's blessing, and may they not be too hard on your arse," was the last thing Rasero heard him say when he left for Paris, sixteen years later. Such remarks and a couple of scoldings for reading too much or for not wanting to go hunting or for refusing to feel up the behind of a housemaid from Madrid were the only memories he had of his father, a "Rasero from the bad litter," as the elder Rasero himself put it.

But the boy wasn't stupid. Besides, even though no one suspected it, he was very happy. He didn't talk, because he saw no need to do so; Angustias understood each one of his gestures perfectly. The boy had only to look at her for her to do whatever he wanted. Her soft breasts were the sweetest and warmest handles in the world to cling to; he could spend hours at a time lying back against them, not thinking of anything, feeling, just feeling. When he was not in his nurse's lap, he spent his time looking at the objects in the house: the old dining-room chairs, plain and heavy, of dark walnut, with the seat and the back upholstered in cherry-colored velvet, the legs carved in the shape of lion's claws and the upper part of the back, also carved, showing the coat of arms of the Raseros: a forearm holding upraised a live-oak club. As a very small child, Fausto used to climb up on them with great effort and touch in awe the coat of arms, wondering how it had been possible to carve that in the wood. And sitting in one of the chairs, he spent a long time contemplating the big painting of the Last Supper that covered half the wall of the dining room. It was bathed in that chiaroscuro which Spanish painters so greatly favored. The figures were rigid and solemn. Jesus Christ, in the center, looked straight ahead with the resigned expression of someone who knows what fate has in store for him and has decided to accept it; Saint John, very young, was leaning his head on his left hand, trying in vain to hide his tears behind it. Peter was looking at the Lord in surprise, his eyes asking him what the devil was going on, and Judas was smiling craftily, looking out the corner of his eye at a handful of coins lying next to his forearm. The atmosphere of the painting was murky, the objects in the background could scarcely be made out, and the only thing that stood out were the thirteen faces barely illuminated by a reddish yellow light, but it looked as though they were meeting in a cheap tavern rather than in the house of the good man who, with his jar of water, came and went on the path of the messengers of the Lord. The painting, which belonged to his mother's family, was not signed, and of course nobody knew who had painted it. Ten years later, in Madrid, when Rasero had acquired the habit of visiting the great Pinacoteca Real each day, it was not hard for him to deduce that the painting was the work of the Sevillian painter Juan de Pareja, a brilliant pupil of José Ribera's, El Españoleto. In the dining room there was also a fine painting attributed to Alessandro Magnasco, *Lisandrino,* showing a lively scene of brigands and gypsies on a spree, and three magnificent paintings by the Dutch painter Melchior Honelecoster, each one of which showed a bird: a robin, a raven, or a falcon. The birds were so well executed that very often, as little Fausto looked at them in fascination, he thought he saw them beating their wings to take flight.

His favorite painting, however, was in the drawing room, above a great hearth. It was a splendid portrait that the immortal Velázquez had done of Fausto's great-great-grandfather, don Fausto de Oquendo. The man appeared almost full face, looking toward the painter. He was dressed entirely in black, with a red cross over his heart and a white ruff round his neck. He was short of stature but thick in build; his legs, short and sturdy, supported him firmly. His left foot, gracefully held forward, afforded a glimpse of the heavy buckle of his sandal. His face, very serious, had a broad forehead that prefigured his precocious baldness; his eyes, set far apart and with large black irises, anticipated those of his great-great-grandson. His nose was long and delicate, with a prominent little ridge down the middle; beneath thin, almost colorless lips, his reddish beard, which he wore trimmed to a point, attenuated the roundness of his face. Seated comfortably in an old easy chair, the child spent hours at a time contemplating his illustrious ancestor's portrait. The face of his great-great-grandfather was exactly the opposite of his father's, which always looked restless and mistrustful, like that of a rat in a cage. Don Fausto, on the other hand, radiated calm and composure, serenity and firmness. As he looked at him, the little boy tried to guess which of the features were also those of his mother, whom he had never known. A short time before, rummaging about in an old little wooden coffer with mother-of-pearl insets that his uncle Luis had brought back from the Philippines, he had found a tiny oval-shaped painting, no larger than a medallion, showing a pretty young girl of about fifteen. Pale, with a slender nose and thin lips, she had big eyes, dark and set far apart; her chestnut brown hair was abundant and wavy, although her hairline was very far above her forehead. It was a portrait of his mother, Angustias told him. "Ah, my Inesita! She was the prettiest and kindest woman who ever passed through this world," his nursemaid said as, deeply moved, she brought the miniature up to just where her generous breasts began. The little boy looked at the painting of his great-great-grandfather and compared it with the portrait of his mother: the forehead and the eyes made them look alike, unmistakable proofs that the same blood circulated in the veins of both of them . . . and through his too, for he recognized the features as his own. He was glad to know that he was an Oquendo, as his father used to scoff, for young Fausto was persuaded that that lineage was much nobler and better than the one whose blazon was the live-oak club. Rasero kept the portrait of his mother with him his whole life, and once he learned that his father's death had left him an orphan, he ordered the painting of his great-great-grandfather, the majordomo and counselor of Philip IV, a close friend of the divine Velázquez, brought to Paris. He hung it above the main fireplace of his town house. There it remained for many years, until he gave it to the painter David. That was at the end of the century, when Rasero, a man far along in years, decided to abandon his beloved city to return to his homeland and the old mansion in the calle Miaja, where he extinguished the lights of his intelligence so as to set them afire once again in the distant future.

The boy was also fond of contemplating many other objects in the house, such as the old weapons that hung on a wall of the dining room: three lances, two of them ending in a point and the other in the form of an ax; four rusty crossed sabers on a frayed escutcheon of cherry-colored velvet; and a fine sword whose ivory hilt had a large gem of a greenish color set in the pommel. He told himself that an ancestor of his mother's, don Anselmo de Oquendo—a man who had been an intimate of Henry of Navarre, the future Henry IV of France (such a close friend, according to malicious gossips, that he shared the royal consort's bed with Henry, and hence many people said that don Anselmo was really the father of Louis XIII)—killed with this very sword none other than a Valois, who had caught him frolicking with his wife, the favors of Queen Marie de Médicis being evidently not the only ones that don Anselmo had sought. A bold man, an adventurer, and something of a charlatan, he was proud of being a learned alchemist, a pupil of the revered Geber, a profound scholar and lucid interpreter of the works of Levy the Cabalist, of the Arab alchemists Rhases, Alphidus, and Khalid; of Roger Bacon, Ramón Lull, Arnold of Villanova, Nicolas Flamel, and a whole pleiad of the sons of Hermes, not excluding, naturally, Paracelsus and Avicenna.

At other times little Fausto played with the tiny wooden sculptures on the mantelpiece. They were quite faithful copies of Michelangelo's David, his Pietà, his Dawn, and his Twilight. Fausto picked them up carefully, gently rubbed his little fingers over the polished forms, and wondered what tools could have been used to execute work such as that. Sometimes, too, he contemplated how the grains the color of old gold slowly fell in the great hourglass. He had discovered that the sand took exactly one day to descend to the bottom of the instrument. From that time on, punctually, just before five o'clock in the afternoon, he always went over to the hourglass to watch how the last grains of sand fell, forming as they did this a little whirlwind in the narrow passage in the middle of the glass. When the upper part of the device was empty, he carefully turned it over—not without great effort, since the device weighed a good fifteen pounds—and left it to its endless emptying of itself, until the next day when he came back to visit it. Or he amused himself with a set of bronze mortars, hard and heavy, which emitted a pleasant-sounding tinkle upon being struck with the pestle. He occasionally handled the ivory paper knife that in days gone forever his mother had used to cut open the pages of the books of poems she had been so fond of. The instrument was light and delicate, surely one from the Orient. It had tiny figures of swallows in full flight carved on the handle, and its edge could easily stand comparison with that of a dagger of Toledo steel. He was wont to while away long stretches of time contemplating the two large vases of blue-and-white majolica with exquisite images of birds and flowers which his uncle Luis had given his mother as a wedding present and which, he said with pride, were the work of the Italian Giorgio Andreoli, the inventor of the technique that was used. What he liked most, though, was the lovely bronze clock in his father's room. It was very old—so old that it didn't have a pendulum. Uncle Luis had brought it from the Philippines, where he had been told that the clock had belonged to don Luis de Velasco, one of the first viceroys of New Spain. Its height was just over the length of a forearm, and it had the shape of a square tower that recalled the lower structure of the Giralda in Seville. On each of two parallel sides it had a face with Roman numerals but no minute hand, only an hour hand. The tower was adorned with eight tiny bronze sculptures of splendid workmanship, representing soldiers on guard on either side of the four little imitation doors in high relief located in the lower part of the tower. The upper part had a little railing topped with a pear at each corner, and in the center of the area the railing enclosed four pillars supported a cupola crowned by a cross with five gems set in its bronze. By pulling up on the railing, the upper part of the clock's housing could be removed, exposing the mechanism inside. It held Faustito spellbound to see the slow turning of the toothed wheels; he watched for a long time the spring of the cord that unwound little by little until finally the movement was interrupted and the monotonous ticktock ceased to be heard. Then with a key, also made of bronze and with large flanges on either side, he wound the clock up as he observed how the spring, the secret of its workings, became taut again.

On certain occasions the boy went down into the cellar of the old mansion. In it was stored the wine from the vineyards his father owned in the interior of the province. The muscatel wines, the reds, the amontillados, and the ordinary white table wine lay resting in the belly of enormous oak barrels. Rows and rows of high shelves held countless dusty bottles patiently dozing so as to make their contents even more precious. The place was damp and dark and permeated with a strong smell of fermented grapes. In the corners were great heaps of corks that the rats were given to gnawing, which became the scene of the bizarre battles he waged with his cousins Matías and José when they came from Macharavialla to visit him. Once little Fausto tried a sip of wine, but he didn't like its taste, at once sweet and sour. He found incomparably better the milk of his beloved Angustias, light, warm, and with a sweet aftertaste, which he continued to suck from her breasts six years after his birth despite the many attempts that the good gypsy woman had made to wean him. And it was precisely owing to one of those attempts that the boy had begun to talk just after he reached the age of six.

He had spent the morning visiting the Alcazaba with Fray Silvestre. Sitting on the railing of a parapet surrounding a large patio, they saw the city, the port, and the sea. Fausto listened to his teacher as he explained how almost ten centuries before, the Arabs, in their powerful territorial drive, succeeded in disembarking on the coasts of Spain. Guided by the intrepid Tarik and his fierce successor, Muza, they soon had conquered the peninsula and with it Málaga, naturally—a "city more than three thousand years old," the old man said solemnly, with the remote hope that the boy would understand what he was telling him. And he recounted to him for the hundredth time the story of those Phoenician seamen, skillful sailors and even better traders, who disembarked in what would later on be called Málaca, where they did not have very great difficulty tempting with their magnificent stock in trade—gold jewelry, alabaster drinking vessels, sumptuous deep purple cloaks, and a thousand pretty trinkets—the uncouth native country folk of this region, then known as Társida, who welcomed the invaders whose servants and quasi slaves they were to become in the course of time. Fausto listened to him attentively as he looked at the leafy trees of the Alameda de Hércules, which began in front of the old cathedral and ran, like an enormous green serpent, down to the docks of the port, where light boats, with their sails furled and their lantern at the end of the prow, were lined up. He saw how they were getting ready to put out to sea at nightfall, to fish for sardines with silver-colored backs and for a smaller variety called *boquerones,* whose tiny bodies, still alive, writhed when placed in boiling oil, as well as for flounder so flat that they had their two eyes on the same side of their bodies but such exquisite flesh, so tender, that it could be eaten raw, seasoned perhaps with lemon juice. "So then, the second caliph of Córdoba ordered this fortress that overlooks the sea, the city, and the mountains to be built. And they built it so solidly that, even though more than a hundred battles have been fought here, just see how its walls look, tall and intact," his teacher said with pride.

While the boy was in the Alcazaba, Angustias had resolved not to nurse him anymore. Six years were too long, even for her, who loved him dearly. What was more, Faustito now had a good set of sharp teeth that were turning feeding time into torture. Besides that, she had often wondered if it might not be her milk that was responsible for the boy's being bald. The memory of her uncle Antonio, who had been left without any hair since he was very small, troubled her. And what if my boy has sucked his baldness from me? she wondered many times with great misgivings. But now her mind was made up: when Faustillo returned from his outing and came into the kitchen holding his little hand out, opening and closing it—the gesture by which he asked to be nursed—she would pay no attention to him, she would pretend to be busy preparing lunch. If the boy insisted, she would tell him no, that he was too old to go around sucking tits, that he should drink cow's milk from a glass, and not hers. Perhaps the boy would cry, have a tantrum, fall into a rage—something that, incidentally, she had never seen him do—but she would refuse to give in regardless of what he did. She was even prepared to slap him if need be—merely thinking of such a thing depressed her—but Fausto wasn't going to get his way, she swore to herself, thinking of the image of the Cachorro, a crude replica of the Christ of Montañes hanging on a wall of her room.

Everything happened as Angustias expected. Almost the moment Fausto came back from the outing, he came into the kitchen with his hand out. The woman greeted him, her mind to all appearances elsewhere, and went on cooking. Surprised, the boy pulled on her skirt, forcing her to turn around as he opened and closed his other hand. "Stop it, child!" Angustias said to him, lifting his hand from her skirt. She doesn't want to nurse me, Fausto thought. For a moment his impulse was to run out of the kitchen to his room, since his feelings were badly hurt, but his gullet, loath to give up that easily, impressed on his head the great urgency of drinking lunch. He pulled on her skirt again and slapped at her with his hand. Her next response was worse: "Stop pestering me, child! What the devil do you want?"

What do you mean, what the devil do I want? Milk, what else? Can my Angustias have gone out of her mind? Fausto wondered, bewildered, as he tugged harder and harder on her skirt. "Look, Faustillo, if you want milk, go and get a glass and pour yourself some from this pitcher. But you won't get any from my tits—not on your life."

She hasn't gone dotty, she just doesn't want to nurse me, the boy thought gloomily. Almost resigned, he was at the point of serving himself from the pitcher when an idea crossed his mind. He thought long and hard. If this didn't work, he'd be saying good-bye to Angustias' breasts forever. At last he planted himself smartly in front of her, looked at her defiantly, and said to her in perfect Castilian, "Angustias, I want you to suckle me."

His nurse could scarcely believe her ears. Her Faustillo was talking! "What did you say, my boy?"

"To suckle me," he answered boldly.

"Upon my soul, I'll let you have what you want," the woman said, weeping for joy as she unbuttoned her blouse and prayed to the Cachorro within her to forgive her for having broken her promise.

From that day on, Fausto spoke more fluently than a lawyer. Fray Silvestre saw with satisfaction that nothing he had taught the child had fallen into a leaky sack; he observed that, on the contrary, the youngster remembered perfectly every one of his words. Furthermore, once Fausto made up his mind to speak, he began to bombard Fray Silvestre with questions, many of them so pointed and so clever that the poor friar was hard put to it to answer and rued abandoning the studies he had begun so brilliantly at the University of Salamanca.

Fausto found speaking an effective way to learn a great number of things. And he soon discovered another way even more powerful: reading. He learned to read with surprising ease, and before he was eight he had devoured all the books in the house. There were, incidentally, not many of them: an old Bible, ten or fifteen books of the Golden Age poetry of which his mother had been so fond, a couple of treatises on geography and ancient history that his uncle Louis had brought, and a *Quixote*—the only book he found in his father's room, and without a doubt the one Fausto liked most, to the point of reading it through at least four times.

Don Enrique received the good news with satisfaction. He has some Rasero blood after all, he said to himself. Thinking that, though the boy didn't have the makings of a gentleman, he could at least be a good canon, he offered a generous stipend to don Joel de Burgos, hiring the learned Jesuit with liberal habits to take charge of the education of his son. Fray Silvestre, very elderly by then and weary of the exhausting work that his pupil imposed on him, decided to go into retreat in a monastery. He ended his days there, his mind gently benumbed by vinous spirits, grateful for the satisfaction of having instructed that child everyone had thought to be an idiot but now saw as a budding scholar.

Don Joel turned out to be an infinitely richer vein to mine than Fray Silvestre; his knowledge appeared to be inexhaustible. Little Rasero spent whole hours listening to his wonderful lessons about history, religion, music, and mathematics. He learned, thanks to him, the secrets of languages: the soft declensions of Latin, the rugged constructions of Greek, and the sensual pronunciation of French, which requires a pursing of the mouth to speak it, as though one were sucking on an apricot pit. They bought many books and consulted the best libraries in Málaga. The boy was happy to immerse himself in a sea of names, dates, symbols, and bizarre stories—some of them tragic, others joyful, most of them violent. He discovered that the world was much vaster than the old mansion where he lived, that the objects he had contemplated in fascination for many long years and that in his eyes were abundant, varied, and enigmatic, were barely a few grains of sand on a vast, limitless beach extending to the horizon. There was then spawned in him a taste for knowing, for getting to the bottom of things, for understanding, for wresting secrets from everything within his reach, that never left him as long as he lived, that on the contrary grew and ramified till it reached every corner of human knowledge.

Now, thirty years later, as you are journeying to Ferney to visit your old friend Voltaire, you wonder whether it was worth it to cram your mind with this glut of knowledge that, even though you realize the extent of the pleasure it has brought, has also kindled in you an enormous anxiety. Being here, in this carriage, fleeing from everything you've learned, seeking consolation from the sarcastic philosopher, is the best proof of this. But you can't fool yourself; it isn't the learning you found in books, in talks with your intellectual friends, in museums and laboratories, that is causing you your deadly dread. It is, rather, those terrible images you carry about with you in your little book—those images which come without your having sought them when, paradoxically, you are enjoying the greatest delight.

"December 13, 1730. The first . . ." You had begun to talk a short time before. Angustias, happy to hear you, and at heart proud of herself for knowing that she was indispensable to your existence, resigned herself to continue nursing you. It was a cold afternoon; you were in your nurse's bedroom, she sitting in the old rocking chair, you on her lap, leaning back against her breasts. The woman stroked your head as she sang a *tanguillo* in a very soft voice. She took your left hand and interrupted her song. "Let's see what this gypsy finds in your little hand," she said to you with a smile. "Well, preserve me, child! You're going to live for many years and you're going to take your pleasure with many women. But you're going to die far away from here, very far. Let's see. Look how big it is! Your hand has an enormous eye in it. You're going to see many things. Heavens above, a whole lot of them! You're going to see places that nobody's ever seen. How strange . . ."

You listened to her while you sucked on her breast. Her milk was warmer and sweeter than ever. You felt an enormous pleasure, in your belly first, and then it descended to your testicles. You felt your penis becoming as hard as a stone and you sucked more and more eagerly. "Don't bite me, child," Angustias said to you. But you didn't hear her. You were feeling something you'd never felt before in your life, a densely concentrated pleasure lodged in every pore of your skin. Your penis, burning, as though alum had been flung on top of it, had spasms and seemed to burst. At that very instant you opened your eyes, but you didn't see Angustias' breasts, or her bedroom, or anything that was familiar to you. Instead you saw a white wall, very badly marred, against which two men dressed in gray with a black blindfold over their eyes were leaning. One of them shouted something you didn't hear, and as though it had been a signal, you heard the sharp discharge of several rifles going off at once. The bullets penetrated the bodies of the men the way a stone enters the water of a pond—except for the bullet that hit one of the men right in the forehead. This bullet didn't pass through his skull but hit it and ricocheted off and embedded itself in the wall, causing spurts of blood and splinters of bone to wash down the face of the unfortunate man. The two men fell to the ground like bundles, their clothes soaked in blood, excrement, and urine. The wretches were still writhing on the ground, pathetically shaking their arms tied together at the wrists. Another man dressed in a tight-fitting beige suit, with a very strange hat in the shape of a plate atop his head, appeared then. He looked scornfully at the dying men. From a black holster that was hanging from his waist he drew out a device that Faustillo took to be a pistol, although the barrel and the butt of it were square rather than round. He aimed at the temple of one of the men who was writhing on the ground and fired. The sound of the shot, very low pitched and muffled, resounded inside your head and woke you. Horror-struck, you rubbed your eyes and could see the delightful flesh of your wet nurse. A frightful howl came from the innermost depths of your being, and you burst into tears like a Mary Magdalene.

"Faustito, my boy! What's happening to you, my darling?" Angustias asked as she covered you with kisses.

The vision made such an impression on the boy that he decided to omit Angustias' milk from his diet forever. Fausto thought that the terrible images were a sort of warning or admonition to cease doing something that wasn't proper for his age. The gypsy woman discovered to her disappointment that the little boy avoided her whenever she tried to come close to him. She felt how Fausto was putting up an impassable wall between them. Her generous breasts, full of milk for so many years, hurt her at night, and the white liquid soaked her blouse. But the pain she felt within her was even greater, and the tears flowing down her cheeks more abundant. My Faustillo doesn't love me anymore, she kept saying to herself, until her breasts and her eyes were dry, and little by little, she learned resignation.

Fausto noted the pain he caused the gypsy woman and tried to lessen it by being affectionate and kind to her. He often told her, for instance, the story of Boabdil, the Young One, the last caliph of Granada, that Angustias was so fond of. He recounted to her the thoughts of the good Moor when he realized that he had been defeated, and the upbraidings he received from his mother, who, despite being a woman, was bolder than the caliph. And he repeated to Angustias the sentence that the energetic lady passed on to her son and to history: "Don't weep like a woman for what you weren't able to defend like a man." Angustias listened to him, smiling sadly. Her blouse and her moist eyes broke Fausto's heart. In moments such as that, he was forced to make a superhuman effort to contain himself, to control the impulse to fling himself into his nurse's arms and nestle his bald head between those two enormous, beloved breasts. But the memory of the visual experience of that man with blood and splinters of bone flowing from his forehead and running down held him back, and he merely said, "So then, Angustias dear, Granada remained without a caliph, and all of old Spain became Christian again."

"What a fine story, and how well my boy tells it!" Angustias said, feeling as spurned as a lover who realizes that the passion of her beloved has burned itself out and that she is unable to aspire to anything but to turn that passion into a homely friendship. She never stopped loving her Faustillo or satisfying the most trivial of his demands, but her smile, which until then had been broad and generous, was veiled first by a halo of sadness and later by one of melancholy—a smile Fausto knew to be that of a woman scorned.

In the carriage, Rasero imagined his beloved Angustias sitting facing him, smiling bitterly, looking at him with her eyes clouded by tears; reminding him of that terrible afternoon on which his lips kissed those breasts for the last time, his body discovered the warmth of sex, and his mind incubated the first of his countless visions. "Ah, my Faustillo! to think that it was my milk that brought on those nightmares of yours. You were just a little boy. My milk couldn't help but do you good. At worst, it could have made you bald, but nothing other than that," the imagined figure told him. And she was right, even though for a long time Fausto thought otherwise—to be exact, for the nine years that went by between that afternoon and his meeting with the Marquise de Gironella in Madrid. He had not had another vision, and that weighed in the balance against the pain it had caused him to give up his nurse's breasts. They were calm and fruitful years. Patiently and carefully, don Joel cultivated the boy's mind, and don Enrique, seeing what swift progress his son's intellect was making, decided to bring him to Madrid to live with him.

He presented Fausto at court just after the boy turned fourteen. The king, Philip IV, an embittered old man, was unable to suppress a smile on seeing before him the only son of the Marquis de Rasero: a skinny, bald boy, with a curious gaze, at once naïve and gentle, looking at him the way an insect trapped in a spider web would. His wife, Queen Isabella, watched the boy with a different sort of interest: her expert crotch told her that that strange youngster would turn out to be a superb lover. Informed by don Joel de Burgos himself of the great intelligence the boy possessed, the sovereigns welcomed him affectionately, gave him recommendations so he could continue his studies alongside the best minds at court, and entrusted don Agustín Montano, the director of the Biblioteca Real de Madrid, with the task of personally supervising the progress of the young scholar's studies.

In the boy's imagination, there was scarcely room for Madrid, with its 200,000 inhabitants, its streets crowded with happy strollers, its criers who loudly called out news of a thousand and one marvels, its countless taverns, jammed full of tipplers placing all their bets and all their hopes on the turn of a card or a roll of the dice, and its Plaza Mayor, imposing and dark, which on days when there was a bullfight was transformed into a gay, brightly lit place, undergoing a change like that of a nun who has made up her face to look like a whore. The deep black bulls, with horns like the trunks of oak trees, were fooled into charging the matador's cape. The bullfighters, graceful and agile, leaped over their backs, and with indubitable courage, tried, face to face with the animal, with only a tiny bit of scarlet cloth between them, to penetrate the bulging muscles above the nape of the bull's neck. They almost succeeded, although on occasion it was the bull that was able to dig one of its horns into the thigh of the brave but unlucky matador. At other times, the plaza became, if possible, even gloomier and darker, as though that nun disguised as a brazen hussy had again changed appearances and turned into a fearsome harpy. That was on the days when the king, seated on a dais, protecting himself from the sun beneath a red-and-gold velvet awning, presided over an auto-da-fé. The condemned, walking in procession, each wearing the penitential sanbenito with flames stamped on it, and carrying an extinguished taper in his or her hands, reminded Rasero of the images created by the divine Dante, with incomparable mastery, in those perfect verses, so solid and so well constructed, so beautiful and so impeccable, that they impelled young Fausto to study Italian day and night in order to savor them in the language in which they had been written. When he could, he spent whole afternoons in the magnificent Biblioteca Real, going over the words one by one, touching with a loving hand the paper on which they were printed, as if he were trying to absorb the poet's inspiration through his fingertips. But the flames that the Florentine spoke of, those that purify souls, tempering them like Toledo steel, leaving them clean and deserving of the Lord's glory, didn't resemble in any way the dark clouds of smoke that rose in the Plaza Mayor, bearing upward the consumed flesh of a heretic, a witch, or a reprobate Jew. The horrors, Rasero discovered in the course of one of those sinister ceremonies, were not merely inside his head.

It had been on a cold afternoon in the autumn of 1739. His father forced him to attend. Fortunately, it was a minor auto-da-fé; no one was being condemned to death. Or to be precise, the only man to have been given the death sentence was to be executed symbolically, for the unfortunate man, a Jew named Simón Mauries, who was accused of relapsing into his former faith, had already died from the cruel torture he received. His remains, in the black sanbenito of those to be burned at the stake, took their place in the procession on a litter borne by four lackeys.

The ceremony proceeded at an exasperatingly slow pace. The king and his courtiers could barely conceal their boredom; all of them were continually passing a hand across their face to hide a yawn. One by one, those condemned to be publicly punished knelt and begged for forgiveness; they were given several obviously gentle lashes, and weeping for joy, saw a bishop light the taper that each of them was carrying, thereby signifying that their soul that had gone astray had returned to the Lord's path. Only the next to the last person condemned (the very last one was the dead Jew), a pretty dark-haired woman with firm flesh and a haughty demeanor, received a punishment of the utmost rigor.

A long list of charges weighed decisively against her. She was accused of belonging to the Garduña, the legendary sect of bandits whose origin went back to the days of the Catholic sovereigns, when the hermit Cal Palinario was visited by the Virgin in person, who authorized him to fight against the Moors and blessed, moreover, any act of robbery or pillage that the holy man and his followers deemed it wise to engage in. María Pastora Torres (that was her name), herself the daughter of bandits, had distinguished herself in the organization from a very early age. When she was barely an adolescent, she was already an expert "siren," the name given to girls who, passing themselves off as whores, led gentlemen on so that their male accomplices, known as "floreadores," "punteadores," or most fearsome of all, "guapos," could attack them without risk. It was said that María Pastora, despite her sex, eventually became a "punteadora" (one who kills with a knife) greatly to be feared, who dispatched to the next world, without the least scruple, more than fifteen Christians. She was also the concubine of the "big brother," or chief, of the Garduña, and as those in the know tell it, she was the real leader of the sect, for she had under her thumb, through both her amatory arts and her iron character, the head "guapo."

As though that weren't enough, she had also been found guilty of being a sorceress' apprentice. It so happened that in recent days María Pastora had almost completely given up her calling as a bandit in order to devote herself body and soul to the service of La Colmilluda, the Fanged One, an old witch known throughout the kingdom. La Colmilluda had taken to living on the outskirts of Madrid in a cave near Manzanares. All sorts of people came to her, and her skills as a healer, a seer, and a reader of omens became legendary in Castile and in many other regions of Spain. The Inquisition could never get its hands on her; every time the terrified guards thought they had her trapped inside her miserable cave, she slipped through their fingers like water. When they entered the cave, it was empty; all they saw was a cauldron on the fire which stank worse than a thousand devils, and an owl that hooted at them derisively. People said that La Colmilluda turned into a raven so as to take wing and escape her persecutors. Finally, during one raid, the familiars of the Inquisition found something more in the cave than the cauldron and the owl. They found María Pastora curled up in a ball on a miserable bed of straw. Her skin was a purplish color and her mouth full of spittle. Pleased with their prey, they handed her over to the Holy Inquisition, convinced that they had got their hands on another body for the stake.

It was odd that the severe tribunal found her guilty of being only an apprentice rather than an outright witch, a verdict whereby her life was spared. They condemned her to receive a hundred lashes and leave the kingdom forever. For many people with a suspicious cast of mind, it seemed that a powerful hand, from very high up, had interceded in favor of the woman. On contemplating her naked torso receiving the cruel lashes, they found it easy to guess why: the woman was extraordinarily pretty. She endured the punishment with contempt, even managing to break out into a mocking smile. But the torturers went about their task with unusual vigor; when they had dealt her no more than twenty lashes, the woman's back was already a bloody mass of raw flesh. After the thirtieth, her smile disappeared and she fainted at the whipping post. Fausto could see an expression of approval on the face of Queen Isabella as she shot a conspiratorial look at doña Milagros de Montellano, the wife of the prime minister, who answered the queen's look with an identical one. Half the punishment was not yet over when a copious hemorrhage spurted forth from the nose and the mouth of the condemned woman. Four lashes more and a violent spasm ran through her body. The woman bandit had died.

Solomon-like, the chief inquisitor decided that, since the condemned woman had died without having abjured her sins and without receiving divine pardon, her remains should be incinerated alongside those of the relapsed Jew. The crowd contemplated in silence the dense cloud of smoke barely illuminated by the last rays of afternoon light. Fausto saw how don José Campillo, the prime minister, tried to hide with his hands the flood of tears falling from his eyes. Doña Teresa Rivera, the marquise de Gironella, stroked the boy's head as she chided don Enrique, "You shouldn't have brought him. He's just a youngster."

On the way back, in the carriage, doña Teresa sat down next to Fausto and settled him comfortably on her lap. "Look how pale the poor little thing is," she remarked to don Enrique.

"Bah! This child has had the color of a corpse ever since he was born."

"Doing that to a little boy. He's a beast," the marquise muttered to herself as she stroked the lad's bald head and pressed his face against her side. The woman's odor, her softness, and her warmth reminded him of Angustias. Little by little, Fausto felt better, until he succeeded in banishing from his mind the image of María Pastora's face bathed in blood. Doña Teresa's soft caresses and the swaying of the carriage made him fall fast asleep. Don Enrique was sitting opposite her, and as he tried to pinch her thighs, she pushed his hand away in annoyance.

"Come on, woman, don't be such a spoilsport, blast it all. I can't believe they're the first infidels you've seen roasted."

"You're a beast, Enrique. Hasn't anyone ever told you so?"

"I'll be damned if they have. And you're an adorable whore. Hasn't anyone ever told you so?"

"Go to hell! And leave me alone, please," doña Teresa said as she again removed his hand, which had now almost reached her groin. She couldn't understand how it had been possible that at one time she had come to love that man so much.

In reality, she loved him because, literally, he had loved her; because he had made love to her as no one ever had before. Her husband, the lord, rest his soul in peace, had married her when he was close to seventy and was burned out, moreover, from having led an extravagantly licentious life. He was unable to give his wife any further signs of affection than a chaste kiss on the cheek. Barely in her twenties, with her life and her beauty in full bloom, she was hoping for quite a bit more than that. It was don Enrique de Rasero who gave it to her—and to the point of satiety, it is only fair to admit, since however great a toper that man was, he was equally potent, and that is saying a great deal. In the beginning, as the young woman's body grew accustomed to those delights, she became mad about that man and did not leave his side for a moment, despite constant scoldings from her mother and her friends, who could not make her see the base deed she was committing by being the lover, and worse still a woman who shamelessly chased after, an obscure nobleman from the provinces. With time, doña Teresa educated her body in the art of love, and in order to confirm the progress she had made, sought out new members for her synod. Her former lover far outdid the first of them, to the point that, after a brief affair, she came back in repentance to the strong arms of the Malagan. But her education went on until she arrived at the refinements implied by a doctorate and learned to be much more selective with regard to her new instructors, and thus contrived to compile a goodly list of lovers who were much superior to the rustic provincial, to whom she more and more frequently denied her favors, until she went so far as to repudiate him and ask herself how it was possible to have once been able to love him. That is usually what happens in the case of apprenticeships.

Meanwhile, Fausto was having a dream. There had come back to his mind the procession of sinners dressed in their sanbenitos. Once again he saw María Pastora's back receiving the lashes. But in his dream, the woman was receiving them with indifference, smiling happily, as though she were remembering the wanton games she had played with Paco el Guapo. Each blow of the lash made a red line in her back, from which a swarm of scarlet wasps flew out. The blows were monotonously repeated, and the wasps, more and more numerous, kept coming out of María Pastora's body. A red cloud then formed, enveloping the condemned woman and her torturers. Many wasps alit on her oppressors, causing their bodies to take on a bright red tinge; it was the color of the insects, mingled with the blood from their bites. The torturers, in a fury, hit even harder, and after each stroke of the lash new swarms emerged. Little by little, the entire square filled up with insects until it took on a color that mingled with that of the late-afternoon sky. The creatures attacked the penitents who had just been pardoned and the expectant crowd and flew up to the platform where the sovereigns and their courtiers were seated. The multitude, submerged in a sea of insects and bathed in blood, milled about frantically; they began to howl like souls in purgatory. Only María Pastora remained calm and content, watching how a swarm of wasps the size of an orange tree came out of her back every time she was struck by the lash. Suddenly, her smile was transformed into a grimace of terror. The cloud of wasps soaked in blood formed an enormous whirlwind whose apex, lengthened now, headed for the woman bandit to penetrate, to be sucked in by her nose and her mouth. The whirlwind, of pure blood now, returned to the woman, who writhed like a fish out of water. At last she remained motionless, fallen face down, with two little red threads, one in her mouth and one in her nose, and a frightful wound to one side of her forehead, in which there could be seen a piece of her splintered frontal bone. It was no longer María Pastora who was lying on the pavement of the Plaza Mayor; it was a man with a black beard at the foot of a whitewashed wall, the same man Fausto had seen from the breast of his nurse. A dry cold settled over the boy's body, and he began to tremble violently. The sound of his teeth chattering brought him out of his dream.

"Look how he's trembling. He's burning-hot with fever," doña Teresa said as she kissed the boy's forehead. "Wake up now, Fausto, you've had a bad dream."

Fausto opened his eyes. His pupils, very dilated, stared at the marquise' face. His gaze, inquisitive and supplicating, intimidated the woman, who felt at once attracted and afraid.

"There, there, darling . . ."

Fausto hugged her, clinging tightly to her as a victim of shipwreck would cling to a length of timber. The trembling gradually ceased, and the warmth that that woman who smelled of jasmine radiated finally drove away the cold surrounding his chest.

The carriage stopped in front of the main gate of the palace of the Gironellas. Two footmen, impeccably liveried, hastened to open the door of the berlin and unfold the little stairway.

"Look, Enrique," the woman said before she climbed down, "Fausto is ill. What he's seen has done him a great deal of harm. Let him stay a few days with me. You're not even able to take care of yourself."

"As you please, woman. But don't get your hopes up. There's nobody who can cure this boy. He was born as feeble and sickly as his accursed mother. He'a a weakling, confound him."

From the door of the mansion Fausto saw his father going off in the berlin. "Good-bye, you damned whore. Good-bye, you fairy," he said, bidding them farewell amid peals of laughter.

The marquise set out a tub of warm water, made ready with salts, fragrant herbs, and flower petals, for the boy. "Come on, Faustito. Soak in the water for a good while. You'll see how good you feel." Standing in front of the bathtub, Fausto didn't know what to do. He was hoping that the woman would leave the bedroom so that he could strip, but he couldn't see in her the slightest intention of doing so. "What are you waiting for, Faustito? The water's going to get cold." And to encourage him, she began to unbutton his shirt. "Don't be embarrassed, child. I'm looking at you just the way a doctor looks at his patient. It's necessary for me to be here while you bathe. You mustn't have a dizzy spell and drown in the tub."

She was lying. And he knew it. She could give a servant the task of bathing him. It was a desire, not a very hidden one, certainly, and one growing by the minute, that was making her stay in the bedroom. A desire aroused gently, almost imperceptibly, when they were at the ceremony, when she began to look at that child, whom she had seen so many times, with a new interest that surprised even her. On looking carefully at the boy, she could see that he in no way resembled his father—except for their ears, which were identical. Good-looking ears, well shaped, not large nor small nor set too close to his skull nor spread out wide like kites. Perhaps it was that detail that awakened her desire. As she progressed in her amorous apprenticeship, doña Teresa had gradually grown fonder and fonder of ears. She delighted in nibbling them; her teeth gave her the sensation of something soft and fragile but at the same time resistant and flexible. They greatly resembled—perhaps that was why she liked them—a phallus that has already emerged from its lethargy but has not yet attained the hardness it reaches when it is fully excited. A penis in that state fascinated her; she could spend whole hours at a time playing with it—something that, usually, was very difficult, for, naturally, it became excited when it was fondled. Ears, on the other hand, remain in that state the entire time. Many of her lovers awakened in surprise, wondering whether the marquise might not be a little mad, when, still half asleep, they felt the mouth and the teeth of their friend on an ear, as with her long fingers she felt about in their groin. Don Enrique's ears, she had to admit, were the reason their romance went on rather longer than she had wished; it was very hard for her to do without them. Even now, when she saw them there, glued to the skull of that odious man, she was obliged to make a superhuman effort to contain herself and not fling herself upon him to nibble them with delight, as she had done as a little girl with the pieces of chocolate sent from Mexico to her home. And this boy, thin and sickly pale, who was looking for a way to hide his nakedness, had his ears there where they should be, on either side of his bald head, ears as beautiful as his father's or perhaps even more so, because the marquise foresaw that they were fresher, softer, and more flexible.

At last the boy got into the tub. Doña Teresa began to rub his back with a sea sponge. It was a delightful sensation. The aroma of the perfumed water that reached his nose, along with the back massage, relaxed him and made him sleepy at the same time that it excited him, as she noted on seeing his skin turn to gooseflesh. He remembered fearfully that long-ago afternoon when he had sucked Angustias' breast for the last time. The sensation was exactly the same: a delicious warmth nesting in every pore of his skin and a warmth, rather more intense, that ran down his back and finally settled in his penis, which he could feel growing bigger by the minute. For an instant he thought of shaking himself like a soaking wet puppy and suddenly leaping out of the water so as to banish that dangerous sensation. But he was unable to do so; pleasure got by far the better of fear, and he allowed the marquise to go on and his body to feel.

In a little while, the woman put the sponge down and continued the massage with her hands, a massage that soon turned into caresses. Her mouth sought Fausto's ear and began to kiss it and gently nibble it. The boy was terrified and happy at the same time; there came to his mind an illustration in a book on natural history, a subject that he was studying with Dr. Ulloa. In the plate there appeared a little white rat with its eyes open wide, paralyzed by fear; in front of it was an enormous python that, with its head raised and its forked tongue sticking out of its mouth, was readying itself to gobble down its prey. "Some ophidians are capable of paralyzing their victim before ingesting it," the caption below the illustration read.

Things happened with incredible swiftness—at least so it seemed to you, Rasero. You did not feel as though more than a few minutes had gone by since you had thought of that book, and then you found yourself naked in bed, with the body of doña Teresa, naked too, next to yours. Much time, however, had elapsed, and many things had happened. The woman was smiling contentedly, and every so often she kissed your neck. Knowing and skillful, she had sensed how timid and inexperienced you were. She then found a way to guide you toward pleasure that was as natural and simple, as gentle and calm, as the way an old sea captain would sail his ship on a warm spring day with the wind astern. Now you were just beginning to enjoy what you felt: the warmth in your phallus increased until it became unbearable; the woman adroitly fit it into her body, and with marvelous movements, brought your delight to the gates of paradise or perhaps of death itself. Then you exploded; the pleasure that you had stored away since you entered that tub broke out in torrents, flooding all your senses. And as had happened to you with Angustias, you had another fleeting vision. You saw men and women wearing strange apparel; many of them had a rifle over their shoulder. They were erecting a barricade with sandbags at a street crossing in Madrid that you recognized. But the vision did not disturb you; you scarcely paid it any attention. Unlike the first time, the enormous pleasure you felt more than sufficed to overcome the anxiety that the vision might have occasioned you. Doña Teresa, satisfied with the aptitudes that she had discovered in you, put you to the test several more times, initiating each new assault by raising her tongue to your outer ear. That greatly excited you, and despite feeling your strength weakening, you succeeded in exploding every time that that was your instructress' aim, reaching orgasm again and again, as there came to your mind the images of a group of panicked people in a street in Madrid.

"Doña Teresa, this has pleased me a great deal."

"I can well imagine. It pleased me too."

"What did you see?"

"What did I see? When?"

"When we made it . . ."

"Look, my boy, don't try to see but to feel. Didn't you feel anything?"

"Of course I did. I felt marvelous . . ."

"You see . . ."

"But I also saw things."

"What did you see?"

"Strange people. They were carrying sandbags . . ."

"You're an odd one, Fausto, that's for sure . . ."

You had discovered something that pleased you mightily. To tell the truth, it gave you more pleasure than anything else that you had ever known. More than reading, more than the interminable talks of don Joel, of Antonio Ulloa, of Agustín Montano, or of any other of your learned teachers, more than the wondrous paintings that you contemplated for hours at a time in the Pinacoteca Real, more than the instruments of glass, bronze, and porcelain, containing colored aromatic substances, in Dr. Ulloa's laboratory . . . more than Angustias' breasts. And, of course, you wanted to repeat the experience. For the two weeks that you spent in her palace, you didn't give doña Teresa a chance to rest; the woman gracefully pursed her little lips every time she saw that you were ready to begin those delightful experiences again. That Faustito, he's more hot-blooded than his father, she thought, pleasantly surprised.

You soon discovered that that pleasure did not lie only in the body of the marquise; you tried things with other women and found it in them too. More intense in some instances, less in others—varied sensations, but in the end the same delectable result. You were really fascinated, so much so that the only time in your life that you succeeded in believing in God was during that period. "It takes a superior talent," you said to yourself, "a supreme intelligence, an absolutely noble one as well, to have granted us this glory." Very young still, you became an expert lover. In each pretty face, in each flirtatious smile, you saw the chance to embark on that marvelous pleasure outing . . . and to contemplate, moreover, strange images.

Because you never failed to have visions each time you reached orgasm. You came to realize that that was as natural in you as it was impossible for others. After a while you stopped asking your paramours if they saw something as they were making love, for experience convinced you that it didn't happen to any of them. You also left off commenting on your visions; a sort of modesty made you feel it necessary to hide those experiences.

They were happy days. And they were even happier once you arrived in Paris at the beginning of the forties. At the court at Versailles you had many more chances to immerse yourself in that pleasure, always identical, always different: since the time of the Regency, mores at court—and along with them, those of the entire kingdom—had been laxer than ever before. Men and woman had finally had the courage once again to indulge freely in their capacities to give and to feel pleasure openly; the prejudices of a withered and puritanical religion, which had turned into a monstrous sin the most noble, natural, and human activity that we are able to feel and to carry out, had been shattered. After more than fifteen centuries of fighting against fear, superstition, and falsehood, Eros was winning out. Women proudly held their bosoms high, bared more and more, before men, society, and history. And after so long a time, they rediscovered their exquisite feminine nature, knowing and vital, the giver and the receiver of love, of pleasure, the only dialectic that makes the world go round, and as if that were not enough, reproduces it. During those five years that you lived at Versailles, you made love to many women and had, of course, many visions—almost all of them war scenes, cruel, full of arms and gunpowder, of soldiers and dead men. But you didn't pay much attention to them; the happiness you felt completely overshadowed them.

They soon began, however, to occupy more space in your pleasure; above all those odious visions of the year '45, which began at Versailles, in the arms of your beloved Jeanne-Antoinette, and continued in Paris, just after you had left the court. It was during that period that you asked yourself for the first time several bothersome questions: Can they be something more than visions? Can I be seeing something that has really happened or is going to happen? Can they be prophecies? Is what I glimpse when I am at the height of sexual pleasure perhaps the future?

More than twenty years have gone by since the Marquise de Gironella obliged you to get into that tub. In all this time, you have had the chance to learn many things, to cultivate invaluable friendships, to involve your mind deeply in the thought of the era, an era so rich in reflections, in critical judgments, immersed in the honest search for truth and stability. You have also had the chance to see many things, in your own time and in the future—because now, on the way to Ferney, about to meet the most feared, respected, and exemplary intelligence of the century, you have long been convinced that it is the future that appears before your mind each time your desire explodes, a future that is either distant or near at hand . . . that you still do not know . . . but unquestionably real. What you know is that it is men like yourself, like your friends, who are the protagonists of your prophetic visions. You have been forced to accept, with profound bitterness, that those dwellers in times to come are capable, as we are—and, alas, perhaps even more capable—of committing savage deeds, of destroying their cities, of designing devices, infinitely superior to ours, to annihilate one another, of having, in a word, a knowledge at hand a very great deal richer and more fecund than ours but one they use, again as we too do, merely to harm one another.

"We're coming to Dijon!" the coachman shouted.

Dijon . . . the only thing that Rasero knew about that city in southern France was that its Academy had protected and awarded a prize ten years before to Jean-Jacques Rousseau, the Swiss misanthrope, famous from that time on, who in his works had undertaken the task of tracing the path that must be followed to be able to turn any society into a model of wisdom, justice, brotherhood, and peace.

III

Voltaire

Ferney, April, 1761

He could see the hand of the philosopher even at the confines of his domains: the inhabitants of Ferney resided in solid stone houses with roofs of fired clay, unlike their neighbors, who lived in miserable hovels made of wood and mud. Every house, moreover, had a well-cultivated and well-stocked garden, and almost all of them a little stable that sheltered a couple of milch cows. Many of them had glass panes in their windows—a real luxury in the countryside—and their sills adorned with pots full of bright-colored flowers. An abundance of hens, ducks, and geese happily roamed about the houses, pecking at the ground in search of food.

That remote region of France, abandoned to its fate since time immemorial, had had the enormous good fortune of being chosen by Voltaire as a site for his residence and for realizing his dreams. For this unusual man, it must be admitted, conjoined in his person two qualities as different as day and night, as difficult to mix together as water and oil: Voltaire was one of the few, the very few people who besides possessing a fierce artistic talent, an unheard-of intelligence, being able to penetrate to the bottom of the most serious and abstract thoughts, to take them apart piece by piece—as the watchmakers in nearby Geneva did with minute screws, springs, and crown wheels—and then put them back together to form magnificent works, also possessed an extraordinary head for business. He made money as easily as he wrote imposing books on history, delightful stories, or Homeric poems. From a very early age, when he grew tired of the study of law and gave up the life plan, linear and boring—of becoming a good bourgeois lawyer—that his father had drawn up for him, he discovered that his vocation lay in letters, art, philosophy. And he also discovered that in order to make that dream come true, in order to be a great philosopher and artist, he needed to be free; he could not subject his intelligence to any dictate, of his father or of any leader, or even of his king. In order to elucidate the great abundance of ideas and sensations that he was beginning to incubate in his head, he needed to be as free as a bird, and being free, it didn't take him long to realize, takes money—the more the better. So he eagerly launched upon this twofold undertaking, and even learned to combine the two; he became the editor, promoter, and publicist of his own works. He learned how to profit from the prohibitions and condemnations that his books became subject to almost the moment that they were published. Unintentionally, his censors were his best financial allies, because they added the spice of the prohibited to the value of the work, thereby increasing the demand and the price for it. He immediately invested the fat profits he earned from his *Henriade* and from the *Lettres anglaises* in a substantial deal: the Paris Lottery. The city government, as always, was very short of funds. Its functionaries then decided to launch an important bond issue backed by the state treasury and, to make the bonds even more attractive to potential investors, organized a monthly drawing that awarded an important quantity in gold coins to the bond that won. The philosopher's keen intelligence soon smelled a good deal within reach. The bonds paid guaranteed interest and could be sold whenever their holders liked. It was like having money in cash which in addition offered a safe return . . . and was entered in lottery drawings. He talked his idea over with La Condamine, a brilliant mathematician, whose qualifications he considered eminently suited for a minute analysis of the plan. La Condamine found nothing fishy about the deal; the money was there for the taking. The reasoning was simple: if they bought up all the bonds for themselves, they would necessarily win the lottery, and in addition to the interest, they would pocket fifty thousand livres a month. Naturally, the young Voltaire did not have enough money to buy up the entire issue of bonds. But he had very good friends who, of course, had no objections to being partners in this juicy deal. So they bought up—under different names—the entire issue and saw their fortunes grow month by month for over a year, the time it took the town council of Paris to realize the mistake it had made and take the pertinent measures to keep it from happening again. By the time the rules of the lottery changed, Voltaire was already moderately wealthy. His precious freedom was assured, and he wasn't yet thirty. He invested his fortune with such unusual talent and such good judgment that the effect of the passage of the years was simply to increase his wealth. When he settled in Ferney, twenty years later, Voltaire was an enormously rich man. He could even boast of having lent money to the kingdom of Prussia, always pressed for funds for its war ventures.

The smiling faces of the peasants, robust, red cheeked, well dressed, who hailed the carriage as it passed by, confirmed the prosperity of their master. For Voltaire, once he had taken up residence at Ferney, used his wealth intelligently, doing his best to see that his workers and his neighbors earned enough to lead a worthy and tranquil life. In a very short time he managed to realize an old dream: creating a tiny republic ruled by reason and tolerance, the old utopia of the wise, paternal, and benevolent governor who ensures the welfare of his subjects. He was finally able to create at Ferney that just and enlightened government he had so strongly urged upon monarchs in his works and upon Frederick by speaking directly into his ear. He taught the peasants to improve their techniques of cultivation and secured posts for their sons, instructing them in the difficult art of watchmaking that his Geneva neighbors were so adept at. Paradoxically, he fortified the religious beliefs of his villagers, for he was convinced that the principles of Catholicism have a wholesome influence on humble people. He gave out work and wealth, trying to involve everyone in the common good. Inspired perhaps by the Jesuit republic of Paraguay, which he so greatly admired, he tried to make of Ferney a splendid showpiece of what a human community is capable of achieving if it is governed wisely and beneficently.

The berlin finally reached the heart of the town, where the philosopher's residence was located. It was an imposing square construction, three stories high. The building, recently restored, had been redone in the purest neoclassic style. The walls, now perfectly smooth, were painted cream color. The trim around the windows and the two little doors that opened at either end of each one of them were painted a luminous green. The imaginary lines that joined the windows and the main door headed, in an impeccable straight line, toward a distant vanishing point. The whole was harmonious and symmetrical; it gave the sensation that if each end of the building were placed in the weighing pans of an enormous balance scale, they would not deviate from their position of equilibrium by the least fraction. A gentle semicircular projection in the center of the west wing of the building broke the regularity of the design. Opposite this facade rose a singular garden, in the literal sense of the word *rose,* for the garden was on an esplanade two paces high. The esplanade was rectangular and was more than two hundred paces long; it ended in a semicircle that formed a counterpart to the one on the facade and enclosed a little circular fountain adorned with a graceful obelisk in the center. One could stroll through the garden on flagstone walkways, bordered with perfectly pruned hedges. The garden was no doubt inspired by the one Le Nôtre had designed at Versailles, which was to win immortality. This one, of course, was much smaller, though more harmonious and more elegant as well.

When the berlin passed through the main gate of the mansion, Rasero could see, to one side of the building, a swarm of masons mounted on large wooden scaffoldings. They were polishing one by one the stones of the facade of what was to be the parish church of Ferney, where shortly thereafter Voltaire, that incorrigible freethinker, the scourge of priests and intolerance, would beatifically receive the sacraments and divulge *Urbi et Orbi* his Christian vocation. "I am terrified by the idea that when I die, my remains will be thrown out of a cemetery," he was to confess a little later to the Malagan. The memory of the corpse of that extraordinary actress he had met when he was still almost a child, the memory of the image of Adrienne Lecouvreur, clumsily shrouded in a coarse cotton cape and thrown in a common grave covered with quicklime, her exposed skin condemned to rot like that of some sort of vermin because she had been a sinner and had died without repenting, had tormented the philosopher ever since. His worst fear was that death—that old lifelong companion—would take him by surprise and force his ailing but beloved body to be a feast for worms without the protection of an oak coffin, or even the company of a few bodies that had received a blessing. Perhaps for that reason he fought so zealously in his defense of poor Joan Calas, accused of making an attempt on the life of his own son. Voltaire did not rest until, four years later, he succeeded in vindicating the honor of the unfortunate Huguenot, although he was unable to save Calas' life, since he was put to death a year later, in 1762. Voltaire himself defrayed the expenses of having his remains transported to a pantheon on consecrated ground. It was for that reason that he built that pretty chapel at Ferney and lovingly cared for it, because that man never believed in God, but always in death, and wanted to be prepared to meet it as clean and pure as a piece of Bohemian crystal.

Longchamp, Voltaire's faithful secretary, was awaiting him at the door, accompanied by two neatly uniformed footmen. He greeted Rasero amiably and affectionately, as though he had known him for a long time. He explained to him that the master was still asleep but that he would receive him in the afternoon "if it please your lordship." Meanwhile, he would see him to his bedroom so that he could make himself comfortable, tidy himself up, and rest a little to rid himself of the fatigue of the journey. As he followed him, Rasero observed the inside of the mansion. It was undeniable that the creator of the sentence "The earthly paradise is where I am" lived there. An exquisite taste was to be found everywhere, as though it were the master of the house. He could see several small, inviting drawing rooms, with graceful Louis XV–style furniture painted in pastel colors, upholstered in velvet the embroideries of which brought to mind delicate flowers. Paintings by Watteau, Correggio, Boucher, and Poussin stood out on the walls. In every nook and corner a detail of good taste suddenly made its appearance: lovely sculptures by Bouchardon, a table with a foot warmer atop which was a large Chinese porcelain vase, a sideboard on which a very beautiful tea set of Mexican silver, at least a hundred years old, gleamed, and a thousand other exquisite touches. Wherever he directed his gaze, it always ended up alighting in a cheerful, pleasant, and harmonious corner, as though he were strolling through Cupid's house on Olympus. Rasero couldn't help remembering his beloved friend, the Marquise de Pompadour, whose taste was so like the philosopher's. If he had not had the recent memory of a journey of several days still lingering in his mind, he could have sworn that he was at the Elysée Palace or in Choissy, or in La Pompadour's own quarters at Versailles. It might be thought that the marquise and the philosopher shared an architect, a decorator, and even a cabinetmaker. What they undoubtedly shared—notwithstanding how far apart, physically and emotionally, the two of them now found themselves—was the spirit of the age. Among the many persons Rasero knew, no one else incarnated as perfectly the élan, the wishes, the dream of that capricious century as those two creatures. No one else loved as much as they did what was beautiful, delicate, balanced, intelligent, light, frivolous. And no one else was as horrified by the crude, the rustic, the vulgar, the obtuse, the heavy-handed. Both of them knew how to use their intelligence—with which they were so generously endowed—to secure the material riches and the position that allowed them to make a world, or at least the world that surrounded them, one that perfectly fulfilled their desires, a world full of wisdom, lively and alert, restless and talkative, a world too beautiful for most of us mortals, who never cease yearning for it as we never cease lamenting our being unable to attain it.

The distant sound of notes from a piano awakened him. He had slept for barely a couple of hours and felt completely rested. He looked, with interest, at a tray laden with hors d'oeuvres and sweetmeats on a little low table, and alongside it a crystal pitcher containing wine diluted with water. He took a sip. It was exquisite. Port wine, he thought. He barely nibbled at a piece of ham, rinsed his face in cold water, and prepared to go downstairs to stroll about the gardens for a while on that splendid April afternoon. Downstairs he could hear the music even more clearly. Someone was playing a piece by Vivaldi, quite well, in Rasero's judgment, and curious to see who was at the piano, he opened the door that led to a little salon and peeked in.

"Monsieur Rasero!" Madame Denis exclaimed in delight and stopped playing the piano. "I can't believe it!" The woman rose to her feet and embraced him effusively. "Ah, don Fausto . . . So many years! But you're still the same. Time has had no effect on you," the woman said sincerely on looking at that strange, dauntless face, without a single wrinkle.

"Nor on you, my dear," he answered politely. "I could swear that I saw you only two weeks ago."

"Flatterer. As though I didn't see myself in the mirror every day! I've become a fat, tiresome old lady."

"Nonsense! You'll never be tiresome. The years have the same effect on you as on a good wine: they make you sweeter and more appetizing all the time," Rasero said as his index finger toyed with the big emerald necklace resting on his friend's generous bosom.

"You rascal. It's you who don't change," the woman said, remembering the enjoyable romance that she had had with that man fifteen years before.

Sitting in a corner, a very young woman was contemplating the scene with a certain reserve. She sensed the excitement that that strange gentleman aroused in the incorrigible Madame Denis, who just a few minutes previously had told her of the "profound despair" she was suffering from because of the irresistible La Harpe, who had robbed her of "all happiness, all hope," because "loving that man as I do, my friend, is like being at the gates of madness." And now that fickle woman appeared to have forgotten her despair. She was trying out her best smile and filling her lungs with air in order to make her breasts, which the man was indiscreetly staring at, appear even prouder and more youthful. Still, on taking a good look at him, she understood her friend. She herself felt strongly attracted by that gentleman, soberly dressed in dark blue, despite the fact that he was far from being a good-looking man, showing off his round bald pate without the least modesty. Perhaps it was his eyes set so far apart, with those enormous black pupils that rather than giving a woman the feeling that he was looking straight through her, made her feel reflected in them. At any event, the vertigo of desire had made a nest for itself within her.

"Ah, my dear! I beg your pardon. The pleasure of seeing this young rogue has flustered me. Monsieur Rasero, this is Marie Corneille. Marie, the Marquis Fausto de Rasero."

"I am at your feet, miss. You don't know how happy I am to meet a descendant of the great Corneille."

In one of his letters, Voltaire had told him how he had had news of that sad girl, the direct descendant of the great dramatist, who had found herself forsaken and was living in absolute poverty. Voltaire adopted her and installed her at Ferney, showering her with every sort of attention and care. In those days he was busy looking for a good husband for her. And not content with doing all that for her, he finally carried out an old plan that, for one reason or another, he had been putting off for a long time: he collected Corneille's complete works and prepared a meticulous edition of them that included, in addition to the prologue, a large number of very precise and penetrating commentaries by Voltaire himself. The philosopher gave the rights to the edition, which was a great success, over to his protégée.

Madame Denis ordered a footman to serve tea and invited her friend to sit down. "You aren't leaving here until you tell me all the latest gossip from Paris," she said with a smile and began to bombard Rasero with a thousand questions. "And dear Monsieur d'Alembert? Is it true that La Pompadour is very ill? How much has really been lost in this war? Denis has finally left his wife, isn't that so? Is it true that Catherine invited him to Russia?" Rasero answered her questions one after the other as best he could. He felt like an undergraduate before a learned doctor of the Sorbonne.

During their chat, the Malagan looked at the girl every so often. On feeling herself observed, Marie lowered her eyes, although she could not keep her cheeks from flushing. As he observed her, a very similar episode he had experienced at Cirey came to his mind.

He was at Madame Du Châtelet's mansion talking with two women as he waited for Voltaire. As now, one of them was very young and timid and the other a mature woman who was beginning to leave her best years behind her. The latter was Madame Du Châtelet, the philosopher's eternal friend, an intelligent and energetic woman, as enterprising and sharp-witted as her lover, and of a certainty more sensual. At that time she was beginning to fall in love with Saint-Lambert, a young officer many years younger than herself, who had managed to bewitch her with his melancholy, languid gaze. It was a love that was to cost her her life, for she died giving birth to a son of his four years later. Voltaire, for whom it was not easy to allow anything or anyone to escape his grasp, knew about his friend's feelings for Saint-Lambert, but to tell the truth, it was not a matter of great importance to him. He himself, to the great displeasure of Madame Du Châtelet, had aimed his amorous batteries in another direction. And they were directed at his beloved niece, no less: at Madame Denis, the daughter of his deceased brother Armand. The young woman had just been widowed and accepted her uncle's invitation to come live with him. The familial love that Voltaire felt for his niece little by little turned into a lover's passion, a love that lasted a great deal longer than anyone had thought it would. Voltaire kept his niece with him, despite her continual infidelities—although admittedly, the philosopher was not very discreet about his relations with other ladies either—until the last day of his life. And this matron, who had already seen her best years go by and who was standing before Rasero, pressing him for news of the court, was the same young girl who fifteen years before avoided his gaze and blushed, as Marie Corneille was doing now.

He remembered that afternoon very well. He never got to speak with Voltaire, for that day the philosopher suffered one of his sudden indispositions. Longchamp, his secretary, came to inform them that the master wasn't feeling well. That morbid fever that had tormented him for more than a month had unfortunately returned. Madame Du Châtelet hastened to her lover's bedroom, and Rasero tried to go on chatting with his niece, who was becoming more and more reserved and dizzied by desire. Her young body, recently initiated into the delights of sex at the expert hands of her uncle, urgently demanded to be possessed by that strange bald young man. Rasero understood the young girl's discomposure. Without a word, he took her by the hand and led her to her bedroom. He remembered that afternoon very well because of the vision that he had had on making love to the girl: with surprising clarity, he saw descending from the sky one of those flying machines that he had already seen several times. But this one was very large, dark green in color, with two darts on each wing. He saw it alight on the ground, gently, smoothly, despite the fact that it must have weighed tons. It landed on a very well paved roadway. Little by little it approached the ground until the squealing of the four pairs of wheels that stood out from its lower body signaled that the vehicle had touched down. It went on rolling over the ground for some hundred paces, until it finally came to a stop. That vision contributed mightily to increase out of all proportion the doubts that were beginning to incubate in his head. It's a machine of the future, was his first thought; but his intelligence refused to accept that his visions were a form of clairvoyance. The memory of those frightful images of the year '45 were too fresh in his memory to allow him to accept a line of reasoning of this sort. He remembered then what he had read a short time before in a book by the great medieval philosopher Roger Bacon. The text read word for word, "Machines could be constructed that would enable boats to sail over the seas more swiftly than by using a multitude of rowers, and carriages with an incredible speed without using draft animals, and, finally, it would not be impossible to build devices with a winged apparatus that would make it possible to fly like birds." He found in this paragraph an explanation. The vision that you had with the appealing Madame Denis, he told himself, is nothing other than a fantastic image from Bacon's text. He thereby only just succeeded in calming his doubts, because, deep within himself, he felt that the vision was too clear and precise to be merely a product of his imagination.

Madame Denis continued her interrogation. That woman's memory was prodigious. She had meticulously filed away in her head names, dates, places, and events that poured out one after the other from her tireless mouth. Rasero could not come up with an answer in most cases. On noting her friend's doubts, as he arched his eyebrows and simply stammered something or other, she answered her questions herself, so that little by little the chat turned into a monologue. "What do you know about the problems that Choiseul has had with La Pompadour?"

"I have no idea, madam. I fear that you know a great deal more than I do about what is happening at court . . ."

Satisfied, Madame Denis began to answer her own question. Rasero glanced out of the corner of his eye at Marie Corneille, who returned his look with a smile of complicity. She was not a pretty woman. Her little, chubby body showed warning signs that she would be obese once she reached maturity. Her round, pale face, dotted with freckles, framed large gray eyes; they bulged slightly and gave her face a look of perpetual fright, like a hare in a cage. Even so, the girl's youth and eagerness powerfully attracted Rasero. And it would not be long before he made her his.

The following morning, after staying awake all that memorable night listening to the philosopher, Rasero decided to stroll in the gardens for a time before going to his room to sleep. In the east, the sky was turning red. A few birds began to sing, announcing the beginning of a lovely spring day. Rasero walked along slowly, mulling over in his mind the things that Voltaire had told him, repeating to himself the question that he had asked himself throughout the night. Why does Voltaire have such a great fear of death? It is no doubt owing to this fear, he said to himself, that a man as frail and sickly by nature as he is, is so energetic and vital. It is this fear that makes him end up undertaking his fantastic projects, undertakings worthy of Prometheus . . . On seeing the little silhouette of Marie Corneille sitting on a bench, he came out of his state of self-absorption. "Good day, miss. We're going to have a fine morning."

"So it seems, sir," the girl barely managed to stammer in reply. She was even more reserved than the night before. In fact, she hadn't slept a wink all night either. Her desire for that man had set every pore of her skin on fire. Several times during the night, surprised by her own daring, she had left her room and gone to Rasero's. Blushing for shame but spurred on by desire, she had entered the visitor's bedroom ready to throw herself into his arms without exchanging a single word. But to her misfortune, the three times that she succeeded in overcoming her modesty to go visit the Malagan, she found his bedroom empty. The last time she did so, as she returned to her own room, she heard through the door of the library the philosopher's high-pitched voice. "To want to live, my friend, is the one thing that gives a person strength; to want to live fully, completely. Then it matters little if our body is feeble; we can get the better of it as often as we like. Provided that our eagerness to live is vastly superior to that hidden urge to die that all of us bear within us . . ." She did not want to go on listening. To a certain extent, she was afraid of Voltaire, and even more afraid of the things he said. Every time she found herself in the presence of that man, who had been so generous to her, she could not help feeling a very uncomfortable sensation, something like being naked before a tribunal of inquisitors. Voltaire's fierce intelligence incapacitated her, made her feel even more dull and stupid; her mind became confused and her tongue clung to the roof of her mouth. He must think I'm an idiot, she told herself when she was with the philosopher and saw the good-natured smile that, invariably, the man beamed at her. She didn't feel like going to her room. She decided to go down into the garden. Perhaps the cool early-morning air would lessen a bit the stifling heat that she felt in her body. Sitting on a bench, she finally managed to relax. She closed her eyes halfway so as to listen to the song of the birds and feel on her skin the freshness of the dew. She sank into a profound lethargy. She was enjoying the delightful sensation of not thinking about anything at all when, on opening her eyes, she saw before her the man who had caused her sleepless night. She felt an emptiness in her stomach that nearly suffocated her. She couldn't understand how she had been able to answer Rasero's greeting, when the latter, gallantly, took her by the hand, and without saying a word, led her to her room, as he had done fifteen years before with Madame Denis.

For the first time in his life, Rasero took more pleasure in his vision than in his orgasm. And for the first time as well, he was not distressed by the certainty that he was looking into the future. He was happy, euphoric. He covered Marie's body with kisses and caresses and made love to her as many times as his strength permitted. Naturally, the girl was also happy. I've never been made love to with such passion, and I don't believe that I ever shall be again, Marie Corneille thought with a certain regret. They scarcely spoke. After the first preliminary maneuvers, they had attained perfect communion. Every time Rasero reached climax, the girl looked at him: she could see a faint, satisfied smile on the man's countenance as he lay face up, with his eyes wide open, staring at the ceiling. He then stroked Marie's reddish hair, as he said to her, "I'm never going to forget you, my child. Never." The girl softly kissed that dear bald head and passed her fingertips over the Malagan's face. Perhaps she was remembering the words of Voltaire that she had heard from behind the library door: "To live fully, completely . . ." Her kisses became more intense until she succeeded in reviving her man so as to begin, joyfully, a new battle. Finally, exhausted, storing up a happiness that she knew she would no doubt cherish all her life, Marie fell into a deep sleep. Taking care not to awaken her, Rasero got out of bed, dressed, and headed for his room. He was not sleepy; he felt in his body a dull, pleasant fatigue, as though he were immersed in warm water. He laughed at himself, at the thought of the expression his face must have, so unaccustomed to displaying any sort of emotion. On finding himself in front of a mirror, he saw his suspicion confirmed. His eyes, usually wide open, were half closed, and his mouth showed a faint, serene, smile, a beatific one, so to speak. He saw the expression of a man in love who has at last secured the favors of his beloved. As he looked at himself, his smile grew broader, although it did not reach the point of changing into a mocking expression, but instead manifested complete satisfaction. And why shouldn't he be satisfied? It had been a perfect day. First of all, that unforgettable evening with the philosopher, during which he had had the good fortune of finding him at one of his best moments: lucid, tranquil, with his imposing intelligence working at full capacity, without casting a pall over his marvelous monologues with the tedious complaints and the insidious gossip with which he usually seasoned his conversation. That night Voltaire was at the apogee of genius, and Rasero had the immense good luck of being a witness to this. He had spent a long evening listening to him alone, to the disquisitions of the greatest man of his time. And afterward, greeting the dawn in the arms of that timid girl who had transported him to the realm of those splendid visions. He didn't want to wait any longer; he was anxious to note down what he had just seen. He took his black memorandum book and his inkwell out of a valise, cut a goose quill pen, and in the section entitled "Curiosities," began to write, departing for the first time from the cryptic, succinct style in which his notes were customarily written:

April 12, 1761. Marvelous day in the arms of Marie Corneille. It is difficult for me to describe what I've seen. The strange images are still reverberating in my head. I have only to close my eyes to immerse myself in them once again. If only I could retain this sensation my whole life long! But I know that that is impossible. Time effaces everything, the present as well as the future. Many of the visions that I have had I remember vaguely, like any other past event. I have even forgotten many more of them. Therefore I want to set down in as much detail as possible what I have just seen, so that these fantastic images in my memory may not entirely vanish.

I saw a strange device floating in empty air. It was a gleaming white and very bright, so much so that seeing it hurt one's eyes, as happens when one looks at snow on a sunny day. Its silhouette stood out clearly against a background as dark as a fish. It had the form of a cylinder, some six paces long and three wide. One of its ends was shaped like a flat-nosed cone. In the cone I could see two rectangular skylights, very close to each other and of the size of a small window. A number of very thin metal rods protruded from the body of the device; two of them were very long and ended in a point, and another one was topped with an odd, intricate wire mesh. I went inside the device. Its interior was very small, the size of a litter. Its walls were covered in their entirety with buttons, small levers, dials like those of a hunting-case watch and any number of tiny little red, green, and yellow lights that kept continually blinking on and off. Occupying practically the whole interior of the vehicle was a man in a sitting position. He was dressed in thick, heavy attire. It was evident that it fitted him very loosely; moreover, it appeared to be inflated, like a bladder full of water. The man's hands, encased in very large gloves, manipulated the buttons and levers in front of him. His head was enclosed in an enormous bubble. Half of it was made of glass, which allowed his face to be seen; the remainder of it was of another material, painted white. I could see the man. His hair was covered with a very tight-fitting white cap, similar to a leather helmet. I saw his features, harmonious and pleasing. His eyes, though wide open, seemed to me to be slightly slanted, yet not enough to make him appear to be an Asian; they reminded me, rather, of those of the Slavs of central Europe. The man was completely engrossed in looking through the skylight, almost without blinking. He was visibly moved, as though he were seeing paradise itself. Then I too looked through the window. I saw the black sky, a deep black such as I had never seen in it before. It was full of stars, a great many more than can be seen on a clear moonless night. And they could be seen with surprising clarity. Some of them were very small, their faint twinkle scarcely hurting one's retinas; there were other more brilliant ones in shades of blue. Venus shone with imposing brightness. Mars seemed within hand's reach, as red as a ruby. To the right, I could see the Milky Way, a long fringe of stars that became lost from sight in infinity. A fine white powder was intermingled with them; it looked like tobacco smoke. On contemplating that swarm of stars, I understood how right the ancients had been to give it that name. It really did look like a stream of milk poured out into the immensity of space. Never, I said to myself, have I seen anything as beautiful—when the moon appeared on my horizon. Round, brilliant, perfect, I could see it down to its slightest detail. The irregularities of its surface deflected the rays of the sun that illuminated it, producing a range of tones, from clear gray to old gold. I could swear that I saw its valleys and mountains, and called to mind the magic names with which the great Galileo had baptized them: Sea of Tranquility, Sea of Storms . . . But seeing the sun was, if that is possible, an even greater spectacle. At first I didn't recognize it. I presumed that it was an exceptionally bright star. It was that same extraordinary, majestic brightness, however, that made me realize that it could be no other star but the sun. The thing is that I had always seen it framed by the soft blue of the sky. And now I had it before me gleaming against a background as black as pitch, dotted with an infinite number of stars. It slowly moved to the left until we lost sight of it. Then, through the window on the right, the arc of a much larger body appeared, which in a very short time covered all our visual field. There unfolded before my eyes a marvelous range of shades of blue, from a very clear, almost greenish one like celadon to a very dark blue that could be confused with black, passing through varied tones of turquoise, sky blue, royal blue, Prussian blue, blending together in a delicate balance that at first sight gave the impression that one was looking at an enormous sapphire. At times, fantastic elongated forms of a very pure white, like threads of raw cotton, furrowed the blue background. Some of them were very large, covering enormous stretches and converging at one point to form a sort of whirlwind. They were clouds, I realized, clouds over an immense ocean that could be no other than the Pacific. Scarcely surprised—at this juncture, my capacity to be surprised was badly deteriorated—I realized that I was observing the earth from an unbelievable altitude, much, very much, higher than the tallest of its mountains. As though to confirm my conjectures, there appeared before my eyes a swarm of little greenish points with a coffee brown tinge, each of them surrounded by a turquoise blue halo. I realized that they were the islands of the Southern Sea, the ones first mentioned by Sebastián Elcano when he returned from his voyage around the world, and that later on were described in greater detail thanks to the expeditions of Fernández Quiroz, Vaz de Torres, the Dutchman Tesman, and so many others. Once again, as though the images read my mind and approved of my knowledge of geography, which my beloved don Joel had forcefully drummed into my head, I could see something that made my supposition an absolute certainty: the outline of an island infinitely larger than the preceding ones, bordered by a pretty fringe that went from sky blue to cobalt wherein one could make out the pink glints of coral. Within it was a whole range of earth colors, from yellow gold at its edges to nut brown in its center, dotted, moreover, with thick dark green fringes that predominated on the right side of the island, covering vast expanses. The green color, as we proceeded westward, grew fainter and fainter until it finally disappeared from sight, leaving visible an enormous stretch of reddish yellow land bordered by dark mountains. It was Australia, the last continent that Western man discovered on earth, a mere century and a half ago. The man at my side was as moved as I was: a while before he had stopped manipulating the apparatuses in front of him and was simply contemplating the panorama with his eyes so wide open that they seemed to be about to break through the folds of his eyelids. Tears flowed from them as he stammered something that I was unable to understand. Whoever he is, I thought, he and the era to which he belongs are obviously not yet accustomed to voyages of this nature. Otherwise he wouldn't be showing such evident signs of excitement. The image of the great desert in the heart of Australia was the last thing I managed to see. The fatigue of my body, and that of my young lady friend, I believe, kept me from setting out on the voyage once again. For I must explain that, although I have written a linear and continuous account of what I have seen, in reality that was not how it happened. What is written here is the result of my having put together bits and pieces of the four visions that I had in the arms of the complaisant Marie Corneille.

He reread what he had written. It did not satisfy him. The text was far from reflecting what he had seen. The images in his head, still fresh, were infinitely more beautiful, more dazzling, than what he had endeavored to express. He was about to tear out the pages and write the whole thing over. But he restrained himself; he realized that it was useless. There was no way to reflect in a text what he had seen. Certainly he was unable to do so, for he was far from being a man of letters. He consoled himself by thinking that at least he had not left out anything important. Perhaps when, many years hence, he reread what he had written, the images described would give his memory an excuse to gather them together and re-create them exactly as they had been, as happens with those likable public storytellers who have in written form only the first paragraph of each story, and once they reread it, can then recite all of it fluently without forgetting a single word.

He was exhausted; he poured himself a generous drink of brandy and collapsed in an easy chair. The images, little by little, left his mind. Their place began to be occupied by reflections on what he had seen.

Where the devil does orgasm take me? he asked himself. How close or how far away is that future? Will mankind be able to go that far, to invent devices that will take it beyond the sky, nose to nose with the stars themselves? What would good Buffon say if he had seen what I have? He would be happy, doubtless. "Here you have science and its infinite power," he would shout to the whole world. "Human inventiveness is inexhaustible. We can do anything we want to. Yes, friends, whatever we want to. We need only study nature, understand its laws, respect its principles, and the world will be at our feet, inexhaustible and generous. We will take from it food, health, riches, whatever we like. That is why I make mock of those who make mock of my work, of my struggle to defend learning, philosophy, and science; I laugh at those who laugh at my style; 'pompous,' they call it. Forceful, rather, I would answer them, vital, beautiful, and richly adorned, because our future is beautiful, because our intelligence is richly adorned by divine gifts. We are perfect creatures, our ability to learn is inexhaustible, our future is sublime. We are called upon to remake, with our own hands, with our intelligence, the kingdom of God in order to return, as an equal to an equal, one day not very far off, to the arms of our Maker."

But what would poor Buffon say, Rasero wondered, if he were to take a look at my other visions, in which science—which is so dear to him—has served only to give men the means to annihilate one another with such cruelty and such power that our own wars seem like children's games? Would Buffon go on writing book after book in which he gives an account of scientific knowledge and makes a sweet little story out of it, in an attempt to make it comprehensible to any mortal who can just barely read? I doubt it. The man who surely would be satisfied if he were able to have a glimpse of the horrible images that have so often entered my head is Rousseau. He would no doubt say, "Here you have your civilized man, able to climb above the clouds . . . without question in order to look for new battlefields, since our old planet will soon be too small for its weapons. Here you have science, gentlemen, creating devices that make us swifter and crueler, devices of destruction that will add several zeros to the right on the final balance sheets of war. Its victims will be counted no longer by the thousands but by the millions, until the blessed day arrives when not a single biped remains on earth to keep an accounting. That is where that accursed obsession to transform everything, to refuse to accept things as they are, is inevitably taking us. That demoniacal inventiveness we so proudly boast of will end up destroying all of us. If you don't agree, look behind you: what do those sad phalanxes of Alexander's with their five hundred men protected behind leather shields, fighting with the same number of Persians armed with their frail bronze-tipped lances, who after a day of exhausting labor succeed in sowing the battlefield with a hundred or two hundred dead, and returning to their camps exhausted, full of welts and bruises, amount to compared with our modern armies, in which a few men in showy uniforms, lined up behind fearsome cannons, manage with just one volley to leave many more dead than the brave Macedonians? And what are—I ask myself—these modern battles compared with those that will occur in the future, when we have perfected our science and technology, when we have mastered so great a fund of knowledge that escapes us today? I don't even want to imagine it."

"If Rousseau had his way, we'd go about naked on all fours and live in caves or in the treetops," Rasero recalled Voltaire to have said the night before. What a shame not to have had this vision earlier! the Malagan thought. It would surely have given François a different slant on my comments."

Madame Denis gave every sign that she was going to talk without a letup for the whole afternoon when, without warning, the double doors of the salon were thrown open. It was Voltaire. Halting in the doorframe, he raised his arms to greet you. You could see how odd he looked: an old man of medium build who had already left his sixties behind, as skinny as a rail and, as was his way, bizarrely attired. He was wearing a pair of old cream-colored slippers and white hose beneath his loose-fitting breeches of red velvet; his body was bundled in a white silk nightshirt as well, over which he was wearing a tight-fitting vest embroidered with showy multicolored flowers. Over all this was a threadbare black tailcoat that was too big for him. His head too was doubly covered, first by a powdered wig with long wavy locks, uncurled and very old, dating from the days of the Regency or perhaps even before. On top of that a nice bonnet of bright red wool crowned his head.

"Come into my arms, dear friend!"

He embraced you effusively and kissed you on both cheeks. Then, with his hands on your shoulders, he stepped back just a little to have a look at you. In his withered, wrinkled face, his angular cheekbones stood out, owing to his thinness as well as to his toothlessness, which made his mouth look like a cruel wound above his strong, jutting jaw. His nose, big and sharply outlined, was rooted amid thick, animated eyebrows, beneath which gleamed his deep-set eyes, seeming to lurk in ambush—doubtless the man's most formidable feature. They were large and almond-shaped; his irises, the color of gray steel, framed dark black, very dilated pupils which, as they observed you, seemed to drill into your head, as if to rummage in the folds of your brain.

"How's that body of yours doing?" he asked you.

"Very well, fortunately, sir."

"You know what, Marie? This man has never been sick a day in his life. I don't understand why I let him into my house, because I know very well that envy makes my ailments worse." You smiled. "It's true. Haven't you heard it said, 'He turned green with envy'? Well, green may be a very healthy color for plants, but not for people. Come on, let's have supper right away, before I too turn green . . ."

They ate in a small salon. Its walls, painted sky blue, were decorated with graceful plaster moldings that framed the delicate engravings of country and worldly life that had come from the screw presses of Boucher, Watteau, and Poussin. The footmen, in elegant livery, glided silently about the room, now serving the soup, now removing dishes from the table, now refilling the wine glasses. Voltaire felt wonderful. He had already discovered in Paris that the presence of the Spaniard agreed with him. He had forgotten his permanent backache for a time; his belly, as if by magic, had stopped rumbling, something unbelievable; his hands scarcely trembled. He ate heartily, forgetting moderation, to the point that Madame Denis had to admonish her uncle when she saw that he was helping himself to a double portion of truffles.

"François, don't overindulge. Remember how they make your stomach burn."

What Voltaire wanted least was to be reminded of those odious burning sensations, the accursed acidity that had taken up residence in the pit of his stomach and that tormented him from the moment he opened his eyes in the morning until he was able to drop off to sleep at night. For some time now not even the carbonate salts prescribed for him by Dr. Théodore Tronchin (his kindly physician in Geneva, who sometimes confessed to you that he didn't understand how the aged body of his patient was able to accumulate so many aches and pains and subject itself at the same time to the very hard work that he forced it to do) gave him relief. The acidity had disappeared now, however; he could eat the truffles and enjoy the delicious wine in which, surely, he was also overindulging, without feeling anything besides a pleasant warmth in his body.

The topic turned to old friends, and Madame Denis, rather than you, assumed the task of bringing the philosopher up to date on their lives.

"Let Fausto answer me, dear. I know that you know what happens in even the most miserable tavern in Paris. Believe me, Fausto, my niece is so well informed that sometimes I forget that I live in the country, in Ferney, two hundred leagues away from Paris, and feel as though I live in an apartment in the rue St-Honoré."

Voltaire learned about Grimm's tireless labors. Now, besides his financial dealings, his negotiations at court, and his literary review, the German was taking steps to bring Voltaire to Paris.

"My good Melchior . . . That's impossible, as you know very well, Fausto. Madame de Pompadour has insisted that I not set foot in the capital. Do you know that three years ago she declared me persona non grata at court? She accuses me of collaborating with the Prussians. What really happened was that she couldn't find anyone better to blame for this stupid war that she, and she alone, started. And do you know why she did so? Because she couldn't resist, like the good commoner she is, a queen's flattering words. Maria Theresa is very clever, there's no doubt about it. In order to rescue her beloved Silesia, which you may be sure Frederick is never going to let go of—he'd rather let his kingdom collapse than see Silesia taken away from Prussia—for that piece of land, as I was saying, Maria Theresa stooped to pleading with a concubine, no less. And since, as you know very well, it's through Jeanne-Antoinette's ears that our beloved king hears . . . In short, I'll write to Melchior nonetheless to thank him for his futile efforts."

You and Voltaire spoke also of Madame Du Deffand, of the Marquis de Pussilles, of d'Argental, and of Duclos, who had replaced Voltaire as royal historiographer.

"And what do you think of Monsieur Duclos?"

"He's a disagreeable man. He works like a mule to inch ahead like an ant. His intelligence is as blunt as a pig's snout; ah, but he thinks he's sharper than a tack."

"Severe judgments, dear Fausto; though I can't help but share them . . ."

In the guest's honor, the desserts were accompanied by a sweet Malaga wine. The odor of the muscatel transported you to the cellar in the old mansion in the calle Miaja. You used to play war games there with your cousin José. You were the chief of the Mexican Indians, and he, of course, was Hernán Cortés in person. Wine corks were the ammunition used in the battle. "Long live God and Our Lady of Remedies!" your cousin shouted, and rained corks upon you.

"Tell me, Fausto, did you attend the premiere of *The Philosophes?*"

The question erased the images from your mind and the smile from your lips. "Yes," you began to reply without knowing how to go on. Of course you went to see it, and enjoyed the work as though you were a child. You laughed till you cried; Palissot's dialogues were really worthy of Molière. And that actor, Pierre somebody or other, was inspired. You had never seen anyone put on such an amusing performance. Walking like an old man, trembling from his ankles to his head, opening his eyes as wide as soup plates, raising his thumb and his index finger to his nose to protect it against the stench given off by his friend, a fat actor with the red face of a heavy drinker, who recited a rosary of stupid remarks that didn't spare Homer, Descartes, Newton, or even Jesus himself. At least twenty times the actors interrupted their performance to accept the applause of the audience, which completely filled the theater. You hadn't seen anything like that for years . . . The problem was to tell Voltaire all this without souring the good humor he'd shown all during the afternoon. It so happened that the work, unusually cruel and corrosive, was devoted to the philosophes, and especially to Voltaire. Palissot had tried—very successfully—to emulate Aristophanes and his *Clouds,* in which the Greek had pitilessly satirized Socrates and the Sophists. To top it all off, Pierre somebody or other, the very funny actor, played Voltaire himself, who was portrayed in the work as a trembling, crippled oldster, the very one who was now facing you, asking you to tell him about the performance.

"Admit that you were amused, you coward!" he said to you. "I've read the text, and although it nettles me, I have to admit it's marvelous. Several times I caught myself laughing my head off at myself. Poor Palissot . . . if his aim was to enrage me, he failed from first to last, because what he succeeded in doing was to make me laugh harder than I have for a long time."

Relieved, you began to give an enthusiastic account of the witty scenes, the remarkable performance of Pierre somebody or other, the misadventures of the plump toper, who was none other than your beloved Diderot. D'Holbach seriously, solemnly discussing with d'Alembert—an actor as skinny as a rail, with his face painted white—the material nature of the soul. D'Holbach insisting repeatedly that "evildoers have a soul of granite, cowards of meringue, the dimwitted of sawdust, the valiant of iron . . . and the philosophes of shit."

"All right, that's enough, Fausto," Voltaire said to you with a smile. "Don't be cruel. You give such a fluent word-for-word account of the play that I'm sure that you've seen it at least four times . . . Three? Ah! I can see how greatly you esteem us. Let's go have coffee in the library; I've had enough of Palissot."

The women excused themselves. Madame Denis still had a thousand letters to write. Marie Corneille didn't tell them what she was going to do, because she hadn't worked up the courage to open her mouth all during supper. Nor did she eat a single mouthful. The wine, on the other hand, aroused her desire. As she drained each glass of it, her face became more flushed and its expression more evasive. She appeared to be studying with scientific interest the weave of the tablecloth, for she kept her eyes riveted on the fabric for more than two hours. You held her hand between yours for a longer time than politeness called for as you bade her good-night. Your lips felt her discomposure as you courteously kissed it; you regretted not being able to accompany her to her room.

The library was the largest room in the mansion. It could easily have held a well-attended masked ball, and the orchestra as well. An enormous oak table occupied the center of it, its surface covered with any number of objects: books lying open, blank sheets of paper, galley proofs, unfolded maps, freshly cut goose-quill pens, several inkwells, two or three paper knives of fine Toledo steel, figurines of fired clay that, you presumed, had come from the New World. Your attention was attracted by a strange pipe made of fish bone with a long fish-shaped ebony stem; the bowl of it was in the form of a naked woman, who looked like a tiny ship's figurehead, and was delicately carved in bone that, because of its lightness, you suspected had to be from a whale.

"It's good-looking, isn't it? Jonathan Swift gave it to me when I was in England. An exceptionally kind man . . . but a very melancholy one."

In the middle of the wall at the end of the room was a great fireplace with a fire that had just been lit. In front of it, on a pretty arras rug, were two comfortable armchairs with a little gilded table between them, and in the corner a small table with a high-backed chair pulled up to it that seemed too large for it. On the table was a long goose quill that had just been cut, two lead inkwells, and a folio of Angoulême paper lovingly cut up into sheets. "This is the philosopher's workplace," you thought. An enormous painting hung above the fireplace. It was a magnificent portrait of Louis XIV painted by Charles Lebrun. Beneath the picture, on the staircase landing, was a row of bronze busts. You recognized Molière, Racine, Colbert, Corneille, and Mazarin. They looked at you solemnly, calmly, beneath the protective mantle of the Sun King. But what would have turned you green if envy could have done so were the high walls absolutely covered with books that you contemplated with admiration. You suspected that this man's library, which had astonished you when you visited it at Cirey, must have been added to as the years went by. But this was going too far: the enormous bookshelves—or bookcases, rather, because all the volumes were protected from dust behind thick panes of beveled glass—displayed an endless procession of titles, each book being exquisitely bound in calfskin, with its name on the spine, engraved in gold letters. Every bookcase, each measuring a good three paces long, extended from the floor to the ceiling, loaded with innumerable books on a single subject arranged in strict alphabetical order according to the initial of the author's last name. And there were at least fifty of those bookcases. You grew dizzy reading titles and names of authors and felt an emptiness in your stomach identical to the one that used to come over you as a little boy, dying of hunger, whenever you saw your beloved Angustias enter the kitchen. You recalled your first visit to Denis Diderot and couldn't help comparing the labyrinth of books all over his house, almost all of them old and worn, piled one atop the other, with these proud volumes, neatly lined up, looking in their impeccable bindings like a marshal in dress uniform. You were so overwhelmed that you were on the point of not taking out the little book that had been in the pocket of your dress coat since morning. You had bought it two years before in a bookstore in Paris specializing in very early editions of old books, with the intention of giving it to Voltaire as a gift, filled with pride at the thought that it would not be one he already had in his awesome library. You weren't so sure now. It's almost impossible, you thought, for this title not to be here: it suffices to look at these walls to be convinced that everything that mankind has written since Homer—who, of course, never wrote a word—down to our own day must be stored in those bookcases, which, alas, would one day be transported with their precious contents to the palace of that nymphomaniac Catherine in St. Petersburg.

You finally made up your mind to give him the book. When you turned toward the master, you caught him unawares with his back turned; he was standing with his right hand leaning on his hip and holding his penis with his left hand. He was urinating copiously on the coals in the fireplace.

"Ah, Fausto," he said to you. "When I was young I put out the fire in no time."

"François, I found this book in a shop in Paris. I hope you don't already have it in your library."

After adjusting his underwear, Voltaire looked with interest at the old walnut-colored leather bindings, opened the book, and read aloud, translating from the Latin, the text on the title page: "*The Image of the World.* A didactic poem, wherein are explained with much skill and good penmanship the fascinating mysteries of the practice of Astrology. Written in 1254 by the illustrious Doctor Gualtero de Metz. Paris, 1494."

"How wonderful! Of course it's not in my library. What do you imagine it to be? A collection of incunabula? Don't overestimate it, dear friend. Ah! if good Jordan were to see this book, he'd leap for joy. He swore up and down that there must be an edition of Gualtero de Metz dating from the 1400s . . . You don't know Jordan, do you? He's Frederick's librarian, an amazing person. He has a love of books surpassed only by his memory. That man's ability is incredible. He knows exactly where every book in the vast library at Potsdam is located. You can take it from me that a number of times I thought there was sorcery involved: all you had to do was barely stammer out the name of an author, or a title, and Jordan would come up with the full name and title, the date and place of publication, and the shelf where it was located amid the sea of books in that library. And that's not all. He proposed to salvage some very old documents belonging to the house of Hohenzollern that he had discovered lying forgotten in a corner of their palace in Berlin. It was a pitiful sight to see the state they were in: the pages fell apart in your hands like crumb cake. So then Jordan, with the patience of a saint, and using heaven only knows what sort of glue that he himself had invented, put together all the pieces of that paper puzzle and glazed them with a little brush soaked with that magic glue that could toughen the folios without making the letters of the texts run even the least little bit. And this despite the fact that almost all of them were written in that very thick ink that was used two centuries ago."

He examined the bookplate printed in the right-hand corner of the title page. It had attracted your attention too. The main motif of the vignette was an architect's compass surrounded with filigree work from which tiny olive leaves burgeoned. The name of the owner was Johan T. Desaguiliers. You had presumed that he was some rich provincial French nobleman.

"How curious," Voltaire remarked to you. "I knew Desaguiliers. Despite what one might think, he was English. I ran across him several times in London. A very erudite, solemn man. He was a physicist, I believe. But what made him famous was being one of the first grand masters of the Masonic Lodge of England. Who could have imagined such a thing?! In those days the Masons were a very small group made up of a few old half-mad bourgeois and a handful of bored aristocrats. You should have seen what success they had! Above all when King George became a Mason. And it appears that the fashion spread like a disease to our good Frenchmen, ever avid for new things. I've been invited several times to join one lodge or another; I've even been made an honorary member of one of them. But, to tell the truth, their proceedings strike me as completely ridiculous and their supposed esotericism as extremely childish. It's the most conspicuous 'occult' group I know of. Have you heard the titles they give themselves? Grand Builder of Pyramids; Knight of the Rose Cross; Confraternity of Templars; Bearer of the Keys of King Solomon's Temple. I ask you! And it seems that there are more than thirty degrees in their hierarchy. I'm not surprised that this little book ended up in Desaguiliers' hands, since the Masons, despite preaching that reason and science are the real driving forces of progress, have an inordinate interest in occult subjects and hoaxes. They extol scientific knowledge at the same time that they forewarn us that the prophecies of Nostradamus will come true. A strange lot, the Masons, there's no doubt about it."

The philosopher sat down in front of the fireplace and began to leaf through the book you'd given him. Meanwhile, you distracted yourself admiring a pretty statue in bronze executed by Pigalle. It was a small, delicate, meticulous piece of work. It represented Zeus transformed into a bull, carrying on his back the beautiful Europa, who appeared to be journeying very comfortably in this fashion, with her eyes half closed and her long arms twined around the neck of the animal. Voltaire read at random from the book on astrology: "*Apotelesmatics,* the knowledge on which the astrology of the Egyptians and Chaldeans was founded"; "the *Sphaera barbárica* of Gemius of Rhodes and Arasti of Soli, the theoretical basis of all astral charts."

The archaic terms awakened his memory, and there came to his mind the delightful image of Olympie Dunoyer, his first love. He was very young, not yet twenty, and had left Paris for the first time in his life to go to Amsterdam as the secretary to the ambassador of France. Young and brash, full of plans, he was prepared to conquer the world. It was Olympie, a young woman approaching the prime of life, who conquered him. Married, although she had few remaining ties to her husband (an old aristocrat who lived in the country chasing wild boars), beautiful, and tireless, she was as happy as a little bird and very much given to learning and to pleasure. She soon took on the task of erasing from Voltaire's conscience that odious feeling of guilt, that revulsion for everything that was carnal that the accursed Jesuits of the Collège de Saint-Louis, with their perverted habits, had insinuated into his mind. Before meeting Olympie, he had fled from sex as from the plague, convinced that in its pleasures nothing lay hidden save filth and suffering. He had sworn to himself to remain celibate all his life. But the charms of that woman, her innate ability to give and take pleasure, made him joyously break his vows to himself and open his senses to new experiences. He even reached the point—although he didn't like to think about the subject—of evaluating the painful experiences he had had at the Collège de Saint-Louis from a totally different angle. Perhaps . . . on second thought—but the one he wanted to think about was Olympie. The woman was a fanatical devotee of astrology. Voltaire was amused when he saw her drawing complicated geometrical designs on paper, with the aid of a ruler and a compass. "You were born on November 21," she said to him, "and therefore on the cusp between two houses: that of Scorpio, the house of terror and death, and that of Sagittarius, the house of piety and religion. That's why you're so odd, François."

"A fine future the stars have in store for me," the philosopher replied. "Terror, death, piety, and religion—my fate is preordained. All that is sheer nonsense. You, for example, were born in the house of Pisces, the house of melancholy and sadness, according to what I read in the charts Cardinal Bembo drew up for you. And it just happens that you're the happiest woman I've ever known."

"That's precisely the reason why, François," Olympie shot back in annoyance, with the expression of a schoolmaster who can't manage to make himself understood. "I *have* to be happy as long as I can, because my destiny has a great deal of sadness in store for me . . ." And the horrible disease that ravaged her for two years before carrying her off to a better life when she was still a young woman was indeed a sad fate.

"Fausto, what sign were you born under?"

"Sign?"

"Of the zodiac, fellow."

"Ah, I see. Cancer, I think."

"Cancer is the house of hidden treasures . . . I insist that you're a fortunate man. You know what? Many years ago I knew a woman who was a real fanatic about astrology . . ."

He began to talk to you about that woman of long ago—Olympie, her name was—and he described her to you with such affection and enthusiasm that it wasn't hard to guess that she had once been his lover. Olympie, Voltaire told you, knew all about astral charts; she herself was able to draw them up, and he had to admit that many times she hit the nail right on the head in the most surprising way. Among the young woman's predictions, the one that had most impressed your friend was when she told him the exact cause and the precise year of the death of his mother. She had also predicted that he would become rich, and fortunately she had been right. During the time he knew her, he told you, Olympie was highly enthusiastic about a little book by Haitze that was all the rage in those days: *La Vie de Michel Nostradamus.* In terror, Olympie told her lover that the world was surely going to end in the year 2117.

"And why does that worry you, dear? I don't believe we'll live to see it."

"François, please, don't be so cynical. Imagine, so many centuries of history, of struggles, of efforts, only to have it all come tumbling down. It's horrible, horrible." There was no way to console her. Her reading of Haitze had convinced her that Nostradamus was infallible; moreover, the prediction was based on the work by Saint John, the holiest of the apostles, the one Jesus loved best. "The power that superstition has is incredible," Voltaire said to you and began to cite to you, taking pride in his prodigious memory, a great number of happenings related to superstition and astrology. Some of them you already knew about, such as that since very early times—more than three thousand years before Christ—in the *Namar Beli,* written by King Sargos and contained in the cuneiform books of King Asurbanipal, rigorous procedures were described for predicting the eclipses of the sun and the moon, and yet since that time these natural phenomena had horrified people, producing a terror that the priests of Egypt took advantage of to save the empire, a fear that even today made many women in the New World, above all those who were pregnant, keep a knife underneath a sash over their belly on nights when there is an eclipse of the moon. Or the writings of the legendary Hermes, in which the influence of the five planets on the five orifices of the head is described in detail. Or how Louis XI consulted sages and astrologers before beginning any undertaking. Or how Anne of Austria, the mother of Louis XIV, ordered, behind her husband's back, the astrologer Morin de Villefranche to stay hidden behind the curtains of the royal bedchamber so as to be able to draw up the horoscope of the prince to whom she had just given birth. Or how Tiberius, exiled on the island of Rhodes, learned, thanks to Trasilus, his faithful astrologer, that he would inherit the Roman Empire. Or how Louis XIII was known by the epithet "the Just"—although there was nothing just about him—because he had been born under the sign of Libra. But he also spoke to you about things you knew nothing about, such as that Catherine de Médicis, the intimate of Nostradamus, saved his life on several occasions when the seer was fleeing from an enraged crowd that wanted to lynch him because they regarded his prophecies as false; or that Charles V of France was so attached to this science that he made it the object of official study and even ordered a college built in Paris to provide instruction on the subject; or that in 1437 the rector of the Sorbonne appointed a commission to pronounce judgment on the influences exerted by the conjunctions and oppositions of the sun and the moon; or that in 1179, Arab,

Jewish, and Christian astronomers agreed that the conjunction of all the planets, which would occur in 1186, would bring about the destruction of the world amid "violent gales and tremendous storms," and that this agreement caused panic all over Europe for seven years; or that the mathematician Stoffler had audaciously predicted a universal deluge in the month of February, 1524, and many people prepared for it by renting boats and a physician from Toulouse, named Auriol, even had a ship built for him and his family that was an "exact" replica of Noah's ark . . .

You listened to him enthralled. The ease and wittiness with which this man expressed himself was incomparable. His erudition, far from seeming dull, presumptuous, as is so common among cultivated men, was fluent, natural, not at all pretentious. Perhaps it was because he was alone with you, free of the court of flatterers who praised him to the skies there in Versailles, whose exclamations and signs of admiration made him as puffed up as a peacock and turned him, minute by minute, into a very disagreeable person, as fatuous and pedantic as the people who surrounded him. Perhaps that was the reason his genius revealed itself fully now. His tongue glided over his words with the same art with which his pen put them in writing in those memorable works that you had never tired of admiring since you were fifteen. You thought of Thieriot, Voltaire's eternal friend. You understood the passion that that man had for the philosopher. How many times Thieriot must have had the opportunity of hearing the master as you were doing now! Serene, happy, allowing his amazing intelligence to function without hindrance. It did not surprise you that Thieriot had devoted his whole life, with genuine fervor, to Voltaire, receiving and writing countless letters, fighting tooth and nail against the court, the city council of Paris, the archbishopric, in order to obtain the permits (so often denied), the approvals and indulgences, that would allow the works of his fecund master to circulate freely. "France has given birth to the genius of this century," Thieriot, drunk and solemn, once told you, "and I have the glory of being his only friend . . ." You wanted to protest, to tell him that that wasn't true, that Voltaire had many friends, yourself among them. But on seeing his sad eyes, filled with tears, you had a glimpse of the tormented soul of that man consumed by a cruel and desperate passion, and you could not bring yourself to contradict him.

As was to be expected, the conversation turned from astrology to science, the only knowledge capable of successfully countering superstition and fraud. "You have no idea what it meant for me to discover Newton. Reason at the order of nature, or perhaps nature at the order of reason. Be that as it may, I don't believe that the world has produced a greater man than Newton. He succeeded in realizing the dream cherished for many centuries by philosophers: explaining the world, the entire universe, on the basis of a few fundamental principles. What a man! Compared with him, we are all dwarfs . . ." Voltaire had had the great good fortune of attending the funeral services for that giant. It was in April of the year 1727; he would never forget it: the procession, majestic and solemn, in Westminster Abbey, headed by the archbishop of Canterbury and King George himself. At the time, Voltaire had already had the opportunity to become acquainted with the thought of the English scholar through the work written by Pemberton, who had kindly had it sent to him before it was published. What great lucidity, what great precision! Ah! and the French savants deaf to so much grandeur. They went on stubbornly clinging to Descartes' whirlwinds. Making it more than a scientific problem, they turned it into a matter of national pride: it was not possible for an Englishman to be greater than the divine Descartes. Only one of them, Guillaume de L'Hospital, stood up for the truth and along with it, Newton. Yet his was a voice in the wilderness. Therefore Voltaire proposed to introduce the work of the English genius to the self-important French; he was even prepared to rub their noses in the *Principia.* "Believe me, Fausto, nothing has cost me as much work. Algebra and geometry are not my strong point; I struggled valiantly to have some inkling of the secrets of calculus." But in the end he succeeded. Confronted with Voltaire's will, the word *impossible* lacked meaning. He reached the point of being able to understand the Englishman and then popularized his work among the French through three of his books: the *Essay on Epic Poetry,* the *Lettres Philosophiques,* and above all, the *Eléments de la philosophie de Newton.* All of these you read with enthusiasm in Madrid with Antonio Ulloa, shortly before you left for France. Thanks to Voltaire, Newtonism won the battle and France hatched several generations of followers of this current, who managed to eclipse the English themselves, "our dear d'Alembert, first of all." You asked Voltaire where he had come across the anecdote, known now in all the schools of France, that he recounts in the *Lettres Philosophiques,* telling how the young Isaac Newton, sitting beneath an apple tree one morning, meditating on the order of the stars, suddenly saw an apple fall and at that very moment had his insight: he understood at once that the force that attracted the apple to the ground is the same one that makes the moon revolve around the earth and the earth in turn revolve around the sun—that this force is, finally, what is responsible for the equilibrium of the universe. "To tell you the truth, I made it up. Mrs. Condouit, Newton's niece, was very kind to me when I explained to her the project I was planning. She gave me a great deal of information, much of it very valuable, concerning the life of her illustrious uncle. Among the information she gave me, she one time mentioned that Sir Isaac used to say that the force of gravitation acted everywhere, from the sun, which thereby forced the planets to revolve around it, to an apple, when, attracted by Mother Earth, it falls to the ground. That is where the idea came to me from. When I wrote the essays, I intended to exalt Newton to the point that he equaled the very greatest men, ones of the stature of Euclid, Archimedes, and Galileo. While I was thinking about that, it occurred to me: what would become of the fame of Archimedes without the bathtub and his *Eureka!* or of the great Galileo without the story—absolutely false, moreover—that has him up in the Tower of Pisa, dropping down two spheres of lead before the astonished gaze of his disciples and colleagues, who see the two spheres reach the ground at the same time even though one of them weighs ten times more than the other, thereby confronting Aristotle and all the Scholastics with a dilemma? It seems to beggar belief, but history has to be embellished with falsehoods in order for it to appear to be true; it has to be given a little informal touch so that we believe in it and it becomes easier to learn. I decided then to place Newton, gravitation, and the apples together in one place. By doing so, I wanted to make his discovery—that one happens to be a real one—unforgettable. And I think I succeeded: little by little the image of the English physicist underneath the apple tree became as classic in the history of science as that of Archimedes in his bathtub." He spoke to you of the prodigious advance that physics had made since then, "so much so that I sometimes think that it is impossible nowadays to aspire to know everything. The way knowledge advances is impressive. From one new piece of knowledge ten or twenty more spring up, like a tree sending out branches. Universal knowledge, so dear to the ancient Greeks, is a thing of the past. Euler, for example, or the Bernoullis, have added so much to our knowledge in the fields of mathematics and physics that it's necessary to devote every waking hour of one's entire life to the task of assimilating it. When I was in Potsdam, I wanted to bring myself up to date on the works of Euler. The kindly Swiss mathematician took a bit of time off—although it irked him more than a little—in order to explain his work to me. I soon left him in peace, convinced that it was useless to try to accumulate so much knowledge." Even so, Voltaire did not allow the opportunity to nose about in that complicated store of knowledge to pass him by, even reaching the point of finding himself involved in the painful argument that arose between two illustrious doctors, protégés of Frederick of Prussia. "I broke with Frederick and left Prussia through the fault of Maupertuis, may he rest in peace, if he can. That man was cruel; he didn't rest till he'd seen poor König reduced to ashes. And all because the unfortunate German had dared publish something quite true: that Maupertuis' famous theory of minimum action had already been proposed by Leibniz sixty years before. I was impartial, believe me. I studied both sides of the argument in detail; I even got help from Euler, an incontrovertible authority, in order to follow the most subtle mathematical reasoning. König was in the right, unquestionably. When I told Frederick so, as my recompense he ordered a work of mine burned, drove König out of Göttingen, and wrote to Maupertuis with satisfaction telling him that he was now ready to toss me aside like an orange from which the juice has been squeezed . . ."

You now understood the cause of that argument between King Frederick and Voltaire that had caused such a stir in France some years before. "That's how life goes, Fausto," Diderot had said to you at the time. "The enlightened sovereign and protector of freedom, philosophy, and the arts orders the most celebrated work of any of his protégés, someone who had fallen into his royal arms fleeing the animosity of the provost of Versailles, to be burned in the public squares of his kingdom. What insane times!"

I shouldn't have mentioned Frederick, Voltaire thought, since despite everything, despite that acrimonious dispute, the humiliation that his being stopped at the border represented, the terrible time the king's guards gave his niece, treating her as though she were a thief, and despite all the bile that that man had poured out against Voltaire, the philosopher went on being fond of Frederick and admiring him. Just yesterday he had received a letter from him. In it Frederick invited him to return to his court; he promised to wipe the slate clean of all the "misunderstandings," as he called them, that had occurred between the two of them. It was a letter written in the style of Frederick the softhearted, of Frederick the philosopher, whom Voltaire knew so well. For that man, like no other, bore within himself two temperaments as opposite as heaven and hell could possibly be, and perhaps that was what attracted Voltaire to him and aroused his deep sympathy and, many a time, compassion. Frederick was a man who had been born with a sensitive, fragile soul, enamored of learning and of beauty, with an instinctive revulsion against violence and evil, one who at the age of eighteen, knowing himself to be the son of a cruel and nearly illiterate soldier, tried to flee and abandon a kingdom that belonged to him as his birthright but was profoundly repugnant to him personally. He tried to escape—he said—to England, a country that at that time offered itself as the mecca of free men, as the last refuge of those who had been persecuted for raising their voices and their pens against the pitiless and unjust regimes of the continent. Frederick was caught in the act of escaping and arrested, along with a beloved friend, an accomplice to his plan. They were sentenced to death, like any ordinary soldiers who desert. The hand of Frederick William, his father, did not tremble as he signed the death sentence; he would gladly kill a thousand sons before anyone might even dare hint that he was a weak and cowardly king. To Frederick's good fortune, his father's advisers succeeded in convincing the monarch that a king doesn't condemn his own son to death because of a simple act of indiscipline. They made him see that, through an act of that nature, the house of Hohenzollern—with its eight-hundred-year-old history—ran the risk of having its bloodline interrupted and, what was worse, that that kingdom of Prussia which Frederick William himself had created with so many difficulties would disappear. The prince's death sentence was commuted, but not that of his friend, whom Frederick was forced to suffer the horror of seeing die on the scaffold. "Since then," he once confessed to Voltaire, "happiness has fled from my life . . ." Four years later, he was married to Princess Elizabeth, a woman for whom he never felt the least liking. In fact, he never liked any woman in his entire life. They were hateful creatures, perfidious, selfish, capricious, mindless, motivated only by animosity and ambition. They were man-eaters—like that countess, Madame Du Châtelet, who sucked out Voltaire's talent like a vampire and did everything possible so that the philosopher wouldn't go to Berlin, for she knew that Frederick was her rival most to be feared. She cleverly used her evil arts to keep him shut up at Cirey, forced him to cool his heels endlessly at Versailles as he waited for the crumbs that that cretin Louis and that harpy of a concubine of his would deign to throw his way. While he, Frederick, offered to make the philosopher the brightest star in the brilliant firmament of great men that awaited him in Potsdam. He had succeeded in bringing Maupertuis, Wolff, Algarotti, Gravesande, Vaucanson, and Euler together at his court. He had managed to gather together the crème de la crème of the European intelligentsia, the minds that were creating a new world, in which ignorance would be a far-distant memory, who were putting down the roots of a future so glorious that no one, with the exception of Frederick himself, had dared even to dream of it. Voltaire, the most resplendent jewel of his store of treasures, put off coming for a long time, too long; his lover had to die before he made up his mind to journey to Prussia and take command of that army of intelligent geniuses. It was too late: ten years of pleading, of fleeting visits, of painful meetings had been the undoing of the moment so long hoped for. No more than three years went by before both of them realized that Sans Souci castle in Potsdam, however vast and sumptuous, was too small to house the two of them; one of them had to go, and it was Voltaire, of course. He left that immense, bellicose kingdom to create his own in Ferney, a small, harmonious one. It nonetheless was hard for Voltaire to leave that tender, gentle, intelligent Frederick, who for so many years had written him such lucid, such amorous, such fearsome letters. That ugly, unsociable man, who spent whole nights in a tiny salon in Potsdam, which he had made into an "oriental paradise," as he himself called it: soft cushions, taborets covered in leather decorated with repoussé work, brought from Turkey, beautiful Persian carpets, curtains of delicate fabrics from Damascus. Everything was a delight: the musicians, discreetly hidden, played soft melodies as Frederick and his friends, lying on the rug, reclining against the cushions as though they were Arabs, read love poems between swallows of sweet Greek wine and nibbles of exquisite sweetmeats. Frederick compared his beloved Algarotti with Antinoüs himself, and with tears in his eyes, felt the warmth of that other body alongside his: a twisted, sick body in his father's eyes. He wanted to love that adolescent physically, something that, alas, his Hohenzollern blood kept him from doing. That same blood that on the morning following one of his sybaritic evenings, gave him the vigor and the energy to preside over a meeting of the Cabinet of State. There, the other Frederick, the cruel, finical, inflexible Frederick, looked over every last item in the accounts of the expenses of his armies and impassibly pointed out on the map some region that, inevitably, would be annexed for the grandeur of his kingdom. He seduced, deceived, and betrayed his colleagues without the slightest scruple. How many sleepless nights poor Maria Theresa cost him with her Machiavellian maneuvers! He seized Silesia from her, and with it an emblem of the millenary pride of the Hapsburgs. Fearless, he allowed all the courts in Europe to look upon him with terror and hatred, like a modern Attila who had overturned an order painfully established after eight hundred years. He continued, with greater discretion, energy, and cleverness, the work of his grandfather and his father; he strengthened, enlarged, and surrounded with an aureole of respect his young kingdom, which yesterday was merely one of many electorates lost in the chaotic sea of the Holy Roman Empire. When he died, Prussia was a large country, feared throughout the world, an admired kingdom of soldiers, of real men. He, King Frederick, had done that, he who at night, surrounded by his intimates, reading Ovid's verses, had dreamed of a republic of wise men and handsome ephebi.

"In any event," Voltaire went on as he tried to efface from his memory the image of the pudgy, taciturn king of Prussia, "and despite all the bad moments that it may put us through, it is necessary to defend scientific knowledge. In addition to allowing us better to understand the world that surrounds us—and that in itself would be more than sufficient—it is undeniable that it has impressive practical effects on our daily life. Really, my friend, we scarcely suspect its scope. A clever and methodically studied observation can change our life, or at least prolong it. Think of inoculation, for instance . . ."

He began to speak to you of smallpox, that fearful disease that threatens everyone from newborn babies to the elderly, a sickness that has cut off countless lives when they have barely begun, that has pitted the faces of a great many people, robbing them of their beauty and their happiness, a sickness that in the New World killed many more people than the keen sabers of the fierce conquistadors, that bore away to a better life the king of the Mexicans himself, and with him the hope of not falling beneath the yoke of the bearded men who had come from the East. "I myself suffered from it when I was around thirty. Fortunately it did not cruelly attack me; it merely left a few scars on my body. Even so, it was something frightful. Death, my friend, standing in front of my bed, winking its eye at me and smiling obscenely, like a whore of the Palais Royal. A hell, believe me; I wouldn't even wish Fréron to have to live through an experience like that . . ." He then spoke to you of Lady Montagu, the "blessed lady!"—the wife of the English ambassador to Turkey in the twenties. That sharp-witted woman had observed that among the subjects of Mahomet IV faces pitted by smallpox were fairly rare, much more infrequent, beyond question, than in European countries (curiously, you had made that very same observation in your visions: you had never encountered a single face with traces of smallpox among the infinite number of people you had seen in that distant world). Intrigued, Lady Montagu made up her mind to unravel that mystery. She soon succeeded. Asking questions here, nosing around there, delving into the customs of that exotic people, she discovered that the Turks had developed an efficacious remedy against that terrible disease. It was a very old remedy that had turned up in Turkey a century before, having been brought there by Afghans, who themselves had learned of it from the Chinese. "Sometimes I wonder if there's anything the Chinese haven't invented . . ." Asians had used a method as old as humankind itself: homeopathy, the art of attacking illness with illness itself. The Chinese took crusts of the eruptions of smallpox, allowed them to dry and ground them up. Then they inhaled the fine powder through the nose. Some people caught the sickness, but many others acquired an immunity to it. In Lady Montagu's day, the Turks had perfected this technique. They had observed that the powder breathed in through the nose turned out in many cases to be excessive; a much smaller quantity was enough to immunize the person who breathed it, and with much less risk of infection. What they did next was inoculate the body by pricking it with a needle. They took a little pinch of the powder and placed it on some part of the body, an arm or a buttock, usually; then they gently pierced the skin with a needle, so that a tiny portion of the substance was injected into the body. Usually the patient treated in this way suffered the symptoms of the disease, but in a far milder form—fever in particular—for two or three days, at the end of which a pustule formed in the place of the inoculation. The patient shortly recovered, and in the vast majority of cases remained safe from the disease. Lady Montagu thought the remedy very prudent and reasonable. She had so much confidence in it that she inoculated her own children. She did not do the same to herself only because she had had the disease as a little girl. She convinced her husband of the virtues of the cure and succeeded in winning his support for waging a great crusade in Western Europe with the aim of making this practice the sovereign remedy for smallpox. "That was more than forty years ago, and in many countries, England first and foremost, the practice of inoculation has become common, whereby, doubtless, many people have been spared from this dread disease . . . But it has not been easy; many people do not accept this remedy. They have a more or less reasonable fear of contracting the disease; many others, and they're the worst, are opposed for religious reasons: 'It would be contrary to the Lord's designs,' the idiots say, as if God saw in science a disloyal rival, as if he had not given us intelligence to fathom the mysteries of nature and thus be able to transform them, and with our reason, reconstruct the Eden from which he banished us with such severity. The saddest part is that the country that has most stubbornly opposed this remedy is France. You can't imagine the fight that my beloved Dr. Tronchin is waging to convince his empty-headed French colleagues of the virtues of inoculation . . . The rejection of it ranges from physicians at court to village healers. For one reason or another, they have fought the remedy as zealously as the disease itself. I think this whole thing bears an aftertaste of patriotism. Our Galens find it hard to accept that the English have been able to invent something that hadn't occurred to them. Something similar to what happened in Newton's case. It saddens me that people as clear minded as our d'Alembert are playing into the hands of those cretins. Yes, Jean doesn't believe in this remedy; he's convinced that the proportion of cases that it prevents as compared with those that it brings on is such that the net number of those who come down with the disease continues to be the same as in the days when nobody was inoculated. He's become involved in a heated discussion with Daniel Bernoulli, who is a convinced believer in inoculation. They've set a deadline of ten years to make a meticulous count of the cases and let arithmetic determine which of them is right . . ."

(Of course it was Bernoulli: in the last years of the eighteenth century—naturally you didn't know this yet—inoculation had become the practice all over Europe, thereby saving many lives and preserving the beauty of many more people, even though at that time the risk of acquiring the disease on being inoculated was still fairly great, as Lagrange, the favorite disciple of your beloved d'Alembert, proved. It was not until the year 1796—when you, a very old man now, having fled from the death rattles of the Revolution, spent the last pleasant evenings of your life in Sanlúcar de Barrameda, in the company of that man, uncouth and somewhat embittered, who nonetheless painted as no one else had since the death of the great Velázquez—that an English doctor, Edward Jenner, after patient observations and studies, had the happy idea of injecting pus from the pox pustule of a cow into a human being. *Vaccination,* as it was called from then on, turned out to be infinitely more effective and reliable than the old method of inoculation and freed those who would live in the nineteenth century of that frightful disease.)

The philosopher talked to you of this remedy with such enthusiasm and vented his rage against "those ignoramuses who refuse to ensure their health out of fear of a ridiculous little prick of a needle" with such vehemence that you felt obliged to mention to him your desire to try the treatment.

"Of course, my friend," Voltaire said to you, a big smile lighting his face. "Before another day goes by, I'll write to Dr. Tronchin to come inoculate you. Everyone in my household has had it done, except for my niece, whom no human force in the world has been able to convince. She's as stubborn as a mule. It's a trait she inherited from my father, I'm certain . . . You're a courageous man, Fausto. You won't regret it . . ."

But words can't tell how much you regretted it! If you'd suspected what was awaiting you, you never would have proposed such a thing to Voltaire. Three days after that night, Dr. Tronchin appeared at the gates of the mansion. He was a robust man, as rosy cheeked as an apple, a person with refined manners and pleasant to chat with, although he had a facial tic that in the beginning distracted you from what he was saying, and later on frankly exasperated you. As he spoke, Dr. Tronchin raised his eyebrows forcefully, as though someone were violently tugging at them. When they had mounted very high, almost touching his hairline, with his forehead furrowed by three broad wrinkles, he blinked, or to be precise, he opened and closed his eyes in a purposeful way, as though a speck of dirt had found its way into them. He did this three times in a row, very quickly. Then his eyebrows returned to their normal position and he blinked as everyone else did. In exactly ten seconds—you counted them in your mind—the process was repeated. On the sixth or seventh time that he did this, you had already lost the thread of what he was saying and you thought of nothing save ending the conversation, or at least blindfolding his eyes with a handkerchief. "You're a fortunate man, Monsieur Rasero. You'll see; you're going to be free of the sinister threat of smallpox."

Yes, you knew that very well, you said to him. "François already told me about it. I think that the sooner you do it the better," you said to him with the intention of putting an end to the prolegomena (Lady Montagu's story, the Chinese, and so on . . .) that Dr. Tronchin enjoyed delivering almost as much as he did inoculating the patient. What you wanted was for it to be over soon, before you too began to raise your eyebrows and blink. Finally, in your room, Dr. Tronchin asked you to lie on the bed facedown and lower your breeches and your underwear a little. "It's not necessary to take them off; all I need is a bit of buttock," he said to you with a smile. The man began taking little glass flagons and bright-colored waters out of his leather satchel. Then an instinctive fear came over you. You felt defenseless, lying on a bed offering your pale buttocks to that trembling Swiss. You were about to leap out of bed, say to hell with everything, and run to tell Voltaire that he should note your name down on his list of the "cretins and ignoramuses" who are opposed to altering God's designs. You would have done so if you hadn't felt at that very moment three painful pricks in your buttock. They were quick and sharp; you were convinced that he inoculated you as swiftly as he opened and closed his eyes in the grip of his tic. A moan escaped you.

"That's all, Monsieur Rasero. You're now protected. You may feel a little indisposed for a few days—a little fever but nothing other than that." You got up out of bed as you pulled up your underwear. You couldn't help looking at him mistrustfully. The doctor withstood your gaze for eight seconds and then he raised his eyelids and blinked: "Come, come, my friend, it's all over . . ."

What did he mean, "all over"? Everything had barely begun. Fortunately Dr. Tronchin left immediately; he had many patients to look after and many buttocks to prick. You spent the remainder of the day in Voltaire's library looking over his books on the subject of the Middle Ages. There was more than enough material to set down in writing that treatise on the thirteenth century in France that you had been incubating in your head for ten years now. Your indispositions began after supper. You ate with the two women, for Voltaire had stayed at Les Délices, occupied by certain financial matters that needed his attention in Geneva. As was becoming the custom, Madame Denis had talked her head off and Marie Corneille, not saying one word, ate heartily as she smiled affectionately at you. "What do you think of the wine, Fausto?" the niece asked you.

"Superb," you answered. In fact, it was a very well aged Bordeaux. "Although they've chilled it too much for my taste."

"Chilled it? Nonsense! It's at room temperature. I ordered it brought up from the wine cellar early this morning. Do you find it cold, Marie dear?"

"Not at all," she answered.

As you raised the liquid to your mouth once more, it felt to you even colder, almost iced, and you noticed that your hand had begun to tremble violently.

"Dear, you're trembling. And you should see your forehead!" Your forehead, your entire bald pate was crowned with tiny drops of sweat. Now the cold had gone from your mouth to your body, just as the tremor of your hands had. "You're burning up with fever! The poor thing, it was that accursed inoculation, I'm certain. Charles! Esther! Help me to take the marquis to his room," Madame Denis ordered energetically as she pulled on the cord to summon more servants.

In your room the footmen undressed you and hastily put your nightshirt on you. Meanwhile, Madame Denis paced from one side of the room to the other prattling and muttering. She sounded like a broody hen that has just been robbed of her chicks. "What a horrible state this man is in! He's going to melt away. Those accursed Turks and that accursed Lady Montagu. As if we didn't have enough sicknesses to contend with without her coming around to us with her remedies! Ah! And François is gone. I'd like him to see Fausto in this state—he looks like a crème brûlée. Maybe he'll leave us in peace now and cease his madness. Because I'll have you know, don Fausto, that there's not a single new remedy, however nonsensical, that he doesn't want to have us take, as though we were little mice. All that's required is for a famous doctor to recommend it, and there Voltaire is, ready to test it on our persons. And to think that he wanted to inoculate me! Ah, my friend, I would never have allowed it, you can be certain of that. At least one person must stay sane in this house of lunatics . . ." You heard her from far away, as one hears people speaking in dreams. The trembling began to go away, and a dull sensation invaded your body. You might almost have been able to fall asleep if it hadn't been for the unbearable heat that the eiderdown produced in your bed. You threw it all the way off three times, and all three times Madame Denis bundled you up in it again. "Don't get uncovered, my friend. Even though you can't bear the heat, you must stay covered. 'Heat is cured with heat,' Dr. Tronchin has told me a thousand times—although now, when I think it over carefully, I shouldn't have paid any attention to him. That man too is madder than a nanny goat. Have you noticed how he keeps blinking? It's as though his head were full of fleas. And he was the one who got François excited about this inoculation nonsense. Did you know they've come close to killing Claude? Pardon me, my friend; I shouldn't have told you that . . . What would you like? . . . Some water? All right, I'll pour you a little, but don't gulp it all down at once." As quickly as it had come, your fever went away and once again you felt an intense cold that pierced your bones. You felt as though they had buried you in the snows of the Alps. You were trembling even harder now; your teeth were chattering so violently that the sound of them hurt your eardrums. You felt the veins in your head pulsing so hard that, through a reflex, you closed your eyes in order not to see when it exploded. "You're very ill. I'm going to call a doctor. After they've bled you, you'll see how much better you feel."

"No!" you cried out in terror, though your outcry came out as barely a whisper. Making a superhuman effort, you managed to utter this phrase: "My dear, I don't feel all that bad. If you let me sleep a little, I'm certain I'll be better very soon." You said it in such a calm voice that you very nearly convinced yourself. And the mere fact of thinking about a bleeding, that odious procedure that you have never understood and for which no one, not even among the eminent physicians of Versailles, has ever been able to explain to you the how or why, gave you enough vigor to fool the woman, who, half convinced, blew out the candles and withdrew backward, with her index finger at her mouth, silencing heaven only knows what phantoms, since for some time only you and she had been in the room.

On finding yourself alone, you felt better. The trembling lessened considerably, and little by little sleep came over you. You slept soundly, lulled by your own breathing, which became slower and slower. You didn't dream of anything; a thick black drop curtain filled your head. Who knows how long you remained in that state, inanimate, unconscious, as though dead, until in the middle of the deep darkness a point of light emerged. It grew larger and larger. You realized with horror that that darkness was deceptive. As in a theater that is totally darkened shortly before the performance begins so as to attract the attention of the spectators and oblige them to concentrate, so the darkness prepared you for the great performance that your senses were putting on. The light, with a silhouette that began to stand out in profile inside it, grew brighter and brighter until it had banished that delightful darkness. The silhouette now stood out clearly: it was Angustias, sitting in her old rocking chair. Her pretty black hair was caught up in a chignon, and her breasts were completely bared. They were enormous, much larger than they had really been—though even in life they had been huge. The immense mounds of firm flesh began to swell up, becoming bigger still, so big that they finally covered everything. You saw that hidden behind them was the face of your beloved Angustias, where you managed to see, shortly before it disappeared, two great tears running down her cheeks. "My little Faustillo doesn't love me anymore!" you heard her say, and when you looked again, practically the whole of her was breasts. To your surprise, you counted three of them, for yet another had appeared between the other two. It was much smaller than they were; furthermore, it didn't have a nipple but was as round and smooth as a billiard ball. It was your head, you realized, caught amid Angustias' flesh. Your body was suspended; you could hardly manage to see your little bare feet kicking in the air. You were suffocating; you realized it as you became aware that the air wasn't reaching your lungs. You were breathing through your nose and mouth as hard as you could, but not the least little bit of fresh air was reaching your body; the only thing that reached it was a highly concentrated odor of jasmine and the gypsy woman's skin. You had to leave this trap of flesh if you wanted to go on living. You managed to work your little hands loose from your face, where your nurse's breasts had them pinned down tightly. You stretched your arms and supported yourself on them as you tried to free your head by throwing it violently backward. You didn't succeed; your hands and your arms sank into the soft flesh, and with the pressure, the only thing you managed to do was to make a fine jet of white liquid spurt out of each breast. You were dying. Your panting filled your lungs with jasmine petals, to such an extent that you could feel them in your throat, which was becoming more and more plugged up. One last effort, you thought, one last effort or I'm a goner. You leaned your hands there where her breasts began, for you knew that that was the firmest handhold you had within reach. You gathered together the little strength you had left and, firmly braced, reared your head back frantically. You easily freed yourself, as when someone flings his entire body against a door to force it open and, at the very instant that it is going to hit against it, the door is flung wide open. You drew away dizzily from Angustias as you felt the fresh air smooth out the wrinkles in your lungs. You saw the woman sitting in her rocking chair, weeping and making herself smaller and smaller until she remained embedded in a patch of light that kept contracting. You didn't know whether it was you or she who drew away. Both of you perhaps. An abrupt blow on your back told you that it was you.

The noise awakened Madame Denis and she came running to your room as she shouted to Marie Corneille. "Good Lord! What's happened to him?" They found you on the floor, at the foot of the bed, on a pretty little Venetian carpet. You were curled up like a fetus and were hiding your face in both hands. "Help me, Marie dear. Poor thing, he must be delirious." The women got you back into bed and covered you up. Madame Denis, very perturbed, did not stop talking. She let out a string of invective, and curses against medicine and doctors of medicine. She went through all the ones she knew and several others that she invented, ranging from old Hippocrates to that "doddering oaf Tronchin. Some poet or other put it very well: those vultures are of no use but to ensure your journey to the other world. The spawn of vipers . . . !"

The women decided to take turns watching over you as you slept. Madame Denis left the room, leaving as she went a wake of blasphemies behind her. Marie Corneille, seated at your side, pressed your left hand between hers. Her gray eyes, slightly nearsighted, looked at you affectionately. Trying to keep your mind a blank, you were looking into her round freckled face when sleep again overtook you. An endless series of images assailed your mind. Your visions, your memories, and your imagination amalgamated to present you with a fantastic spectacle. You saw not only those crude carriages with no draft animals that moved swiftly over smooth highways, but also Damiens' mouth, with his beautiful teeth, thanking the Virgin for her favors; first the cruel smile, and then the expression of amazement, of Pierre, the hangman; the bald, starving men, who held out their bony arms toward the leader of the soldiers. At times, the swarm of scarlet wasps that came pouring out of María Pastora's back reddened the landscape. When they disappeared, you saw Denis Diderot submerged in the water fighting against the odor and the rats. Very far in the distance, Voltaire was talking. His precise, high-pitched voice was speaking to you of death: "It's at our side from the time we're born. Lying in wait, hoping for a moment's inattention on our part. I know it well. Sometimes I feel that it lives in the pit of my stomach . . ." You saw the agreeable Annette, her round curves traced on a wall, who stretched an arm out toward you but could not make it come off the wall. And again Voltaire's voice: "There it was, at the foot of my bed, as perverted and obscene as a Palais Royal whore . . ." Marie Corneille smiled at you and, dressed in a white suit with her head encased in a glass bubble, was accompanying you on high, above, very far above the clouds, in order to contemplate the enormous sapphire that the earth is. As you came down, you saw that huge city spread out on an island grow larger and larger. The tall buildings, seen from above, looked like gigantic needles pointed at the firmament. Beneath them, a dusky pink belt was forming. On the roof of the tallest building you saw a man. He seemed to be about to throw himself into the void. You went closer to him. He was bald. He was expressionless. He was you. You accompanied yourself as you fell. Vertigo made your stomach rise to your mouth. "In the pit of my stomach," Voltaire was saying, "I feel an emptiness, a terrible emptiness. I know that it is death. Because death can't be anything but emptiness. Like a knife without a blade and without a handle, that's what death is, my friend. Nothingness, much less than nothingness. And it's always there. Watching. Smiling. Waiting for a moment's inattention . . ." Dr. Tronchin, with a needle in his hand, looked at you with a smile. In ten seconds there was his tic, but now, besides blinking, he folded his ears over double and wrinkled his nose. "You're protected now, my friend," he said to you, and you finally fell from that building; you fell into a yard surrounded by a barbed-wire fence. Men and women as emaciated as death, wandered about murmuring something that you didn't understand. Their hands grabbed you with unexpected force; they seemed like grappling irons. Their fingernails buried themselves in your skin. You resisted, tried to free yourself, shook your body, but it was of no use. Between all of them, they lifted you up and carried your body stretched out above their heads, as though they were playing with a rag doll. They carried you inside the building. The irascible man with the absurd mustache smiled at you slyly from his portrait. They opened one of the ovens; you felt the wave of heat and saw inside it the bluish white color of the ovens at Sèvres. Horrified, you tried to escape, but the emaciated men held you down by force, as though their hands were tongs. They managed to put you into the oven. The heat was frightful, like falling into the heart of the sun. You remembered Diderot's bathtub, and you imagined it full of icy water—extremely cold water, thawed snow brought from the Sierra Nevada. You wanted to weep, but the heat evaporated your tears. "Don't be afraid, cousin," José said to you as he masturbated. "Pull on your foreskin. You'll see how good it feels. Pull, Faustito! Don't be a fairy . . ." You wanted to explain to him that you weren't in the mood to masturbate, that you weren't a little boy anymore and you weren't in Macharavialla, that you were inside an oven, damn it! being baked like a loaf of bread. You were sweating copiously; you felt the drops of sweat run down your face. But it wasn't sweat, it was yourself: you were melting like a wax candle. You looked at your hands in horror and saw that, little by little, they were becoming smaller as a viscous little puddle formed under where they were. You wanted to cry out, but again the jasmine petals plugged up your throat. "Don't worry, friend," you heard, "when one is completely melted, one starts to feel very good . . ." It was an Asian, perhaps a Chinese, with very slanting eyes and skin the color of parchment. He was slowly melting away. The oven became enormous and was filled with Chinese, many of them melted completely; only a tuft of hair on a shapeless heap marked their presence. Others appeared to be unaffected by the heat; they looked fresh and smiling. All of a sudden, one of them began to turn red and swell up like a balloon, until it exploded and disappeared in a sphere of light. "Aren't they marvelous?" Madame de Saissac said in your ear. "They look like little balls of phosphorus . . ." One after the other, the Chinese exploded. "In as little time as a sigh, everything goes to the devil," Voltaire said to you. "In a fleeting instant, death snatches from us what has belonged to it since we were born . . ." Your eyes hurt because of how tightly closed you had kept them. It was useless, though; the images were inside your head. You didn't know how to flee from that horror. Pray, you thought, that's it, pray. And then you recited the only thing you knew by heart, verses from the Book of Revelation: "And the fourth angel sounded, and the third part of the sun was smitten," you said in a very loud voice as, one by one, the Chinese exploded. "Woe, woe, woe to the inhabitants of the earth by reason of the other voices of the trumpet of the three angels, which are yet to sound." You were no longer praying; it was Saint John. The saint, naked, facedown, with a beautiful Jewish woman astride his waist fornicating vigorously with him, was praying, "And there came out of the smoke locusts upon the earth: and unto them was given power, as the scorpions of the earth have power." You heard Marie Corneille say in a very loud voice: "Monsieur Rasero! Please, wake up." She showed terror as she shook your body. You opened your eyes; you saw the woman's face. Tears were falling from her bulging eyes. You tried to smile at that kind woman in order to calm her anxiety. You saw her again, but she was not weeping now. Nor was she Marie Corneille. She was a mature woman and extremely pretty. She smiled at you as she looked at you and joined you in prayer: "And in those days shall men seek death and shall not find it; and shall desire to die, and death shall flee from them." She approached your bed, crawling on the floor. The face of that woman was that of the Marquise de Gironella—you recognized it now—but her body was that of a giant serpent. She climbed into your bed. She slowly drew closer to you as she raised her head. She looked lustfully at you. Her body, cold and clammy, coiled about yours. Her face was very close now. "Ah, Fausto! How strange you are," she said to you as she fixed on your eyes her gleaming irises, as dark blue as the sea. She opened her mouth; it was enormous, with long pointed fangs. Her forked tongue, very red and barely moist, licked your neck and your ears. You were petrified. A thick vapor like fog came out of the back of her mouth. It smelled of peaches. The aroma penetrated your body, a body that felt to you as tiny and trembling as that of a little mouse. She squeezed you more and more tightly; you could feel your bones being dislocated. You lost your rigidity; you were a rag. The tongue of the marquise–boa constrictor was licking your bald pate when her mouth opened even wider and swallowed you completely. Inside her there was nothing; it was like being in a tomb. You were accompanied only by a strong odor of ripe peaches. Relieved, you allowed yourself to drift off to sleep. You spent a long time in the marquise' cool belly. You slept soundly, oblivious to everything, when a strange sensation awakened you. You felt someone staring at you intently. On opening your eyes, you noted that you were still enveloped in darkness, although it was not as pronounced now; you could just barely see, almost make out an outline. Little by little it filled in. In front of you, very high up, you saw an imposing Gothic statue. Elongated and almost rectangular, its limbs were embedded in the stone. On seeing that square face with a thick beard and its eyes sunk in the granite, you realized that it was Saint Joseph, for you noted the expression of a resentful husband on his face. His eyes took on life and looked down with infinite tenderness to one side of you. You looked there too and saw four newborn babes, covered with wool blankets, who were weeping copiously. They were lying at the foot of the staircase of a temple. Their little hands and feet had freed themselves of their covers and they were anxiously twisting and turning to the rhythm of their bellowing. When you went over to them, they stopped crying. The first of them, a robust child with pretty gray eyes, looked at you with curiosity. It was d'Alembert, there was no doubt about it; his melancholy and intelligent look could not be that of any other orphan. The other two at his side closely resembled each other. Their skulls were covered with a fine reddish down; they looked fearfully at you with their big blue eyes. "The Emiles," you thought. They were the sons of Jean-Jacques Rousseau, the great pedagogue, who had abandoned them almost as soon as they were born. Their little pink bodies, their anxious looks, moved you deeply. You felt, as you hadn't felt for a long time, the sorrow of orphanhood. The other baby was you yourself. Your round head and your black eyes set very far apart from each other made you look more like an Oquendo than ever. When you saw yourself, you began to cry again, still louder; you writhed and kicked, asking yourself with your shrieks why your mother had abandoned you when your life had barely begun. You wept torrents; you inundated the temple with your tears, a sticky, transparent liquid like anisette. "Come, come, child, don't cry. Calm down, my darling," she consoled you in a very soft voice. You quieted down, stopped kicking, and looked about, with your little mosquito eyes, for the woman whose voice it was. "That's better, Faustito. Much better," she said to you again, when you finally found her. She was in a street along which swift vehicles without draft animals were passing by. She was on the edge of the sidewalk, sitting on one of those strange devices with two big thin wheels that you had seen so many times. One of her feet was resting on the ground and the other on a sort of pedal in the midsection of the apparatus. Her legs were encased in a pair of very tight black breeches that hinted at her well-shaped curves. She was wearing a white shirt, very tight fitting as well. She straightened from her narrow waist upward, affording a glimpse of her firm, erect breasts, whose nipples could be seen trying to break through the cloth. It was obvious that she was wearing nothing underneath, not a corset nor a girdle nor a camisole. Her neck was long and delicate, supporting an adorable head. Her chestnut brown hair, very fine, was loose, falling over her shoulders. In her face, a perfect oval, with cheeks that were generous but did not quite make it round, were splendid eyes beneath thick, well-defined eyebrows. Her eyes were big, and her irises shone with a curious color, bordering at once on green and coffee, that reminded you of the color of the mountains of Australia when you saw them from the heights of your coupling with Marie Corneille. Her nose was long and pointed, slightly aquiline, just enough not to make her face look hard but giving it, on the contrary, greater graciousness. Her skin, smooth and bright, was the color of marzipan. She was not wearing rouge or paint. It was her mouth, however, that captivated you: large, though not excessively so, with delicate, well-outlined, glowing pink lips—"the color of her nipples," you thought. Her lips hid a marvelous row of teeth, as white, perfect, strong, and healthy as those of a young mare. You could see them all, even the molars, when the woman let out a great peal of laughter on seeing that you were ceasing to be a child and becoming a man again. You had never before seen anyone whom a laugh made beautiful in that way. A jovial laugh, full of life, love, impishness, and tenderness at the same time. You wanted to say something, but you couldn't get a word out; the jasmine petals were still clogging your throat. You went over to her. She stopped laughing and looked at you affectionately. "We'll see each other again, my seer," she said to you. She began to laugh again and to infect you with her happiness; she gave herself a push with one leg and set the device in motion. Moving rhythmically, she drew away from you with unexpected speed. You tried to catch up with her, but it was useless; she was going on ahead much faster than you. Her hair buffeted by the wind and her ample thigh, with her firm buttocks solidly perched on the little seat, were the last you saw of her. You began to cry again; you could feel the dried anisette running down your cheeks. "Life, dear Fausto," Voltaire was saying to you, "is the only antidote. It is the negation of that eternal negation that death represents."

"To want to live, my friend, is the one thing that gives a person strength," the philosopher told you as he paced from one side of the library to the other. "To want to live fully, completely. Then it matters little if our body is feeble; we can get the better of it as often as we like. Provided that our eagerness to live is vastly superior to that hidden urge to die that all of us bear within us . . ."

The candles had almost burned down and were beginning to gutter; the soft light of the new day was starting to come through the windows. Voltaire was excited. He poured out two more glasses of brandy and handed you one. *Life, death.* Those two words summed up his obsession, the meaning of his existence. Ever since he was a very small boy seeing his mother on her deathbed, ever since he saw her close her eyes and never open them again, the idea of death had settled for good in the consciousness of that man. A profound fear, or more than fear, perhaps dejection, an oppressive sensation of impotence, of futility, of absurdity, laid waste to his thoughts night and day. To be here, to be conscious of all of this, the philosopher thought many times, to enjoy so many pleasures, to suffer so many sorrows, only to end up closing one's eyes and never opening them again . . . And, as he told Rasero, in life, in the eagerness to live, to think, to love, to touch, to fornicate, to listen, to touch, to taste, to create, to hit out, in every vital act, he had found the antidote, the answer to that overwhelming uncertainty that death is, that nothingness is. Voltaire believed, perhaps rightly, that as long as he was active, as long as he used the strength, however great or small, that he had stored up, he would be conquering his enemy, that Palais Royal whore, cruel, treacherous, and empty. By understanding this, it was easy to understand Voltaire's life, and there was little astonishing in the extraordinary activity that this skinny, sickly man manifested down to the very last day of his life.

"Life, the Chinese say, is a victory over death. As long as a living being exists, however minuscule or miserable it may appear to be, life will go on winning. We must not give in to despair; we must fight to vanquish not only death but history. Because just as a little plant or an insect is a palpable proof of the triumph of life, our actions, what we succeed in constructing with our intelligence, are proofs of our victory over the past. What I mean by that is that in the future, which in the end is the result of what we do today, there must be a place only for better things than the ones we have today; there must be men kinder and wiser than we are, whose nobility and wisdom must in some way have been sown by us, in the same way that the ancient Greeks sowed them and today, ripe and harvested, they are our most precious values. The future must be much better than our present if we truly follow the example of life . . ."

On hearing these words, a great number of cruel images came to your mind. Images of men nearly dead of hunger, of wars, of bombs, of Chinese burning to cinders, of cities without vegetation, with their crude, shameful vehicles pouring forth clouds of gray and nauseating smoke . . . but of war, above all of war—images you now knew were of the future and were the result, doubtless, of the struggle in the present against history. If Voltaire could see them, you said to yourself, would he think as he does? Rousseau, however, has foreseen them in some way. Like a coward, you put your own doubts in the Swiss philosopher's mouth: "Rousseau states precisely the contrary: our acts lead us to a worse and worse future; it is history that defeats us. The difference between us and our predecessors is that we are now crueler and much better armed . . ."

"Ah, Rousseau! Don't speak to me about that man. If it were up to him, we would go about naked on all fours and live in caves or atop trees . . . Still, I admit he's a very intelligent man. Have you read his *Discourse on the Sciences and the Arts?* It impressed me as a fascinating essay, though I don't agree with anything it says. It seems interesting that a person as clear-minded as Rousseau has a point of view diametrically opposed to that of most philosophers. He's a sort of counterpoint. I believe that this is salutary for thought. If we all agreed, we'd run the risk of not getting very far: we'd spend too much time and talent praising one another. But Rousseau's vision of history—which is profoundly repugnant to me—has obliged me to improve my arguments in order to refute him, to hone, so to speak, my intelligence, to poke about more carefully in the arsenal of my thought. And that is good: progress is fascinating, but we must be alert to the risk of its deforming us, so that we're not led astray by its sweet song, as Ulysses' men were by the call of the sirens. Rousseau is a good tocsin, it must be admitted. As a human being, though, he's unbearable. I have never experienced his company personally, but I need only read his letters to know that he's insufferable. You know him, don't you?"

"Yes, I met him in Paris in 1757. I had very little contact with him. He's an extremely unsociable and mistrustful person. His intelligence is truly dazzling, but as for being on intimate terms with him, you're quite right: he's nearly impossible. He bears, for some reason, a rancor, a contempt toward his fellows that makes him repulsive. He gives a person the feeling that he lives in two worlds—that of his ideas, which he sets forth so fluently in his works, and the real one, which to his misfortune has nothing to do with the world of his ideas. This contradiction overwhelms him."

Voltaire listened to you with interest. Fausto's keen-witted, extremely clever, he thought. I can't understand his passivity. Why is his pen idle when his head is so active? Besides being clever, he's odd, very odd . . . He felt the heat of the brandy in his throat and a heaviness in his eyelids; sleep was beginning to get the better of him.

"In a word, my friend," he said to you, trying to hide a yawn, "Rousseau is a closed subject with me. It's curious: without ever getting to know him, I've definitely broken with him. And don't get the idea that it was because of his letters, many of them as bitter as they were bizarre. I was always ready to ignore this; it's well worth the trouble of putting up with his reproaches, his complaints, his protests concerning matters I had nothing to do with, as long as one reads his reflections on philosophy, art, or politics, which, I insist, seem to me to be very brilliant, even though I don't share his views. What I can't stand is the way he treated our dear d'Alembert because of a matter as trivial as Jean's article on Geneva in the *Encyclopédie.* In the last analysis, what is it that Jean asks for in that article? For a community of men who claim to be civilized not to prohibit an artistic expression as old, as useful, and as generous as the theater is. Can you imagine Greek culture without the theater? Would Spain have given rise to that generation of titans of the Golden Age if the theater hadn't existed? Could the Sun King have civilized and refined France without theater, without dramatists? The theater, my friend, has for centuries been a school, a source of news, a crucible of ideas, the most lively and effective contact between the people and its learned men. And those idiotic Calvinists have forbidden it in their cantons! 'The theater is immoral,' the hypocrites maintain. 'It corrupts man, whose one destiny, prescribed since the beginning of time, is to read the Bible, fear God, and copulate with some puritan woman once in a while so she'll bring into the world new Bible readers who will fear God. Attacking this imbecility is a minimum obligation on free men, on thinking men. And that is exactly what Jean did, and did very well, with that delightful talent that providence gave him. And what does Rousseau do? He attacks our mathematician as though he were little less than a monster that embodied all the vices and corruption of the Western world. And the one who pens this fierce criticism is none other than the author of several works for the theater and a vulgar little sentimental novel. How can such cynicism be possible? Rousseau made me indignant, Fausto. Very indignant. Reading those insults written by a man who couldn't even tolerate an innocent joke by Diderot is something scarcely to be believed. You should have seen how thin-skinned he was with Denis. 'One does not insult a thinker,' he said to him. And, a little while later, he truly showered d'Alembert with insults. He insulted reason so as to defend that gang of prigs . . . I don't want to hear anything more about that embittered man. I'll learn about his ideas from the books he publishes, but I'll never again write him a single letter. That unfortunate is carrying out the moral duty he's taken upon himself: he's become more isolated these days than Robinson Crusoe on his island . . . May it prove useful to him."

Obviously angry, with a trembling hand, he drained in one swallow the brandy still left in his glass.

"Well, my friend, let's leave that Swiss in peace and retire. Please believe me when I say I've had a most pleasant night," he said with a smile as he searched about on the oak table for something. You replied that you too had been very pleased, that you had spent a delightful evening, and you went on with other such courteous remarks. Meanwhile the philosopher, sitting in the high-backed chair, wrote something on the frontispiece of a book. "Here, Fausto. A modest souvenir of this bounteous night."

He handed you the book and kissed you on both cheeks. You saw him go off, walking slowly on his bowed legs, his left hand resting on his lower back. "To my very dear Fausto Rasero, a modern Prince John Casimir. Yours, François Voltaire," you read on the flyleaf of the book. It was a first edition of *Candide et autres contes,* handsomely bound in chestnut brown leather. On the way to your room, you wondered who Prince John Casimir might be. Many years later, in your mansion in Málaga, alone and advanced in years, reflecting on your memories and preparing for the long journey, you saw that name again when you reread Voltaire's *Le Siècle de Louis XIV:* "John Casimir, king of Poland, weary of the difficulties of governing and desiring to be happy, chose to return to Paris. . . . Paris, having years before become the seat of all the arts, was a delightful dwelling place for a king who sought the enjoyable pleasures of society and loved letters."

Dawn heralded a warm, clear day. You decided to go out into the garden for a stroll before going to bed. You were thinking of death, that "Palais Royal whore," when you saw the silhouette of Marie Corneille sitting on a bench. She was waiting to take you up there, far above the clouds.

IV
Mozart

Paris, December, 1763

"Check," Philidor said with a smile.

His opponent looked at the chessboard in astonishment; he couldn't believe what he was seeing. Just five moves before he'd have bet his own hand without hesitation that he'd win, and in only three moves that devil Philidor, attacking the king in apparent desperation, even sacrificing a rook and leaving a bishop unprotected, had put his opponent's king and his queen in check at the same time. How did all this happen? he wondered as he went over in his mind the last moves.

"Ah, François! You're a devil." Diderot, sitting to one side of the chessboard with a glass of brandy in his hand, had followed the game with interest. He sincerely admired the master's skill at moving the pieces. He was very fond of playing chess, although he realized that he was a rather mediocre player. His anxiousness, his eagerness to end the game in a hurry, almost always betrayed him and kept him from carefully watching his adversary's moves. He concentrated too much on annihilating the enemy king and didn't pay attention to what was going on against his own. Hence he almost always lost. Just as he calculated that in two or three more moves his adversary would be defeated, he would hear, "Check!"—the way that Melchior Grimm had heard it a moment ago—and would finally direct his gaze once again at his own position, where he'd find his king irremediably lost. "Dear Melchior, there's only one move you have left: resigning your king," he said, between hearty peals of laughter.

Reconciled to losing, Grimm resigned his king and held his hand out to his opponent.

"At least I was close this time."

"Much closer than you imagined," Philidor answered. "To tell the truth, I saw myself about to lose."

"Nonsense! It's always the same with you, François. You play with your opponents the way a cat plays with a mouse. You're cruel, my friend; you let them become puffed up and vainglorious, feeling victory at hand, so that their downfall will be all the harder for them."

"Would you like to play?"

"God spare me! I'll never play against you again. The longer I watch you, the more convinced I am that it would be as simple to beat you as to go to Syria and back. No, my friend, I know my limitations. Since I'm never going to get to be a good player, I'm resigning myself to being a good onlooker."

"Well, let's say you're not a very good one," Grimm remarked. "I almost feel that you were the one who made me move my queen. You looked at her so compellingly."

"You don't say! So it turns out now that it was my fault you lost. Having master Philidor as your opponent didn't have anything to do with it; it was my yearning glances. Come off it, Melchior!"

Rey, the owner of the café, called to Philidor. He was being invited to play a game at another table.

"Let's go and watch," Diderot said to Grimm. "I've been told that that boy is as good as Legàs. It's going to be an interesting duel." With the bottle in one hand and the glass in the other, he walked over toward the swarm of onlookers gathering at the back of the room. "Let me through, please . . . François, put a chair aside for me, will you?" he shouted. He held the bottle aloft as he tried to elbow his way through the crowd.

"There he is," Rasero thought. He was arriving just in time, for if the game had already begun, he'd have had to wait until it ended to be able to talk with the philosophe.

"Denis!" he called out urgently.

"Hello there, Fausto," his friend answered. "Do you want to watch the game?"

"No, I don't have time. Come with me."

He had been looking for him all afternoon. At the Academy, at Grimm's house, at the Procope, and at the Gradot. When he didn't find him at the latter café, he was certain he'd be at the Régence. He had deliberately left it till last: the place got on his nerves. It was always full of languid fops, eternally aspiring philosophers, who between one swallow and the next, kept resolving the situation of the kingdom and of the whole of Europe, of gossipmongers and schemers who arrived at the café eager to pour out their poison, of elegant prostitutes, giving themselves the airs of great ladies, who listened, bored to death at the tedious talk of their future customers, to conversations that they didn't understand in the slightest and weren't the least bit interested in understanding either. As they listlessly observed their table companion, who kept endlessly talking and drinking, they whiled away the time calculating how many louis d'or they could get out of him. With a couple of swallows more, they told themselves happily, I won't even have to surrender my body to him. And the chess players. They were the worst of all. They spent hours at a time with their eyes riveted on the chessboard. They would begin the game in a carefree mood, telling each other jokes between one move and the next. But as the game went on, they would gradually become serious, anxious, drumming on the table with their fingers and casting furious glances at their rival. When the game was nearing its end, those who had been joyous contenders turned into mistrustful, irascible players, with just one thought in mind: Beat that cretin, or at least, not lose the game. Not allow that wretch to humiliate me by forcing me to resign my king. Many of those games ended at dawn, under the elm trees in the Champ-de-Mars. Going so far as to knife each other over a stupid game . . .

"Come on, Melchior. Let's go see what our Andalusian wants." As they headed toward an empty table, far from the chess players, Diderot saw a customer who was reading with interest Fréron's *L'Année littéraire.* He gave the paper a resounding whack. Annoyed, the customer raised his eyes. "Don't read that rubbish, my friend! It'll numb your brain," he said with a smile, and went on his way.

"Denis, leave him alone."

"It's that it's disgusting to see them reading that pig swill. Damn! They ought to send that swine Fréron off to Martinique. He knows how to do only two things: grovel and slander. I hope he drops dead."

They finally reached the table, where their friend was already waiting for them.

"So then, Fausto, what news do you have for us?"

"I've now gone over the articles you gave me last week. Here they are."

"What did you think of them?"

"They're fine, for the most part. Although in the article on Oceania there are several inaccuracies: there are many more islands 165 degrees to the northeast of Samoa. I indicated this on the map . . . Oh! the Fiji islands aren't in the right place either. In reality, they're farther east of Australia, by four or five degrees. I corrected that too."

"I'll be damned, Fausto; you never cease to amaze me. I thought those calculations were current. Where did you get your information?"

From Marie Corneille's legs, Rasero thought to himself as a faint smile crossed his face.

"I was looking over some very old documents of Roggeven's that I stumbled on by sheer chance," he lied. "Among them are some fragments of his ship's log from the years '21 and '22. I had no doubt that his observations had been misinterpreted."

"Are you certain? Look, if we're not perfectly accurate, the Academy will eat us alive."

"I'll cut my arm off if I'm wrong. And if the Academicians don't believe it, let them go down there . . . even by sea."

"What do you mean?"

"They'd get there faster if they flew, don't you think so?"

Grimm smiled when he heard this.

"Fausto, leave off your joking. This is quite a serious matter. The article was written after all the most modern maritime charts had been consulted . . ."

"Modern? Come off it, Denis, The most recent cartographic survey is at least fifteen years old. Trust me. Those island are there as surely as the sun is in the sky. If you don't believe me now, leave the map the way it is. When all is said and done, I don't think it means much to people where in the devil those islands are. Going there isn't exactly a pleasure jaunt."

Diderot looked intently at Rasero as he made up his mind. The Malagan's assertion is doubtless correct, he thought. I can't remember a single piece of information of his—and there have been a great many of them—that was wrong. What he refused to accept was the reason his friend had given him. It is easier to nose around in the secret library at the Vatican than it is to rummage about in the documents of the Dutch navigators; they guard them as though they were the apple of their eye. Where did he get that information? It was incredible. He'd known Rasero for more than ten years, and he continued to be as strange and mysterious to him as on the first day they met. He remembered perfectly how the mere presence of that man was enough to banish the horror into which the memory of Vincennes had plunged him. The moment he saw him, he began to feel better. In fact, every time he saw him he felt fine, even if he had a terrible hangover, like the one that had been torturing him until a moment before. Rasero was the first to suspect that d'Alembert would abandon the *Encyclopédie* project. He had hinted as much to him one night, a month before it happened: "The Damiens affair is going to complicate things vastly, and I don't believe our dear Jean will resist the pressure . . ." Rasero was also the most solid support he had at hand when his life took a 180-degree turn—when with profound pain (it still grieved him to remember it)—he left Antoinette and their children (who had finally come into their lives, though only after a long wait) to enter the arms of his adored Sophie. He had never felt so bad, so guilty, so disloyal. The stench that so often pervaded his senses was transformed into disgust at himself. He found it impossible to tolerate himself. Not even when he was submerged in warm water did that revulsion, that total repudiation of his person, leave him for even an instant. He felt calm only in Sophie's arms. When he was with her, nothing else mattered; time stopped, and the whole world could go to hell. But it was impossible to spend his entire life in that woman's lap, and to leave it was to begin to die. He thought openly of suicide, although he lacked the courage to go through with it once and for all. He preferred the slow way: instead of poison, alcohol, which in the proper quantities amounts to the same thing. He alternated frantic activity in behalf of the *Encyclopédie* and interminable bohemian nights, drinking till dawn. Antoinette had initiated legal proceedings against him, while Sophie demanded his company more and more. He was going mad. His mistress reproached him for drinking the way he did. He smiled. "I'll get over it," he answered and went on drinking. He reached the point of having fits of delirium: fearful monsters visited him in his dreams at daybreak. That was the state Rasero found him in one of those mornings. With his face contorted, his eyes filled with terror, trying to swat to death with blows of his hand the countless nonexistent cockroaches that had invaded his bedroom. "Fausto!" he shouted. "Help me! They're trying to eat me alive!" It wasn't easy for Rasero to calm him. He shook him violently, shouted to him to wake up, to come out of his dream; he even had to cuff him. Once he was awake, Denis was not very convinced that the evidence of his senses was fictitious: as he talked with Rasero, he kept casting sidelong glances around the room searching for some of those insects that he knew were hiding there hoping that his friend would leave so as to come out again to drive him mad. "What's happening to you, Denis?" Rasero asked, genuinely worried. "You're killing yourself; why the devil are you doing it?"

Diderot looked intently at his friend. He saw reflected in those eyes—so strange, so black and set so far apart. He observed himself in them: pale, his hair in a tangle, his eyes bloodshot. He looked at himself for a long time, till finally he burst into a loud fit of weeping. "Ah, Fausto!" he said, and wept in torrents. Rasero let him give vent to his feelings. Every so often he stroked the nape of his friend's neck and felt in the palm of his hand the spasms of his sobbing. Finally Denis calmed down, the tears stopped coming, and he began to speak. At times he interrupted himself because of the mucus running down from his nose that he sucked back up with loud snuffles. In a voice so low that Rasero was obliged to put his face right next to his friend's, Diderot spoke for a long time. As though he were on the point of dying and Fausto were a sort of judge of the lower world, Denis went over his whole life, starting with his happy childhood in the fields of Langres and in his father's workshop, where he observed with fascination how they tempered steel by heating it red-hot and them immediately plunging it into ice-cold water. He told him about his arrival in Paris, about the enormous impact made on him by that magnificent city the moment he set foot in it, about Louis-le-Grand, the secondary school where the Jesuits taught him so many things. It was there, he confessed to his friend, that he had fallen in love with knowledge. "Everything they taught me seemed very little to me; I always wanted to know more and more. Books have been my most faithful companions ever since. And though you may not believe it, Fausto, I was still there in that school when I set out to be an Aristotle of the eighteenth century. I paid the same attention to the arts as to philosophy and science. Great days, my friend . . ." He spoke to him of his first writings, of the enormous effort that they required of him and of the deep disappointment that they caused him when he read them, serene now, from a distance. "How devilishly difficult it is to write, Fausto." He was on the point of saying to hell with the whole thing, of returning to Langres and devoting himself to forging steel like his father, "but I couldn't abandon this city." He then met Antoinette and fell in love with her with all the impetuousness of his young years. "My parents were opposed; they considered her beneath me." Nonetheless, he stubbornly—if there was an exemplary trait in that man, it was stubbornness, for his spirit was more malleable and at the same time more resistant than the knife blades his father made—held out for his first love: against every obstacle put in his way, he married Antoinette. Those were very happy days. Around that time, overcoming his first doubts, he began to feel that his writings were improving. Besides marrying Antoinette, he had married his pen and books, and in contrast to his abandonment of her, he was never to abandon these latter.

His life was going well. As his faith in knowledge and in the joy of existing grew, his religious faith—which had never been very great, certainly—lessened by the day. After passing through a stage of very intellectual and not at all mystical pantheism, his faith had finally died out altogether. After having denied absolutely the existence of God, he arrived at a more mature conclusion, which accompanied him the rest of his life and made him a brother in spirit to that strange, inexpressive bald man. "The existence of God, I discovered one day, is not a problem. Whether he exists or not doesn't affect us in the slightest, and there's no reason to worry about something that doesn't affect us." But religion, on the other hand, does affect us; it's stuck its pointed nose into even the most hidden depths of our lives. Like an invisible policeman, it has tried to keep our existence under surveillance, to regulate it with a cruel, cold, hypocritical logic. "As Jupiter castrated Saturn, so the church has tried to castrate all of us . . ." That was why he had begun to fight against it. An uneven battle, no doubt about it: just a few intelligences against the entire apparatus of the state, which manipulated the priests of the Sorbonne as though they were little lap dogs. He had no sooner begun this fight when the horrors began: the publication of his *Lettre sur les aveugles* earned him the eternal hostility of the church, a "thing I wouldn't wish on my worst enemy." Others who thought as he did fled; Paris was no place for agnostics. But Diderot, bound by a mysterious and invisible tie to the old city of the Franks, remained in it, prepared to be the victim of reprisals, which came soon enough: the inferno of Vincennes. He spoke to Rasero of that horror, of those sinister days locked up in the tower. "It was very shortly before we met, remember?" And he spoke to him of the stench and of the rats, of the interminable hours submerged in a bathtub correcting the first galley proofs of the *Encyclopédie.* "The *Encyclopédie!* Ah, Fausto, I thought I saw my liberation in it, and what I found was a cruel and unyielding master that squeezed me till I was left as dry as a raisin." A courageous undertaking. To want to compress in those hundreds of folios all the knowledge of his time. "And that of all times, what the hell. In those days that undertaking seemed to me to be not only possible but even simple, I must confess, within reach of my lofty pantophilia, and far, far below my stupid vanity." He put in almost twenty years on that madness, getting into squabbles with booksellers, with readers, with philosophes—"They're the worst"—mediating between a thousand interests, many of them opposed, irreconcilable (alas, how dearly it cost him to discover it), certain others worse than irreconcilable. When the first volume came out, it was an enormous success. Everyone wanted to subscribe. Orders came to the publishers from places as distant as Russia and even far-off America. The aristocrats of Paris—the most exquisitely refined, cultivated, and vacuous aristocracy in the whole world—vied for Diderot's presence at their soirees. It became fashionable to organize readings of the work. If some of its authors attended them, better still, and if the editor in chief was present, best of all. Diderot could scarcely believe that there were so many ladies of ancient lineage interested in his person. Letters, invitations, and even love poems piled up on his work table. He was submerged in a dizzying whirl of elegant salons, exquisite wines, powdered faces, of affected speech, wealth squandered to the point of extravagance, "and of stupidity, dear Fausto, torrents of stupidity." In the beginning, the priests and other inquisitors scarcely bothered him. "My vanity, swollen to infinity, told me that I'd pulled the wool over their eyes, that I'd left them as disarmed and powerless as a bride before the altar." Of course that wasn't how things really were. Not too much time went by before little notes containing veiled threats began to slip into the correspondence he received. In a short time, they were no longer veiled, they were real pamphlets, whole rosaries of slander, promises of horrible punishments. Finally he began to receive summonses, from the archbishopric first, and then from the court. Those same cretins who praised him to the skies in their ostentatious salons, celebrating his genius as that of a "modern Thucydides," those same wretches on the very next morning, still suffering from the hangover of the night before, signed summonses, injunctions, orders for seizures and censorship. "That's the way those bastards are, like spiders that hold their prey spellbound before injecting them with their poison . . ." The problems grew like a snowball: "I came to believe that the fourth volume would never be published." The resistance of the clerical party and of the ministers of the court was fierce.

They took advantage of the slightest legal sophistry to suspend its publication: "Whole days cooling my heels in anterooms, pleading with that bunch of idiots . . ." But despite all obstacles, the work went ahead; the fourth volume finally reached print. And it was precisely at that time, as it was being presented at a soiree organized at the mansion of the Duchess de Mailly, that he first met Sophie Volland. They were listening to Buffon, who in his pompous style was reading an article on equines, when their eyes met. "It was something to see her and fall into her trap. Eros pierced my heart." And the same thing happened to her. It was not long after that meeting that they began to share the same bed, which they would turn into the scene of real amorous battles. "Everything that woman had, inside and out, enchanted me. Even her toenails seemed marvelous to me." Antoinette soon realized that she had been cast aside. Denis kept coming home later and later and reached the point of not coming home at all for two or three days in a row. The sad woman saw her husband becoming more and more distant and her children growing, those children she had wanted so much. A few years before, she had begged the old wooden Christ that she visited every afternoon in the church to perform the miracle of letting her offspring live. In return, she swore to devote herself entirely to him, over and above her own husband. And that is what she did: as those hours went by, those endless days when she kept looking inside the cradle, not taking her eyes off the little child sleeping peacefully in it, meanwhile praying to the Savior, reminding him of her promise, she was so anxiety ridden that many a time she awoke her daughter, fearing that death would snatch her away as she slept. She shook her roughly until the little thing burst into tears; only then did she sigh with relief. When, finally, the days turned into months and the months into years, when she saw the miracle with her own eyes and her intuition told her that that little girl would not meet the fate of her brothers and sisters, then Antoinette donned the habit, so to speak. She divided her life in two: her daughter and religion. There was no room left for Denis. There was nothing strange, then, in an intruder's stealing him from her. At first it didn't matter too much to her; instead, she felt relieved. She could devote herself entirely to her children and to her God. Meanwhile, her husband would have someone with whom to distract himself a little, taking time off, even though only occasionally, from that *Encyclopédie* that was sucking his brains out. She was confident that Denis would soon tire of his mistress and return to her arms, like a repentant prodigal son. No one knew Denis as well as she did, Antoinette thought; no one listened to him so patiently, knew how to cheer him with a mere look, knew all about his doubts, calmed his anxieties. She had been his companion for too many years for anyone to be able to take him away from her. Denis would never get over his need for her. He would come back to her arms as a wave returns to the shore it belongs to, even though it must go all the way around the world. But the wave didn't return; it remained trapped in another port. Diderot found his new mistress not only a welcome distraction, he found a great deal, a very great deal more than that. "Sophie is the other half of my androgyne. I wonder how I could have lived without her for so many years . . ." Loath in the beginning to accept the situation, Antoinette eventually convinced herself that her husband had undertaken a journey from which there was no return. A deep sadness came over her. She went back to living those frightful days when her first children breathed their last in her arms. In a short time, however, her sadness turned to fury, an implacable fury, for the hatred that she began to feel for Denis and his new woman was compounded by her self-contempt: I shall never be a whole woman, she told herself. When I was a lover, I was unable to be a mother, and when I was a mother, I ceased to be a lover. Deep feelings are always selfish: when Antoinette realized that she was doomed not to be happy, she couldn't bear the idea that her husband might be. So she used a whole battery of evil arts (surprised at herself when she discovered that arsenal) to drag Denis down. Complaints, threats, demands, fits of hysteria, hints of suicide—she used all that and much more to secure for her husband a place in the hell that she was experiencing. And she succeeded, she succeeded completely. Denis sank like a swamped boat. Children, a wife, a mistress, and the *Encyclopédie* were a burden impossible to bear, "and something worse, a fear," because the wound of Vincennes, which after four years appeared to have healed over, opened up again with a vengeance. He discovered to his regret that the scab that had formed over it hid decomposed tissue. Once the scab was removed, blood and pus came pouring out in torrents: "Since then, I've been storing my writings away. I don't have the courage to publish them." Writings that were better and better. His keen intelligence had taken him even farther afield as time went by. The church and religion were no longer the only object of his criticisms.

He had discovered that this institution was only a small part of the interlocking mechanisms of a much more complex entity. It was the state—its conception, its aims, and its methods—that was really responsible for an unjust order imposed down through the centuries by means of the sword and the stake. An abominable structure had been built, supported on the backs of millions of men who lacked everything save for their ability to work. And above them were a handful of the privileged, parasitical and useless, who enjoyed all the good things, all the pleasures of this world, by virtue of the supposed valor of their ancestors of four centuries before. The church was only a means resorted to in order to oppress those down below, to kill their spirits as armies massacred their bodies. It was a diabolically unjust and perverse order, in which the supreme instrument for subjugating those down below was not even religion, "it is ignorance, dear friend. As they have immersed our people in ignorance, they can go on feeding on it like leeches." He had seen this very clearly and began to say so in his writings. Just as the earthquake of Sophie took place, as his wife almost went mad with jealousy, as the *Encyclopédie* was threatened, he was beginning to discover the real cause of injustice in this world that he so abhorred. But he felt unable to publish his writings: "I don't have Voltaire's courage."

"Voltaire writes for his time, and from Prussia. You write for the future, Denis," Rasero replied. Love, repentance, and fear had finally brought his friend to that state in which alcohol had already begun to hatch insects in his mind. A little while longer and everything would be over. "To hell in order to rest." Rasero contemplated him. His face dared to express concern and affection. "Denis, pardon me for speaking to you in this way, but you're an idiot. As far as I can see, you're killing yourself because you love and because you think. And, I ask you, isn't that what distinguishes us from animals? You who claim to be an atheist, what obscure Christian sentiment do you have embedded in your soul so that loving makes you feel like a sinner? You've found life in Sophie, the life that Antoinette could no longer give you because she gave it all to her children and to her God. You've found life, and your response is death. You've found, after seeking it for so long, a generous wisdom, a wisdom that will bring light to many lives . . . and your response is death. Look, my friend: Socrates has already drunk the hemlock, and Christ has already died on the cross. We don't need more martyrs of wisdom or of love. What we need is to go on fighting against those cretins who are building a frightful future—and who will keep on doing so as long as we allow them to. I know that very well; I could swear to you that I've seen it. Drink wine to the point that it sharpens your intelligence and brings your senses to life, but no more. Don't dull your mind with it, don't destroy yourself, I beg you. You're intensely in love, and that's the best thing that can happen to a person. Enjoy love, damn it! Enjoy it while you can. Love Sophie; don't make her a widow. Antoinette will get along all right; she'll eventually understand. She's a good woman, and you know it. And write, for the love of God! don't stop writing. But don't publish it. Keep your writings, polish them, let them age. Now isn't the time to publish them, because they'd lock you up. And in prison you couldn't write, as I know very well. I needed only to see you in that tub to realize how much harm being imprisoned can do you. You can't flee either, you yourself have told me so. You belong to this city as much as the stones of Notre Dame do. Don't destroy yourself, my friend," he said to him, his eyes dimmed by tears. He embraced Denis and kissed his broad forehead. "Love, don't be a coward, love with all the strength you can muster," he repeated to him in a very quiet voice.

That night sealed their friendship. Rasero's words penetrated to the depths of Diderot's mind. He began to keep his distance from alcohol and discovered to his satisfaction that when one is resolved to confront a problem, it turns out to be much less complicated than it appeared to be. Antoinette, as his friend had foretold, gave in little by little until she finally stepped aside altogether. She stopped harassing her husband and devoted herself body and soul to the care of her children. Sophie's love went on maturing and growing deeper until it reached the point of turning into a friendship, a meeting of minds, a harmony of spirits, that was to last all their lives. He went on writing, better and better each day. He liked not feeling pressed to bring out his texts. This gave him the opportunity of revising them as many times as he cared to, of lovingly polishing them, as though they were precious gems. He had decided not to publish them during his lifetime; Sophie and Melchior Grimm had instructions to bring them to light as soon as he passed on. The *Encyclopédie* went on being published, despite the innumerable obstacles it encountered. He even managed to face those problems good-humoredly and learned to make friends with its censors. He used to go out for a night of drinking once or twice a month with Joseph d'Hémery, a member of the Paris secret police who was in charge of keeping an eye on the doings of the philosophes. D'Hémery turned out to be an invaluable source of information for Denis, and thanks to him, he found himself protected from the hostility of his enemies. It so happened that the kindly d'Hémery, a serious, honest man, had taken a liking to the philosophes after reading their works—in the beginning, out of strict fulfillment of his official obligations. He came to appreciate the keen-mindedness and the courage of those men whose biographies he kept carefully locked up in his archives. At once scrupulous and generous, he turned out to be a key piece that enabled many works to be published that up until then had been prohibited. Owing in large part to the prudent intervention of d'Hémery, the *Encyclopédie* had already progressed as far as the fourteenth volume, whose galley proofs Diderot saw on the table, with notations written between the lines in sepia ink in the sensitive, minuscule hand of his friend Fausto Rasero.

"All right, we'll put the islands where you say. I'll find a way to get around the members of the Academy. But I warn you that I don't believe one word of what you've told me about Roggeven's log. 'I stumbled on it.' Of course. You're a demon, Fausto, or a sorcerer at least. Don't think I haven't heard about your dealings with the Rosicrucians . . ."

"All nonsense."

"Yes, nonsense, that's what I think . . . but you're in on something."

"Come off it, Denis."

"Very well, then, don't tell me where you get your information. When all is said and done, friends aren't for babbling secrets to, right?"

"Don't be childish, Denis. There isn't any secret."

"Now it turns out that I'm a child," Diderot said with a smile as he looked at Grimm. "Bring us some brandy!" he shouted to the waiter. "Brandy to celebrate my childhood." He went on, "To your good health, friend!" clinking glasses with Grimm. "To your good health, gypsy! This volume is almost ready. We ought to celebrate the occasion, don't you think? I invite both of you to Madame Chantal's place."

"I can't come with you, Denis," Grimm said. "I have to go see the Mozarts."

"So the child prodigies are already here," Diderot said mockingly.

"Yes, they arrived at the end of last month. They're staying at the von Eycks' palace."

"Are they really as good as people say?" Rasero asked, remembering a recent letter from Voltaire: "Don't fail to see that child for anything in the world. Providence didn't hold back a single gift from him."

"Better. The boy especially. I've never seen anything like it; I swear that the first time I heard him I was spellbound. He's really wonderful. That boy is full of music to his very fingertips."

"Come on, Melchior, you're reciting your article from the *Correspondance littéraire* to us."

"But it's true, Denis. I don't believe a phenomenon like this has ever before existed in the history of music. That child is barely seven, and he's already signed several compositions."

"Really?"

"I assure you it's true. Moreover, they're impeccable. Simple pieces, naturally, but very pretty. Just imagine what he's going to compose when he's twenty!"

"If he manages to live that long," Diderot interrupted. "Because, according to what people have told me, his father makes him work like a donkey."

"They're exaggerating. The real story is that Leopold—a great musician, incidentally—is more aware than anyone else of his son's genius and intends, to our good fortune, to share it with the world."

"And also take in his share of some good doubloons. For the love of heaven, Melchior, don't be naïve."

"All right, I don't deny it. The father is interested in money, as who isn't? But he's been good at teaching his son, and it's my opinion that he takes care of money matters quite well. The youngster is happier and livelier than a little bird. To that child, performing isn't a form of work but a game—a game that fascinates him, because he's in love with music."

"And how about the sister?"

"She's a virtuosa. I've never heard anybody thirteen years old play the harpsichord the way she does. What happens is that she disappears alongside her little brother. She's a virtuosa; he's a genius."

"Well, then, we'll have to see this genius," Rasero put in.

"On Friday, they'll be giving their first concert. It'll be in the von Eyck palace; I'll be happy to reserve seats for you."

"Two for me. I want to bring Sophie."

"Of course, Denis. Well, friends, have a good time at Madame Chantal's. Say hello to her for me . . . Ah, Denis! Don't forget to send me your *Salon;* without it, the *Correspondance* is left limping. It's not easy to placate the subscribers when it doesn't appear."

"I don't think it's all that important . . . I'll give it to you on Friday, don't worry. There's no lack of flatterers around."

"I don't think it's flattery, Denis," Rasero said as he watched the German walk away from the table—tall, a good fellow, impeccably dressed in dark green, his eternal smile lighting his calm face. "Your articles are really interesting. You have a very original way of looking at art. I like it very much. I confess I'm even beginning to like Chardin's paintings. I would never have believed that I'd reach the point of finding an old dish, a few pieces of fruit, and a dead duck charming, but they are, really charming . . ."

"It's necessary to see the atmosphere of those paintings; it's necessary to know how to see everything they show. That's what's magnificent about Chardin, though very few people see it. Stupidity, my friend, is more firmly seated on its throne than our Beloved Sovereign is on his. Nobody understands art anymore. They wait for the opinion of Fréron or of Saint-Yenne to know whether a work pleases them or not. Penny-a-liners are the arbiters of good taste today. And the way they lavish praise on rubbish! It's disgusting. What's happening, Fausto? By acting like those ignoramuses we've become like them. Figurines decked out in powder and rouge, with our skulls emptier than a table during Lent—that's what our masters are. There they are, strolling like royal peacocks through the charming little salons of their mistresses, generously exuding their scandal-sheet wit, and being as careful as surgeons not to utter, even by mistake, one phrase, one single intelligent, exactly right word. Everything must be light, facile, stupid . . . Do you know what? Sometimes I think I ought to take Voltaire's advice and clear out of here to found that republic of philosophers that he's proposed to me. Has he spoken to you of it?"

"Yes. It's a fine project, but one totally impossible to carry out. A select group of thinkers set down in a little German electorate, with the countryside three steps away, without palaces, or theaters, or cafés, or soirees, or operas, or even brothels. How many days do you think they could stand one another's company? It would be an unbearable place. Admit it, Denis, Paris has filled up with ignoramuses, but even so, it's still the most livable city in the world. I can't imagine you anywhere else."

"Don't you believe it; sometimes I get fed up with it. But you're right about Voltaire's idea: it'd be impossible to live surrounded by pedants. But maybe I'll clear out of here when I finish the *Encyclopédie*—if I ever do finish it. Queen Catherine has invited me to Russia, and I'm thinking of accepting."

"You in Russia? Come off it, Denis . . . There's nothing there but cold and savages, my friend. I insist that I can't imagine you anywhere except Paris."

"Didn't Voltaire go off to Prussia? And mind you, he's more of a Parisian than I am."

"So he was once . . . Look at him now. In his precious Ferney, sighing for Paris like an abandoned bride."

"Incidentally, have you had news of him?"

"Yes, I've just received a card from him. He's all right. He's still fighting the case against Calas."

"And what's his point in doing that? Because that man is dead and gone."

"To vindicate his honor. For the time being, Calas' family is out in the street. Everything they owned was seized. If they succeed in vindicating him, they'll recover all of it. Still, the most important thing is the fight François is waging against intolerance, against that odious Edict of Nantes."

"Voltaire has courage. I think the passage of the years has agreed with him. He writes better and more calmly all the time. I feel that he's even less vain."

"A great deal less, without doubt. So then, have you already forgotten my invitation? I'll pay for supper."

"All right, then, let's go. We'll have supper there; this place is filling up with fops."

They didn't have to walk very far to reach Madame Chantal's house, the facade of which overlooked the gardens of the Palais Royal. They spent a pleasant evening in the company of the wards of the place, charming, refined women who knew very well how to deal with educated men. When Diderot made love, he thought about Russia, and you, keeping to custom, saw a hair-raising war scene in a tropical city full of Chinese.

Melchior Grimm had done his work well; the main salon of Baron von Eyck's palace was completely full; the audience numbered more than a hundred. The elite of Parisian society had an appointment to meet there to hear the Mozarts' concert. The men, elegantly dressed, effortlessly bore the weight of their resounding names, names belonging to the aristocracy of the sword, which symbolized entire generations of fierce warriors, of proud knights who crossed Europe to rescue the Holy Lands and fought for more than a hundred years against the Anglo-Saxons to wrest the jewel of the Franks from the English crown. What lamentable descendants those brave knights had: svelte popinjays, walking shakily on their high heels, slightly rearranging every so often the curls of their powdered wigs, giving little sneezes like well-brought-up young ladies as they raised their lace handkerchiefs to their mouths after taking a pinch of snuff, or exchanging criticisms in their affected, highflown speech about how uncomfortable the place was or the terrible taste of the person who had had the idea of hanging those "frightful" paintings by Chardin on the towering walls. "Poor Germans," the Duke de La Vallière remarked to Madame de Sassenage as they contemplated a still life, "they have all the delicate sensibility of a porcupine."

"Can that youngster be as good as they say?" asked the Countess de Pons, a fat woman who had passed the half-century mark some time before, although she insisted on affecting the dress and youthful manner of a girl of twenty. Her green silk dress—it was impossible to understand how she managed to get into it—pushed up, over the edges of her generous decolletage, a pair of mammaries that lacked nothing compared with Angustias' when it came to size but everything when it came to firmness, for they were as soft as an uninflated ball. When the lady walked, her breasts trembled like pâté that hasn't set, and at times it seemed as though they would overflow her low neckline like milk boiling over. Rasero contemplated in fascination the big beauty mark the woman had painted on her right breast. When the lady moved, the beauty spot traced fantastic trajectories, like a blowfly when it bumps into a windowpane.

"I don't believe so, madam," answered the Baron de Boyer, the havoc wrought on him by the Naples disease being concealed neither by his wig nor by his rouge and powder. "The boy is German, and as we all know they're a people who lack any sort of cleverness. The only thing they know how to do is drink beer and work, nothing else. Music is too much for them; it's like setting a donkey to reading Homer. If the boy were Italian or French . . . or even Spanish, for that matter, I could believe what they say about him. But German . . ."

"You're right," the whale replied. "On the other hand, who is it who says all these marvelous things about the youngster?"

"Melchior Grimm, another German . . ."

"Ah, my dear! I greatly fear we're unfortunately wasting our time . . . ," she said to empty air, for just as she reached the middle of her sentence, the syphilitic stopped listening to her and went off like a shot to the entrance to greet the Marquis de La Forté-Imbault, who had just arrived.

The Marquis de La Forté-Imbault did not belong to the aristocracy of the sword; he could boast only of being an aristocrat of the robe. Nonetheless, that was the nobility that had been gaining power since the days of the Regency. For lack of blue blood, the new nobles tinted theirs gold, a color that revealed a shorter lineage but was much more highly coveted. The marquis, like many others of those present there, belonged to the aristocracy of money. His forebears were not valiant warriors or intimates of kings. They were, rather, mere bourgeois. Hard-working men, intelligent and greedy, who little by little, just as cultivated fields take over woodlands, were wresting their riches away from the feudal lords who, having become useless once matters leading to war had ceased to be domestic affairs and become reasons of state, led lives stultified by idleness. The monarchy took away their arms, the bourgeoisie their money, and they used their name—the one thing they had left—as a sort of net to catch the daughter of a banker, a great merchant, or an industrialist, a spouse with whom, once they had settled down, they would father a new noble, a fancy-dress noble, an aristocrat of money.

Of course the high-ranking clergy were also present. The Lord's representatives came and went solemnly through the vast public rooms of the palace, showing off their splendid, impeccably cut black vestments adorned with the finest lace, which must have cost many a nun of the Convent of the Assumption her eyesight. The secretary of the archbishop of Paris (their patron declined to attend the concert, for he considered it disrespectful that those wretched Austrians should perform in the city before having rendered the king homage at court), a man as bulky as an armoire, with a round, fleshy face cruelly ravaged by smallpox, Puglier than hunger, but more lustful than Tiberius—he was said to have as many concubines as the sultan of Persia—was indiscreetly eyeing Mademoiselle de Roure. He was looking at her long neck, her breasts, round and firm, her slender, perfectly white arms, her eyes with great long lashes and thick eyelids that made them look sleepy. Above all he saw—or was trying to see—her legs, hidden beneath the ample skirts of her dress. As it happened, the girl was the niece of the Countess de Luaraguais, a woman as beautiful as she was frivolous, who had once shared her bed with him. As he tried to make out the girl's figure beneath her dress, the secretary remembered what a lamentable spectacle it had been to see the countess nude. After having frantically desired her for a long time, he had finally succeeded in getting the lady to grant him her favors. It was in the countess' castle, on a gray, rainy afternoon. With their nerves on edge, since the count might return from the city at any moment, they stole away to the woman's bedroom. The man, young and ardent, took off his cassock in the wink of an eye and began to undress his future lover, who, to his surprise, was violently opposed. Instead, she lay down on the bed and raised her skirt. With her legs bent and wide open, she offered her private parts to the curate, who contemplated in fascination the spectacle before his eyes and wondered when and how the countess had taken off her underthings. Then he mounted her and made love to her in a frenzy; engulfed in a sea of cloth, he felt like a bee that had been caught in the heart of a rose. When they finished, the countess sat up and put her garments back on. She gave every sign of being ready to return to the salon. But the man wasn't at all satisfied. He had wanted that woman too much to be satisfied with so little. Coitus had calmed the vertigo of desire, and now, calm once again, his sensibility, which had grown refined, so to speak, impelled him to make love to this woman gently, as though he were enjoying a sweet dessert after having eaten heartily. He began to caress her and kiss her neck, tenderly, warmly. In the beginning, the woman tried to resist, although she soon gave in. She too was afire with eroticism, but it had not exploded by the time the curate had finished. She let him do as he liked, and she herself began to do as she pleased, until the two of them ended up naked on the rug like two little toy pigs. They made love again, although with greater calm now. They rocked their bodies in cadence and in perfect harmony. They climaxed at the same time, happy at being alive, grateful to Eros for the delights that he is capable of bestowing on us. On the floor, in each other's arms, they let time go by, as, through contagion perhaps, it passed slowly and sinuously, pursuing an elusive nothingness, its eternal lover.

The creaking of the wheels of a carriage brought them out of their reverie. "My husband!" the countess shrieked in alarm. She leaped to her feet and went over to the window. The curate, still enthralled by the pleasure she had given him, looked tenderly at the woman, who had her back turned to him, clinging with both hands to the folds of the curtain, looking out the window. He saw her pretty reddish hair that fell in waves, like spilled honey, down her back. He saw her waist, as narrow and svelte as a stalk of maize; two pretty dimples showed where her buttocks began, there where they curved outward, firm and generous, from her hips. He could see underneath them, between her legs, the little hairs of her pubis, of the same color as her hair and coiffed into a point; they were reminiscent of the beards of gentlemen of a century before. How different her private parts looked now! Timid, barely hinted at, slightly moist from the little liquids of pleasure. How different from those swollen, inflamed lips, crowned by black curly hair, that the countess had offered him, lying face up in the bed, only a short while before! "Hurry up and get dressed, for the love of heaven!" the woman begged him from the window. But he was not ready to move until he had finished his amorous visual reconnaissance. After having contemplated once again for a good while longer those delightful buttocks, he lowered his eyes and . . .

In heaven's name! Who put that there? How horrible! he thought. Not believing what he had just seen, the man abruptly rose to his feet and focused his eyes, blinking a number of times, as though trying to moisten his eyes so that the veil that distorted objects in such a way would disappear. But no, there was no veil. He looked again and saw the same thing: a pair of legs, long and strong, though more bowed than the flying buttress of a church. They began there where they should begin, where the groin lies. They were there together, as they ought to be; but as soon as they extended farther down, they drew apart from each other, forming an ample curve. The great est distance between them was at the height of her knees, where there was a gap so large that a Spanish mastiff could pass through it without even grazing its back. A mastiff! An entire bull! the curate corrected himself. Then the two limbs came closer together again to touch again at the ankles. The empty space between the countess' legs was shaped exactly like a Gothic window. The curate thought of the Chinese and of that absurd habit of theirs of tightly bandaging the feet of women from the time they were little children so as to atrophy them and turn them into something resembling stumps, smaller still than their hands. He said to himself, They mounted this woman astride a horse;

they tied her feet underneath, and left her in that position for at least twenty years . . . The surprise had bowled him over.

The woman began to get dressed as she tried to hurry him up: "For the love of God," she said to him, "get dressed this minute. Do you want my husband to kill you?" It was all the same to him: he'd already given himself up for dead. He had the horrible sensation of having fornicated with a monster. He thought of Europa raped by a bull, of Perseus in Medusa's bed; he thought of himself and the women he had loved. Can they have felt, he wondered, the way I feel now? For he himself was ugly, and knew it, as ugly and as big as a monster. How could they have loved me, he kept wondering insistently, how can they love a monster?

Without knowing it, he was asking himself the same question that many years later Count Mirabeau, a man who resembled him so closely that he could well have been his son, would ask himself. It made a great impact on Rasero when he made friends with the great tribune, shortly after the memorable days of June, '89. And that great impression was not caused, as Mirabeau believed, by his incomparable gifts as an orator nor by his fierce intelligence but by his absolute loyalty and by his amazing resemblance to the secretary of the archbishop of Paris, whom Rasero had met so many years before, on that evening as they awaited the performance of the Austrian musicians, and who had powerfully attracted Rasero's attention because he was so tall and so ugly, and because he didn't take his eyes off the skirts of Mademoiselle de Roure, who, incidentally, had been in your arms not long ago and had taken you—the woman was passionate—to a bullfight several times. The spectacle, you discovered, though much changed, had survived into the future and produced the same magical, somber effect on the multitudes—much larger than those of today—that contemplated, drunk and ecstatic, the sacrifice of the noble beast.

Rasero was strolling along with Diderot and Sophie Volland when they passed by the secretary. "It smells bad here," the philosophe said in a loud voice. Without knowing why he was doing so, Rasero stopped and went over to the priest. The man's gaze remained fixed on Mademoiselle de Roure. "Don't worry, sir," he said to him, "the woman isn't knock-kneed."

Surprised, the secretary turned around to see the man who had spoken to him. He watched him as he walked away: erect, impeccably dressed in dark blue, his head—bald, round, and shiny—reflecting the golden glow of the candles. "Who is that man?" he asked Abbot Gorde, who was standing alongside him.

"Fausto Rasero. He's a Spaniard, an eccentric. They say he's a Mason or a Rosicrucian, or something of the sort."

"Well, he's also a sorcerer," the secretary replied and determinedly approached Mademoiselle Roure to place himself at her orders.

There's that miserable scoundrel again, Abbot Maudoux thought. He was an old prelate, the confessor of King Louis. "The idlest man in France," the courtiers used to say jokingly of the abbot. The man was well acquainted with the secretary's womanizing and found it altogether repellent. Maudoux, along with the late Mallet, was one of the very few French clergymen who still feared God and who lived their lives according to divine precepts. Intransigent with his body, which received caresses only from his mother, he kept it pure and chaste till the last day of his life. A laudable effort in and of itself, it became an immense one in the case of this man, for he had—though only he knew it—a prodigious mind, much given to fantasizing, crammed since the tenderest years of his childhood with all the obscene, lascivious, and even pornographic images that have passed through men's minds through the whole of their long history. Brother Maudoux' body had never known pleasure, but in his mind—this was the work of Satan, who else?—there was not one woman, except for his mother, who, having once passed before his retinas, he had not fornicated with, by way of all the orifices of her body. It was quite something to have a woman before him, already naked, lying on her hypothalamus, tied down by the wrists and ankles, receiving in a daze everything that a woman can receive from a man, or to be more precise, everything that a female can receive from a male. And despite that fantastic zoo of images that the good man was burdened with, he was able to remain chaste, to the point that in his entire life he had never once uttered a blasphemous word. If his fellow clergymen had suspected what this abbot had kept bottled up inside his head, they would surely have canonized him, for only a saint—and a major one—would be able to lead an existence such as the one that this man led having a mind like the one that this man had. Who better to shrive the king? With a body as pure and limpid as springwater and prepared at the same time to understand the confidences of a monarch who, unlike his confessor, had an unsullied mind, incapable of thinking up even one blasphemy, and a tireless body—that is the work of Satan, Louis said to himself—when it came to giving and receiving pleasure. A playful and sensitive body that writhed like a clam when lemon juice is poured on it whenever it came into contact with the soft, fresh skin of a fifteen-year-old girl. Insatiable and open-minded, like a philosopher face-to-face with knowledge, Louis XV never failed to take pleasure and to learn—as good teachers do—but in the eternal labyrinth of the flesh. That was why poor Maudoux had no work to do: the mind of his lamb was too pure to dare to confess the excesses of his body; an instinctive modesty blocked it. Furthermore, if Louis were one day to decide to confess to Abbot Maudoux the countless filthy acts (filthy acts to his mind, delights to his body) that he had committed with such a great number of women, and such beautiful ones—if some day he confessed all this to enable his pastor to grant him forgiveness, the priest would demand that he stop doing such things, would make him swear before God that he would renounce sin, that he would enjoy no other flesh save the withered and long-forgotten breasts of Marie Leszczynska. And if Louis swore to God, he would be obliged to fulfill his vow, his conscience would not allow him to deceive the Lord; the abbot would remind him of the frightful torture that awaited him down below, in the ninth circle, next to Judas and Satan, if he failed to keep his promise. If he were to confess, he would have to live as pure and chaste a life as his pastor. Better death, his body told him, and finally he made a wise decision: I'm going to confess very soon now, the king told himself, now that my body is growing weary of so much lust, and then I shall live free of sin and die in peace, and my spirit will go to glory, alongside the throne of my ancestor, Saint Louis. And, as always when he had to make a troublesome decision, he postponed the matter: Very soon now, he would insist, very soon now . . . Meanwhile, his confessor, knowing that he had him cornered, waited; the poor man waited as he suffered in his mind what his lamb enjoyed by way of his body.

Intellectuals and artists rounded out the soiree. The Austrian youngster's influence had been able to bring the two opposites of the Parisian intelligentsia together in the same place. It was curious to see the group of the Encyclopedists and Fréron's clique together—though not mingling. They occupied, naturally, the corners of the salon the farthest apart from each other and pretended not to see each other, although from time to time Rasero noted the furious looks (Palissot) or contemptuous ones (Marmontel) that passed from one group to the other. Diderot, the unquestionable head of the Encyclopedists, presided over that group's conversation. Smiling, sarcastic, and a little tipsy, he spoke with his friends of the armistice recently signed at Versailles that put an end to the Seven Years' War, as it was beginning to be called.

"Those who are going to come out the winners are the English of America, you'll see," he said to them. "The European kingdoms tear each other apart for pieces of land that have changed hands a thousand times, whereas in America those Quakers and Puritans stealthily invade Canada and Louisiana. They have within their reach a territory much larger than all of Europe put together, and according to what they say, one overflowing with riches. They are creating an enormous country, and they have the great advantage of not bearing the burden of a history full of crimes, selfishness, idiot kings, corrupt and petty churches, like that of our old Europe. Over there, my friends, everything is new. They wiped out the poor Indians that inhabited those regions and welcomed with open arms any adventurer, thief, troublemaker, or pauper who arrived in their domains. How long will they remain loyal to the English crown? Not long, I'm sure. Why pay tribute to an island that is much worse off than they are? You'll see: North America will be the monster born of this war."

"And what about Spanish America?" Marmontel asked him.

"That's something else again. The Spaniards have been there for a long time. Moreover, they have been able to dominate and to live amicably with the peoples they encountered. They didn't exterminate them, or at least they allowed many of the ones who now share their cities to survive. The Spaniard doesn't have the commercial spirit and the diligence of the Englishman. As long as there's wealth in those lands, he'll exploit it without scruple and will go on sending ships laden with gold and silver to Europe. It never occurs to him even for a moment to expand those countries, because he doesn't feel that they belong to him. When you have a piece of beef for dinner, you don't begin to reflect on the sufferings of the steer that contributed it; the steer exists to die and give you beef. It's that simple, since to the Spaniards, America is turning into the same thing as a steer, a steer that gives silver instead of beef. On the other hand, because they did not completely wipe out the original inhabitants of those countries, as the English did, the Spaniards remain continuously afraid, and always will, that they'll lose that wealth. In their heart, they know it doesn't belong to them. They exploit those lands and care for them, but they don't feel that they're theirs, as their neighbors to the north do. This has caused Spanish America to become weaker by the day—like an animal being bled to death—whereas the part of the continent to the north keeps growing stronger and stronger. I very much fear that if the Spaniards cease to despoil those lands some day, it'll be the Anglo-Saxons who'll continue to milk them. Moreover—and Voltaire explains this very well in his writings—religion plays a fundamental role in what I'm telling you. In the north they're Protestants and therefore permitted by their religion and by their pastors to annihilate the infidels who inhabit the lands that they now are enjoying the fruits of, and they're encouraged also to developed their individuality and their selfishness to be rewarded by their God with all the wealth that they're capable of producing and carrying off. At the same time, it's only fair to admit, living—as they do—like brothers in their communities, they fight together to better their living conditions, fearful of authority and believing only in their own strength and that of their comrades. In the south, on the other hand, they're Catholics. They're not allowed to exterminate the Indians. They're obliged to evangelize them and inculcate the Christian faith in them and, above all, submissiveness, which is so Catholic, in order to be able to exploit them then without burdening their conscience. The Spanish colonists are not accustomed to working with their hands; their Indians, once they have been baptized, are the ones who do that. And as if that isn't enough, they feel an absolute respect for authority, whether it be that of the pope, of the king, of the viceroy, or of whoever represents it. They give everything to authority and expect everything from it. Their entire organization comes from above, from agreements between those with power, and like it or not, they must obey their masters. The priests are very careful to instill this feeling of submissiveness in their conscience from the time they're children. The same thing happens with our peasants, although I believe it's worse over there, because no people are as fanatical as the Spaniards. That's why they're such good soldiers ('God guides them') and such bad administrators ('God will tell us . . .'—and God always says that the big fish gobbles up the little one)," he concluded with a smile.

D'Holbach seized on the chance to speak up. He was working on a theory concerning fear, submission, respect, and things of that sort, and his tongue burned to talk about it. The philosophe soon lost the thread of what he wanted to say. He wound up his remarks with such abruptness, such haste—distracted, perhaps, by the thought that the concert would begin and he would have to break off his peroration—and the concepts he employed were so complex and abstract ("The mind is nothing besides sensations. It probably comes from the glands of the midbrain that are the source of these latter," you managed to hear) that you simply didn't make the slightest effort to follow what he was saying. Discreetly, you left the group in search of a place to sit down. On the way, you greeted Philidor, who was having a lively chat with Gossec, Duport, and other musicians. You felt a great liking for that man: despite the fact that he was a great chess player—the best perhaps—and a remarkable musician, his person radiated the unaffected manners of a village baker. He had the gift of making things appear to be simple, be it a matter of moving the pieces on the chessboard or giving a concert, asking for a loan or speaking offhandedly of the financial situation of the kingdom—which you suspected he didn't have the least notion of—with Berryer, the secretary of the Ministry of the Navy. Philidor was everyone's friend: just as he had animated conversations with Diderot and his group, and participated in their binges and their scandals in the brothels, so he remained silent and taciturn with a little glass of liqueur in his hand listening to the interminable disquisitions on the fashion of the moment at one of the soporific soirees organized by Madame d'Egmont, where the presence of Fréron and his bunch of hypocrites was indispensable. Nonetheless, he was the intimate of no one. "My great love," he confessed to you that day, "my only love, is the black queen," and he burst into loud laughter, spitting everywhere little bits of the canapé he was chewing. You also greeted David Hume, the great Scottish thinker who was living at that time in Paris as the secretary to the ambassador of England. Hume was a ruddy-faced, robust hulk of a man, whose eyes shone with intelligence and kindliness. You had met him a short time before, at a gathering in Versailles where the superintendent had introduced you to him, allowing you the opportunity of a long talk with the Scotsman. (Beginning in 1749, Count de Buffon had been appointed superintendent of the Royal Gardens, gardens that soon became the most important museum of natural history in France and perhaps in the entire world. Since that time, Diderot had come to address the great scientist as Superintendent, something that didn't please Buffon at all, as he told his friend often enough. What he got from him, though, was an answer of this sort: "Very well, Superintendent, I won't call you that again." Of course, he went on doing so, until he got all the group of Encyclopedists into the habit of calling the good Buffon

Superintendent.) Hume was pleased to discover that you knew his works well, something that encouraged him to explain to you the projects that he had in mind. His ideas on human understanding left you openmouthed. They were sober, precise, and elegant, like Cupid's darts. You understood then why this great man had come to France: his intelligence was in perfect harmony with that of French thinkers, and nothing was more promising than exchanging his ideas with them. Perhaps that was why he looked a bit tense to you at that gathering, nodding respectfully at the observations that his employer, the ambassador, was making to the Baroness de Hausset, an extraordinarily beautiful woman, though rather vulgar, who listened to him with little interest as she fanned herself flirtatiously. Hume looked out of the corner of his eye at Diderot's circle as a little boy might look at a cookie jar he is forbidden to approach. When he greeted you, he looked at you imploringly: Get me out of here! he said to you with his little slanting eyes. You could not refuse him this favor: you greeted the diplomat and politely told the baroness that you placed yourself at her feet. She greeted you with delight, making a graceful curtsy that somehow allowed even more of her splendid breasts to show.

"Ah, my dear. You're an ingrate," she said to you. "I never have the pleasure of seeing you at my soirees"—or in my bed, her gesture underlined. "Promise me that you'll come have supper at home with me tomorrow."

"Can anyone deny you anything, my lady?" you answered gallantly. If you had had moustaches, you would have licked them like a satisfied cat. The woman held promise—though she was rather vulgar, but what difference did that make to you?—of succulent battles in the soft marriage bed of the Baron de Hausset. "I'll be there tomorrow, madam . . . Mr. Ambassador, might I steal your secretary for a moment? The other day he told me so many things, and such interesting ones, that my head has been a well of doubts ever since, and nobody except him, who in the last analysis is the guilty one, can rescue me from such confusion."

"Of course, marquis. Go and talk together all you like. Don't be offended, but with company such as I have," the ambassador said, making sheep's eyes at the woman with him, "I don't need anyone else."

"I'll be expecting you tomorrow, dear," the baroness said to you as you left.

With long strides, David Hume made for the group of Encyclopedists, as Diderot raised his hand from afar to greet him. (D'Holbach went on talking, although nobody appeared to be paying any attention to him.) "Thanks, friend, I owe you this favor," the Scotsman said to you with a smile as he left you to go give Denis a friendly embrace. "You may be sure I'll pay you back for it!" His letters, so lucid and poised, so stimulating, were a real haven of peace and calm when, a year later, you would plunge into the anguish of going on living despite yourself. Thanks to him, moreover, you were put in touch with English chemists whose advice, experiences, and knowledge were your most intimate companion during the interminable years that succeeded that earthquake that gave your life meaning, only to fling you later into an immense vacuum that you futilely tried to fill with your visions, your reading, and the study of chemistry, that strange science full of odors, colors, and magical ideas which that young scholar at the Court of Madrid had given you such a liking for so many years before.

Sitting close to the improvised stage—a wooden platform (underneath a large window and lit by more than forty candles arranged in a semicircle), toward the center of which stood a magnificent harpsichord, and a little farther back an Italian pianoforte finely decorated with country scenes—Rasero passed the time before the music began by leafing through the pamphlet that Melchior Grimm had given him at the entrance. It was illustrated with the picture of a very small child, no more than five years old, decked out in a full-dress suit with all the trimmings and his tiny white wig. He was shown sitting in front of a harpsichord with his eyes blindfolded. "Wolfgang Amadeus Mozart," the legend at the bottom of the illustration read, "the prodigy of our century. This creature of genius learned to play the harpsichord before he could talk. At six years of age, he had already signed a dozen exquisite compositions for this instrument and for the violin, of which he is also a skilled player. The courts of Central Europe that have already had the good fortune of becoming acquainted with his genius have been deeply moved by his talent, simplicity, and enormous personal appeal. Wolfgang can play the most difficult pieces with his eyes closed. He needs only to hear a few bars of any work to improvise marvelous variations on it. Accompanying his sister Nannerl, a lovely young girl, as well as a virtuosa of the keyboard and the possessor of an angelical voice, he contrives with her to make of any aria or popular song a real work of art. Little Wolfgang has accompanied, as first or second instrument, Europe's best musicians in memorable sonatas. Gluck, Nardini, and Reutter, among others, have shared and attested to his genius. We will be eternally grateful to Leopold Mozart, Wolfgang's father and teacher, the author of the *School of the Violin,* the best musical textbook of our time, to whose vision and generosity we owe the immense privilege of listening to his son, that sublime creature who has stolen the heart of the empress of Austria."

Good heavens, Rasero thought, our worthy Melchior didn't run short of generous words.

At eight o'clock on the dot, the ushers closed the doors of the salon. The audience took their seats. Standing in the middle of the platform, Melchior Grimm coughed gently to clear his throat. Elegant, as always, he greeted the people he recognized in the audience with a pleasant smile. He began to speak. Fortunately it was a brief introduction, sensible and intelligent. He praised the Mozarts, and young Wolfgang in particular, as the musical high point of the era. He read several passages from the commentaries he had written about this family of musicians of the stature of Gluck and Reutter and of critics as exacting as Maria Theresa of Austria or the Palatinate elector Charles Theodore. "I do not wish to expatiate further," he finally said, "and shall allow you to be witnesses to the prodigy to whom I am referring and then tell me if I have exaggerated in the slightest." More politely than enthusiastically, the audience applauded Grimm when he finished his introduction and went on applauding—very indifferently, it must be admitted—when it saw the Germans mount the platform. While Grimm was speaking, Rasero had distracted himself by looking around for the Baroness de Hausset, who was seated to the right of him, two rows farther back. The woman smiled at him—why is it she's so vulgar?—as she fanned her face and neck, the latter circled by a magnificent necklace of yellow and white diamonds that triumphantly cascaded down her proud bosom. The deep cleft formed between the two mounds of flesh fascinated Rasero. If only one were able to plunge into it, he thought, to disappear into that blessed place that smells, as no other bodily part does, of the essence of womanhood . . . If only one could nestle down in that flesh. As he felt more and more at ease, seated in that perfect place, a fleeting memory of the delirium he had suffered from several years before in Ferney, when he had subjected himself to Dr. Tronchin's cruel procedure, came to his mind as if by magic and made him shiver. He abruptly turned his eyes away from the woman's body and, blowing his nose into his handkerchief, tried to expel a concentrated odor of jasmine that had settled in his nose. The sound of the applause brought him back to reality. Relieved, he tucked his handkerchief into his sleeve once again and joined in the ovation. The Mozarts were already onstage. Leopold improvised a brief speech to thank people for their kindness, "above all, Baron and Baroness von Eyck and the most excellent Monsieur Grimm." Rasero looked at the Mozarts in curiosity. The father, a middle-aged man of average build, was well dressed, though his attire seemed just a little old-fashioned. He had an imperturbable, austere face, a "perfect match," Rasero thought, "for that of a strict Jesuit professor at Louis-le-Grand." His voice—he was speaking now, between one expression of thanks and another, of his book on the violin—was energetic and resounding, although his French was very bad, "worse than mine," Rasero thought. During his speech, Leopold referred several times to his son, and as he did so, Rasero observed that he looked at him in a very special way: with admiration, with fervor, almost with fear, as a saint would look upon the image of his god, as Angustias had looked at Rasero himself when she heard his first words or when he told her the story of the last caliph of Granada, as the Marquise de Pompadour looked at her lover and monarch, Rasero thought, or as Marie Corneille looked—when she dared to do so—at Voltaire as he chatted happily at table. The Austrian's gray eyes, gazing fleetingly but intensely at his offspring, caused a warm feeling for the musicians in Rasero. How lucky that man is, he thought, and how unlucky . . . He still hadn't heard him play, and already he felt greatly attracted by that youngster who was able to exert such an influence over his father. The sister, Nannerl, listened attentively to Leopold, although it was obvious that she didn't understand anything he said. She was a young girl of fourteen or fifteen, but she might easily have been taken for one of ten or eleven, for her face, pale and serene, with big, noble eyes, very much like those of her father, and her body, slender and svelte, in a pretty dress, very tight at the waist and with a high collar that modestly hid breasts barely showing beneath the cloth, were more those of a little girl than of an adolescent. Her pretty powdered hair was caught up in a chignon in which little violets were tucked. It resembled—without the little flowers, naturally—the style in which the empress of Austria always arranged her hair. Each time her father uttered her name, her cheeks flushed, and when he mentioned that of her brother, she turned around to look at him with a smile and gazed at him with the same almost religious look that her father did. The boy, standing between the two of them, scarcely came up to Leopold's waist. He was seven years old, but he looked no older than five; he was small and slight of build and perhaps seemed even more so because of his attire: a full-dress evening suit exactly like a grown man's, of fine blue satin with pretty white lace trimmings at the lapels, the pockets, and the cuffs of the coat. Underneath it was a shirt, white too, with showy frills and stiffly starched cuffs. His feet were shod in brightly polished ankle boots with heavy buckles. His silk hose were fastened tightly to his breeches (perhaps the right one was a bit droopy), and he was wearing a curious little scarlet sash beneath his coat. A ribbon of the same color was tied around the pigtail of his wig, which was white and very heavily powdered, with two curls over each temple. That attractive outfit, Rasero learned later, was a gift from the Empress Maria Theresa, who had been charmed—like everyone who heard him—by the talented little gentleman. Wolfgang's head, perhaps because of the wig or the small size of his anatomy or perhaps both things together, looked too big for his body. "He looks like a little dwarf," Diderot said to Rasero in a low voice. His face was not especially remarkable, very pale, like his sister's, though perhaps a little more prepossessing. His eyes, though very small, were much more vivacious and amiable than Nannerl's. As Rasero contemplated the youngster, very erect, with that round, oversized head, smiling as he listened to his father, and in that attire of an adult, he couldn't help feeling that the figure before him radiated something at once partially ludicrous, sordid, and obscene. For an instant, his gaze met Wolfgang's, and Rasero sensed that the little boy was thinking exactly the same thing he was. That bald man with the pointed face and eyes like a mosquito's is odd looking, he thought the boy must be thinking. This certainty made him like the youngster even more; they both smiled at the same time, and although only the two of them could see it, since they did so in their minds, they slyly winked at each other, like two accomplices.

Leopold ended his speech, which, to tell the truth, hadn't done a great deal to increase the musicians' reputation. "If he plays the way he talks, we're in for it," Diderot commented. The applause was even more lukewarm than what had greeted their arrival onstage. Finally, they set to work. The little boy sat down in front of the harpsichord (it was odd to see his little legs hanging halfway between the floor and the keyboard), the father tucked his violin underneath his chin, and the little girl placed herself in front of a music stand. To begin the concert, they had prepared a well-known aria from the ballet-opera *Roland,* by Jean-Baptiste Lully. With exquisite diplomacy, they had chosen a musician they detested but who was a national institution in France, nearly as venerable as the Sun King, in whose service he had been throughout his life. Nannerl had a pretty soprano voice, with good tessitura and modulation, although it revealed much more training than talent. On the other hand, she had a fairly good accent in French. Her brother accompanied her discreetly. They were showing off Nannerl's voice and not the little boy's skill, and he knew very well how to make himself unobtrusive. Diderot gave Rasero a sidelong glance and raised his eyebrows when their eyes met. The gesture was eloquent. Rasero played dumb and pretended to focus his attention on the girl's singing. In all truth, his mind was distracted, thinking about Jean-Baptiste Lully. Voltaire had once told him about that unusual Italian who had come to France as a humble cook's helper and eventually became a respected noble, the secretary of King Louis XIV and the supreme arbiter, whose judgment was not to be questioned, of music in the days of the Sun King. "He was a despotic and ambitious man," the philosopher told him. "He was not a great musician, but he was a genius at arranging music, singing (he used the rhythm of our language better than anyone else), and dance to form a perfectly harmonious whole." But the remarkable thing about Lully—which is what Rasero remembered now—was the way he died: "They were rehearsing, as they had done so often, one of his ballet-operas. He was in the habit of pounding the floor of the stage with his big baton so as to set the rhythm for the ballerinas. When he fell into a rage—which happened very often—he pounded so hard that on several occasions he broke the boards on which he was standing. The last time he did so, doubtless during his very last fit of rage," Voltaire said to him with a smile, "he moved his foot between the baton and the floor of the stage, with the result that he broke his big toe to smithereens. He never recovered. The fracture affected his entire foot until the whole thing rotted; then his leg rotted, and in a few days he died. As simple as that. The whole thing was absurd, my friend . . ." Nannerl ended her song. She had performed it fairly well, and the audience' applause, much warmer than at the beginning, told her so. The applause was dying down as the boy began to play his instrument again. It was the melody of the aria that his sister had sung, but as Wolfgang interpreted it, the cadence was much more languorous and much more sensual (saying, "much more," is hyperbole, because the melody was not at all sensual; it began to be sensual in the hands of that youngster). Now the keys resounded forcefully, no longer hidden behind Nannerl's singing; their sound filled the vast room, and the audience reacted as though it had had a bucket of cold water thrown on it. A murmur, an *ah!* of admiration competed for an instant with the harpsichord music, only to die down immediately and give way to total silence. The joyous notes frisked about the immense salon, as the listeners, concentrating to their utmost, their eyes opened wide, paid the sort of attention that is usually paid only by a criminal as he listens to his sentence. That was how the prodigy began . . .

Once the melody by Lully was over, without giving himself time to take a breath, the boy began to execute a joyful piece by Vivaldi. His sister, sitting at the pianoforte, accompanied him. Little by little, Wolfgang changed; the tiny person turned into a giant. He hit the keys with unexpected vigor as a big smile came over his face, a slightly demoniacal smile, Rasero thought. The Italian's music rang out, brilliant, lively, like a whirlwind of pleasure and desire. The torsos of the listeners could be seen to undulate rhythmically, following the beat of the music. The boy's smile had infected them: they all smiled gently, calmly, as though a spirit of good fellowship, of affection, of composure had taken hold of them. Time, obeying other laws, seemed to have stopped, as though it too had taken a rest to listen to the marvelous child. The sound of the notes gave Rasero a sensation of pleasure and happiness that up until then he had been able to experience only during orgasm. And like orgasm, it transported him elsewhere. Though not to the future: he could see, as though they were at his side, his cousins José and Matías, strong, energetic, full of life, bearing with them their precocious adolescence. The two of them were in the countryside at Macharavialla, happily chasing a lizard. He too was there, a little boy still, with his bald white head, running with tiny steps, trying in vain to catch up with his cousins. The breeze smelled of jasmine and olives. In the distance rose the mountain range, tinged a dark green, a color it seemed to have stolen from the sea. The notes intermingled, or better put, melted together in the song of the dark little birds flitting restlessly from one olive tree to another. "Don't let it get away, Matías!" José shouted with his rasping Andalusian voice (which was nothing other than Vivaldi's melody), "Don't let it get away, Matías!" over and over again, until a grave, vibrant note like a clap of thunder frightened the birds, which took off in large flocks from the olive trees. Startled by the sound, Matías let go of the reptile and Faustillo fell flat on his face, only to sit up again immediately and find himself elsewhere (and in another melody: now Wolfgang was interpreting Gluck; it was one of his best sonatas, the little boy giving it a very lilting interpretation, with the serenity of a mystic, and his father's violin coming in, precise, clean, exquisitely marking the tempos for his son). Rasero then found himself in his Angustias' arms, rocking in her lap. The good woman was singing a pretty gypsy ballad to him in a very low voice. It was a very sad story that he never tired of listening to: Adela, the daughter of the king of the gypsies, had lost her mother when she was very small. Her goodness and her beauty *shone like a sun* . . . Carmela, her stepmother, who was *more evil than Eve's snake,* took all her rancor out on Adela, all the wrath that the memory of her dead adversary had stored up in her soul, *darker than soot.* She obliged her stepdaughter to do the most tiring and basest tasks, in the hope of lessening thereby the girl's charms. But Adela grew, and along with her, her beauty, *which the very flowers envied* . . . In desperation, the stepmother tried to kill her; one night she entered Adelita's tent armed with a dagger that she did not hesitate to plunge into the child's little body . . . But *Saint Gabriel did not allow that infamous deed;* the archangel entered the tent *in all his glory* and took the dagger out of the body of the orphan; he then passed *his blessed fingers* over the wound, which disappeared *as night disappears when day comes* . . . Satisfied at having fulfilled his duty, *because God does not abandon his creatures,* the archangel, in the form of light, *which was not something to look upon, because it left you blind,* returned to heaven. The young girl, knowing nothing of this miracle, arose early in the morning and began her daily tasks. *She was in the river, beating the clothes,* when Carmela saw her. The wicked woman, on seeing the girl, immediately supposed that it was a ghost. "*Leave my side, shade from limbo,*" she said to the girl as she made the sign of the lizard with both hands. "*What is troubling you, my lady?*" Adela answered. Horrified, the stepmother ran off. She ran without stopping; she felt behind her back the breath of what she thought was *a soul in pain* . . . Driven mad, she reached the top of the ravine and when she tried to stop, *by the will of God, who never forgets,* she stumbled over a rough stone and fell into the abyss, *and much lower still, because they say she ended up in hell* . . . Adelita could finally be happy and, a woman now, married a gypsy *as tender as a dove,* who loved her as much as we must love the Virgin . . . The story, then, had a happy ending, to the rhythm of a *tanguillo:* and *Adela and Juan, her man, were the best king and queen that the gypsies have ever had,* Angustias declared again in the voice of the harpsichord when the child prodigy played a piece by Telemann—a happy vivacious piece that condensed in its notes all the tanguillos of the people of the pharaohs . . .

When the piece ended, Leopold wanted to magnify still more his son's virtues. As though what they had heard amounted to very little, he invited Raupach and the violinist Gacinièrs, who were in the audience, to accompany them as they played several pieces by Bach. The musicians did so willingly, and spurred on by the boy's genius, "played better than they had in their lives," as Melchior Grimm was to comment later in his *Correspondance littéraire.* The high point came when the little boy held his arm out to Lois-Claude Daquin, inviting him to come up onto the platform.

Lois-Claude, a little old man, was moved by the ovation he received. It so happened that he had been the greatest child prodigy that France had given the world. He was six years old when the eighteenth century began, and his reputation as a harpsichord player was already legendary throughout the kingdom. King Louis XIV attended many of the little boy's concerts in person and was captivated by his genius. He made him a noble and arranged for him to receive a generous pension, proud at having discovered in the twilight of his reign a star so bright that, in a way, it symbolized the seed containing all the glory of his era which was destined to germinate and flower in the future to testify to the eternal grandeur of his rule.

In obedience to nature's inescapable dictate, the little boy grew up and attained adulthood. He did not fulfill as inevitably, however, the expectations that he had created in the mind of the Sun King: Lois-Claude was a good musician but no more than that. Perhaps on seeing him reach manhood, the muses wearied of him and abandoned him. In any event, the musician had to resign himself to the bitter pleasure of living off the memories of his past grandeur. That was the reason Lois-Claude was so moved now. It was not the warm and sincere applause of the audience that brought great tears to his eyes; it was that blessed child in whom he saw himself. He was himself reincarnated, and seeing himself face-to-face made him feel such emotion, a pleasure and a pain so profound, that had it not been for the fact that his heart was as sound and strong as a bull's—Lois-Claude lived to be almost a hundred years old—it would have burst like a grenade. Little by little the musician calmed down; he said something in Leopold's ear, the latter nodding, sat down at the harpsichord, and began to play a melody that Rasero was unable to identify. Leopold accompanied him as first violin and little Wolfgang as second with his tiny instrument. It was a mournful sonnet that in a short time filled the room with a pleasant drowsiness. If the first notes that Lois-Claude played were a little harsh, as though his fingers and the keys of the instrument were too tense, so to speak, their nerves on edge, after a little while they had become soft. His hands began to move agilely over the keyboard and to caress the keys rather than drum on them. The violins, willing partners, frolicked around the harpsichord music, like a pair of flirtatious damsels whose charm obliged their gallant suitor to show himself off at his best. Their ensemble playing was perfect. Beauty, disguised as music, shone in all its splendor. Rasero, like the rest of the audience, felt himself transported to that kingdom of the sublime, to that region inhabited by sounds and silence, by lights, splendors, brilliant colors, and dark shadows, by soft, svelte, burnished, curving forms, now with sinuous and lilting movements, now in total repose, their dense volumes having settled in places reserved for them since the beginning of time. He was transported to the world of art, to that space that has no fixed point in the universe, which in fact doesn't correspond to it, because it exists only insofar as man exists—that singular creature, able to surpass any other by far when it comes to cruelty, ferocity, selfishness, and wickedness ("Man, the shame of the animal kingdom," Denis had once said to him) but also capable of creating that world of art in which now, borne by the skillful hands of the three musicians, Rasero was floating in ecstasy, like a cork in a calm pool. He was happy, euphoric at knowing that he was alive, at having palpitating senses, able to capture such beauty, to bear it to the depths of his soul—and sad, utterly sad at the same time, perhaps at knowing how ephemeral everything is, how fleeting and fragile beauty is, much more delicate than the wings of a butterfly, which, once caught in the spiderweb of our consciousness, disappears, turns to dust like a 65,000-year-old skeleton. Also sad perhaps at knowing that he was alone, at not sharing that world, that magical and human world, with anyone other than the inseparable consciousness within himself that spoke to him in a muffled voice, as in dreams, from the moment he had opened his eyes to the world, only to see his mother's close forever. His soul harbored an acute pain (as high-pitched and penetrating as the note that came forth from the little finger of Lois-Claude, who was now playing as in his childhood years, or perhaps better: the man had received the last visit of genius and was, while the melody lasted, the leafy tree in the sap of which flowed, energetic and vital, all the grandeur of old France, exactly as dreamed of by the one who had reigned over it from his solitary throne for so many years), a pain that filled the emptiness that he had just discovered. Can this be love? Rasero asked himself for the first time in his life. Can this be the implacable yearning not to be alone, to cross the immense desert of existence with a brother spirit, to be with someone when arriving at a blessed oasis where the greenery, the clear water, life deceive us sometimes, telling us that something more exists besides the terrible uncertainty of nothingness?

Love up until then had meant to you a receptive body, a pleasant smile, caresses to sharpen the senses and finally explode in a cruel and instantaneous enjoyment that dragged along in its wake, as well, the frightful images of a future that, alas! is undoubtedly looming. Love . . . you turned around and fixed your eyes on the Baroness de Hausset. The woman was listening ecstatically to the musicians. She was visibly moved. She was breathing anxiously, heaving her magnificent breasts in abrupt spasms, like a trout out of water. The power of the music was so great that, you thought, it succeeded in banishing the vulgarity that that woman radiated. Love . . . could you love her? Doubtless you would sleep with her tomorrow night; she had already told you as much by the look in her eye. You will gambol about, you will feel each other's bodies, you will smell each other's essences, you will couple, you will melt into a single being for an instant and then explode, she toward vertigo, toward a fierce and dangerous sensation, like falling into an abyss; you, however, as you fall into that abyss, will see, as you have always seen, some scene out of the future—with a bit of luck, something pleasant, such as a park full of people strolling about or sitting on benches idly allowing time to pass, or else something odious (unfortunately, that was more likely), such as men killing one another with impossible weapons in a dense jungle or in the dunes of a desert. Love . . . is that all it is? you said to yourself for the first time. You had to think that it was much more than that, as a beach is much more than a grain of sand. Love . . . you remembered how you spoke of love to your friend Diderot when, caught in its trap, he nearly lost his life because of it. You spoke to him wisely, self-assuredly, like a professor at the Sorbonne: "Love!" you said to your friend, "love with all your strength!" You had said that, you, Fausto Hermenegildo Rasero, a forty-year-old émigré, bald, taciturn, and a Rosicrucian, a man who never before now, never before this very minute when the magic of three musicians obliged you to do so, had thought about love, had felt love. You giving advice to Denis: an absurd paradox. Nobody, nobody, you said to yourself, knows as little about love as you do. You had endeavored—with what pain you were discovering it!—to fill that vacuum with knowledge, with visions, with caresses . . . Lois-Claude had stopped playing some time ago. Mechanically, without having any clear awareness of what you were doing, you applauded him enthusiastically along with the rest of the audience. But your mind was still elsewhere; it kept on asking itself why you hadn't been able to find company, to meet someone who would journey with you to love, to that oasis, to that glory of the human being which is the only one, if such a thing is possible, that can give meaning to existence. Wolfgang began to play the pianoforte. The last piece of the concert was a sonata that he himself had composed, a piece too elegant and well balanced to have been written by a seven-year-old child. Love . . . can it be that it exists? Your lips were parched, and your eyes tried to shed tears, but they were unable to; they hadn't learned how to, they had never done so. Could there exist something capable of filling this emptiness, this complete emptiness, this loneliness, this absence so final, so overwhelming that death itself seems like a fiesta alongside it? The concert was coming to an end. It had taken you to heaven and to hell. You had had a glimpse of the sublime, only to discover your inability to share it. You had encountered yourself as you really were: strange, indifferent, solitary, unutterably alone. The final movement was repeated a second time. A strange fear took possession of you. You didn't want the little musician to finish, as though your entire existence depended on those notes. Death, you said to yourself, will come for me when this youngster is through playing . . . There was only emptiness, only those last notes that presaged the throes of death. Truly frightened, you opened your eyes wide, fought in your mind against this fateful idea. Naturally, you didn't want to die; indeed, you didn't even want to feel what you were feeling. Life, however empty it might be, was something, something you wanted to cling to desperately. You turned around again to look for the Baroness de Hausset. It's emptiness, it's nothing, but when all is said and done it is also pleasure, you said to yourself hopefully as you looked for the woman with the eagerness of a sailor looking for land after a three-month voyage. You did not find her: the chair that the Baroness de Hausset had been sitting in until a moment before was still occupied . . . but by another person. You cleared your vision by blinking quickly, as the little boy lifted his hands from the keyboard. You didn't understand what you were seeing: another woman was occupying the baroness' place. A very beautiful woman. You contemplated her profile. She was tense, sitting very straight in the chair, with her eyes as wide open as possible; great tears were falling from them. The woman was looking at the youngster with an intensity and an emotion that revealed themselves in an expression of love, anxiety, happiness, and deep grief at the same time, as Mary might have looked at Jesus atop Mount Calvary when he reproached his Father for having abandoned him. The child rose to his feet, as did the woman. She applauded frantically, she applauded furiously, she wept, she smiled, she wiped away her tears, she applauded again, minute by minute she was more beautiful, closer, more dearly loved. You applauded enthusiastically too: the child, his genius, and that marvelous woman whom you at last recognized. Her nose, slightly aquiline, but above all her mouth, her incredible teeth, her marvelous laugh, were unforgettable. Without understanding why, and without asking yourself why, you knew that you were face-to-face with the woman of your life.

V
Mariana

Paris, December, 1763

"Hurry up, girl, make up your mind. It's getting late."

This was said by Jacinta, a mature, robust woman, with a firm-fleshed body the color of old copper. Mariana contemplated her faithful maidservant, who was carrying over each forearm a dress, one white, the other pale blue. She couldn't decide. The two dresses pleased her a great deal, but in a certain strange way they frightened her as well. A modesty that she still hadn't completely got the better of advised her not to wear such clothing. She had bought the dresses, along with the yellow one that she had worn the night before, as soon as she arrived in Paris. A French dress! It was an old dream that went back to her adolescence, when, in the old mansion in Taxco, she looked at herself in the mirror with dissatisfaction, trying on one of those old-fashioned heavy velvet dresses, dark-colored and altogether seemly, capable of hiding any feminine charm, no matter how prominent, that she had inherited from her mother.

Of course, when she became part of the court in Mexico City, her wardrobe improved noticeably. Her husband, the viceroy, was incapable of denying her the slightest caprice. Each month she eagerly awaited the royal stagecoaches that arrived from Veracruz filled with things made in Spain, in which there was always a large trunk meant for the Marquise de las Amarillas. Mariana opened it excitedly, the way a little child would open a present. The cherry-colored dress had arrived at last, with its sleeves, its neck, and half of the wide skirt embroidered in black thread, the dress she had seen the Duchess de

Osuna wearing in that print that had reached her only a year before. Aided by Jacinta, she eagerly removed in no time the clothes she had on and donned the new garment. Her maidservant grumbled, "Those men who make ladies' dresses in Madrid are certainly stupid. The waist is too big again. But I'll fix it in the time it takes to recite a rosary . . . It's adorable, my child!" In fact, Mariana did look very pretty in it. As she looked at herself in the mirror, she smiled in satisfaction: she was the best-dressed woman in New Spain; there was no doubt about it. She could already imagine the expression of envy that would come over the face of the Marquise de la Borda when she saw her at the palace wearing that dress. Confound that young woman, she thought the marquise would think, she keeps getting ahead of me. I ordered that dress just two weeks ago. It's not going to be of any use to me now.

Mariana had good taste and the best of ladies' dressmakers. She was able to prove it to herself when she arrived in Spain bringing with her her voluminous wardrobe—consisting exclusively of black garments, strict mourning attire, since the unfortunate death of the marquis that terrible morning in Cuernavaca required it. Spanish ladies, accustomed to looking contemptuously at those from America ("Poor provincials," they were in the habit of saying, "they're at once vulgar and heedless. You won't believe me, but I've seen several of them wear gold around their neck and silver at their wrists, pearl earrings and diamond bracelets. How dreadful! Though it's to be expected, living as they do in those jungles, surrounded by savages"), could not keep themselves from admiring that young widow in an imposing black silk dress with marvelous lace insets that opened like fans on the sleeves down to her wrists, and at her neck, as svelte and proudly erect as that of an Egyptian queen, as she made a graceful curtsy to King Carlos in receiving the monarch's sincere condolences over the death of her "most upright and most beloved" husband. The lovely widow of Spanish lineage born in the New World soon made herself popular at the Court of Madrid. Her large dowry, which came for the most part from the diligent efforts of her father, who spent many years of his life in a continued struggle to rob the bowels of the arid mountains of Taxco of their silver and, above all, to defend that wealth from plunder by the man who was first his partner and then later his enemy, don José de la Borda. What he was able to save from the claws of that bastard, which in reality was quite a substantial sum, was bequeathed to his daughter, the only person he had left in the world after the death of his wife, who had been consumed by sadness on learning that her only son had given up his life, the victim of the fierce Apaches, in a far-distant place almost lost in the wilderness, which, cruelly, was named Santa Fe. The large dowry of the girl and her beauty, elegance, and winning personality, had sown dreams and hopes in numerous suitors at court, as well as envy and rancor in no fewer ladies of noble birth. And it inflamed even more hearts and aroused more envy when, after two years, Mariana ceased to wear mourning and began to wear bright colors once again.

Young and mature at the age of twenty-five, a more charming creature—and a sadder one—would have been hard to find. For, despite everything—her wide acceptance, her circle of admirers, the little library of love notes that she was assembling, knowing herself to be pretty and admired—that happiness which had accompanied her during almost her entire life, since she had reached the age of reflection, a happiness that did not abandon her either when she learned what had happened to her brother, or when her mother died, or even when her father, the person whom she had loved the most, kissed her on the forehead and said to her, serious and taciturn, "Farewell forever," and climbed into the carriage that would take him to Acapulco in order to embark there on the China schooner and disappear forever into the enormous belly of legendary Asia, that happiness, until then firm and resistant, fell apart like unfired clay that morning in Cuernavaca when the Marquis de las Amarillas, after having eaten a hearty lunch, feeling happy, stretched and said to her, "Darling, I'm going for a stroll in the gardens. I don't know why, but I'm in a very joyful mood; perhaps it's this splendid morning . . ." Full, smiling, he set out among the ash trees. He was listening with nostalgic happiness to the song of a mockingbird, when, surprised by death, he suddenly fell into a pond as though struck by lightning, lifeless already and hence not drowned. What really drowned was Mariana's happiness. She realized then that the marquis, an astute man as well as a kind-hearted one, had robbed her of her happiness; he had taken it with him. Because that sad old man, until that fateful morning, had never known what it was to be happy . . .

Don Agustín de Ahumada y Villalón, marquis de las Amarillas, a serious, shy, and unbelievably responsible man, never understood—or had not understood, alas! until that morning—that there is another world, wide and varied, full and inexhaustible, beyond duty, beyond the rigid path his father had marked out for him first, and his stern Jesuit teachers after that, a world that opened up before him, although it was extremely difficult for him to realize it, when for the first time he saw that likable girl acting with grace and talent in a comedy by Lope de Vega that was being put on in the Palace of the Viceroys. The man took an interest in her and entrusted his astute secretary to find out everything he could about the life of the young actress. In a few days' time the report was on his desk:

> Doña Mariana Francisca de Paula Rodríguez de Lassaga y Barreiro was born in Real de Minas de Tasco, Kingdom of Méjico, on the fourth of March of the year 1738 in the bosom of our Holy Catholic mother church. She is the daughter of don Federico José Rodríguez de Lassaga y Bojórquez, a native of Oviedo, Spain, a nobleman, the third heir of the Baron de Bojórquez and second cousin of the Marquis de Salvatierra, don Ignacio Rodríguez; and of doña María Cristina Barreiro y Nesta, a native of La Coruña, Spain, and also of noble birth.
>
> Doña Mariana is the third of five children, the first and fourth of whom died at birth and the last of whom died when he was a small child. The only one of her brothers and sisters to reach adulthood was the second, don Guillermo, born in Madrid, Spain, who discharged his duties in the Royal Army of His Majesty in these lands of the Viceroyalty of New Spain and in the Philippine Islands, where he attained the rank of first cavalry lieutenant, distinguishing himself by his valiant deeds in the fight against the Chichimeca Indians, who people and lay waste the south of this kingdom. He was outstanding for his deeds of valor in Zacatecas, Guamuchil (where he obtained the rank of lieutenant), San Blas, and finally, Villa de Santa Fe, the capital of the province of New Méjico, where he had the misfortune of losing his life, after fierce and courageous skirmishes, at the hands of the Indians called Apaches, on a day in the month of October in the year of our Lord 1756.
>
> Don Federico J. Rodríguez took the proper steps and obtained at the court in Madrid a royal letter-patent, dated in the year 1743, in which he was granted the right to exploit the mineral wealth of the mountains of Güatepec, close by the Villa de Tasco of the Kingdom of Méjico in this New Spain. He invested in this undertaking all the property and goods that he had in the Spanish Peninsula. He arrived in this kingdom in the year 1736 and took up residence in the aforementioned Villa de Tasco. He successfully exploited the silver-bearing lodes of Nta. Sra. del Pilar y la Purísima in the aforementioned mountains. Don Federico soon joined forces with don José de la Borda, who had been working the mines of the nearby mountains for twenty years. Around the year 1750, the aforementioned associates separated, however. It would appear that

don Federico did not approve of the methods that don José employed to exploit the mines, especially with respect to his treatment of the Indians, with whom, as is well known, he deals in a notably pitiless and cruel manner. Whether for this reason or some other that we did not succeed in discovering, the partnership was definitely dissolved in the year 1752, when don Federico ceded the rights to exploit his mines to don José de la Borda in exchange for one hundred sacks of silver.

With this respectable fortune, don Federico and his family came to reside in this very noble and very loyal city of San Francisco de Méjico in the spring of the year 1753. They took up residence at Number 5 of the calles del Espíritu Santo. It was at that time that don Guillermo enlisted in the Royal Army and departed to fulfill his first mission at the presidio of Zacatecas. Doña Mariana became a boarding student at the girls' school of the Sisterhood of Mary in order to continue and advance in the studies appropriate for her feeble sex which, with such good omens, she had begun in the Villa de Tasco in the care of the Sisters of Saint Brigid. Doña Mariana soon distinguished herself as an eager and intelligent pupil, excelling in particular in verbal composition. It is said that she was so ingenious and clever at composing lovely verses and poems that there was no lack of those who saw in her a future Tenth Muse, like our immortal Hieronymite nun Sor Juana Inés de la Cruz.

The year 1756 was a fateful and terrible one for don Federico: first, because he had to defend himself against a lawsuit brought by don José de la Borda; second, because, as we have already noted above, his son, don Guillermo, died at the hands of the Apache Indians in the presidio of Santa Fe de Nuevo Méjico; and third, because, informed of such fatal news, doña Cristina, his wife, found her strength ebbing, consumed by the sadness of losing her only surviving male offspring and by the tribulations confronting her husband, until she thought it fit to leave this sinful world on the ninth day of March of the year 1757. Doña Cristina died in the arms of our Holy Catholic mother church after having received the blessed sacraments.

As for the lawsuit, the following developments took place: it would appear that don José de la Borda dusted off in his archives a very old royal letter-patent signed by don Felipe V and endorsed by the viceroy don Juan de Acuña, marquis de Casafuerte, in which don José was granted the right to exploit a vast zone adjoining the oft-mentioned Villa de Tasco. Among the sites granted him, he believed he found, albeit under another name, the mountains of Güatepec, which, as we have indicated above, were granted to don Federico Rodríguez in the year 1737 by King Felipe V himself, may he rest in peace. For this reason, don José requested that the sacks of silver be returned to him, as well as the interest accrued, which he had paid to settle rights that he now considered his. (We know that Your Excellency is familiar with a number of details of the aforementioned lawsuit, but we have made bold to put them before you for your consideration, since, as will be seen below, they are very important in the life of doña Mariana, the subject of this report.) The request was handed on to the royal tribunal of this very noble City of Méjico, which, as a first step, decided to freeze the aforementioned funds and accrued interest and place them in the custody of the order of Augustinian brothers until the case is settled. More than a year has gone by without a decision's being handed down in favor of either party, for which reason the royal tribunal has recently decided to transfer the case to the tribunals of the Cortes de Indias in Seville. Don Hernando Rodríguez de L., don Federico's brother and a resident of the Peninsula, has taken on the task of looking after the interests of his relative, and for the purpose of pleading don Federico's cause has hired the distinguished lawyer don Joseph de Gálvez, who despite every effort has not succeeded in unraveling this complicated matter.

Finding himself without a fortune, a wife, or an heir, don Federico felt his spirits flag and even his reason diminish, according to what certain people say, and decided to embark for the Far East in order to lend voluntary aid to the Jesuit missions that are established in those far-distant lands. He embarked on the Day of the Name of Our Lord, in June of the year 1757, and since then nothing has been heard of him.

As for doña Mariana, her father, before departing, entrusted her to the care of the family of don Antonio Bassoco, which resides at Number 8 of the calle de la Acequia of this most noble city. Don Antonio, a man very well known in these parts for his piety and noble heart, has treated doña Mariana as though she were his own daughter, and being aware of the talents with which she is blessed and her great cleverness, has seen to it that her education is prosecuted with painstaking care. Meanwhile, doña Mariana is hoping that the lawsuit will be settled, for she is the sole heiress of her father's estate, which consists of nothing beyond the sums held in trust by the Augustinian brothers. She needs to have such an unjust situation resolved, for she requires this estate so that she may have at her disposal a dowry that will permit her to marry a man worthy of her, or else to enter, in a sound financial state, the Hieronymite Convent, one that she admires and longs to enter, influenced perhaps by the brilliant aura of our American Muse. Meanwhile, she is advancing in her studies in letters, music, and singing, and is also helping doña Angelina Bassoco in household tasks. At the same time, spurred on by Tomás Bassoco, don Antonio's son, a young man of outstanding talent, a scholar who is greatly respected in our Royal and Pontifical University despite his youthful age and who manifests an unusual love for and interest in our Castilian letters and its incomparable geniuses, to the point of amassing in his library and in his memory an immense collection of their works, many of them—especially the unforgettable comedies written in that most brilliant seventeenth century—being the ones that have led him to organize and direct a charming theatrical company made up of illustrious members of the best families of this New Spain, doña Mariana Rodríguez participates in the company, occupying a most distinguished place in it as the young leading actress.

The company has delighted many of us with its graceful and masterly performances of the comedies, tragedies, and *autos sacramentales* of our classic authors. It has achieved such great success and such renown that not long ago it staged a performance to commemorate the feast day of the resurrection of our Lord, in this Palace of the Viceroys of New Spain, where Your Excellency had an opportunity to appreciate and be moved by the talent of the young actors and to meet that young girl, a virtuosa, who has quite rightly awakened your sovereign interest.

With the hope of having fully complied with your sovereign instructions, the present report was drawn up on the ninth day of the month of May in the year of our Lord 1758, in the very noble and very loyal city of San Francisco de Méjico.

Crisóstomo García de Valdepeñas,
Secretary of His Most Illustrious Excellency . . .

As the wind fans a flame, so the reading of the report fanned the viceroy's interest in the girl. A profound sentiment that he did not succeed in understanding at all impelled him to do as much as he could to aid that helpless creature. Discreet and diligent—as he had always been—he skillfully pulled the long strings of his power that extended beyond the sea to the Court of Madrid and the offices of the Council of the Indies in Seville, in order to accelerate the legal formalities and obtain a positive decision in favor of doña Mariana in the lawsuit that the Marquis de la Borda had brought against her father. To his satisfaction, the viceroy discovered that don Joseph de Gálvez, the lawyer of the Rodríguez de Lassaga family, was an honest and intelligent man and that his fame and influence were expanding, like bread left to rise, in the corridors of the Royal Palace, thus making a verdict favorable to the daughter of the Asturian foreseeable. But "the time things take at court is never short," as the proverb has it, and unfortunately this one is truer than most: the lawsuit might well have gone on for another two years, and the viceroy, concerned because the kindness and the patience of don Antonio Bassoco had not drained her cup of sorrow and in the end had left the girl at fate's mercy, tried by all the means at his disposal—which were many—to make don Antonio see, implicitly and at no time explicitly, that the fate and the future of doña Mariana were very dear to his royal person. He therefore did his utmost to flatter don Antonio and smoothed his path in everything he undertook, while at the same time inviting him more and more often to share, together with his wife, son, and protégée, in the splendid luncheons and dinners at the palace.

Don Antonio, who had never lacked intelligence, soon discovered what was hidden behind the viceroy's kind treatment and took great pains to care for Mariana and spoil her as though she were his own daughter, and perhaps even a bit more. As was to be hoped, the viceroy's fondness for the theater, which had been very slight if not nonexistent up until then, increased at the same pace as his admiration for the girl. Not a week went by without, on one pretext or another, a theatrical performance at the palace being organized. Tomás Bassoco was happy: the sovereign's sudden interest in the art that he so dearly loved permitted him to prepare and present the most difficult and inventive works, for the viceroy did not spare a single real in ensuring that the costumes, the stage machinery, and the set would all produce an absolutely magnificent effect, carefully supervised down to the last detail. He even reached the happy extreme of authorizing the purchase of revolving scenery for the little palace theater. It was a dream within reach of very few dramatists.

Meanwhile, doña Mariana developed her art and enhanced her beauty. She spent entire afternoons reading so as to be able to fix in her memory the dialogues and monologues of the innumerable characters she played in the palace theater. She was thus the energetic and courageous queen doña María in *La prudencia en la mujer;* she was the timid and trusting Jacinta of *La verdad sospechosa,* the audacious and noble Rosaura of *La vida es sueño,* the Elvira who "still has large shields in the now-effaced coat of arms of her portal," of *El alcalde, el mejor rey,* the very beautiful and impulsive doña Inés of *El caballero de Olmedo,* and a thousand other characters. Among them, it could be said that she represented her own person in the character of doña Ana, the protagonist of *Quien vive para la plata . . . ,* a delightful comedy Tomás wrote in her honor on her twenty-first birthday, in which the eager university student did not make much effort to hide his esteem for his father's beautiful protégée.

The plot of the work was a complicated affair revolving around a lawsuit that don Pelayo (an obvious allusion to don José de la Borda), an avaricious, ambitious man with few scruples, has brought against don Anselmo, Ana's father, a kindly noblemen, taciturn and too naïve. Don Pelayo, after buying off witnesses, corrupting judges, falsifying documents, and involving with his specious arguments the comendador himself (who is none other than the viceroy de las Amarillas), nearly sees his wishes fulfilled, for the judge hands down a decision in his favor, stripping don Anselmo of his possessions and even sending him to the galleys. The daughter, whom up until then the comendador had regarded as a disloyal and scheming woman—an image with which don Pelayo's machinations had left him—is sentenced to be cloistered in the convent of the Discalced Carmelites and live on charity. After the verdict, the final curtain begins to fall. When the play is presented, the audience, surprised, squirm in their seats, and some of them even begin to hiss and boo such a loathsome ending. At that point there hurries onstage—the setting of which represents a tribunal—Ramiro, the young male lead, who during the entire work has tried to defend the interests of don Anselmo and his daughter Ana, for whom he feels a tender affection. Ramiro enters in the company of Gervasio, the comic character in the play, a tiny figure, very talkative and quick-witted, one more instance of the innumerable simpletons that invariably have a role in Spanish comedies. He asks don Ramiro to raise the curtain again, and addressing the comendador, rather than the judge, since he has already discovered that the judge's moral conscience was bought with don Pelayo's riches, begs for his attention in order to unravel the complicated situation. It turns out that Gervasio, armed with his cleverness and guile, has been an invaluable collaborator of don Pelayo's in carrying out his maneuvers, in the execution of which he has made the most of his reputation as a simpleton. But in the end he doesn't turn out to be all that simpleminded. His intelligence and guile are much greater than don Pelayo suspected, for Gervasio has always been loyal to don Ramiro and has pretended to help the avaricious don Pelayo in return for a handful of coins only to amass proof of don Pelayo's infamous machinations. In a charming ballad, Gervasio explains the entire matter, leaving the stern comendador completely satisfied. Feeling remorse for his severity toward the honest Anselmo, he turns with even greater fury against don Pelayo, whom he condemns to hand over all his possessions to the one who up to that point has been his victim and to row as a galley slave in the China schooner alongside his accomplice, the corrupt judge, though not before the two of them have received a goodly number of sound lashes.

At the performance for the viceroy, the audience, content with that, enthusiastically applauded, and it applauded even more heartily when doña Ana, turning to the spectators, ended the work with this ten-line stanza:

> Through silver the good man is carried away,
> he does not recognize his friend
> and lives like a beggar.
> He who lives for silver
> has a soul of tin.
> I say to you, audience, do not turn a deaf ear:
> since this metal is of no use for fattening,
> it is better to store up corn in the barn
> than to throw your salvation overboard
> for ambition's sake.

Almost everyone enthusiastically celebrated the genius of Tomás Bassoco, whom they could envision as a worthy successor to the great Juan Ruiz de Alarcón. I say almost everyone, because in the audience was don José de la Borda, who could be accused of many things but not of being an idiot. Deeply offended, he left the theater without performing, for the first time in the more than forty years that he had been in Mexico, the ritual of kissing the viceroy's hand. That was how deeply the poem that Mariana had recited had pierced his pride.

When the performance ended, the viceroy had ready an intimate supper to entertain the girl regally. Attending it in addition to Mariana were don Antonio, his wife and son, and don Crisóstomo García, the faithful secretary of the Marquis de las Amarillas. In a little salon, waited on by silent footmen and sampling exquisite dishes from both sides of the Atlantic, they spent an enjoyable evening during which reactions to the work that had just been put on dominated the conversation. The quality of the dialogues, the ingenuity of the plot, and Tomás' great acting in the role of the comic character Gervasio gained much praise. There was also talk about the anger of the Marquis de la Borda. "He was so angry he turned yellow," don Antonio commented with a smile. "Green, you mean," his wife corrected him, "because he's always been yellow. That man is the color of parchment; it must be on account of the sourness of his soul . . ." When the time came for toasts, the viceroy improvised a little speech in which he politely praised Mariana's charms. "To a most unusual young lady; she is proof that there is room for beauty, cleverness, an virtue in one and the same person, however difficult that may appe to be," the viceroy said with his glass raised and his eyes fixed o those of his admired young lady. Once he had ended his toast, whic received the sincere applause of those present—except for Marian who, rattled, could hit on nothing to do other than to smile as he eyes searched about for somewhere to look without embarrassment– the viceroy's secretary handed his employer a tiny object that h employer in turn placed in front of Mariana. "Accept, my girl, th modest gift. I hope that it will oblige you always to remember th enormous good feeling and admiration that this old man feels f you." It was a small silver locket suspended from a thick chain of th same metal. Its workmanship was Moorish, and it had the form of walnut. It was made with just one strand of silver that plaited itse and curled about to form whimsical filigreed figures. It had a min uscule door in the form of a heart that on being opened allowed on to see the jewel inside. The locket had belonged to the viceroy's famil since time immemorial. In it the viceroy had kept for many years lock of the hair of his first grandchild, whom he had hardly known for he had lived for only two years. He had replaced the curl of ha in the locket with a small but very pretty yellow pearl he had ha sent to him from the Philippines, his intention being that the colo of the jewel would serve to remind Mariana of the title Marquis d las Amarillas belonging to the one who had given her the gift. O seeing the present, the girl, deeply touched, put the locket aroun her neck, and in a spontaneous gesture, went over to the old ma and kissed him on the forehead and both cheeks.

When the banquet was over, the men took their leave of th women and withdrew to an adjoining salon to smoke their pipes an drink cordials. Meanwhile the women waited for them in a littl drawing room, where they passed their time observing in fascinatio the tiny figures that the skillful hands of the Moorish craftsman ha made with the strand of silver in the brand-new gift to Mariana fron the Marquis de las Amarillas.

The viceroy, reclining in a comfortable armchair, felt with satis faction the sweet fire of the liqueur go down his throat and savore with pleasure the acrid tobacco smoke. Don Antonio paced from on side of the room to the other, muttering something to himself. It wa obvious that he was ill at ease. Several times, turning to the viceroy he was on the point of beginning a sentence, but then, regrettin having gone that far, he coughed and began his pacing back and forth again.

"What's the matter, my good friend?" the viceroy asked him. "Either I'm imagining things or you've been wanting for some time to tell me something that you don't dare to. Come on, my good man, tell me in all trust what's troubling you."

Don Antonio looked at his son, who nodded his head, and finally he decided to speak up.

"I very much fear, Your Excellency, that the news I have to give you is not going to please you at all . . ."

"Stop beating around the bush, my friend, and tell me once and for all what the trouble is."

"The trouble, sir, is that the last mail from the Peninsula brought me news as happy as it was unexpected . . ."

"And what's so bad about that?"

"Wait. It's truly happy news, but not for everyone . . ."

"Come on, don Antonio, you're wandering off the subject again."

"Believe me, Your Excellency, if there were any possible way, no matter how difficult, for me to avoid putting you through this unpleasant experience . . ."

"Out with it, my good man, tell me once and for all what's happening. You're making me edgy."

The little old man looked the viceroy in the eye; he grew flushed and did his best to hold back tears. He couldn't work up the courage to continue the conversation. He stammered something unintelligible and coughed once more to clear his throat. Don Tomás, his son, who knew his father very well and knew how hard it was for that good man to express himself when an emotion held him back, intervened: "Father, if you will allow me, I can explain the matter to His Excellency."

"Yes, son, certainly."

"Well, then, my lord. The happy news to which my father is referring is that his distinguished uncle, don Aniceto Bassoco del Barrio, may he rest in peace, before leaving this sinful world thought it wise to name my father the sole heir of his estate, which is no mere trifle, naturally."

"Well, then, allow me to congratulate you, don Antonio. But apart from the unfortunate death of don Aniceto, I find no misfortune for anyone in this piece of news."

"Wait, we're coming around to it. It so happens that the main estate left by my great-uncle consists of a good hundred fanegas of the best parcels of land in La Rioja, all of them vineyards cultivated down to the very last corner. He possessed, moreover, stills, wine vats, and cellars where his forebears first, and then he himself, produced one of the best wines of the region—and when I say that it's one of the best wines of the region, that is tantamount to saying one of the best in Spain, for in no other part of the country are better and finer ones produced than there . . ."

"That's certainly true! Indeed, this inheritance is no mere trifle, my friend."

"My father, as you are very well aware, has been in love with wine and its production since his tenderest years. It is not without cause that he is the best producer and distributor of wine in this New Spain. You can understand, then, that since he received this news, he can scarcely wait to go off to Spain to take possession of his inheritance."

The smile on the viceroy's face that up until then had been noticeable disappeared as if by a spell.

"So you and your family are thinking of leaving, don Antonio?"

"With Your Excellency's permission," answered his friend, who, relieved of the most difficult moment of passing on his news, decided at last to speak. "You will understand that I cannot leave these possessions in God's hands. Moreover, they bring in an ample income, which will allow me to send my son to the University of Salamanca so that he can complete his studies and earn a doctorate. It greatly grieves me, dear marquis, to have made this decision, but I view it as impossible and even impious to rebuff the favor that providence is granting me."

"Of course . . ."

The viceroy was able to conceal his vexation only with the greatest effort. He rose to his feet and poured himself more liqueur. Now he was the one who began to pace up and down the room and clear his throat without working up the gumption to speak. Tomás understood the anxiety that the marquis was experiencing and smoothed the way.

"We're thinking of taking Mariana with us."

"And does she already know this?"

"Yes. My father told her as soon as he decided that we'd be going to Spain."

"And does she agree?"

"To be frank, she is not very excited by the idea of going off to live in such a small town; these lands are more to her liking. But she is ready to follow us. She considers herself, as she has told us, my parents' daughter, and as such will obey their decision."

"She could stay here . . ."

"With whom, Your Excellency?" don Antonio interjected. "Since her father died, we're the only people she has in the world—or at least in America, since another possibility is that once she arrives in Spain she can go live with her uncle Hernando in Madrid."

"She could enter a convent. I've heard that she admires the Hieronymite sisters. The dowry wouldn't be a problem; I could help her while the lawsuit is being settled . . ."

"To tell you the truth, she herself suggested that," Tomás said. "But it sufficed to see her face when she said it to realize that she didn't like the idea at all. Frankly, sir, I believe that the spirit of our Mariana does not accord well with the customs of a convent. There are birds that are born to be caged; others, however, need more space and would rather die than find themselves shut up. And I believe that Mariana is much more like these latter . . ."

"That is true, young man. I can't imagine Mariana cloistered in a convent . . . There's no question about it, don Antonio, everything points to your decision as the right one. When are you planning to leave?"

"In two or three months, Your Excellency. I must settle my business affairs and auction off certain properties. We have sunk deep roots in this territory; it is not easy simply to take wing. My son will leave next week. He is going on ahead to look after the formalities required by the will and to enroll at Salamanca."

"Well, have a good journey, my boy," the marquis said, embracing him warmly. "And may God permit you to achieve all the success that your talent deserves. So then, don Antonio, you were certainly right! That happy piece of news has left me very sad. You are well aware that I have held you in the greatest esteem; in all truth, all of you have been the only family I have had in these lands. But good fortune is not to be disdained. Go to La Rioja, though, mind you, I order you to produce the best wines in Spain; if not, I will never forgive you for your having abandoned me."

"God willing, I'll do precisely as you order, marquis," the robust older man said. His face had flushed again and tears fell from his eyes. "I swear to you that in my heart there will always be a place for this Mexico and its beloved viceroy . . ."

"Calm down; calm down. You're not leaving tomorrow. We'll still see each other, if God so wills, many times. And I have many requests to make of you."

"I shall not live with my conscience at ease if they are not fulfilled to the letter, Your Excellency."

"I know, my friend, I know. We'll talk about the matter later . . . For the moment, let's offer a toast, let's offer a toast in honor of the success that awaits all of you in Spain," the viceroy said, raising his glass as in his mind he saw, as if branded in red-hot fire, the image of his cherished Mariana.

The days that followed were terrible for the viceroy. He realized in sorrow that the bitter solitude in which he had lived for the previous twenty years, since the death of his wife and the departure—which took place shortly thereafter—of his son for the kingdom of Naples, a solitude he had succeeded in banishing since he had met the pretty young girl, was returning once again to the depths of his soul and would accompany him for the rest of his days. Curiously, today—when he was twenty years older and infinitely wearier—he was far less prepared to accept his destiny with resignation. His spirit rebelled as he was confronted with the panorama of spending his last days sunk in reviewing documents, listening with badly concealed ennui to the complaints, pleas, demands, petitions, and even threats of his subjects, presiding over ceremonies as solemn as they were boring, and heading processions through the main streets of the city at the head of the town council, of the tribunal, and of the religious brotherhoods, accompanied by the sanctimonious archbishop, who, after the procession, once inside the cathedral, would deliver from the pulpit a pedantic, dull sermon, full of quotations from the classics—as was the fashion—with a reference or two to pre-Hispanic Mexico in order to please those Creoles of Spanish blood born in these lands who had been fighting for more than a hundred years to give New Spain an indigenous history as heroic and as respectable as that of the Old World.

He had had to live for more than sixty years to discover something within himself that did not accord at all with what, up until then, he had thought of as his character—something that greatly troubled him while at the same time filling him with delight, that obliged him to cut ceremonies short, to be indolent when it came to affairs of state, to drink two or three little glasses more of spirits than discretion dictated, to organize, more and more frequently, fiestas, soirees, social gatherings, excursions to San Agustín de las Cuevas, to Tacubaya, on the pretext of bidding farewell to his friend and his family. He surprised himself by taking an interest in playing cards on a quiet afternoon beneath the age-old *ahuehuete* trees of Chapultepec, or encouraging, in such a loud voice that his cries were frankly shouts, the red cock that mercilessly attacked the yellow-plumed one in the pit of the arena he had set up in the courtyard of the palace, to the horror of the archbishop, to celebrate the Day of the Cross in the month of May.

But the Marquis de las Amarillas was also anxious; he was counting the days on the calendar like a man waiting for the sentence of death to be carried out. In those few days he saw Mariana more often than in all the time before that, perhaps with the hope of saturating himself, of growing tired of her appearance and her presence so that, when the fateful day arrived that she would undertake the journey to Veracruz—or instead to Europe, since in all likelihood he would accompany her to Veracruz, why not?—he would be sufficiently weary of her and could resign himself to her absence. But not at all! The more he saw her, the more he wanted to see her, and the time he spent without her became more and more distressing to him. Reaching the point of falling in love at your age, you old fool, he said to himself, because the more his old conscience, disagreeable and disciplined, fought to rid him of that idea, the more furiously his heart, awakened for the first time in his life, beat, threatening to burst if he let the girl go.

Philosophers say that time upholds physics, but the marquis knew very well that that was a big lie, because against all the laws of nature, time is something that, when a strong force is applied to stop it or at least to make it flow more slowly, does the very opposite: it speeds up dizzyingly. Its passage is not immutable, as poets think; ever treacherous, it goes by faster to precisely the degree that we would like it to slow down. Hence those two months went by as if they were no more than a passing sigh.

The marquis was thinking about that on that gray morning in July as he saw heavy raindrops hit against the windowpanes of his office. Don Antonio, red faced and well dressed, brought his enormous bulk to its feet, approached the viceroy's desk, and said to him, "If God does not decree otherwise, we'll be on our way to Veracruz on Friday . . ."

If Don Antonio, instead of saying these words to his friend, had plunged a dagger into his back, it would have hurt the viceroy less. He felt an emptiness in the middle of his body, so violent that it made him think that he was smothering to death. He made a superhuman effort to regain control of himself and still had enough energy to rise to his feet, embrace his friend, and contain the tears that welled up in his eyes.

Don Antonio had just left the office when the viceroy did likewise. He told his secretary that he felt indisposed, canceled all his appointments for the day, and shut himself up in his quarters. He sat down in his old armchair with his legs stretched out on a footstool. With his eyes half closed, he allowed time to go by, vainly trying not to think of anything at all. The rain, which was now coming down harder still, hit the windows violently, and a couple of blowflies, determined to pester him, alit again and again on his forehead or on his cheeks as his distracted hand tried to swat them. He poured himself a generous glass of spirits in the absurd hope that that liquid fire would extinguish the blaze that was consuming his insides. Naturally, the only thing he accomplished was to make the blaze flare up even more, though it is also only fair to recognize that the alcohol made the fire within him more bearable: after the fifth or sixth glass he felt a bittersweet drowsiness, as though he were floating on a cloud, that made him exquisitely aware of an intimate, dull, almost sensual pain. The flies kept on pestering him. He raised his hand to his cheek once more, and unlike before, his fingers this time came in contact with something: they were wet with the great tears that were slowly running down his face. The viceroy smiled on discovering that he was weeping. How long had it been since that had happened to him? He truly did not remember. His soul, dry and barren as dunes in the desert, had not been refreshed by that fertile liquid, full of yearnings, of longings, but above all of life, that tears constitute. Happy, euphoric almost, he opened the floodgates that for so many years had been kept closed by his fear, his terror, of the unknown, of feelings, of emotions, and allowed the warm tears in his eyes to flow in torrents. "Mariana, Mariana," he said again and again. "Mariana, don't leave me; don't leave me, my beloved," he kept repeating.

A long time went by in this way. He wasn't in a state even to pour himself another glass. With his face buried in the palms of his hands, he listened to his breathing, which, somehow, was following the same rhythm as the images that came to his mind. He saw Mariana smiling, dressed as a page boy, playing with exquisite charm the role of Rosaura in *La vida es sueño;* now he saw her serious, rigid, solemn, as the queen doña María in *La prudencia en la mujer.* Then he felt her lips, dry and pliant, on his forehead when the girl, grateful for the gift, dared in an unconstrained gesture to kiss him. He saw her neck, as long and cool as a tree trunk without bark, that contained at its top, just where her ear began, an unforgettable aroma that had reached his sense of smell once when Mariana whispered a joke in his ear: an odor of pine, or rather, of a pine box containing oranges, jasmine, and roses—an odor that at the same time delighted and tormented his sense of smell and his memory. Useless to live without that fragrance, without that presence. The same day the ship weighs anchor, he thought, I'll give my old body into the hands of the Creator.

Everything in this life has a limit, even despair. When the viceroy reached that point, when he cursed his lungs for continuing to consume an air he no longer wanted to breathe, when he discovered that not even being alive was an act that depended on himself, when he almost dared to utter a blasphemy aloud—"Lord," he began to say, although the rest didn't come out of his mouth, despite the fact that it crossed his mind, "are you God or are you the devil? Are you good or are you evil? You are . . . you are very cruel, I swear . . ."—at that very instant, a very odd idea went through his mind, like a swallow flying across the sky in the middle of winter. Its having occurred to him made him smile. People are right to say that love makes a person go mad, he thought, and tried to turn his mind back altogether to his discontent. But the new idea would not leave him; it fluttered round and round in his mind like a moth around the light of a candle.

After a while, the idea no longer seemed so absurd to him. Shortly thereafter he realized that, if not an inspired idea, it was in fact the only alternative, the last recourse he had at hand if he was to go on valuing his existence. His mind made up, he rose to his feet, and staggering a little—he realized then that he had drunk a fair amount—went over to the call bell and summoned the butler. He ordered him to light the candles and bring him a snack along with some wine diluted with water. He ate slowly and without appetite. In reality he was marking time, he was working up his courage to do what he had made up his mind to do. The wine was too weak; he opted once again for spirits and drained a generous amount in one swallow. The invigorating alcohol spurred him on. He walked around the room several times trying to draft in his mind what he would have to write, although he was unable to put a single sentence together. Finally he went over to his desk, dipped the pen in ink, and began to write. His pulse gave him away: when he wrote Mariana's name, the pen leaped about between his fingers as though it had a life of its own. He was obliged to squeeze his right wrist with his left hand to control the violent tremor. He tore up the first sheet, for the name that he had written on it was obviously illegible to anyone but himself. He began again:

My dear one,

I trust you will excuse the disorderliness of these lines, which are being written not by my hand but by my heart. Just this morning, don Antonio informed me of his intention to leave this Friday. Believe me, daughter, if he had told me that he was taking my eyes away with him, it would not have hurt me as much as knowing that you are leaving. Moreover, why would I want to retain my eyes if they can no longer contemplate you? Mariana dear, I have realized that without you the little life I have left is going to become a premature hell. That is why I dare write you this nonsense—because, my girl, I have lost my senses, your eyes robbed me of them, they lost their way as they followed your presence. I have been mad for some time now, and I am fighting against it. What I am unable to fight against is the solitude in which you are leaving me . . .

But, finally, to get around to what I wish to say. Amid this anguish, dear, an idea came to me. It is surely madness, but, believe me! it has been a dim ray of light within so much darkness; it has been like the dove that, bringing an olive branch in its beak, told Noah that the world was saved . . . Again I am wandering off the subject of what I have to tell you. Ah, my girl! My fingers burn at the mere thought of writing it to you, because what would you think of an old man like me if he were to dare to ask for your hand in marriage so as not to lose you? No, never fear. A flower as beautiful and as fresh as you would wither the moment I put my old, clumsy hands on it. No, I would never permit that. I therefore offer you a chaste marriage, like that offered to Our Most Blessed Mother by Saint Joseph. I offer you my protection and my company. My life is not going to go on for very long, my daughter, and I would like to sweeten my last days with your adorable presence. I will be, I swear to you, patient and kind; there will be nothing that you desire that I shall not place within your reach. I shall respect and revere you as a virgin. I ask nothing in return, save for your company, which to me is everything . . .

Hence I have been bold. What I had to say I have said to you, and dared to go this far. I am sending you this letter immediately, before, obeying my impulses, I tear it into a thousand pieces.

I await your reply, a prompt and calm one. What you decide will be, without doubt, what is right. From one who worships you,

Agustín

The viceroy was very far from imagining the happiness that that letter caused Mariana. The girl has resigned herself to her fate only with great difficulty. She had no desire to abandon her beloved country, her cherished Mexico City, to go off to live in a little town in La Rioja. Nor did the idea of cloistering herself in a convent appeal to her. Even though that perspective had greatly attracted her, when she was a little girl, influenced perhaps by her reading of heroic nuns such as Saint Teresa or Sor Juana, the idea gradually ceased to occupy her mind as she grew to adulthood, learning the ways of the world—to the point that it became something frankly disagreeable. So vast a world and so beautiful! To end up between four walls doing embroidery and baking little cookies, she thought when don Antonio proposed that alternative to her. She preferred, despite all the pain it caused her, to abandon her much-loved Mexico. In the final analysis, she thought with resignation, destiny has not been very generous to me, but what is there to be done about it? She would have to bury her dreams, the longings of her youth in which she had up till then blindly believed. Perhaps there in La Rioja she would meet a good and agreeable man who would love her, as a companion. They would buy a pretty little house, in the countryside, and raise a dozen children. Dreaming again, she said to herself regretfully, on discovering that her new dreams were quite a bit more inane and prosaic than the ones she had previously dared to cherish. From a woman of the world to a gardener . . . Good heavens! But on reading the nervous hen scratches of the marquis, her confidence in her hopes was restored. It was wonderful! She would not have to leave her country and would live with a very good man whom she was genuinely fond of. The uncertainty of her life would end: she would have a husband and a roof over her head, she would stay in the city and would lack nothing. And what do I think of his boldness? the good man asks me, she said to herself with a smile. I thank God for giving him the courage! She went off happily in search of don Antonio and doña Angelina to tell them the news and seek their approval, as she thought with contentment that now she was really certain she was not going to leave her beloved country as long as she lived. She was far from suspecting that she would do so less than a year later . . .

The wedding took place on August 12, 1759, for the viceroy wanted his new wife to be at his side as he presided over the innumerable ceremonies that would take place on the following day, when yet another anniversary of the surrender of Tenochtitlán to Cortés and his conquistadors would be celebrated.

Beneath the imposing Altarpiece of Kings, on the high altar of the cathedral in the capital, the archbishop of Mexico, don Manuel Rubio y Salinas, officiated at the ceremony. A robust and unfeeling man, with a penetrating, accusing gaze, he was convinced that each and every one of the faithful listening to him on their knees without understanding his oration in Latin was an inveterate sinner, a soul condemned to hell. In his heart of hearts, the archbishop knew that heaven ought to be emptier than the deserts in the north: few, very few, people were capable of garnering a sufficient number of merits to earn eternal glory. Perhaps not even he himself, he often thought in dejection—and it must be said that he did his utmost to live a chaste and upright life, devoutly obeying the Lord's commandments. But he recognized his weakness: pride—a mortal sin—overcame him again and again. The more he fought against it, the more arrogantly it reared its head when he least expected it. He was unable to avoid feeling superior to all those dolts. Yet again . . . forgive me, Lord, he thought as he raised his eyes and fixed them on the enormous oil lamp midway down the center aisle of the church. Who am I to judge these unfortunates? And lust . . . alas! that was the worst. Sensual by nature, don Manuel had lived a real hell fighting against his instincts and against his memories. Because only once, one single time in his life, the devil got the better of him. He was very young at the time—"I pray you to understand, Lord," he said a thousand times—and had just begun his ecclesiastical studies at Alcalá de Henares . . .

Ever since he had entered the seminary, he had been strongly in the grip of the example of Pablo Montes de Oca, who was a slender, dark-skinned lad, a little older than he. As serious and diligent as they come, he spoke Latin and Greek more fluently than a learned scholar. Often the stern masters remained silent or babbled some sort of nonsense when Pablo asked them a question so penetrating that it went beyond their knowledge. He did all his assigned tasks, no matter how worthless, with dignity and modesty. He never made fun of anyone, even though it was obvious that he surpassed all of them in one way or another. This man will get to be pope, Manuel often thought. Hence he sought out his company, trying to emulate his conduct, to learn to comport himself with the dignity and the poise that radiated from his companion. Pablo accepted this in a friendly way. He began to help him with his studies and the tasks given him. "No, brother, don't cut that branch like that," he said to him as they were treating a diseased orange tree. "If you cut it in the middle, the disease will still be inside it. Cut it down to where it branches off. Make a smooth, slanting cut in it, and when you're through, wet the stump with limewater. If you don't, the disease will get down into the trunk."

"And how come you know all that?" Manuel asked his friend, genuinely surprised.

"When I was little, I liked to watch the men who took care of the orchard. Thus little by little a person learns lots of things . . ." And Manuel was no less surprised when he heard Pablo elegantly recite whole passages from the *Iliad* or—this did not please him as much—erotic poems by Ovid in perfect Latin. "And where did you learn that?"

"In books, Manuel. Almost everything is to be found in books . . ."

One afternoon, after the rosary, Pablo came to get him in his cell. "Come with me," he ordered, "and put on a doublet, because it's cold out."

"Where are we going?" Manuel replied, a little taken aback.

"Come on! Put on your cape, and don't ask any more questions."

Manuel obeyed, put on his outer garment, and followed his friend, who, taking great strides, entered the seminary garden. "Are you crazy?"

"Shhh, shut up, dummy, the concierge may hear us."

At the far end of the garden was a high wall of whitewashed stone. At one end of it was an old door. Manuel was surprised to see his friend take a large key out of his doublet and open the door. "Where did you get that key, Pablo?"

"Saint Peter gave it to me," his friend answered with a smile.

They began walking down a poorly paved narrow street as the west devoured the last of the light of day. Manuel, who couldn't believe what he was doing, followed his friend like a puppy.

"Look, Manuel," Pablo began as he pointed to the seminary wall, "inside there is heaven, one might say, or purgatory at least. They're preparing us there to be shepherds of souls, and that's something very serious. So one has to behave accordingly. I can't imagine a soul in heaven or in purgatory being unruly. Doubtless everyone behaves very well there, as we do in the seminary. Ah! but here outside it's the earth, even, if you press me a little, hell, or something very closely resembling it. The earth, as our Lord already said (though in different words), is the great laboratory of sinners. In it it's not only necessary but advisable to sin, and the more the better. Imagine if people on earth behaved like the souls in purgatory! As long as that lasted, we'd have no work: it would be useless to shepherd shepherds. Moreover—and this is much graver still—our beloved religion would lose all its meaning. Would our Savior have descended from glory if there were no sinners on earth? To whom would he have addressed his marvelous parables? For whom would he have sacrificed himself on Mount Calvary? How, finally, could we enjoy the happiness of redemption if we had never sinned? No, friend, God is wise; he knows very well what he's doing. That's why he made the devil and allowed us to eat of the forbidden fruit: to make his work dynamic. Because, in addition to his infinite wisdom, he also possesses experience, which is far from useless when it comes to honing the understanding . . ."

"Don't be blasphemous, Pablo . . ."

"We're now on earth, I tell you, we've left the seminary behind. Don't be a pious hypocrite, for the love of God, or we'll go back this minute."

Yes, go back to the seminary, that was what he had to do. His friend was carrying things too far. He wanted to stop right then and there and turn around. But he couldn't; something kept him from it. It was a far-distant breath that reached his consciousness and demanded of him that he go on with the adventure.

"All right, I'll shut up. Go ahead . . ."

"Go ahead . . . where? . . . Oh, yes, I was telling you that God had the experience of creating a world without sinners: the world of angels and other celestial creatures, right? And what happened? What happened was that our Lord was utterly bored. His subjects apparently worshiped him, but in reality they didn't give a hoot about him, for they had nothing to thank him for. That was why he prevailed on Lucifer to rebel . . ."

"But, Pablo . . ."

"Yes, that's right. Who else would have put such ideas in the rebellious angel's head? But it didn't work out very well for God. We have already seen how, except for a very few, all the other angels turned their backs on their Creator and followed Lucifer, the ingrates. What's more, since they were immortal, there was no way of threatening them with death as a punishment. Things didn't turn out well for God, and he had to resign himself to keeping his first creatures in hell. Once that experience was behind him, he created humankind."

"Where did you get this whole bunch of nonsense?"

"From the Bible, my friend, and also from John Milton, the Englishman. Haven't you read his *Paradise Lost?* It's a marvel."

"I don't read books by heretics or by infidels."

"Well, you're missing a lot then. Almost everything worth reading is the work of infidels."

"For heaven's sake, Pablo!"

"Come on! Weren't Homer, and Virgil, and Cicero, and Aristotle infidels? And I'd better stop saying, 'and.' Otherwise I'll go on all night long."

They stopped in front of the door of a tavern. Its name, El Lobo Azul—The Blue Wolf—could be read on a painted signboard hanging from the front.

"My good friend," Pablo said, "let's leave theology for later and begin to sin in good time. Here inside they serve such delicious suckling pig that I guarantee you, Manuel, not even Simon the Stylite could keep himself free of the sin of gluttony once he tasted it . . ."

"Must you blaspheme?"

"Come on, you pious hypocrite!" his friend answered as he pushed him inside the tavern . . .

I should never have gone into that damned tavern, the archbishop said to himself as he stretched out his arms and raised his head crowned with the white-and-gold miter, the symbol of his investiture. The bride approached the altar leaning on the arm of don Antonio Bassoco, her guardian. She looked very beautiful in that ample white dress lovingly embroidered on the sleeves and at the neck. Don Manuel, instinctively, kept his gaze from meeting that of those eyes that were the color of the plains of his native Extremadura.

"Don Pablo! God be praised for permitting your presence in this humble house!" a fat woman said to them.

"Come on, Alfonsina, stop buttering me up, and bring us a pitcher of wine. Did you make suckling pig?"

"Of course, master Pablo, and it turned out so well you'll lick your fingers. You'll see."

They drank a rough wine of the region and partook of the pig with gusto, for it really was delicious.

"You'd like another helping, wouldn't you, you rascal?" Pablo said with a smile on seeing how his friend was gobbling up the last bits on his plate. "I told you so: when it comes to this meal, if a person doesn't commit the sin of gluttony, it's because he's dead."

Although he regretted having to admit it, Manuel felt very comfortable. The good food and the good wine had relaxed his body and his mind, which were almost always tense and alert, like a caged rat. They spent a long time in the tavern. Pablo joked with every customer he saw come into the place. He gave the impression that everyone knew him and liked him.

"Don Pablito," a toothless old toper said to him. "Do me the favor of praying for the soul of my Dorotea! And if you can—and of course you can, you're a very good man—dedicate a mass to her. We'll see if that way she'll leave me in peace. I can't close my eyes without Dorotea showing up in my dreams . . ."

"And is that bad?" the seminarian interrupted.

"I'll say it is! My Dorotea, may she rest in peace, was never a very pretty woman, let's say. And now that she's passed on, she's got even uglier. You can't imagine how it scares me to see her. And the worst of it is that she wants to take me with her. 'Don't open your eyes anymore, Pascualito,' the scary ghost says to me. 'Leave them closed once and for all, and come with me.' God keep me from going off with her! I put up with her for more than twenty years while she was alive, and now she wants me to keep her company in eternity, the conniving devil!"

"Well, it's said and done, Pascual. I'm going to pray more Pater Nosters for Dorotea's soul that she ever prayed in her whole life. And I'm going to recite as well—it's because I hold you in great esteem, Pascual—the prayer with which Saint Cyprian put to flight an army of souls possessed by devils who were trying to take possession of Burgos. It's a very powerful and effective prayer, though it has its dangers. Look, if for example instead of saying, 'Sanctum factorum,' a person says, 'Sanctis factorum,' some twenty souls more are let loose on him. That was why Saint Cyprian had so many problems: he didn't know the prayer, he was inventing it, imagine! For every mistake, more souls in pain. The poor man reached the point where it wasn't only Burgos that he filled with evil spirits, it was all of Spain."

"How awful!" Alfonsina said.

"It wasn't until the Lord enlightened the saint and he could recite the complete prayer that the phantoms began to flee. But so many of them had come that he had to repeat the prayer without stopping, night and day, for more than forty years."

"You don't say!"

"Tell me if that man didn't deserve to be a saint . . . As for the mass, stop worrying about that too, Pascual. Now that I'm going to Toledo, I'll ask my uncle, the bishop, to officiate at a solemn mass in the cathedral, with acolytes and five altar boys. You'll see if Dorotea rests in peace or not!"

"Ah, don Pablito, you're a saint," the old man said, genuinely moved.

"Not yet, but we'll see," the young man answered in a serious voice. "For now, you can sleep in peace tonight, because as soon as I finish eating, I'm going to my cell to recite those Pater Nosters."

"And Saint Cyprian's prayer?" Pascual asked anxiously.

"All right, I'll recite that too. May God keep me from making any mistakes!"

In good spirits, the old man left the tavern, not without having first stood the youngsters to a pitcher of wine.

"Why do you lie that way, Pablo?"

"I've already told you that we're on the earth, and here one must practice sinning . . ."

"But lying is frightful in God's eyes . . ."

"Come off it! Lying, on the contrary, is something very useful, so useful that it ought not be considered a sin. Look at Pascual, for instance. See how happy he was when he left. You can be sure he'll sleep in peace tonight, after who knows how many sleepless nights. What's a lie for us is the truth for him, and that's enough. What's more, this little white lie doesn't do any harm to good Saint Cyprian, who, when all is said and done, is a saint. How much work will he have to do to let that poor man sleep in peace? A miracle like that is a mere nothing to him."

"You're a sophist," said Manuel, who, despite everything, couldn't hide his admiration for his friend's cleverness.

"You're calling me a sophist? Well, taking the risk that you'll consider me a cynic afterward, I'm going to follow your line of reasoning. The problem is that with all that breast-beating those pious prudes at the seminary force upon us, our heads rumble too much to give them a chance to reflect calmly. Take a good swallow of wine, stop beating your breast, and give your head a chance to think a little . . . You say that lying is a frightful sin. I'm going to give you another example so that you'll think carefully about the rubbish flowing from that mouth of a future priest you have: didn't our beloved Peter lie—three times at that—when they arrested the Savior?"

"But . . ."

"Shut up. Listen and think. Peter lied despite himself because, I regret to tell you, he was rather like you: he didn't think things through. He followed the Master just as he would have followed any of the charlatans that abounded in that era. It was doubtless Jesus who steered him to lie: as a matter of fact, he had already informed him that he would, during the Last Supper. And now, to get to the point: Imagine what it would be like if good Peter had unthinkingly followed his impulses. Well, he didn't, and when that Jew asked him whether he was a disciple of the Nazarene's, if he'd answered, "I'm his most faithful follower," what would have happened? They would have arrested him and tried him, and our beloved painters would have had to portray four men who were crucified on Calvary instead of three. And what's worse, Peter, the Rock destined to be the foundation of our church, would have died alongside his Master. There wouldn't have been any bishop of Rome, nor a Catholic church, nor would you and I be dressed in these absurd black garments, nor would we be speaking of a sin that, if there were no church or religion to point it out, wouldn't exist . . ."

"You're right, Pablo; I see now that you're a cynic. Note that I've listened to you and reflected on what you've told me. The only conclusion you cause me to arrive at is that the church is founded on a great lie . . ."

"Shhh! Shut up, dummy. If that's your way of reflecting, you're going to end up being roasted at the stake. I don't understand how you passed the courses in logic; you reason like an ass. Excuse me for pressing the point, but you're exactly like Peter: you're fated to obey, not to think . . ."

How right his friend was! To obey . . . his parents, his teachers, his superiors, his confessor . . . A lot of good it had done him! Because he obeyed the pope, he now found himself here, a long way from his native land, in a country of scoundrels and savages. The few Europeans here were as selfish and rapacious as vultures. The poor Creoles were trying in vain to create a history of grandeur when in reality the only thing there had been was robbing and plundering. The half-breeds, with their countless castes, were like horseflies: they were bothersome and they stung, but they didn't do anything useful. And the wretched Indians: silent, rancorous, they didn't forget their humiliation. Nor did they forget those odious idols they adored the minute nobody was paying attention. How many times people had reported to him that inside the sculpture of a saint, of a Christ, or even of a Virgin, horrifying paintings of those savages with their diabolical drawings had been found. They'd hidden their monstrous figurines even inside the walls of churches so as to worship them as they pretended to be venerating a Christian saint. Who knows what they might have hidden beneath the foundations of this cathedral! Who knows how many idols slept the sleep of the just in the bowels of these lands, at peace because they knew that they were worshiped by those men and women with copper-colored skin . . . Pride again, he said to himself. "Forgive me, Lord . . ." The bride was radiant, and the marquis, filled with emotion and eager, appeared to be before the gates of paradise. An ill-assorted couple, the archbishop couldn't help thinking. It's like marrying spring to winter. He elevated the host and offered it to the heavens. Can that old man make love to her? To my mind, he's already entered the climacteric, he thought with a certain satisfaction . . .

"What you're telling me isn't right, Pablo," Manuel said in self-defense. "Your reasoning leads to that one conclusion, which naturally strikes me as preposterous."

"Listen, friend," Pablo answered, making an annoyed gesture. "Who is wiser, kindlier, more important for our faith, Peter or Jesus?"

"Jesus, of course."

"Well, then, Jesus didn't lie: remember that he was the one who prophesied that Peter would lie, and Peter did. So then, what Jesus decreed turned out to be true. In any case, the church is founded on a great truth—the one the Savior proclaimed—and the only possible way for that to have happened was for his disciple to lie. Do you realize how important lying is?"

Disabled by his friend's cleverness, Manuel could only smile.

"You're a demon, Pablo. I understand poor Eve now: what was the unfortunate woman to do when confronted with the devil's rhetoric?"

"Eat the forbidden fruit, without doubt. Very good, Manuel, very good . . . ," Pablo said, amid peals of laughter.

It was late at night when they left the tavern. They were very happy and a bit tipsy. Pablo was singing an old ballad as his friend told himself how many more things there were in the world, right there in front of his nose, without his even suspecting that they existed. And as though he had read his mind, Pablo said to him, "Well, Manuel. We now have our bellies full and our minds dulled by alcohol." As he spoke he began to urinate copiously against a wall. When he saw him do so, Manuel felt an urge to urinate too and imitated his friend. "We're ready, I think, to practice greater sins, what do you think?"

"The right thing to do, exactly right."

"Not a word more, then. Follow me."

Taking great strides, he entered a labyrinth of narrow back streets. Manuel almost had to run to catch up with him. An absurd fear had come over him. He felt that if he lost sight of his friend, he would remain lost forever in that dark and miserable place. After walking for what seemed to Manuel an eternity, Pablo stopped in front of a door not at all different from the many others on those streets. He hammered on the door very hard with the knocker. After he had knocked several times, a woman's voice was heard inside, asking timidly, "Who is it?"

"A couple of Christians, woman. Come on, open up, it's Pablo Montes de Oca."

"Pablo!" the woman shouted in joy as she unbarred the door. She must have lit a good fire inside the house, for once the door was open, Manuel saw a bright yellowish red glow that was in violent contrast to the darkness of the street.

"Come on in, friend," Pablo said to him. "Welcome to hell . . ."

On that long-ago day he entered hell, and since then he hadn't been able to get out of it. More than forty years had gone by since all that had happened, but he still retained it in his memory with perfect clarity, as though it had taken place only yesterday. From the pulpit, he looked down at the parishioners below. As was to be expected, the elite of New Spain were gathered together there. In the front rows, in the places of honor, the members of the royal tribunal, in formal dress, were readying themselves to listen to the sermon like obedient children. The hypocrites! the archbishop thought. Just look at them! A fine breed of schemers and egotists. I'll never know their secrets . . . Ah, Lord, what a punishment you inflict on your servants by obliging us to hear the confessions of all these dolts. He remembered having once read in a book by Sigüenza y Góngora that the ancient Mexicans had a goddess named . . . her name failed to come to mind: he had never been able to master that accursed language of the Indians. The thing was that the function of that goddess was to listen to the confession of the Indians shortly before an important ceremony so that they might participate in it in a purified state. Generally the confessions were of a sexual nature (whether they had copulated with the wife of a friend, with their sister-in-law, and even with their daughter), or else they had to do with breaking the law (whether they had stolen maize from the community granary, whether they had failed to pay their debts, etc.). The idol listened to their confessions, and after that their minds and their consciences were pure and clean. *Eater of excrement:* he remembered that that was what the name of that goddess meant. Precisely the right term: *eater of excrement.* That was exactly what he was: an eater of excrement, of filth. As the Indians did with their goddess, so the Spaniards hastened to their priests to unload their shit and go off at peace with themselves to commit more sins. And the priests . . . what about them? . . . and what about him? What to do with the immense burden of shit that kept piling up in his conscience? He could confess his own sins to a colleague, of course, but the confessions that he himself heard could be talked over with no one; that would be anathema. He was condemned to retain that fantastic parade of filth in his memory. And what was worse, he had to dissemble, he had to act as though everything he heard he had thrust out of his mind—as though that were possible! as though it were a matter of documents that, once read, were consigned to the oblivion of archives. But that was his fate: he would have to dissemble and smile beatifically when, at the end of the mass, the Marquise del Valle Ameno—who was now listening, serious and absorbed, to the sermon, like a devout believer—bowed before his presence and kissed his hand. He would smile at her and give her his blessing as there came to his mind the scenes that she related to him barely a week before, when, with a wealth of detail, during her confession she informed him of her love affair with her husband's coachman. She had copulated with that lad any number of times and in every imaginable fashion, "even by way of the wrong place, Father . . ." And he would not even feel compassion for the cuckolded marquis—who was now kneeling with his hands clasped together on his chest, with a mystic's expression on his face. He would not feel compassion for him because he would remember what this man in turn confessed to him: "I cheat miners, Father. I have adjusted the balance scale so that a pound weighs a little bit less . . ." He had also cheated the king himself, since the shipments of silver carried as cargo by the China schooner weighed much less than was recorded in the ship's documents. A little here, a little there, this wretch accumulated riches like a Croesus at the expense of friends, partners, hired hands, and clerks. But the marquis confessed his thefts to him, recited a few Ave Marias, ordered the altar of a church gilded, and thereby felt more pure and clean than a baby just arrived in this world. He on the other hand had lived in a state of impurity for more than forty years. He had not been able to rid himself of that stain. Lust, which his spirit knew on that accursed day, remained harbored within him; it had become something as much his as his arms and his legs. And this was owing to the fact, as he knew very well, that he had never had the courage to confess that sin. He had kept it like a punishment so that it would corrode his conscience. Or perhaps he had kept it all this time because—"Oh, Lord, forgive me!"—the memory pleased him so much, because it was the only thing that had happened to him in his petty existence that was worthy of being treasured, because it pained him a great deal to remember it but it also—"Do you understand me, Lord?"—caused him infinite pleasure to know that he was capable of doing what he did, at least once in his life . . .

The dwelling was mean. In fact, it was a single room, though quite large. In the back, a fire was lit. The flames heated a cauldron suspended over them. It hung from a crude hook suspended from a chimney vent that did not suck up the smoke at all well. In the middle of the room was a square table with thick pine planks. Four crude chairs of the same wood surrounded it. In one corner, there was a narrow cot with a straw mattress and a few very dirty, threadbare blankets. A large crucifix over the head of the bed was the only adornment hanging from the walls, whitewashed long ago, for they were blackish rather than white and covered with damp stains.

"Pablo darling!" the woman said as she effusively kissed her friend's cheeks. "You're a devil . . . casting me aside for such a long time." She frowned, though without showing any signs of real anger. "What have you brought me? Jewelry perhaps?"

"You've guessed it; jewelry is what I've brought you." The woman gave little leaps for joy as she clapped her hands. "But first say hello to my friend; don't be rude. Manuel, this is doña Ignacia Salazar, the phoenix of the whores of Alcalá," Pedro said caustically. "Ignacia, this is don Manuel Salinas, the distinguished holder of the baccalaureate, and the future bishop of some corner of our beloved kingdom."

"Delighted to meet you," the woman said, making a ridiculous effort to be elegantly polite. "Make yourself at home."

It was hard to imagine that she could consider this hole-in-the-wall her home. The wretchedness of it was like a heavy weight on his chest and cut short his happy drunken spree. In its place, strong waves of nausea brought a thick acid taste to his mouth. He didn't feel able to control the retching that he knew would soon begin.

"But what a face, my friend! You're paler than a corpse. Sit down and rest," Pablo said as he brought a chair over to him. "Don't be scared, you're getting over being drunk, that's all. You'll feel better in a while."

Pablo looked fresh and calm, as though he'd just got out of bed after a restorative sleep. As he spoke, the woman looked at him anxiously. She was hoping he'd finish talking once and for all and give her the jewelry he'd promised her.

"Yes, woman, I'm going to give it to you now. But don't look at me like that, you remind me of a hare." With a smile, he raised his hand up inside his doublet and took it out again, waving a bottle of wine in the air. "Here it is! A real jewel: wine from Valdepeñas, the elixir of the gods, and all of it, well, almost all of it, just for you alone, darling Ignacia."

"Well, clear out of here with your jewel, and go somewhere else," the woman said, very annoyed. "I don't want any drunks here. This is a respectable house."

When he heard these last words, Pablo broke out in a loud guffaw. Manuel, despite how bad he felt, couldn't keep from joining in the laughter.

"Clear out of here, I tell you." The woman, in a fury, gave them a look filled with hate. In desperation, seeing that, far from paying any attention to her, the two young men were still laughing, she took a big knife that was lying next to the fire along with some dirty kitchen utensils. "We'll see if you don't get out of here now, you roughnecks," she said, as she brandished her weapon.

Suddenly, Pablo became very serious and looked at the woman with cold disdain. "That's enough out of you, you whore!" he said to her very slowly. The woman felt a shiver go down her back. She put the knife down on the table and, suddenly docile, cowered in front of him, her eyes filled with tears. Pablo smiled again. "Come on, woman, things aren't that bad. Look what I've brought you," he said as he dangled in the air a tinkling pair of magnificent gold earrings with a purple stone set in each of them.

"Pablo! Oh, Pablo darling!" Ignacia, transformed by delight, went over to the young man and embraced him as she covered his face with kisses. "My boy! You're a saint. A saint . . . that's what you are . . . ," she said between one kiss and the next.

"Stop it now, woman, keep a few for later. And open the bottle now, because my throat's drier than Christ's on the cross . . ."

"Pablo!" Manuel broke in, genuinely indignant.

The woman went over to the stove to look for something to open the bottle with. As she moved happily along, she never once took her eyes off the earrings. She raised them to her mouth several times and bit them carefully to see if they were really gold.

"They're gold, woman, don't be so suspicious," Pablo said, smiling, and went on, addressing his friend: "They belonged to my grandmother. Family treasures, you know. What my grandmother would say if she saw her amethyst earrings dangling from a whore's ears!" He gave a hearty laugh. "Because my grandmother, I must confess, was a sinless woman. Lord almighty, was she ever sinless! I still don't understand how she was able to bring seven children into the world. If you'd known her, you'd see what I mean. Often, very often, I've tried to imagine my grandfather, as skinny and withdrawn as that poor little man was, mounted on top of my grandmother, and I simply can't. Alongside my grandmother, a marble statue would seem more alive, more hot to trot than our Ignacia. Really. If it hadn't been for her offspring, I'd have sworn that that woman had no other openings except her ears and mouth . . . and the latter hardly counted, because it was unbelievably tiny. She spoke less with it than a Capuchin monk reciting vows. My grandmother's accursed mouth was so small that she had to eat soup with a demitasse spoon; an ordinary spoon wouldn't go into it, I swear . . . Even though the log between my grandfather's legs fit inside her very well down below . . . ," he said thoughtfully, as though he were involved in a well-argued academic discussion.

Even now, so many years later, the archbishop shuddered when he remembered his friend's coarse words, and he wondered, as he had wondered forty years before, how it was possible that this Pablo Montes de Oca was the same young man whom he had known in the seminary and whose example had held him so strongly, what with his excellent manners, his discipline, his spirit, ever open and generous. He began the sermon: "The Lord wished to test the faith of the man whom he had chosen to be the seed of a blessed people . . ." Not without guile had don Manuel chosen the story of Abraham as the subject of his sermon. He spoke with delight of the patriarch's venerable age as he looked at the bridegroom out of the corner of his eye. The Marquis de las Amarillas, however, did not take it personally. In fact, though his eyes were riveted on the pudgy figure of the archbishop, he was not listening to what he said. He was too happy to pay attention to his oration. Even the figure of the archbishop, stuffed into his ceremonial cassock, struck a chord of fellow feeling within him, because at that moment he was filled to overflowing with love. He felt capable of obeying to the letter the second commandment: he loved everyone, he loved his neighbors more than himself, he even loved the archbishop, for whom he had always felt contempt because of his selfishness and his sanctimoniousness. But he was not fulfilling—and he was not distressed by the fact—the first commandment. He did not love God above all other things. On the contrary, he loved this girl, this sun he had at his side who looked more beautiful than ever, radiating such splendor that it illuminated even the farthest corner of his consciousness. ". . . And Sarah, already very old, for she was almost a hundred, smiled in disbelief when she heard from the archangel the good news sent by the Lord. 'How am I going to be a mother,' she said with a smile to God's messenger, 'if I am almost a hundred years old and my good Abraham'—the archbishop fixed his eyes on the viceroy—'is more than a hundred and forty?' 'Do not mock, my good woman, the words of the Lord. The Lord is infallible,' the messenger said to her very seriously, 'and as a proof of it, you shall call your firstborn Isaac'—which means *smile* in Hebrew," the archbishop pointed out didactically. The priest noted with annoyance that his words had not had the least effect on the spirit of the viceroy, whose imperturbable expression did not change, barely hiding a smile of enormous satisfaction. Pig, lecher! the archbishop thought. He already sees himself in bed with that beautiful girl. Pig! he repeated and was unable to banish from his mind the thought that followed: . . . How I envy you! . . .

The woman placed the bottle of wine and three big clay mugs, dirty and chipped, on the table. Pablo, in a very light mood, served the wine, and taking the woman by the waist, sat her on his knees.

"I wish you good health, by my grandmother's impossible hole!" he said, and downed the liquid in one swallow.

The woman, not understanding the toast, shrugged and drank too. Manuel looked dubiously at the mug, feeling that if he raised it to his mouth, he was sure to vomit.

"Come on, you prig! Drink it down, once and for all," his friend ordered him imperiously.

He swallowed it. He had a hard time getting the warm sour liquid down his throat. He felt that he was about to retch and kept himself from it, but when, finally, the wine reached the pit of his stomach, he began to feel better. He felt the color coming back to his cheeks, and his nausea went away. He took another swallow. In better spirits, he looked at the woman for the first time. She was in front of him, sitting on Pablo's knees. She leaned backward with abandon. Laughing, Pablo held her by the nape of the neck. "You're going to fall, woman!" he said to her, but she went on with the game, raising her legs that were peeking out from underneath her skirt. Finally she straightened up, and taking Pablo's cheeks in her two hands, gave him a resounding kiss on the mouth.

She was a woman who had already crossed the threshold where youth begins to decline and turns, little by little, into old age. She was wearing a dark green dress, very shabby and threadbare, especially where the lace of the sleeves and the flounces of the wide skirt had been. Surely some great lady wore that dress with pride some twenty years ago, Manuel thought. Later on, worn and out of fashion, it had ended up in the hands of an old clothes peddler, who probably gave it to this woman in exchange for a few caresses. He looked at her neck, dark-skinned and strong, with her hair pulled back and caught up in a heavy round chignon the color of a fly's wings. A few rebellious curls fell over it. Her ears were pretty, medium sized and well defined, although they were an intense flaming red that gave them the odd look of not belonging to that dark-skinned head, as though they were borrowed. Her face was common and hardly attractive; her forehead, small and slanting, was blotched by the roots of her hair, especially at the temples, which were covered by a dark fuzz. Her eyes, though good sized and of a pretty honey color, were too close together, as though they had started out on the ridge of her nose—on which, incidentally, a little protuberance showed, as though someone had hit it—and hadn't had enough time to move completely apart. Her mouth was small, but with fleshy, sensual lips, as flaming red as her ears. Her tiny slanting chin, along with her forehead, gave her face a very curious look: forehead, chin, and cheeks receded abruptly, as though they had been forcefully pulled from behind. Hence the tip of her nose—also bright red—along with the middle of it, was the prominent part of her face; all her features uniformly regressed and slanted back from that point. She looks like a *perinola*—one of those tops people use to gamble with, Manuel thought.

When the woman laughed—and she did so very frequently, because of who knows what things that Pablo was saying in her ear—Manuel could see yellowish teeth, large and uneven, like an ear of corn. She was missing one eyetooth, which, strangely, gave her bursts of laughter a certain fierceness. Her robust little body was that of a peasant woman from La Mancha. As a matter of fact, she had no waist: a straight line descended from her shoulders to her hips. Her breasts, of which Manuel could see almost all the top half because of the loose neckline of her dress, were very generous, and from the way they shook when the woman guffawed, Manuel calculated that they were still quite firm and full. Her legs, which he saw each time the woman raised them as she leaned backward, allowing herself to be held up by her friend in a game that to Manuel, without his knowing why, seemed very stupid, were short and chubby. But they looked hard and energetic, like the trunks of two little fir trees. Her ankles helped to give them that appearance, for they were almost as thick as her calves, as though the woman's whole body—save for her breasts—were seeking to escape the curvilinear: everything about her body was straight and cylindrical. She was wearing a pair of very old rope sandals tied with a colored ribbon laced up almost to her knees. Manuel couldn't see her thighs, but he imagined them to be short and thick as well. And so they were. He saw that his guess was correct when his friend's large hand slid up one of them, the back of it rolling her dress up into the woman's lap.

"Look, Manuel: the flesh of sin," Pablo said as with delight he felt up her thigh, sinking his fingers into the soft folds of flesh. "Food for men that the Lord bestowed on us so as to put us to the test. Touch it, come on, touch it!" Manuel looked at him fearfully. "Come on! You're not going to burn your hands, you coward. Even though maybe you'll burn some other part of you, isn't that right, Ignacia?" The woman, cheerful and drunk, still had her arms clasped around Pablo's neck and was kissing him again and again. "Well, then, come and get it, you prude. What a priest you're going to be! If you aren't acquainted with the sins of the flesh, how are you going to counsel your faithful? How are you going to be able to understand what they feel? You must do some studying, young man, you must do some studying."

Manuel poured himself another drink. Although he felt awful and very ill at ease, he couldn't keep his eyes off his friend or, rather, off his friend's hand, which was gently going up and down that thigh. It reached the knee and gave it a little squeeze. Slowly, tightly clutching the woman's skin, the hand descended, describing tiny circles, till it arrived at the place where the buttocks start. There it turned aside, toward the inside, toward the woman's groin, where it lost itself between her thighs. It remained there for some time. The tendons tensing on the back of his hand were a sign that he was moving his fingers, like someone strumming a cittern. His hand stayed there for a while and then came out and began its descent, which in reality was an ascent, for the woman's knees were now raised.

The more he drank, the drier Manuel's throat felt. An unpleasant empty feeling settled in the pit of his stomach, and the nausea, although he no longer felt it in his body, lingered in his mind. He wanted to get to his feet and clear out of there, but a force stronger than he was kept him riveted to his chair—a force he knew was responsible for the feeling of suffocation his body was experiencing, as though he were being roasted over a slow fire. He passed his hand over his forehead and felt thick drops of sweat.

"Look, Manuel. I'm going to teach you something you're going to like a lot." Pablo took his hand away from the woman's thigh and raised it to the neckline of her dress; he plunged it inside and took out her left tit, as though it were a big ladleful of butter. It was a big round breast. The nipple, very dark, was surrounded by tiny tough, straight hairs. "This, my friend, is a magic demijohn: you suck and suck"—as he spoke he raised his mouth to the nipple and sucked at the tip of it—"and nothing comes out. But, what the devil, you go on sucking and sucking, as though you were drinking nectar"—and he sucked now for a long while. "Ah! Nothing and everything. That's why it's magic. No doubt you drink an invisible but very potent liquid, because it gives you gooseflesh and a cock that's harder than a rifle."

"Let's have a look . . . ," Ignacia said as she straightened her torso and raised one hand behind her to feel between her friend's legs. "I can't believe it! Pablito, my boy, it's right on target!"

"Never mind where it's aimed. In a little while it'll be exactly where it should be," Pablo said, laughing. "Do you want to have a try, Manuel?"

Manuel didn't answer. He looked at them with his eyes bulging, unable to hide a violent tremor in his cheeks. As though he'd taken a turn sucking too, he could feel that his cock was very rigid and about to explode. He crossed his legs and tensed his muscles, as though controlling an urge to urinate, and he felt a sharp pain, but at the same time a pleasant one, in his groin.

"Well, come on or you'll lose out on it."

As he said this, Pablo got to his feet with the woman in his arms and began to whirl rhythmically round and round, as though he were dancing. Ignacia, amused, stretched out her legs and let her head dangle. Pablo turned faster still.

"Be careful, you idiot, we'll fall!" the woman said between great gales of laughter.

They reached the cot, onto which Pablo dropped the woman like a bundle. There was a crashing sound as she came down on the wooden frame and a little cloud of dust rose from the straw mattress.

"You brute! You nearly broke my neck," Ignacia said, rubbing her neck and pretending to be in pain.

Pablo, standing at the head of the cot, looked at the woman for a moment. A serious, almost sober look came over his face, as though he were pondering something crucial. All of a sudden, he began to laugh, raised his hands to his waist, and with swift, nervous movements removed his underwear, which remained coiled around his ankles. He had strong, muscular legs with thighs darkened by abundant downy hair. His member, rigid and pulsating, was pointing slightly upward. The woman looked at it in delight and, with a satisfied smile, settled her buttocks firmly in the bed, as she lifted her skirt to her lap, opening her legs and bending them so as to offer her private parts to the young man. Pablo was ready and waiting; in a jiffy he was on top of the woman with his waist gripped between her heavy thighs. He penetrated her easily, and when he could feel that he was well inside, began to thrust firmly and rhythmically with his hips. Manuel, sitting at the table with the mug of wine in his hand, watched the scene in fascination. He didn't miss a single detail. He had seen the woman's lustful gaze fixed on his friend's member; he had seen how she settled down in the bed with circular movements as she tucked up her skirt. But above all he had seen the woman's sex, shameless, surrounded by thick hair as black as coal, with dark lips of a color between bright pink and purple that formed a violent contrast with the pale pink of her inner lips, which were moist and swollen. A powerful force attracted his gaze to that point, a force so intense that he felt pain in his eye sockets. The vision of that strange place with folds of live flesh, which hinted at an orifice that gave every sign of being deep and endless, had aroused in him the uncontrollable desire to leap up and plunge his entire body into that mouth. But what had entered it was his friend's penis. He had seen it advance, slowly, sixteenth of an inch by sixteenth of an inch; he had seen how the woman's folds of flesh enveloped it like thick cream. An unbearable feeling of emptiness nestled in the pit of his stomach, and his temples began to pound furiously, as though they were about to burst. He wanted to close his eyes, but the image that he had before him kept him from it. Now Pablo's thrusts were more and more violent. The same was true of the palpitations in his own head. With a trembling hand he raised the mug to his mouth to put out the fire in his insides. At that moment the woman gave a deep howl that Manuel felt came from the very depths of hell. He could stand no more; he threw his mug violently against the stove, stood up, and stumbled to the door. With a great effort, he unbarred it and ran out into the street.

Like a man possessed, he ran as fast as his legs could carry him. For a long time he ran like a madman in those narrow back streets dimly lit by the light of a waning moon, not knowing, not even thinking about, where he was going. Finally, exhausted, he stopped, looked around him, and confirmed that he didn't have the slightest idea of where he was. He felt very dizzy and still had a bad pain in his head. He raised his hand to his forehead as he leaned against a wall. Rubbing his face hard with his hand, he discovered that his cheeks were bathed in tears, and as though that had been a harbinger of what was to come, he began to weep in torrents, aware now that he was doing so. Not even his spasm of weeping could shake off the images that whirled about in his mind: Ignacia's privates, absolute and open; Pablo's frantic thrusts; the muscles of his buttocks that tensed every time he swept forward; the woman's half-closed eyes, as she bit her lower lip with her incisors; and the cry, that cry full of lust and of pleasure, which reverberated in his ears, as though it had arisen from the middle of his head. Afflicted, he lifted his hands to his ears, trying in vain to drown out a sound that came from within him. Then he himself let out a blood-curdling howl as if to cover the one that was tormenting him. It was so long and shrill that it surprised him, for never since his voice had changed and was now that of a man had he been able to produce such a high-pitched note.

"Quiet, you fool! You sound like a wolf."

When that thick, unpleasant voice reached his ears, he thought he was dreaming, but when he opened his eyes, he saw in front of him a grotesque figure. It was an old woman, very small and hunched over, wearing a heavy black dress and with her head bundled up in a shawl of the same color. He could scarcely see her face, from which a very big aquiline nose and thick eyebrows joined together protruded. Her bright little black eyes, like a rat's, could hardly be seen behind her thick eyelids, ringed with wrinkles. Her toothless mouth, with dark down at the corners, looked like a badly healed wound. Manuel could have sworn that it was Celestina, who had stepped straight out of that abhorrent novel in order to torment him. For there were few things he hated more than that novel and in particular that character, a procuress in whom he saw incarnated all the vices and moral corruption of the human species. He was deeply repelled and tried to get away from the woman.

"Wait, handsome, don't be afraid." A long, bony hand grabbed his arm and squeezed it with unsuspected force. "You want a woman, don't you?"

A woman! Manuel thought. That old hag is really out of her mind: she comes across a man in the street in the middle of the night, weeping and howling like a wild animal, and the only thought that occurs to her is that he wants a woman. I'm going to tell her off . . .

"Yes," he answered, surprised at himself, as though someone else had spoken through his mouth and kept him from letting loose the string of insults that he had thought of hurling at the old woman.

"Well, if you'll give me ten reales, I'll get you a girl who's much more beautiful than the sun and cooler than the dew. You'll see whether or not she sheds her light on you and refreshes you!"

These deliberately poetic words annoyed Manuel even more, since he thought that such a repugnant creature had no right to utter beautiful words. Avoiding the woman's eyes, he searched about in his pouch and gave her the money. The old woman snatched it up greedily, as she gave a horrible smile. "Follow me," she ordered, and began to walk ahead with very swift little steps.

Manuel followed her, taking long strides. The old woman surprised him once again: it seemed inconceivable that she could move about so agilely. When she reached the end of the street, she turned to her right and entered a very narrow alleyway, so narrow that just by stretching one's arms out, it was easy to touch the walls on both sides. At the end of the narrow passageway was a big wooden door. When they reached it, the old woman ordered him to wait and disappeared behind the door. Manuel waited for some time, so long that he came to suspect that the woman had tricked him out of his money and was escaping by way of some secret exit somewhere in those crude constructions. He felt almost relieved on arriving at that conclusion. The nightmare's going to be over now, he said to himself, and began to walk away from the door.

"Young man! Where are you going? Come here." The old woman imperiously held out her skinny arms. "How impatient these young men are, I swear! Come with me," she grumbled. They went inside the building, and the old woman grabbed him by the hand. "Be careful, it's very dark. Don't let go of my hand."

They went up a wooden staircase which, from the way it creaked under their footsteps, must have been at least a hundred years old. It was totally dark—like approaching hell, Manuel thought, expecting that Cerberus would leap out at him from one moment to the next. The air was thick and foul; it smelled of dampness, urine, and something that Manuel was unable to identify but that was no doubt very old, as though time, itself stagnating, had begun to smell. They climbed many steps and made their way past at least two landings. Finally, the old woman stopped and pushed a door open. They went inside a dingy cubicle dimly lit by a tallow candle stub. Manuel had only to take a quick look around to be convinced that, compared with this room, Ignacia's dwelling was a palace. In one corner, he managed to make out a bundle on the floor covered with a couple of threadbare blankets. He felt his nausea return.

"Blow out the light," he ordered the old woman. "I don't want to see anything."

"As you like, handsome. There's your flower," the old woman said, pointing to the bundle. "May you enjoy yourselves."

This said, she blew out the candle and disappeared along with the light. The room was now plunged into such deep darkness that Manuel decided that it was even darker than the stairwell. As though there could be different shades of darkness, he said to himself, surprised for the hundredth time at the trivial, stupid details that distracted him. A voice bought him out of his reflections.

"Come on over here," he heard.

It was a delicate feminine voice that was in noticeable contrast to the old woman's hoarse voice and to Ignacia's, roughened by cheap spirits.

"I can't see a thing," he answered.

"Over here, follow my voice; follow it, that's it, that's it . . . Well, here you are."

He felt a hand take his. How can she see me? he thought. Even a cat couldn't see its own nose in this place.

"Get undressed," the voice ordered.

Obediently, without objecting, as though the order that he had been given were the most natural thing in the world, Manuel began to undress. Perhaps this relaxation, this absence of anxiety that he was feeling, was due to the hidden certainty that he had been dreaming for some time now; to be precise, ever since he had left the prostitute's house at a run. This is all a dream, he said to himself, and you have to leave dreams alone; if you try to repress them, they turn into unpleasant nightmares.

"Have you finished undressing?"

"Yes, just about," Manuel said as he tried to take off his high-laced shoes with one foot lifted and hopping about on the other.

"Come here," the woman said and pulled him by the arm. Manuel fell facedown on the straw pallet. "Come, come here by my side." The woman guided him till he was lying next to her. "What's your name?"

"Manuel."

"Manuel . . . a nice name. That was the Savior's name, wasn't it?"

"I don't know," Manuel replied in annoyance.

He didn't want God to enter that dream which was becoming more pleasant by the minute. He was lying face up. He felt the woman's naked body clinging to one side of him. Its true, she's nice and cool, he thought with satisfaction. The sensation of having his eyes wide open and seeing absolutely nothing, as though he had them tightly closed, pleased him a great deal; without his understanding why, it made him feel calm and free, as though he had just come into the world, with his conscience cleaner than the tears of the Virgin (not even that minor blasphemy troubled him). The woman stroked his chest. Her hands, cool and dry, were soft and delicate. Manuel could feel her fingers playing with the hair that had begun to sprout on his chest. Suddenly he felt the woman's lips on his mouth. They gave each other a long kiss that seemed delightful to Manuel. Without removing her lips from his, the woman settled herself astride the young man so as to receive his penis. He penetrated her gently and easily, as though he had always belonged in that place that felt wide, moist, and cool to him, and—without his being able to understand how that was possible, but understanding it with his senses—at the same time narrow and warm. Kissing each other again and again, they coupled for a long time. Manuel felt he was in heaven. Only one cloud threatened the intense brightness that illuminated his spirit: the fear of awakening from that dream that he desperately wanted to be eternal. He had a long, profound orgasm, the first in his life, and he felt all his life in it, ridding himself with that happy explosion of all the burdens he had been carrying since he first became conscious. Fears, anxieties, doubts all vanished, along with the stern faces of his father and his teachers. His spirit expelled them with amazing ease, without violence, without rancor; they simply went away, thereby lightening his soul, which frolicked about like a soap bubble. Everything vanished. Last to withdraw from his consciousness, so painful till then, was the crude and lubricious scene of his friend and the prostitute fornicating like animals. Even those dreadful images that he had thought indelibly branded on his innermost being went away, defenseless, agile, like salmon returning to the sea.

When they had finished, the woman moved gently aside and held the young man's hand. Manuel, lying face up, enjoyed the contact of the body at his side but, above all, the deep darkness that his sight was unable to penetrate. He was relaxed and satisfied: he felt limpid, transparent, light as a feather. He wasn't thinking of anything at all. For the first time in his life he allowed his sensations to flow freely, without trying, as he had always done, to sift them through his reason. They spent a long time in that way. Time, Manuel understood without thinking—although he felt it, curiously, in his sense of smell, which was suffused with an odor that was sour and pungent, though very agreeable, the smell he'd have recognized to be, had he been thinking, that of a woman's flesh—time was passing at another rhythm, unhurried, as if with a lazy unwillingness to proceed, satisfied with how things were going without the slightest wish for them to change. Hence Manuel refused to let it go on flowing; he wanted, in a word, for the whole thing never to end.

"Turn your face toward me, I want to see you," the woman said.

Manuel thought that the girl wanted to have light in the room. This thought caused him an odd uneasiness, something very much like what he had felt as he went up the stairs behind the old woman and, on reaching the last step, flexed his leg to go up one more stair that wasn't there; a feeling of vertigo and emptiness invaded his body for an instant. He felt the same thing now.

"No, please, don't light the candle," he pleaded.

"And who said I was going to light it? I don't need my eyes to see you; my hands are enough," the woman said in a conciliatory tone, as though speaking to a frightened child. "Don't you know that hands can see better than eyes? Let's see . . ." As she spoke, she raised her hand to the young man's forehead. "You have a broad forehead." Her fingertips slid gently over his skin, barely touching it. "You're very young; there aren't any wrinkles in your forehead. Your hair is limp and fine . . . it's dark brown, almost black, isn't that so?"

"Yes," Manuel replied. "But how did you know?"

"Shhh . . . your ears are nice, but because you're very shy, they redden easily. Well, well, you have very delicate eyebrows, they seem like a young woman's." Now her fingers were exploring his eyelids, describing little circles each time they came into contact with his skin. "Close your eyes . . . that's it. They're big and slightly slanted." She kept the tip of her index finger on his eyelid and pressed gently down on it. "They're the same color as your hair; they're a very dark coffee color, almost black . . . Your nose is large and long . . . it ends in a definite curve, like the beak of a bird of prey. Your lips are very thin; the upper one especially, is scarcely more than a line . . . You have a slightly receding chin, and there's a dimple at the tip of it . . . Your cheeks are plump and very smooth; you have good skin, did you know that?" As the woman spoke and explored his face, Manuel felt better and better. As though those tenuous contacts were in reality an energetic massage, his body was invigorated and his sensitivity, which had been dormant for some time, came slowly to life, warm and soft, like a cushion filled with goose down. "I came to know your body before, while we were making love," the woman said as she raised her busy hands from one side of the young man's body to the other. "It's plump, like your cheeks. It's obvious you don't exercise much; your muscles are flabby and padded with flesh, like a woman's. You have a priest's body," the woman said and laughed very softly.

I have a priest's body . . . what other kind of a body could I have? Manuel thought without annoyance.

"Don't you want to see me? Try it, it's very pleasant," the girl said as she raised one of Manuel's hands to her face.

Now it was the seminarian who delicately slid his fingertips over the other's face. Manuel's hands, as though they had a life of their own, found sustenance in the flow of sensations that descended from his fingertips and formed, there in his palms, images that, in some strange way, reached his head. And so it was that he saw—that was the right word—thick, wavy hair the color of old gold; delicate, arched eyebrows above big almond-shaped eyes, of a pretty green color (that was what he felt when the woman placed his fingertip on her eyelid); a fine long nose; lips that were fleshy and cool, the lower one turned just a little downward; a soft pointed chin; and an oval face with smooth, olive skin.

"You're very beautiful," he exclaimed in surprise.

Suddenly he had the sensation that he had already seen many times before that face his hands had pictured for him. He searched about in his memory until an image appeared that was unquestionably identical to the one that he had discovered in the darkness: it was the face of a life-sized wooden Virgin in the chapel of the seminary. Manuel had a special veneration for that statue. He spent many afternoons on his knees before the image, apparently praying—apparently, because in reality he merely looked and looked at the painted figure, his mind a blank. And now, without understanding either how or why and without being in the least troubled by the enormous blasphemy that that thought implied, he felt that it was that Virgin who was lying naked beside him.

"Your name is María, isn't it?" he asked the woman, certain of her answer.

"Yes, how did you know?"

"I don't have any idea . . . it just came to me," he lied as he went on exploring the woman's body with both hands. He felt her long, thin neck, her small, delicate shoulders, almost like a child's, her firm

reasts, also small, with their sensitive buttons wide awake, her round
nd lustful belly. He skirted her sex and went on to her thighs, long
nd firm, covered with a down that reminded him as he touched
hem of the skin of a peach. As he explored that body, young and
mooth, a feeling grew in his consciousness, one absolutely new to
im, which dazed him, distressed him, and at the same time made
im infinitely happy. It's love, he realized. He was making love to
hat creature as he had never made love in his life. The strange cer-
ainty that he was dreaming that he was making love to this unknown
voman (which freed him from all prurience), who in reality was the
irgin herself, whose body of wood and plaster had been transformed
y enchantment in his dream into that pretty girl, ardent and delicate,
nflamed his spirit to the point that he realized, without the least hint
f fear, that he was on the verge of madness. It mattered little to him;
e was determined to go mad, even to die, if only he could savor that
narvelous sensation till the end. Now he was the one who settled
imself on top. He penetrated the woman with the same ease he had
he first time, as though it were a matter of a rite repeated for cen-
uries, and began to move his waist rhythmically up and down. The
irl gently followed, like an expert ballerina. As the urgencies of love
ccelerated his movements, there came to Manuel's mind the image
f his friend fornicating with Ignacia, and he wondered in confusion
vhether, when all was said and done, that was love, if that feeling
vhich was so beautiful and so profound that it almost drove him
nad finally leads to these savage thrusts, as he thought with a certain
egret. But his pleasure was a great deal stronger than his reason. His
houghts were diluted in the act of love like salt in water. They
eached orgasm at the same time; Manuel discovered this because at
he very moment that he abandoned himself totally, he heard a sharp
noan from the woman. Now, perhaps because he had nothing more
o empty out of his conscience, completely purified for the first time,
he profound sensation of orgasm was accompanied by a strange suc-
ession of images. A dream within the dream, Manuel perhaps
hought. He saw himself, now a mature man, fatter and a bit bald,
vith deep wrinkles on his forehead and cheeks, wearing a cassock
nd sitting in a handsome confessional of exquisitely carved walnut
vood. He was hearing a confession. The penitent was a very young
ad, almost a child. He was thin, with delicate features, and elegantly
lressed in dark blue velvet. Yet there was something very strange
bout his face. Perhaps it was his eyes, very black, almost without

any vitreous surface, bright and set far apart, like those of an insect
Or perhaps it was his head, round and well proportioned but withou
a single hair on it.

"How long has it been since your last confession?"

"I don't remember, Father. A long time, perhaps not since my
first communion."

"And why haven't you been to confession?"

"Because I didn't believe in God."

"You didn't believe in God? . . . And now you do?"

"I don't know."

"Why have you come to confess then?"

"Because my father ordered me to."

"So then . . . ?"

"I fornicated with a widow."

"And . . . ?"

"And . . . ?"

"And what happened . . . ?"

"The usual thing, I believe. We did it three or four times."

"And . . . ?"

"I liked it very much."

"That is a great sin."

"I know. But I liked it . . . What's more, I saw things."

"You saw things? . . . When? What things?"

"When I reached the climax of pleasure. They were strange images. People in the street running from one side to the other. Man
of them were carrying sandbags to block it, as though in preparatio
for an uprising . . ."

As he listened to the boy, Manuel thought in surprise that, in
certain way, the same thing had happened to him: many years befor
he had seen strange images when he reached the climax of pleasur
with a girl whose face he was never able to see but which was identica
to that of the Virgin in the chapel of the seminary where he ha
studied . . .

But that isn't true, Manuel said to himself. Nothing ever happene
with that girl, much less with the Virgin. It was all a dream . .
Relieved, he heard María say, "You must go, Manuel; day is alread
beginning to dawn."

The young man saw a tenuous glow in the upper portion of th
wall. It was a little window with thick bars that let the first light o
dawn in. He got up and dressed quickly, avoiding turning his head

since there was now enough light to see the girl. When he finished dressing, he walked over to the door and couldn't help contemplating the lamentable state of the cubicle. As if the odors had slept in the darkness, they awoke with the light of day and aggressively made their way to his sense of smell, where he distinguished a number of odors, though all of them had in common the odor of poverty. He stopped at the door, fearfully turned his head, and saw on the straw pallet a bundle of threadbare blankets in which the woman was hiding. He tossed a doubloon in that direction.

"Here! Many thanks," he said, and left.

Once he was in the street, he began to run as hard as he could. As though an invisible hand guided him, he made his way through the labyrinth of narrow back streets and reached the seminary in no time. He knocked furiously on the door, and when the old concierge opened it for him, he fell in a faint at his feet.

He came to in the afternoon with a bad headache. A friar came into his cell bringing him hot chocolate.

"Drink this, brother; drink and rest," he said to him.

The thick, sweetish liquid went down slowly, heating his whole body. Serenely, he went over, with delight almost, what had happened to him. He concluded that everything that had taken place with Pablo, from the time they left the seminary until he left the house of that prostitute, was real. What happened afterward was doubtless a dream, as he had kept telling himself at the very moment that it was happening to him. Despite all the horrors he'd experienced, he concluded that the balance was positive: he had known sin; he had seen with his own eyes two bodies copulating like animals and felt profound repugnance. He was almost grateful to Pablo for having given him the opportunity to learn all that. He had no doubt about it now: lust is infernal. It surprised him to think that so many men proved so weak when it called to them. To him, the matter was very simple: avoiding those sins was like avoiding the sting of a poisonous insect. He did not hold it against his friend, but from then on he coolly kept his distance in his dealings with him. Pablo Montes de Oca noted it, and little by little parted ways with the fat prig. On the other hand, the dream didn't distress him either. He tried to see in it a message from providence. In some way the Virgin—whom he now visited and venerated more than ever—intervened in his dream to cleanse, with her divine presence, whatever filth there might be in his spirit. Love like that, just as I dreamed it, despite its profound sensuality, cannot be anything but pure and chaste. Only in a dream, and with divine intervention, can the pleasures of the flesh mix in that way with those of the spirit, he told himself.

He ended his studies brilliantly and was ordained a priest in a solemn ceremony that took place one spring morning in the year 1727. He devoted all his efforts and talent to his calling and soon stood out as a well-balanced, serene, and just man who lived an exemplary life. These merits—despite the envy to which they ordinarily give rise—earned him continual promotions, to the point that, when still very young (he was not yet forty), he was named parish priest of one of the main churches in Madrid. And one afternoon he found himself in that church, seated in the imposing confessional, content and satisfied because he had just eaten a good portion of tripe, his favorite dish. His drowsiness and the heaviness in his belly troubled him a little, since on several occasions he had fallen asleep while listening to the sins of some penitent because of the hearty meal he'd eaten and the carafe of wine he was in the habit of drinking with it. Forgive my gluttony, Lord, he thought with a smile, and give me the fortitude to fulfill my duties.

It was at that point that he saw a young man dressed in blue, thin, with dark eyes and a bald pate, approaching. A massive terror took possession of his soul. He wanted to stand up and take off for somewhere else, no matter where, far, far from that young man who he knew was going to be his perdition. But he contained himself, waited riveted to the bench, sweating heavily. He rubbed his soaking wet head and hands, and they gave off a sour odor of rancid tripe, an odor that, like the young man, brought back memories.

"How long has it been since your last confession?"

"I don't remember, Father. A long time . . ."

As he listened to him, the priest's mind remained fixed on that same scene of fifteen years before in what up until then he had presumed to be a dream. Because now, who knows by what strange paths, he had arrived at the certainty that, alas! he hadn't dreamed all that, that it was as real as what had happened with Pablo. Once he had confessed it to his pastor, shortly after it had taken place, he had completely forgotten about it. But now the cruel, sharply focused images came back to his mind, as though he were living the entire episode at that very moment. He hadn't dreamed anything: the old woman existed, as María existed and . . . that love existed.

From that time on, the man's life took an entirely different turn, as though it had been banished, along with the first father and mother, from Eden. Still, saying that his life took another turn was not completely accurate. To appearances, he was the same as ever; the routine of so many years led him to go on as he had comported himself up until then, although admittedly only by an enormous effort. He climbed the rungs of the ladder of the complicated church hierarchy and was one day appointed archbishop of New Spain without anyone's suspecting the titanic struggle that was taking place in his conscience. He never showed anything on the outside. Perhaps a keen observer would have seen that after that encounter with the boy, don Manuel's face had grown stern and abjured smiles, and that his body, although he continued to be obese, weakened like a church from which the wooden structure hidden inside its thick walls has been removed. The priest became taciturn, bitter, and irascible, though the majority of those who knew him attributed it to the weight of his duties. No one ever knew what that poor man had on his conscience. He had enjoyed carnal pleasure, and so much, so very much, that he confused it with divine pleasure. That revulsion against sex, which he had so easily acquired through the memory of his friend and the prostitute copulating, disappeared completely, replaced by a morbid eagerness, a desire to experience again what he had felt with María on that long-ago night. From that time on, he couldn't lay eyes on a pretty woman without having the greatest difficulty controlling the impulse to pass his fingertips over her face, to touch her flesh with his hands, to feel again what, up until then, he thought had been a dream because it had been so impossibly beautiful. From that time on, the eagerness to make love, lust, tormented his spirit . . .

It's been exactly twenty years today that that bald young man came into the church, the archbishop thought as he raised the host to the bridegroom's mouth. Twenty years, Lord! Twenty years paying for that sin. Twenty years purging the insufferable torment of knowing that the more he despised what he feared most, what he hated most was also what pleased him most, the only thing worth being experienced in life. He raised the host to the bride's mouth. He saw, from above, the girl's features as she received the sacrament on her knees—those delicate and neatly traced eyebrows, her big eyes the color of verdant earth, her long slender nose . . . Mariana . . . the Virgin . . . her body, those movements . . . Pablo and the whore, María . . . the bald young man . . . These were the last images that came to his mind before he fainted and fell full length at the foot of the main altar, where the Christian sovereigns, surrounded by fanciful gilded vegetation, looked upon him indifferently . . .

The sacristan, alarmed, raised his eyes heavenward begging for aid. Four robust guards lifted up the archbishop's bulky body and carried it to the sacristy. Distinguished doctors hastened to examine him as the worshipers remained silent and in suspense. Domingo Pantaleón Alvarez de Abreu, bishop of Puebla, took over and from the main altar cast an energetic look toward the choir, indicating to the organist that he should go on playing. The chords of the fugue reverberating in the vast church helped to calm people's spirits. A doctor went over to the bishop and said something in his ear. Smiling, don Pantaleón announced to the faithful that don Manuel Rubio y Salinas, "our beloved archbishop, is all right. He suffered only a slight dizzy spell, doubtless because of his untiring activity. But he's fine now; there is no need for you to worry, brothers. Let us pray to the Lord in thanks for this happy news." He knelt to begin the prayer in a low voice. Afterward, he himself prepared to bring the ceremony to a close. Mariana could not help comparing the thin, nervous figure of the bishop of Puebla, with his long, lean face, whose straight and fine-drawn nose cast a shadow over a hard and energetic mouth and chin, with the archbishop's plump body and ruddy face.

Don Pantaleón carried out beautifully the last duties of the sacrament, satisfied perhaps at feeling himself, though only for a moment, the supreme head of that cathedral and, hence, archbishop of the largest archdiocese in the world—a dream that he had cherished in his heart for many years but that God had never been willing to make come true.

Many of the faithful saw in the incident a fateful omen and hastened to cross themselves and murmur the holy names appropriate for driving bad luck away as they looked out of the corner of their eye at the couple and selfishly thought that the calamity that had occurred should be attributed to them since, when all was said and done, they were the ones responsible for that ceremony. The viceroy, for his part, paid scarcely any attention to the occurrence. Not even the resounding impact of the archbishop's body against the marble floor succeeded in bringing him out of his self-absorption. His long-suppressed desire was finally being realized, and it was not going to be the fainting spell of that fat hypocrite that would bring him out of his inner delectation. If his soul was at all disquieted by such indifference, its uneasiness vanished altogether when he heard the calming words of the bishop of Puebla.

Once the ceremony was over, the viceroy was the host of a splendid banquet in the palace. It was a happy, though restrained, gathering. Perhaps that moderation on the part of the guests, who after a couple of glasses of wine refused to allow the footmen to fill them again, was owed to the still-fresh memory of the fainting of the archbishop, whose place alongside the bride was occupied by the smiling Pantaleón, who was one of the few guests who did not refuse the drinks the footmen were offering. The bishop joked with the marquise and told her savory anecdotes of his adopted land. "Don't let His Excellency hear me, my lady, but I guarantee you there is no city in all of New Spain more beautiful than Puebla. Are you acquainted with the chapel of the Virgen del Rosario? . . . No? For the love of heaven, my lady! That is almost a sacrilege," he said smilingly. "Promise me that you'll come visit our city."

"Of course, Your Reverence, I shall do so as soon as I can. And you in turn must promise me you'll be the one to guide me so that I may become acquainted with all those marvels you've mentioned to me."

"My lady, I could ask for no loftier honor . . ."

The viceroy listened patiently to the mayor's wife as she spoke in an affected voice of the Court of Madrid. The marquis was amused to see the "killer" beauty mark that the woman had painted on her left cheek. She was one of the very few respectable ladies of the country who dared use this daring cosmetic touch, so much the fashion at the court at Versailles. She looks like a whore, the marquis though good-humoredly. Several times his eyes met don José de la Borda's. It was not by chance; the miner kept looking anxiously at the viceroy, hoping for a kindly gesture, like a little dog nuzzling his master's hand in order to be petted. But the viceroy at times pretended not to see him and at others, worse still, gave him an ice-cold look, capable of slicing through the air between the two of them. Don José was very worried; he knew very well what the source of the viceroy's annoyance was and was ready to remedy the situation as soon as the occasion arose. Despite his great fortune and his undeniable power, he could not offer himself the luxury of being on distant terms with the supreme authority of the country, thereby risking seeing, as was already happening to him, his wealth and privileges diminish. He was the one who gave the bride and groom the most costly wedding present: an impressive silver table service for twelve guests. It must have cost at least ten talegas, the viceroy thought when don José's messengers presented it to him. That's how frightened the wretch must be . . . Nonetheless, he hadn't yet given them the really big present. Don José de la Borda anxiously stroked the rolled-up document lying on the table as he impatiently waited for the wedding feast to be over at last. When it finally ended and the last guests were saying good-bye to the couple, tendering all sorts of good wishes, the miner planted himself before the marquis and the marquise, and after making a slow bow, said, "My lady, allow me to offer you this humble present, which I hope will forever close the painful wound it meant for me to part company with your beloved father, one of the best persons I have ever known in my life, please believe me." This said, he held out the parchment scroll and placed it in the woman's hands.

Mariana listened to him seriously, aloofly. It was nearly impossible for her to hide a grimace of disgust when she heard those flattering words for her father from that despicable man. Nevertheless, despite everything, she was happy: both she and the viceroy guessed what the scroll contained without having to read it. It was a document signed by the Marquis de la Borda in which he gave up the lawsuit brought against don Federico Rodríguez and therefore gave up all claim to the sum that he had paid for the mine in the mountains of Huatepec. He authorized the Augustinian brothers to give doña Mariana the capital that they had kept in trust when she decided to turn it over to their safekeeping.

"Many thanks, marquis. God will find a way to repay your noble gesture," the girl replied, and bade him farewell.

The gift came as a profound relief to the Marquis de las Amarillas. The old miner's decision effaced as if by magic the one concern that cast a shadow over his happiness, namely, that his fortune was not very large and almost all of it was promised to his only son. He could bequeath very little to his new wife, and that disturbed him, for he knew that his life would end soon and he was unable to find a way of offering his young wife financial security in her widowhood. Now, with this happy news, he could feel at ease. Mariana's future ceased to be uncertain, since the sum that Borda was giving her was quite large if one took into consideration, besides, how skillfully the Augustinian brothers had handled her affairs, for in a short time they had considerably increased the capital that had been entrusted to them. Hence the viceroy accompanied the old miner to the door of the drawing room and bade him farewell with the affable smile that he had denied him for several months and the absence of which had kept the ambitious Marquis de la Borda on tenterhooks.

The months that followed the wedding were, beyond the shadow of a doubt, the happiest in the viceroy's life. He had the gift—he told himself with satisfaction—of creating a pretty spring in the winter of his life. He realized this above all on the day following his marriage, when, accompanied by his brand-new wife, he presided over the solemn ceremonies with which the society of New Spain celebrated yet another anniversary of the fall of Tenochtitlán to the Spaniards. It was an especially warm and bright Saint Hippolytus Day. As though the clouds were in league with the viceroy, on that day they departed from the sky. They could scarcely be made out on the horizon, to the east, waiting serenely for the newlyweds to enjoy the fiesta, to return the following day with their raging summer storms.

In the main square of that ancient country, beneath the imposing volcanoes, those who attended the procession resembled a colony of industrious ants. As though the entire population of Anáhuac had agreed to meet at that spot, a motley mosaic of human types could be seen, dressed in the most dissimilar attire, from the haughty Spaniards of the town council, who, with their black capes and the red crosses on their chests, arrogantly cleared the way for the open carriage of the viceroy and his wife, to the Indians, hieratic, taciturn, and stern, with eyes blacker than coal, dressed in their homespun cotton trousers cleaner and whiter than the snow of the volcanoes, and including an endless variety of mestizos. Castes whose very names evoked the irrationality of the racist spirit: *saltapatrás, mulato, chino, morisco, lobo, jîbaro, zambarzo, cambujo, calpamulato, alborregado, ténte en el aire, babarino, torna atrás, barocierna, coyote, chamizo, allí te estás*—everything from a "Chinaman" to a "Moor" to a "wolf" to a "rube," down to a forthright *no te entiendo:* "I don't understand you."

Although all of them were gathered together in the enormous square, in some way every group was perfectly identifiable because of its attire, customs, and attitudes. Hence, whereas the Creoles and the Spaniards, dressed in their best, milled about as close as possible to the passing procession, happy but solemn, so as to get a look at the dignitaries, admiring the beauty and charm of the new viceroy's wife, and fervently crossing themselves when the image of the Virgen de los Remedios passed before their eyes, the mestizos watched the procession indifferently in clothing that reflected what they themselves were, dressed as they were in a combination outfit with cotton trousers topped by a short embroidered jacket, and wearing on their head a broad-brimmed sombrero whose fanciful form didn't come from any sort of headgear worn in Castile, much less from the rolled-up headcloth of the native Indians. Every so often the fine attire and the costly jewels the Spaniards were wearing attracted their attention, sparking their greed and their envy at the same time. Others frankly planned an imaginary escape route they would take to get away after snatching some lady's necklace or filching some gentleman's bulging money pouch. "Over here, guards; I've been robbed!" It was a shout as frequent as the amen that brought to a close the litanies recited by the fat priest walking in front of the Virgin's platform borne by many who were carrying crosses on their backs. The Indians, keeping their distance from the center of events, scarcely paid any attention to them. Their inexpressive faces gave no hint of what inner feelings they were keeping to themselves, although it was not difficult to suppose that it was rancor bordering on hatred: for them there was nothing to celebrate. The victory won over their forebears by those men who came from across the sea represented for them nothing but oppression, pain, and misery. The Spaniards were celebrating the origin of what for the Indians was a nightmare from which they had long since resigned themselves never to awaken.

The viceroy didn't notice. As though in some way his state of mind were reflected in the crowd, he saw only happy, noble, serene faces. A perfect harmony, he thought, swearing to himself that he would be the most just, kind, creative governor ever known in this marvelous kingdom that now, thanks to the force of love that was too great to find room within his breast, was receiving his uniform and generous affection as the fields receive the water of an abundant rain. And in some way he fulfilled his vow: during that brief but intense last stage of his reign he was energetic, just, generous, and tireless. From early in the morning on, he was in his office attending to urgent matters, and when there were none, he ordered his secretaries to search in the archives to take care of petitions, claims, and problems long neglected that, had it not been for these new bursts of energy of the governor's, could have been doomed to sleep the sleep of the just. He ate with good appetite and returned to his duties, which he did not leave until late in the afternoon. Then, and this was what pleased him most, he shut himself up in his quarters with his wife and sat down in a comfortable armchair, allowing the fire in the fireplace to warm his body and letting his two big mastiffs play with his sandals. He sipped a bit of sweet wine and listened to his companion as she read, now passages from plays, now novels, but above all, poetry. He especially liked hearing the rhythmic verses of Bernardo de Balbuena in his majestic *Grandeza mexicana* as he felt, minute by minute, a greater love for that pretty girl who, in a sweet and well-modulated voice, read the description of that country which, as he did his wife, he felt himself loving more and more each day:

> All year long here it is the months of April and May,
> pleasant weather, discreet cold,
> a clear, calm sky, soft breezes . . .

"True, very true . . . ," her husband murmured with satisfaction as she read and he rapturously contemplated her, the way an artist contemplates his masterwork.

Never in his many years of life had the marquis ever felt as well. His ill health, with which recently he had been more and more gravely afflicted, improved as if by magic. His physicians could scarcely believe it when they saw their patient rosy cheeked, energetic, possessed of a good appetite, and walking with firm and unfaltering steps, like a stripling. Unobtrusively, he paid less attention to them and to their irksome treatments. He ordered a servant to get rid of all the little bottles of a thousand sizes and colors, containing all sorts of cordials, syrups, and pomades that he kept in the bureau of his bedroom and that, with the passage of time, had become more necessary to his body than bread itself. But if the improvement of his bodily health was almost a miracle, beyond a doubt that of his spirit was also one: melancholy, perennial sadness, petty fear of death, pessimism, uncertainty, which for a very long time had been his guests, now, along with the vials of medicine, severed themselves from him forever, making way for opposite feelings that up until then had been forbidden any possibility of inhabiting that embittered spirit. Thus, optimism, happiness, confidence, an absolute faith in the joy of being alive, a conscious lack of concern about the possibility of death occupied their new home, dusting it off, opening its windows to let in the fresh air of enjoyment, turning what had once been a prison into a pretty and cheerful little country house. Among these new guests an unexpected one stole into his spirit. Unassuming at first, it sought no great attention; it was content to settle down in a distant corner of his consciousness. Nonetheless, with the passage of time it little by little became more conspicuous and, arrogant and capricious, began to demand more and more attention, until it finally became the new and most fearful tyrant that his spirit had ever harbored: desire. The marquis was unable to understand that feeling, nor was he able, as he had tried to do at the beginning, to avoid it without attributing any importance to it. You're an old man, he said to himself. Moreover, that never particularly mattered to you . . . Indifferent to his reflections, desire goaded him more and more violently. The sweet kisses with which he said good-night to his young wife every night began to burn his lips. He could scarcely keep control of his hands, which avidly sought to stroke those soft contours when his wife embraced him, contours that in his imagination his hands ran over a thousand times, encouraged by the fleeting images he retained in his memory of his wife combing her hair, dancing, or laughing, of the initial curve of her breasts which he caught a glimpse of when, as he was seated, Mariana leaned down toward him to kiss him on the forehead. Love, the marquis realized on one of his sleepless nights, the immense love he felt for his wife, demanded its physical counterpart, for just as the soul cannot be torn away from the flesh, so desire cannot be separated from love. The more he loved her and the more pure and lofty he knew his feelings to be, the more his body, his penis even, asleep these many years, pressured him to caress, to kiss, to make his flesh one with that of that blessed woman. But he was incapable of even hinting at his feelings to Mariana. He had pledged to respect her and to take care of her like a daughter, and despite the enormous impulse of his sensations, he contained himself, consoling himself with the thought that it would be almost an outrage to unite his old, withered body with that fresh young woman's. Perhaps at heart what kept him from carrying out his desires, the enormous strength capable of holding back the torment that shook his soul—which he succeeded in containing even on that afternoon when he entered Mariana's bedroom without warning and caught her by surprise naked in her bathtub, barely getting a glimpse of her slender back and her long neck with her abundant hair caught up atop her head, the woman turning toward the door as she heard someone come in and offering to the eyes of the marquis the profile of an impeccable breast, so that the cone of pneumatic flesh, crowned by an aureole tinged an old rose color, was close to vanquishing the viceroy and his feet, as though they had a life of their own, started to make their way closer to the bathtub, the palms of his outstretched hands forming a hollow, already prepared to receive those breasts, but he restrained himself, closed his eyes in a fury, and walked back toward the door full of resolve, with the enormous strength of will that Eve had not had for overcoming Satan's temptations—perhaps that tremendous force, he went on to himself, did not come so much from the desires and uprightness of someone who had given his word as from the unspeakable fear that the woman would reject him, that Mariana, surprised and indignant, would feel contempt for his advanced age, his lack of honor, his cowardice, and cease to love him. It was that profound fear that held him back that day and practically all the days that followed, for from that time on, desire, once inflamed, had uprooted all the other feelings of his spirit and despotically made him suffer infinitely more than his former sorrows, while at the same time, paradoxically, giving him a strange pleasure and almost a feeling of joy, perhaps a hidden pride, to know that, despite everything, he was so full of life.

In a certain way, the same thing happened to Mariana. The affection she felt for her husband had been gradually maturing along with her body, which after she turned twenty, had reached its prime and began to demand that she no longer be treated as a young girl but as a woman. On the other hand, the image she had of the viceroy grew more pronounced by the day. His rectitude, his integrity, the subtle and kindly way he treated her slowly but inexorably seduced her until the affection that she had originally felt for the man turned into love, and along with it, into scarcely contained longings to give herself to him, to become his real wife. Despite the extraordinary vigor she discovered in that new feeling, capable of affecting her even physically, since dizzy spells, lack of appetite, and even fever devastated her more and more frequently, she had enough strength of character to hide it. For something very similar to what was happening to the marquis was happening to her too: she was ashamed to feel that desire for a person who looked upon her and treated her as a daughter. What would he think of me if I were to tell him what I feel? she asked herself and didn't dare answer. She almost considered herself to be a perverted, incestuous daughter. And she feared nothing more than that a shameless and immodest forwardness on her part would be unfair to a man she idolized. And so, with him fearing to offend the person he thought looked on him as a father, and she terrified at the possibility of hurting the person she believed looked on her as a daughter, they spent their days loving each other more and more and also suffering more and more, fighting the irresistible attraction by force of will, avoiding each other the more they wanted to be together, fleeing each other the more the yearning to embrace goaded them on. They were like two moths circling a candle flame, incapable of flying away from it but also incapable of throwing themselves into the fire and burning their wings once and for all.

Curiously, it was the intervention of don José de la Borda—an individual of ill omen in Mariana's life hitherto—that broke the vicious circle. They had been married for eight months when the viceroy finally accepted the invitation that the miner had many times extended to them to come for a time to take a rest at his house in Cuernavaca. They arrived there at the end of April of the year 1760. Mariana had to admit that, this time at least, don José was honest in what he had said and had even understated the truth when he described to them how pretty the place was and how inviting his house was. It was situated near the center of town, to one side of the old walls with battlements which surrounded a venerable Franciscan monastery dating from the sixteenth century, which itself included an enormous and austere church that without dispute bore the honor of being the cathedral of this warm city in the hotlands. The house was simple and unpretentious. The high adobe walls were covered with stucco and whitewashed; they held up thick cedar beams that gave off a pleasant smell, a little like a forest and also a little like a jungle. Above them were large fired-clay bricks and smaller ones that held up heavy Spanish-style roof tiles curved in the form of the thigh on which they had been molded. The prettiest part of the place, however, was the gardens. Vegetation from all over the world grew luxuriantly. The imposing trees seemed to hold up the sky above their cool, damp leaves that gave off metallic gleams as they reflected the afternoon light. There were flowers everywhere, in flower pots, in borders along the garden paths, around the fountains and ponds, on bushes around the trees. Even between their branches there were orchids that gave off lusty fragrances at daybreak.

"It's curious," the viceroy said to Mariana as they watched dusk fall, sitting in wicker chairs on a cool covered balcony whose roof was supported by columns of quarrystone above which thick live-oak beams rested, "I have the sensation that I know this place, as though I'd been in it many times. Perhaps it's the flowers . . ." Mariana didn't understand this last part, nor did she make the slightest effort to. She was, so to speak, somewhere else. To her, this gorgeous garden brought paradise to mind. At least that was how she had imagined it when she read in the Bible the austere description that Moses gave of Eden. And like Eve in paradise, she felt more tempted to sin than ever. She didn't dare turn her face to look at her husband, for she wasn't at all certain of being able to contain herself. That sight, that sun that, although about to set, was still able to send forth a warm and penetrating light, like darts of fire, and that sweetish odor that the night-blooming flowers were beginning to give off, were together making her feel dangerously drowsy and languid. Frightened, she drank down in one swallow the wine still left in her glass and apologized to her husband. "I'm very tired," she said to him. "I think it's because of the journey," and rising to her feet, she went over to him to give him, as she always did when they parted company, a kiss on the cheek. Distracted, the marquis was not aware of his wife's approach. At the very moment that she was about to kiss him, he turned his head so that, for a fleeting instant, their lips met. The shock to both of them was identical; they felt this tenuous contact with the same intensity as if someone had placed a red-hot brand on their lips. The woman withdrew toward her bedroom almost at a run. There, lying on the bed, she waited for darkness to come in the hope that it would make her fall asleep.

Far from making her fall asleep, the darkness that invaded the room allowed the images whirling inside her head to light up and become impossibly clear and real. With the heat of that unexpected kiss still on her lips, she saw her husband's calm, perpetually melancholy face. She thought dreamily of his hands, long and delicate, surprisingly fresh and young for those of a man of his age. She dared to remember, encouraged by the intense heat, by the penetrating smell of the flowers, by the disturbing chirping of a thousand crickets, and above all, by the call that a teasing bird was addressing to her. "Psst!" she heard, and every time the bird made that sound, her first thought was that it was someone calling her; then she realized it was the bird. "Psst!" again, and as a bugle guides armies, the bird's call guided in her mind the images that were obsessing it: there she was, bathing naked in the tub, when she heard someone come into her bedroom and surprised the marquis, who, abashed, turned his head. Then she discovered with the utmost clarity what she had not wanted to see then: the fleeting look that the viceroy gave her before turning his eyes away was in no way paternal; she was sure of it now. He was looking at her like a man, the way a male looks at his female. She knew it, and a secret pride warmed her body. A pride and a pleasure that, as she now realized, made her turn her waist coquettishly so that her husband could see her breasts. "Psst!" the bird repeated, and she took heart. He looked at me with desire, she thought. I'm certain of it; I can't be mistaken now . . . Because she had been mistaken, she realized. In truth, the two of them had been mistaken, hypocritically playing their roles so as to safeguard an image that surely did not suit them; she didn't feel like his daughter, nor he like her father. They were simply a man and a woman. An old man and a young woman, it was true, but a man and a woman impelled by the profound love that they had for each other to make love like any other couple. Because she now understood that too: the marquis was able to make her fall in love by dint of an affection and a devotion—as he had promised in his letter—that had a more powerful effect on her than the vain and selfish gallantries of a young man sure of himself ever could have had. "Psst!" It was clear; if the slightest doubt remained, the vivid memory of that recent kiss dissolved it completely.

She felt the same as I did, the marquis said to himself, also lying abed and listening to the crickets and the playful bird. "Psst!" he heard and on opening his eyes saw, at the threshold, illuminated by the silvery light of the moon, the delightful body of his wife, showing clearly and perfectly through the light nightdress she was wearing.

The next day, very early, the viceroy de las Amarillas strolled smilingly through the gardens of the house of the Marquis de la Borda. Serene, happy, still amazed at this sweetest of miracles that had turned him, at the age of sixty-some, into a new, young man, perfectly different from the man he had always been, he contemplated with delight the vegetation that now, illuminated by the first rays of the sun, shone with silvery glints unlike those of late afternoon, when its glow was more golden. He listened to the birds that had taken the place of the nighttime crickets. A mockingbird was trying its best to drown out the others by giving forth with a loud song, incredibly beautiful to the viceroy's ears. He walked unhurriedly toward a large pool full of lilies and water lilies. His mind was a blank. He left it deliberately empty, cherishing his memories, which were nothing but the caresses of his Mariana. There were flowers everywhere, of a thousand forms, colors, and sizes, although their aromas were stored up, awaiting nightfall to be given off freely, to fill all space and madden flying insects with lust. The marquis understood then why the age-old inhabitants of these lands loved flowers so much, to the point of making of the word denoting them the synonym of beauty and of wisdom. Really, he thought, the best and most noble sentiments of humankind are contained in those soft petals . . . There came to his mind, gliding quietly by, charged with a meaning that he had never before discovered in them, the verses of his admired Bernardo de Balbuena:

> The loving and delicate clover,
> the clicie or sunflower ever restless,
> the tender jasmine, the royal purple gilly flower;
> the blue lily, the violet cárdena,
> the happy lemon balm, pungent thyme,
> mirla, fresh myrtle, the white wild rose . . .

In a pool, full of green lilies with polished, fleshy leaves, crowned or, rather, crested with pointed blue flowers reminiscent of fragile plumes, he discovered a lovely water lily in bloom. It was bright vermilion, the color of fire. Enormous, it spread its petals in the water to received the warm rays of the morning sun. He contemplated it for a long time until he decided to cut it to offer it to his wife. "I place my heart in your hands," he thought of saying to her as he handed it to her. As he tried to reach the flower, an acute pain in his head foretold his death. He understood immediately. Curiously, he was not frightened; his one concern was not being able to reach the flower. I'll never be able to reach it, he said to himself, and fell full length into the warm water that received his body already devoid of his soul . . .

She decided on the white dress. After more than two years of dressing in mourning she still was not used to wearing bright colors. She was somehow inclined toward the white one because she had read somewhere that it was the color the Chinese wore for mourning.

"You don't know how pleased I am that you've finally decided to accept an invitation," her faithful Jacinta said to her as she helped her dress. "You're a very pretty woman, Mariana. You can't live cloistered like a nun; that's an offense against God."

Mariana listened patiently to the eternal litany of that good woman as she looked at herself in the mirror. She was almost ashamed at what she saw in front of her: a young woman, extraordinarily beautiful, with a serene face and a distant and melancholy gaze. One's face is the mirror of one's soul, she thought. What a terrible falsehood! That young and attractive woman in no way resembles my soul, which, if it could be seen, would look old, in pain, tired, like an aged woman who has lived a long and very difficult life . . .

The bells of Notre Dame announced noon.

"My lady," a young maidservant announced to her, "the Marquis de Rasero has arrived. He is awaiting you in the drawing room."

Coquettishly, she gave her hairdo the last finishing touches, allowing two or three curls from the chignon that held her hair back to fall over her neck. She thought of the man who was waiting for her, and once more there came to her mind that image which, she now understood, had become obsessive: the man, with his serious and taciturn face, listening in rapture to the music of the child prodigy, the furtive tear that ran down his left cheek and which he dried immediately with the sleeve of his coat but that she, only she, could see. That detail disarmed her. Hence she accepted the invitation that the man offered her when they were introduced. Perhaps also because she knew that he was Spanish and spoke the same language she did. Although she spoke French fairly well, she found it unbearable. Or perhaps because that man was a relative of don José de Gálvez, the good-hearted lawyer who had done her so many kindnesses in Madrid. No, it was definitely on account of that tear, on account of that obscure message that he sent her with his inexpressive face and that she understood immediately, for as they say that Masons have secret keys for recognizing each other, lonely people also have them.

She was going to go out with that man, and that pleased her. The smile she saw in the mirror, which denoted hope, longing, and a faint uneasiness, came to contradict the reasoning that had seemed so solid to her just a moment before: her face reflected precisely what her soul felt . . .

VI
Madame de Pompadour

Paris, March, 1764

Everything there was in the little drawing room seemed to have been deliberately planned to astonish her: the light armchairs, with their finely carved curving forms, their comfortable and graceful backs with the silhouette of a medallion, upholstered in blue damask with tiny embroidered flowers forming charming bouquets like the ones—these latter of real flowers—in the large porcelain vases that showed, in addition, framed in an oval against the dark blue background, rural scenes, delightful maidens and rosy cherubs that had come from Boucher's delicate paintbrush; the gilt clock with four winged horses that appeared to be bearing aloft the girl who was walking her little Pekingese on a leash, the two of them inside a bell jar under which, discreetly, the dial showed the passage of time; the huge fireplace chimney, topped with an exquisitely polished marble ledge from which, surrounding the entire recess, there led ribbons of gilded plaster whose straightness was interrupted every so often as they twisted into capricious knots, little bells, and bunches of grapes, and framed the paintings and engravings hanging everywhere on the walls. It's incredible that two towns so geographically close can be so different . . . , Mariana thought as she remembered the pieces of walnut furniture, dark and heavy, the thick wine-colored curtains, the severe and somber paintings (of martyred saints and imperturbable gentlemen), hanging from blank, austere walls, that customarily decorated Spanish houses and palaces.

Of course, she had already heard of the Marquise de Pompadour's good taste. It was legendary. For many years, that woman had been the unquestionable arbiter of the fashion and tastes of the French court. But it is one thing simply to hear about something and another to confirm it directly: Choissy was the loveliest little palace that Mariana had ever seen in her life. What must the Elysée Palace be like? she thought, or her rooms at Versailles . . . ? She fixed her attention on a large painting hanging above the fireplace. The oil was a portrait of a little girl of about ten. She was dressed in a pale pink spring dress with a heavy dark blue ribbon at the waist. A woolly little dog was playing with her, leaping up to take the little ball that the child was holding in her hand. They were in a pretty garden filled with plants, in the shade of a large oak tree from which a swing hung, its ropes adorned with pink and yellow flowers. The little girl had a pretty face and a graceful figure, svelte and elegant, with long, soft arms. Her eyes were enormous and took up practically the whole of her oval face; her mouth was small and a bit puckered, as though on the point of smiling at the animal's charm. Tiny wild flowers adorned her long hair.

"It's by Droidet. I don't like that painter. He's very mannered, almost insincere," Rasero said on noting that Mariana had her eyes fixed on the painting.

"And who is the little girl?"

"Alexandrine, Jeanne-Antoinette's only daughter. She died nine years ago. She was a delightful child."

As she looked at the little girl's soft features, Mariana thought about the strange impression that the picture had made on her, an impression she understood on hearing Rasero's words, for as she was contemplating that serene, sad figure, the thought had come to her that doubtless the little girl was dead, as though paintings were capable of reflecting the absence of life. She had noticed this several times, above all with regard to the portrait of her husband that had hung, ever since their marriage, in all the rooms that she had occupied. She liked to look at it. Even though it was not a very good painting, with a brushstroke that was obviously clumsy, the artist had managed to capture that half-melancholy, half-benign expression of the Marquis de las Amarillas which she herself had discovered in him on the day they first met and which she was extremely fond of. Before her widowhood, on many mornings she looked at the portrait before she looked at her husband, and she always greeted it affectionately; indeed, it became a custom that bordered on superstition—as happens with many habits—and she spent the day feeling upset and preoccupied if for some reason she had not greeted the image of her husband when she got out of bed. She remembered now in fact that on that fateful day when she became a widow she had not greeted the portrait, for the simple reason that she hadn't slept in her own bedroom, since she'd spent the night, for the first and only time, in the viceroy's bed. From then on, she had continued to greet it, but no longer with the happiness and the carefree attitude with which she had done so before; now it had turned into a bitter rite with a sad association, and even though the painting was obviously the same, it no longer reflected the reserved and good-natured face of the marquis but the image of someone who had gone away forever, leaving an empty place in her soul—an empty place that until a short time ago she was convinced would never be filled but that this bald, hermetic man, who at the very moment was looking at her, not only had filled many times over but had filled to levels whose existence she had never suspected possible. Rasero's thoughts were similarly appreciative as he contemplated that woman who in a few months had become the center of his life and his reason for being.

"Fausto, dear!" the Marquise de Pompadour exclaimed from the threshold. "Fausto, dear!" she said again, her eyes dimmed with tears she had difficulty holding back. "Come into my arms!"

Mariana saw how Rasero embraced the mature woman, impeccably dressed in a white satin dress with very sober embroidery that had tiny cream-colored pearls as the finishing touch. The woman's face, like her whole body, was a little bloated, with puffy cheeks and a rather conspicuous double chin. Yet it was not a healthy pink face or a handsome one; on the contrary, its fullness betrayed ill health, as though it were not muscles and fat underneath the skin but thick, malignant humors. Her eyes, which should have been very large and haughty, were almost hidden behind eyelids that looked as swollen as the rest of her body. They barely afforded a glimpse of the marvelous old-blue irises that, perhaps because of the tears that she was holding back, gleamed intensely, reflecting an enormous vitality, a vitality that the rest of her anatomy was very far from confirming.

Those bright blue eyes are all that remains of the beautiful Diana the huntress who impressed me so when I saw her for the first time at a ball at Versailles almost twenty years ago, Rasero thought with a certain sadness. Nevertheless, after kissing the woman on both cheeks, he drew away from her with a smile. "What's your secret, Jeanne-

Antoinette? Every time I see you, I find you more beautiful and attractive."

The marquise answered him with a bitter smile. "Ah, Fausto! What wouldn't I give if only your flattering remarks were true! But the real truth is that if you'd waited just a little longer to come visit me, besides finding me beautiful and attractive you'd have found me stone-dead."

"Shhh, woman! Don't talk nonsense. Let Voltaire think of death; you have a long life ahead of you," Rasero answered emphatically, although, within himself, he couldn't help feeling that the woman was right. She really looked very ill . . .

You were grateful to Mariana for insisting that you go and visit your friend; had it not been for that, you probably wouldn't have come back to see the Marquise de Pompadour, and you would never have forgiven your negligence after having accumulated any number of letters and messages from Jeanne-Antoinette in which she literally begged you to visit her, for she felt death to be "as close to me as my shadow . . ." But you, for one reason or another, continually put off keeping your promise to visit her. In all truth, it was for only one reason, and not for others, that you didn't want to go to Versailles. The last time you had visited her there, almost three years ago now, you witnessed much unpleasantness: Jeanne-Antoinette wasting her health in order to support an idiotic war lost from the moment the first battle was fought; Choiseul, with his whims, destroying her nerves; the king, with his lack of will and his melancholy, demanding of her frivolous and absurd diversions day and night so as to distract him from his boredom and offending her in her heart of hearts by his insatiable sexual appetite, a veritable gluttony, which was placated only by virginal dishes fifteen years old brought by his procuresses to the little house that he had bought near the Deer Park. Jeanne-Antoinette knew about the whole thing and looked the other way. In fact, she had ceased many years before to be the king's lover—in the literal meaning of the word, since officially she remained that until the very last day of her life—but on the other hand she was his only friend. If at the beginning she felt relieved when she discovered that the king demanded less of her in bed, although he did not stop demanding, perhaps even more, her presence (since the duties of love, never something that pleased her, were like a heavy burden that at first her ambition, and then later an enormous affection, obliged her to bear uncomplainingly so as to make her beloved sovereign happy), she soon discovered that it was much simpler to satisfy her lover in bed than outside it, because Louis, as though he had turned the compass of his existence upside down, behaved more and more like an ill-mannered child as he grew older. In his desperate war against the tedium and melancholy that tormented him, he made Jeanne-Antoinette the supreme commander of his armies. Of her he demanded pleasure, delight, diversion, above all diversion, and the poor woman consumed the little good health she had left thinking up ways to entertain her lover: little theatrical works, musical performances, evening gatherings that lasted far into the night, when she had to talk and talk but only about pleasant, witty, and clever things—nothing about war, nothing about politics, nothing about intrigues. He nodded, seriously and silently, if what he heard didn't satisfy him, or else he deigned to smile faintly when he heard something that he considered amusing. As she spoke, the woman studied the monarch's face, avidly hoping for one of those contented expressions which, alas! were more and more difficult to get out of him.

That last night you were in Versailles you felt deep scorn for Louis, his crown of Charlemagne, and his pure blue blood that, it was said, ran in the veins of the proud Sun King, of Louis the Just, of the intrepid Henry of Navarre, of Charles the Mad, and even of Saint Louis, because that night Louis XV was merely a miserable Capetian—as they were to call his grandson at the foot of the scaffold—who despotically imposed his sadness on the palace as though he were the only one with the right to feel sad, to scorn life, to lament his fate. You saw his poor lover, loaded with makeup to hide the vestiges on her face of her tears for the death of her only daughter—tears also for the destiny of France, which was sinking like a swamped boat in the absurd battles of Central Europe, where Frederick was playing cat and mouse with the wretched French armies, mangled even before entering combat by their own generals, who knew as much about war as Mars about commerce yet stole so skillfully that alongside them Ali Baba and his thieves were like schoolboys. Jeanne-Antoinette, however, did not stop talking, did not stop saying pleasant things. She squeezed her inventiveness like a fruit so as to extract its tasty juices. Louis was unappeased. He was not satisfied. Are you trying to make my melancholy go away with that string of stupid remarks? his look said to his lover. Jeanne-Antoinette, in deep distress, smiled—the more upset she was, the more she smiled, because it was forbidden her, as it was to everyone in the palace, to show discomposure outwardly—changed the subject of the conversation, searched for an amusing anecdote, but it was useless, like trying to get water out of a stone: Louis remained sad and taciturn. You suspected that, at the bottom of his soul, that man profoundly detested his lover. And you were not wrong. If you had been able to enter Louis' conscience like someone entering a pantry, you would have found yourself with an impressive collection of guilt and doubts, nothing else—guilt at believing in God and being a sinner, at being a king and not loving his kingdom, at being a husband and feeling contempt for his wife, at being a father and not loving his children, at being intelligent and at the same time terribly lazy, at not knowing how to enjoy his status, at envying all those people whom, supposedly, he ought to be looking down on, at dreaming of the grandeur of France and being incapable of moving so much as a finger to achieve it, at wanting to be, finally, a virtuoso and not being anything but a billy goat. And a good part of the blame for his having to put up with so many guilt feelings was owed to that woman, the Marquise de Pompadour, whose mere position in the palace—as his official mistress—was demeaning to his person. She was a woman who had not even—this Louis knew very well—enjoyed his caresses, who felt very superior to him, to the point of being the one who strummed the strings of power, who dragged him, him and all of France, into that stupid war merely to earn the respect of Maria Theresa, who had known how to play with Jeanne-Antoinette as Frederick had played with the empress of Austria herself. A bourgeoise, the daughter of a banker and a woman with a more than dubious reputation, wanted to decide the destiny of France. That was why he detested her. No, he detested her, rather, because he was unable to get rid of her, because she was as necessary to him as the heart in his chest. After the death of Cardinal Fleury, when Louis moved through this sad world like a bird without wings and found her—beautiful and irresistible, dressed like a pagan goddess—it was as if he had found his wings, as if the breath of life, the spirit, of the cardinal had been reborn in her. And he loved her, and tried to live, and tried to be loved by his kingdom, and won battles and dispensed justice, and won his subjects over and had them call him the Beloved, and believed in life and believed in his body . . . and she didn't. Jeanne-Antoinette never loved his body—him perhaps but never his body. This distressed him. His spirit, like a cask with a hole in it, little by little lost its energy, its desires, its illusions, the plans it had in store, until it was as barren as a desert, perhaps retaining the arid rocks of despair, the storms of impotence. That was why he detested her: because she gave him a great deal and took from him a great deal more. That was why he tormented her by showing on his face that expression of boredom and sadness that pained the woman so and annoyed you, Rasero, so. When you saw that odious expression, the roast goose that you were eating stuck in your throat and not even the big swallow of wine you took was able to push it down—as though it were stuck in your esophagus waiting for you to spit it out violently into the face of that cretin of a monarch who did not hide his eagerness for the evening to end as he looked, again and again, at the time on the standing clock, which showed on its dial the moon and its phases, its profile adorned in its wanings and waxings by a big dreamy eye with very long eyelashes. When, finally, the two hands came together, marking the beginning of a new day, Louis got up from the table and excused himself. "The duties of state fatigue me more and more," he said very cynically, and withdrew. Jeanne-Antoinette and you knew very well where he was going. First, of course, he would go to his quarters so as to go through with the absurd rite of the *coucher,* which his pompous great-grandfather had invented. The royal steward, the lord chamberlain, the first gentleman of the bedchamber, and other blue-blooded idiots would help the monarch, assisted by his footmen, to don his nightclothes and then put him to bed—which, meanwhile, had been heated with a copper bed warmer. Once their lord and master was in bed, they would lower the colors and the entire court would withdraw, walking backward and trying not to make any noise. A footman would then put out all the candles and lamps, except for the tiny candle that lit the image of Saint Louis, and would also withdraw so that, once the door was closed, he could lie down on the floor at the threshold to sleep, protecting his master as a dog might.

As soon as Louis found himself alone, he would hop out of bed like a hare and go to a little antechamber where his faithful Luynes would be waiting for him—the man who could rightfully be called (it was a shame the office hadn't existed in the vast inventory of royal posts drawn up by Louis XIV) the royal pimp. There he would get dressed again, though in simpler and more comfortable clothes; he would don the black cape with royal purple trimmings that was his favorite and furtively steal, like some common thief, down the discreet little winding staircase that he had ordered built in other times so as to have access to the rooms of his former lover. Now, he would give Jeanne-Antoinette's door a wide berth and go on downstairs till he reached the esplanade, where a carriage would be waiting for him to take him to the charming little house that he had bought not long ago, just a short distance from the palace, three shots of a crossbow away, in the Deer Park. There he would await a pretty young thing whose mother had let herself be persuaded to allow her daughter to be seduced by an "important gentleman" prepared to pay generously for favors received.

At the beginning, the girl was uneasy and a little afraid: they had brought her to that elegant house, put her in a big bedroom, and stripped her of her poor rags and left her there naked, and then put her in a tubful of hot, perfumed water, where a sour-faced woman rubbed her skin so hard with a sponge that it seemed as though she were trying to skin her alive. Then she was dried off with very fine sheets, her body was rubbed with wonderfully fragrant perfumes and colognes, and she was dressed, from her undergarments to her handkerchief, in new, freshly ironed clothing, lovelier and more elegant than she had ever dreamed of. By then, the girl was happy. She looked at herself in the great mirror in the drawing room and could not believe what she saw in front of her: a pretty girl dressed from head to foot like a noblewoman, with jewelry around her neck, at her wrists, on her hands, and hanging from her ears—jewelry that, unfortunately, she would be obliged to give back afterward unless she succeeded in giving uncommon pleasure to her beau, who would not hesitate then to give them to her as a gift (so the old woman with a sour face had explained to her as she dressed her). She was impeccably coiffed, with her bright red hair caught up atop her head, allowing a few rebellious curls to fall down her fresh neck, thus making it even more fetching.

In fact, without even moving a finger, without her even having seen him, Louis had already almost seduced the girl; such is the power of wealth. The girl was uneasy once again, though not frightened. She began to become impatient, for she was eager now to meet such a splendid beau and throw herself in his arms to thank him for his favors and try—she would do everything possible—to make him very happy, to give him all the pleasure that her young body was able to offer him, and, would to God, she might thus earn the fine jewel that adorned her and that she was already beginning to feel were hers.

Finally the man arrived. The girl discovered to her satisfaction tha he was much younger than she had imagined and . . . much handsomer. Tall, erect, and elegant, his body showed his nobility; his broad forehead crowned large, haughty eyes the color of cedarwood. His nose, straight and generous, reminded the girl of the one of the monarch's that she had seen—in all truth, very seldom—on the gold coins called louis. That scapegrace of a Luynes has done a good piece of work, Louis thought as he contemplated the girl. For, despite having made love to so many women, beauty still surprised him; it intimidated him and attracted him powerfully, as though he were a celibate stripling. Subdued, the man remained standing, as silent as Tancred, the leader of the First Crusade, was reputed to have been. It was the girl who took the initiative by offering him a glass of wine and a smile much more intoxicating than the alcohol. Little by little the drink and the magnificent spectacle he saw as he observed the girl made him twice as timid. He approached her, began to compliment her with gallant remarks and kiss her warm cheeks. In a little while they would be frisking about in the bed, where Louis would happily discover that the girl had little skill at playing love games. Patiently, like a good teacher, he would lead her through the labyrinths of flesh with such wisdom and dexterity that, as day broke, that girl would have ceased to be an innocent maiden and become an avid lover, ready to become an expert. Louis would be satisfied: by Jove, he'd have had a splendid time! He'd have forgotten for a while the boredom that was gnawing at his vitals . . . For a few hours he'd have been no more than what his body wanted to be: sensations, enjoyment, delight, bliss at feeling himself alive. He'd have forgotten his worries, the wars in the colonies, the balance at the state treasury—eternally showing a deficit—Jeanne-Antoinette's illness, the death of his son, the mockery of his people, who had stopped calling him the Beloved and instead were now calling him the billy goat, the Pervert, the Unloved. For a short time, an exquisite time, all that would not exist. Louis XV would be nothing but a simple man who had enjoyed, as anyone else would have done, that delightful creature. He'd be so satisfied that he'd order the girl to be paid twice as much as usual and, furthermore, he'd give her as a gift the jewels that adorned her.

The girl, who was beginning to be a woman, could not have been happier. She saw the sky grow lighter through the window as she fondled, with nearly the same lust as that with which she had fondled her lover, the handsome necklace that he had just put around her neck, for good now. But Louis had given her as well, although she would not know this until some months later, the seed of a child. The girl's fresh belly was beginning to harbor a new life. A new bastard of Bourbon blood would certainly be born. Perhaps there would run through his veins the ardent blood of his father or of his great-great-grandfather Henry IV, perhaps the phlegmatic and calculating blood of Louis XIII or, then again, the dense, absolute, implacable plasma of the Sun King or—God forbid—the languid, easy-going, lazy blood of his nephew, Louis XVI, Citizen Capetian (perhaps your very own blood, Rasero, since that business about your great-great-granduncle, don Anselmo de Oquendo, who it was said crowned with a nice pair of cuckold's horns the royal head of Henry of Navarre, has never been quite clear).

In the carriage, on the return to the monumental palace, Louis' relish and happiness began to slip away like water through his hands. Boredom, melancholy, sadness came home to roost because of his arrogance—and with even greater force, as though in some way they were punishing him for having had such a good time. He was paying, with interest, for the little that he might possibly have gained a short while before. He was coming back older, more tormented, readier than ever to make a martyr of his old companion because—even though he wasn't sure how—she and nobody else was the one responsible for his pitiful state.

Meanwhile, you remained in Jeanne-Antoinette's quarters with some friends. After supper, the marquise invited you to play faro. She wasn't much amused by card games, it was obvious. In truth, this was only a pretext to be with you, to tell you with the look in her eyes, her marvelous blue eyes, of the anguish eating her spirit away. She told you about it with her look much more clearly and eloquently than she would have been able to tell you in words—something that, besides, she would never have done: that woman of plebeian origin was much prouder and more reserved than any lady who bore a musty old title that went back eight centuries. So she talked to you about her daughter, the being that she had loved the most—after her sovereign, of course—about the disaster of the war, about Frederick's animosities, about Maria Theresa's childish pranks, about her enemies, Richelieu, d'Argenson, and Maurepas, who tirelessly sought a way to snatch Louis' favors away from her, with little success, fortunately, even though it was harder each day for her to wage that battle against those cretins and the lovely women they put in front of the monarch in the hope that one of them would usurp her place as his favorite, about her health, the fits of coughing, more and more frequent, the little drops of blood that showed on her handkerchief after the crises, about her insomnia that not even the strong poppy tea was able to overcome, about the deep sadness caused her by the continuous and irremediable degradation of her lover and monarch. She saw herself in your eyes and knew that you understood her and pitied her. Despite her pride, she thanked you and showed her gratitude by way of that one tear that dimmed her eyes but that she had the control not to allow to fall. I'm never going to set foot in that accursed palace again . . . , you said to yourself that day. And you've kept your word, because now you're not at Versailles. Fortunately, you've been able to see your dear friend in her palace at Choissy, far away from all those good-for-nothings who upset her so, although close, alas! very close to death . . .

"So you're from the New World," Madame de Pompadour said. "Good heavens, that's a long way from here! I've read that it's very pretty, but to tell you the truth, it's very hard for me to imagine. Sometimes I feel that nothing except Paris and the surrounding countryside exist in the world . . ."

"Well, something else does exist, I assure you, madam. And in all truth they are magnificent lands, very different from Europe, no doubt, but magnificent," Mariana said with a certain pride.

"Do tell me about them."

"What can I tell you? They're enormous, and except for the center of the country, they're scarcely inhabited. One can travel for days, even weeks, on end without seeing a single stretch of cultivated land. There are very high mountains, and several of them have their summit covered with snow year-round." You observed that Mariana was growing excited as she talked; her cheeks were turning a bright red, and a bluish vein in her neck was throbbing. She really loves that country, you thought. "The climate is marvelous, warm without ever becoming suffocating. You can take my word for it that it's hotter in Madrid during the summer than in Mexico City. Winter, which is so terrible here, is perhaps the best time of year there, however, because it doesn't rain and the air takes on a delightful coolness that never, except very early in the morning, becomes truly cold. This very day, for example," she said, turning her eyes toward the huge fire in the fireplace that was barely able to heat the room, "if we were in the town where I was born, we would be talking together on the terrace dressed lightly, without capes or heavy coats, and we would see both green trees and trees that have dropped their leaves. Ah! and some enormous red flowers that open only during the winter."

"I can't believe it. A winter like that . . . Doesn't it ever rain there?"

"It certainly does! A great deal, but in the summer. And it rains, madam, in a way that I've never seen it rain here—as though the sky were falling all of a sudden. Enormous warm raindrops, one after the other, like a waterfall. And it can go on raining for three, four, even five days like that, to the point that it's hard to imagine how the sky can hold so much water. Then all of a sudden it stops, the sun shines brightly again, as though it had just been washed, and all the plants glow, as though they'd been dipped in a bath of gold."

"How lovely!"

"And so much . . . I could also tell you of the plants, the flowers, the animals that exist there, and it would seem as though I were telling you fantastic tales, believe me. The flowers, for instance"—now she was truly excited, as Jeanne-Antoinette noted, giving you a complicitous, pleasant look—"the variety of flowers that grow in my country is unimaginable. They don't have as strong a scent as the ones here, it's true. Their fragrance is much more discreet. My husband explained to me that this is because of the altitude, since as you know, madam, Mexico City is situated on an altiplane, high above sea level. That's why its climate is so pleasant even though it's located a great deal closer to the equator than any city in Europe. But the altitude produces a very subtle air, much more transparent, so to speak, than the air one breathes in this part of the world. For that reason the flowers are less fragrant, although for the same reason there are practically no consumptives there." Mariana felt a little sorry after uttering these last words. She realized that in all likelihood the Marquise de Pompadour was suffering from that terrible disease, but the latter, intelligent and tactful, allowed the remark to pass, pretending not to notice.

"Go on, my dear," she said to her.

"They have less fragrance," Mariana said to her. "But on the other hand, a great deal more variety. There is no color, from white to black, that cannot be found among our flowers. Their very names are a delight to one's ears: *cempaxuchitl* . . ."

"Cempa . . . what?" the marquise interrupted.

"*Cempaxuchitl.* It means 'countless flowers,' for the word *flower* was *xuchitl* in the old Mexican tongue and *cem* literally means 'four hundred,' and in the figurative sense, 'many, a great many.' They call this flower by that name because it has many petals. It resembles the carnation, but it's larger and a flaming yellow color. It's a sacred flower for the Indians; they use it in the offerings they make to their dead once a year. There is also a tree with a twisted trunk whose leaves are replaced during the month of November by enormous flowers, as white as cotton and soft textured, as though they were made of thin paper: *cazahuate,* they're called. There are *anacahuites,* in the form of a bell and with the color of an orange; the fragrant, velvety *curnito,* which is purple; the *flor de maravilla,* or 'wonder flower,' which opens only after dark; the *chilpantlazolli,* red and yellow, that cover enormous expanses of open countryside; and the *flor de fuego,* or 'fire flower,' which I mentioned to you before and which opens in December and January. It is enormous, the size of a large plate with its large flaming red petals and its yellow center; it is one of the most beautiful flowers. And what to tell you of the orchids that live as parasites on tropical trees? It's impossible to describe them, madam; only by seeing them can anyone believe that such marvels exist." Spurred on by her own words, by the images, so beloved and so far distant, that came to her mind as she described the delights of her land, Mariana spoke faster and faster and more and more enthusiastically. Somewhat drugged by her memories, her French, which was correct though stiff, made it harder and harder to express herself. Without her realizing it, Spanish words now and then replaced French terms she didn't remember or wasn't sure how to pronounce correctly. She spoke to the marquise of the maguey, a strange, pitiful-looking plant, able to give the Indians food, drink, roof thatching, clothing, and even medicine.

"That's not possible!" Jeanne-Antoinette exclaimed, obviously interested.

"But it is, my lady. Honey water, which is their name for the liquid they extract from the heart of that plant, besides being very tasty and nourishing, is the best remedy there is against stomach ailments . . ."

She told her of iguanas: "They look like a lizard or a chameleon, but they're the size of a dog and a yellowish green color."

"They sound awful!" the marquise interjected.

"They're not all that awful, madam. When one sees them for the first time, it's true that the creatures' ugliness is impressive, but when one gets to know them, one ends up having a high opinion of them. They're docile and shy. In addition, they keep the house clean and free of pests, for they devour any insects and other harmful vermin within their reach. They're an excellent food, besides. Their flesh is really delicious."

"Don't tell me that, Mariana. Eating a lizard? How disgusting!"

"With all due respect, madam, pigs and lobsters are in no way less ugly than iguanas and yet they're eaten with gusto. It's all a question of what a person is used to."

"That's true, my dear," the marquise said as she remembered the profound disgust she'd felt when she'd been served at table—she was barely twelve—a plate full of garden snails still in their shells, bathed in a thick reddish sauce, a dish that was now one of her favorites.

You listened, much engrossed, to Mariana, Rasero. Perhaps you felt a little jealous, since she had never talked to you of her country with such passion. Every new thing you heard, as now, when she referred to a magnificent bird with an enormous tail that for the ancient Mexicans "was a hundred times more valuable than if it were made of pure gold," was like a prick to your vanity, which had told you that, after being on familiar terms with this woman for almost three months, you knew her better than anybody else in the world did, better than her own mother who gave birth to her. You now realized that that was not true; your dear Jeanne-Antoinette had been capable of eliciting from Mariana a pleasant commentary about her Mexico, about which you knew almost nothing. You felt aggrieved, and a little stupid when you took note of your ridiculous jealousy. "Love is possessive, Fausto, terribly possessive . . . ," you remembered Diderot telling you on that long afternoon when he was on the point of being shipwrecked in a sea of alcohol and despair. "I can't exist without my Sophie. It torments me to think that she was born, that she has grown older, that she has lived far away from me for years, without my intervention, so to speak, and I am being driven mad by fits of jealousy, my powerlessness, my stupidity at letting my mind work in this way, but I can't help it . . ." You couldn't keep from smiling when you heard your friend, despite his lamentable situation. The smile was identical to the one on your face at this moment as you were thinking about those stupid jealousies and listening to your beloved woman speak of Mexican serpents. "There are as great a variety of them as there are of flowers," she was saying to the marquise, "beginning with certain thin ones, brightly colored in shades of red, yellow, and black, that are called coral snakes. They are timorous, ever so easily scared, but if for some reason they bite a person and inject their poison, there is no effective remedy: the unfortunate victim has no more than three hours to live . . ."

Just look at that face! Jeanne-Antoinette thought. Who could have imagined that Fausto had that in him? She had known him for almost twenty years and had never had the occasion to see any expression on that oval face, with its skin as smooth as an adolescent's; now, on the contrary, he was looking at this woman with the typical expression, the smile and the idiotic expression and all the rest, of a love-smitten man. But she understood it, and it made her happy. Really, Mariana was a very lovely and very likable woman; her appetite for life was contagious. She had even made her forget for a time the wretched d'Argenson and his little friend who were coming close, very close, to taking her Louis away from her . . .

A little embarrassed by the enthusiasm she had shown, Mariana stopped talking, took a sip of tea, and turned her eyes toward the portrait of Alexandrine. She had been surprised at herself as she heard herself talking about her country with such fervor. Up until then, she had avoided remembering it. She had never even wished to speak of it with Fausto. Every time the man questioned her about her homeland, she changed the subject and spoke of other things. The pain she felt when she called it to mind was still very sharp. Now, however, she was finally able to speak of it at length with pleasure, without feeling those pangs of nostalgia and rancor. I have found my country again, she thought with satisfaction.

"And what has been your impression of Paris, Mariana?"

"I must confess to you, madam, that the first days I was here I didn't like it at all. To tell you the truth, its climate makes me sad. It is painful to see the days go by with no chance of coming upon sunshine, just a gray sky and a soft, dreary rain. That weighed heavily on my heart. But Fausto has had the kindness—and the patience—to show me the city. Thanks to that, I've discovered many of its secrets and have become acquainted with the enormous beauty and vitality hidden beneath this so conspicuously gloomy and somber sky. Paris is marvelous, or so I now think. Very different from my homeland—the two countries couldn't be more different—but Paris is as beautiful and as magical . . ."

Thanks to Fausto . . . , you thought. When she had been the one to show you Paris! You had been in this city for more than twenty years, and in barely two months you discovered that Paris was as unknown to you as those remote lands that Mariana talked of so enthusiastically. You remembered the first time you went out together. You were very nervous, waiting in a little drawing room of the Gramonts' town house, where Mariana was staying. The memory of the night before, when you saw the woman for the first time, just as the concert of the Austrian child prodigy was ending, was still fresh in your mind. (Yet saying that you saw her for the first time was not altogether accurate. You were certain that you had seen that woman before, although no matter how much you delved in your memory, you couldn't remember where. In some strange way, that woman brought back to your mind a dream or perhaps a prophetic vision.) In some way or other, Mariana's presence supplanted that of the Baroness de Hausset, whom you had watched all evening long, convinced that she would not be long in granting you her favors. (Incidentally, what had happened to her? Only now did you recall that you had arranged a rendezvous with that woman. That had been almost three months ago, and you hadn't even sent her a message to apologize. She must be furious—as though it mattered to you in the least.) From the very moment you saw Mariana, everything round about you—even that marvelous child—was effaced from your surroundings; there existed only that beautiful woman with the long, soft neck who wept with emotion as she tried to reach the little musician to kiss him on the cheeks out of sheer pleasure. What happened from that moment on until you were finally able to speak with her was very confused. People were applauding, greeting each other, embracing each other. Leopold Mozart was happily signing copies of his books; Denis was speaking without pausing for breath with Sophie, Philidor, and you about the grandeur of that little boy. You weren't listening to him, you were nodding like an automaton as your eyes remained riveted on that unknown woman. You saw with genuine consternation how she left the hall accompanied by a gentleman and various ladies. "What did you think of the interpretation of Duport, Fausto? You've never heard it performed in that way, have you?" Denis asked you. You looked him in the eye for a moment trying to understand his question and then, as though someone were leading you by the legs, you headed in great strides toward the door. Diderot smiled and let Philidor answer his question. Passing over the threshold, you stumbled upon

David Hume's bulky anatomy. "Fausto, my friend, what a splendid concert!" he said to you happily. You didn't answer, for your eyes were searching for that woman. You didn't see her anywhere. Desperate, you were about to start running toward the street to peer, if necessary, inside each of the many carriages awaiting their owners. At that moment, Hume grabbed you by the shoulder to stop you. "Wait, Fausto. What's your hurry? I want to introduce you to a lady from your country." Annoyed, you turned your head. A quick greeting and then I'll excuse myself, you thought. With enormous surprise you discovered that the woman David Hume wanted to meet you was none other than she. How did she get here? Why didn't I see her before? you asked yourself pleased, thinking, moreover, of how the Scottish philosopher was beginning to pay you back with interest the favor you had done him in getting him out of the clutches of the ambassador before the concert began. "Fausto, allow me to introduce to you doña Mariana Rodríguez, the marquise de las Amarillas. A charming woman." Mariana: it was the first time you'd heard her name, pronounced with the Scotsman's peculiar burr. "Madam, Marquis don Fausto Rasero."

As you kissed her hand—which, had you been able to, you would have devoured—you heard, "Fausto Rasero: you must be related to don José de Gálvez, if I'm not mistaken?"

"He is my cousin, madam."

"Ah! I'm meeting you at last. If you are José's cousin, you are already my friend. You may believe me when I say that don José is a wonderful person."

"I believe it indeed, madam."

"He suggested that I meet you. In addition, he entrusted me with some correspondence for you. I'll be happy to send it to you if you'll tell me where to address it."

"Certainly not, madam. I shall be happy to come get it wherever you say. So you are Spanish?" you asked her in your native tongue with the hope of prolonging the conversation, for now that you had her before you, you were even more fearful of losing her.

"Not exactly. I am from the American colonies." A Creole, you thought. What a big world it is, and what a small one. ". . . But I've been living in Madrid for three years. And now I've made it away to Paris in order to see this prodigy. It was truly worth the effort. He's a marvelous child, don't you think?"

"Of course." You were nervous; it was hard for you to get a word out. The more you feared not being able to do so, the less able you were. You'd never before experienced that feeling of stupidity. The same thing happened to Mariana; the presence of this man unnerved her. But unlike Rasero, who felt a knot in his throat and could barely utter a word, she, in her nervousness, began instead a rather incoherent speech, one word following another in a rush that made practically no sense. She too had no wish to end the conversation. "Even though the price of seeing this child is heavy, since Paris, sir, has such a horrible climate! I've been numb from the cold ever since I arrived. I don't understand how there can be trees in this city. On first sight, it seemed as though the only thing that could grow in this soil, so cold and damp, was mushrooms. Of course, I'd heard many good things about Paris, though I don't believe that I am going to be able to enjoy them. Look how vapor is coming out of our mouths right this minute as we talk. One really has to take great pains just not to freeze to death. I should have come in the summer; perhaps if I had, I would have been able to enjoy this city a little . . ."

"It's not completely bad, madam. Anyway, the worst of winter hasn't come yet . . ."

"How dreadful!"

"Look, as the adoptive Parisian that I am, I must do something to mend the ugly image you have of the city. Allow me to be so bold as to invite you to become acquainted with it. You won't regret it."

"With great pleasure, sir. Though I warn you that I'm not certain I shall be very pleasant company: I don't see a way to shake off the cold that has settled in my body ever since I arrived."

"We'll search for a way, madam," you answered with a smile.

She finally arrived in the drawing room. She was dressed in a pretty white dress. If you had thought her beautiful when you saw her yesterday, today she was dazzling. Your throat clogged up again when you tried to speak. A man forty years old as timid as a Piarist monk! you thought. So this is what love is like. Truly curious.

"I'm ready, sir."

"Doña Mariana, you look splendid," you said, genuinely moved. As though the sky had heard the Creole woman's complaints, that autumn morning could not have been more pleasant. The clouds went away and finally allowed the sun to appear; a bright yellow, it bathed the entire city in a warm, gentle light. When the two of you went out into the street, Mariana, in a happy mood, stretched her arms out to greet it.

"There's nothing more beautiful than the sun," she exclaimed joyfully. You did not go very far. You thought that the best place to begin to know Paris was the Ile de la Cité, which in fact had been the original city. You stopped at Notre Dame, in front of the great facade with its three enormous doors with pointed arches, topped with the twenty-eight saints marvelously carved in gray stone, who for more than six hundred years had serenely held up the second level with its windows also topped by ogival arches and the rose window imposing and radiant in the center. Mariana turned her neck around as far as it would go so that her eyes would also take in the two huge towers, square and massive, that seemed to float above the very delicate pilasters that appeared to support them. Her attention was attracted by the exquisite way in which each stone had been worked. The adornments, discreet and faultless, enveloped the imposing edifice in their beauty. "Even the capitals the highest up are decorated," she said to you, "but they can barely be seen."

"It's so that the angels can see them," you answered with that phrase as well known to Parisians as the Seine. As Mariana contemplated the bas-reliefs on the main portal and tried, in vain, to take in all the details, the secrets they contained, you told her that that sober building had been begun in 1163 and had not been finished until 150 years later. Animated by that subject—the French Gothic—which had been of passionate interest to you for so long, you saw your shyness gradually vanish and your tongue emerge at last from its paralysis, to move happily and pronounce a long disquisition on the subject of that Paris of the Goths that existed more in your imagination than in reality, for there were few buildings dating from that period that had survived. "The origin of this city," you explained to her, "is lost in the shadows of time. It already existed in the Roman period, although it was nothing more than a little village inhabited by barbarians. Its grandeur began in the thirteenth century, when the decline of southern France began after Spain's great trade shifted to Italy and Holland and when the Capetians, after having conquered the powerful feudal lords of the center and the south of France, the Plantagenets, of Avignon and Poitou, decided to fortify themselves on this island, which in a short time became the capital of their kingdom, displacing its proud and, up until then, superior rival, the city of Orléans. An obligatory point of passage in transporting by river the merchandise destined for the commercial fairs of Champagne, Paris became a powerful trade center. On top of that, attracted by the king's power and the wealth that was increasing by the day, a great number of learned scholars and doctors of the church came to settle here, so that the city became a sort of Athens of the Christian world. So three great powers—political, economic, and cultural—were concentrated in one and the same place." You continued to speak to Mariana as you went up the steep staircase that led to the terraced roof of the cathedral. "Paris became the largest and most prosperous city of the Lower Middle Ages . . ." The sacristan listened to both of you with a smile on his face as he showed you the way with a lighted torch. That bald man's an amiable sort, he thought. He's come here so many times, and he always pays me the same generous bribe. He doesn't realize that I'd offer him a good discount. From the railing of the roof terrace, flanked by the two enormous towers that "were finished in 1230," as you explained, the view was magnificent. It was possible to see the great Ile de la Cité, with its silhouette of a boat run aground in the middle of the river, which, green and calm, flowed northward, like an enormous boa constrictor. "This island was the whole of Paris; everything else was swamps and tilled fields. For many years, enclosed within a wall, of which there are a few remains nearby—if you like, we can have a look at them later—the court, shops, and schools set themselves here. Right over there," you told her, pointing toward the end of the island, "where the city hall is now, was the king's palace. Alongside it, Saint Louis ordered the Sainte Chapelle built, which fortunately still stands. Behind it, where those old mansions can be seen, there was a hostel, the Hôtel Dieu, for lodging students who arrived from every corner of the globe to learn from the Parisian teachers. The king defrayed their expenses. For a great many years there were always at least eighteen students at the Hôtel who were protected by the state. Ah, what days those were! . . ." Mariana looked at her companion out of the corner of her eye. His profile was fine and delicate, with a small straight nose; his eyes, a deep black, seemed to be seeing much farther than what they were focused on. They're seeing through time, she thought. "Although, of course, this island soon turned out to be too small for a dynamic city. It began to spread out toward the Right Bank . . . over there . . . above all after 1180, when Philip Augustus expelled the Jews from the Cité. They then established themselves on that bank and, by dint of hard labor, drained the swamps and set up their businesses. In a short time their quarter became a commercial area, the Ville, more important than the Cité itself. Paris spread out in all directions from the Grand Pont. The kings themselves had another palace built off the island, the Louvre, which fortunately still exists, although it has undergone many changes. It's that building over there . . . ," you said, pointing toward two o'clock on a dial.

"It's huge!" Mariana commented.

"It wasn't that big in the beginning, of course, and it mustn't be confused with the farthest end of the building, which isn't part of the Louvre but is the Tuileries. That building was erected barely a century ago . . . There behind it, though from here we can't see it, the Temple was constructed, the place where the kings kept their riches. Farther in the background, where those old houses with the lead roofs can be seen, was the Innocents, which marked the outer limit of the city. Just to our right is the Grève, which at that time was an enormous warehouse where all the merchandise that went to or came from Champagne had to pay customs duties. After a while the Left Bank too, which up until then had been cultivated fields around Saint-Germain-des-Prés, right over there, gradually became populated. Many tradesmen went over to that side of the river, especially those whose activities were bothersome and unhealthy for their neighbors, such as butchers, tanners, rope makers, and many others that can still be found working there. But not furriers. In the last days of the reign of Louis XIV, they went much farther away, to an island that's on the outskirts of Paris. It was a very sensible move, because the stench that their work gives off is intolerable. Much the same change occurred with regard to the schools. They came to have so many men and women students that there was literally no room for them on the Cité, so they moved to the Left Bank, around Sainte-Geneviève. I think that, in proportion to the inhabitants, Paris has never again had as many schools. Did you know that they date from the thirteenth century and that the first bookstores came from here, from Paris? People came from all over to buy manuscripts in shops that specialized in selling them. Two centuries before printing was invented, there were already numerous bookstores here . . . It seems unbelievable!" Of course, Mariana did not know that—neither that nor so many of the other things that that strange man was telling her. She admired his erudition. It sounded odd to her and even amusing to hear things such as, "But the one who founded a great school, a school that made Paris famous all over the world, was a friend of Saint Louis', Robert de Sorbonne, who made his name more renowned than that of many kings. His school excelled in theological studies and attracted all the finest minds of Europe. But he had to get around certain problems, especially the enmity of the Parisian bourgeois, who saw with mistrust how that school attracted its best men. In order to defend it from them, the teachers, the graduates, and the king's men formed a defensive fraternity, a 'conjuration,' as they said in those days. In 1208, they gave the name *university* to this conjuration, and ever since that time all higher centers of education in the world have been called universities." He told her too how "faculties have been known by that name since 1219, the date when it was agreed to separate the teaching of the four basic branches of knowledge: the arts, law, medicine, and theology, of course, the queen of any curriculum . . ."

"And the woods that can be seen in the distance?" Mariana asked, pointing straight ahead.

"Ah! That's the Champ-de-Mars. There's a great military school there, although in those days it was only a forest on the outskirts of Paris." As you said this last, you realized that for a long time you had been showing Mariana a city that did not exist. Enough of your lectures, you said to yourself. Show her the Paris of the eighteenth century.

You left the cathedral and headed for the Tuileries. You went through the lovely gardens designed by Le Nôtre, although Mariana did not appear to be overly impressed by them. On the other hand, she liked the Place du Roi very much, with its beautiful equestrian statue of Louis XV—still of plaster, since in those days Gabriel was supervising the casting of it in bronze—and the four virtues watching over it. You recited to the woman the ingenious epigram that the people of Paris, inspired by this square, had made up: "Grotesque monument, infamous pedestal; / The virtues on foot and vice on horseback."

She thought it very amusing. What upset her, however, were the cruel jokes that, also inspired by the statues and a thousand other pretexts, popular wit had inflicted on the Marquise de Pompadour. "You wouldn't believe how many scurrilous pamphlets have come my way in the few days that I've been here. I don't think she deserves it," Mariana said. "Admittedly, I don't know that woman, but the little I've learned about her pleases me."

"I for my part have the pleasure of knowing her, and I can tell you that you're not mistaken. She's an extraordinary woman," you replied.

You walked down the Allée des Orangers in the rue St-Honoré, you visited the Opéra and ate in a small café near the gates of the Palais Royal. Tomorrow I'll take her to the Champ-de-Mars and the Jardin d'Histoire Naturelle, you thought. With a certain embarrassment you realized that that was all that you could show her of Paris, because really it was the only thing you knew. You'd lived twenty years in this city, and you'd never left that narrow ambit! Your curiosity was focused on the past; you'd never paid the present much attention. When you returned, you went through a poor neighborhood near the Pont Neuf. It consisted of countless narrow back streets, badly paved. There were many shops, modest ones of course, and even more taverns.

"Fausto," Mariana said to you, "could we stop here for a while? I like this neighborhood. It reminds me of the little back lanes of Dolores in Mexico City." You sat down, feeling a little anxiety: dusk was falling, and it was not at all safe to venture into this neighborhood, particularly as elegantly dressed as you were. Mariana in delight began to go down the narrow alleyways. You looked around in all directions, fearful of being assaulted. Every so often you looked behind you to see if your coachman and his boy were following you. Reassured, you noted the presence of the burly man and the lad at a prudent distance. Mariana was holding a lively conversation with a woman selling roasted chestnuts who was sitting on a corner alongside her stove. The woman's head was covered with a heavy wool shawl, and she was speaking emphatically with the Creole. She gladly gave her a handful of chestnuts and roundly refused to accept payment for them. "Humble people are noble," Mariana said to him. "Sometimes I believe that they're much nobler than those who are supposedly so by birth."

"You find everything everywhere," you answered sententiously. The woman bade you farewell with affectionate gestures and tears in her eyes. "What did you say to her?" you asked Mariana. "Why are you so touched?"

"Poor thing. She's desperate. They conscripted her son and sent him to fight in Germany. That was three years ago, and she's had no news of him. She's convinced he's dead. I told her he wasn't, that her boy is very much alive, to have faith; I assured her that by Christmas she'll see him again."

"And why did you tell her that?"

"I don't know. But I'm certain that the boy will come back. Believe me, I didn't tell her that only to console her."

You walked a good while longer through narrow streets that became darker and gloomier. Mariana insisted on entering a cheap tavern to try the house wine. "Ah! I have to admit that French wine is excellent. Try it, Fausto, do."

You took a good swallow from the glass that the woman offered you. It really was good. It was a strong, rough wine but warm and pleasant. "I think it's time for us to leave, madam. It's getting dark, and this neighborhood is very dangerous at night, especially dressed as we are." Mariana agreed reluctantly. On the way back to the house where she was staying, you invited her to continue the outing the following day. She agreed with delight and even proposed to you that the two of you dress more inconspicuously so you could be more at ease in exploring the back streets of Paris, which "I'm really enthusiastic about."

The next day you went on with your outing, an outing that lasted more than two months, Rasero. In it you truly came to know the city you'd lived in for so long, but you especially came to know that marvelous woman. Dressed simply, you felt freer and more at ease, and as if by abandoning the formal way of dressing you had also renounced the rigid code of worldly etiquette in your behavior toward each other, you began to address each other in the familiar form. You explored the old city from one end to the other. You were as likely to stroll along the elegant rue St-Honoré, with its luxurious jewelry shops and exclusive fashion houses, as along the narrow back streets of Les Halles, where the fishwives prepared the fresh fish eaten all over the city. You visited the Saint-Antoine quarter, where the master carpenters and cabinetmakers turned out the stunningly handsome pieces of furniture whose style set the entire fashion of the day. Mariana observed attentively as a craftsman created curved forms from the large piece of wood revolving on his lathe. She bombarded him with questions, many of which seemed inconsequential to you at the beginning, though you later understood that you had no idea what the answers to them were, that they encompassed a knowledge you had long ignored, the knowledge of the everyday, by which almost everything that surrounds us is made, a knowledge you were contemptuous of, regarding it as inferior, absorbed as you were in unearthing the history of five centuries ago or in understanding the secret mechanisms whereby substances are composed and decomposed, or worse still, in making sense of that extensive succession of images you've recorded in your memorandum book and that tell mere fragments of a future you detest.

"How long do you leave the wood before you carve it?" Mariana was asking an elderly, gentle-mannered cabinetmaker.

"That depends on the wood, miss. Some of them, the most delicate ones, such as peach, have to be left to dry for several years at least. Pine can be used after six months, though it's advisable to allow it to dry for at least a year . . . ," the man answered as he rubbed a cloth soaked in aromatic varnish back and forth, again and again, over the highly polished surface of a commode.

You still had the penetrating and agreeable odor of the varnish lodged in your lungs when it began to be mingled with the unpleasant and pungent one of the glue that bookbinders employ to attach calfskin to the pieces of cardboard used to make book covers. Mariana looked with interest at the curious work tools of the binder, who, like the cabinetmaker, was patient and amiable. "How many folios can that knife cut through?" she asked, or then again, "How long do you leave them in the press?"—pointing to a bundle of books as tall as a person piled up in four rows, each with slabs of wood at the top and bottom, tied down firmly with two heavy chains. ". . . Two days, miss," the young man answered, without taking his eyes off his five apprentices, who, standing in front of a long table, were applying the boiling-hot glue to the calfskins with a little brush and then affixing them to the cardboard covers. In the back, a husky man was turning a screw on a threaded shaft to compress another bundle of books. Not without great effort, he managed to make the two ends of the chain meet and then fastened them together with an open link. Exhausted, he let go of the big wheel-like screw and, together with a young apprentice, moved the enormous bulk alongside the bundle they had seen before. The pile of books gave off a pleasant smell, a mixture of skin, cardboard, and glue. "That's how it's done, miss. They must be allowed to dry under much pressure, otherwise the covers will become warped and make the book look awful . . ." As Mariana went on nosing about, you thought, somewhat surprised, of the enormous work that lies behind a book, that object you hold in such high esteem, hoarding it like a miser. And that's only part of it, the last part, you said to yourself. First it must be printed, and even before that, the paper for it has to be made . . .

It didn't take long before you learned about the steps after the papermaking, for a few days later you visited a printshop located in your own town house, no less, in the basement. When you bought the building, the printer already had his shop set up there, and it wasn't hard to reach an agreement by which you continued to rent it to him. Monsieur Michel Gautier was a serious, hardworking man; he was your renter for more than twenty years, and never, even in the hardest times, did he fail to pay the rent on time. When he died, his son, whom you had known since he was a little boy, took over his father's business. He was doubtless much more ambitious and diligent that his sire, who had been satisfied to do simple work—calling cards, invitations, leaflets, little posters, and so on—since his printing press was very old and that was all it could handle. Even so, Monsieur Gautier could support his family and the three or four apprentices he always had in his workshop. And in addition he was able to save a few louis, because his son, Marcel, almost the moment he took over the business, had the money to buy a printing press that, although it was secondhand, was much more modern and much faster than the old-fashioned equipment his father had used, and would become, in time, the tireless press that reproduced the incendiary tracts of the men of the Revolution. (A likable lad, this Marcel . . . Who would ever imagine today, as you were exploring the dimly lit place with that splendid Creole lady, who in pleasure dilated her nostrils to take in the sweetish, faint, suggestive aroma of the ink, that this youngster, who treated his elderly father with such veneration and respect, would become the husband of your beloved Annette and the father of an extraordinary boy who, with the passage of the years, would become one of the lions of the Revolution of August 10, 1792—the faithful assistant of the eager Camille Desmoulins—dooming good Annette to become childless and a widow at one and the same time and almost to go mad, for she came very close to losing her mind because of that grievous event. Fortunately, she did not take complete leave of her senses and once again became the companion of her former employer, whose eyes she closed for the last time, having reached by then a ripe old age.) But today Marcel was still a shy boy who listened attentively to his father as he explained to Mariana how an alloy of lead and tin had to be melted together to form the type, and how ink had to be applied to the rolls of the press so that the printed letters were not too fat, "like blowflies," or too thin, "like spider legs," the good man said with a smile. Naturally, you had never visited the shop your renter ran. Though it was down below your house, it could have been in Siberia—that was how far removed it was from being of interest to you, you who so dearly loved books. Perhaps it was a bit painful to get to know Paris. It was painful because you also discovered your blindness to experience and your indolence. You could hardly understand how you had let forty years of your life go by without learning about so many things, and worse still, you were convinced that if you hadn't come across this woman, you would never have known about them.

You wouldn't have known about the windmills of Montmartre except for their outward appearance—their strange silhouettes with their enormous arms creaking when driven by the breeze. Up until then, those mills had reminded you only of Don Quixote. Deep down, you knew that they were really monsters in disguise or something of the sort. What had never crossed your mind—though you thought you knew it—was that they were used to turn dry grains of wheat into flour; of course, you had never in your life seen grains of wheat either. "What impressive force the wind can work itself up to!" Mariana said to you as you watched the enormous millstone grind the grains. You had taken her to Montmartre to view the city from the hills. You were convinced that the impressive sight would make a deep impression on your friend. But that wasn't what happened. Mariana contemplated the panorama for a short time. "It's quite grand . . . ," she said to you and immediately headed for one of the windmills, drawn by the mechanism she suspected was kept inside. "Let's see how they work," she said to you. "In Mexico there aren't any windmills, and the ones in Spain seem much cruder and heavier than these . . ." As you approached the mill, you tried to understand what sort of person this pretty Creole woman was who scorned the view of Paris—the most beautiful city in the world—and preferred instead to become acquainted with the workings of a windmill. (What you didn't know then, Rasero, was that Mariana was treasuring in her memory the sight of the Valley of Mexico when she saw it for the last time from the foot of the volcanoes that had to be crossed in order to reach the coast. The city, amid an enormous lake, surrounded by thickets of cypresses and *ahuehuetes,* boldly disclosed its huge buildings. Convents, churches, and palaces, made of stone the same deep color as aged wine, emerged, like very pretty mushrooms, between the houses, as white as milk, with roof tiles the color of fired clay, Mexican clay, Rasero, which has the color of the earth and sky as dusk falls and which gives off bright black glimmers where the torch pine that fired them stained them with their dark and pungent smoke. It's a city bounded by gardens located in the water, like huge barges, a city, Rasero, a great deal, a very great deal, more beautiful than this Paris—at least as seen from up high—which is too dark, too sad for the eyes of someone who has seen Anáhuac from the foot of Ixtaccíhuatl.) The miller, a little, nervous man, covered with flour from head to foot, looked like an elf just escaped from a story for children. He answered with the seriousness of a university student the many questions that Mariana asked him. "My flour," he said proudly, "is as white as snow; I sift it three times, and only the best bakers in the city buy it. Not even Gonesse' bread is as good as that made with my flour. If you don't believe me, go to the Marais; they sell it there . . ."

And, of course, you went to the Marais and to many other bread markets: the one of the Augustines, to Saint-Michel, to Maubert, to the ones in the Place du Carousel, to Les Botchers, and to the cemetery of Saint-Jean, where Gonesse' famous bread was sold, which, despite what the personable miller on Montmartre had told you, was the best in Paris: white, soft, baked to perfection. Every piece of that bread was a feast in itself. Not to mention Gonesse' rolls that had a little piece of chocolate inside. "They're marvelous," Mariana had to admit as she sampled one of them with delight. You also became acquainted with the big bread market at Les Halles. There enormous loaves of a dark and pliant bread, with a slightly acid flavor, were sold. It was the dark bread that most of the populace of Paris ate and on whose price and abundance the peacefulness of the kingdom depended, for humble people are prepared to put up with many shortages, to work from sunup to sundown for miserable wages, but they are not prepared to stop eating even though their only food is those loaves of black bread accompanied by cabbage and boiled potatoes. In times of scarcity, when the wheat harvests are not sufficient and bread is hoarded and the price goes up, enraged mobs attack the markets, the customs barriers at the gates of Paris, and even the big storehouses, in search of bread for their children. You have seen such uprisings several times, and you know the degree of ferocity that can be reached by those previously peaceable but ravenously hungry people who proliferated in the popular neighborhoods of Paris, working industriously, patiently, in a thousand and one crafts and labors that the inexhaustible curiosity of your friend allowed you to become acquainted with during those last three frantic, hallucinatory months . . .

As you listened to Mariana explain to the Marquise de Pompadour how in her country the staple of the diet of most people was a bread made of corn, which in no way resembled bread made from wheat, since it was "as thin as a plate and has an exquisite taste, much more flavorful than wheat bread," and how from the grains of that plant any number of dishes could be prepared—the mere names of which brought back to the marquise the memory of her readings as a child, full of legendary beings, indomitable dragons, wicked witches, and captive princesses—there came to your mind the endlessly varied images of that strange, almost fantastic Paris that you had discovered during those unforgettable outings . . .

You visited the Gobelin tapestry makers, responsible, refined men who did not conceal their pride at practicing such an esteemed craft, whose fame had spread throughout the world; the stonemasons of La Motte, who looked happy and satisfied. This was owed, Mariana affirmed, to the fact that they had not lacked for work lately. "Very much to the contrary, miss," she was told by a big, sturdy man so downright ugly that, curiously, his ugliness bordered on sweetness, "what's in short supply are men. There are day laborers and apprentices who arrive from the provinces and never lack work," since Paris in that period was undergoing a feverish construction boom. The old swamps and coppices that a short time before—you could still see them when you came to Paris—practically poked their noses as far as the Champs-Elysées, quickly disappeared, their space soon being occupied by elegant town houses that the rich, both the new and the old, built in order to enjoy residence at the same time in the city and in the countryside and thus to avail themselves of a nature that up until that time had been avoided but that Jean-Jacques Rousseau's clever pen painted in such vivid colors that it seduced a great many aristocrats and no fewer rich bourgeois. You met tradesmen from Saint-Denis, from the rue des Lombards, and from the rue des Gravilliers, prosperous and grasping men; tireless blacksmiths; pretty laundresses who pounded with vigor, and not without a certain gracefulness, huge sheets on the smooth stones along the banks of the Seine. You spoke with gendarmes and police—the best in the world, as Choiseul boasted. You met butchers, chimney sweeps, tavern keepers, footmen, milkmen, barge loaders, men delivering bread in their *plumes,* water vendors, shopkeepers, street musicians (violinists, guitarists, drummers, flutists, and even a player of an ancient horn without keys), florists, confectioners, locksmiths, town criers, hostlers, traveling companies of actors—at once pathetic and dignified—and seamstresses, workers from Saint-Martin and Saint-Denis, makers of glass, of fabrics, of tools . . .

You observed the delicate and precise work of the watchmakers of the Place Dauphine, who cursed their luck and their longtime Swiss competitors because they had managed to make movements and springs of an impossibly small size. "How do they do it?" an old watchmaker wondered, sincerely surprised on seeing the mechanism of a hunting-case watch he had just opened. "It seems like magic . . ." But the Paris watchmakers were able to create mechanisms that, although larger, no one, not even the ingenious Swiss, could equal for beauty and complexity. Mariana saw, for example, a tiny ballerina whirl round and round with mechanical grace—if such a thing is possible—to the rhythm of the little music box, and she couldn't help remembering that exquisite clock that the Marquis de las Amarillas had given her shortly after they were married. "Look, Mariana," the viceroy, impressed by it, said to her. "Isn't it precious? It's French. The man who sold it to me assured me that it had belonged to the Duke d'Orléans—as though that makes it more valuable! . . ." Meanwhile Mariana listened, enthralled, to the notes of a gay Baroque popular song that set the beat for a pair of dancers who tirelessly went round and round inside the bell jar. With the same pleasure—perhaps accompanied by a tinge of sadness you did not notice—she was now looking at that pretty object the watchmaker of the Place Dauphine was proudly showing her.

No, Rasero, you didn't believe that there was a single craft that had escaped the attention of this beautiful Creole who at this very moment was holding your beloved Jeanne-Antoinette spellbound with her stories about her country. Her conversation was so agreeable that every so often she managed to light up the Marquise de Pompadour's withered, sick face, allowing the last traces of her extraordinary beauty to appear. Her blue eyes sparkled as she listened to Mariana tell of the protocol of the viceroy's court, so rigorous, austere, and solemn that it seemed like something out of another century. The marquise could scarcely believe that the Spaniards were so conservative, so sanctimonious, so worshipful of God and of his mother that they wore strict mourning, as though a king had died, each year during all of Holy Week. "The city seems deserted," Mariana explained to her. "People leave their houses only to go to churches, where masses follow one upon the other like the beads of a necklace and vigil is kept for Jesus Christ as he lies stretched out, just after the descent from the cross. In certain churches they have very well carved and painted images, which a person could swear are alive—or rather, that they are images of a living man who has just died. I have known women"—whenever she spoke of the subject, there came to her mind the obese and unpleasant image of the Marquise de la Borda—"who didn't stop weeping all week long, as though their son had died. I swear . . ."

There was no workshop or studio that did not attract Mariana's curiosity, the way a magnet attracts iron. You spoke with the prostitutes who appear as dusk falls, like swallows who have lost their way, in the vicinity of the Palais Royal. Then you visited a workshop where candles were made: incredibly, you had never suspected what technique was used to get the tallow or the wax to stick to the wick, although you had read about this process in an article for the *Encyclopédie* that Denis had given to you to edit. The thing is that reading about it wasn't the same thing as seeing it. Not even the illustrations for the article allowed your imagination to grasp the real process that has nothing to do with how it's described in writing even when the writing deals with the same subject. That's how you learned about the world, Rasero: in books, disentangling it from between the letters and, alas! that's not how it is. Or at least not exactly. The whores of the Palais Royal, for instance, knew another world, knew of other kinds of tiredness, of other efforts, which they were pleased to describe to Mariana. Those women that you've used, in the unthinking way that at table one uses a knife or fork, so as to attain the pleasure of orgasm and then be sent to that odious future, those women were something more than implements, Rasero, they were beings who thought, who felt, who suffered, who knew a reality that you, an expert on the Middle Ages, didn't even suspect, just as you didn't suspect the knowledge that can be amassed by an armorer, who needs only to look with his expert eye at the barrel of a rifle to know whether the bullets that it spits out are aimed straight at their target, or by merely passing the tips of his fingers over the string of a crossbow will tell you without hesitation what its exact range is, just as you did not suspect the misfortunes, the vicissitudes, and anxieties endured by night watchmen as they engaged in their occupation, risking their lives, night after night, for miserable wages—all of which they related to Mariana in heartfelt terms, as though she were a royal functionary—nor the fatigue of the water vendors who looked so picturesque as they went about the streets carrying those enormous leather skins full of water. It was hard to imagine that those skins weighed more than eighty pounds, Rasero; it was hard to understand that there was so much stamina behind those colorful figures, a stamina also possessed by the rowers on the Seine, who tirelessly dipped deep down into the water again and again as you explained to Mariana, while you sat on soft cushions, what the oldest bridge in Paris is (which, curiously, is called the Pont Neuf) and when it was built. Nothing, no one escaped her. Not even the humble stable boys, who knew animals so well that a person could swear that they could talk with them. "This is a very noble animal, miss," an old, toothless coachman told Mariana, referring to a mule as far along in years as he was. "I can say that for certain, since I've reached such a ripe old age. Ah! miss, I've known very few persons who have even a little bit of the nobility of this mule . . ."

Not even the unbearable stench kept you from talking with a collector of human excrement. You came across him in one or another of the narrow back streets of the Saint-Antoine district. People turned aside the moment they saw the little old cart approaching, drawn by a fat donkey of the same color as the load it was pulling. "Wait! I want to talk with that man," Mariana said to you, pointing at the little figure of the excrement collector.

"For the love of heaven, woman," you protested firmly, "that man stinks like a thousand demons."

"Wait," she repeated without paying the slightest attention to you. She approached the excrement collector and had the strangest and most curious talk with him that you've ever heard with your own ears in your entire life. They spoke, of course, about shit. And it so happens that shit too bears with it its special knowledge, which, generously, the little man proceeded to pass on to the Creole.

"No, it's not all the same, miss," he said to her very seriously. "The price of the load depends on where it comes from. The excrement from a first floor is worth much more than that from a fourth floor, for instance. It comes from better-fed people, their waste matter is heavier, it enriches the fields far more . . ."

However incredible it may seem, shit too costs money. "So you pay for it then?" Mariana asked in surprise, for such a possibility had never occurred to her. She had often seen the barges full of dung in the canals of Mexico City, whose load she knew would end up in the floating fruit and flower gardens of Chalco and Xochimilco, but it had never crossed her mind that they paid for it. And if they did so here, then surely they did in Mexico City as well. Because if something had become clear to her at the end of these two months in which she had been able to become acquainted with this beautiful city, it was that more or less the same thing existed everywhere; certain customs, certain traditions, certain details varied, but in essence the bustle of life in all cities was identical. "And if you didn't want to pay, what would people do with their excrement?"

"Oh my, miss! You have no idea how many others would buy it. There's more competition all the time . . ." So that shit was valuable, and people even fought for it. A curious world. "Yes, miss. You get to have an educated sense of smell, and it's not easy to pull the wool over my eyes: I can tell right away who ate rice and is trying to convince me that he ate meat. It's not easy to hoodwink me. There are shit collectors who taste it, but I don't need to do that; my sense of smell is enough. Besides, when I've actually tasted it, I've got sick. It takes a strong stomach to put it in your mouth, believe me! . . ."

Even rich people's shit is more valuable, Rasero! Not even their excrement makes men equal, not even their shit. Only death—that's the only thing capable of making us all equal. What would Voltaire say if he were to scrutinize what you're thinking? He, so terrified of death, would immediately reject, in indignation, the thought that's forming in your head as there parade past inside it hundreds, thousands of images, of faces of this good, humble people of Paris whom you've just discovered and as you sadly contemplate the withered face of your dear Jeanne-Antoinette that tells you with resignation of the imminent end of her life: Death is a blessing, the only real act of justice that God—if he in fact exists—accords to men. Death awakens us from that presumptuous dream which life is, in which we act as though we are eternal, as though we are different, as though we have the right—the same right that kings claim, "divine right" they call it—to feel ourselves superior to other men, who for that very reason, because they are deemed to be inferior, are obliged to serve us, to wait on us, to carry out the thousand and one labors that mold our lives, lives of men like you, Rasero, rich and indolent, to make them pleasant, so that we do not lack a good wine on our table, warm covers on our bed, a candle to light the darkness, a book to relieve our idleness, or a toilet for our buttocks to sit on in order to evacuate our shit, our shit, Rasero, which, of course, is much more valuable, "worth at least four sols more, miss," much more valuable, than the poor excrement of those starving slaves that we've condemned to wait on us, to work like swarms of industrious bees so that Madame de Stainville can show off her finest dresses before the envious gaze of Mademoiselle de Marigny and smugly listen to the piquant remarks of the Duke de Luynes, a sybarite more exquisite and useless than anyone else in this world: "Darling, I swear to you that I can see the expression on the face of that imbecile Jeanne-Sophie when you arrive at her mansion. Shocking! Poor thing, she's uglier than a spider. Ah! my girl, even if she were decked out in diamonds, she'd look like a broken glass . . ." Tireless ants that build our houses, adorn it with handmade furniture, harvest our food—thanks to them, to those tiny ants, you can sit in a café to discuss with your illustrious friends the problems that are swooping down on the kingdom, to discuss ideas that were first conceived countless centuries ago and that return again and again, elaborated and torn apart and again elaborated in our minds, whereupon they pass fluently down to our mouths, make our tongues wag, and emerge resoundingly, as if they had been just discovered: "All men are equal," we say, or else, "Selfishness is innate in humankind," or, "Reason has always fought against superstition and ignorance. Reason makes us human, ignorance animals." Whole endlessly long discourses, tireless devourers of pages, impassioned, brilliant, the secret props of our self-complacency, we repeat such notions again and again, feeling the gratification of the onanist, because however often we repeat them, the enjoyment it brings us to know that we are rational and wise is always the same: a warm, intimate, delightful pleasure at feeling ourselves just a little superior to an industrious bee.

But death makes us equal. You realized this on that morning, just a few days ago, when you visited the catacombs beneath the cemetery of Montparnasse. Hundreds, thousands of skeletons, of human skulls looked at you from dark hollows without eyes, with their horrible, grimacing, indifferent smile. There they were all equal, round-shaped pieces of calcium, all smiling and distant, stripped of their flesh and, above all, of the breath that once made them live. Mariana talked to you of a city in New Spain. She told you its name, an odd name you no longer recall, and she also told you that there the dead do not decompose, or at least not enough to turn them into bones. They keep their withered flesh, "frightful, believe me," because of heaven only knows what properties of the earth that shrouds them. "There the earth does by itself what took the Egyptians so much work," Mariana said to you with a smile, although you didn't pay much attention to her: keeping you from hearing your friend was that impressive parade of death, those skulls, so serene, lined up like a well-disciplined army, that smell of damp earth, that lugubrious and eloquent vision of nothingness—showing itself shamelessly, gnawed by rats, with its bared teeth, with its mute smile, as if it were happy to have vanquished time, to have succeeded in being indifferent to whether the hands of a clock moved to the right or to the left or whether the water in a clepsydra went up or down. Death, like an utterly just *rasero*—a leveling stick—is like a mushroom in the woods, Rasero: water, yearning, causes it to spring up and grow, and then to die when the water, when the yearning, begins to grow scarce. Implacable death, death the equalizer, there it is, sketched in the face of your dear friend. In that same face where many years ago you encountered life, young and fresh and strong, the mere sight of which was enough to banish from your senses the frightful images that devastated your mind, there it is, crouching behind those beautiful eyes that try so hard to go on gleaming, to trap a little of the enormous strength that in other days nourished that ambitious and prodigal, gentle and energetic, astute and sentimental, noble and selfish creature, the Marquise de Pompadour . . .

". . . a great deal, madam. The actors are stupendous and the stage sets couldn't be better. We saw a Molière comedy and several others by modern authors. Comparing them becomes inevitable, and I greatly fear that here in France the same thing is happening as in Spain: modern authors are not even the shadow of what those of the past century were. They repeat with little inventiveness the same plots, and except for the stage effects, which are dazzling, their works are thoroughly mediocre . . ."

They were now talking about the theater. Jeanne-Antoinette unquestionably displayed exquisite manners toward a person when the person pleased her. She knew how to listen patiently; she showed her approval with a soft smile when she heard something clever; she never interrupted, and very often she summed up in a felicitous phrase the idea that the one with whom she was speaking couldn't quite put into words. She was very different when she did not find a person to her liking. She listened coldly, distantly, subtly showing indifference and sometimes even scorn. You could almost still see her, nearly twenty years before, extremely pretty, dressed like a queen, sitting in a box at the Opéra, conversing with, or rather, listening without interest to, the Duke de Richelieu, who was spending his magazine of ingenious phrases—quite a well-stocked one, incidentally—in his attempt to please this beautiful woman who was undoubtedly aiming at becoming the new favorite. But he did not succeed: Jeanne-Antoinette, looking at him without seeing him, barely hid her weariness of him, going to the length of concealing—or pretending to conceal, since everyone saw it—a yawn behind her fan. It was difficult for Richelieu to contain his irritation, but he made one last effort. Knowing the passion that the young bourgeoise had for the theater, he said in a very loud, solemn voice, "Madam, theater is the passion of my life."

"My dear duke," the woman replied, "I would say, rather, that the theater *is* your life . . . ," and beamed a charming smile at him. The duke could no longer suppress his anger, nor the rest of those present—you included—the laughter that came to their lips. Only Jeanne-Antoinette remained aloof, indifferent, as though those around her were speaking a language she didn't understand. That night she sealed a pact of enmity with the duke that has lasted all these years. Richelieu, faithful to his rancors though never faithful to anything else, had not rested for a single day since then in his vain attempt to destroy his enemy. He had not succeeded in doing so, yet on the other hand he had managed to harass her, to torment her, forcing her to be ever on the defensive, tense, fearful of falling into one or another of the many traps he had set for her. Richelieu had not succeeded in separating that woman and the king, but on the other hand—and the accursed obese duke must have been very proud of the deed—he had succeeded, through his continued hounding, in driving his enemy's good health away.

". . . Do you know Antonio de Zamora? There can be no better example of what I'm saying. The very least he brings onstage is a coach drawn by two horses. If not that, it's enormous towers that burn down with real fire or rivers with running water or little angels that descend from the sky or devils that disappear before our eyes behind a column of smoke. His staging is really impressive. But with such commotion, such stupendous effects, his real achievement is to distract the audience to the point that it doesn't listen attentively to the lines, which, you can take my word for it, are lamentable. Forced rhymes, commonplaces, extremely poor dialogues . . . it's embarrassing to hear them. The one richness in his works is in the stage effects, and in my opinion that is not what theater is or ought to be . . ."

In addition to that exquisite manner of dealing with people, there was no denying that Jeanne-Antoinette possessed excellent insight. She had guided the conversation toward subjects that made Mariana wax enthusiastic. First she had had her talk about her country, and you yourself were surprised by the fervor and the affection with which Mariana expressed herself concerning it. Now she had led the conversation to the theater, a subject—as you knew very well—that was of passionate interest to the Creole. You had discovered that only a few days before . . .

You were in the Café Procope, taking time out to rest, for you had gone on a long excursion though the neighborhood of Les Halles. Mariana amused herself watching the people who lived there, while your attention was absorbed by her. You felt, your pleasure mingled with fear, how that woman was gradually becoming an intimate part of your life, how she was banishing that anxiety, the profound grief you felt as you listened to the music of the child prodigy, how she had little by little been filling that unbearable emptiness that assailed you that night, that same night you met her. You hadn't touched her yet, you hadn't yet placed your lips on that long, delicate neck which you knew contained a fragrance of flowers, of fresh woods, of a woman's flesh at its prime; you had not yet kissed those cool, barely moistened lips, that kept watch over the most beautiful teeth you had ever seen in your life; you had not yet savored that fresh, agile tongue that happily moved about to form a thousand and one ingenious, pleasant words; you had not yet bitten those firm, proud breasts, covered with a skin that glistened like dew; you had not yet penetrated that sex which—it could not be otherwise—was the entrance and the exit, the end and the beginning, of your existence; you had not yet made that woman yours, and already you were so enthralled by her that you could not imagine yourself without her company. Desire had never been so devastating to you. You could scarcely restrain yourself; you could barely contain the longing that impelled you to fling yourself into the arms of the Creole, to intertwine your body and hers and be commingled with it once and forever. Mariana noted the twitching of a nerve in your cheek, a twitching that mounted to your temple. She had already learned to read it as a symptom that something was upsetting you.

"What's the trouble, Fausto?"

"The trouble is that you're the most beautiful woman I've ever seen in my life," you answered, relieved at allowing your words at least to caress the woman.

"Body full of truths / yours is rightfully called / for not a single truth escapes it / though every possible lie comes forth from it," she said to you, smiling.

Her answer disconcerted you. This was the second or third time that she had answered you in verse. Just yesterday, when she suggested going to Saint-Marcel to see how tanners did their work and you hesitated and then proposed that you wait instead for the Museum of Natural History to open—in all truth, you didn't want to go to Saint-Marcel, the legendary stench of that neighborhood (which, of course, you were not acquainted with) not attracting you at all—Mariana, seeing you hesitate, said, "You are hesitating a long time, my hope grows fearful, for procrastinating is a form of saying no." Her speaking to you in verse intrigued you a little, but you let it pass and, acceding, ordered the coachman to go to the stinking neighborhood.

"What does what you said to me mean?"

"It means you're a liar. There are many women in Paris more beautiful than I am."

"No. What I mean is, Why did you answer me with a poem?"

"It's an old habit . . ."

It was a habit she had lost a long time before, and it surprised her too to have taken it up again. In fact, it had begun as a sort of mnemonic exercise to fix in her memory the dialogue of the plays she was going to interpret on the stage. After a time, she developed an unusual ability to intercalate into her conversations fragments of the dialogues of the text that she was studying. She used them sometimes to ask a question, sometimes to answer one, or else to complete a sentence that she had said or heard. This talent of his wife's delighted the Marquis de las Amarillas. It was a sign of impishness and cleverness, he told her and encouraged her to keep it up, to which end he often brought about in their conversation situations that would enable her to insert exactly the right fragment of one of the speeches of Juan Ruiz, Calderón, Tirso, or another of the great dramatists. Since the death of the marquis, Mariana had stopped doing that. She was in no mood for clever wordplay, much less for joking. Up until now, she had believed that her happiness was as dead and buried as her late husband; she had resigned herself to live accompanied by a perennial sadness, sweetened at times with pleasant memories but almost always embittered by a profound nostalgia. The happy images that came to her mind from time to time, such as those in which she was a little girl playing with her old china doll in the patio of the mansion in Taxco shaded by the bougainvilleas and the ivy that climbed up the old columns of quarrystone, with the constant murmur of the stream flowing from the spring, and the cheery warbling of the canaries—her mother had had a real passion for them—that flitted restlessly from one end of their cages to another calling with sweet songs to the females or with threatening trills to other males, were immediately, almost the moment that they began to delight her, blotted out by the frightful image of the marquis floating facedown in the pond, surrounded by a sea of green lilies, brilliant and crested with their blue flowers, and terribly indifferent. Much the same happened when she remembered the happy occasion in the girls' school of the sisterhood of Mary when a stern jury chose her poem from more than two hundred as the winner of the contest that was held each year in the school and that, on this particular occasion, was doubly important, since the winning poem was to be read before the viceroy on the occasion of the ceremonies to inaugurate the hospital for the poor that the sisters of Mary had built for the city. Mariana, very young, standing in the middle of the patio, with the sun beating down on her shoulders, was thankful for the ample skirts of the pretty blue dress that doña Angelina Bassoco had had made to order for her for such a solemn occasion, for they hid the violent trembling of her legs that was so intense she could barely remain standing. She felt the penetrating looks of her schoolmates, of the nuns and the priests all around the patio, but above all of the viceroy and his court, who were seated on a high dais in front of her. It was the first time in her life that she had seen the Marquis de las Amarillas, and she was especially pleased by the fine manners of that mature man, the soft and even sad look in his eyes, and even more, the serene and understanding smile that formed on his lips when he noted the nervousness that was consuming the delightful fifteen-year-old girl. The viceroy's smile calmed her and gave her the courage to begin reading her poem. Absorbed in the sheet of paper trembling in her fingers, she finally began:

> It was God's will, beneath this limpid sky
> to place innumerable goods . . .

But at this point, the poem and her memory irremediably changed:

> The jasmine bursts into bloom
> and with beautiful Flora and her garland
> the woods are crowned and enhanced . . .

Mariana read, and the marquis, with his old and affable face illuminated by the reddish glow of the fire, closed his eyes to re-create in his mind the images heard a thousand times, evoked a thousand times, of the poet Balbuena, his favorite writer. As dusk fell, they sat on either side of the fireplace to rest from the tiring events of the day and allow all the verses of that Castilian poet—who, like the viceroy himself, had fallen in love with the territory called Mexico—to lull them like the song of an affectionate nursemaid. Hence, what had begun as a happy, strengthening memory, ended with a sad recollection, full of nostalgia. This had been happening to her for the last three years, and she had now become accustomed to it. Mariana was trapped within her sadness as a philosopher is in his thought, and she did not make the slightest effort to flail her way out of it. It was only with difficulty that she was convinced by the repeated pleas of her uncle Hernando and the lawyer José de Gálvez to take advantage of the opportunity to hear in Paris that Austrian child whose fame had already spread all over Europe. "A change of air will do you good, darling," said her uncle, sincerely worried over how the young widow was consumed by melancholy. "Moreover, Madame de Gramont is a magnificent person, you'll see. In the last letter she sent me, she tells me she is eager to meet you, to show you that city full of marvels. You'll see how happy you'll be in Paris . . ." And lo and behold, it was true! But it was not the dense and freezing air of Paris that banished sadness from Mariana's soul, nor Madame de Gramont, a wonderful woman as kind as they come, though too French—too frivolous and overconfident—and though the thought was painful, a bit too stupid to be able to cheer the soul of the Creole. It was, on the contrary, that youngster, that wan child with haughty manners and the look of a surgeon, who succeeded, with the magic that flowed from his hands, in awakening the enormous happiness lying in slumber in Mariana's spirit; he contrived to revive her sense of enjoyment, her delight in knowing that she was alive, in being young, in still being able to absorb happiness, pleasure. Mariana understood, as she allowed the chords of the music to penetrate her consciousness, that, like it or not, she was still alive, that her body and her soul rebelled against being precociously withered, victim of a selfish sadness, that she still wanted to enjoy, to be surprised at, to marvel at everything that life offers. No, she was not going to remain perpetually gloomy, sad, secluded. The vigorous blood that ran through her veins refused to tolerate that. How could she give up the good that existence might offer her when she had scarcely sampled it? How could she renounce love when she had scarcely had a taste of it, no more than a lightning-swift flash that fed her desire? That was why she cried that day. Tears flooded her eyes, although this was the first time in many a day that she was not weeping in sadness, that she was not weeping at the memory of the pathetic figure of the marquis floating in the pond. She was weeping out of happiness, as though the liquid that flowed from her eyes had first cleansed her brain, ridding it of the very last mote of dust of nostalgia, of the ugly refuse of self-pity. And for that reason too, because of the magic of that immortal child, she was able to notice that bald man who, like her, was also weeping, also removing the mold from his brain, also washing out his spirit. For that reason she had been able to notice him and, much more than that, she had been able to love him, she had been able to confer upon him that enormous accumulation of tenderness that she was hoarding like a miser in some dark corner of her soul. That was the reason she had been able to enjoy this city that was old, gray, freezing, but full of marvels, of simple and industrious creatures just the same as, just like, the ones that abounded in her beloved Mexico City. That was why she felt happy, and as before when she was so happy that she didn't even notice that she was, she began to use ingenious pet phrases in verse in her speech; she again took up that old habit that had so greatly pleased her late husband, that good man whom now—a tremendous joy—she recalled with loving sympathy, with affection, but no longer with sadness . . .

"It's an old habit. Because you surely must know, Fausto, that I was a great actress . . ."

She said that to you with a mocking gesture, and began to talk to you of the profound influence that poetry had exercised over her from the time she was a very little girl. As far back as the days in the convent in Taxco she had enjoyed enormously listening to Mother Amparo read, in her grave and well-modulated voice, the strikingly beautiful passages from the works of the poet Fray Luis de León, the amorous invocations of Saint John of the Cross to his God, the cruel paradoxes of Saint Teresa, the ingenious sonnets of Quevedo, and the diaphanous poetry, limpid as springwater, of the divine Lope de Vega. She found even more pleasure when she did her first composition exercises. She spent hours at a time absorbed in racking her brains to come across, in some corner of her head, the word, the phrase that would fit into the poem she was working on. Patiently, "as though I were a watchmaker in the Place Dauphine," she counted on her fingers the syllables that, obediently, formed simple verse with relative ease. "But major verse forms were something altogether different; the fiendishly difficult hendecasyllables slipped out of my hands like a fish just taken out of the water; now there were ten, now there were twelve of them, or worse still, when they came out at exactly eleven as they should, it turned out that the accent of the verse was oxytone or proparoxytone and I found I either had one syllable too few or one too many." But after a time she was well on her way to mastering words, and when she arrived in Mexico City, a little girl still, she already had in her repertory a goodly number of quatrains, octosyllabic stanzas and sonnets, ballads, madrigals, "which are very difficult, believe me," Christmas carols, and even two or three sonnets, "my greatest success." She also had with her "what I took the most pride in," a letter from the mother superior of the convent in Taxco, where she had gone to primary school, recommending her highly "as a willing, alert pupil and one with a great love for learning, especially those things having to do with the pen." The mother superior was earnest in her advice that anyone who continued to educate this child take great care to polish those qualities "that God, our Lord, has found fit to bestow generously upon this clever creature." And it was there, in the great city, that she discovered something that pleased her and impressed her even more than poetry: the theater. Though saying that it pleased her more than poetry was not altogether correct. In the final analysis, she maintained, the theater is a form of expressing poetry; it is a happy combination of the world of verses and of situations taken from life. The theater, so to speak, gives substance, a home and a form, to poetry. She spoke to you with enthusiasm of the theatrical company formed in Mexico City by a group of friends directed by Tomás Bassoco, a "very talented young man, who lived for nothing but literature and the theater . . ." The first role she played was that of Rosaura in *La vida es sueño.* "It was the greatest challenge I've ever faced in my life. I believed that it was going to drive me mad. I read the speeches once and a thousand times and was unable to fix in my memory even three words. The nervousness that got the better of me once Tomás had offered me the role was like a huge sponge: it absorbed everything that came into my head, leaving it emptier than a public square at midnight . . ." The rehearsals were even worse. They were a real disaster; her turn to recite invariably meant an interruption of the rehearsal. She began out of turn or spoke up too soon, cutting off the last words of her partner's speech, or else she waited seeming centuries as she worked up the courage to speak, searching fearfully in her memory for the dialogue, for she hesitated to begin until she was sure of remembering the words exactly. This took interminable lengths of time, while the other actors stood there waiting, making anxious gestures, as though they would have liked to wrest the words from her mouth once and for all. "I gave up several times. I told Tomás that it was useless, that he should look for another actress. But he reassured me: 'That happens to all of us,' he said to me. 'You're going to be surprised at how well you do.' And I really did do well . . ." Down to just a few minutes before the play began, she was certain that it would be a disaster. She felt that she had forgotten every bit of it, even its name. Standing in the wings, she did not move even her eyelids; she was convinced that her legs wouldn't obey her, "as though I were dead while still alive . . ." She listened as from a distance to the dialogues of the actors who were onstage and cursed herself for not being able to fall into a faint—the one expedient that would save her from the inevitable ridicule that awaited her. Finally her turn came. "My legs obeyed me, and my head responded too. It seems incredible, Fausto, but once I entered onstage, the speeches came to my mind, smooth flowing and exact—and not only my own: I remembered the whole play perfectly. I didn't look at the prompter even once. Everything was there, sharp and clear, as though I had the text inside my head. I believe that I worked so hard to memorize it that it was engraved there as with a red-hot brand. Even today—and keep in mind that all this was almost ten years ago—I remember the play from beginning to end, without a single word having escaped my memory. Our minds are very strange . . ." What she forgot at that point was all the anxieties and worries she had gone through; the enormous pleasure that acting was blotted them out completely. "The only thing I thought about was a new play. Of course, I never lost my nervousness completely, the terrible fear that comes over you when you're about to start performing your role, though I learned to control it . . ."

"Well then, if you're so fond of the theater," you said to her, "what would you say to our going to the Comédie Française on Friday? As a matter of fact, they're going to begin the season with a work by Molière—*L'Avare,* I believe. The company is excellent; it's really worth seeing them."

Mariana accepted with pleasure. You took advantage of her enthusiasm to invite her to dine at your house after the theater: you had finally resolved to ask her. "Denis says I have the best cook in France, and I think he's right. We'll see what you think of her . . ."

During the following three days, you were the one who behaved like a novice actor. You alternated outings with Mariana and preparations for the dinner. You had to make a great effort to hide the nervousness that consumed you as you explored the neighborhoods of Paris with that pretty woman. With poor Annette, on the other hand, you gave free rein to your anxiety. The moment you saw her, you bombarded her with repeated, stupid questions. You didn't want to think very much about it, but even so, something told you that you had never behaved so absurdly in your whole life. "Yes, don Fausto, I've ordered the mushrooms," Annette said to you, mustering all the patience she had. Had she not already noticed the feelings of her master toward that likable little Spanish lady, she would have felt very offended. Since when had don Fausto ever doubted her abilities? After all, she had been the one who put everything in order in that house which looked more like a tavern than a real home when she saw it for the first time. Wasn't she the one who had persuaded her master to buy some decent furniture, to hire a chambermaid and a footman? "Sir," she had said to him courageously, knowing it might cost her her job, "you give the impression of being a miser. A marquis cannot or ought not to live like a petty clerk. If you'll allow me, I can put this house in order." Fortunately, her master answered her with an amiable smile: "Do whatever you think best, Annette." And she certainly did just that! This house naturally isn't the Elysée Palace, but few town houses in Paris are as comfortable and pleasant as this one, Annette thought with satisfaction. And now he's coming round to ask me if I'm sure I've prepared the crepes properly, as though I hadn't made them countless times. But never mind: be patient. The poor thing has been pierced by love's darts, and between a man in love and a babe in arms there's no other difference than the beard that is still to crop out on the younger one's face. In any case, don Fausto deserves my patience and a great deal besides . . . I'm going to take greater care than ever. On Friday that woman is going to dine on exquisite dishes that only angels have tasted . . .

Nonetheless, on Friday, just before going to get Mariana, you made a last careful inspection of the house and you appeared—I think it was the first time you'd done so in your whole life—in the kitchen to see how the cooking was going. The exquisite aroma in the place reassured you; even so, you wanted to get a whiff of what was in a big cooking pot hanging above the stove, when Annette, frankly annoyed, spoke up: "Sir, for the love of God, get out of here, or I swear to you that I'll burn the dinner . . ."

"All right, Annette, I'm going. But are you certain that . . . ?"

"Clear out of here, for heaven's sake!" she said to you, almost shouting, and you didn't dare say anything back.

The theater was completely full. There is no denying that Parisians are never going to be bored by their beloved Molière. Onstage, amid splendid sets, the actors took scrupulous care in interpreting their roles. They seemed just a little stiff—that almost always happens on the first night of performances—as though they were taking such pains to do things well that, despite their success in achieving what they sought, they sacrificed just a little of their spontaneity. You hardly noticed it, however; to you, the spectacle was at your side and not in front of you, and that was the way you kept your head turned during the two hours that the performance lasted. You had never seen Mariana look so beautiful. The blue silk dress seemed to have been painted on her body, as though she had been born wearing it. (Finally she's made up her mind to wear the blue dress, Jacinta thought happily when Mariana asked her to bring it out. It was no doubt the prettiest dress she had and the one that looked best on her, although her mistress had never made up her mind to wear it. When she tried it on, it pleased her very much, of course. She couldn't deny that it was a marvelous fit. But when she saw herself in the mirror, with the close-fitting sleeves and the tightly cinched waist and, above all, with that very low-cut neckline that allowed her firm breasts to show, she felt embarrassed. The dress was too daring, too French for her, and even though she had seen many Parisian ladies shamelessly wear décolletés like that or some even more daring—many of the women showing flaccid, withered breasts, yet as proud of them as if they were fresh, firm flesh—she was never going to dare to show off her body so brazenly. But that night she decided to do so, sheepish and happy at the same time but, above all, ready to please the Malagan. I've changed more in a couple of months than I did in three years, she said to herself as Jacinta buttoned the last buttons down the back.) Her hair, caught up in a tall coiffure dotted with little wild flowers, bared her long neck, which three or four rebellious curls made even more delectable. As though she wanted to show clearly that she was from the New World, Mariana did not adorn her neck, ears, wrists, or hands with gold jewelry and precious stones, as was the fashion among Parisian ladies. Her jewelry was all silver. Her earrings were hoops, from which large, whimsical little ribbons of metal dangled. Solid bracelets with little opals set in the silver adorned her wrists, and around her neck was a heavy chain from which hung a locket of Moorish filigree work, resting placidly in the cleft between her breasts.

The dialogue of the actors, the laughter of the audience, the chords of the music reached your ears as if from a distance, as if coming from a dream. Your five senses—and even more if you had them—were absorbed in the being at your side. You saw that profile, with the smooth, slightly prominent forehead; the long, thick, clearly delineated eyebrow; the enormous eye, very wide open, absorbing the light that came from the stage and reflecting a curious more or less yellowish red glow from its iris of the color of fertile soil; the nose, long and elegant, slightly aquiline, just enough not to mar the beauty of her face but to give it, rather, greater grace; the cheek, generous and smooth, that invited you to bite it like a ripe fruit; and the mouth. Its delicate corner, its tender, fresh lips, of an old-rose color, of the color of her nipples. Never quiet, they sometimes pursed—depending on the plot development—sometimes they relaxed and smiled, sometimes, best of all no doubt, they broke out in a resounding burst of laughter, affording a glimpse of the row of perfect white teeth, as beautiful as those of that unfortunate, Damiens, and perhaps even more beautiful. Every so often she turned toward you and asked you to translate for her some bit of dialogue that she hadn't managed to understand. You leaned closer to her ear and whispered it to her. The sight of that ear, small and delicate, as though a meticulous craftsman had fashioned it, of that marvelous neck, of that hidden place where her hairline began, and above all, the sensation of that aroma she gave off—an aroma that you knew so well but that you never tired of sampling—which you had never smelled so close by (you were discovering that it smelled infinitely better there, since, without losing its subtlety, it gained enormously in intensity) caused you great excitement. Dizzied, making a superhuman effort to control yourself, you explained the dialogue to her. You did so in such a low voice that she was unable to hear you. "What's that again?" she asked you, turning her face toward you. Her mouth was then so close to your own that the wing of a butterfly would not have passed between them. "In what an odd state I find myself, Forsina . . . ," you translated, while at the same time, out of cowardice, you moved your head back. Why didn't you kiss her? It was really strange. That timidity was as alien to you as hair on your head would be. You had taken your pleasure with a great many women, and it never cost you a great effort to seduce them—as though in some way the longing you had inside you to attain pleasure, pleasure and those hateful visions, communicated itself to your future companion, making the preliminaries to the carnal act so simple and clear that you almost didn't notice them but perceived only the acquiescence in a woman's look so that in almost no time you were romping in bed with her. It was that simple. It was just the opposite of what happened to you now, at the moment when, paradoxically, you most desired a woman.

At intermission, you chanced upon Diderot and Sophie Volland. Denis was a bit tipsy and in a good mood. He took advantage of the break between acts to drain three or four glasses of champagne and deliver to the two of you, between one swallow and another, a roundly amusing commentary on the play.

"Dear friend," he said to you in a very loud voice, so that all the fops and snobs swarming about the place would hear him, "in the face of the overwhelming confirmation of the facts, it is possible to extract only two conclusions: either Molière was illuminated and used as he pleased that gift, so prized by Nostradamus, of looking into the future, and was able to see with the minute vision of a naturalist our beloved functionaries and their distinguished ladies, portraying them to us with an abundance of detail in this work, as a sublime painter would have done; or else, and I believe that this is more likely, human stupidity is eternal, preserves itself intact down through time, and reproduces itself prodigally for century after century in the heads of our long-suffering governors, who are not one whit less stupid than those who were closest to the Sun King—and I suspect that the same thing goes back to the dignitaries of Charlemagne. For instance, the appealing Harpagon is Richelieu in person, did you realize that? . . ."

He went on in this vein for some time, comparing the characters in the comedy to those "protagonists who act in the tragicomedy of real life." His witticisms were so clever and delivered with such humor that it would not be an exaggeration to say that people laughed more during intermission than they did during the play itself. Denis gave them no rest; they had barely recovered from one burst of laughter when he had already launched another dart, even more penetrating than the one before.

Mariana, her eyes brimming with tears of laughter, said to him, "Please stop, Monsieur Diderot. I swear to you that my sides already ache. You know what? You ought to write comedies; really, your wit isn't a jot less than Molière's."

"I have written some, madam, indeed I have," he answered with fake seriousness, "although, as you can imagine, they were not very well received by our beloved nobility. But I have no quarrel with men of the cloth. My works pleased them so much that they haven't hesitated to burn them whenever they get their hands on them—wishing, I suppose, that the smoke that, doubtless, the spirit of the words contains may reach without impediment the most remote corner of the heavens, where the Almighty dwells, so that the savory acquaintance with them may enable him to fight off, if only for a short time, his immortal boredom."

The ushers announced that the play was about to resume. When you went into the amphitheater, Denis took you by the shoulder and led you off to one side of the door. "Listen, Fausto," he said in your ear—and there reached your nose a strong odor of doubly distilled grapes—"if you let this woman get away, I'll split that big bald pate of yours in two, I give you my word . . ."

Annette has gone too far, you thought when you saw Claude, your footman, standing alongside the door, as rigid as a soldier on guard duty and dressed in ridiculous bottle green livery with silver trimming. Where could she have got that uniform? And as if that weren't enough, he was wearing on his head an enormous wig covered with more powder than there is dust on a hundred-year-old bottle of wine, and with two enormous curls hanging over his chest. The white silk tie—clumsily knotted, by the way—was your own, as was the gold coat. What was not yours, nor Claude's, were the enormous patent-leather boots that it was plain to see could accommodate both of the boy's feet in a single one of them with room left over; the same disproportion was true of the limp, wrinkled white gloves he was wearing, as though the hands inside them had shrunk.

"Your house is really pleasant, Fausto," Mariana said to you as Claude took her cape.

"My dear, we're going to skip the politeness of the aristocracy. I can't bear it," you replied with a poorly hidden surliness.

You were really annoyed by that idiotic protocol of the nobility which considered it very good taste to spend fifteen or twenty minutes praising the host's house. It was almost an obligation to inspect the drawing rooms, take a close look at the draperies, thoroughly examine the upholstery of the furniture, or lift up a large porcelain urn so as to look at it against the light—all of this accompanied by phrases that, contrived to be clever, clearly belonged to the immense world of clichés: "This is by Watteau, isn't it? Ah! There are no hands more delicate than those of that man . . ." "It's incredible what they've succeeded in doing at Sèvres. Look, dear, anyone would think that this urn is Chinese . . ." "What a pretty rug! Just look at those birds, so perfect they could take wing this minute . . ." "This is a real table service; no matter what La Pompadour keeps insisting, a meal ought to be served on silver and not on crude earthen crockery . . ." "What a splendid fireplace! And so enormous! You could warm a whole army with it, my girl . . ." There were a thousand other ridiculous remarks of the sort. The phrases that those same guests, so delighted and so surprised by the mansion they had just visited, would come up with when they arrived at their own would be much more inventive. Cruel, mordant phrases, belonging to that other world—as vast as the previous one—of animosity and envy: "How awful! Two hours sitting on that divan; my back feels as though I'd wallowed about in an anthill. And that rug, for heaven's sake! It would hardly do even for making burlap bags . . ." "Did you see her table settings? With her uncle's initials. Poor things, so much effort to hide their poverty when all Paris knows very well where all their money went . . ." "What a woman! That's what we've come to by selling titles of nobility as if they were roasted chestnuts. I swear to you I could hardly eat; just seeing her, with all that rouge and powder, with that beauty spot she'd pasted on her breast, with her little finger as stiff as a corpse and talking with a piece of bread in her mouth, as though she were kneading it—it turned my stomach. I've heard that her husband hired a Russian prince and a Polish countess to educate her. An utter waste of money; it's easier to teach a deaf mute to give public speeches than to educate that awful creature . . ." "The only difference, darling, between the Marigny mansion and Madame Chantal's brothel is that the latter is decorated in better taste and, of course, the whores are much better looking . . ." Denis was right; idiocy is eternal, "and God in his infinite wisdom," you would add, "bestowed it on a much greater scale upon those he chose to bless with wealth."

"Monsieur Rasero, you have offended me," Mariana said with a smile. "There wasn't the least hint of adulation or hypocrisy in what I said to you. Hasn't it ever occurred to you that certain people can be sincere? This drawing room really pleases me. And now, as a punishment, you're to show me the whole house, and you're going to have to tolerate my compliments or criticisms, as the case may be."

Resigned, you allowed her to do as she wished. She began to nose about in the little drawing room with the careful attention of a tax assessor. She liked very much a small painting by Chardin hanging from one of the walls. It was a rather dark still life. You had been all but forced to buy it by Denis, who insisted that you were acquiring a jewel at a giveaway price. "It doesn't look to me like something from the next world," you dared to say when, after hanging it on that wall, you stepped a couple of yards back to have a look at it.

"For the love of heaven, Fausto, what do you keep in that big bald head of yours besides Gothic puppets and chemical formulas? Anybody would think there wasn't anything inside. That still life is marvelous, my friend. Look at it carefully."

You tried to hone your senses so that they would receive that extraordinary message your eyes were incapable of apprehending. Perhaps that ripe, lascivious peach, of a dull yellow, with its two big reddish spots that were reminiscent of a schoolgirl's cheeks? Or the outstretched wing of the dead wild duck which had whitish Grecian frets, barely visible, geometrically distributed amid the grayish black? Or the eyes of the animal itself, already lifeless, but which still denoted enormous sadness, as though looking toward a very distant place where the bird would be safe from the hunter's shotgun? Or the bottle of wine, green and uncorked, showing the thick dark liquid filling it halfway up? Or the candle, already burned almost all the way down, whose flickering flame tinged the whole with its reddish light, like that of an oven that has just gone out, leaving everything barely visible, blurring it, as though it were disappearing? Yes, that was it, the candle. The candle gave the painting great charm. Proud of your discovery, you told Denis about it. "It's the candle; it's really marvelous."

Diderot smiled. "Bravo, my friend, you've hit the nail on the head. I'm pleased to note that you're a sensitive person. I wrote in one of my *Salons* pieces, very clearly, it seems to me, 'Chardin's greatness does not lie in what he shows but in what he suggests; it is not in the objects but in the atmosphere.' But few, very few, have understood me the way you have. In fact, that nonexistent candle is the most beautiful thing in the painting." At this, you were confused. You looked at your friend's face to see if he wasn't pulling your leg—something he was in the habit of doing very often—and the expression you found in it convinced you of the seriousness of his words. Intrigued, you took another look at the painting—which, incidentally, you liked more and more—and you had to contemplate it for quite a while to notice anything extraordinary. The duck, the bottle, the pieces of fruit were there; they were serenely continuing to disappear. What was not there within the frame was the candle. Just the semicircular shape of the small copper candlestick was visible in the lower left-hand corner of the work . . . The admiration you felt for Denis Diderot grew enormously that day . . .

"What a magnificent painting!" Mariana said in sincere admiration when she saw the splendid portrait of your great-great-grandfather hanging above the fireplace. "It reminds me a great deal of Velázquez' portraits . . . That stern gentleman surely must be a relative of yours; it seems as though I'm looking at your eyes."

"It's my great-great-grandfather, don Fausto de Oquendo, and in fact it's a painting by Velázquez," you answered without hiding the trace of pride that accompanied your words whenever you mentioned that much-loved painting.

You invited her to sit down and began to tell her the story of your illustrious forebear. Meanwhile, Claude, who had taken on his role with the seriousness of a judge, had uncorked a bottle of champagne that he placed inside a very elegant silver bucket (Where could they have got hold of it? That Annette is really incredible), along with two glasses of fine Bohemian crystal. He left the tray on a little table and vanished like a shadow.

"He was a great man. He was cut from cloth that doesn't exist in our own day." Without realizing it, you were repeating, almost word for word, what you had heard so many times from your uncle Luis when you were a little boy and spent hours at a time curled up comfortably in that old armchair listening to him as he paced from one side of the room to the other, telling you with his exuberant and fluent chatter, full of piquant anecdotes, of the misadventures of Philip IV's majordomo. "He had the misfortune of being the counselor of Philip IV and a confidant of the Duke de Olivares. And I say the misfortune, because that king, wan and sickly, as hypocritically devout as his grandfather but infinitely more of an imbecile," Uncle Luis said, "was doubtless the one responsible for the breakdown of the Spanish Empire. Don Fausto de Oquendo, who had a spirit tempered by other nobler and more glorious eras and who had been an invaluable help for a strong and resolute king such as Charles V or Philip II himself, found himself obliged to collaborate with that decadent Hapsburg, who was as sensitive to his advice as a wall is to wailing . . ."

As you spoke, you gradually abandoned the carefully chosen words of your uncle and began to express, from deep down inside you, what you thought of that remote ancestor for whom you felt a strange sympathy, a mixture of piety, admiration, and envy: "Ever since I was very young, I had no other goal than the grandeur of Spain. I dreamed of being a heroic soldier, a fierce conquistador of the stature of Alexander or Julius Caesar or, at least, Hernán Cortés . . ."

You had imagined him many times. The fascination that that portrait had exerted on you since you were a small boy had obliged you to delve into the life of that man. You used many of the hours you spent in the Biblioteca Real in Madrid studying the exploits of don Fausto de Oquendo. Moreover, in the small little ebony coffer—the same one in which you found the portrait of your mother, a real Pandora's box that filled your adolescence with magic and ghosts—you came across, tied with a frayed royal purple ribbon, a packet of letters written by don Fausto and addressed, from countless places in old Europe, to doña Carmen, your mysterious great-great-grandmother. In these letters, much more than in the thick documents you nosed about in at the Biblioteca, you found the indelible traces of that unusual man, shaped by the idea of grandeur and doomed to failure. Don Fausto de Oquendo, young and high-spirited, practiced sword handling for four or five hours a day and then, scarcely taking time to rest, devoted himself to reading for the hundredth time Plutarch's detailed description of the life of the great Caesar, or Caesar's campaign diaries, or else the fascinating accounts of don Hernán Cortés, the *Cartas de Relación,* in which the native of Extremadura describes in his incisive and zestful style the marvels of that exotic country the mere names of whose villages are a challenge to pronounce, a country—a strange world—that was the birthplace of that strikingly beautiful woman who at this moment was listening to you attentively as she cast sidelong glances at the black, indifferent eyes of don Fausto de Oquendo himself, whom you were seeing embarking, begging Aeolus to blow mightily so that the galleon would reach America as soon as possible, that continent where the Dutch infidels, blond and meanspirited, were going to test the temper of his steel. "But destiny is not always attuned to our desires: he first saw action in the naval battle of Matanzas, in Cuba. There the Dutch inflicted a tremendous defeat on the Spaniards . . ." The Spanish naval forces, just recovering from the debacle of the Invincible Armada, suffered yet another setback in Cuba and were left reeling, "finally falling—and not getting up again—at Las Dunas, ten years later. Don Fausto was there too and endured the terrible humiliation of surrendering to Tromp . . ." Yet these reverses did not crush his spirit: he worked tirelessly with the Duke de Olivares to restore Spanish power. He followed the battles of the Seven Years' War attentively and advised the duke and the monarch again and again to support the Austrian Empire without reservation. "The triumph of Protestantism would be the end of Western civilization," he wrote in his letters. One by one, his plans fell apart. The Swedes advanced in high spirits through the north of Germany, where the Reformation spread like wildfire in a dry forest. The French, a fickle people, flirted with both sides, always ready to share the booty of victories and avoid the cost of defeats. The foundations of Spain itself were collapsing. The Portuguese, the Catalans, the Navarrese, and even the Andalusians—don Fausto himself was a native of Andalusia—wanted to have nothing to do with centralized power; they named their own kings and declared war on Castile. Don Fausto was involved in all these chaotic defeats, and though his lips tasted just a sip of the nectar of victory, as when they beat the Duke de Medinasidonia in Andalusia, or don Miguel de Iturbide in Navarre, they experienced the bitter taste of defeat till they had more than their fill of it. He saw how the Portuguese—backed by the perfidious English—succeeded in breaking off their ties with the kingdom, how they reduced the Spanish infantry troops to dust at Roseoir, and how (alas! this was perhaps what pained him most) the Duke de Olivares fell from the king's graces and saw his place taken by none other than a nun. The accursed woman: her person was a compendium of all the vices and defects typical of her feeble sex, along with a large part of those of the opposite sex. On the other hand, there did not exist in her the slightest trace of virtue, either masculine or feminine. "My dear," the Marquis de Oquendo wrote to his great-great-grandmother, "what have we come to! I know that I have committed many sins in my life, but I do not believe that they were so numerous as to oblige me to endure this torture to expiate them. And it is a torture to be forced to see and to suffer what I am seeing and suffering: the sovereign in the hands of a harpy, our Spain collapsing like a house of cards, our language, our culture reduced to nothing and reviled by all those churls, and our empire incommunicado, unable to reach America without being attacked by Saxon pirates . . . Everything worthwhile, my darling, foundering before our eyes, and not being able to do a thing because that accursed witch has turned into an insurmountable wall! I have requested an audience with the monarch five times now, and five times he has denied me one. Is it possible to endure any greater martyrdom?" Yes, yes, there was: the Peace of the Pyrenees was a greater martyrdom, and poor don Fausto no longer held out against it . . .

". . . He died a few days after that shameful peace was signed, as though by signing and sealing it he had signed and sealed the end of his life as well . . ."

Seeing him in the portrait, erect, haughty, with his foot thrust forward, as though threatening to start walking, still a vigorous man—he was probably no more than thirty years old when his portrait was painted—you felt the irresistible impulse to raise your glass and drink to the health of the old warrior. "To your good health, Grandfather! And courage, you still have many failures ahead of you." Mariana smiled when she heard the toast, but she could not suspect what was going through your mind. For now, after speaking a good while about don Fausto, you suddenly understood the reason for the sympathy, the ever more irresistible attraction that the man exerted upon you. Above all, it was that you identified with him, and not only because of the obvious physical resemblance but on account of something much more profound: just as your eyes resembled his, just as one grain of sand looks the same as another, so your fates resembled each other, both of them doomed to end in failure. He dreamed of the grandeur of Spain; you, more ambitious, of the grandeur of humankind. He prepared by training himself in the use of arms and of political intrigue; you by reading and visions. You both found in war the origin and the cause of your despair—he in that endless Thirty Years' War that had gone on for half his life, you in equally endless warfare . . . How many years had it been? The first time you saw the warfare you were six years old; that is to say, it was thirty-four years ago, and without doubt it had begun some time before then. This was so, this was true, if the time in which your visions took place flowed at the same pace as the time in which you lived. You were not certain of this, but neither were you certain that it didn't. And logic told you that if in fact you saw the future—and that's something you no longer doubted—that is, if you saw the same world you lived in except for a difference of who knows how many years (one hundred? two hundred?), there was no reason at all to suppose that the time of that world ceased to flow when you were not observing it. That would have been absurd, as if a group of actors were waiting to perform as soon as you reached the theater and then suspended acting once you had left. So it was certain, so far as anything could be, that in the future that inflicted itself on you, time went by in exactly the same way as in the present. On that premise, you'd been immersed in a war for thirty-four years—in this respect, you'd outdone don Fausto—a war that gave no sign of ever ending. It had been a little more than two months since you made love for the last time . . . as long as that? Ever since you met Mariana the Creole, you had completely forgotten about sex, orgasm, and even the future. It was true that you were in love. With that famished little whore you met in the Marais and took to bed more out of pity than out of desire, you saw a hair-raising war scene, one of the most unpleasant you've witnessed—and that's saying a great deal. It developed that those enormous flying machines were dropping from very high up, like an eagle whose prey escapes its grasp, twenty or thirty iron tubes that exploded with incredible violence on reaching the ground; the spectacle that your senses afforded you might be called "bombs from heaven." Needless to say, what was down below—mud huts, worn and threadbare objects, Asian men and women (in the future, it seemed unquestionable that wars would have spread much beyond Europe and its colonies)—was reduced to shards beneath an immense cloud of fire, smoke, and dust . . . Unlike your ancestor's war, yours lay in the future—although, of course, there were wars in your present too, and an abundance of them: it was barely a year ago that the Seven Years' War ended. But frankly, compared with what's swarming in your head, these seem insignificant. There were wars in your present, but you were not immersed in them; they were of as little moment to you as the question what the sex life of the inhabitants of Sirius might be like. On the other hand, the fighting you saw in the future affected you deeply. Why? Who knows? The scenes made you a participant in them, and above all they made you aware of your failure, of the profound despair that rendered you a brother in spirit to your great-great-grandfather. Why this sensation? Perhaps because you realized that this war of at least thirty-four years was a consequence of all the stupidities that we were working so hard to commit nowadays and that no matter how hard you had tried to find the way to avoid them, you have done no better than Sisyphus with his rock, or the vulture gnawing at Prometheus' vitals.

"Madam, sir, dinner is served," Claude said in a pompous voice. There was no doubt about it: he was at his most appealing that night. The sight of his solemn, grotesque figure made your somber thoughts disappear as if by magic.

Before going into the dining room, Mariana insisted on carrying out her intention of familiarizing herself with her friend's house. "There's not much to see," Rasero said in advance.

"I'll be the judge of that," she answered with a smile.

The apartment was quite large: in fact, on the upstairs floor, with a surface area identical to that of his own quarters, Rasero had rented out four comfortable apartments. Yet the layout of his own apartment was very simple. It consisted of two long wings of rooms—the large windows of one of them overlooked an inside patio and those of the other the street—with two adjoining bedrooms at one end. The doors of the rooms opened out onto a wide hallway painted a pistachio green and decorated with plaster filigree work and a delightful collection of engravings by Watteau and two or three little tables against the wall with majolica vases on top—filled now with enormous, showy bouquets of red flowers. At the end of the hallway was the front door. The drawing room the two of them were in was to the right of this entrance, in the inner wing of the house—a wing that no doubt was Annette's territory, since she was the one who had furnished it and decorated it: before the young woman had come to that house, those rooms had remained empty save perhaps for a number of crates with furniture, books, and bibelots that Rasero had ordered sent from Spain and hadn't yet got around to unpacking, to the satisfaction and feasting of the little mice that overran the place. Next to this drawing room there was another, almost identical. "Anyone with any self-respect ought to have at least two drawing rooms," his young housekeeper had explained to him with exactitude. Its furniture was more modern than that in the first room, an old salon dating from the Regency. This little drawing room was in the purest Pompadour style—even if the history of style, as capricious as the marquise herself, was later to refer to the style, light and cheerful although perhaps a little uncomfortable, by the name of her royal lover. There was also a magnificent Italian boudoir grand piano that had been there no more than a week: motivated by the splendid concert of the Austrian child prodigy, Rasero could not resist the temptation of acquiring the piano when he, along with Mariana, saw it in that elegant shop in the rue St-Honoré. The next room was very spacious; it had two big windows with damask draperies. Annette had turned it into a game room. There were three little round tables for playing cards, as well as a very odd piece of furniture, made of cedarwood, with rounded contours, its two large doors each with (really awful) brightly colored paintings of thick clusters of flowers underneath their varnish. When Annette brought the ugly and cumbersome hulk into the house, she explained to her master with great self-congratulation that she had acquired it at a giveaway price in a shop in Saint-Antoine. "It's for storing bottles, glasses, cards, scoring books, and other paraphernalia for gaming," she told him, making no attempt to conceal her pride. At the back of the room, there was a large billiard table with its heavy feet covered in gold leaf. In all truth, this was the one object in the room which Rasero liked, and he spent many more hours than anyone might have suspected playing with the polished ivory spheres there. While they were in the game room, Annette, who grasped the young Spanish woman's intention of becoming acquainted with the entire house, ordered Claude to hurry and light some candles and oil lamps in the other rooms. At the opposite end of the hallway, from which Claude emerged like a thief on the run, was a guest room. "A noble person must always have a roof under which to provide lodgings for his friends," Annette had announced sententiously when she decided to furnish that room.

The furniture was of the same Louis XV style as that in the second little drawing room. The pieces were lacquered in a grayish color that went well with the fabrics of the bed canopy, the draperies, the counterpane, and the upholstery of the chairs, all in shades of sky blue. That bedroom was at the root of the one quarrel Rasero had had with Annette. For it was really very expensive. When the bill arrived, Rasero thought he was being sold an entire town house. "But, sir, it's the handiwork of the king's very own cabinetmaker . . ."

"Regardless of whether it's the work of Saint Joseph himself," Rasero replied in a rage, "it's going to cost me at least a vineyard. What do you think I am, a Richelieu?"

The girl burst into tears and began to mutter. It was hard to understand what she was saying: you caught something like "ungrateful" and "I'm going back home to where I came from . . ." She said this latter very seriously, and the annoyance you were feeling turned into apprehension: the idea of losing that delightful creature who had made your life so pleasant alarmed you.

"Very well, Annette, you win. The bedroom stays, but please don't cry any more . . ." She hardly seemed to hear Rasero, but went on weeping and muttering, raising her arm, threatening heaven only knew what phantoms. Finally, Rasero embraced her and kissed her cheeks drenched with tears. In a little while, the two of them were calmly recumbent on the newly acquired bed. Annette, happy, gave her master a concluding hug and let sleep overcome her. Rasero, on the other hand, looked at the canopy above the bed and smiled in thinking about the strange vision he had just had, of three people sitting on a sofa looking toward a wooden box. One of its sides was of glass, behind which could be seen tiny colorless people who looked as though they had been sketched with a pencil but who moved about nimbly all over the place.

Now that he was showing the room to Mariana, however, he had to admit that Annette's idea had been a good one. He had lodged many of his friends in that room. Denis had found in it an ideal refuge for his casual trysts; David Hume had spent three or four days in this house, happy to be free of the ambassador; and even that unsociable creature Rousseau sometimes took shelter beneath its roof. Next to this room, there was another of exactly the same size, and it was the first room in the opposite wing of the apartment. But this one was nearly empty; the only things in it were a big pine table and a couple of shelves of the same wood on one of the walls. There were also several wooden crates on the floor. When Mariana saw the room, dimly illuminated by an oil lamp that Claude had just lit, she looked at Rasero quizzically. "I'm thinking of setting up a chemistry laboratory here," he answered her. It was an old plan of his. In fact, he had been thinking about it ever since coming to live in the house, twenty years before. For one reason or another, he had kept putting his plan off. Almost twenty years, he thought in surprise. I've finally acquired a table and several shelves, and there's a fair amount of equipment in the crates. There'll still be enough time to set it up, he said to himself, as he had been doing for nearly twenty years. In any event, his resolve seemed firm. At least so it appeared to Annette when she suggested to her master that he set up a music room in there. Rasero didn't say one word in reply; the furious look in his little black eyes was enough for the young woman not to insist. She realized that that wing of the house was don Fausto's domain, and presently withdrew from it.

The next room was Rasero's bedroom. The dark, somber furniture and the draperies of heavy wine-colored velvet formed a sharp contrast to what was in the other wing of the house. A person is in France there, and in Spain here, Mariana thought. Rasero's bed, the one he had had in Spain and had ordered brought to France once his father died, was placed lengthwise along the wall, beneath a heavy, delicately carved canopy. It was a magnificent piece of cabinetwork in dark walnut. The headboard showed pretty carved nymphs who were smiling as they avoided being caught by a robust satyr with goat hooves who was chasing after them. On the footboard, the same nymphs, naked to the waist, were peacefully gamboling around a pond. Great oak trees, among which tiny sparrows flew back and forth, completed the rustic scene. His uncle Luis had explained to him that this bed was made by the great Malagan master don Francisco Hurtado and that, along with the pretty carved bureau based on the same theme, it was given to don José de Rasero, Fausto's paternal grandfather, in thanks for certain favors of his having to do with landholdings. The set of furniture was completed by two large easy chairs upholstered in the same velvet fabric as the canopy and the draperies. They were placed facing the hearth of a small fireplace. There was, finally, an old secretary underneath the window. Rasero's study came next, where Mariana could see, barely lit by two candles, a large work table littered with papers, open books, chemical apparatus, and other objects in utter disorder: Annette and Louise, the chambermaid, had strictly forbidden any of the staff to touch the master's things. All the walls, except for the one opposite, where there was a large window overlooking the street, were covered with bookcases of dark wood. Mariana caught just a hint of the agreeable aroma of books stored away that always aroused in her a warm sense of pleasure and in this case a barely restrained yearning to settle down comfortably in one of the two easy chairs on the magnificent Persian rug, prop her feet up on the footstool, and begin to read in peace and quiet one of the works of the master writer Calderón de la Barca. In the other chair, curled up in a ball, was Nostradamus, an enormous cat—he looked as though he had been altered, but he hadn't been—with a long dark coat and black tiger stripes. Annette had brought the cat to the house just a short while after it was born, with the intention of getting rid of the rats that infested the empty rooms. Very soon the good Nostradamus—Why did don Fausto give it such an ugly name? Annette had often wondered—had rid the house of the rodents, at the same time growing as fast as well-watered ivy. To such a point that Annette came to think she'd been given a lynx rather than a cat. When Mariana saw him, she went over to him at once and clasped him in her arms. Rasero didn't have time to tell her that Nostradamus was terribly unsociable and that, except for Annette and himself, didn't allow anyone to touch him. In surprise, he saw how Nostradamus rubbed his whiskers on his friend's lap, purring with all his might. "Pretty kitty, what's your name?"

"Nostradamus," Rasero answered, not without a certain envy when he saw how the animal settled comfortably upon his friend's bosom. "He's not only a splendid hunter; he's my confidant, companion, and friend." Mariana left Nostradamus on the chair and at last headed for the dining room, which was the final (or the first) room in the house, just opposite the drawing room where she had been received. The dining room furnishings were the ones that had been in the old mansion in Málaga for many years. The extremely heavy chairs, with their legs ending in lion's claws and with the Raseros' coat of arms on their backs, were imposing. So were the large painting of the Last Supper by Juan de Pareja and the magnificent birds by Honelecoster, the Dutch painter.

Annette had carefully decorated the table. She decided not to put the place settings at either end of the enormous table, as etiquette counseled, but instead to position them facing each other across the center of it; and Rasero was grateful to the girl for that subtle detail.

The table settings were of pure silver, as were the large flat service plates that held the pretty Sèvres porcelain dishes decorated by the unsurpassable hands of Rasero's friend François Boucher and given to him by his beloved Marquise de Pompadour as a gift just short of a year before. The set of glasses was of Bohemian crystal, cut simply and delicately. In the middle of the table a large candelabrum with five candles lit the room. Claude, standing as rigid as a soldier behind Mariana's chair, seated the lady. Louise, whom Annette had decked out in an attractive bottle green dress on top of which her immaculately white apron gleamed, did the same for Rasero. Another gesture of his diligent employee made Rasero smile anew. In front of each plate, leaning against one of the glasses, was a white card with a coral-colored filigree design in the corners; on it was printed, in letters of the same color and in characters that looked handwritten, the menu they were about to enjoy. It was surely good Marcel Gautier, the son of the printer who lived downstairs, who had made the card, obeying, as always, the slightest whim of Annette, on whom he looked—as Rasero had already discovered—with the same devotion as that shown by Ares for Aphrodite.

Hors d'oeuvre
Anchois de Catalogne
Pot-pourri au vinaigre de Maille

Entrées
Pâtés de palais de boeuf fourrés aux truffes
Ailerons de poularde en compote

Rôtis
Langues fourrés de Troyes

Entremets
Epinards à l'essence de jambon
Macaroni de Gênes au parmesan

Dessert et fromages
Buisson de gâteaux
Petits fours mêlés
Brie de Coulommiers
Figues fines d'Ollioules

Boissons
Vin de Madère sec — Vin de Bousy — Vin de Chambertin
Vin de Chablis — Vin d'Asti — Vin de Málaga
Café de Martinique — Café Moka — Liqueurs

"Mmm . . . ! How delicious! But who's going to eat all that?" Mariana said after reading the card.

"It's best if we do. If we don't, I suspect that Annette will never forgive me."

Mariana raised a slice of anchovy to her mouth. "Exquisite!" she commented as she felt on her tongue a pleasant salty flavor that had the virtue of awakening in her a voracious appetite. From that point on, it was easy to do honor to the delicious dishes that Annette had prepared. They ate calmly, allowing their palates fully to enjoy every mouthful. Every so often, a good swallow of wine—which was smooth as velvet and very dry, barely hinting at a discreet and evasive sweetness, like the fragrance of jasmine—helped clear their palates and leave them receptive to new delights. Mariana felt very good; the meal and the wine invaded her body, lulled it, relaxed it, as though she were submerged in a tub of water, warm, dense (if water can be dense), and scented. Little by little, with the same slowness with which light gradually replaces shadows at dawn, an even more pleasant sensation, though at the same time a more overwhelming and violent one, gradually came over her. She recognized it immediately, not with her reason but with her senses, which took her, as though it had been only yesterday, to the terrace of the Marquis de la Borda's house in Cuernavaca on that warm afternoon filled with fragrances. Suffocating—as on that afternoon—she raised a good swallow of wine to her lips and began, as always when she was perturbed, to speak rapidly, perhaps hoping that the flow of words that came out of her mouth would take away with it the oppressive sensation. She spoke then of a thousand things: Of the play that they had just seen, which "really filled me with enthusiasm. Even though, to tell the truth, I think your friend Denis made me laugh even more. What a nice man! And so intelligent . . . One has only to look at his eyes to realize how enormously intelligent he is, and feel like a worm alongside him—it's terrible! . . ." From the theater she jumped to the subject of Les Halles, the district in Paris she liked best of all. "The fishwives who tend their stalls are the fiercest women I've ever met in my life . . ." Rasero, who was more familiar with desire than his friend was, let her go on without trying to stem the flood; every bite she raised to her mouth transformed itself in his imagination into a nibble of that adorable body. He listened, to all appearances attentively, but in reality he barely followed the meaning of what she was saying; rather, he received her words as though they were soft kisses placed on his cheeks. Like Mariana, desire had perturbed him—something that, except for the Marquise de Gironella, had never happened to him with any other woman. But unlike Mariana, who kept talking on and on, he was more silent than a stone, sometimes nodding his head, at others smiling, with his coal black eyes opened very wide, riveted on the Moorish locket that was indifferently resting between his friend's breasts. "He's really a good-looking man, a truly handsome one," she said. "I now understand why his fame has even reached as far as Spain. Nonetheless, I didn't like him. His person radiates something very irritating, a sort of cynicism, of indifference, or even worse, of falseness. That's it! I think that man is a charlatan . . ." She was referring to Casanova, the Italian adventurer who had become a legend at the court at Versailles through his countless amorous adventures with who knows how many ladies of the aristocracy and no fewer chambermaids of their town houses. In addition to being a woman chaser, he was, rumor had it, also a swindler and a confidence man; Voltaire had hinted at something like that in a letter to you: "Monsieur Casanova is involved in the Paris Lottery scheme. May God warn my dear peasants of what lies ahead . . ." In all truth, that man interested Rasero very little. He had seen him two or three times in the drawing room of some nobleman or other and had always been immune to his charms. What had just been said by Mariana, who, out of curiosity, had wanted Rasero to introduce him to her when they ran into him as they were leaving the theater, conformed to his own impressions: Casanova was a fraud and nothing else. But attractive, devilishly attractive . . . He had noticed it when the Italian kissed his friend's fingers after making an elegant bow; he looked at her with his big languid eyes, as though consumed by an old and stormy love for her. Mariana smiled, and Rasero, frankly jealous, interrupted the chat that the Venetian had begun with her. Coldly, he took his leave of him and left him with his words still in his mouth. He's a viper, he thought, terrified at the idea that his dear Mariana might succumb to his charms. "He's the sweetest man that I've ever known in my life," Rasero heard to his distress. "Without exaggerating, I could tell you that it was thanks to him that I survived in Madrid. He showed me nothing but kindness and infinite patience, because when I arrived in Spain, I regret to say, I was unbearable, overwhelmed with melancholy. There was nothing that pleased me enough to want to go on living, not even the theater . . ." Relieved, Rasero realized that Mariana was now talking about his beloved cousin, José de Gálvez.

He was embarrassed by the stupid jealousy he had felt, which Mariana had noticed when she saw how his face suddenly turned red and how he broke his silence and began to talk of his beloved relative.

"They were the only friends I had when I was a little boy." He told her of their games in the cellar of the mansion in Málaga and in the fields of Macharavialla. He explained to her how José had always defended him against the enmity of the neighborhood children who lived in the calle Miaja and detested the bald little gentleman; they had made him the target of their jokes and of all the cruelties children are so fond of. But when José was with him, the little urchins hid like frightened rats. "Hey there, you scoundrels! How come you don't come to me and say those things? You little pantywaists! . . ." José's brother Matías, who was older and more serious, didn't intervene in such matters. "Only once, in Macharavialla, he broke the arm of the son of the overseer of the farm when he caught him just as he'd finished smearing my head with honey and feathers."

"And what did you do?" Mariana asked.

"What could I do? The wretch had tied me to an olive tree," he answered with a smile and went on, happily, as he raised to his mouth a helping of the famous Langues fourrées de Troyes. He told her about the last time he saw José, shortly before leaving for France. Fausto had spent several days at Macharavialla; he was an adolescent, his cousin almost a man. But the two of them ran in and out among the olive trees as in the good old days; they spied on the women bathing in the river and even organized one last lizard hunt. Sweating and happy, they arrived at the overseer's little house, a small dwelling that had always fascinated Fausto: whitewashed, its high-pitched roof covered with red tiles, its four windows protected by badly made iron gratings. The big double door of thick pine, with its crudely carved grapevines, was beneath that arch of pink quarry stone that crowned a niche containing a tiny Saint Gabriel with his sword on high, a miniature copy of the imposing statue that guarded the main entrance of the Gálvez mansion and represented the family's patron saint . . . They then went up, as they had done so many times, to the top of the bell tower of the parish church. From there it was possible to see out over the little valley buried amid the peaks of the great Sierra Nevada. To the south were vast stretches of vineyards surrounded by, as though they were their shepherds, old olive trees with their gray-green foliage—an odd color that could well have been stolen from the sea—and their dark twisted trunks, which, who knows why, always reminded Rasero of the martyrdom of Christ. "Look, Fausto," José said to him, "however far you can see and much, very much, farther, to the Atlantic if you look toward the west, or to Russia if you look to the northeast, everything you see is already conquered: it has belonged to Europe for thousands of years. There is nothing left to do here except to participate in those idiotic wars to divide, or rather, to change owners, for the hundredth time, of mere handfuls of land, kingdoms or principalities that have always been apathetic toward their new rulers, ever since the fall of the Roman Empire. On the other hand, over there," he said to Fausto, pointing westward, "there are enormous lands, unknown and unexplored, where tribes of savages live who have not even received the light of the Gospels. I must go there, cousin, there is still a great lack over there of men who believe in God, in Spain, and in its sword . . ." As time ages wine, so those childhood longings to be a conquistador had also matured. The blood of the great-great-grandfather that ran through Fausto's veins and his came to life once more in that cousin who had the gaze of a falcon. Obediently, he studied law at the University of Madrid; he thereby reassured his father and also gained knowledge that could be useful to him some day (weren't Cortés' studies at Salamanca useful to him?): "I'm going to go to America, you'll see, dear cousin, and if God and Saint Gabriel allow me to, I shall enlarge the geography of Spain with new, vast, and very rich lands . . ."

"Well, I believe he's going to do just that," Mariana said to Rasero, "because I've heard that he's going to New Spain again this year. It seems that the Council of the Indies is about to name him inspector general . . ."

It pleased Rasero greatly to hear that, although it saddened him a little too, for he was convinced that if his cousin went off to America, he would never see him again.

"Who was Angustias?" Mariana asked, intrigued by the name she had heard several times as Rasero was telling her about his cousin.

"My wet nurse . . . or rather, my mother," he answered as he felt the sweet almond liqueur that Claude had just served slide gently down his throat. The name Angustias and the flavor of the drink became one and the same thing. He spoke for a long time about that good woman. It's hard to remember what was said, but doubtless it was something very emotional that came from the innermost depths of his being.

Mariana listened to him attentively; she could see that gypsy woman with her sweet smile, her enormous breasts, and her hair, blacker than pitch, caught up in a pretty chignon. The wine and the conversation having made her feel tipsy, the Creole's spirit had never been so sensitive. She saw the delicate mouth of that man and listened to the tender words coming out of it. She already felt herself loving Angustias as though the gypsy woman were her own mother; already she wanted to grasp her breasts and suck that milk whose flavor was even better than the delicious almond liqueur evaporating on her palate. With her eyes moist with tears barely held back, she asked him, "And what has happened to her?"

"I don't know. She disappeared when I decided to come to Paris . . ."

"No, my son, no," Angustias said to him with her eyes swollen from weeping. What the devil would she do among the Frogs? "I'm an Andalusian, my darling. I'm scarcely able to stand the Madrileños, and only for your sake, mind you. But the French, never. Ah! Faustito, ask me to tear out my eyes and put them in your hands. I'd do it gladly. But don't ask me to go to France . . ." Two days before he left for Paris, Angustias disappeared. She left a letter on his dresser: "Fausto, my son: Go wherever you must, and may God bless you. I'll never see you again, my darling; I don't have the heart to go back to Málaga without you, or to stay among these screeching Castilians. I'm going far away, to my kin. I'll be all right; don't worry. Swear to me you won't forget me, flesh of my own flesh within me. Angustias, your mother . . ."

"She joined up with a tribe of gypsies that was making its way to Barcelona. I never found out anything more about her . . . But, do stop crying, woman!" he said to Mariana when he saw the flood of tears. "She's all right; Angustias is immortal, I swear to you," he said, forcing himself to smile as, with his eyes, he gave Claude one last instruction.

The footman disappeared from the dining room like a shadow, only to return immediately and remain standing in the middle of the room, his eyes fixed on the Christ of the Last Supper, who returned his gaze reluctantly, a bit annoyed perhaps at Saint Peter's slow-wittedness. Claude was holding a fair-sized object in his arms, covered with a blue cloth. He placed it on the table and discreetly withdrew. Mariana, still sobbing, stared, intrigued, at the package.

"Please accept this gift as a souvenir of this night that I wish would never end."

Mariana raised the cloth and could see, protected by a bell jar, a tiny ballerina in the proper position to begin her dance. At the ballerina's feet, the dial of the clock mechanically indicated midnight.

"Fausto dear!" the woman said in excitement as she stood up to come over to him. He rose as well, and the two met halfway. She embraced him affectionately, and he felt her delightful warm body fit itself to his. He kissed her on both cheeks with pleasure, as with his left arm he clasped her waist and with his right hand took her firmly by the chin; he turned her face toward his so that they might meet in that eternal kiss, the happy conclusion of those desires contained for so long a time.

Rasero distracted himself by looking at the nymphs frolicking around the pond, carved at the foot of his bed. He had seen them a great many times, but they had never looked so pretty to him before—above all, the one who, on her knees, was looking at the water trickling from one of her hands, as a sparrow, beating its wings, seemed to fly closer to drink from her palm. The nymph had a long, delicate neck, like her torso, though this latter was adorned with firm, uplifted breasts. Like those of his Mariana, who was sleeping soundly at his side. Rasero could see her back, with her thick black hair spread out over it. One of her very slender arms was bent in such a way as to form a pillow, on which the woman's forehead was resting. How long had he lain like that, contemplating the nymph and his companion? Who could say? Time itself had lost its meaning. It was going by, of course, at the feet of the ballerina enclosed in the glass jar standing on top of the bureau, the clock tirelessly moving its hands, indicating with them—had Rasero cared to notice—the break of dawn. But time had stopped in the Malagan's mind. In it the memories of that night returned again and again—memories he enjoyed as he recalled them almost as much as when the events they recorded had really taken place. The long kiss in the dining room. Then, standing next to the bed, he saw Mariana's naked body. Young, fresh, slender: subtly widening out only at her bosom and her hips. What a dress can hide! He suspected, of course, that that body was a lovely one, but he had never imagined that it was as lovely as that. He regretted, on seeing those long limbs, as firm and flexible as cornstalks, not having the skill or the talent of his friend Boucher to immortalize the impressive figure on canvas. Then, later, the long embrace, the reconnoitering with their hands, with their lips, and with their sense of smell, exploring each other like meticulously observant naturalists. And finally, the explosion; the freeing of those longings that had been contained ever since their eyes met for the first time during that unforgettable concert. When they made love to each other, the man felt incredibly good. Too good, perhaps. Having just finished, as he was leaning against the headboard of the bed, still panting and his heart pounding in his chest, Rasero wondered what had happened that had been able to fill with happiness, with inconceivable pleasure, each pore of his skin, each nerve of his body, in short, each particle of his existence. He knew his body, he knew, naturally, the pleasure of orgasm; he also knew, because he had been agitated by it ever since he met Mariana, the intensity of love. Nonetheless, there was something more. He tried to consider this with his senses, since he knew that reason was of no use in finding an answer, when Mariana lightly brushed one of his eyelids with her lips and they began their love play once more, perhaps with even greater eagerness. And it was then, precisely during that second orgasm, that his senses found the answer. (It was a more prolonged and enjoyable orgasm than the first, for their bodies had already been freed of the tension, the anxiety, that invariably accompanies the first act of intercourse. Moreover, they had begun to know each other. Like diligent pupils, they were learning each other very swiftly; guided by their instinct, they were finding the places, the caresses that delighted them most.) It was at the height of pleasure, in that fleeting instant when we cease to be what we are and turn into divinities, that Rasero, with enormous jubilation, found the answer: for the first time in his life, the future had not come to interfere with his pleasure. The odious visions of a world to which he did not belong did not appear in his consciousness; in it there were nothing more than his pleasure . . . and his Mariana, because during that happy moment he saw her, very beautiful, smiling, showing those perfect teeth for which he would give his life. That was what pleased him most to remember as he gazed at his companion, at the marvelous sorceress capable of performing such a miracle, as she slept at his side. The future did not assail him; he didn't exhaust himself thinking about it. He felt, also for the first time in his life, like a normal man, a man without any other responsibilities than those toward his own era, toward his present. It was as if a hunchback, after a miraculous operation, found that they had removed the lump he had carried about for forty years.

Now he could walk erect, happy, with his back as straight as a ruler; he would be a real man, he would no longer be a counterfeit. They made love yet again. A little anxious, Rasero plunged into what seemed like a dangerous adventure; it even cost him a great effort to become excited, since the nerves that were responsible for the fear of tempting the future again chilled his spirits. But the love he felt for Mariana and her great beauty were more powerful than all his fears, and in the end their bodies were able to couple once more. And again it was the same: nothing of the future about it, only her, only Mariana, with her eyes tightly closed, biting her lower lip when he looked at her, or smiling, with her chestnut brown eyes gleaming like stars just before he closed his own eyes, during the rush of pleasure.

I'm cured; I can finally walk erect, he thought, when the crowing of an early-rising rooster awakened the woman. With her eyes a little swollen from sleep, she looked at him with a smile; she leaned her elbows on the bed and shook her head several times. The sight of her rounded breasts, barely kissing the bed with their buttons, and the aroma that reached his nose when the woman moved the sheets—a warm aroma that contained traces of the fragrance of her perfume, of her body, and a distant hint of their sexual encounter—inflamed him. He kissed her ardently. "Good morning, dear marquis," Mariana said to him, a placid smile appearing on her face.

He contemplated her in ecstasy. "Mariana, marry me."

"Dicen que me case yo; no quiero marido, no . . . ," Mariana happily answered the Marquise de Pompadour's question. "Pardon me, dear marquise, it's a proverb that's an old joke. It means, *They tell me I should marry, ho, ho, ho, but I don't want a husband, no, no, no . . .* But we're really seriously considering it, aren't we, Fausto?"

"Well, you should get married. I've known few couples as well matched as you two."

She said this sincerely. Jeanne-Antoinette knew Fausto Rasero very well, of course, so far as it was possible to know that extremely hermetic man, and she had never seen him look the way he did now. He seemed like another person. In his face, which had impressed her so on seeing it for the first time, when he took off his disguise at that long-ago masked ball, she had never caught a single expression, of happiness, or of annoyance, or of irritation. Many times she had felt that that man spoke from behind an impenetrable mask. But now, one should see him! He was looking at his companion with that unmistakable expression of stupidity that comes over the faces of lovers, in the same way that she still looked at Louis, with whom, despite everything, she continued to be deeply in love. A fit of coughing brought her out of her self-absorption. The storm is approaching, she thought with resignation. For this afternoon at least I was able to forget it completely . . .

"You're really adorable, Mariana," she said after clearing her throat with a rasping cough.

"Jeanne-Antoinette, we're leaving. You must rest. I'm leaving in a very happy frame of mind after seeing how much better you are," Rasero said, and went over to his friend to kiss her.

Mariana also affectionately embraced the marquise and kissed her on both cheeks.

"Madam, it's been a tremendous pleasure to meet you."

"As it has been for me as well, Mariana. It's a real pity we didn't meet sooner . . . Ah, my girl, I have so little time left," she said, looking with deep sadness at the couple. "If I don't see you again, I want you to know that I'll always remember the two of you as among my most precious treasures . . ."

"Jeanne-Antoinette, please," Rasero said, "drive those gloomy thoughts from your head, or they'll end up doing more harm than your illness. You'll see how soon you recover. And after that, promise me you'll go with us to Fontainebleau. I want Mariana to know a real Amazon. Because truly, Mariana, nobody rides a horse better than Jeanne-Antoinette."

"Yes, Fausto dear, I promise both of you." They kissed her again and bade her farewell, for notwithstanding Rasero's smiles and his cheerfulness, the three of them knew that they would never see one another again.

The days that followed this visit were the best Rasero had spent in his life. Mariana, along with her faithful Jacinta, came to stay in the house in the rue St-Jacques. Now their time was altogether theirs, and they could finally enjoy it. They continued their outings in various parts of Paris. Sometimes they ventured farther, to Versailles, for instance, to Melun, to Chantilly, or to Fontainebleau, where Mariana fell in love with the country surroundings. They decided that after they were married they would buy a house there for times between their stays in Paris. On other days they stayed home making plans for their wedding, or else Rasero devoted his afternoons to his old project on Gothic France, as Mariana delved into French poetry. Rasero finally had decided to write that history and buried himself in his reading with real application. Sometimes they went to the theater or to the Opéra, or to the Café Procope, where they spent pleasant afternoons listening to Diderot, whose clever wit seemed inexhaustible. Naturally, a great part of their time was devoted to lovemaking. In the morning, afternoon, or evening, a gesture, a look, was enough for them to change their plans and end up frolicking in bed. The pleasure of feeling each other, of reconnoitering each other, of exploring each other again and again, seemed never to end. And in Rasero's case, that enormous pleasure brought him a twofold happiness, for he proved to himself, again and again, that those terrible phantoms of the future had definitely parted from his life. To the jubilation, the euphoria, of loving his Mariana was conjoined the no less considerable bliss of knowing he was freed from that torment. Now, at last, orgasm belonged to him alone; there was nothing save enjoyment, and the superbly beautiful face of his lover, when he reached the full blossoming of his senses.

The pleasure of love was followed by another, which, though more serene, was no less intense for that. This was when they spent a long time resting in bed, allowing their bodies to recover their strength, their senses delighting in the caresses just received, recalling memories, agreeable sensations. Like almost all men, Rasero became very eloquent after making love. As she listened to him, Mariana felt that she was penetrating the life of that man as a miner penetrates the bowels of the earth. She could see the old mansion in the calle Miaja, in Málaga; she strolled through the garden in search of ripe figs; she felt Angustias' warm lap as she sang her gypsy *tanguillos;* she met Uncle Luis, an indefatigable traveler; she listened to his engaging stories and wept when she learned that the ship taking him to the Philippines sank, the toy of a violent typhoon, as it was sailing through the China Sea; she played with José and Matías amid the olive trees of Macharavialla; she listened attentively to the gentle conversations, full of wisdom and perhaps a touch of irony, of Fray Silvestre; she learned with alacrity the difficult declensions of the Latin that don Joel de Burgos patiently taught her; she studied in the Biblioteca Real of Madrid, beneath the stern and vigilant gaze of don Agustín Luyando; she often visited the laboratory of Dr. Antonio

Ulloa and never ceased being fascinated and surprised when that young scholar revealed to her some of the secrets about substances. She saw how gold dissolved in aqua regia and then reconstituted itself, even yellower and more brilliant, when don Antonio added an ocher powder to the mixture . . .

Were those long talks of your teacher don Ulloa what led Mariana to ready that great surprise for you, do you remember, Rasero . . . ?

The noises you heard in the hallway ended your sleep. What the devil is happening out there? you wondered, annoyed, for you had slept very little; the study of Jean Froissart's *Chroniques* had kept you up until almost dawn. Mariana wasn't in the bedroom. Where can she have gone this early in the morning? you said to yourself, as you splashed ice-cold water on your face to wake yourself up. "Be careful, you idiot! If you break that big glass jar, I swear I'll send you to the Temple," you heard Annette shout. When you appeared in the hallway, you saw four or five big, strong men laboriously carrying several enormous wooden crates. At the end of the hallway, Annette, with a threatening gesture, was showing them where to set the crates down. "There, at the end of the hallway. And be careful, for heaven's sake," she said, pointing inside the room that you had intended for twenty years to set up as your chemistry laboratory.

Furious, since you were convinced that Annette, defying you, had finally decided to carry out her plan to furnish that room as a ridiculous music room, you went over to her. "Annette, what does all this mean? . . ." The girl smiled when she saw you, and instead of answering, looked mischievously inside the room. You did likewise, and found Mariana standing next to the window, giving instructions to the movers.

"Over there, please," she was saying to them, pointing to a corner where at least twenty crates were already piled up. Your annoyance changed into perplexity. Halting in the doorway, you gave Mariana a questioning glance. She didn't pay you the slightest mind and went on with her work. You started to open your mouth, but one of the men came into the room carrying a crate and bumped you so forcefully that you nearly fell flat on your face. "Be careful, Fausto! Come over here, don't get in the way of those poor men. They've enough to do, carrying their load." Submissively, you planted yourself alongside her and asked her, as you had already asked Annette, the meaning of the hubbub. "Ah! It's a surprise. It's a pity you woke up; I wanted everything to be ready by the time you got out of bed. But there was no way; it's hard to tell these men not to make a sound. Just look at the size of those crates!"

"Can't you explain to me what's going on?" you insisted.

"No. Not till they've finished bringing everything up. It won't take long now," she said as she looked out the window. "Look!"

You peered out too and saw three carts, each drawn by two mules. Two of the carts were empty and the third had only four or five crates left in it. There was nothing else you could do but wait acquiescently for the men to finish their work. Finally, they set the last crate down. Mariana spoke with one of the movers, whose stern and superior countenance indicated that he had to be the one in charge of the others, and handed him a little pouch full of coins. "Now you'll see what's up," she said to you with a smile as soon as you were by yourselves. "Do me the favor, Monsieur Rasero, of opening a crate."

"Which one?"

"Whichever you like."

You opened the smallest within reach and, when you raised the lid, saw several packets very carefully wrapped in cotton cloth. You took out one of them and unwrapped it. It was a magnificent set of magnifying glasses, made in Holland, you presumed. Eagerly, you unwrapped the other packets. As each wrapping came off, an object appeared before your eyes, the mere sight of which filled you with a tremendous exhilaration. You felt like a pirate who has just discovered a buried treasure. But instead of pearl necklaces, it was a retort that your hand stroked, not a golden goblet but a set of porcelain crucibles, bronze mortars, flasks of a thousand shapes and sizes, cork stoppers, alcohol lamps, oil burners; there wasn't a single piece of equipment that wasn't there. You spent the whole day unpacking those marvelous objects. A whole laboratory! You could hardly believe it. To top it all off, the last three crates contained books, all of them on chemistry, and even two or three handwritten notebooks that you leafed through, finding in a tiny, nervous hand a large number of notations, drawings, descriptions of experiments, and progress reports. Elated, you shuttled between unwrapping the objects and tendering kisses and squeezes to Mariana. "Darling, it's unbelievable. Where did you get all this?"

"It was simple. Last week, while paging through a back number of the *Annales scientifiques,* I came across an advertisement of a certain Mademoiselle Geofroy. She was offering to sell the entire laboratory of an 'illustrious chemist.' I remembered this empty bedroom, the good Dr. Ulloa, and my bald dreamer. So I went to see her. She's a charming woman. Her father, she told me, had been a great chemist, Dr. Claude-Joseph Geofroy. Did you ever meet him?"

You answered that you had indeed, that you had met that good old-timer more than ten years ago, shortly before his death. Buffon had taken you to visit him. "He's a great man," the regent told you. "He's spent his fortune on science. He has a splendid laboratory, and what's more, he has created one of the most complete botanical gardens in France." It was none other than Buffon, the creator of the most important *jardin botanique* and *musée d'histoire naturelle* in the world who had said that to you. Claude-Joseph, very ill and almost blind, was, as your friend Buffon had told you, a most agreeable person. Patiently, he showed you his garden and his laboratory. When he spoke of the work he had done, his eyes shone once again and he looked twenty years younger; filled with pride and enthusiasm, he told the two of you of his experiments with tartaric potassium, borax, and prussic acid.

"So Mademoiselle Geofroy found herself in a difficult situation financially and was determined not to give up the botanical garden her father created. Because of that, she decided to sell the laboratory—although, in fact, she agreed only to sell it whole, and to someone who really loved science. That will help her cover the expenses in keeping up the garden. It was not hard to persuade her when I described your fondness for chemistry. We came to an agreement . . . and here it is. Now you won't have any excuse for not going on with the studies Dr. Ulloa drummed into your head."

"But all this must have cost a fortune."

"You're worth much more than that, dear friend . . ."

. . . Mariana saw Paris as you arrived full of illusions; she lived at Versailles and endured the ambassador's irritating assignments; she was mortally bored in that great palace watching the days go monotonously by, with no news except vicious gossip, without any work to do except to write stupid letters; she was at the masked ball and met the Marquise de Pompadour, very young and beautiful, disguised as a pagan goddess; she met, thanks to her, the good d'Alembert, the fearsome Voltaire, and the lovable Diderot; she returned happily from Fontenay to settle in this magnificent town house in the rue St-Jacques, where she was now listening to you, who were at her side, lying in bed, with your eyes fixed on the canopy, and talking to her for hours on end about your life.

It was on one of those afternoons, after a clamorous love battle—for you were celebrating the first three months of becoming lovers—that you spoke to Mariana of the future.

After finishing making love, you fell sound asleep. When you awoke, you saw your companion sitting in an armchair in front of the fireplace. She was wearing a light nightdress, and over her legs, which were resting on a footstool, was an open book she was engrossed in. You went over to her and could see one of the handsome illustrations that your friend François Boucher had executed. Mariana had recognized that the manuscript was in your handwriting.

"It was you who transcribed it, wasn't it?"

"Yes. A long time ago."

"Do you like this text a lot? It seems very gloomy to me, and even gloomier with these illustrations. They're beautifully done, but they're also frightening."

"I think it's the work of Boucher's that I prize the most."

Mariana raised her face and looked at you with a question in her eyes. She failed to understand why you had transcribed that very odd book. Nor did she dare ask you, for the perturbed expression she observed on her friend's face made her think that you had no desire to talk about it. You understood Mariana's forbearance. You were very well acquainted with her insatiable curiosity, and therefore grateful for her tact. Nonetheless, you felt an impulse to answer her, to speak once and for all of those odious visions you had had for almost your whole life. In fact, it was the one aspect of your existence of which Mariana had no knowledge whatever, and you didn't want to keep secrets from her. On the other hand, a modesty that had become a habit over many years paralyzed your tongue. After reflecting for quite some time, you poured yourself a glass of wine and sat down alongside her. Nostradamus settled himself comfortably between your legs. Stroking the cat, with your eyes fixed on the flames in the fireplace, you at last began to speak.

You told her the story from the beginning. From that long-ago day when you sucked the breast of Angustias for the last time; from the day that the Marquise de Gironella bathed you in Madrid. "After that, I've never once been free of those visions when I've made love . . ." You spoke to her of the frightful visions of the year '45, of the Book of Revelation, and of Boucher.

As Mariana listened to that strange story, she wondered if she wasn't dreaming. "And how do you know that it's the future?"

"At the beginning, naturally, I didn't know. For a long time, I thought it was my imagination, a sort of cruel joke that my senses played on me. But in the end, I've gradually been able to see through that. I have no doubts now: what I see is the future, as though I were observing it through a window . . ." He rose to his feet and went over to the secretary. He took a black memorandum book out of one of its drawers and handed it to Mariana. "Look at this."

She spent a long time looking through the small book. The phrases she read were extraordinarily disconcerting. Many of them she did not understand, but all the same they frightened her. "August 5, 1745. Impossible light. Thousands of Asian men and women are burned to ashes in an instant."

This can't be, the woman thought. Not even the Book of Revelation is that terrifying . . . She raised her eyes and saw her friend's profile. You were absorbed in contemplating the fire. She felt a greater tenderness toward you: There's a cause for his being so strange. Having to carry all those images around in his head . . . the poor man. She felt a deep sadness settling over her outlook, but she rebelled against it. She could not allow herself to become downcast. On the contrary, she had to keep up your spirits, instill happiness in you—now more than ever, now that she knew of the enormous burden you were bearing.

"Well, you must like that future a great deal. Just think of how many times you've looked at it!" she said to you, smiling, as she leafed through the pages of the memo book. "Heavens! I never imagined that anyone could make love so many times."

You returned her smile; you had immediately understood Mariana's noble intentions.

"Even though you may not believe it, I don't like it at all. Almost everything I've seen has been thoroughly unpleasant. It's sad to have confirmation that the human species is going to go on behaving as stupidly as it does today or perhaps even worse: if I've found any difference between that future and our present, it's that the ability to annihilate one another is infinitely increased in the years to come . . ."

Mariana again gave you a look of interrogation.

"Why do I do it if I find it so abhorrent? you ask me. You may find it hard to believe, but I've asked myself the same question many times. I can come up with two reasons, perhaps three. The first is that, in spite of everything, I get pleasure out of making love. My pleasure is identical, I believe, to the kind anyone else is able to feel. It has absolutely nothing to do with the visions, however odd that may seem. Two sensations are involved, even though they occur at the same moment. I'm able to distinguish them perfectly from each other. And one of the sensations is so agreeable to me that, despite the risk of an awful vision, my body impels me to go ahead. The second reason is that, like you, I'm very curious. It would be hypocritical of me to tell you that when I'm on the threshold of a love adventure, I'm thinking only of pleasure. I'm also thinking of the visions. It's a sort of sickness. Every time I get involved in such an adventure, I know that I'm going to see something that may be unpleasant; nonetheless, curiosity leads me on. Anyway, sometimes I see very interesting things—such as those apparatuses that fly. They're really fascinating. Or I see amusing things, such as when I saw a couple making love, or things that are frankly marvelous, such as when I observed the entire earth from up above, from much higher than the clouds . . ."

"Is that possible?"

"It would seem so. According to what I've seen, our successors are going to be terribly clever. You can't imagine the number of vehicles, artifacts, and devices I've seen. It would appear that science and technology have no secrets for them. How many times I've thought of good Buffon when I see those marvels! Unfortunately, I've also thought of Rousseau's writings, and I greatly fear that that man is right. Our cleverness can make gods of us, as Buffon maintains . . . or demons, as Rousseau says. And I believe that we're going in the second direction: our successors will be much more skillful, and more knowledgeable perhaps, but they won't be one whit more human than we are. Read what I've noted down in the section entitled "War," or worse still, the one I've called "Horrors." The future, so far as I've been able to see it, is full of conflicts, of slaughters, and I've observed civilians die there just as often as soldiers. They don't fight on battlefields, as we do now. Cities, with their enormous buildings, and miserable villages seem to be the places where their wars take place . . . which are terrible, you can believe me, Mariana, terrible . . ."

"And do you know when they'll take place?"

"Absolutely not. If the visions are strange, the form in which I perceive them is even stranger. I see the persons, their cities, their vehicles; I hear noises, and I've even heard them speak, but I don't understand what they're saying, as though they were speaking Chinese. Though often I recognize—I don't know how—that it's French or Spanish or English they're speaking. The same thing happens to me with what's in writing: I've seen countless posters, books, and newspapers; I recognize the alphabet, the numbers, though I can't understand what the writing says. It's discouraging. I'm certain that I've often seen some date written down, but I haven't been able to assimilate it; hence I don't have the least idea when what is depicted will occur. Naturally, I've made a few conjectures. Because of how advanced their techniques are, I'm convinced that it's a very distant future, perhaps three hundred years or more from now. But from people's attire, and from the habits and customs I've been able to observe, it would seem that it's no more than fifty years away. I suspect that it's a time that's more than a hundred and less than two hundred years from now."

Mariana did her best to make sense of what she was hearing, but she was unable to. The sensation that she was dreaming continued to hold sway over her consciousness. What she was hearing was too fantastic, too absurd. But every time she looked at the serious, somewhat sad face of her lover, she realized that, impossible though it was, it was all true.

"And the third reason?"

"The third? . . . ? Oh, yes! I imagine that now that you've heard all this, your mind refuses to accept it. It's too absurd, too fantastic, and you can't find a way to come to grips with it rationally. Or it's a nightmare or some sort of madness. A person's intelligence finds it hard to accept an unaccustomed line of reasoning."

"That's precisely what I thought," said Mariana, who was beginning to suspect that you were really a seer.

"He appears to be a sorcerer, you're probably thinking. But I'm not; there's not a trace of sorcery in what I'm telling you. Really, it's very simple. It's easy to guess what you're thinking, because I've been asking myself those same questions for more than twenty years, Mariana. My mind, like yours, refuses to accept something that fantastic. For many, a great many, hours I've racked my brains to make sense out of all this. In the beginning, as I told you, I came close to convincing myself that it was my imagination. Perhaps my imagination was a little more fertile and active than that of an ordinary man, I told myself, but that was all. As time went on and the visions came again and again, though, more and more clearly each time, more eloquent, more real, one might say, my first conviction didn't hold up and I was forced to accept that it was not a question of imagination but that, in fact, what were coming into my mind were scenes of the future. Nonetheless, I was back where I started from, because, even if I accepted the nature of the visions, I was—and am—very far from explaining to myself why they happen to me. And it's here that thinking has been of very little use to me: neither have I managed to work out a rational theory capable of explaining why I see into the future every time I reach orgasm, nor have I found such a theory already formed, because I'm convinced that nothing like it exists. I've had to be satisfied with working out other, absolutely irrational, hypotheses. There are several. The first—and it is the one that seems to me, despite everything, the most plausible—is that what's happening to me is a nightmare, a bad dream. Some day I'll wake up, perhaps younger or perhaps older, with a woman at my side, and rubbing my eyes, I'll banish the last memories of my dream. I'll get up out of bed, wash my face with cold water, and say, "What rubbish a person can dream." I'll forget the whole thing and continue a normal human being. The second hypothesis—and many are the times that I've feared it's the right one—is that the only cause of all this is madness and that, in the way of what people always say about madmen, I don't realize it. It's my imagination, in fact, that has given rise to all this—even though it's a great deal more than visions. My unhinged imagination has created this illusion of my existence, which I fulfill as seriously and as thoroughly convinced of my sanity as those unfortunates who wander aimlessly about the courtyards of asylums believing that they're the incendiary Nero, the implacable Alexander, or the irresistible Cleopatra . . ."

"You're not mad, Fausto. Or if you are, then I am too."

"Perhaps I'm imagining you as well; perhaps, as Plato said, nothing exists outside of what we imagine. Though it's hard to accept that . . . There are two other hypotheses, but they're so absurd that I almost never think about them. I'm afraid to, for I see madness, true madness, very close at hand the moment I begin to probe into them . . ." You took a big swallow of wine. You were lost in thought for a long time, as Mariana looked at you anxiously. Then you went on. "At times I've thought—just look how far absurd reflection can take a person—that I really live in another era, in the future, of course. I've thought that sometimes, perhaps when I dream, or when

I make love, I see myself in my real era. Perhaps I'm an admirer of this earlier, eighteenth, century and, crammed with the study of it, my imagination takes me here, to the France of Louis XV. When I reach orgasm, somehow I meet up with my own time again, the one to which I belong, in which I live my daily life, even though here in the imagination of the past, I'm not conscious of it . . . But there's one more hypothesis, still worse: I simply don't exist. My existence consists in the fleeting visions that some man who lives in the future has when he reaches orgasm. I, you, Voltaire, Denis, France, our whole familiar world, are only part of the amorous spasms experienced by some inhabitant of a century beyond the second millennium." Mariana smiled, and you smiled along with her. "Yes, darling, such are the conclusions a person arrives at when wanting to explain the inexplicable . . . When all is said and done, whoever we are, we're together, and that's what counts."

"You haven't told me the third reason for doing it. Remember?"

"Ah yes, I haven't made that clear. I believe I've gone on making love not so much for the pleasure of it or out of curiosity as because I've always suspected that there, precisely at the moment of orgasm, I was going to find the answer, the explanation of all this. And believe me, dear," he said with a smile, "my intuition hasn't failed me. I haven't found the answer in love, but I've now found repose. It surprises me that you, a woman so full of curiosity, haven't asked me what I've seen when the two of us make love."

"I was afraid to ask you."

"Well, do you know what I've seen? Nothing," you said, almost shouting, "absolutely nothing. The pleasure of loving you, and you yourself, have been my only companions during orgasm. Darling, thanks to you, I've left behind everything that, whatever it may have been, I'm now content to regard as having been a bad dream."

"Is that true?"

"Absolutely true!" You took her in your arms, obliging her to get to her feet, and held her tightly. "Darling, all that is over and done with, I'm convinced of it. What it was and why it was will remain a mystery. But there are many mysteries in the world, and even so we can live in peace. I left that nightmare behind ninety days ago . . ."

Touched, Mariana kissed you again and again, until you ended up in the bed joyously making love. Once more, you felt a pleasure free of that odious and now long-gone burden.

Love also felt very good to Mariana, for it helped dissolve the complicated thoughts that had lodged in her head building pressure. All those were effaced, and she was convinced that you would never rouse them in her mind again. You had put it well: there were just the two of you there, alone . . . and your children. She wanted, as she never had before in her life, to have a child with the man who was so dear to her, and she allowed that sweet dream to occupy her mind. You, for your part, kept your eyes fixed on the canopy of the bed. You looked serene, satisfied, happy. As she contemplated that delicate profile she was so fond of, there came to her mind those pleasant afternoons that, as a little girl, she spent counting syllables in order to do her homework. She remembered one particularly difficult assignment: to compose a ten-syllable poem with two hundred letters in it. She never managed to do what was prescribed. The tyranny of arithmetic implacably fettered her imagination: either the poem was a nice one but had either more or fewer than the two hundred letters required, or it had precisely that many but was no longer pretty.

"Fausto. I'm going to do a portrait of you in ten verses and two hundred letters. What do you think of the idea?"

"I think it's a good one, darling," you answered, a little taken aback.

Mariana leaped out of bed, put a shawl over her shoulders and sat down at the desk. Rasero spent the morning in the laboratory putting the instruments in order and trying to decipher Dr. Geofroy's records. Many times he wanted to speak with his lover, but there was no way to get her to listen. "Later, darling," she said to him, "leave me in peace now." And he would leave her in peace, with her pen in one hand and counting on the fingers of the other. Rasero was unable to see her until lunchtime, when she arrived in the dining room, impeccably dressed in that green dress he liked so much, an enormous smile on her lips.

"Sir," she said to him cheerily, "kindly contemplate your portrait." And she handed him a sheet of paper on which were written the words

> I met a Señor Rasero,
> black eyed, bald headed;
> he never sleeps till break of day,
> and yet I love him anyway.

He's a sorcerer, I've heard tell,
because he's doubtless odd;
a forehead ten fingers broad,
a magus of alchemy
(this isn't an absurdity).
And a seer as well.

The Malagan really liked the poem. "It's splendid, Mariana," he said, touched.

"And it has ten verses, two hundred letters, and fifty words," she explained proudly, without mentioning that she had arrived at that last result by chance, without deliberately aiming for it. "It's curious; I've wanted to write that ten-line verse for a long time, but I never could. I couldn't find the right word to rhyme with *tell,* because the line 'He's a sorcerer, I've heard tell,' came to me just a few days after I'd met you. What you talked about to me last night gave me the key. I never would have suspected that you're a 'seer as well.' "

"*Were* a seer, Mariana," Rasero interposed, a little edgily.

Mariana perceived his discomfort and felt sorry, though, in all truth, what she had learned the night before was not easy to digest. No matter how hard she tried to forget it, it kept coming back to her, over and over, like an irritating blowfly. So she'd decided to compose that poem, and in fact she managed to keep her mind busy for some time. But now the strange confession came back to her, and she knew she wouldn't be able to let go of it until she had cleared up a doubt she hadn't had time to question Rasero about. "Fausto, I don't believe I'll ever bring up this subject again; I understand how much it must trouble you. But before I drop the matter altogether, I'd like you to clear up one last doubt for me. I promise you that after that I won't ever say a word about it again."

"Go ahead and ask, darling."

"Have you kept your secret all to yourself for these many years? Haven't you ever confessed it to anybody?"

"Two persons, apart from you. The first was the Marquise de Gironella, the woman with whom I made love for the first time. I remember that I very much enjoyed doing that even though the images of terrified men and women in a street in Madrid interfered with my pleasure. Naturally, I didn't understand this, and I had to ask myself if the images could be normal, if they could be part of the act of making love. The simplest thing was to ask the marquise, for

I had no doubt that that woman was an expert in matters of love. So I asked her what she had seen. 'See? . . . When?' she replied in surprise. 'When we made it . . . ,' I said. She looked at me as at a very odd creature and answered that there was nothing to see; the point was to feel. That struck me as very strange. When I made love with other women and visions kept appearing, I was very careful not to tell them so, though sometimes I asked them if they'd seen anything, perhaps in the hope of finding someone to whom that same thing was happening that was happening to me. When they heard my question, I always received the same look as the one from the marquise. Some of them said I was crazy, and others simply laughed. It wasn't long before I discovered that nobody, except for me, ever saw anything in making love . . ."

"And the other person?"

"He was a priest . . . It's a rather odd story. I was about to leave for France, and my father ordered me to make confession before taking off. I did it completely willingly. I had had that experience with the Marquise de Gironella not long before, and I was really deeply moved by my discovery, so moved that a religious fervor suddenly came over me—something I've never again felt. After tasting such delights (besides the marquise, I had also made love to a couple of housemaids), I was convinced that God existed. Only he, I said to myself, is capable of offering us this. I understood Christ's insistence on love. I had no doubt that love was the one thing capable of putting an end to human hatred. Everything seemed clear to me: love was salvation. And of all the religions, none has placed as much emphasis on love as Catholicism. So I thanked heaven for having been baptized in its church. I even thought of becoming a priest. Of course, I soon pushed that idea from my head, for I realized that carnal love—which was the only form of love I was acquainted with—was forbidden to priests, at least to honest priests. My fervor was so great that I found religious significance even in the visions that I had had, which were beginning to become more and more disagreeable. I am one of the elect, I said to myself. It has pleased the Lord to bestow this gift on me. It is his will that I should see suffering and human misery at the very moment that I attain the greatest carnal pleasure. That is, without doubt, in order to remind me of our insignificance, so that, in addition to loving a woman, I may love my neighbor, have pity on him, as I ought to pity myself for being a sad mortal subject to a thousand vicissitudes, though also capable of loving, of being for an instant equal to him, my Father, with whom I shall become one some day if only love and compassion guide my footsteps. Such were the foolish thoughts flying around in my head. I was happy, therefore, to make my confession; I was eager to cleanse my conscience before the serene gaze of one of our Lord's shepherds. I went into the first church I came upon. It was a very old one, in the center of Madrid. It was nearly empty, for it was siesta time. The summer sun entered pitilessly through the tall windows. The scattered rays of light reflected by the adornments on the altar, along with the terrible heat, gave the place a sinister aspect, more like entering the antechamber of hell than the house of God. Relieved, I saw, beneath the curtain of a large confessional, a pair of patent leather shoes and the long skirt of the cassock above them. Just as I reached the confessional, a woman dressed in black rose to her feet, and crossing herself, left the bench. I knelt down. I was unable to see the priest's face through the curtain of black tulle. His sour sweat mingled with the disagreeable fumes that wine produces when, after it has been drunk, its vapors mount to the mouth after warming in someone's belly for God only knows how long. I must admit that by that point my religious dedication had moderated, but even so, it was strong enough to keep me from being deterred. I began to enumerate my sins. The man listened to me in a bored way; I could see him nodding his head drowsily. I felt pity for him: It must be terrible to be listening to sinners at this hour of the day, with this heat and a belly full of food. It didn't matter to me that he didn't pay very much attention to me. I felt very good knowing that I was purifying my spirit. In the end it's God who must hear me, I said to myself, and he never sleeps, nor does he suffer from indigestion or hangovers . . . I finally came to my greatest sin, which I nonetheless felt as proud of as a new holder of a bachelor's diploma does his piece of parchment. I knew that what I had done was a sin, for the Marquise de Gironella was a widow and we had shared the marriage bed without the Lord's blessing, even if I was also well aware that love purifies everything. I was prepared to repent for having fornicated, and to make amends for it I was willing to recite all the Pater Nosters and Ave Marias that the good priest would choose to impose upon me, but naturally I was not prepared to repent for having experienced love. There was no need to pardon it, since it wasn't a sin at all; instead, it was the best way of following the commandments of the Son of God. When I spoke of the marquise, the priest roused himself and began to bombard me with questions, almost all of them indicative of an unwholesome cast of mind. It was then that I spoke to him of the visions. The man rose to his feet abruptly, with such vehemence that his head hit the ceiling of the confessional with a terrible blow. 'What are you saying, you wretch?' he said to me in an imposing, thundering voice.

" 'That I've seen strange things,' I answered fearfully.

" 'Out of here, you son of Satan!' he shouted wrathfully, having fled the confessional. I'll never forget his robust body, his dark, wizened face, with its aquiline nose and slightly slanting eyes."

Mariana, of course, thought of the archbishop of New Spain.

" 'But, Father . . . ,' I said to him.

" 'Out with you, I said, spawn of Lucifer!' he shouted, wiping with his sleeve the big beads of sweat running down his forehead. 'Vade retro, Satanás! I don't want to see you!'—and he hid his eyes—'Monster of lust, violator of virgins, loathsome abortion of Satan . . . ' I was indignant; I didn't deserve those insults. But I was also thoroughly frightened: the man was very tall, and he was threatening to strike me. 'Out of here, out, you infamous fornicator. Sacrilege.' I edged away and ran for the door. 'You'll burn in hell, you wretched worm . . . daring to place your impure hand on the body of our Most Holy Mother! Pig, wretch! . . .' He said these last words with tears in his eyes. We exchanged a final look. The man, his face contorted, his eyes holding back the tears they were close to shedding, flung one last curse at me—'May you rot in the underworld, you abortion of the devil!'—and hurled a bronze candelabrum at me as well, which I very nearly failed to dodge. It was so big, Mariana, that if that raging fanatic had hit his target, I wouldn't be here to tell you all this . . . After that horrible afternoon, I've never again gone to confession, nor have I spoken with a priest inside a church. I prefer to talk to priests in their houses and in drawing rooms, and to restrict myself to French priests, who are a great deal more cynical but at the same time more civilized. I stopped believing in God shortly after this. But I certainly am left without the slightest doubt about the rabid fanaticism of Spanish men of the cloth. May God deliver us from them!"

"They are awful," Mariana agreed, as she allowed a long procession of priests in cassocks whom she had known in New Spain to pass through her head. Few of them, if any, had escaped being rabid fanatics, as Fausto had said . . .

You were just finishing your meal when a messenger arrived from Versailles, in time to make your desserts taste bitter. It was a note from Gontafout, an old friend of La Pompadour's, in which he let you know that the marquise was dying. Mariana burst into tears, and you ordered Claude to ready the carriage at once. You embraced your Mariana, who couldn't stop weeping. "I'll be back as soon as I can, darling," you said to her and gave her a quick kiss.

The horses struggled to make headway, for they had to go through heavy mud, which came above their hooves, and ford the many streams down which turbulent water was rushing toward the river. It was raining buckets, and the afternoon was very cold. We're halfway through April, and it seems like the middle of winter, you thought. It's this damned weather that's killed her. You remembered that, when the two of you visited her, at the beginning of March, Jeanne-Antoinette had just recovered from a terrible crisis that had kept her with one foot in the grave for several days. "She was so ill," Soubise told you at the time, when you ran into him at the Opéra, "that she couldn't even lie down, because her cough suffocated her. She sat upright in an armchair for days at a time . . ." But the weather improved, and with it, the marquise. March began splendidly, as though spring had decided to arrive a few days ahead of time, and Jeanne-Antoinette, feeling much better, began to cling to life once again. She had the energy to observe from a terrace at Choissy the eclipse of the sun that took place at that time. This was the same phenomenon you watched with Mariana, along with countless others, on the Champ-de-Mars. The strange happening was not at all to your liking, Rasero. You regarded it as a bad omen. Seeing the sun hidden when it was at the zenith gave you the melancholy sensation that a life was being cut off abruptly just as it was reaching its full strength. When that imbecile Louis noticed that Jeanne-Antoinette's health had improved, he could think of nothing better than to commission Codin to write a vulgar little poem, in which the rebirth of the sun after the eclipse and that of the marquise after her terrible crisis were conjoined. Yet that wasn't the worst part. A poem, no matter how bad it might be, wasn't going to damage the health of your beloved Jeanne-Antoinette. What could make it worse, however, was forcing her to go to Versailles. That confounded palace was colder than a grave. The Sun King's extraordinary pride made him order such enormous rooms built, with such gigantic and imposing windows, that there was no fireplace on earth able to warm the vast expanses. When winter was the coldest, going three or four paces away from the hearth was like venturing onto the steppes of the Ukraine; the cold, the absolute master of the palace, enveloped a person from head to foot. There was good reason why so many dauphins and princesses died before reaching puberty. Pneumonia was as common among the Bourbons as a prognathous jaw among the Hapsburgs. Louis XV's own blood paid harsh tribute to the delusions of grandeur of the son of Louis the Just. But stubborn and self-centered, he had his old lover brought to the gloomy palace. Jeanne-Antoinette had just arrived when the much-heralded spring took sudden leave and winter, returning, settled tyrannically over France. Those were terrible days. The ice-cold rain seemed to want to go on till the end of time. And it was that unseasonable winter weather, those extremely cold days—which, paradoxically, were the best ones you'd spent in your life, Rasero, since basking in the warmth of the hearth, shielded from the cold by the warm body of your lover, you eluded that freezing winter you could see pounding against the windows, which seemed to you as far away as a star, and beneath your roof you felt a warm, comfortable atmosphere, quite like the one, no doubt, in that beautiful country where your Mariana had been born—it was those terrible days that finally robbed Jeanne-Antoinette of her life.

At last the carriage reached the road to Versailles. Dusk had fallen, and the rain beat insistently on the roof and the little windows of the carriage. You couldn't see a thing outside; darkness had consumed the countryside behind the curtain of water. But you had little need to see it. You knew this landscape like the palm of your hand. How many times you had traveled the road in both directions! Thinking about that, you realized that, even though obviously the road and the landscape were precisely the same whether you were going to the palace or coming from it, to you they had always been two very different things. You remembered the road as being pretty, joyful, sunny, with luxuriant fields and smiling peasants, whenever it was taking you back to Paris. In the early days, when you were still living at Versailles, going to Paris was something that delighted you utterly. A day before leaving you were already as eager and excited as a bride on the eve of her wedding. Going to Paris! Leaving behind all those dolts; visiting your friends; going to Notre Dame to contemplate from its terraced roof the cherished sight of your beloved city. You smiled on remembering yourself young and happy, full of dreams, ordering the coachman to whip up the horses in order to shorten the trip that in your eager impatience seemed eternal. The road back to Versailles was very different. You remembered it as dark, with night falling, the countryside desolate, and always some laggard peasant driving his team of oxen home with boredom stamped on his face. You felt dejected, gloomy, as though that same bride had suddenly turned into a widow: Back to that odious palace, to put up with that cretin of an ambassador, to feel the enormous weight of the decadence of the Bourbons, to endure the company of that whole pack of foppish snobs, to enter, in a word, the kingdom of hypocrisy.

But the road had never been as ill omened as now, because now it wasn't a bunch of imbeciles awaiting you but the lifeless body of your best friend. After having played cat and mouse with each other for more than twenty years, death and Jeanne-Antoinette had finally met. You had seen death in that very dear woman from the moment you first met her. You saw it hunched over, still very small, behind the pallor that had so impressed you. You also saw it in her mother's face, already mature, the very nearly absolute mistress of that existence she led, as would be the case later on with her daughter, when she did not live long enough to reach her fifties. You saw it in Jeanne-Antoinette's own daughter, that adorable creature who inherited the virtues of her mother enhanced a hundred times over, though she also inherited, greatly accentuated as well, a deadly disease that did not allow her to reach even her fifteenth birthday. You had also seen death when you made love to Jeanne-Antoinette. You saw it disguised as the cadaver of a man whose body vainly awaited being reduced to ashes in an oven that, perhaps tired of consuming so much human flesh, had gone out forever. And just a short time ago, you saw death when Mariana and you visited her. But now it had grown in size; it was imposing, so imposing that it hid Jeanne-Antoinette. The terrible face of death scarcely allowed even a glimpse of your friend, whose life, gone into hiding, barely managed to appear in the brightness of her eyes . . .

When you arrived at Versailles, you were informed that the marquise had just passed away; at that very moment they were transferring her remains outside the palace, to a residence in the rue des Réservoirs, where a wake was being hastily organized. Despite the enormous sadness that came over you, you couldn't help being glad that Jeanne-Antoinette had passed away in Louis XIV's palace. Violating the code of etiquette that the Sun King had imposed, the Marquise de Pompadour, without being a member of the royal family, had died at the palace of Versailles. A bourgeois lady, the daughter of a banker with a dubious reputation, she had died beneath the same roof that had witnessed the birth of the great-grandson of the greatest king that France had ever had. You reflected, even by her death she was able to give the nobility that detested her and humiliated her every single day she lived in that obscene palace one last slap in the face . . .

Your friend reposed in the middle of the four tapers. Death, perhaps satisfied, abandoned her face, which, serene and relaxed, still showed the enduring traces of her former beauty. Friends and enemies surrounded her corpse. D'Alembert made no effort to hide his grief; Richelieu, obese and as eternal as the plague, seemed the most wretched man on earth. Choiseul embraced you, downcast: "She was a great woman, Monsieur Rasero. The greatest woman I have known in my life . . ." They were all there . . . save for the man who had molded the existence of that creature as though it were clay in his hands, the man whom Jeanne-Antoinette wanted above all else, for whom she had sacrificed her husband, her daughter, her health, and all of France when necessary, the man whose image occupied, despotically, the mind, the consciousness, the senses of that woman, so that she was unable to free herself from the image for a single day in more than twenty years' time. That man was not present; he was unable to render a last homage to Jeanne-Antoinette's remains. He was unable to be with his old lover, for a disgusting code of etiquette, prescribed by his great-grandfather, would not allow it. He had to be alone with his grief in some room or other of the palace, weeping bitterly and swearing to himself for the hundredth time to purify his being, from now on and forever. If you still had an ounce of sympathy for that man, sensual and solitary, selfish and tormented, it disappeared forever on that winter night in the middle of April.

Two days later, they buried the marquise in the Capuchin Convent in Paris, in the Place Vendôme, thereby fulfilling her express wishes. It was one of the most lavish and solemn funerals the old capital of the Franks had ever seen. All Paris paid a last homage to that capricious woman whose kindness, beauty, happiness, cleverness, and exquisite taste had made her the symbol of an entire era. She was the feminine side—Voltaire was the masculine—of the spirit of an enchanting century, perhaps the most luminous that humans have known, one that perished along with her and, like that woman who had died before her time, scarcely past forty, also perished before its time, when it still lacked more than thirty years before its end should have come.

You did not attend that funeral, Rasero. Those two gloomy days between the wake at Versailles and the solemn mass at Notre Dame were to you like two centuries in which horror, uninvited by anyone, entered your existence and, alas, from then on never left it . . .

VII
Lavoisier

Scellières, June, 1778

In the abbey of Scellières, in Champagne, at dusk on the last day of the month of May, a small group of people heard the Abbot Mignot's poignant words bidding a last farewell to the philosopher's badly embalmed remains. In the end, Voltaire, as usual, had had his way: the earth covering his coffin was consecrated. But it had not been easy, despite all the measures he took in his last years, and above all during the last days of his life, when he realized that death would finally vanquish him. After receiving communion in an elaborate ceremony at Ferney thirteen years before, he had confessed his sins and his repentance—although very ambiguously—for the continuous attacks he had mounted against the Catholic church throughout his life. And on his deathbed he had as his last companions two of God's shepherds, the good Mignot and the abbot of Saint-Sulpice, Tersac, whom Voltaire had chosen as his confessor. It was they who in sadness heard his last words, in truth not at all pious ones: "Let me die in peace!" The church, moss-backed and vengeful, convinced for many years that Voltaire—the Antichrist, as it had come to call him—was its worst enemy, was not mollified and therefore made every effort to prevent the body of its old adversary from being shrouded by hallowed ground. The archbishop of Paris threatened to excommunicate whoever dared bury the philosopher in any church or pantheon in the city and sent instructions to his colleague in Troyes to do the same. That malevolent man knew very well the terror that Voltaire had of being buried in a common grave, outside a cemetery: the image of the body of the actress Adrienne Lecouvreur, wrapped in a sheet and flung into a hole lined with quicklime, which Voltaire had seen almost fifty years before, and the horror with which he remembered it, had remained with him until the last day of his life.

But Voltaire was cleverer than his enemies. A few days before dying, with his health definitely broken, he used what little strength he had left to work out a plan with his intimates that would protect his remains from the archbishop's antagonism. Meticulous and precise, as though he were conceptualizing another book, he thought it all out down to the last detail: once he had passed on, the minister of police would ask the town council for authority to remove the body from Paris so that it could be buried at Ferney. Only after it was outside the city would they embalm it in order to transport it on to the crypt that awaited in the parish church at his country mansion. Everything would have to be done in the strictest secrecy; Voltaire's body had to be outside Paris when the archbishop learned of his death. It was even necessary to buy the silence of the journalists.

All this went as he planned. Voltaire passed away at midday, but no one learned of the death—apart from the small circle of his closest friends and the chief of police—until late that night. They put an old nightshirt on his body, with a nightcap on his head, and transported his remains to the carriage of a friend, the Spaniard Fausto Rasero, who was to take the body to Scellières. At the same time, in another carriage, loaded with a trunkful of old newspapers, Madame Denis left for Melun. They did that because the philosopher did not altogether trust the chief of police. They told him that the corpse would leave by way of the road to Melun in Madame Denis' carriage. If the official double-crossed them—something, incidentally, that did not happen—the soldiers at the tollgate at Vincennes would find a big pile of old newspapers instead of the philosopher's body. When Voltaire came up with the plan, his toothless mouth smiled on imagining that scene. Meanwhile, Rasero would leave by way of the Montrouge gate, and once in Scellières would wait for Madame Denis and other friends. They would embalm the corpse on the spot before going on to Ferney.

You went through customs without mishap. A soldier peeked out the little window of the customs booth. "What's that?" he asked, eyeing the bundle a thick woolen blanket covered in the front seat.

"A pile of old clothes," you replied. "I'm going to give it to the nuns at the Convent of the Assumption to hand out to the poor." They let you through the gates without asking more questions. A pile of old clothes, you thought. What that blanket was concealing was the body of France's greatest thinker, who, precisely because of his prodigious ability to think, was sneaking out of his native city, as though a wretch of a thief. Once the danger was past, you uncovered your friend's face; you wanted to look him in the eye to apologize for passing him off as a ragbag. "There was no other way around it, my friend," you said to him as you looked at that incredibly wizened countenance, as though death, before giving his body the coup de grace, had dug its fingers into it, slowly tearing his flesh away ounce by ounce until it had left him as you were seeing him, looking like a skeleton barely covered by an old yellowed skin, like old parchment. Nonetheless, when you saw him that way, in his nightcap, his eyes closed and his mouth shut very tight, he seemed to be sleeping peacefully, perhaps dreaming of his long-ago glories at Versailles, generously distilling his inexhaustible wit and fatuously receiving the false flattery and fawning of his countless admirers. He appeared to be smiling in his sleep, although it was the same smile, cruel and indifferent, that you had seen on the skulls at Montparnasse. He's smiling because he managed to put one over on his enemies, you thought, because he is seeing realized his fervent wish to be buried with dignity, in some plot of ground consecrated by the church he so thoroughly detested. An odd sort: a man who could state in all seriousness a few months before his death, "I die adoring God, loving my friends, without hatred toward my enemies, abominating superstition." What else, if not superstition, was his fear of being buried just anywhere, a fear arising from the foretokening he detected in the burial of a stage actress so many years before?

Abbot Mignot was waiting in Scellières. The abbot was very upset, for the archbishop of Paris had learned of the death of the philosopher and had sent messengers at once to every corner of the kingdom with the order—under threat of excommunication—not to permit Voltaire's remains to be buried in ground consecrated by the church. "It is impossible to bury him at Ferney," Mignot told you. "The bishop of Lyons is going to stop it, I'm certain. It's best to bury him right here; we can do it before the interdiction arrives from Paris."

You agreed, but it was necessary to await Madame Denis' decision, and she hadn't yet arrived. Meanwhile, the corpse was embalmed. In a short time, the niece arrived. She too was very worried, since on the way she had learned of the order of the archbishop of Paris. When the abbot explained his idea, the woman agreed immediately. "But do it at once, for the love of God, before the messenger from Notre Dame gets here. If my uncle is buried in a common grave, he'll never forgive me . . . The poor man was so terrified that that would happen."

They barely had time to dress up the corpse. They put Voltaire into his elegant royal librarian's uniform. It was a beautiful outfit of white silk with gold embroidery, but even over his nightshirt, it looked very loose fitting on the emaciated body. It's incredible how thin he'd grown, you thought, remembering the day you saw your friend appear in that costume for the first time, more than thirty years before . . .

He looked impeccable in the immaculate white uniform and his plumed tricorn, but what most ennobled him was the splendid smile that lit up his face. It wouldn't have been humanly possible to receive all the greetings, embraces, and congratulations of those present. That day François was the lord and master of Versailles; even the king seemed insignificant alongside him. Louis looked at the writer with a certain envy, for he understood that all those homages, signs of respect, and gestures of admiration with which his courtiers were paying tribute to Voltaire were owed to the man's incredible talent. He, on the other hand, received those same tributes not because he was an outstanding man but simply because he was the great-grandson of Louis XIV, who in turn was the grandson of Henry IV, and so on. His courtiers respected him and did him homage for what the blood running in his veins represented, not for his merits, which, as he knew very well, were extremely few.

Perhaps it was this envy, so ill concealed by the king, that was responsible for Voltaire's exile. You imagined what Louis was thinking as he observed the new nobleman: He is greater than I am, greater than any other man. Nonetheless, I am more powerful. As he plays with ideas, I play with fates, and I am going to prove that to this man, who says that he loves Paris above all else; I shall condemn him to leave the city and never set foot in it again. In any event, the fact was that, shortly after that ceremony, Voltaire found himself obliged to leave his native city and begin a period of exile that lasted almost thirty years . . . But he returned: even in the game of playing with fate he turned out to be more powerful than the monarch. Not four years had gone by after the death of Louis, eaten away by smallpox, when his old rival came back to Paris victorious, like a Roman general who returns to the metropolis after a successful campaign in the East. He returned old and ill, it is true, but possessed of an amazing vitality, determined to find in his beloved city the colophon of a life that, like many of his creations, was a work of art. "I'm very ill, Fausto, really ill. I know it, because for the first time in my life I don't fear death; instead, I'm beginning to see it as a blessing . . . ," he said to you when he returned to Paris, six months before, and underwent a terrible crisis that everyone thought would be fatal. But it wasn't. He summoned the strength of spirit to recover in just a few days: "I don't intend to die without first harvesting what it has taken me such great pains to plant in this city . . ." And what a harvest it was! All Paris turned out to hail its hero, who, when he was in far-off Potsdam or the mountains around Geneva, never broke his tie to his native city. As if through a long umbilical cord, his works nourished the active minds, eager for knowledge, that abounded in Paris; similarly, he was nourished—by letters, newspapers, and magazines—by the cultural juices that, despite the church, the courts of justice, and the police, flowed abundantly in the capital of the Franks. Once recovered, he squandered prodigally the impressive forces his iron will had helped him amass during the recent years of awaiting his longed-for return. He made the rounds of the salons, visited the Academy and the museums, gave lectures, and pursued projects, including the longstanding one of compiling a dictionary of high quality though small size and easy comprehension, suitable for a much larger readership than that of the *Encyclopédie.* "If the Gospels, my dear friend," he told you on that memorable night in Ferney, "had been written in thirty-seven volumes of fifty pages each, you may be certain that Christianity would be as familiar to us as the rites of the Bushmen . . ." He formally proposed his idea to the Academy and even offered, despite his eighty-two years and the multitude of responsibilities he had taken on, to write the section under the letter *A.* And he did so. He also brought out a play and personally supervised its rehearsals and staging. He received all those who sought to see him, including Benjamin Franklin, the prepossessing ambassador of the brand-new republic of the United States, who was perhaps the one person whose fame and popularity could be compared to the philosopher's. The big bear hug that these two men gave each other, along with the affectionate colloquy that Voltaire had with the ambassador's little grandson, was unquestionably what most gripped Paris' imagination in those days; their meeting was celebrated to the point of exhaustion, and was immortalized by a painter. Paris was proud and happy at welcoming back its most illustrious figure, like a loving mother receiving her son after he has been away from home too long.

The apotheosis, however, took place at the Comédie Française on the night of the premiere of *Irène,* the last work Voltaire wrote for the theater. The ovation lasted for more than a half hour. The audience, the crème de la crème of French society—among which, like merely another spectator (for that night her charm, and her beauty, and her impressive attire did not divert in the slightest the attention everyone present was paying the philosopher) was Marie Antoinette, the young, winsome queen who, in an unusual mark of respect, noted down in her program her observations as she watched the play—applauded till their palms turned red when a bust of the philosopher was unveiled in the middle of the stage, and it applauded even more when an actor planted himself in front of Voltaire's box with a crown of laurel in his hands. The artist modestly handed the crown to the Marquise de Villette, but at the insistence of the audience, she was finally obliged to have it placed on her temples by the hands of your beloved friend Jean d'Alembert. Like everyone else, you applauded madly. At your side, your friend Antoine Lavoisier, happy and moved to a degree that you had seldom seen in him, also applauded as he shouted, "Bravo!" at the top of his lungs. It's strange to see Antoine in such spirits, you thought, as it's also strange to see me in them—so happy, so moved, that the tears I'm holding back are clouding my eyes . . .

It was strange because happiness and emotion had not visited you for many years, Rasero. But the happiness of Voltaire, your old mentor, was so great and so sincere that he generously shared it with everyone present. You had never seen that wizened and incredibly aged face look so pure; paradoxically, it reminded you of that of a newborn babe, for that was how innocent, how serene it looked. Voltaire, like a good wine, had finally rid himself of his impurities, or better and more precisely put, he had like wine, transformed them, making the bitter sweet, the rough noble, the sour smooth and gentle. Having rid himself of vanity, of petulance, his spirit, for which there was no longer any room inside that exhausted body—a formidable spirit that fought tirelessly through who knows how many years against superstition, fanaticism, and ignorance and that sought, as never before, the light of reason, the power of ideas, the limits of intelligence—shone brightly, illuminating all those who were willing to see it and many, many others, illuminating his own time and all times. On seeing him at that moment, a tiny, sick man, stealing extra time from life, you realized that the soul of that man was immortal, like that of Descartes or Newton, Plato or Aristotle, Pascal or Leonardo, like that of all who, as rebellious as God's angels, refused to accept their fate as mortal beings and dared to defy the very heavens so as to steal from them a portion of their glory. It was useless to resist in the face of that extraordinary strength; a mere smile of the philosopher was enough to hold your perennial sadness at bay. The seemingly contrary marks of laughter and tears showed in your face and in the faces of the spectators: everyone was laughing self-consciously or weeping happy tears in a rather absurd way—perhaps because our faces have still not learned to manifest, in a clear, definite expression, feelings as contradictory as admiration and envy, joy and sadness, veneration and pity.

"He's a great man, Fausto," Lavoisier said to you, infected by the collective enthusiasm. Of course he's a great man, you thought, as is Antoine himself . . . And at the very moment that this thought crossed your mind, you had a better understanding of the philosopher's greatness, because a person like Lavoisier, whose intelligence, energy, and discipline had never ceased to amaze you, a person like Lavoisier, you were thinking, along with so many other young men you knew (Lagrange, Berthollet, and many others), a real pleiad of talent, would be unthinkable without Voltaire. It was he who inspired them, he who through his penetrating works showed them the fertile path of reason. His persistent, stubborn, and at times heroic fight to see scientific labors recognized, to place philosophy at the service of science, was the generous seed from which these men had sprung and from which many more would doubtless also rise. Ah, Rasero, at times you thought that that future which has never ceased to devastate your existence would arrive long before you suspected it would, especially when you noted the dizzying progress that science was making in the hands of those young men. ("He's a great man, Fausto," your friend insisted without leaving off applauding.) But of all that luminous generation, your favorite, by far, was Antoine . . .

Place in a very clean retort eighteen ounces of pure dry saltpeter, reduced to a fine powder; pour over it six ounces of pure highly rectified vitriolic acid; place the retort at once in a sand hotbox; and fit it with a large

> glass receiver, hermetically sealing all the joints with a mixture of mortar and a little sand. Very soon a little heat and a red vapor will be produced; then apply a moderate fire, and the receiver will immediately be filled with red vapors, as a liquid begins gradually to drip down.

Rasero reread Boerhaave's text, hoping to discover any omission on his part in following the prescribed steps. But no: he had done precisely what the author had specified. Then why in the devil doesn't it come out the way it should? he wondered as he observed the results of his experiment. The retort had indeed been filled with a red vapor that went duly into the receiver . . . and then went out through all the joints of the apparatus, filling the laboratory with an acrid and very penetrating odor. What he failed to see anywhere was the liquid that "begins gradually to drip down"; the top of the receiver had merely been coated with a faint gold-colored dew. At this rate, it'll take me a year to obtain the quantity of spirits of niter that I need, he said to himself as he put a handkerchief to his mouth, since the reddish gas had ended up permeating the room. It was a very difficult experiment, and Rasero knew it. That was why he had decided to perform it. He could secure spirits of niter at the laboratory of one friend or another, or else make it himself through a much simpler process the Scotsman Joseph Black had developed with which he was very familiar. But by carrying out complicated experiments he had found a sort of anodyne for his mind. The more attention, care, and precision the steps in an experiment required, the more the experiment was able to draw his mind from the memory that tormented it. Who knew if he would have survived had he not had that old book of Dr. Boerhaave's in his house?

After spending a long time in hell, so to speak, his faculties despite everything found the courage (or the cowardice?) to combat the madness in which he had sunk just one step away from losing his mind altogether, and once he overcame it, there was nothing for him but to go on living, even though he was still not brave enough to go out of the house or see his friends or go to a café, much less to a theater or even less to a brothel. He decided then to shut himself up in his library, but his mind, during his convalescence, could not assimilate what he read. Almost the moment he finished reading a paragraph of any sort of book, he would find himself thinking aimlessly about it, and after a time his wandering thoughts had nothing at all to do with what he had read, and a little while later even his wandering thoughts ceased. His uncontrolled intellect, like a mare in a fury, took off on its own to visit the future without any need of the pleasure and consolation of orgasm. And to think that once upon a time he thought he'd freed himself forever of that nightmare! There was no need now to excite his senses in order to make visions come to him. They came all by themselves, when they felt like it, in the midst of his reading, in the depths of sleep, or in the course of a conversation. Little by little, he learned to tolerate them; he even succeeded in enjoying this new situation, for he never lost the hope of finding, precisely there in one of those visions, in that remote future, the answer to that mystery, and also perhaps—that was really what he hoped to find most of all—his Mariana, there somewhere far off in the distance, heaven only knew how. In the beginning, however, the visions aroused a profound anxiety in him and he fled from them—to no avail, naturally—as he would have done from the plague. Hence he substituted the laboratory for the library. The first time he went there, all ready to set to work, he hadn't the slightest idea what he was going to do. He leafed through the notebooks kept by Dr. Claude-Joseph Geofroy, but the man's handwriting, minuscule and skittish, required a great effort to decipher. He then picked up a book, *Elementae cheimia,* by Dr. Hernamis Boerhaave and read passages in it at random until he came to a paragraph that attracted his attention. Dr. Boerhaave, in addition to being a great chemist, was without doubt a gentleman of impeccable manners, for only courtesy and consideration could explain the uncommon solicitude he showed for his hypothetical reader, whom he led, step by step, along the intricate paths of chemistry with the patience and the tender affection, one might say, of a benevolent and generous father:

> The following is the description of the work I have carried out to obtain absolutely pure spirits of wine (alcohol) without a trace of water solvent, so as to be able later to carry out highly interesting experiments with this marvelous, modest liquid, which has the faculty of catching fire in such an energetic, absolute, and clean way that I have never found any substance that can even be compared to it. But first I must warn you, kind reader, that the procedure here described is extremely laborious and full of difficulties. I can aver that I struggled for more than six months against the residues of water solvent, which despite my distilling the spirits of wine more than twenty times, resisted expulsion from the alcohol. So then, do not be dismayed if the first results are not encour-

> aging. In the art of chemistry, failures provide as much knowledge—and even more, I sometimes believe—than do successes.
>
> A sort of oven was constructed for a heat bath that did not allow the temperature to fall below 214 degrees Fahrenheit, and within it a large alembic was placed, into which the spirits of wine were poured until it was approximately two-thirds full. Then a cover was placed over the alembic at the end of a long thin tube introduced by way of the serpentine . . .

Rasero decided to carry out this experiment. It appealed to him for two reasons: on the one hand, the author warned that it was "laborious and full of difficulties," and thus it promised to absorb his mind for some time; and on the other, he couldn't help thinking that performing his first formal experiment in chemistry with spirits of wine was symbolically fitting, after saturating his body with wine for more than three months. So he began without delay. He searched about among Dr. Geofroy's gear and found, to his relief, that everything he needed was there, although the instruments, unused for so many years, were very dirty and dusty. He carefully laid out the ones he was about to employ and summoned his faithful Annette.

"Annette dear, bring two pails of clean water and help me wash this equipment." The woman, happy to see that her master had decided to occupy himself with something, hastened to bring him the water. "Oh, wait!" Annette heard as she reached the threshold of the door. "Bring me four bottles of wine as well."

The young woman's happiness vanished from her face. "But, sir, are you about to begin again?" Rasero looked at her in surprise, although he understood her at once. "No, woman, I'm not going to drink them. I need that wine for an experiment I'm about to perform."

Not altogether convinced, Annette went off in the direction of the kitchen.

It took Rasero several days to prepare the alembic and set up the receiver. When he finished, he contemplated with satisfaction, like an artist before his painting, the device that he had put together. The serpentine was no doubt the star of the entire system; it looked mysterious and beautiful and gave the equipment a serious look, as if to say, Only the sons of chemistry and the grandsons of alchemy are capable of using such strange and twisted, yet beautiful, instruments. Finally, he lit the bain-marie and prepared to observe the process. The water had not yet come to a boil when he saw dew forming on the walls of the serpentine; a little while later, a thin thread of vapor as subtle as dew came out through the mouth of the apparatus. It had a pleasant aroma, fresh and penetrating. Shortly after that, the receiver caught big drops of spirits of wine accompanied by the residues of the water solvent. Naturally, it didn't take Rasero six months to obtain dehydrated alcohol; in the end Boerhaave himself had provided the key for obtaining it much sooner ("Add to the second or third distillation a half pound of calcined salt"). Still, Rasero needed a good two weeks to get it—two weeks that he spent with a tranquil mind, keeping close watch on his experiment, preparing the salts, cleaning the new receptacles, and reading Dr. Boerhaave's work, where he found many interesting experiments that he could carry out later on with the alcohol. The visions scarcely bothered him; the future visited him only a couple of times—once as he was watching the wine distill and another time while he was sleeping. As usual, what he saw was not at all pleasant: "November 4, 1764. Huge tunnel full of people. They are all crowded together at the edge of what appears to be a public square. Suddenly, braking hard, a strange vehicle appears, without draft animals, of course. It is dragging ten or fifteen big boxes that are all rolling on strips of iron. Inside the boxes—I can think of nothing else to call them—a great many people can be seen, for the boxes have large windows. When the artifact stops, many doors open onto the public square; the people who are inside want to get out and those who are outside want to get in, so that a terrible disorder is created at each door. The people push one another and look at one another with hatred. (Why are they traveling underground?)"; "November 10, 1764. A man on his knees with his hands tied by the wrists behind his back. He looks badly beaten. Another man approaches. Both men have Asian features. The second one takes a pistol out of a leather sheath; he aims it at the temple of the man who is kneeling. He fires . . ."

He poured the anhydrous alcohol in a glass vessel and contemplated it, fascinated, for a long time, the way a mother contemplates her newborn child. He brought his nose closer to the vessel and breathed the penetrating odor of the alcohol. Then he took a small portion of it and placed it in a watch crystal. He next brought over a small piece of paper that he had lit in the oven, and he was able to see the pretty sight of the spirits of wine burning. The flame, pale blue in color, almost invisible, twisted and turned, while still retaining the aroma of the alcohol; it truly was a "marvelous, modest" liquid, as Dr. Boerhaave had described it. Rasero gave extended thought to choosing an experiment to perform with that substance. He caught sight of one of the bottles of wine he had used in the experiment, still half full. Taking care not to spill any, he poured the alcohol into the bottle until it was full. He shook it, using his thumb as a stopper, and then drank it down in three swallows . . .

The "marvelous, modest" liquid soon took effect: a dull stupor took possession of his senses. It was as if he had drunk ten bottles of wine all at once—and in fact, he had used almost ten bottles of wine to obtain the distillate. His sexuality, which had been asleep for so many months and which the innumerable bottles of wine he had drunk during that time hadn't done the least to excite, now suddenly awakened however, as though a pail of cold water had jarred it alert. The intense sexual urge he felt forced him to stand up—not without great effort, since everything around him was frantically turning round and round—and head for the door out of his house, which he reached only after having broken three or four large flower vases on the way. In a thick, deep-throated voice that he himself did not recognize, he ordered Claude to ready the carriage.

He hadn't visited Madame Chantal's place for more than a year. When she saw him come in, the woman greeted him warmly. "Monsieur Rasero! I can't believe it; I thought you'd abandoned us forever . . ."

Rasero listened to the woman rattle on, without understanding what she was talking about. First she appeared to reproach him, and then she asked him about his health and described the wondrous charms of her new ward, a "delightful creature," according to what she said. "Do you want me to call her?" Madame Chantal asked as she looked at her old customer's face. It looked worn-out and paler than usual. She also noticed that don Fausto had grown visibly thinner and, most disturbing of all, deep wrinkles had appeared in his face, on his forehead, at the corners of his mouth, and alongside his eyes. Moreover, the marquis was obviously drunk; a person had only to see the lost look on his face and the way he was standing, swaying gently back and forth as though he were on the deck of a ship. She had never seen him in such a state. Don Fausto, always so serious and so elegant . . . what can have happened to him? the woman wondered as she went on talking about Charlotte's charms and talents with a well-nigh maternal pride.

"Very well, madam, I shall be most pleased to meet that creature," Rasero replied in the thick voice that continued to surprise him.

In all truth, Charlotte not only did justice to the warm praise of her employer but even surpassed it: she was an extraordinarily pretty girl. Although a bit blurred from the "spirits of wine," Rasero's eyes registered an enchanting image of her. The girl's face, rosy cheeked and dotted with freckles, could not have had finer or more delicate features, as though straight from Boucher's palette; her eyes, enormous and almond shaped, of an intense green, like that of the leaves of an ash tree when struck by the light of midday, were too pretty, Rasero thought. It's unfair that something so beautiful is doomed to disappear, to be turned into dust in just a few short years. Ah, you devil of a God! What's the point of creating so much beauty if later on you weary of it and allow it to wither and rot like a fruit fallen to the ground? . . . I'm very drunk, he said to himself. Marvelous, modest liquid. That's certainly true! . . .

What pleased him most about Charlotte, and that is saying a great deal, was her hair, long and soft; when the girl unpinned her chignon and let it fall, it spread out over her back and hung down, like a silk curtain, as far as her buttocks. The color of it was marvelous. It had a reddish cast, but not the opaque color tinged with orange of nearly all redheads. Hers had exactly the same color as a brandy aged for at least twenty years. It has the color of spirits of wine, just before another distillation turns it into that marvelous, modest liquid, Rasero thought with a smile.

And you loved that girl, Rasero. You loved her passionately, almost desperately. Your body, after a long time, awakened and gratefully received the intimate pleasure she caused it to enjoy. Still, it was no longer the same; you discovered that before even touching the adorable woman. Something of you, of your spirit—I say of your spirit, because your body hadn't forgotten how to take its pleasure—disappeared with Mariana on that fateful day when Jeanne-Antoinette's remains were transported from Versailles to Paris. You'd lost something forever. Or perhaps not: perhaps you'd find it, surely you'd find it when your lover appeared. Perhaps at this very moment—why not? you asked yourself as you caressed that fresh young body. But no, it didn't happen that way at all: Mariana did not appear. On the other hand, your old visions did show up, punctual and solicitous, like a faithful servant. There they were, like so many other times; there the future was just as your senses exploded. It was a miserable village on the edge of a luxuriant jungle. The huts were made of palm fronds and mud. The inhabitants, Asian men, women, and children, almost all of them with beautiful features, were running in terror. Above them, flying at the level of the treetops, was a small machine: this one had no pod at the end of it, Rasero. Who knows what drove it. Perhaps it was the tubes it had under its wings. Be that as it may, it must have been very powerful, because it flew very swiftly and made a deafening noise. It released a curtain of water on the village. No, it wasn't water, Rasero; it looked like a more viscous liquid. Besides, it caught fire the moment it touched the ground or the huts or the skin of one of those unfortunates; as it burned it produced huge flames, not blue ones or faint ones, like those of spirits of wine when they're set on fire, but yellow and reddish ones, like those of wood. In a little while—two or three orgasms with Charlotte—the whole village was burning down. Many of its inhabitants were lying on the ground burning like human torches. A few of them reached a little stream close-by, but, despite submerging themselves in the water, they went on helplessly burning . . .

This was how his first chemical experiment ended: in a settlement burning down in the middle of the jungle. But he didn't lose heart; in the final analysis the visions had nothing to do with chemistry, or with alcohol—or even, alas! with orgasm—for they had become part of his nature, like the lungs inside his chest or the ideas that skipped about in his mind. So he went on with his experiments, which, in addition to diverting him, increasingly held his attention. He prepared new batches of anhydrous alcohol and performed many fascinating experiments with it. Spirits of wine were a splendid solvent, particularly of those substances that Lefèvre described as being of animal and vegetable origin. He prepared countless elixirs, extracts, cordials, and liqueurs, especially of plants, whose effects he very soon tested on himself or on Claude, Annette, and Louise, whom he often used as guinea pigs.

"Come on, drink it down. Nothing's going to happen to you." Claude, half scared to death, was staring at the glass containing a mysterious green-colored liquid that smelled worse than a thousand demons. "There's nothing better for stomachache than the extract of aromatic balsam flowers and camphor," Rasero said to him, "and please note that I'm not the one who says that, but Dr. Le Febure, the greatest apothecary who has ever lived . . ."

The distinction of Dr. Le Febure failed utterly to reassure Claude, who stubbornly resisted drinking the elixir.

"Look, you coward," his master said as he took a generous swallow of the potion. "You see? Nothing's happened to me. Drink it and be done with it!"

The servant finally did as he was told. He downed a liquid with a very bitter taste that burned his stomach as though he had swallowed live fire. He turned very pale; something deep within his soul told him that he was doomed to die. He collapsed full length in an easy chair. "A priest, right away!" he dared order his master. "A priest . . . I'm about to die!"

"What do you mean, you're about to die! Lie there quietly for a while; you'll soon feel fine," Rasero replied, smiling.

A little while later, the burning sensation that Claude felt in his stomach disappeared, along with the pain that had been tormenting him in recent days. He really did feel better. The marquis is a magician, he thought.

"Sir, excuse me for what I said to you before, but I was very scared. I feel much better now."

"Didn't I tell you so?"

He not only felt better, he began to feel very, really very, good, far better than he had felt for a long time: full of energy, happy, and even a little tipsy, for Rasero had acquired the habit of adding a generous proportion of spirits of wine to all his preparations, since he'd discovered that it helped considerably in almost all treatments. I swear to God that this man is a magician! Claude repeated to himself.

Shortly after that, when his master summoned him to the laboratory to show him an experiment he was performing, Claude had no doubt that don Fausto was an incomparable magician and, what was more, a real genius.

"Take a look at this substance, Claude . . . Don't be scared; you're not going to drink it."

Claude saw a large glass receptacle containing a pretty, transparent red liquid. It's the color of rubies, he thought.

"A nice color, isn't it? It's an extract of rose petals dissolved in spirits of wine as a solvent. Now take a look at this other substance . . . What do you suppose it is?"

"Water," Claude answered without hesitation on seeing the contents of the second vessel.

"That's what it looks like, it's true, but really it's a very powerful compound capable of reviving someone who's fallen into a faint and to cure any number of illnesses. It's sal ammoniac dissolved in water," he said in a very serious voice. Rasero realized that the young man didn't understand one word of what he was telling him, but it amused him to see Claude's frightened face, with his eyes wide open and his body rigid, ready to take to his heels if his master suggested that he try one of the substances. It made him feel like Merlin giving his amazing demonstrations to the knights of the Round Table. "Smell," he ordered as he brought the vessel up to the servant's face.

Extremely apprehensive, Claude brought his nose closer and cautiously dilated his nostrils, like a mistrustful mouse. A strong and very penetrating odor entered his nose and seemingly reached the back of his head as well, which he abruptly thrust rearward.

"Ouf! It smells awful . . ."

"I've already told you that this substance is able to bring an unconscious man back to his senses. Its strength lies in its smell. Now watch," he said to him, and immediately poured a little of the sal ammoniac into the red liquid and stirred the mixture with a wooden spoon. Claude could hardly believe his eyes: as soon as the red liquid was mixed with the ammoniac, it began to lose its color, until it was no more than a faint pink. "A bit more is needed," Rasero said, and added two or three drops to the vessel. He stirred it a little once again, and the pinkish tone disappeared; the liquid was now as colorless and transparent as water.

"But . . . ," Claude stammered.

"Yes, the ammoniac took the color out of the mixture."

"It's unbelievable . . ."

"And that's not all. We're going to see what happens if I add a little more to it."

And he did so. As he added the ammoniac and stirred the mixture, the liquid began to take on color once again, although now it had a greenish tinge. After a time, Claude saw a transparent liquid, like the one at the beginning, but of an intense shade of green. His fear had disappeared, and he was beginning to become excited.

"How pretty . . . ! But I liked the red better."

"I did too. I think it's possible to restore the original color of the liquid. To do that, we're going to use a very dangerous substance, Claude. We must be very careful." He showed him a bottle containing a viscous yellowish liquid. "Do you know what this is?"

"No sir," Claude replied in a very grave voice.

"It's oil of vitriol, a very strong acid. It attacks practically any substance, except gold. To give you an idea of how powerful a solvent it is, if you were to drink half this bottle, not a trace of your stomach and intestines would be left; they would be completely dissolved by it. We're going to try it . . ."

"No sir!" Claude answered, terrified.

"Don't be frightened, Claude. I didn't mean for you to try it. What I'm going to do is demonstrate the strength of vitriol to you. Watch." He poured a portion of the liquid into a porcelain receptacle. "Do you have a copper piece?" Claude rummaged through his pockets and took out several copper coins. "One is enough. Put it inside the vessel; be careful not to get any liquid on your fingers."

Trembling, Claude flung the coin in the acid. Once it came in contact with the liquid, there was bubbling all around the coin and the liquid gave off vapors with a yellowish cast and a penetrating odor. Little by little, the liquid took on a light blue color. After a while the acid stopped cooking and the coin disappeared; all that was left in the receptacle was a sky blue liquid.

"Do you see what happens?"

Of course Claude saw; he couldn't have opened his eyes any wider. That oil had devoured his copper coin in no time. He didn't care to imagine what would have happened to his insides if his master had forced him to drink the substance.

"And what about my coin?"

"Your coin no longer exists, Claude. It's always necessary to pay a price for knowledge. Now watch this."

He added a spurt of vitriol to the green liquid. As soon as the liquid entered into contact with it, it gave off tiny bubbles, as though it were boiling in that spot. Then Rasero gently stirred the mixture. The green color slowly lost its intensity until it finally disappeared. The mixture again looked as colorless and transparent as water. "We're already halfway there. Now we'll add a little more vitriol."

As he stirred with the little spoon, the mixture took on a pinkish color; soon it acquired the pretty ruby color it had had at the beginning.

"Bravo!" Claude exclaimed. "You're a great expert, sir."

"Thank you, my friend. Now touch the wall of the container and tell me what you feel."

Claude placed the palms of his hands on the sides of the glass vessel and felt a very intense heat, as though the mixture had been over the fire for some time.

"It's very hot," he said in surprise.

"That's because two quite opposite principles have interacted: sal ammoniac and vitriolic acid," Claude's master stated, continuing to play the role of instructor. "When there's contact, the conflict that results gives off a great amount of heat. That's what happens."

"Ah . . . !" the lad exclaimed without understanding one word of the explanation. Nonetheless, he felt very proud of himself. He had no doubt whatever that his master was a great man, one of those magnificent luminaries for whom nature has no secrets. He remembered hearing it said that, among such men, certain of them were even able to turn other metals into gold.

"Do you know how to make gold?" he asked in all seriousness.

"Of course. To tell the truth, it's very simple . . ."

Claude looked at him dubiously. He had just had proof that the marquis was an extremely learned man, but from there to being able to make gold . . . and to saying that it was a very simple process . . . He was aware of his own ignorance, but he also knew that he wasn't an utter idiot: making gold couldn't be a simple matter for anyone.

"I don't believe it."

"You're right not to. The first attribute that a good philosopher must have is to be skeptical and incredulous. Only in that way, by doubting, continually doubting, can knowledge be attained. Our dear Descartes has already said as much."

"I don't know who that Monsieur Descartes is or what he's said. But with all due respect, sir, I don't believe that it's a simple matter to make gold."

"Do you want me to show you that it is?"

A bit frightened, the lad nodded.

"Very well. But first I must warn you of something, Claude," Rasero began, evincing a serious aspect. He felt a little ashamed of the way he was pulling the lad's leg, though it also amused him a great deal, and when all was said and done, he wasn't going to do him any harm. "The gold we chemists prepare is very special. It's much purer and more valuable than ordinary gold, but sadly, there's no way to put it to any practical use."

"Why is that, sir?"

"The reason is not known for certain, although the majority of experts who have studied the problem agree that the phenomenon stems precisely from the material's purity. As you'll see, the gold we're going to obtain will separate out from the water solvent, but it's not akin to ordinary gold . . . The problem is that, when one tries to separate the gold from the water, the gold disintegrates, turning into an amorphous, unpleasant substance. It would appear that it is air that spoils it, but you'll see . . . Ah! There's another very important thing." He looked intently at the lad as though he were revealing to him a closely guarded secret. Listen to me now: never, never let it enter your mind to describe to anyone what you're about to see. A terrible curse weighs upon anyone who dares reveal these secrets. Truly terrible, Claude . . ."

"Is that true . . . ?" The lad was beginning to feel alarm.

"To give you an idea of how terrible it can be, I'm going to tell you a story. The great Alexander Seton, the Cosmopolite, one of the most notable alchemists who have ever existed, died in a dungeon, the victim of cruel torture, for having publicly revealed the procedure to be followed. The same thing happened to Anton Berdemann, a poor German apothecary who in 1647 dared to exhibit alchemical gold in Paris, and to Seton's disciple, the Pole Michael Sendivogius, and to a great many others. Helvetius himself, perhaps the greatest chemist of the last century, despite taking great care not to apply his knowledge of the process, was nonetheless on the point of doing so once, when providentially Artist Elias, the supreme master of the sons of Hermes, appeared to him and warned him of the fearful end that awaited him if he went through with the experiment . . ."

"You'd best not perform it, sir. You might be punished . . ."

"Who, me? Don't worry; I'm not running any risk—unless you divulge . . . The one who taught me this procedure—I can't reveal his name to you—gave me permission to demonstrate it to just one person. He recommended that I choose that person carefully, for if he has a loose tongue, the two of us, and my teacher as well, will be punished. That is why I chose you, Claude; I have the utmost confidence in your discretion."

"I thank you, sir. I will take the secret to the grave with me."

"I believe you, my friend . . . Well, then, let's begin. Bring a pail of cold water while I prepare the equipment."

When Claude returned with the pail, his master was lighting a fire under a sand oven. "Everything is ready. First of all, look at this piece of metal," he said, handing Claude a bit of lead.

The lad weighed it in his hand, observed the color of it, and even carefully bit into it. "It's lead," he concluded.

"Very good. That's precisely what it is, Claude. Now, I'm going to place it in this porcelain vessel and attack it with aqua regia, the most powerful solvent there is." When he added the liquid, the lead, as had happened before with the copper coin, began to give off bubbles. They were of a penetrating, yellowish gas, and after a time the metal disappeared in an amber-colored solution. "Now we're going to transfer it to this retort and add a little water to dilute the strength of the acid . . . Very good . . . Please bring me that dark-colored flask on the shelf." Rasero uncorked the flask and poured a little of its contents into another porcelain receptacle. It was a white crystalline powder that looked much like salt. "This substance is marvelous, Claude. It closely resembles salt; even its taste is nearly identical. But it has very strange and powerful properties. With this substance countless medicines are prepared. In order to obtain it, it is necessary to evaporate enormous quantities of sea water, where it is found in solution, along with many other salts. Truly, it is very difficult to prepare, although that doesn't matter much now, does it?"

"No, it doesn't," Claude answered, captivated.

"It's necessary to dissolve this salt in water so that it can act at its greatest strength," Rasero said as he poured a little water in the receptacle. "There. Now pay close attention." He gradually poured the salt solution into the retort. The moment the two liquids came in contact, an earthlike substance of an intense yellow was formed and deposited on the bottom of the receptacle. Claude looked on in fascination as the powder the color of an egg yolk slowly settled. "Very well, we have now removed the mercury from the lead; all we have left is sulfur, do you see?"

"Yes . . ."

"This, Claude, is nearly gold. All we need to do is extract the excess of humidity from it. For this, we're going to use fire." He placed the retort in the sand oven and allowed it to heat for a fair while. When it was good and hot, he stirred the mixture. The yellow powder dissolved in the liquid, which took on the precise look of white wine. "We have now extracted the humidity. Do you see the gold?"

"No sir."

"It's there nonetheless. What happens is that the grains are so fine that they can't be seen; they just barely give the water that golden color . . ."

"So that's alchemical gold?" Claude asked, frankly disappointed.

"Wait a bit. Pick up the vessel with a cloth so you don't burn your hand, and take it out of the oven." Claude obeyed. "Now we have to wait till it cools down a little, because if we put it in water the glass will break."

They waited ten or fifteen minutes, which Rasero spent describing to Claude, with a wealth of detail, the torments suffered by the hapless Seton the Cosmopolite, in the dungeon in Dresden.

"I think it's time now. Take the flask and plunge it in the pail of cold water. Be careful that no water gets into the receptacle." Claude held the mixture in the water for a while, until Rasero ordered him to take it out and place it on the table. "Look!"

Claude could scarcely believe his eyes: a very fine gold powder was suspended in the liquid. The tiny golden particles scattered the light with incomparable brilliance.

"It's gold, marquis!"

"Naturally. Alchemical gold; there is none purer . . ."

"And it's certain that I can't take it out of the water?"

"Absolutely certain. I've already told you, my friend: unfortunately this gold serves no purpose besides being stared at . . ."

"It's so pretty . . ."

"And so dangerous. How many deaths, how many wars the ambition to possess it has caused. And you've now seen what it is: a piece of lead properly treated. Nothing more than that."

"It's a shame we can't remove it. We'd be so rich . . ."

"Would we? . . . Be careful, Claude. If we were to try to use this gold, what we'd be is a couple of corpses. Remember what I told you."

"You're certain the curse is real?"

"As certain as I am that what you have before you is gold."

Rasero smiled at the thought that this last remark was the only true thing he'd said to the lad that afternoon.

"Don't worry, sir. Anyway, I thank you for your confidence in me. Your mind can be at ease; I'll never speak with anyone about what I've seen," the lad promised solemnly, proud of having witnessed a miracle and, above all, of having been worthy of his master's trust.

The experiment aroused Claude's interest in chemistry. On the slightest pretext, he went to his master's laboratory and whiled away spare moments observing how Rasero manipulated substances. Little by little he began to help him, until he finally became a true assistant. To tell the truth, he learned many of the secrets of science—among others, that of the marvelous alchemical gold that had so greatly impressed him. Unburdening his conscience, Rasero explained that he had been playing a joke on him. The tiny golden grains Claude had seen floating in the water were not gold but an odd lead compound, that was all. Claude was not overly distressed to learn the truth; in fact, he felt relieved, since he had found it harder and harder to keep a secret like that. Two or three times he had been on the point of letting the cat out of the bag to Annette, but at the last moment the memory of Seton the Cosmopolite's tortures deterred him.

Shut up in the laboratory for four or five months, and with the aid of such a diligent disciple, Rasero's knowledge of chemistry increased by giant steps, to the point that he finally decided to carry out the experiment of obtaining Gauber's spirits of niter according to Dr. Boerhaave's instructions. The operation was unusually complicated, though, and he hadn't yet brought it off despite reading heaven only knows how many times the explanations of the learned German . . .

The laboratory had filled with reddish smoke that kept pouring out of all the joints of the apparatus, everywhere but the place it should have come out: the mouth of the alembic.

"Close it up, Claude, or it's going to fill the entire house with smoke," Rasero said to his assistant when the young man came into the laboratory.

Coughing violently, Claude barely managed to say, "A gentleman is looking for you," and handed a calling card to Rasero.

> Dear Fausto,
>
> The bearer of this card is Antoine Lavoisier, my best pupil. I will be as grateful for all the courtesies you may show him as I would be had you shown them to me personally. Yours,
>
> Jean-Etienne Guettard

"Show him in, Claude. But open that window first."

Good Guettard, Rasero thought as he watched the reddish cloud partially pass through the window; that prompted him to remember the nightmare he had in Madrid on that long-ago afternoon when his father forced him to attend an audo-da-fé. It's been almost two years since I last saw him . . .

He had met him five years before, during a gathering at the palace of the Duchess de Mailly at which the tenth volume of the *Encyclopédie* had been displayed for the first time. Buffon had introduced him: "Fausto, this is Dr. Guettard, the greatest geologist in France and in my opinion the entire world . . ." What most impressed Rasero about the man was his lack of affectation. Despite being highly esteemed as a scholar and one of the most influential Academicians in the kingdom, he comported himself with the modesty and mild manner of a village schoolmaster. Rasero had known few as devoted to their work, either. The moment Guettard discovered the interest of his new acquaintance in geology, he launched into a passionate monologue in which he described his main ideas. "The animal, vegetable, and mineral worlds form a unitary whole," he explained to him. "Therefore I intend to demonstrate the unambiguous and direct relationship that exists between the vegetation of a site and the composition of its terrestrial crust . . ." It was an exceptionally interesting theory, and he had worked out a major part of it. "But there is still a great deal more to do . . . Why don't you come with me on one of my field trips? You won't regret it. It is necessary, marquis, to be out in the field, far from men and their depredations, to appreciate how much more beautiful and enigmatic nature is than we usually imagine it to be. On Tuesday, I'm going to the Soissonnais. I'm thinking of spending two weeks there. Come with me. I'd really be delighted if you did," Guettard said sincerely, since he felt a strong liking for the bald Spaniard that he wouldn't have been able to explain. "What do you say to that?"

Rasero accepted gladly and went with his new acquaintance to the Soissonnais region, where he had a pleasant stay. The countryside, as his new friend had maintained, turned out to be full of beauty and mysteries. Rasero had never suspected that such a great variety of plants could exist, from tiny weeds to imposing trees and including an infinite range of species of the most varied forms, sizes, and methods of reproduction imaginable. The same thing proved true of the rocks. At first sight, they were all the same or almost so: grayish or dull brown, hard and amorphous, haphazardly scattered about. But, to an expert eye such as Dr. Guettard's, the apparent uniformity barely concealed an unexpectedly abundant variety. For one who can distinguish granite from basalt, limestone from marble, ferrous minerals from cupriferous, meteorites from terrestrial metals, quartz from rock salt, and a thousand cases more, the old earth is a real cornucopia, containing as many beauties and secrets within as on its fuzzy dark and light green surface. Only an expert eye such as Jean-Etienne Guettard's could divine the marvelous nature of the object in Rasero's hands that he had just picked up off the ground in the hope of coming upon a specimen that the Academician's rigorous opinion might deem worthy of a closer look. It was a round, dark-colored stone. Disappointed, Rasero saw nothing special about it, and in irritation he was about to throw it as far away as he could. "Wait, marquis!" Guettard shouted as he rushed to the Spaniard in great strides. "My friend, you've found a wonderful stone . . ." Rasero smiled timidly, like a youngster who receives an unexpected prize, and handed the stone to him. "What a beauty!" Guettard said in ecstasy. "It's very nearly perfect; isn't it a lovely thing?"

"Frankly . . . ," Fausto began to answer him, not at all convinced of the beauty of that round, rough uncut stone of a very dark coffee color and an irregular surface. "I for my part find it ugly."

"Ugly?" He looked at the Malagan in indignation. "Ah, marquis! You've found one of the most beautiful and strangest stones that exist on earth, and it strikes you as ugly," he said, with an enigmatic smile. "Perhaps after you see this, you'll change your mind . . ." He picked up a hammer and chisel, and leaning the piece of rock against a great basalt monolith, he struck it a hard blow exactly in the middle. The rough stone split in two. Guettard took one of the halves and showed it to Rasero. "And how does this look to you?"

"It's very beautiful," Mariana said when she saw the stone on your desk that blessed night. "I once saw a very similar one in Taxco, though it was much larger . . . ," she said as she rubbed her long fingers over the polished inner surface of the stone, with white crystals around the upper edge of the hollow in its middle ("Something like half a melon," Guettard had said to you), of a lovely royal purple color. "Where did you get it?"

The memory caused Rasero a sudden sharp pang. He didn't feel up to receiving the gentleman, even though he came recommended by his dear friend Guettard. In fact, in the last year, he could not bear to see anyone except Denis, who visited him rather frequently. He went over to the door of the laboratory to tell Claude to send the visitor on his way. But when he reached the door, he realized that it was too late: he saw standing on the threshold a man scarcely twenty years old dressed in a very well tailored wine-colored frock coat and breeches. His appearance testified to his serenity and was of an unusual handsomeness. His facial features were delicate and well proportioned: perhaps the nose was too large for those eyes, set quite far apart and very wide open, giving every sign of the young man's superior intelligence. The mouth, with its thin and slightly puckered lips, appeared to disguise a permanent smile, and curiously, that made his face look even more serious.

"Good afternoon, marquis."

The man had a rather hard time speaking, for the smoke in the room had brought him to the edge of a coughing spell. Arriving at the front door of the house, he could smell that someone was working with spirits of niter, but he didn't suspect that they had been doing it so badly. He had only to take a look at the joints of the alembic to understand the catastrophe: the mortar was very dry and hence was not sealing them correctly. It was obvious, besides, that they had been using much more saltpeter than necessary. Probably they're following Dr. Boerhaave's directions, he thought.

"Come in, come in. Please excuse this disaster. I've just put out the oven."

"Don't do that, marquis. I presume you're trying to obtain Gauber's spirits of niter, aren't you?"

"That's right."

"I carried out that experiment some time ago, and the same thing happened: my entire house was filled with fumes," he said with a smile. "But I discovered the problem. What happens is that the vapor dries out the mortar. I don't know why this didn't happen to Boerhaave; he no doubt used lime and gypsum. But the solution is very simple. Will you allow me?"

"Of course."

Lavoisier slowly removed his frock coat and hung it on a chair. He rolled up his shirt sleeves and set to work.

"Would you like an apron?"

"I don't believe I'll need one. May I use these candles?" Antoine asked, referring to three candles in an old tin candelabrum.

"Go ahead."

He brought the candles up close to the heat of the oven to soften them and made a dough of them. With a knife, he removed the mortar from the joints of the alembic and combined it with the wax until the mixture formed a thick paste. With it he resealed the joints, and immediately the gas stopped escaping.

"The wax helps keep the mortar from drying out . . . Did you use the quantities Boerhaave gives?"

"Yes . . ."

"That explains all the gas. Really, only twelve ounces of saltpeter are needed, not eighteen."

"An error of that magnitude by a chemist like Boerhaave is remarkable."

"Yes, I thought so too. It's occurred to me that maybe in Boerhaave's time what was called pure saltpeter was a mixture of several substances—maybe they had not yet purified it as thoroughly as we do nowadays. That would explain the difference in weight. But since you've already put in eighteen ounces, all we can do is add more oil of vitriol. Do you have any on hand?"

"Here it is."

"Thank you . . . I suppose you used six ounces?"

"Yes."

"Very well. In that case we'll add four more . . . Raise the heat of the oven, if you will."

Rasero fanned the oven and discovered to his surprise that thick drops of a yellowish liquid were beginning to fall into the receiver.

"There you are!" Lavoisier said with satisfaction.

"Many thanks," Rasero replied, still amazed at the man's skill. "And now, tell me, in what way can I be of service to you? To tell the truth, after having seen what you've done, I doubt very much that I can be of any use to you whatever."

"Don't say that, marquis. Acquaintance with a procedure makes it very simple to carry out. The problem is to interpret instructions that are usually very obscure. It took me nearly a week to obtain spirits of niter . . ."

A week, Rasero thought, crestfallen. It took me more than two weeks . . .

"I hear that you've acquired Dr. Geofroy's laboratory."

"Yes indeed."

"Well then, the reason for my visit . . . apart from the pleasure of meeting you—you can't imagine how often Dr. Guettard has mentioned you to me," he hastened to correct himself, "—the reason for my visit, as I was saying, is to ask a favor that I hope won't inconvenience you."

"Tell me."

"A few days ago, in looking over some articles in back issues of the *Annales scientifiques,* I found one by Dr. Geofroy, dated 1750, that struck me as especially interesting. In it he describes a balance he had a Swiss craftsman build. The apparatus, he says, is astonishingly precise, capable of measuring down to the half grain. I've had several balances made, but they fall short of a precision on the order of even two grains. If Dr. Geofroy's apparatus is still around, I thought, it must be in his laboratory. I went there, and the doctor's daughter—a very kind person, incidentally—explained that she had sold it to you about a year ago. Our shared friendship with Dr. Guettard brought my footsteps to your door, and here I am, asking you to let me see that marvel—if it exists, that is. I'd even like to ask you to lend it to me for a time so that I may finish an experiment that in several months' work I haven't been able to carry out successfully because my instruments aren't precise enough. If I can get hold of the balance, I'd like to study its mechanism, and if you'd allow it, have an identical one made for my own use."

"You can be happy, my friend. I believe I have this balance, and of course I'll lend it to you," Rasero said as he searched among a heap of crates piled up in one corner of the laboratory. "Let's see . . . I think this is it."

He took to the table an ordinary-sized box, exquisitely decorated and varnished. (It looks like a musical instrument, he had thought the first time he saw it.)

"Will you allow me?" Lavoisier said, visibly moved.

"Certainly."

The man opened the box and found inside it, fitted into wooden compartments and carefully wrapped in velvet, countless pieces of gilded metal. The pans, the support, and the bar of the balance were of fair size, but there were also many tiny pieces, like those used in watchmaking. Arrows, crowns, screws were little by little unwrapped and deposited on the table by Lavoisier's loving hand. "What a marvel!" he kept exclaiming every so often. "Look at this, marquis!" he said, pointing to a minute screw. "I don't doubt that it took them more than a year to make it; it's incredible . . ."

Finally he unwrapped the last pieces: several long, thin bronze chains, no doubt intended to support the pans, Rasero thought, pleased to discover at least one tiny piece whose use he understood among the endless number of them lying on the table.

"May I assemble it?" Lavoisier asked diffidently.

"Certainly, my friend, go right ahead," Rasero answered with a smile, as he bade Claude light the laboratory candles, for dusk was falling fast. "I suspect, though, that this is going to take some time. So won't you please stay for supper."

"It's an honor, marquis. With great pleasure."

"Now it's for me to ask a favor of you. I'd be grateful if you didn't address me as marquis."

"Very well, Monsieur Rasero," Lavoisier replied, eager to get to work.

It took about two hours to set up the instrument. Those were very pleasant moments, especially for Rasero, who stood watching, altogether engrossed, as the young man went about putting the balance together. Lavoisier's hands, as soft and sensitive as those of a violinist, picked up, with perfect delicacy—with gentleness, one might say—each of the pieces, suspending it between his fingers for several minutes, time enough to scrutinize it slowly and to ponder with consummate care exactly where it belonged. Each tiny part appeared to achieve a goal in finding its rightful place in the instrument once again and awaited its companion piece, which, held above, was awaiting its turn. Rasero looked at his new acquaintance as a kindred spirit. Thank goodness there wasn't time to ask Claude to send him away, he said to himself as he listened to the young scientist's string of remarks.

"The way they fixed the shape of the bearing is ingenious in the extreme, isn't it?"

"It certainly seems so to me."

"In this way, the support required by the bar is minimal . . . I definitely expect that this instrument will have the precision Geofroy claimed for it."

Finally, the apparatus was ready to be used. It looked magnificent and even graceful—the gleaming pans in particular, which hung from long, elegant little chains that seemed to be made of pure gold. Above them, in the exact center of the balance, the very slender arrow pointed to the zero on a semicircular scale that was marked in tiny painted characters, "1/2 grain," underneath each one of the five dividing lines on either side of the zero.

"Very well, let's give it a try," Lavoisier said, and cast about for something to weigh. He finally hit upon some of the old newspaper that Claude was accustomed to use for lighting the ovens of the alembics. He cut off a small snip of paper, so tiny that it easily fit on the tip of his index finger, and placed it in one of the pans of the balance. The arrow moved slightly to one side, stopping just short of the first mark to the left. Lavoisier cut off another snip of paper, perhaps even smaller than the first, and placed it in the same pan. The arrow stopped at the line that indicated a half grain. "Half a grain! It's unbelievable . . . Monsieur Rasero, this instrument holds the future. You have no idea what a piece of equipment like this will be able to do for chemistry."

Rasero clearly had no idea. He was unable to comprehend the extravagant euphoria of his new acquaintance. It's a balance a bit more precise than the others, that's all, he said to himself. I don't see how it's going to revolutionize chemistry.

Many years had to go by before Rasero saw. But in a way it all began that afternoon.

Claude came to tell them that supper was served. As they left the laboratory, Rasero noticed that the receiver was almost full of the yellowish liquid, with a thick cloud of reddish vapor floating above it. Not the slightest trace of gas was escaping the apparatus now. I have met a great chemist today, he thought.

During supper, Lavoisier explained the work he was doing. "It's a study of gypsum. What I want to prove is the relationship between the application of heat to the substance and the capacity of the substance to hold water and thus to form a mass. Gypsum heated to a certain temperature gives off the water that has been mixed in with it and hence loses weight. If water is again added, the gypsum will form a new mass with no problem. But if it is heated further, until it becomes calcined, it also loses its capacity to hold together with the aid of the water. I suspect that the heat causes a change in the composition of the substance, as happens with metals when they are calcined, although in the case of gypsum, the substance loses mass rather than gaining it as metals do. It follows that the principal element of gypsum must have properties opposite those of metals, in the way sulfur has. It hasn't been easy, however, to prove this. The changes in mass are very small, and my balances haven't been precise enough to be certain of my results. With this balance, I'll be able easily to bring the experiment to a definitive conclusion . . . and to carry out many others . . ." He explained to Rasero that he was thinking of entering that study, along with another he was well along in performing, concerning the lighting of the streets of Paris, in the annual competition of the Academy of Sciences. "It's a very important study. I believe I'll win the prize," he said very soberly, without the least sign of vanity.

And a year later, during a stately ceremony in celebration as well of the first centenary of the famous institution, founded in the days of the Sun King by the tireless Marin Mersenne, Antoine Lavoisier received from the hands of Louis XV a gold medal attesting to the talent and originality of his work. Among those in attendance, Rasero applauded enthusiastically. His young friend was beginning a dazzling career that would one day come to a tragic end because of the implacable workings of human stupidity.

A firm friendship between the two men sprang up that afternoon, a friendship that time would broaden and deepen.

Rasero devoted those years, so sad in other ways, entirely to chemistry. He spent hours at a time shut up in his laboratory, or in that of his friend Lavoisier, whose tireless work was little by little turning it into the best-run laboratory in all of France. Together with Lavoisier, Rasero was one of the first chemists in France to give extended attention to the study of air and gases, a study the importance of which Mayow and Boyle had already pointed out more than a hundred years before but which the prevailing theory of phlogiston had completely overshadowed. Only now, some ten years later, did the British chemists Black, Cavendish, and Priestley—many of the works of whom they had learned about through the intermediary of the philosopher David Hume, that splendid gentleman to whom Rasero felt he owed his life and his hell—focus their work on gases, and their results, many amazing and disconcerting, were laying the foundation of a new science radically different from and infinitely superior to the old iatrochemistry and phlogistics.

They were peaceful years, despite the perennial sadness that accompanied him, and the odious visions that came more and more frequently to him and at times when he least expected: that war going on in some jungle in the East seemed to be lasting forever, for again and again the terrible images of what was undoubtedly genocide came to Rasero's mind. Despite this, he experienced pleasant moments, above all in the company of his friends Diderot and Lavoisier. The former, thanks to his indomitable will, had managed to bring the

Encyclopédie to a successful conclusion. More than twenty fat tomes condensed all the knowledge of its time and attested to the unbelievable genius and the no less incredible capacity for work of Rasero's beloved Denis. As with Voltaire, the passage of the years was kind to Diderot: it polished his virtues and ground away at his defects to the point of almost causing them to disappear. His good humor and exquisite sense of irony kept him faithful company, as did his dear Sophie, till the very last day of his life. Rasero was completely surprised when, after having finished the *Encyclopédie,* Denis finally accepted Empress Catherine's persistent invitation and left for Russia. "We'll see how the Slavs treat me," he said smilingly to his friend shortly before climbing into the berlin.

They treated him badly, Rasero. It was not difficult for you to discover that when you saw your friend a year later. He looked worn-out; he had lost many pounds and aged many years. "Ah, my friend!" he said to you when he realized what was going through your head. "You have no idea what the climate of Russia is like. Frightful, absolutely frightful. It was a miracle it didn't kill me." But he recovered. The good climate of Paris was partly responsible ("It's a paradise by comparison with Moscow"), as well as the better food (which Louise doubtless had a large hand in, for she had learned from Annette the art of cooking, and Diderot was not at all stingy with his praise of her skills—praise that took a concrete form when he asked her for second and even third helpings: "How I envy you, you rascal!" he said to you as he raised to his mouth a succulent bit of salmon cooked in lime juice). In a few months he had recovered his corpulence and his vitality, and despite his more than sixty years, he went on tirelessly with his work and his womanizing. But something was no longer the same about him: his jokes were perhaps just a touch more sarcastic, more mordant, as though they concealed a deep-seated rancor; the look in his eyes was veiled by an aura of sadness that reminded you a great deal of the one the face of your beloved Angustias bore so many long years ago, when you made up your mind to keep your mouth away from her breasts. It was beyond question that something of the spirit of this great man—though you never discovered exactly what it was—remained forever buried in the snows of Catherine's Russia.

The relationship of the Malagan with Antoine Lavoisier was also full of pleasant memories. They spent hours at a time in the laboratory contemplating the dripping of liquids into the receptacle or collecting nonvolatile gas that, bubble by bubble, displaced water so as to occupy its volume. "You see?" Lavoisier said to him after placing a lit candle inside a bell jar full of gas. Once he covered it, the candle went out. "It's different from air, yet it forms part of it. Air, my friend, with all the respect I owe Boyle, is not an element; I suspect that it is made up of several constituents . . ."

Lavoisier, for his part, also was fond of listening to the Andalusian's disquisitions. His knowledge is very much of an earlier time, he often thought as he listened to him, but it is full of mystery and magic. And it was true that Rasero talked to him of authors of long ago whose names and exploits—which had lain dormant in some fold of his memory for so many years—came back to him when he looked at apparatuses and substances. He would then reminisce about delightful conversations with Dr. Antonio Ulloa. He talked to him about Julián Damián, the colorful Italian adventurer—or was he French?—who arrived at the court of the king of Scotland at the beginning of the sixteenth century and managed, through his ingenious experiments, to win the respect and the admiration of everyone around him. "He was an extraordinary sort," Lavoisier heard him say. "Who knows what evil arts he used, but the fact is that he held King James IV enthralled. He managed to get the monarch to spend fabulous sums to equip his laboratory, and you know the Scottish are not exactly famous for their largess. He was obsessed with obtaining the 'quintessence,' which was sort of a combination of the philosopher's stone and the elixir of life. Julián was convinced that it was from spirits of beer that he would be able to extract it. I don't believe he succeeded, but what is beyond doubt is that he was the inventor of whisky, which he made in prodigious quantities (if the figures he noted down for the royal treasurer are accurate), enough to get an entire army drunk. But his major distinction had nothing to do with the 'quintessence' and a great deal to do with birds: Julián convinced his patron and monarch that it was possible to fly the way birds do. All that was required was to construct a proper pair of wings, the design of which he already knew, by way of information he had from a supposed descendant of Michael Scot, who, as everyone knew, crossed the skies of Scotland, headed for Paris, on a magic black horse with wings, in order to carry out an important mission to the French king. Julián Damián built his pair of wings and had the courage to fling himself from the top of the walls of Stirling Castle (which, according to what people say, are a good twenty yards high), determined not to end his flight till he reached Paris. Inevitably, his mission ended a great deal sooner: at the foot of the wall. But like his courage, his good luck was also outsized. He merely broke his hip. What's more, he never admitted that he failed. He explained to the monarch that the cause of his misadventure was the treachery of the craftsman he had commissioned to make the wings: 'Despite receiving from me enough money to build a pair of wings with the best eagle feathers he could get his hands on, the dolt built them of hen feathers. And Your Majesty knows very well that those creatures like to stay on the ground; they never dare soar to the heights.' People say that Damián had already readied a new pair of wings, made of eagle feathers this time, when death took his sovereign by surprise. So he was unable to make a second try. It's a shame; the experiment might have been a success," the Malagan concluded with a smile.

Next he was speaking of Seton the Cosmopolite and, as he had done for Claude, he described for Lavoisier the tragic existence of that mysterious fellow who was capable, "at least, so they say, of fabricating a yellowing agent, which, when just a pinch was added to a crucible full of melted lead, turned the metal into purest gold beneath the eyes of astonished observers. You can't imagine, Antoine, the great number of documents that exist, many of them signed by people of spotless reputation, attesting to that miracle . . ." He explained how the Cosmopolite, shortly before a death resulting from the cruel tortures inflicted on him, bequeathed to his great friend Sendivogius, the German Hermes, a generous portion of his magic agent and the guardianship of his beloved young wife, who in the end was the unwitting cause of Sendivogius' misfortune. "Possessed of such a marvel and married to the young widow, he traveled all over Europe performing his miraculous demonstrations until he was exhausted; his passage left gold everywhere in its wake. The emperor himself, Rudolf II, had him come to Prague so that he might personally witness his talents. The ruler must have been thoroughly convinced, for he lavished favors and riches on the man of learning and did him the homage of unveiling a plaque in his honor in an old section of Prague, which has been known ever since as the alchemists' quarter. But although Sendivogius' teacher had left him a sizable quantity of the magic agent, he had been unwilling—or unable—to reveal to his friend the formula that would have enabled him to make it himself. Hence the poor man saw his reserves dwindle by the day.

He sought a way of using less of the agent each time he performed a transmutation, but he knew very well that sooner or later it would give out, and that his fame and perhaps even his life would come to an end along with it, for there was sure to be some monarch who, out of disappointment, would shut him up in a dungeon until the alchemist could make him the gold he craved—exactly what had happened to his unfortunate teacher. Sendivogius' last days were so grim, terrified as he was that his agent would give out—the remnant of which he kept in tiny flasks, one of which hung suspended from his neck until the hour of his death—that I suspect they were the inspiration for that wonderful children's story set down by a great German teller of tales. Although in Grimm's version, of course, the magic agent became the elixir of life . . ."

Calibrating a balance, Lavoisier was glad to listen to his friend, who continued, "Van Helmont himself once stumbled upon that marvelous agent. He describes it in detail in his memoirs: a yellowish powder, very similar to sulfur (identical to the Cosmopolite's powder), and swears to high heaven that he saw how lead was transformed into gold right in front of his nose. It's very odd, especially coming from someone like van Helmont. He was a very serious scientist. Do you know his experiment on water?"

"No," Lavoisier lied. He was perfectly familiar with the experiment, but he enjoyed listening to the Malagan.

"It took him several years. What a patient man! He planted a little tree in a flowerpot, weighed everything, and put it on his window sill. He didn't allow anything but rainwater to fall into the pot. Periodically he checked the weight of the plant. After a couple of years, its weight had doubled. It's the dust in the water that's making the plant increase in weight, he concluded, embracing a tradition whose origin is lost in antiquity. You can't imagine how many men of learning among the ancients were convinced that water contains dust!"

"Ancients and moderns, Fausto," Lavoisier replied. "There are still a good many who are convinced of it. If water is distilled a sufficient number of times, the cretins maintain, a fine, colorless, and inactive powder will be obtained. Water without wetness, they would have to call it in order to carry the absurd arguments of the alchemists of five centuries ago to their logical conclusion."

"I too think that that is absurd, but as long as it can't be disproved, there will always be some who believe it . . ."

"Why don't we prove that it isn't true, Fausto?" his friend interrupted, obviously excited. "We have a fine balance," he said, pointing to the splendid instrument he had had the craftsman Chemies make for him following the design of the scale Rasero had lent him, "and this glass couldn't be more inescapable," he noted as he struck a large retort with his knuckles.

As amused as two little boys bent on a mischievous prank, they set to work. They set up the alembic, and Antoine very skillfully developed a system whereby the water, after having been evaporated and condensed, returned to the original receptacle, which was heated by a sand oven. They carefully weighed the receptacle and lit the oven.

The days went by and the water showed no propensity to transform itself into dust. After a month, there was a tiny deposit of very fine dark powder in the bottom of the receptacle. Rasero looked at it in surprise.

"Don't worry, Fausto. I'm convinced it's residue from the glass of the retort."

In order to leave no room for doubt, the apparatus was kept working for 101 days without interruption. When they finally put the fire in the oven out, the water looked unchanged; transparent and serene, as though it had nothing but disdain for the incredible quantity of heat to which it had been subjected. The disturbing residue of fine sand in the bottom of the receiver had increased, but even so the quantity was infinitesimal. When they weighed the apparatus again, amid boisterous bursts of laughter and toasts with champagne, they no longer had the slightest doubt: the mass of the system was unchanged. The fine powder that had formed, as Lavoisier had conjectured, was nothing but a residue of the material of the receptacle.

"To your good health, my friend," Lavoisier said joyfully. "We've exploded a myth that's more than two thousand years old . . ."

This happened at the end of the year '68. Seventeen sixty-eight: ten years ago already . . . , you thought as you watched the last shovelfuls of earth fall on Voltaire's coffin.

It was a very special year, Rasero. Annette, convinced that you had recovered when she saw you so engrossed in chemistry and so far removed from wine, finally decided to return the immense affection shown her by Marcel Gautier, the printer who lived on the ground floor of your town house. They were married in January. Shortly after that, you had the enormous satisfaction of attending the ceremony in which your young friend Antoine Lavoisier was welcomed by the

French Royal Academy of Science as an associate member. The prestige and renown that your friend was acquiring were such that he was admitted into the Academy at twenty-three, though ordinarily the youngest members of the institution were past fifty. He had received a much larger vote than Dr. Jars, an elderly, much-respected scientist who had rendered countless valuable services to the Crown, and the king, with Solomon-like judgment, ordered both men admitted to the Academy, with a temporary seat created—something that had never occurred in the more than hundred-year history of the institution—that would be lost as soon as a member passed on, so that the membership could revert to its original number. In that same year your friend Lavoisier entered another institution, very different from the Academy but, like it, very well known. The reputation of this one, however, was unsavory; it may well be that the provosts of Versailles and Paris neither had a reputation as black nor were as detested by the people of Paris. This institution was the Ferme ("the Farm"—a curious name for the office that collected indirect taxes for its own profit after paying the government a fixed fee for the right). "Why are you doing this, Antoine?" you asked him when he told you he was going to join the Ferme as the assistant to François Baudon. "It has a terrible reputation . . ."

"All that is utter nonsense, my friend. Somebody has to collect taxes. The kingdom wouldn't survive without them. Besides, it's a magnificent way to build extra funds. I intend to invest in my laboratory whatever profit I make on the taxes I manage to farm. You know how important it is to be able to count on good equipment, and you know too how devilishly expensive it is . . ." And so he became a farmer-general. It did not take long for you to discover that Antoine, like Voltaire, belonged to that small and very select band of individuals who conjoin talents as dissimilar as coming up with philosophical and scientific ideas and making money. And Antoine made piles of it. His capacity for work, like that of the old philosopher, who seemed indefatigable, allowed him to wrest secrets from nature with the same skill with which he extracted the savings of the Parisian bourgeois. His ever-prospering fortune permitted him to set up a laboratory that was by far the best in France, and perhaps in the entire world. The work that he carried out in it earned him the admiration and the gratitude of scientists all over the continent . . . and of the prime minister of the State Cabinet, for it's only fair to acknowledge, much of Antoine's effort was directed toward bettering the economy and financing the institutions of his country. "Science, my friend," he once said to you, "ought to serve us to understand what surrounds us better, but it should also be useful to make our life fuller and more pleasant . . ." The people who thoroughly disliked the young thinker—and that had been worrying you for a long time—were the residents of Paris. Unfortunately—and especially after 1774, when his associate died and he was named one of the tax collectors for Paris—his name was as well known among them as it was in scientific and political circles, but for Parisians it had a very different connotation. "He's a leech, like all the damned farmers-general! They live, and live like princes, off our work. With all due respect, Monsieur Rasero, I can't bear that man," you were surprised to hear good Marcel, Annette's husband, say one morning when, in despair, he came to ask you for a loan, "since the wretched farmers-general have left me without a single sol in my pocket . . ."

But the most memorable event of that year, by far, was the birth of Faustillo, Annette and Marcel's son. How you loved that child! Since when he was very small, you were drawn by his unusual beauty (his big green eyes, his ruddy, freckled complexion, his strong and flexible limbs), his excitable, alert character, and especially his enormously likable nature. He has made you feel like a grandfather without ever having been a father, since you never scolded him or upbraided him—Annette took very good care of that—but, on the other hand, obeyed the most trifling of his commands and catered solicitously to his every whim. You never tired of watching him play, running about the laboratory, observing any object within his reach, bombarding you with questions, many of them very intelligent, as you yourself used to do with Fray Silvestre there in the old mansion in the calle Miaja.

Faustillo was ten years old now and hadn't lost the least fraction of his virtues. On the contrary, without changing his likable nature, he had turned into a serious and diligent youngster who kept his schoolmates from winning any of the honors for studiousness—though not for comportment—in the Collège Mazarin, the best primary school in Paris, where you enrolled him when he was seven years old. He was born at the beginning of October, '68. It was a long and difficult birth. You and Marcel spent many anxious hours at the door of Annette's bedroom. The midwife kept going in and out of the room. They searched her face, looking for news that the woman refused to concede them. Her face was as mute as her mouth;

a Gothic statue would have been more expressive. The one person who never left the room was Dr. Jardel; his dry, rasping cough barely betrayed his presence. You couldn't keep images—did you really see it all, or did you dream it much later?—of your own birth from coming back to your mind. "Things are going very badly," the midwife said. Your mother was howling like an abandoned wolf cub, and your father was hammering on the door. "What the devil is going on?" he kept shouting, yet, finally, a very intense light blinded your eyes and a great mouthful of air rushed into your lungs. Before you heard your own wail, you heard a very high-pitched, endless cry. It was your mother dying, Rasero. She died with a thin cord of flesh still joined to your body. Another cry brought you out of your self-absorption; it was Faustillo, who had decided to abandon once and for all his warm refuge. "The two of them are fine. You may come in to see them, but don't make a lot of noise. The woman is very weak," the midwife told them with the seriousness of a sergeant. Overcome with emotion, Marcel and you embraced.

"A son, Monsieur Rasero!" he said to you, proud and happy, as though nobody in the world would have been able to do what he had done. "A son!" he repeated.

You decided to go to Madame Chantal's to celebrate. Denis went with you. Antoine was too young and, as is apparent, too serious minded to visit a brothel. Diderot too had been celebrating something, though you no longer remembered what it was. I hope I see something pleasant, you thought as you headed to the bedroom with Charlotte. Your hope was not unreasonable: that year, alternating with the frightful images of the war in the East that seemed never to end, you had a number of visions that you considered, if not enjoyable, at least reassuring. You saw great crowds, joyful and unruly, marching though the streets of many cities; among them you recognized Paris. Almost all the participants were young people, of both sexes, although it was difficult to tell them apart, since most of the girls were wearing pants like the boys. They were walking along arm in arm and shouting slogans you didn't understand but suspected were ribald and daring, given the big grins you saw on countless of the faces after each slogan was shouted in chorus. Many of the marchers were carrying paper or cloth placards, with messages you were unable to make out, and in most cases they were illustrated with amusing obscene drawings. You realized that something important was happening in that remote world of the future, for it was not difficult to see that those marches, festive and arrogant, were taking place in very different places. You could tell this because of the appearance of the different crowds: at times the majority of the participants were white and fair-haired, Europeans no doubt; at other times they were dark-skinned and had very black hair, or sometimes were Asians. At other times whites mingled with blacks. The cities where these marches were taking place and the faces of the marchers varied widely, but the spirit, the self-assurance, the rebellion, the pride, and the grace of the young people were everywhere the same. Perhaps they're protesting against so many wars, you thought once, when, in the middle of an experiment with prussic acid which you and Lavoisier were conducting in his laboratory, you were seized with the vision of a huge column of those young people, hundreds of thousands perhaps. Now, however, they were marching solemnly, hieratically; no one in the enormous crowd was uttering a single word. They were advancing slowly and grimly; many of them were holding their arms up with a Roman numeral five formed by two of their fingers. The silence was even more imposing than the clamor you had heard earlier. It gave enormous weight to their protest, or whatever their demonstration was. Sometimes the silence was broken by the sound of the applause the column received from spectators on both sides. Many of the spectators stopped applauding and joined the procession. Deeply impressed, you too applauded. Never—except for that memorable occasion at Voltaire's country mansion at Ferney—had a vision pleased you so much. In that distant future a hope exists, you thought as you went on applauding. "What's up, my friend?" Lavoisier said to you, intrigued. "I don't see much reason to applaud. The mixture has decomposed again . . ."

And your desire was fulfilled: in Charlotte's arms you had one of those visions. It was a huge public square, filled with people, almost all of them young, like the other times. They were sitting on the ground, laughing and joking. The afternoon sun beating down lit their faces, many of them copper colored. Someone was speaking from the plaza of a large building; the people were listening attentively to him. Every so often they broke into loud slogans they shouted in unison. Even very small children, who could barely walk, were taking part in the activities; they too were shouting and laughing happily. That vision pleased you a great deal, Rasero. You considered it a good sign, above all when you thought of Annette's son who had just been born. Within a few years, that baby will be like those children, rebellious and cheerful, proudly confronting a cruel and selfish world . . .

Charlotte too was in a good mood. She liked this customer, always so attentive and so grand. Besides, he was very good at making love, which made her work a pleasure. She talked to you—as she had on many other occasions, for she had discovered that you were a good listener, able to spend hours at a time quietly listening to her without interrupting, nodding your head every so often in agreement with her remarks (this was very much to Charlotte's liking; it allowed her to put her ideas in order and reflect on her anxieties and plans, as though she were writing a diary)—about the Gironde, the region where she had been born, about the stream where she liked to bathe when she was a little girl. "There was something special about that stream . . . there's no doubt about it. I was deflowered alongside its waters," she said in a natural, even tone of voice. "Maybe that's why I think of it whenever I've just made love . . ."

"Well, let's go back to the stream," you suggested to her with a smile. You wanted to go back to that public square. Charlotte surrendered docilely to your caresses, and in a little while, to your satisfaction, you returned to the square. Those young people were still there. But now they weren't sitting down or laughing or joking. There were signs of fear on all their faces, intense fear, terror. They were running in all directions in a panic, with the result that they very often knocked others down and trampled children and the weakest underfoot. It was pandemonium. You soon understood why: the place was surrounded by men dressed in green—soldiers, no doubt—armed with rifles that spit out bullets at an astonishing rate. They fired on the crowd, as though the people were ducks trapped in the middle of a pond. The festive and irreverent shouts had turned into piercing laments, into hair-raising screams. In less time than it takes to tell—can orgasm last any longer than that?—the square was covered with blood, with abandoned clothing, with books and magazines, and scattered in the debris, like seeds sown at random on the ground, there were cruelly wounded bodies, some of them still writhing, many others lying in the stillness of death. So that was how it was? you thought. Not even an hour had gone by before that pleasant vision, which you had seen as so auspicious, turned into a nightmare. The death and war that devastated that era could not exempt those youngsters; they too had to suffer their share . . . The good sign was now a fateful omen. You thought once more of that baby who had just come into the world and asked yourself if he too would have his life snatched away from him almost the moment it began to flower. "Accursed future! It's hopeless," Charlotte, somewhat frightened, heard him say . . .

Abbot Mignot delivered a brief, heartfelt eulogy. Those present knew only too well what sort of man they were burying; it wasn't necessary to dwell on his greatness. Rest, dear friend. Truly, no one deserves to rest as much as you do . . . , Rasero thought as he saw the workers place the heavy marble slab above the grave. The burial service ended as darkness was falling. Soon a long line of carriages began leaving for Paris. Rasero remained behind in the church. He had decided to spend a few days in Scellières to keep Mignot company. The priest was sick at heart; the burial service was no sooner over than a messenger arrived from Paris: the archbishop informed him that he had been suspended from his duties and even went on to threaten him with the possibility of an ecclesiastical trial.

"They're going to excommunicate me, don Fausto," his friend said, his eyes dimmed by tears.

"No, Mignot. They won't dare. What sort of Christian would punish a pastor of his church for fulfilling his duty? Anyway, you're not alone, Mignot. You can appeal to the Vatican. I'm sure many people would support you. That idiot of an archbishop isn't going to risk a trial in such circumstances. You'll see."

Though he was far from convinced, the priest thanked him for those words with a sad smile. "Let's say no more. It will be as God wills . . . I'll order a room readied for you, marquis."

Rasero remained still for a long time, contemplating his old friend's tomb. It was dimly lit by a curious reddish glow, coming from the enormous plate of a moon that was beginning to rise in the east. The aspect of the philosopher came back to him: thin, frail, restless, pacing with quick little footsteps, like a hungry rat, from one end of the library to the other. "To want to live, my friend, is the one thing that gives one strength; to want to life fully, completely . . ." And you did that just as it is to be done, François dear. You drank life to the dregs . . . But everything, absolutely everything, even an existence such as yours, comes to an end . . . , Rasero thought, his eyes still on the tomb, which was much brighter now, tinged with that cold and metallic color the moon imparts to things when it's full and at its zenith. He imagined François inside the coffin in his impressive white uniform. He was smiling, satisfied and very comfortable. The coffin fit his shrunken body amply. That Palais Royal whore also fit in, looking much prettier than your friend had told you she was. The happy woman never left off looking at the philosopher from the sockets of her empty eyes, kissing him with her fleshless mouth, embracing him intensely, fatally.

"Your room is ready, marquis," Mignot announced.

Rasero left his friend resting with his eternal lover. He was still upset at the thought that the body of a man like Voltaire reposed in a little out-of-the-way village, hidden almost, through the fault of people of immeasurably lesser stature than he. (Several years would still have to go by for the remains of Rasero's friend to receive the homage they deserved. They were finally able to rest, forever this time, in the heart of the city he had been born in.)

Two weeks later, Rasero was in his study looking through the correspondence that had piled up during the time he had been away. He read with interest a letter from Lavoisier:

> Dear Fausto,
>
> I enclose with this letter the copy of an article I have just published. In fact, it contains almost the same material as the memorandum I presented at the Academy in 1775 regarding the eminently breathable portion of air, with which you are thoroughly familiar. I have, however, added new observations, and above all I have attempted to be clearer. It is no easy task to persuade those donkeys. Nonetheless, I trust that now they will not raise any more objections, since I have proved, beyond the slightest doubt, that nonvolatile air is a compound composed of carbon and the breathable part of air. The procedure to prove it couldn't be simpler: it is much easier to prepare oxygen (do you like the sound of the name I've thought up for this element?) than to cook any of the marvelous dishes that our dear Annette makes. This is the only way to convince those cretins. Phlogiston is as firmly rooted in their heads as a cyst! Just a few days ago I performed the experiment as Dr. Macquer looked on. On seeing the gas (or more accurately, its effects), the man turned livid, as though he had found himself face-to-face with death itself. His brain could not make up its mind to accept what his eyes were seeing (not even Saint Thomas was that stupid). He reminded me of Galileo's colleagues when they refused to look through the telescope to observe the satellites of Jupiter. "Ptolemy clearly established that there exist only seven planets," they said unyieldingly to Galileo, who answered, "And what about those satellites?" "They're the work of the devil," they replied, proud of knowing how to answer. In the very same

way, Macquer refused to accept the evidence. "When metals are calcined," I said to him, "they increase in weight because they combine with oxygen. It's that simple, doctor; it has nothing to do with phlogiston, with negative weights or other nonsense of the sort." "But, sir," he replied, "how would we have gotten anywhere with our old chemistry if it were necessary to construct a totally different edifice? Don't you appreciate everything that has been built?" "I appreciate the truth, my friend," I answered him, "and I greatly fear that we'll have to construct that totally different edifice you speak of just as soon as possible . . ."

In short, Fausto, I'll soon be able to give you all the particulars about this. Kindly read the article and tell me sincerely what you think of it (though I'm certain you're going to think it's very good). Ah! my friend, I'm happy; that accursed theory will soon be deader than Charlemagne. Yours,

Antoine

Not until now, old ass that I am, Rasero thought, not until now have I realized what that balance meant . . . Antoine, Antoine, how diabolically clever you are!

He then read another letter, so different from the first that it could be said that all the two had in common was the epistolary genre. It was written by the director of the Collège Mazarin and addressed to Rasero in his capacity as the tutelary mentor of the young Fausto Michel Gautier. He had to read four long pages, querulous and prolix, explaining something that deserved but two paragraphs: young Fausto Michel had been temporarily expelled from the school for hitting his Latin teacher over the head with a heavy lead inkwell. "Master Junot, on ascertaining that young Fausto Michel had not fulfilled certain assignments related to the declensions of that beautiful language, resolved to order his pupil's approximation to the teacher's platform so he might deliver an incontrovertibly condign punishment. Instead of ambulating forward, however, the boy remained intractably seated in his place, and from there pronounced before his teacher, in a stentorious voice, so that all his classmates could apprehend the affront, 'Go to hell, you hypocritical befrocked son of a b——!' (I am dismayed to have to convey to you that that was his exact usage.) As you will have the facility to appreciate, Master Junot was grievously vexed, to the point of manifesting his disquiet in unconstrained gestures of his own, in having to breast the boisterous indecorum of his pupils, many of whom had begun insolently ejaculating at him, 'hypocritical son of a b——, hypocritical son of a b——.' The master directed his person toward Fausto Michel's seat in order to require the instigator to leave the room and to present himself to my purview. But the hapless gentleman was scarcely able to take two steps before he sustained upon his forehead, just above his organs of visual perception, the formidable impact of an inkwell of eminent weightiness that the boy projected at him with, I regret to say, inerrant aim . . ."

That little devil. I must have a serious talk with him . . . , Rasero thought, although he realized that he was of no mind to scold the boy. He almost felt like congratulating him for his deed. Those damned priests—they have it coming to them, he thought, remembering Voltaire's account of his misfortunes at Saint-Louis. Though naturally, I can't congratulate him; I must be severe, he said to himself with distaste, and make him understand that he can't spend his life tormenting friars. It was not, by a long shot, the first time the director of the Collège Mazarin had complained about the unruliness of Rasero's protégé. Well, I'll have a talk with him tomorrow, he reflected. I don't feel up to reprimanding him today. What I'll have to do is warn him not to say anything to his parents. He mustn't do what he did the last time he misbehaved, when he proudly told them all about it, as though he'd won a prize. His prize became a terrible thrashing. When Annette's angry, she's a veritable fury.

Finally, he read a letter from his friend Diderot:

> Dear Fausto,
>
> Enclosed is an article about our Voltaire that I've just written. I hope you like it,
>
> Denis

Rasero took the article and settled down in his old easy chair. Denis, with that sober, direct style of his free of the slightest affectation, a style that always pleased the Malagan, rendered sincere homage to the beloved philosopher. He wrote of the enormous vacuum that his absence meant for French letters. "Your name . . . will reach the remotest posterity and will disappear only amid the ruins of the world . . ." He also wrote of Voltaire's tireless work in practically every field of knowledge and art. History, literature, politics, religion, and science kept no secrets from him. How many great men of the entire world came to be known thanks to the patriarch of Ferney! Locke, Newton, Shakespeare, Swift, Pope, and so many others. At the end, Diderot wrote, with greatest feeling of all, of the titanic struggle that Voltaire waged against intolerance throughout the last twenty years of his life, of his heroic defense of those poor wretches whom religion made the object of fierce persecution. Calas, La Barre, and many others drew the interest of the philosopher, who acted tirelessly as their advocate; he fought with his bare fists, one might say, against a stone wall, out of sheer intransigence. He fought like a brave warrior from his little Ferney, that pretty village that his drive, his inexhaustible energy, created virtually out of nothing. Diderot ended the article with a sentence whose modesty was truly moving: "Which of us would not give his life in exchange for just one of his days?"

You, Denis, you answered, ought not give your life, because it's as valuable as Voltaire's . . . With profound sadness, suddenly aware of the dizzying passage of time, you allowed a striking procession of images to run through your head. They were different and at the same time identical. There was your friend Diderot, young still, lying in a bathtub, sick to death of the filth of the world and of the men who came brutally to his mind through his delicate sense of smell. Then you saw him—a little older—happily drinking in Madame de Mailly's drawing room. He had just read aloud a few paragraphs of the introduction to the *Encyclopédie* and was receiving with a show of modesty the praise showered on him. Next you saw him, rather drunk, smiling with pleasure, clinking glasses with two of Madame Chantal's girls and talking to you about the cathedral of Puy, where "they keep the most valuable relic that exists, there's no doubt about it, dear friend. I'm talking about the remains of Saint Prepuce, no less." After that, you saw him on the bed, stewed to the gills, his eyes filled with tears and dead tired, tormented by the insects swarming about in his mind, and in love, totally in love. Then you saw him as an older man, but recovered now and brilliant. He was causing your Mariana to split her sides laughing at his quick, pointed, slightly poisonous phrases, like Cupid's darts. You saw him a little later, next to your bed, with you in as bad shape as he had been six years before, and in as permanent a stupor from alcohol. How long had you been like that? You had no idea; it was Annette who knew. When she saw that you were ending your second month shut in your room, drinking without stopping and almost without eating a single bite of food, she turned to your beloved Denis, for the good woman knew he was the one person who could save you. You saw him there, at your bedside, with his enormous calf's eyes on the point of bursting into tears. "Clear out of here, once and for all!" he was saying to the old beggar who, in one corner of your bedroom, was playing a sad popular ditty on his violin, completely out of tune.

"Do you hear him, Fausto?" Mariana had asked you. She was standing in front of the big window, the dawn light slumbering on her face. "Poor thing! . . . Give me a louis," she said to you.

"If we give him a louis, we're going to have him down below that window every day."

"That strikes me as marvelous. That way we'll wake up to music every morning." She threw him the coin, and as you feared, Rasero, at the exact moment the sun came up in the east, the old man could be counted on to begin playing the same eternal popular tune. When Mariana disappeared, you spent a sleepless night drinking all the wine that's ever been since Noah invented it, and weeping, weeping all the tears your insect's eyes held back all your life . . . and then you heard the beggar's music. I don't believe poor Damiens suffered from his tortures as much as you from listening to that music. Hoping perhaps that the pain would in the end kill you, you went to the window and told the aged man to come upstairs. You installed him in a corner of your bedroom, and asked him to play his instrument. And there he stayed, as wordlessly faithful as your Nostradamus, for more than two months, playing over and over the song that tore pieces of your soul from you just as Pierre Brachet's tongs tore pieces of Damiens' body from him . . .

Diderot moved toward the old man to chase him off, threw cold water on your face, shook you like a rag doll, and even gave several cuffs to bring you out of your stupor. "Fausto!" he shouted vehemently, "Fausto!" He looked at you with deep affection; he looked at you from his own unhappiness and saw in your eyes a desolation he knew well. He recognized in what you smelled the stench that tormented him . . . and he said not a word more; he just burst into tears and put his strong arms around you. Who knows how long you remained like that, in each other's arms and weeping your hearts out like a pair of despairing lovers? But it was that embrace, Rasero, and that silence, so eloquent, so full of ideas, anxieties, hopes, and above all, affection, that made you decide to go on living . . .

The afternoon was extraordinarily hot. Rasero decided to go for a stroll to get a breath of fresh air but, above all, to try to banish his sadness. Walking along slowly, he went up the rue St-Jacques and then went across to the Ile de la Cité. He passed in front of the old cathedral and took the Notre Dame bridge to the Right Bank, reaching the quarter of La Ville. He stayed there a long time, walking round and round like a foreigner who'd lost his way, until the first night shadows drove him toward the wide avenues that surround the Louvre, impressively lit owing to the genius of his friend Lavoisier.

Although it was fully dark by now, the heat had not abated. On the contrary, it was even more intense. That was perhaps because the stones of the streets and the houses, though no longer under the intense pressure of the sun's rays, were allowing the heat they had absorbed during the day to escape. Because of that, or for other reasons, the heat was stifling. Rasero raised one hand to his brow and discovered to his surprise that it left his hand wet. Seldom had there been sweat on his head, his bald head. The sight of the wet hand somehow affected his mouth and throat, for all of a sudden they seemed to him drier than a Dominican's sermon on Sunday. He descended into the first tavern he came across. He literally descended, for the tavern, like many others near the Palais Royal, was below ground level, in the basement of a four-story town house. The place was quite pleasant. Though not very well lit, the cheerful paintings on the walls were well visible. They were large oils, much darkened by the bad quality of the varnish coating them, by the smoke from the tavern's candles, which remained lit both day and night, and above all, by the passage of many years. Even so, the pretty, robust women in the paintings—some in Roman tunics, but most of them nude, their generous, rosy flesh, which the great master Rubens had been so fond of, completely exposed—were able to excite the blood of any young man. Badly composed and painted even worse—More likely than not, they're the work of the apprentices of some great artist's studio at the end of the last century, Rasero thought—the paintings had a charm anyway, perhaps because they went especially well with the atmosphere of the place: like the women on display, who made no pretense of being Venuses, the tavern made no pretense of being an elegant café, but just as the women portrayed on the walls were more attractive and seductive than the elegant, haughty highborn ladies in other paintings, so one felt much better in this place than at the Procope.

Though there were a fair number of customers, Rasero found a table in a far corner. The waitress, a large woman with salt-and-pepper hair, with breasts and backside more ample than human desire and more often caressed than the relics of a saint, seemed to have stepped out of one of the paintings. Without waiting for him to order, she set down on the table a pitcher of chilled wine, an earthenware mug, and a big earthenware plate on which there were fried whiting. "Anything else?" she asked with a come-hither smile; she knew very well what this bald man, he and all the others in the place, wanted. "Nothing else then. Thanks very much," he heard the woman say, with just a slight tone of disappointment, as she buried the coin he'd given her in the deep cleft between her breasts.

The walk had made Rasero feel good, as good as the cool wine gliding into his stomach. Strolling along the streets freed his mind of the sad thoughts that troubled him. He remembered his casual glance at the old Franciscan monastery a few steps from his house; he had seen the groups of students making a great racket as they passed by, heading for the Sorbonne, in the Latin Quarter. He had watched the river's flow, its thick, greenish water carrying along, as always, its peculiar smell, an emanation resulting from the combination of a thousand odors so intimately assembled that not one of them could be identified, not even the smell of poverty, which without a doubt was the most powerful of them all. He had seen the facade of Notre Dame, with its rose window as enormous as a wheel of Apollo's chariot and its slender pilasters effortlessly supporting the two massive towers. He had not wanted to see more of the cathedral; he had seen, however, the women walking the streets, smiling, noisy, and flirtatious: the little dark-haired thing standing on a street in La Ville, leaning on the door of a tavern, was really pretty. He had looked at the shops, stores, and display windows without seeing them, and—this he saw very well—a little carriage painted a bright, incandescent orange that made his eyes hurt just to look at. It's a mad world, he thought.

You were draining your second glass of wine when you saw a man enter the tavern who powerfully drew your attention. He was very young, not over twenty, dressed simply and neatly. He was not wearing a wig; his fine brown hair was tied back in a pigtail. He was of normal height, rather thin, and very pale. What caught your attention, Rasero, were his eyes; they were wide open and vivacious, and they radiated a strange happiness. The man sat down across the way from you, and the ample waitress plunked the wine, the mug, the fish, and her proposition down on the table. Like you, he accepted everything but the last. The woman, very sober faced, went off with another coin stuck in her bosom.

The man occupied himself looking at the paintings. That allowed you to stare at him frankly without running the risk of being taken for a pederast. What is there about this man that catches my attention? you wondered. As though the young man had heard you, he turned his head and his eyes met yours. He smiled politely. That's it! you thought once you saw the smile. I know this man. I'm certain I've seen him before; I know him well . . . but why can't I remember who he is? You closed your eyes and rested your head in the palm of your hand. You made your mind go blank in an attempt to get the memory to come back.

It didn't, at least not at that moment. What appeared was the future. You had a very strange vision, perhaps the strangest you'd had in your life—and that's saying a great deal indeed. You saw the little house of the overseer of the Gálvezes' farm in Macharavialla. It was very run-down. The whitewash on the walls had stains from the dampness and had turned a greenish color from mold; in many places the stones the house was built of were visible, for the stucco had fallen away like a dried crust. Almost all that was left of the Saint Gabriel who watched over the main entrance was his legs with the laces of his sandals twining up above his ankles. Inside, you saw a vast bedroom. Its walls were white too, and full of damp stains; the oak beams, very old and worm-eaten, that held up the roof were threatening to give way under the weight they bore and to collapse once and for all. There was a big bed with a brass headboard, a desk underneath the window, and several portraits of people, done in pencil or black ink, some from the torso up and others full length. Among them, your attention was held by that of a mature man who was holding, one in each of his own hands, the hands of a boy and a girl; they were walking down the street of a city you identified as one of those of the future. On the desk, you saw a black wooden coffer decorated with mother-of-pearl insets. It was not hard for you to recognize it. By it stood a man who was opening one of its drawers and taking from it a book with wine-colored cardboard covers. He was leafing through it with interest. As if sensing your presence, the man turned toward the door. He was still young, surely not over thirty. He was tall, skinny, and a little ungainly. His hair, very short—like that of almost all the men you had seen in the future—was brown. His little eyes were fixed upon the text, and a deep furrow was forming between his eyebrows, which arched above his slightly protruding eyes. His nose was short and straight. It's me, you thought absurdly. The man raised his eyes and looked toward the door. You had the feeling that his eyes met yours. He didn't see you, of course; he smiled in a very odd way and went back to his reading. For a moment you felt that his eyes were your eyes and that you were looking at the book through them. There was a short handwritten passage on the page and underneath it, occupying two-thirds of it, a splendid drawing. For the first time, you managed to read something in the future you visited, though only the last lines of the paragraph: "Selfishness and its faithful spouse, Stupidity, will be your gods. And they will be loved and respected as never a god was adored on earth."

He read, and you read. Then both of you lowered your eyes and saw the illustration: a horrible man, wrapped in a great ermine cape, with a cruel and pitiless laugh that showed his enormous, repugnant mouth, with the few remaining teeth eaten away with decay. He was sitting on a throne. He had a heavy crown laden with jewels on his head, a staff topped by a skull in one hand, and a big, heavy pouch of coins in the other. He was receiving on his withered, hairy cheek, the kiss of a no less repulsive little woman, as tiny and skinny as a reptile, and like him, with round, bulging eyes covered as far as the middle of her eyeballs by swollen, sticky eyelids. Her nose, long and pointed, recalled that of a ferret. She was wearing a very tight dress decorated with capricious Grecian frets. She looked like a juggler or a harlequin, and like either, she was wearing on her head a cap that ended in three long points, from each of which hung a small bell. It was at once a horrendous and a beautiful image. This was unquestionably due to the enormous skill of the hand that had painted the figures, with a regular-sized brush soaked in sepia-colored diluted ink, on that yellowish paper. How strange! he thought, you thought, and the two of you raised your hand to your head. For the first time in your life as well, Rasero, you had the experience of having hair; your fingers sank into a shock of it, softer than you had imagined. And it was firm and well anchored, for despite picking up a lock with your hands and pulling very hard, you were unable to dislodge it.

"Excuse me." The young man was standing in front of your table. You roused yourself from your absorption. In your left hand, raised up, you could no longer feel the shock of hair; the only thing left on your head was the heavy sweat. I'm going mad, you thought.

"Excuse me," the young man said insistently, transfixed by the peculiar expression that had come over the bald man's face.

"Yes?" Rasero was finally able to answer.

"Aren't you the Marquis de Rasero?" the young man asked in a strong German accent.

"Yes, I am."

"Ah sir. It's an honor to meet you," he said as he smiled in a way that Rasero found winning. "Allow me to introduce myself: I'm Wolfgang Mozart."

Mozart? Rasero thought. He sat there for a moment fondling that name in his mind until the memory finally surfaced: he saw that marvelous little boy, dressed from head to foot like a grown-up gentleman, with his tiny sword hanging from his waist, sitting before a harpsichord from which he was drawing out the most beautiful notes Rasero had heard in his life. He recalled how the young boy met his gaze for an instant, smiling with amused and conspiratorial eyes at the Malagan.

"Of course, Monsieur Mozart. The honor's mine. Do sit down, please. I hope you'll let me buy you a drink," he said as he summoned the waitress, ordering a bottle of champagne, "and make sure it's well chilled. Ah! And bring us the right glasses." The woman went off pleased, with a heavy louis inside her peculiar pocket. "So you're back in Paris . . . Really, I hadn't heard the news."

"That's the problem," Mozart replied ironically. "It seems nobody's heard I'm here . . ."

The effect of the wine soon enlivened their conversation. Mozart was a very affable and likable person. Notwithstanding the complicated situation he was passing through ("My mother is very ill. I don't know which has done her the greater harm, the climate of Paris or her son's failure . . ."), his mood, fated as he was to being as happy as a bird, had not given way to despair; it was instead irony, and occasionally sarcasm, that held sway. "Ah! Monsieur Rasero, I'm relieved to learn that you're Spanish. It will let me rail against the French as much as I please. They're unbearable. I've never known a people more tyrannized by fashion and stupidity, believe me. They refuse to forgive me for growing up. Every time I present myself at the palace of some nobleman, he looks at me, throwing his head back as though he's seeing me through opera glasses, as though I were some strange creature. Are *you* Wolfgang Mozart? he says to me, half incredulous, half disappointed, and from that simple reaction, I can see that the wretch, like many others, is not going to take the trouble to put my abilities as a musician to the test. He's a grown-up, they think scornfully. What can he offer me that none of my musicians can? And so, if things go well for me, they hire me to teach their pampered daughter to play the harp or the harpsichord. And those girls, usually, have about as much talent for music as a stutterer for public speaking. So that's how I spend my days: going from one end of Paris to the other to teach empty-headed girls that the harp is played by plucking the strings and not by hammering on them as on an anvil, or that the bow of a violin is not an arrow meant to be shot at a target. If it's not that, it's worse still: teaching them to sing in this language that's so pompous and affected. Believe me, sir, there's no language that's worse for music than French; the idea of composing an opera in French petrifies me. This language is an endless rosary of monosyllables expelled from the middle of the gullet. Making music out of that is impossible. Of course, Lully or Rameau can do it, if you consider what they do music . . ."

It was a genuine delight to listen to that young man. His genius is not only musical; he could have been a great philosopher, Rasero said to himself, for many of the things he heard the musician say reminded him of the conversations of his beloved Voltaire and Diderot.

"How was I able to recognize you, you wonder? Ah sir. It wasn't hard. Your shining pate led me to you the way a lighthouse guides a ship to port," he went on, bursting into peals of laughter. "Don't be offended, sir, but in this world of men who wear wigs, your bald head is highly conspicuous. Besides, though you may find it hard to believe, I remember you very well. We met at a concert at the von Eyck palace, when I came to Paris for the first time. You were there, near the platform, weren't you?"

"Yes, I was."

"I liked the look in your eyes, and your bald head. My music pleases that man, I thought, and his bald pate pleases me." He laughed again. "When I came back in '66, I asked Melchior Grimm if he knew a bald man with a likable air about him. 'Of course,' he said to me, 'that's the Marquis de Rasero. A splendid person; I have the pleasure of being a good friend of his.' I wanted him to introduce me to you, but it was impossible. It seems you had sealed yourself up in your town house and didn't want to see anybody. Later on, to tell you the truth, I forgot about you and your bald head, until I saw you a while ago scrutinizing me as though I were a half-remembered flame from your village. He's trying hard to recognize me, I thought, so I'm going to spare him the agony . . ."

The waitress put a second bottle of champagne on the table. Mozart downed big swallows of it with true pleasure.

"Ah! French wine is excellent, though it pains me to admit it." His cheeks had become slightly flushed, and his nose had turned bright red. "Of course I tried at Versailles. I presented myself there just two days ago, dressed in my best, wearing a heavily powdered wig, and carrying countless musical scores under my arm. Among them I had a symphony that I've just composed and that I've dedicated—a trifle hypocritically, I must confess—to this city. Though it's immodest of me to say so, it's a splendid symphony. But it did me no good at all; no one even took the trouble to leaf through it. The only connections I have at Versailles stem from the proposal of marriage I made the present queen of France when I was six years old, and the scolding I gave the Marquise de Pompadour when she wouldn't kiss me . . . Of course, that happened when I was a child, and hence a prodigy. Since I'm no longer a child, and therefore no longer a prodigy either, no one showed the slightest interest in me, even if I was bringing the very music of the spheres with me under my arm . . ."

When they finished the second bottle, Rasero invited the musician to have supper at his house.

Mozart ate with a voracious appetite, accompanying his mouthfuls with generous swallows of wine, and he took advantage of the intervals between the courses to speak freely to his host of his adventures in Paris. "Ah, dear Melchior . . . to tell the truth, I can no longer bear him. He's conspired with my father to make me return to Salzburg. Do you know the date I set for that? Never! Believe me, I'll throw myself headfirst into the Seine before I go back to Colloredo's palace. Ah, Monsieur Rasero! You don't know how infinitely lucky you are . . ." Rasero looked at him without understanding. "You're lucky because you don't know Colloredo. Seriously, anyone who has dealings with that man, even if only for a couple of hours, can testify to what I say. After seeing that man, you find nothing the same again—as if your spirit had become begrimed with soot and not even a thousand bleachings could make it clean again. That's the contamination he is. Imagine the tragedy I've suffered," he said between great bursts of laughter, "I, who have been on intimate terms with him all these years. I don't understand how I've managed to survive. Don't laugh; it's true. I swear I even had blasphemous thoughts that are the fault of that cardinal. God is quite perverse, I tell myself at times. How else explain his giving life to a monster like that? Fortunately, the devil exists, the one who in the final analysis must be held responsible for creations as odious as that. But, believe me, I'm convinced that even Lucifer must be very sorry for having done what he did . . ." The loud guffaw with which he ended his sentence kept Rasero from catching the last words. The Malagan listened with amusement. The young man's wit and his jokes—which were even funnier because they were uttered in appalling French with that odd accent of his (What I can't imagine is an opera in German, Rasero thought, but he kept his own counsel with the musician)—had managed to divert him, and he was able to escape momentarily the profound anxiety that his bizarre vision had caused him.

Mozart had a second helping and repeated the proposal of marriage that he'd made to Louise the moment he'd tasted the soup. "I beg you, miss, say yes to this poor musician. We'd make a fine couple: you'd delight my insides and I your ears. Can you ask for anything more?" The young woman, proud and a little embarrassed, answered with a squeaky little laugh that must not have been very pleasing to the highly educated ear of the Austrian.

When they'd finished dessert, they withdrew to one of the drawing rooms to have coffee and liqueurs. Mozart, very tipsy, kept making nonsensical remarks and laughing uproariously at his own witticisms. "Ah, my friend! the stupidity of Parisians is like the coiffures of their queen: there's no limit to either of them. To the health of my beloved countrywoman!" he said, raising his glass of brandy. "May God give her the strength and the courage to have her hairdos reach higher than the tower of Babel . . ." On lowering his glass, he spied the pianoforte in one corner of the room. Rasero noted that the mere sight of the instrument was enough to cause a look of seriousness to come over the young man's face for the first time since he had approached his table in the tavern in the rue St-Honoré.

"It looks terrific. May I try it out?"

"I'd ask for nothing better."

Mozart sat down at the keyboard. His fingers, agile and lively, ran frantically up and down it. In no time he had sounded each key three or four times. Suddenly he stopped playing, except for the ring finger of his left hand, which kept repeatedly striking one note.

"It may be slightly too low pitched," he thought aloud. "Otherwise, it's perfect; very well tuned. I like your piano, Monsieur Rasero; it has a superb sound. Ah! it's a pleasure to play it," he said as he gave out with a joyful little tune. "Can you believe that since I've arrived in Paris I've been without a piano for three months? There wasn't any that would fit in the miserable garret we were renting, even though we were paying forty pounds' rent for it. We have better lodgings now, and I have a piano I can use. But it's quite a bad one; there's no comparison with this one!"

"If you give me your address, I'll be glad to send it over to you. You can return it when you leave Paris."

"But, sir . . ."

"Do take it; I want you to. The piano is mere decoration here. I never play it."

"With my most grateful thanks!" Mozart exclaimed in delight as he improvised a pleasing melody.

Rasero sat down in the easy chair to listen to his new friend. With his glass of brandy between his hands, he threw his head back and closed his eyes so as to take in the full intensity of the music issuing from that man's hands. As Mozart played, he was thinking about the offer he had just received. A good piano for me alone, and for as long as I wish . . . marvelous! On it I'll compose the grand opera I've been dreaming of—and in French. Those blockheads will see what a real musician is. If someone were to commission it, if I were to get an advance . . . I could get rid of all those silly girls I have to teach . . . triumph in Paris . . . This last thought led him, as invariably happened recently, to Eloise Weber. He could go back to Mannheim with his head held high, free of Colloredo, of flighty pupils, of petty commissions: he wouldn't be needing them anymore. His fame would be much greater than when he was a child, because now his music was infinitely superior; he knew that very well. His new fame would make people vie for his creations. No money troubles ever again. The world, generous and prodigal, flung wide open, to enjoy it to the point of exhaustion with his beloved Eloise. He would compose the most beautiful arias ever written for her to sing in her marvelous voice, the most beautiful voice Mozart had heard in his life. Not even that castrato he remembered from Italy had a voice like Eloise'. She's an angel, he said to himself as he accompanied on the keyboard the sweet, serene, pure song of Eloise that was resounding inside his head . . .

You weren't listening to Eloise, Rasero, but you were indeed listening to the melody this man was playing. It was too beautiful; it had an exasperating rhythm. As though the notes had fallen asleep in his fingers, they took an eternity to follow one upon the other. It was almost silence rather than music. So, with that slowness that can occur only in dreams, there came to your mind the fond image of your Mariana. She was weeping with emotion as she listened to that magic child; she was weeping nervously, barely smiling. In rhythm with the music, you saw her features. The notes stopped first on her eyebrows, then on her eyes, and finally on her mouth; there they hummed lingeringly, like bees meeting, and then went on, one by one, particularizing for you your memory of her . . .

She also wept the last time you saw her, Rasero. She was weeping for Jeanne-Antoinette, or perhaps for everything. You kissed her before you left for Versailles—a hurried kiss, barely brushing her lips. If you had only known it was the last one you'd give her! . . . At this point the melody dragged you away; you didn't have the strength to prevent it . . . it took you to that carriage as you were returning from Versailles at dawn, after having spent the night keeping wake over your old friend. The morning was cold and gray; for the first time you felt that the way to Paris was as sad and gloomy as the one going to Versailles. You had only one consolation: Mariana was waiting for you in Paris. Thinking about it, you fell asleep; the jolts from the road and the fatigue of the sleepless night finally overcame you . . . Aye! that music, that terrible music brought to your mind that dream, that vision, Rasero . . . Who knows how long you remained asleep? All of a sudden, you woke up; you woke up in the middle of a huge city. There were many vehicles without draft animals hurrying along its wide streets in both directions. You saw the tall buildings with an exterior surface of glass windows on all four sides. You saw the people, in their peculiar attire, walking hurriedly in either direction. I'm dreaming, you told yourself, terrified at the thought that this was another vision. But you knew for certain that it was a vision when you saw Mariana there, at the edge of a street, sitting on that curious two-wheeled device. She was dressed as she had been the first time. You at last discovered when it was that you had first seen her: it was in the nightmare following the vaccination by Dr. Tronchin. As she had done that time, Mariana looked at you. But you weren't smiling now, Rasero, you were weeping, weeping bitterly. You wanted to come closer to her but were unable to. Never as much as on that day did you mind your inability to make contact with the world you visit during orgasm. "Mariana! Mariana!" you shouted to her, as the notes from your piano were now shouting.

"Good-bye, my seer!" she said to you, and rode off. Her image grew smaller and smaller by the second. You ran after her, but you didn't move forward a single step. You knew that it was useless, that the only thing that would help was to wake up.

For an instant, an absurd hope crossed your mind: Perhaps, when I open my eyes, I'll find myself in my bed, with Mariana at my side. But no. You opened your eyes and found yourself inside the carriage on that fateful morning in April. A sinister presentiment occurred to you. You ordered the coachman to pick up the pace; you wanted to get home as soon as possible. The man did the best he could, for the streets were terribly muddy. The journey seemed to last forever, just like this melody . . . When you finally arrived, you went up the stairs with foreboding. "Mariana!" you shouted while you were still outside the front door. In alarm, Annette came to let you in. "Where's Mariana?"

"I don't know, sir. I imagine she's in her bedroom . . ." You headed there like a sigh. You didn't find her. You didn't find her anywhere in the house, not her, nor Jacinta, nor her clothes, nor her jewels . . . nothing. It was as though she had never lived there. Like a man possessed, you went into the street to look for her, though you knew that what you were doing was useless. Once you woke up, a terrible certainty hammered at your mind, as now the bass notes coming from Mozart's left hand were doing . . . I'll never see her again, you told yourself in despair. Of course, you didn't want to accept that. You went all over Paris, from one end to the other; you went to all the city gates, to the terminals, to the places with carriages for hire, to the docks, everywhere. A frantic and absurd coming and going, as the notes were coming and going in your head . . . until you returned to your house, three nights later. I'm going to write to Matías, you thought, though you knew—you knew, but you wouldn't admit it—that this was going to prove just as useless. I'll never see her again, you kept thinking. Exhausted, you threw yourself on the bed and began to weep . . . A grief that lasted for months, Rasero, and that still hasn't ended. You knew that, because at this very moment your eyes were wet with tears. The musician hadn't noticed because he too was weeping, Rasero, he too had his own burden to bear . . . You spent a long time like that, lying on your bed, weeping all the tears that you hadn't wept in your life. I must look for her . . . , you thought. When you got up from the bed, you saw her; you saw her adorable face. It was on your desk. It was an oval-shaped miniature, done in pencil or in black ink. The face of your Mariana, with her hair loose, smiled at you from her portrait. "Mariana! What's happened?" you said to her. "Where are you, in heaven's name; where are you?" you asked the image, when, below it, also on the desk, you saw one of the sheets of Angoulême paper with something written in the middle. You recognized her handwriting. The hope that this paper aroused in you was extremely cruel, Rasero. For a joyful moment you believed that your fateful premonition was fading. With trembling hands, you picked up the sheet of paper and read that sonnet, Rasero . . . You recalled it now, it came back to your memory accompanied by that incomparable music reaching your ears:

> As today is yesterday, yesterday will be tomorrow.
> Cruel time caught me in its labyrinth
> where I met a man very different
> who filled with passion my life dulled by sorrow.
> I return, Fausto, to my American land
> (but to a time when they tell, my instinct says to me,
> how it was discovered by the fifteenth century);
> your Mariana awaits you there and then.
> The love that lights your path may let you see
> in time a way to come to me,
> a fruit ripe and sweet,
> and burst there, deep within my womb.
> Aye! I now but obey my fate's decree
> that only in the future will we meet . . .

You did not want to understand that poem, Rasero. You still didn't want to understand it now—as you also still didn't understand the nature of that miniature portrait you wore on your breast, in which you had not found a single clear mark of the pencil or the brush with which it was composed and which your tears had been unable to mar. No, you did not understand. You would with time . . . The one thing that was clear to you on that terrible day was that you would never see your Mariana again . . .

The last notes bore your recollection away with them. "Ah! Monsieur Rasero, it was a splendid evening," the musician said to you. Deeply moved, with great tears running down your face, you embraced that man; you embraced him and kissed him on both cheeks. "You're a marvelous being," you told him . . .

VIII
Robespierre

Paris, December, 1794

"Citizen Fausto Rasero?"

The lieutenant didn't like the looks of the old man who came to the desk. He's a damned aristocrat, he thought. The officer was perceptive, since the old man's attire had nothing at all aristocratic about it. He was wearing a somber black frock coat with trousers, a white shirt, very clean, buttoned to the neck, and no tie. But his bald head, which he was trying to hold erect, his yellowish face furrowed with wrinkles, and above all, his black eyes, wide apart and bright, that appeared to look through a person, radiated that elegance, the accursed hauteur of noblemen, with which the lieutenant was well acquainted. He's doubtless a nobleman. The only thing he's missing are those ridiculous knee breeches, he was compelled to think.

"Citizen Robespierre will attend to you when he has time," he said in a surly voice. "Wait here." His eyes pointed out a bench against the wall.

The bench, without a back, of rough wood that had scarcely been planed, much less varnished, was in curious contrast to the wall behind it. The wall was very high, painted a sky blue, and decorated with costly moldings of plaster covered with gold leaf. In the middle of it there were still the marks left by the large painting that had hung there a long time. This was just one of many contrasts Rasero saw as soon as he entered the Tuileries: he remembered, for instance, the highly polished marble floor, of colored slabs arranged with exquisite taste in geometrical shapes, over which, not long before, elegant young ladies had passed in their panniered dresses of silk and crackling satin and their fantastic coiffures that raised their powdered white hair to unimaginable heights and in addition had pinned on, by heaven only knew what artifice, fruit, flowers, and trinkets abundant enough to supply a market. The floor had borne the tread of pompous gentlemen, with their snow-white powdered wigs and their bright-colored attire adorned with ruffles and embroidery, and of footmen and ushers more elegant than their masters, with livery edged in gold and silver, who glided about like ghosts to fulfill the wishes of their lordships . . . Now, on the other hand, uncouth soldiers wearing blue-and-white uniforms with a tricolor cockade pinned to their hat, or better yet, to the waistband of their trousers, wandered over the same floors. Many of them had been, until only a short time ago, petty clerks or apprentices of a thousand trades who saw their life go by beneath the roof of a workshop or the faint sun of Paris. There were also politicians, most of them dressed soberly: in outfits of black trousers and white shirts and wearing their cockade proudly over the heart. Almost all of them were obscure provincial bureaucrats; their clothing still had the sour and stale smell of notaries' studies, of small-town libraries, and of sordid business offices. There were also, of course, the women of the Revolution. Full of themselves and noisy, they came and went, as the footmen had once done, from one end of the place to the other, making a racket like a flock of hens as they passed by. Some of them looked at themselves in an enormous mirror in a gilded frame that miraculously remained where it had always been. They straightened the kerchief or the liberty cap that covered their head, or with fingers wet with spit, they groomed their eyebrows so their eyes would in their fury look even colder, often giving a little downward tug to the neckline of their white blouse to show off more of the firm flesh underneath.

As had happened with the people frequenting it, the furnishings of the palace had also changed. The charming little drawing rooms, the dining rooms, the large windows, the heavy pianos, the coquettish chaises longues had disappeared. Revolutionary austerity had settled implacably over the place; the only furniture that could now be seen were work tables all about, square and clumsy, which had multiplied everywhere—along with uncomfortable straight-backed chairs and benches—like mushrooms in autumn. It appeared that the former lawyers couldn't get along without their desks, their inkwells, and their files. The lavish palace of the Bourbons has turned into a gigantic notary's office, Rasero thought. The military spirit was also still noticeable, however: pennons and standards of the glorious legions that had stopped the Austrians at the Rhine or turned the English back at Toulon filled every inch of the high walls. Underneath, as on an altar, countless rifles, leaning on their breeches and fitted with bayonets, gave the appearance of firewood stacked for the holocaust.

The Revolution was everywhere. But above all on the walls: where there had once hung a large portrait of Henry IV, young and absorbed in thought, perhaps deciding whether he would accept Paris in exchange for a mass, a large poster was now suspended. In the middle of it, were two heavy pages, spread open to form a diptych, as though they were the tablets of the law; each was supported by an angel, which had no air of the celestial. The look on the angels' faces was identical to that of the urchins who played in the waters of the Seine. On the two pages, in big clear letters, with the beginning of each paragraph marked by a capital letter more baroque than in Gutenberg's Bibles, the Declaration of the Rights of Man appeared. CITIZEN, printed in bold letters above the pages, served as an invitation to read the tablets. All the old paintings had been replaced by posters such as this one, bombastic and rather pretentious, reminding those who walked by of the glorious assault on the Bastille, of the angry, decisive storming of the Tuileries, or of the unforgettable days of August '92. One poster, didactically, listed the months and days by the absurd Revolutionary calendar's names.

Rasero couldn't decide whether this palace, and this world, were worse off when they sheltered hypocritical, corrupt fops and frivolous and empty-headed young ladies or now that they teemed with illiterate militiamen, fishwives from the markets, and ambitious bureaucrats. Just, wise, good men—dreamers on either side who had sincerely fought for a better world—were not to be found here. They did not go into the Tuileries. They filed by, however, in the Place de la Révolution—in the very spot where Gabriel surrounded vice by four virtues—to have their heads lopped off. Rasero felt a shiver run down his spine at the thought, because he was sitting where he was, waiting to be received by the most powerful man in France, in order to plead for the life of his beloved Antoine Lavoisier, whom he could already see, with complete clarity, beneath the sinister shadow of the guillotine . . .

It was the winter of '83. A group of eminent scientists had assembled in the huge laboratory set up by Antoine Lavoisier in the Arsenal, which he headed. Like a good stage director who before the first performance of a work has gone over all the details minutely—the voice and the frame of mind of the actors, the costumes, the stage setting, the lighting, the stagehands, and even the uniforms of the ushers at the entrance—so Lavoisier, aided by Marie-Anne Pierrette, his faithful wife and companion, had prepared for the demonstration down to the last detail. There was indeed much that was theatrical about the whole thing. But Antoine knew very well that circumstances required it: the competition between the British chemists and him was fierce. Many ideas, many experiments that no one had thought about for more than a hundred years, had begun to occupy the minds and the laboratories of a number of investigators at the same time. In places as far apart as Sweden, Scotland, and France—and almost concurrently—three men performed the same experiment, knowing that by carrying it out successfully they were revolutionizing chemistry but still not aware of what their distant counterparts were doing. Publications followed later, and accompanying them, fits of jealousy, quarrels, insults. Treacherously, the knowledge that for centuries had eluded everyone was suddenly within reach of several men at the same time.

That was the reason Lavoisier was doing things as he was: he did not want to see repeated the sort of painful altercation he had had with Scheele over oxygen. Antoine had behaved badly, and he knew it. Selfish and cowardly, when he published the summary of his experiment, he did not reveal the contents of certain letters the Swede had sent him. What was recorded in those letters was definitive: in all fairness the discovery should have been attributed to Scheele. But the man didn't realize what he was discovering, Lavoisier told himself to ease his conscience. Unable to free himself of the old theory, he called oxygen dephlogistized air. Although I didn't discover oxygen, I did explain what its discovery means for science. And in the last analysis, this is what is important . . .

With the demonstration he was about to carry out, the same thing was not going to happen. The prominent scientists gathered there—among whom (completely by chance) was Dr. Charles Blagden, an influential English scientist, who was soon to become the secretary of the Royal Academy of Sciences—would irrefutably testify that he, Antoine Lavoisier, was the only discoverer of the chemical nature of water, despite the important approximations Dr. Cavendish had arrived at with regard to the phenomenon.

Lavoisier at last delivered, weightily, his remarks to open the meeting: "Gentlemen, you are about to enjoy the privilege of witnessing one of the most fascinating phenomena ever to have taken place in this—kindly forgive the redundancy—fascinating science that is chemistry: the synthesis of water. With a certain fond bow to the past, I must remind you that water was first conceived as an element by the acute mind of Thales of Miletus but that its nature remained unexplored for many centuries, without even such brilliant talents as Dr. Robert Boyle (to whom we owe the modern notion of an element, among many other things) suspecting its true composition. Water, my friends, is not an element; it is the synthesis of two substances, both of them indeed elements, which manifest themselves as light, colorless, and odorless gases when they are in their free state. To a certain degree, Anaximenes, the disciple of Thales and also an Ionian, was closer to the truth when he maintained that air is the fundamental element in nature. Of course, that isn't true either, as we know very well today, but there is a certain poetic fitness in its being gases—or 'airs,' as they were called until recently—that form that marvelous, absolutely essential substance for life, water . . ."

Dr. Blagden looked skeptically at Lavoisier. What's all the fuss about? he thought. Dr. Cavendish has performed this experiment many times . . . After Lavoisier completed his introduction, he presented the actors: a piece of zinc, a handful of cinnabar, sulfuric acid, a powerful magnifying glass, an electrostatic generator, and—the leading actress—his magnificent balance. Several glass flasks, retorts, and apparatuses for collecting gases through the displacement of water constituted the stage props. Aided by his wife, the chemist activated his protagonists: the zinc bubbled merrily on contact with the acid, and the gas it gave off little by little displaced the water in the receptacle. Inside a bell jar, the cinnabar twisted and turned and was scorched under the intense beam of light from the magnifying glass. The vapor it gave off was, like that from the zinc, collected in a receptacle. When the metal disappeared and the cinnabar had been completely turned into mercury, they carefully stopped up the flasks containing the gases. By an ingenious system of glass tubes, Marie-Anne mixed both gases in a single receptacle and took it over to the balance, leaving on one of the pans a tare that represented the weight of the receptacle. When, using the electrostatic generator, Lavoisier produced a spark inside the receptacle, an impressive explosion ended the drama. The receptacle that had contained the two gases showed little drops of dew on its walls now and a minuscule deposit of pure water in the bottom. In an epilogue, the flask with the obtained water was taken to the balance; the tare, very well disciplined, indicated that the water's weight was identical to that of the original gases. Those present couldn't help applauding enthusiastically. Lavoisier modestly received their homage with a slight bow from the waist.

"Now, gentlemen, I beg you to sign this document," he said as he produced a memorandum book. "What is written above is simply a description of what you have just seen. I would be very happy if you testified by your signatures to what you have just seen on this memorable day."

The men agreed, although Blagden and Rasero did so extremely unwillingly. When the Malagan's turn came, he barely scribbled a signature on the paper. The truth is that he was very annoyed. He did not understand why Lavoisier had made such a drama out of an experiment that, although unquestionably very important, was already quite familiar to everyone: Cavendish had reported it a long time before. Rasero was concerned by this attitude on the part of Antoine, who was also so ambitious for glory, so eager for his name to go down in the history of science. It was not the first time that he had seen his friend act in a wholly unworthy manner in stealing the credit his colleagues deserved—with the same greed he showed in seizing the profits of the working people of Paris. Blagden couldn't reconcile himself to Lavoisier's conduct, and he spoke aloud what Rasero was thinking to himself: "This demonstration has been very interesting, Monsieur Lavoisier. But to tell you the truth, I can't understand the reason for all this excitement. With all due respect, I must remind you that all of us gathered here know very well that this demonstration was successfully performed by Dr. Cavendish several years ago."

Marie-Anne looked at the Englishman with hatred in her eyes. But Antoine smiled serenely; he had been waiting for this remark for a considerable time and had prepared a faultless reply: "I understand your concern perfectly, Monsieur Blagden. Naturally, I too am familiar with Dr. Cavendish's experiments. In addition, I might venture to mention that before him, Dr. Priestley had synthesized water, and even Dr. Mayow reports this experiment, which he performed more than a hundred years ago. But that is not what's important.

The essence of the subject lies in what I explained to you at the beginning, and in the corroboration of the final mass of the system that we provided as we ended the experiment. Allow me to remind you that, although Dr. Cavendish managed to synthesize water, never—never, do you follow me?—did he indicate (because, as I shall demonstrate, he was unable to do so) that water is a compound. Dr. Cavendish—and you are well aware of this, Monsieur Blagden—at no time succeeded in freeing himself from the phlogiston theory, and within that theory, the experiment we carried out has a very logical explanation (although looked at from another perspective, it couldn't be more nonsensical): oxygen is nothing but 'dephlogistized air,' the theory tells us, and the gas produced by zinc is, quite simply, 'intensely phlogistized water.' On this theory, when the two gases enter into contact, it is only natural that the first should take on the phlogiston of the second (which is manifested by the intense heat that it gives off), and that the latter, free now of phlogiston, should return to its original state of water. Water, then, *continues to be* an element, according to the phlogiston theory. Nonetheless, several parts of the theory are weak, and that is the importance of the calculations of mass we have carried out. Only by supposing that phlogiston has a negative mass can the increase in weight of a metal when it is calcined be explained: on losing phlogiston, the metal paradoxically gains mass, behaving in a way contrary to that of ordinary masses. And they call this theory scientific, for heaven's sake! But let's return to the experiment. If the gas from the zinc is phlogistized water, it ought to increase in weight, when it combines with oxygen and loses its phlogiston, as metals do when, on the theory, they lose phlogiston. I have clearly demonstrated—and I was the one who did so, not Cavendish, or Priestley, or Mayow, or anyone else—that there is no variation in mass during the phenomenon. This proves, beyond the shadow of a doubt, that oxygen is an element, inflammable gas (or hydrogen, as Cavendish calls it) is another, and that together they compose water. I have invited you to this meeting because I know that you have the expert knowledge to understand the tremendous implications that this original, yes, *original,* demonstration has for the theory of chemistry."

There was nothing for those present to do except applaud once again. This was the real import of the demonstration, Rasero thought when he heard his friend, and he couldn't help feeling great regret at having dashed off his name in signing the document that attested to the event. His name would forever be illegible alongside that of Blagden, Laplace, Vandermonde, Fourcroy, Meusnier, and Legendre on a document that, he now realized, would be a historic one.

Satisfied, the men left the laboratory, except for Fausto Rasero, who remained behind to help Marie-Anne and Antoine gather their instruments together . . . and to tell his friend something that had been weighing on his mind for several days.

"What did you think of it, Fausto?"

"Stupendous. I have to admit that at first I reacted the same way Blagden did. But there's no question about it; you've convinced me. And I believe you've convinced him too, although it's a terrible blow to his Anglo-Saxon pride."

"Quite true," Marie-Anne said happily.

"Frankly, what strikes me as boding no good is the other project you're involved in, Antoine." Lavoisier looked at him without comprehending. "I'm referring to the damned wall. Where did you all get that idea? Antoine, you're becoming more unpopular with Parisians than our Unloved Sovereign in his worst moments. Look at this." He showed him a leaflet that was circulating like coins of small value among the inhabitants of Paris:

To haul in a bigger take
And cut off our horizon
La Ferme is ready to make
Us all live in a prison . . .

"Yes, I already knew about that. And I'm aware of others much worse. In one of them, they suggest that the wall be inaugurated by hanging me from one of its tollgates," Lavoisier said with a smile.

"Well, I don't think it's funny. It's a preposterous plan, Antoine. You farmers-general are going to have all Paris out for your head . . ."

"Didn't you tell me that the people already despise me?"

"This is going to make it much worse. You'll risk getting knifed to death by some fanatic. This is no time to test the people's patience. You know very well how hard conditions are for them. Their restiveness is spreading like fire."

"Ah, how naïve you are, Fausto, my friend! Never, do you hear me, never, have the bourgeois of Paris and of all of France been as prosperous as they are now. You have no idea how much their profits have increased in the last few years . . ."

"So you're saying that the discontent I see the minute I go out in the street is the work of my imagination?"

"Of course not. What happens is that the bourgeois are playing a very treacherous game, a perverse one, I'd say. They've grown richer than they'd ever dreamed of being, but they've been very careful not to share their wealth with the state, which is becoming poorer by the day. And it's the state that takes on the responsibility of setting prices, of helping the poor, and of building public works. That's the origin of the discontent: an impoverished state that, as if it didn't have enough problems, must bear the tremendous load of an idle, parasitical, and incredibly extravagant court. A state such as that can't, obviously, fulfill its obligations to the people . . ."

"But . . . ," the Malagan stammered. It was his Spanish nature, so given to arguing, to never agreeing with the person he was speaking with, that brought that *but* to his lips. His intellect, however, told him to keep his mouth shut, that what his friend was saying was right and well reasoned.

"That's why we decided to build that wall. The amount of smuggling in Paris is scandalous. Goods and money come in and go out of the city without regulation. That affects us tax collectors, of course, but it also affects the state, which finds its revenues tremendously reduced, and it's unfair to the few honest tradesmen who pay the taxes they owe. When all is said and done, though, the ones most affected are the humble people of Paris, who find the aid that the government can offer them more and more limited. Nonetheless, the bourgeois have been very good at rousing the people to rebellion, as though the wall were going to affect the people's wretchedly meager incomes. We're not thinking of building that enormous wall to stop petty clerks, craftsmen, and fishwives, Fausto. The rich tradesmen know that very well, even though they take great care to tell the people something else. They've had the fiendish cleverness to hoist the workers onto their own boat and make them protest and fight for interests that, in the long run, do them harm. The situation is very touchy, we know; it's very difficult and even dangerous, like walking on a razor's edge: on the one hand, there are the nobility, corrupt and stupid, who expect nothing from us but more wealth so they can go on living their idle and frivolous lives, and on the other are the bourgeois, industrious and clever—there's no denying it—but terribly selfish as well. For them we're nothing but a bother, and they'd gladly destroy us. Between the two of them are the people, who are doubtless the ones who benefit most from our work, but paradoxically, they're also the ones who detest us most. There's no other way out, however. The state needs resources, Fausto, and if it doesn't get them, we'll end up being devoured by our neighbors."

"Enough. You've won me over a second time. It's obvious that you're persuasive today. But in any case, be careful; this matter is much more serious than the argument with Dr. Cavendish. The hatred of the people can be very dangerous, Antoine."

The famous wall was built, and as the Malagan feared, the hatred of the people of Paris toward the tax collectors increased many times over. That became perfectly clear to Rasero five years later, at the time of the terrible explosion in the gunpowder factory, in which Le Tort, the director of the enterprise, and the unfortunate Mademoiselle Chevraud lost their lives. The lives of the others were miraculously spared . . . Antoine had performed one of his spectacular demonstrations with gunpowder enriched with a new substance that Berthelot had discovered. The experiment was witnessed by Berthelot himself, Madame Lavoisier, Rasero, Chevraud, his niece Mademoiselle Chevraud, and Le Tort. After preparing a fair quantity of the new gunpowder, Lavoisier took a pound of it and a slightly greater amount of ordinary gunpowder and set fire to both at the same time in order to compare the results. The new powder exploded violently, so violently that the other sample seemed like merely some burning wood. The chemist then took the observers to some storerooms to show them the great quantity of the new compound that had already been prepared. Le Tort and Mademoiselle Chevraud remained behind to clean up the laboratory and ventilate it. "Those dreadful nets to collect saltpeter in people's houses will no longer be necessary," Lavoisier explained as he pointed to some barrels full of salt. With the new compound . . ." At that very moment a tremendous explosion reverberated. The shock wave threw all of them to the floor, and a multitude of objects mixed with shards of glass spun about in a great whirlwind.

No one ever found out exactly what had happened in the laboratory; those who might have lived to tell the tale died in the explosion. Still, this tragedy was a cause for jubilation among the good people of Paris. Like a trail of the gunpowder Rasero's friend had invented, the news spread through the poor districts of Paris. In a little while, there was a crowd in front of the doors of the gunpowder factory. Rasero remembered the people there in the street, singing and dancing as though it were carnival time. "The tax farmer exploded and spattered us with shit!" they chorused jubilantly. When they found out that Lavoisier hadn't died in the accident, their spirits fell just a little, but even so they went on celebrating. "He didn't explode, that's true. God wanted him to live so the people can blow him up . . . ," they were now saying.

A year later, when all of France exploded much more violently than the gunpowder factory, Lavoisier took another step that would finally seal his destiny: he refused to open the Arsenal so that the enraged masses could take gunpowder from its storerooms during the insurrection of the summer of '89. Since then, *traitor* was the chemist's nickname . . .

"I couldn't be an accomplice to a massacre, Fausto," he said to you scarcely six months later, when you went to visit him in prison. "You know what they did at the Bastille, at Versailles, at the Tuileries . . . Lafayette himself congratulated me on how I acted. Of course, today nothing can harm me more than being congratulated by Lafayette . . ."

"I'm going to speak with Danton. I'm certain he'll be able to help you . . ."

"Danton? Come off it, Fausto. Do you really believe that Danton, however great a friend of yours he is, is going to risk his reputation as a tribune of the people, as an implacable revolutionary, to defend a tax collector? Be realistic. Anyway, from what I've heard, he may be worse off than I am. Or do you suppose he left Paris for a rest because he doesn't want to know anything more about public affairs? I suspect he's having very serious problems with the Committee. The way I see things, his head will soon roll . . . It'll be his or Robespierre's. Power, my friend, doesn't permit ruthless guardians. You'll see."

"Well, in any event I'll go to him, and even Robespierre if need be. What matters is getting you out of here."

"I'm grateful to you, Fausto, but I'm very afraid that it's going to be useless. Sometimes I think that not even divine providence can save me."

"Please, Antoine."

"It's true. I've thought a great deal about it. One of the few advantages of being shut up in prison is that you have a great deal of time to think. That's let me arrive at conclusions that will likely surprise you. In the beginning, I was persuaded, as you are, that I landed in this wretched presidio because I'd been chief tax collector—that somehow the hatred that mounted against me was exacting its tribute. I remembered your warnings. We should never have erected that wall, I said to myself, or, I trusted too much in my reputation as a learned man, for a tax collector is despised, however learned he may be. But after giving the subject extended thought, I'm convinced that that's not the reason I'm here—or rather, that if it were a question of only that, I'd soon be out of prison (which I don't consider likely). In fact, the case they have against me is a very feeble one: as for the 'exorbitant profits' they attribute to me, and worse still, as for the brazen fraud they're trying to pin on me, I have answered such accusations easily. The hearings I've been put through leave it plain that I do not have ill-gotten gains; quite to the contrary, those cretins had to admit that, in the four years of the monarchy, far from piling up a fortune for myself, I put up very solid louis for the government out of my own pocket . . . As for the wall, it's obvious I didn't build it all by myself. Many of us reached the decision together, beginning with Calonne, the prime minister. Of course, that doesn't help me much, but if you consider that among the eager participants in the project were at least three of the brand-new deputies of the Convention, things start to look different. They wouldn't like the subject to come up for discussion. The best proof of what I'm telling you is that nobody is in prison because of that wall, not even me: that accusation doesn't weigh against me in my dossier. Nor do I owe my fate to my refusal to open the Arsenal to the multitudes during the events of '89; Robespierre himself ruled in my favor on that occasion. Don't allow yourself to be taken in by appearances, Fausto. That sinister petty lawyer fears the people more than he does us, no matter how much he colors his speeches with demagoguery. So if it were a question of only that, my skin would be safe, as I'm sure that of many farmers-general is safe."

"Well, then?"

"The oddity is that, in my opinion, my fate springs from my being a scientist. Some years ago, it was my bad luck to have a little article with scientific pretensions, frankly a shoddy piece of work, fall into my hands. It was signed by Dr. Jean-Paul Marat. I don't believe I ever told you about it. And I know very well why I didn't: it just wasn't worth discussing. Monsieur Marat, with a presumption and an arrogance that only his ignorance could equal, dared, in his words, to make it clear to everyone, once and for all, what a 'most unfortunate interpretation Dr. Newton made of optics.' He crowed, in effect, I shall not attempt to plug up the leaks in it, for it has such a large number of them in so many places that it is better for it to sink for good. What I propose is a new and absolutely faithful interpretation of the facts . . . The piece, in short, was a bunch of insults strung together. As you can imagine, in my capacity as director of the Academy I often had the misfortune of receiving writing of that sort. So I did as I had done on similar occasions. I leafed through the article and ended up throwing it where it belonged: in the wastebasket. Ah, but Monsieur Marat was extremely offended. In his demented frame of mind—I can't think what else to call it—he was certain I was driven by envy, and envy (what else?) must have been behind my stout opposition to nominating him for the Academy. Dr. Marat was convinced that he was of the stature of an Academician, Fausto. He was furious when I turned down his candidacy without bothering to bring it up for discussion. Where would we end, I asked myself, if candidates such as he were seriously considered? I soon forgot all about this, but, obviously, Marat didn't. You know what happened later on: our deplorable scientist turned into a famous politician, adored by the plebs, and he spared neither effort nor resources to get even for the affront I had dealt him. The "friend of the people" turned me into enemy number one of the people and nourished better than anyone else the soil in which all that slander and those lies thrived later. The worst, however, was when they killed him. Take my word for it, Fausto. When I learned of the murder, I had a fateful presentiment. My feeling was that his death sealed my destiny, that inevitably he would drag me with him to the grave. And so it has come to pass: you can defend yourself against the "friend of the people," but there's nothing you can do against his ghost, a ghost that cries out to the four winds for my head . . . I'm firmly convinced that if I had admitted that man to the Academy, my life would not be in danger today, even had I been a thousand times more a thief than they say I am, or had I built five walls around Paris . . ."

"Friend of the people. The people, friend, will never forget you . . ." The words surrounded the oval of the portrait. Putting the face of Marat in profile did not mitigate his ugliness, although David's clever hand had managed to give him a certain grandeur, making him look like a venerable Roman censor. The portrait was hanging from one wall, just opposite where Rasero was sitting. The guard looked at the old man out of the corner of his eye. Let him rot! he thought and smiled in contentment on seeing the darkness outside the windows. Robespierre is a great man, he said to himself. Rasero stood up and went over to the desk. The lieutenant looked at him mistrustfully. The officer was a young man; he couldn't have been more than twenty-five, but he had already acquired the look of a veteran of the Revolution: his eyes reddened by fatigue, the deep wrinkles furrowing his brow, the suspicious and fierce expression on his face, but above all the big scar—a memento of the revolutionary struggles—on his left cheek that his ill-shaved beard did not manage to hide.

"Lieutenant, is there somewhere I can go to empty my bladder?"

The man looked him up and down, grimacing in disgust, as though he had before him a repulsive specimen from some zoo. He looked straight at him and sat there thinking for a long time; it was as though he had been asked a complicated question concerning advanced metaphysics. Finally he answered, "All you want to do is urinate?"

"That's all."

He thought for a good while longer.

"Do you see that door?" His very hairy hand pointed to it. "It leads to an outer courtyard. You can piss there," he said reluctantly.

When Rasero came back, there was a woman in front of the soldier's desk, chatting cheerily with him. She was a woman past her prime, though her curves could still rouse the interest of many a man. She was standing at the edge of the desk, leaning both hands on it and bending her body forward so that the lieutenant could not help seeing her magnificent tits about to leap out of her low neckline.

"Give me that key, woman!" the man demanded.

"If you want it, take it," the woman answered, flirtatiously and defiantly.

"Marie, I'm on duty. This is no time for jokes. Give me that key . . ." The man was becoming very nervous.

"Take it, I said. If you don't, I swear I won't give it back to you."

The guard sat there thinking for a long time, his eyes riveted on the woman. It seems that his mind works very slowly, Rasero thought. The lieutenant finally made up his mind. He looked about anxiously in all directions. (Rasero was careful to avert his eyes when he felt the man's on him.) Then he raised his right hand, very quickly, as though he were about to hit or stab someone, up to the neckline of the woman's dress and plunged it between her breasts. Having her fun, Marie grabbed the man's wrist with both hands. "Search about, search all about, soldier," she said to him.

The lieutenant's face turned scarlet, and big beads of sweat broke out on his forehead. "Marie, please."

"Search all about, lieutenant," the woman repeated, laughing loudly.

Finally he found the key and removed his hand from the neck of her dress even more quickly than he'd placed it there.

"Bye, dearie. I'll be waiting for you, you know where . . ." She threw him a kiss and went off happily.

The man's face was still as red as an apple, and he was sweating copiously. His trembling hand gripped the key tightly, as though it were a very precious jewel. He turned his head and stared hostilely at the old man, who responded with a pleasant smile that disarmed the soldier. Without knowing why, without even thinking about it—obviously, that would have taken him a while—all of a sudden he felt a pronounced liking for the gaffer. He gave him a frank, generous smile in return; his face took on the expression of a grown-up child, at once ingenuous and noble. The effect was enhanced by the scar on his cheek and his big, wide-open mouth, which, perhaps because he was missing an incisor, evinced an almost irresistible tenderness. He's Michel's age, Rasero thought . . .

Despite the run of problems he had along the way, owing to his rebellious nature and the visceral hatred he felt for everything smacking of religion, Michel—for this was what Rasero began to call Faustillo when he saw he was becoming a man—finished his schooling at the Collège Mazarin with the highest honors for academic achievement and the lowest marks for discipline. His mentor had a great deal to do with that, for besides paying the expenses at the most expensive school in Paris, he had to invest just as much—if not more—to pacify the director of the school every time the boy misbehaved. It's true that the Latin teacher, to cite but one example, had been close to the grave as a result of the brutal blow to his forehead from the inkwell. There was no way to relieve the pain in his head or the resentment in his breast: he had sworn not to set foot in the school again if the boy returned to it. He even threatened to take the matter to court. The doctors found no way to ease the terrible migraine that tormented the poor man, and as if that weren't enough, the big lump that had formed above his eyes, despite the prodigious number of remedies attempted, would not subside. They applied pieces of fresh meat to it, ice bags, unguents with frightful odors, cold compresses, warm compresses, burning-hot compresses, fruit rinds, and even a cloth soaked in cat's urine. All in vain: the promontory stayed there on his forehead, as lofty and intact as Mont Blanc. There was the same intractability to the teacher's attitude: he would not yield an inch in his resolve, despite the pleas and even the threats of the director, whom Rasero had already managed to convince—through a donation to the college worthy of Croesus—that in the final analysis the whole episode was nothing but the mischievous prank of a lively child. The teacher remained firm: "A few more days of this monstrous headache," he kept saying, "and I'm going to court." When the time he had set was almost up, Rasero finally found the remedy. A real panacea, the heavy pouchful of louis that he gave Master Junot was able to make the swelling go down, get rid of the migraine, and even abate the resentment of the illustrious teacher: "Ah, that Faustillo is a rascal, but he's the best pupil I've had. I don't believe that even Cicero expressed himself with Faustillo's grace when he declaims in Latin . . ."

In the Faculty of Law, where Michel enrolled later, his behavior improved noticeably, as though he had decided on a truce with the professors. On the other hand, his academic effort lessened by a fair amount. In fact, he barely worked hard enough at his studies to get by. Unlike the classes at the Collège Mazarin, where, despite the priests, he learned many things he found exciting, the classes he took at the university couldn't have been more tedious and dull. As though in obedience to a guiding principle, the teachers went to zealous lengths to make their pupils see that the law was unbearably dry. They took great care to skirt any subject that might have been at all stimulating. Even the courses in history—which were the ones that interested Michel the most—did not depart from the pattern: with really enviable adroitness, the professors managed to turn the meatiest and most interesting subjects (the uprisings of the Huguenots, for example) into a barren succession of names and dates, into a sterile and boring fund of knowledge, as foreign to the students' interest as the sexual inclinations of termites. Real knowledge, critical knowledge, exciting and suggestive, the knowledge a sharp mind cries out for as the thirsty man cries out for water, was forbidden at the school; for it, it was necessary to look elsewhere.

Michel found it in his mentor's library. He spent more time there than at the university, devouring the works of the great thinkers, both ancient and modern. Thus he followed Erasmus' ingenious and elegant critical arguments, as well as the subtle reasonings of Spinoza the pantheist, and Voltaire's delightful disquisitions. As happened to all the young thinkers of his generation, daring, irreverent ideas, logical above all, began to spin about in his head—but also hopes and utopias. It did not take Michel long to reach the point where Montesquieu's ideas, which in the beginning had filled him with enthusiasm, began to seem timid and fainthearted. That peaceful system of a constitutional monarchy, upheld and at the same time watched over and preserved by the division of powers, in the end seemed very naïve to him. It's impossible to attain that balance, he told himself. Inevitably, one power will end up taking over the others, and as always, it will be the worst one that does so . . . Not even Voltaire's ideas, concerning the skillful rule of a generous, enlightened, and benevolent monarch, managed to convince him. Such men don't exist, he said to himself when he thought of the barbarous deeds of Frederick and Catherine in Central Europe. And if such a monarch did come along, he would immediately be annihilated by his enemies, who would refuse to shoulder the burden of generosity and benevolence . . .

Rousseau, on the other hand, sparked his enthusiasm. Michel read *The Social Contract* over and over, with genuine devotion. After the third reading, the book had so many annotations in the margins that they competed with the text itself, and there were so many underlinings that the only part of the text that stood out was what wasn't underscored. He also read *Emile,* the *Confessions,* and even *Eloise,* although he abandoned the last at the halfway mark. After studying Rousseau, squeezing the meaning out of his ideas, trying his best to understand him, Michel arrived at the conclusion that the Swiss philosopher was the greatest man of the century. He said as much to his mentor one afternoon: "Don Fausto, did you ever know Jean-Jacques Rousseau?"

"Let's say I did . . ."

A long series of images came to Rasero's mind, all of them unpleasant: Rousseau at the marquis' house, furrowing his brow when he saw the furniture Annette had just bought for the guest bedroom ("Very well, if there's no way round it, I'll sleep here." Really, it's almost as if I ought to thank him for deigning to sleep at my home and eat at my table, you said to yourself in indignation); Voltaire in a fit of rage, in his library at Ferney ("Rousseau is wicked, believe me, Fausto. To play such a nasty trick on Denis!"); d'Alembert beside himself with fury, at the Procope ("Have you read that letter, Fausto? He made our differences a personal matter, and I won't tolerate that"); Denis at the Opéra ("Have you heard that Rousseau-Cato, public enemy number one of the theater, of sentimental literature, of life, in a word, of anything that has to do with human emotions, has just published—under a pseudonym, naturally—a short novel for young ladies with vulgar tastes? These are insane times!"); a letter from David Hume ("I trust you will forgive my tardy answer, but to speak the truth, I've been through several hard days. I don't want to fall into an indiscretion, but allow me, I pray you, to vent my spleen a trifle: Rousseau is driving me mad! . . ."); the Swiss philosopher's five sons, whom he abandoned on the doorstep of an orphanage just after they were born, he of all people, the great pedagogue, the author of the *Emile,* a veritable educational epic of the eighteenth century . . .

"What was he like?" Michel asked.

"Look, Michel. I'll put it this way: You've read every one of his books, haven't you?"

"Of course."

"Well, go on reading them; they're the only good thing that that man has ever done in his life. Whatever else I tell you about him will be unpleasant, and in all likelihood you won't want to believe it. I'll merely say this: never judge a man by his writings, and still less judge writings by their author. If I were to think of Rousseau's books what I think of the man, you wouldn't find a single book by him in my library."

Michel was disconcerted. He had never doubted the intelligence and wisdom of his mentor, who up until very recently seemed to him the wisest and most just man in the world. But to say what he had said (to say . . . : actually, he had said nothing)—well, then, to insinuate what he had insinuated about Rousseau—Michel wouldn't tolerate that even from don Fausto.

"I'll go on studying him, since I didn't have the marvelous opportunity you did of knowing him . . ."

Michel spent part of his time helping his father in the printshop. His father would have preferred him not to, since he was more concerned about his son's studies than Michel was himself.

"Go on, go study. I can do it alone," his father said to Michel when he discovered that he had slipped into the workshop like a shadow, had put his cotton apron on, and was cleaning the printing plates and putting the type away in its cases.

Actually, Marcel was very proud of his son. Faustillo—he never stopped calling him that—was a healthy, strong, and very bright young man. What was more, despite his inclination to rebellion and fits of temper, he had a good heart. He's like his mother even that way, Marcel often thought—because it might indeed be said that his son was the male version of Annette. Like her, he was rather short and robust, without being downright stout. He had the same greenish eyes as his mother and her fair hair and rosy complexion, and also like her, he had wits that were sharper than hunger and he had the fiery temperament of a thousand devils. Nothing could please his father more, for he still loved his wife as intensely as when he had first fallen in love with her, from the blessed day that he had first met her, twenty-five years before . . .

"And who are you?" the adorable girl asked him with a frown.

"Marcel, the son of Monsieur Gautier, the printer."

"Well, listen to me, honorable son of the printer Gautier: if I hear that accursed machine making that frightful noise after ten at night again, I swear to you that you and your father are going to be thrown out into the street on all fours."

"But, miss, we're doing a print job that's urgent. And the marquis has never complained about our working late . . ."

"Do I look like Monsieur Rasero? Am I bald? No sir, I have neither his pate nor his patience. And I'm going to live here"—on hearing this, the young man smiled happily—"What are you laughing about?"

"Nothing, miss . . ."

"Well, it's only idiots who laugh over nothing. In a word, I'm going to live here, I told you, and this is going to be an orderly house from now on, do you understand?"

"Whatever you say, miss," Marcel answered with a smile on his lips.

"You really do look like an idiot, my good man."

"If you say so, miss . . ."

If there was one happy man in France, he was to be found on the basement floor of Fausto Rasero's town house. As Marcel saw his son giving him a helping hand in the printshop despite his protests, he asked himself, as he had done many times before, why fortune had been so generous with him. He had a good woman for a wife, energetic and hardworking and, on top of that, the best cook in the world, he had no doubt. His son would soon be a great lawyer, something that Marcel's father had never dared dream for him. Véronique, his daughter—she was ten years younger than her brother (in between the two of them, three other children had been born, but none had lived till its first birthday—was an adorable young girl, as docile and affectionate as a little lamb. Just as Michel resembled his mother, the little girl was very much like Marcel, both in her peaceful and industrious nature and in her physical appearance: she was dark-skinned and slender, with very dark, almost black, hair and big light brown eyes—"You have honey inside your head," Michel used to say to his little sister—as well as a long, fine-drawn nose. What was more, Marcel's shop had prospered wildly. In fact, the machinery he had acquired ended up occupying the entire space that for many years his parents' living quarters and the business had shared. He and Annette now lived on the floor above Rasero's quarters, in a pretty apartment—a wedding present from don Fausto—and in the printshop they kept only one bedroom, for the apprentices. The rest of the space was chockablock with machinery: among the machines was the old press his father used, which had kept food on their table for a long time. Although Marcel no longer used it, he was unwilling to get rid of it; he felt enormous affection for that machine. Presses, type fonts, inks, and great bundles of paper took up the whole area. If, in fact, he had been lucky, Marcel never left off suspecting that he owed his luck to the Marquis de Rasero. Ever since that strange man had bought the town house, when Marcel was still just a little boy, things improved considerably for the entire family. His mother recovered from that terrible illness that had kept her in bed for almost a year. Shortly thereafter, they received news from his uncle Eugène, who five years before had gone off to Martinique as a colonist and whom they had given up for dead, since they hadn't heard a word about him in that time. Perhaps the most striking thing was the sudden improvement in the business, just when he had been on the point of going under. (What Marcel didn't know would have confirmed his suspicions. Shortly after moving into the town house, Rasero became aware of the difficult time the printer was going through when his tenant came to him: "Marquis, please give me two weeks more; I swear I'll pay you. I'll even pay you interest. I beg you . . ."

Rasero had taken a liking to that man: he didn't doubt that he was honorable and honest. He sympathized with his situation and not only gave him a grace period for paying his rent, as he had asked, but also persuaded his friend François Voltaire to send the printshop several poems the poet-philosopher had written in honor of Louis XV on the occasion of the victory at Fontenoy. That commission, along with the many others that the Malagan went on to secure for him, allowed the good Marcel Gautier to build his income.) In any event, the fact was that don Fausto never ceased to be a sort of bald guardian angel to Marcel.

"Leave that be, I tell you. Go study."

"But, Father, I don't have any homework today."

"Well, go play with your friends then. The exercise will do you good."

Michel liked playing handball almost as much as he liked reading Rousseau. Two or three times a week he went to a handball court near the house, in the neighborhood of the Cordeliers. He was a formidable player. His lightning-quick rushes and the fury with which he hit the ball made him almost unbeatable; very few of the lads frequenting the place were able to boast of having defeated him. That morning—it was the summer of '87—a man no more than thirty, of average height and slender build, turned up at the handball court. He was very good-looking; his big eyes dominated his face, giving him the expression of a taciturn poet. His looks in no way accorded with his reputation as a great handball player or suggested that that was what had brought him there, for at the court where he usually played—which was in a neighborhood on the Right Bank—he had heard that near the Cordeliers there was an unbeatable player and he was impatient to pit himself against him. Once the stranger's identity became known—his fame had already crossed the river—there was great anticipation in the gymnasium. Nobody wanted to miss the match. The friends who had come with the challenger were pleased to accept the bets of the people who lived in the neighborhood. Very happy, Michel hammered out an agreement with the stranger about the terms of the match; they even bet some good louis of their own, in order to make the contest more exciting.

It was a great game—so great that long after it was over those who had witnessed it continued in animated give-and-take about it. Every so often their arguments turned fierce, as though their lives depended on settling the disagreement. Michel was much the more agile and the stronger player; on the other hand, his opponent had the gift of ubiquity, so to speak. As though he could read his adversary's mind, he was always in exactly the right place to catch the ball. He didn't respond very forcefully but instead directed his shots to a spot a long way away from his adversary. It would be no exaggeration to say that Michel ran ten times as much as his rival in the course of the match. In the end, though, he came out the winner; his strength, in the extended competition, prevailed over the will of the champion from the Right Bank. The spectators—most from Michel's neighborhood—applauded madly. Perhaps their ardor had an influence on the result of the game. If we had played in his court, with the spectators cheering him on, I probably would have lost, Michel thought. So when the game was over, when he went over to his opponent to shake his hand, he said to him, "If the idea suits you, we can have a rematch in your neighborhood."

"Delighted, sir," the other answered, still panting from the effort, though very satisfied with the great game they'd played. "But for now, allow me to stand you to a drink. Defeats like this one should be celebrated too . . ."

"So you're a law student?" the loser asked as the waitress plunked another bottle down on the table. They were attacking the wine with the same gusto they had shown in going after the ball a while before. "Never mind, my friend, nobody's perfect. God deliver us from lawyers!"

"And how about you? What do you do?" Michel answered.

The man looked at him as if joining in an intrigue, turned his head in both directions, giving the appearance of making sure nobody was listening, leaned closer to Michel's ear, said, "I'm a lawyer," and burst into laughter.

As he came to know him better, Michel realized that he had encountered someone who was much more than a worthy rival at handball. He was an amazing person; his culture seemed to be too big to fit his young years. Camille Desmoulins—that was his new friend's name—was animated by the wine and jabbered on without stopping, as though at last giving free rein to a speech he had been simmering in his mind for a long time.

"The notables . . . bah! They're a bunch of idiots. Expecting them to solve France's financial crisis is like expecting a eunuch to father a family. They're the ones who have driven the kingdom into bankruptcy. There's wealth around, a great deal of it. The Treaty of Versailles left the country in an enviable position: we've tripled our trade with the colonies, and there's no one on the Continent who can compete with our textile industry; in addition, this year's harvests have been especially abundant . . . The trouble is that there isn't enough wealth to support the army of parasites making up the court. Anyway, as long as the nobility refuses to contribute even a small part of its revenues to the state treasury, it will be impossible to improve the kingdom's finances. Really, Calonne wasn't wrong to propose that the nobility and the clergy pay taxes too. We're a good way into the eighteenth century, my friend, and it's absurd for such feudal privileges to be maintained. But you can see what's happened: Calonne ingenuously called the Council of Notables together to ratify his proposals. He couldn't have been more ingenuous: asking those leeches to sanction measures that aren't in their interest . . . I ask you! By pursuing that course, the only thing the prime minister accomplished was to lose his post. He deserved it for being so stupid. I don't see much of a future for Abbot Brienne either. He's actually in the same situation as his predecessor, whom he criticized so fiercely. And the fact is that there's no alternative: either taxes must be made more democratic or there won't be way out of this predicament. At least the new minister did the right thing in ending the meeting of notables. But he miscalculated when he thought that the Parlement of Paris was going to support him. If the 'nobles of the sword' are useless idlers, the 'nobles of the robe' are much worse. They're not as useless, but they're terribly selfish and couldn't be more treacherous and scheming. Just think of the game they're playing: they refuse to accept Brienne's financial edicts and demand, instead, that the States General be convoked. They're very clever: instead of opposing the minister's measures purely and simply because their interests are affected—as the notables did—they're doing so in the name of the people of France, as if the people had an interest in seeing the feudal prerogatives of the ennobled judicial authorities of the Parlement preserved. And though it seems beyond belief, the people applaud them roundly. Weren't you at the Gate of Vincennes when they left the city?" Michel shook his head. "It was a great spectacle. The bourgeois of the city came out en masse; they hailed them as though they were victorious generals. Even more than at Troyes, they looked as though they were departing to conquer the Rhine Basin . . . I must admit, though, that I'm in complete agreement with them on one point: if we want to change the structures of the kingdom, it's necessary to convoke the States General. Brienne, of course, is adamantly opposed to that, and the king is too, I believe. But they're in a blind alley; sooner or later they're going to have to do just that . . ."

On the fifth of May, 1789, a long procession, headed by Their Most Catholic Majesties, entered Notre Dame by way of the main portal. The men representing the States General of the thousand-year-old kingdom of France solemnly marched into the venerable edifice, there to receive the Lord's blessing and pray for him to crown their historic mission with success. The crowd, on either side of the procession, clapped in support. They cheered the king with a lot of enthusiasm, the queen with quite a bit less; they grudgingly applauded the clergy and were silent as the nobility filed past. On the other hand, when the final contingent passed, the crowd became delirious. The representatives of the Third Estate, marching along with serious, stern faces, listened proudly to the great ovation the people offered them. They were by far the largest group, having approximately the same numbers as the other two groups combined. Unlike those orders, whose members marched in imposing silk uniforms, adorned with a thousand lace and brocade insets—the nobles in showy pastel colors, the abbots in lustrous black, scarlet, and purple—both estates resplendent, plumed and bejeweled like Oriental satraps, the members of the Third Estate were almost all in very austere attire, in black and dark colors with very few decorations. A few were wearing a silver medal pinned to their breast, a medal small in size but charged with great meaning, for it testified to the wearer's honesty, diligence, or valor. A stout man marching in one of the first rows of the group stood out. Like the nobles, he was in an elegant wine-colored silk costume with silver adornments. Neither his majestic bearing nor the splendor of his apparel lessened by a jot his ugliness, for it was as absolute as death. A heavy, enormous head, reminiscent of a cannonball, showed beneath the white wig—so large that it seemed made of the wool of an entire Merino—a mere glimpse of a face as flat and full as an October moon. Eyes, a nose, and a mouth made their appearance as little round mounds, protruding and obscene, indifferently glued to a skin ruined by smallpox. It was none other than Count Mirabeau, a man who at that time was a living legend in France—a legend he himself fed through his scandalous conduct, his fierce spirit of rebellion (which led him to firsthand acquaintance with a goodly number of the kingdom's prisons), and his propensity for the good life and for complete dissipation (which he often did not have enough money to satisfy, so that he was obliged to swindle, cheat, and compromise anyone naïve enough to fall in his hands, and even to spy for his country in the kingdom of Prussia). But above all, his enormous éclat stemmed from the spicy and piquant novels he had written: *L'Education de Laure, Hic-et-Haec,* and *Ma conversion,* among others, had become part of the zoo of erotic imagery of the era. Very daring, written with an eloquence that left very little if anything to the imagination, but set down in a sober and elegant style, these works caused a veritable furor at court and in aristocratic and bourgeois circles all over France. Mirabeau marched, shoulder to shoulder, with the deputies of the Third Estate. He had dramatically renounced the privileges he enjoyed as the noble he was and had been the winning candidate in a vote to choose the delegate from Aix, his native province, as just another representative of the common people of France. By his action, he increased the admiration his many followers had for him, and the antipathy of his still more numerous enemies.

Not very far from Mirabeau, another man was marching who couldn't hold a candle to him when it came to corpulence. He was actually even taller than the aristocratic tribune, though much younger and less ugly. He was dressed in black, and his formidable head of hair was tied in a pigtail. He was striding along energetically, furiously almost, as if cleaving the air as he passed by. His eyes, large and haughty, looked with contempt at the nobles who were heading the procession and had turned at a right angle to enter the church. But he gazed with pleasure, a broad smile on his lips, at the crowd hailing them.

"Bravo, Danton!" Michel shouted in a rasping voice.

It seemed unbelievable, but there was Georges-Jacques Danton, as a deputy of the people, representing the district around the Cordeliers, with the *cahier de doléance,* the list of grievances in his district, underneath his arm . . . They had pulled it off. Camille and Michel embraced with joy as they lost sight of their idol. And they unquestionably deserved to celebrate his victory. For more than eight months, ever since the States General was convoked, they had worked tirelessly for Danton's cause. Hundreds of meetings in the district. Endless discussions in the cafés of the Palais Royal. Going to and from the town hall: every time they handed in what they believed met the last requirement, they came back with yet another new decree and were obliged to begin over. Far from being annoyed by all of this, Michel found his ardor heightened. Ever since he met Camille, his life had taken a radical turn that made him happier than he had ever suspected he could be. Michel had finally found his way—the possibility of giving his existence a meaning. This went far beyond the routine at the university, beyond his work at the printshop, beyond games at the handball court. Camille had taught him the way . . . no, that was not quite true. It was not Camille, to be fair, it was Rousseau who had shown him the path, as Rousseau had opened the path to Camille, Danton himself, and many of his other new friends. What happened, in a manner of speaking, was that Desmoulins showed him how to make his way along that path. It was he, with his brilliant eloquence, with his indomitable spirit, who had launched him on the marvelous adventure of fighting for his ideas. "Life isn't in a book, Michel," his friend often said to him. "It's to be found in this filthy pigsty that those wretches have turned France into. Living and fighting to change it have become the same thing—living to fight and fighting so that all of us will live better. That's quite clear. We already have the ideas, they're there, in the books, and have been for a long time . . . And even if they weren't, we'd invent them; can there be any doubt of that, my friend? Today we must pay for the air we breathe; we won't be worth a thing if we aren't able to bequeath to our sons a world just a little better than the one we inherited . . ."

In a sense, Michel brought the Revolution to the town house in the rue St-Jacques. He spent a great deal of time in the printshop, along with Camille and his other friends, setting galleys, correcting proofs, and printing countless speeches (almost all of them by Danton or Camille), proclamations, manifestos, notices of meetings, and even a twelve-page weekly. In order to get use of the printshop, Michel had to work patiently to persuade his father, who refused to believe that the rash of disturbances taking place in the city could ever justify the financially wasteful way his machinery was being put to use, for Michel's friends paid Marcel so miserably for their print orders—when they paid at all—that the money was barely enough to cover the expenses he incurred on account of them.

"Look, Father. It's the future of France that's at stake."

"And meanwhile, I'm making nothing," Marcel answered. "So how in the devil am I supposed to give a shit about the fate of France?"

"Well, even though you may have doubts, the measures that Necker, the minister of finances, has proposed are going to improve it . . ."

"Yes, yes, I've heard all that before . . ."

"Please listen. Necker is ready to force the nobles to pay taxes. In exchange, he'll suspend the indirect tax. Just think of how much more revenue that's going to bring in!"

"I'll believe it when I see it . . . Calonne and Brienne said the same thing, and you see what's happened to them. The damned nobles are going to end up giving Necker a boot up his Swiss behind. You'll see . . ."

"Nothing doing. The Third Estate won't let them do something like that . . ."

"The Third Estate, bah! For the love of God, Michel! Who constitutes the Third Estate? A bunch of provincial pettifoggers, more ambitious than Herod and more selfish than a Norman. You'll see how long it takes to corrupt them. Once the nobles meet their price, they're going to stop screaming like madmen and start behaving like little lambs. And everything's going to go on as usual, with the poor working like mules and the privileged scratching their balls . . . It's always been the same story . . ."

"Father," Michel replied, very annoyed, since he felt an almost religious veneration for the deputies of the Third Estate, "those men represent the best of France. They don't have a dishonest bone in their body. And if someone did fall into corrupt ways, he'd be accountable to the people who elected him. The punishment they'd mete out to him would be terrible, believe me . . ."

"The people . . . and who are the people? Are the people those urchins who teem in the streets like famished rats, forever on the lookout for an incautious man to assault or, in the best of cases, to sell a bottle of river water that they pass off as wine? Or are the people the fishwives at the markets who sprinkle lemon juice on rotten fish so they don't smell to high heaven and can be sold as fresh to the dupe who lets himself be taken in? Or the whores of Saint-Antoine or Les Halles, who freshen their rotten cunts infected with the Naples disease in order to get a few coins out of the unlucky fellow who sticks his cock in one of them? Or are the people the apprentices in the workshops, always ready to stop work, swindle their masters, and if they can, seduce their wives or their daughters? Or are the people the schoolmasters, embittered and incompetent drudges who teach only one thing to their miserable students: the gleam of the ruler they beat their little bodies with because they can't learn what their masters have failed to teach them? Or are the people the lawyers, keeping a ferret's eye out for the good lawsuit that can fleece some widow or rob a bastard of his inheritance? Or are the people the shopkeepers who cunningly fix their scales so as to steal just a little bit every time they weigh a sale—just a little bit that becomes an enormous nest egg if you add up all the petty thefts they get away with over the days, the months, and the years? Or are the people us, the printers, who calculate the price of our work by multiplying by at least three the expenses involved, among which we count the wages of the apprentices when in reality very few of us pay them anything at all, considering them adequately paid if they're given a corner to sleep in and a few crusts of bread a day? Those are the people, my son, not one whit better than the deputies who represent them . . ."

"But father, don't you believe in anything?"

"Wait till you're my age, and you'll see if you're still inclined to believe in anything."

"You may have a point. But as long as I haven't reached your age, I have a right to believe in many things. Despite everything you've said, I'm altogether convinced that our fight can succeed in turning this cruel and pitiless world you yourself have described into something much worthier of being lived in, where selfishness, usury, and injustice will cease once and for all to be the most powerful influence on our behavior . . ."

"Stop delivering sermons. When you talk that way, you sound exactly like your friend Camille. You know what they used to call people like you two in ancient Greece? Demagogues . . . So enough of your speeches. Just tell me what you want."

"We have to get out a manifesto. Camille's already written it. All we need are five thousand copies."

"A trifling five thousand?"

"Really, Father, it's of the utmost importance. In it we come out strongly for the Third Estate's vigorously refusing to accept votes by orders, since there'd always be a disadvantage to us in having two against our one. Votes must be cast individually. The manifesto is terrific; it matches the patriotic resolve of the deputies of the entire Third Estate . . ."

"Enough, enough. Do whatever you like. But tell your friends to pay me just four or five pistolas more. Almost all the last manifesto was paid for out of my pocket . . ."

"Thanks, Father!"

Michel kissed his father's cheeks effusively and was off like a shot to the café to tell his comrades the good news. As Marcel watched him go, he thought proudly of the great man his son would some day be. I wasn't honest with him a while ago, he thought. There's something I do believe in. I believe absolutely in my Faustillo, in his youth, in his nobility and generous spirit. Perhaps it's true; these youngsters just might change the future of France and the whole world . . .

Rasero was much more patient with Michel and less critical of him than his father. Almost every night, when he finished his exhausting day's work, the young man came upstairs to his mentor's to let him hear about what was going on. In the library, accompanied by the fourth Nostradamus—who looked nothing at all like the founder of the dynasty, since this one was a small cat, entirely black—and between sips of hot tea, the two men reviewed the situation of the kingdom. Dawn often surprised them still deep in conversation.

". . . The king has kicked them out of the palace, as though they were footmen. Yet they haven't given up. Do you know what they did? They met again, right there at Versailles, at a handball court. They've stayed shut up inside it for three days now. They've proclaimed a National Assembly and have sworn not to let up until they've given France a constitution. Isn't that terrific?"

"A National Assembly? Strictly speaking, Michel, they don't represent the entire nation . . . What have the other orders done?"

"What do you expect of them? They condemned them and made them out to be Satans. The archbishop of Paris threatened to excommunicate them, and the notables to lock them all up in the Bastille. But they no longer have the strength to do that. Fortunately, they're deeply divided. There exists a group of diehards, who appear to have the upper hand, mostly courtiers belonging to the queen's circle. But there are also others who are more moderate, support Necker, and are prepared to yield on several points, such as in renouncing certain feudal privileges and in being subject to taxes, though they're not prepared to join the Assembly. They're listing from side to side like a ship at sea; sometimes they side with the courtiers and sometimes with the members of the third contingent, who are, one might say, the most radical. This group—almost exclusively priests—is ready to undertake a total reform of the structures of the kingdom, and that brings them closer to the position of the Assembly. Indeed, I hear that at least three priests have left their order and have joined the people's deputies. And there are going to be many more like them, I'm certain. Count Mirabeau's eloquence is directed toward them, and believe me, don Fausto, that man's eloquence is irresistible. When he climbs onto the rostrum and begins a speech in that booming voice that God gave him, flies don't even dare buzz. He begins in a very deliberate way, so slowly that it's almost exasperating, as though he were having trouble getting each word out. That succeeds in making his hearers tense and expectant as they try to guess the word that's coming next, and sometimes a few deputies anticipate what it is and murmur it in a low voice. But as he goes on, the time between one word and the next gets shorter, and the volume of his voice increases at the same rate. When he gets to the high point of his speech, his words come frantically pouring out, almost in a shout, and the big, roly-poly man by then has the Assembly spellbound. He at that point seems like a Moses haranguing his Jews. His orations are so marvelous that last week, shortly before the soldiers threw them out of the place, Mirabeau delivered such a powerful and emotional speech against the king's decision that when he'd finished, the deputies from the nobility—and the courtiers among them—seemed to be vying with the other orders to applaud loudest. It was worth seeing. Believe me, don Fausto, it's been a long time since we've laughed as hard as we did when we saw the bright red faces of the courtiers as they applauded like mad. When they realized what they were doing, they stopped short, with the palms of their hands still apart and their arms outstretched, arrested in the middle of their ovation. Their faces flushed, and they began booing the tribune to make amends for their slip, but by then it was too late: the laughter drowned out their hoots . . ."

It was hard for you to imagine Mirabeau's grotesque, imposing figure on the rostrum before the people's deputies. You had met him ten years before in a radically different situation. Mirabeau was in his drawers, his shirt unbuttoned and an empty wine bottle in each of his big fists. Plastered to the gills, he was leaning on two of Madame Chantal's pretty girls, as though they were crutches. "Eustache! Pierre! How come there's not a little wine for this poor thirsty man?" he was shouting to the four winds. You were surprised to note the impressive resemblance between this man and the secretary of the archbishop of Paris, whom you had met fifteen years before at the von Eyck palace.

They were two peas in a pod. Or rather, two dribbles of pease porridge, you corrected yourself, for peas struck you as being too ideal in form to give the figure of speech the proper effect. This has to be his son, you thought, and gave way to the impulse to ask him about the abbot. "No sir, I don't know him. To tell you the truth, I don't think I've ever known a priest in my life. I wouldn't want one of those vultures to be in my company even on my deathbed." He let out a loud guffaw. You spent a very pleasant evening with that big hulk of a man, who turned out to be not nearly as drunk as he had given the appearance of being in the beginning and to have great intelligence hidden behind that incredibly ugly face. Later on, you saw him several times more—always at Madame Chantal's. You even received letters from him and a goodly number of invitations to dine with him and to attend meetings where there would be a reading of some of his works. You never responded. In view of your indifference, he stopped writing you a long time ago. Despite what he told you the day you met him, you remained convinced that he had to be a relative of the canon who kept looking so lustfully at Mademoiselle de Roure at that memorable concert by the little Austrian boy, when you saw your Mariana for the first time.

Michel was alert to the sadness that appeared on the face of his mentor. Here it is again, he said to himself. In fact, that expression of melancholy was as characteristic of his uncle as his bald pate. Since he'd been a very young boy, when his reasoning powers were just beginning to develop, Michel remembered don Fausto that way: silent, taciturn, staring into space, as though he were seeing behind his person. Making his beloved uncle smile became a real challenge for Faustillo. He racked his brain in search of a funny phrase or planned some bit of mischief that his mentor might find amusing. Hence, his victories in games at school and the delicious blackberry sweets his mother made, and even the first kisses he stole from the girl who lived across the way, didn't make the boy as happy as seeing don Fausto happy. And he often succeeded—though, to be fair, his success was often unintentional.

After a time, Faustillo gradually identified certain words that weighed heavily on his mentor's spirits. He was very careful not to use them in front of him. America, Mexico, New Spain, the theater, poetry, and war were words and subjects that Michel had forbidden himself to approach in his talks with his uncle. What have I said now?

he thought, on seeing the sadness that had settled over don Fausto's face. Mirabeau? How can it have made him sad to hear that name? . . . He was on the verge of asking Rasero if he knew the great tribune, but he contained himself; it might complicate matters.

"The deputies of the Third Estate are going to achieve what they set out to do, I'm sure. This third contingent of the high orders that I mentioned to you before will end up joining the Assembly, and I suspect that they're going to bring with them many who are still undecided. The courtiers are doomed to remain alone . . . And that's only right. Actually, they're the group that receives the most from all of us and in exchange contributes absolutely nothing; they're sharks. The kingdom will never get out of trouble if these parasites encysted in the court are not extirpated. Necker knows this, and I believe the king does too . . . The problem is that damned Austrian. She's the one who really rules at Versailles; she has poor Louis in the palm of her hand. If he had at least inherited a little of his grandfather's energy! . . ."

"Listen, Michel. Don't believe a word of what they taught you in school. History is written by the powerful in order to justify their acts; that makes it as fantastic as a work by Swift. I knew Louis XV, for example, and I can tell you that that man had no energy except to fornicate—though I must admit he had a lot of that. As king, he wasn't worth a hill of beans. His grandson is a much better man, even if that surprises you. However much the scandal sheets overrunning Paris make him seem an oaf who only knows how to take watches apart and hunt wild boars, he's really a far more responsible and sensible man than his ancestor. Louis XV, particularly in his last years, took a livelier interest in erotic acrobatics than in the economy of France. He used the energy that you've mentioned to persecute his critics. Didn't he even go so far as to shut down the Parlement? His excesses and indifference were responsible for the bankrupt kingdom his successor inherited, with its army of resentful soldiers and its impressive zoo of ass kissers. Nothing less than a powder keg about to explode. And remember that he himself had succeeded to the most powerful kingdom in the world . . . So to me it doesn't seem fair to attribute to his poor grandson all the calamities that are happening today. Louis XVI lacks energy, he is too taciturn and phlegmatic to rule over this insane asylum, it's true, but at least he tries. You have to admit that if your revered people's deputies are shut up inside a handball court swearing to bequeath to the kingdom a constitution in the image and likeness of the one that the young republic of America has, they owe to the king their chance to do that: Louis XVI had the courage to reopen the Parlement, to name Necker minister of finances, and above all, to call together the States General, even at the cost of losing a large part of his power. Do you know what his grandfather would have done in his place? Increase the indirect tax so as to bring in more revenue, and put anyone against that measure in the Bastille. That was his way of going about things . . ."

"But the Austrian woman . . ."

"Hold on. I'm just getting to that. I was saying that Louis XV would have thrown all his critics in the Bastille. If you don't believe me, take a look at the rolls of the prison. You'll see that twenty years ago it was more crowded than a slum in Saint-Antoine. In those days, *lettres de cachet* fell on Paris like snowflakes. But go to that prison today, and I'll be glad to give you ten pistolas for every prisoner over a dozen you find there. In short, with this king, who's plump, myopic, and inane—if he had the dignified bearing and hauteur of his grandfather, half his problems would disappear—we're freer. And in the last analysis, isn't freedom what your esteemed people's tribunes are crying out for at the top of their lungs? As for Marie Antoinette . . . to be fair, that catastrophe shouldn't be blamed on the king either. (Of course, I agree with you that it's a catastrophe to be married to her.) Like everything else, that too is the work of his grandfather. Wasn't he the one who arranged the marriage with her? Louis XV was luckier even in that respect. He couldn't have found a more submissive, reserved, and discreet wife than poor Marie Lesczynska. That unhappy woman passed through the kingdom, through life, with the same humility and discretion that a mole living out its days in a garden has. Sometimes I find it hard to credit that that Polish woman ever really existed. Marie Antoinette, on the other hand, has taken great pains to ensure that everyone is aware that she exists; she's like a rhinoceros in the garden. Like so many others, she's decided that her husband is totally incompetent, and she's taken it upon herself to save—as she sees it—the kingdom of France. The problem lies in the idea this woman has of what a kingdom is. To her, France is nothing except Versailles, the people are applause and cheers, work is wealth, history is fashion, and wisdom is the theater, period. It's not fair to expect her to think anything else. Since the day she was born, her little head has been crammed with such patterns of thought. You can't begin to imagine how much stupidity is concocted in a royal palace! Alas, the woman is energetic—much more so than her husband—and is prepared to fight for that little world like a cat that's pinned down. To her, all those meetings of bourgeois quibblers, and those impassioned speeches of that monster Mirabeau, are simply menaces to the kingdom she considers as much hers as the earrings that dangle from her ears. And to a certain extent, that's natural. What would your father think, say, if tomorrow a committee of masons from the rue Mouffetard were to come to the printshop and tell him that they're taking over his business in the name of the Supreme Mason, who has just revealed himself to be the only true God? Marcel would fly into a rage and boot them out of the place; that's without doubt what he'd do. Well, the queen is in a similar position. The woman is convinced that she has in her veins a blood blessed by God for more than a thousand years and that that gives her the right to claim as her own entire nations, including their applauding people, their creators of wealth, their history-making dressmakers, and their learned men, as well as their comedies and operas. So she too will kick out all those who dare to dispute her ownership of them. And there is no lack of people who'll lend her a hand in her undertaking. I agree with you: those who are behind her are the worst scum of the kingdom. Those parasites at court . . . ah, if only you knew them! You'd be even more to be feared than your friend Danton. But that isn't Louis' fault either. On the contrary, those swine are his worst enemies—and if he doesn't know it yet, he soon will. They're his worst enemies, and the kingdom's . . ."

"Really, Uncle, it's a pleasure to listen to you. I don't understand how you do it, since you always seem to be shut up by yourself, but to my mind you're one of the people who understand France's situation best. You have no idea the influence you could have on us. Forgive me for insisting, but you really ought to agree to what I ask. A simple meeting. I'd invite only my closest friends. Believe me, they're dying to meet you. I admit it's my doing: I've talked so much about you. They can scarcely believe that you were friends with Voltaire, with Diderot, and with Rousseau . . ."

"Rousseau wasn't my friend; I've already told you that."

"All right. But you knew him. You can't deny that."

"No, it's a shame, but I can't."

"Do you know what you mean to us?"

"Yes. I'm sort of a living fossil. Do they think that merely because I knew those men, I picked up their talent and wisdom? Please,

Michel, you make them seem like saints. They were men of flesh and blood, like you and me. They weren't demigods. If what you're looking for now are anecdotes, you have Condorcet, the last of the Encyclopedists, another living fossil. And as far as I know, nothing gives that man more pleasure than talking about bygone days. Why don't you turn to wringing him out like a sponge and leave me in peace?"

"We're fed up with Condorcet. He repeats his stories like a parrot. If they removed stupid memories and astronomy from his head, it'd be emptier than a beggar's belly . . ."

"Look, Michel, you go wage your battles and leave me by myself, and both of us will be happy . . ."

"To me, that doesn't seem quite fair. 'Leave me by myself . . .' Do you think I haven't heard of your visits to Madame de Staël's salon to meet with the cretins in attendance there?"

"You shouldn't call them that. At bottom, they're fighting for the same cause you people are. I don't see that anything good can come of the fight if those of you who are supposed to be on the same side begin trading insults."

"I'm sorry, Uncle, but in no way are we on the same side. We're fighting for the people of France, whereas those fops are fighting to defend their own petty interests."

"Now it's you who are being unfair, Michel. I don't think the Marquis de Lafayette, for instance, went to America to fight in a war that wasn't his, at the risk of having his belly ripped open on the battlefield, in order to defend his own petty interests . . . But enough. I don't have the least desire to get involved in a Byzantine discussion. Anyway, I'll tell you, if it will ease your mind, that I went to only a couple of those gatherings, and I don't think I'll go again; they are a deadly bore . . ."

In point of fact, it was Lavoisier who took you to Madame de Staël's. "No excuses, Fausto. Put on your frock coat and let's go there. This is no time to allow yourself the luxury of being a hermit . . ." You acquiesced reluctantly, more out of the affection you felt for that man than because of any possible interest the gathering might hold for you. It had been a long time since the future of France or that of the whole world mattered to you in the least. All you wanted was to be left in peace. All you asked was to be left alone in your laboratory to busy yourself with aromatic substances, subtle and discreet, that docilely permitted themselves to be worked with and, without demanding anything from you in return, revealed their secrets one by one, changing their colors and states. Now the red powder of cinnabar, impelled by the intense heat of the magnifying glass, calcined, twisted, and turned, gave off a stinging vapor, and was transformed into a splendid silver liquid, and that same substance then dissolved in gold, amalgamating itself with it and taking from it that golden color which made it so magnificent. Now you played about with the oxygen your friend Lavoisier had discovered, which, aggressive and penetrating, attacked, corroded, ate into, and set on fire any element that fell within its invisible embrace. Or to be left alone so that you could go on writing your history of Gothic France. You had more than a thousand pages already drafted, and you had no idea when you would reach the end of it. You were never going to finish it, you knew that very well, Rasero, nor did that bother you; what mattered to you was accompanying Saint Louis on his adventures, following him to Asia to see him fight in vain to rescue the Holy Lands, becoming involved in endless talks with Albertus Magnus and Thomas Aquinas, advising Dr. Sorbonne to take prudent steps to save his university (which ought to be immortal and eternal) from the enmity of the bourgeois, and calculating along with master masons the magic measurement above which, even if it was only by a few inches, the enormous ogival vault of a cathedral was doomed to fall to the ground (this happened to all the architects who, out of vanity, tried to raise their vaults higher than the one at Chartres, because they didn't know, or wouldn't accept, that the vault there was constructed exactly to the unsurpassable height). What did the troubles of Necker's daughter matter to you, or the question of whether the monarchy should be a constitutional one and feudalism abolished? What did the pompous and ridiculous heroism of the Marquis de Lafayette, who strutted about in her salon as though he were the only man in the world who had ever fought in a battle, mean to you? Of what interest to you were the avid glances that Madame de Staël shot from her ugly visage out over her robust breasts toward the phlegmatic Benjamin Constant, who returned them with resignation, calculating the effort it would take to place a new adornment, cuckold's horns, on the head of Ambassador Staël? What the devil did Marie Antoinette's necklace matter to you, or the stupidity of Cardinal de Rohan? What in tarnation could there be of interest to you in the elegant and sensible conversation of that American, Jefferson, who was already looking scornfully over his shoulder at Europeans, from the lofty height of a country that had existed for only ten years, and pitying them for their "utter inefficiency" . . . ? To be left in peace—that was all you asked. To be allowed to brood about your memories, to recall, every so often, the cherished, intimate image of your Mariana when you saw her supinely naked in your bed, panting with pleasure, when you brought your nose up close to her neck or her genitals. To be left alone so you could decide once and for all which aroma pleased you more. You wanted to remember the times she talked to you, the times she laughed—aye, when she burst into peals of laughter . . . To be permitted to loom once again in that mouth, to lick her marvelous teeth and bury your phallus there, yourself there—to plunge into that mouth headlong forevermore, once and for all. You wanted to be left in peace to think about that odious future that took her away from you. Not only to think about it but to visit it. You preferred even the visions to listening to that imbecile Chinon when he said to you, "I greatly fear that we're in the same situation as Perseus: we must have it out with any number of monsters, but the people and the courtiers are by far the worst . . ." Lord almighty, he was unbearable! If a vision had assailed you then, you at least would have been delivered from listening to such nonsense. You'd have preferred passing your time observing slaughters, famines, excesses, wealth, and wars—even the wars of the twentieth century. At least all that was far away; it would fall to the lot of other unfortunates to suffer through it. Whereas you were obliged to listen to that idiot Chinon and nod every so often, as if the nonsensical things he was saying were very clear-sighted and meaty. "I've heard that an important edition of Diderot's works is being prepared; what do you know about it?" the ostrich asked you. The only thing you knew was that Diderot had been dead for five years. Even in that he had been more fortunate than you, for his lover was with him until shortly before his death and he was deft enough to pass on when he was beginning to be bored with life . . .

"Hello there, young man! So you've finally come to say good-bye to your old friend?" Denis said to you in a very feeble voice from his sickbed.

The passage of time had shrunk his body, which looked tiny and frail swallowed up by that white nightshirt. He was leaning back against a big white pillow, his yellowish face raised, the cheeks of which, always so ruddy and glowing, had disappeared forever. His eyes, however, were as beautiful as always, for they stood out, proud and bright, as if they still held great reserves of life in that sick and withered face. His head was now almost as bald as your own.

"Don't talk nonsense, Denis. You may not want to, but you're going to have to see me many times more," you lied.

The doctor, before you had gone into the bedroom, had warned you, "Be very careful not to excite him. He won't live through another attack. I'm very afraid he has one foot in the grave."

Only a few months ago, Denis had still looked robust and strong. He still had the vitality to work and to bear the loneliness into which his ideas, more and more radical and irreverent as time went by, were leading him. His vehemence and his free ways eventually alienated many of his friends, who ended up warier of him than of the plague. "The cowards!" he said to you on that occasion. "Who needs them? . . . Ah, my friend! I don't know which hurts me more, the loneliness that those bastards have consigned me to or the stupidity that led them to behave toward me as they did." What he was unable to withstand, however, was the death of his beloved Sophie Volland. When it came about, your friend collapsed like a wall without foundations. "She's gone, Fausto," he said to you at the funeral. "My only consolation is knowing that I too will very soon be leaving this world . . ." And as always, he was as good as his word: when you saw him lying in the bed, more dead than alive, you knew that you would never see him again.

"Come off it! Whom are you trying to fool, you gypsy? I'm no longer to be counted among the living; you know that very well. And don't get the idea that I give a damn. On the contrary, I'm very happy to leave this filthy world forever," he said with a faint smile that moved you deeply.

His enormous calf's eyes alit on the face of the Malagan. He still looked so much like that young man he'd known more than thirty years ago! As in those days, he was dressed in dark blue. He had the same bald head, the identical mosquito's eyes and inexpressive face, though now his face was full of wrinkles and suggested not a search for something, an anguish for it, as it once had, but instead a deep and final sadness. But what was most important was that Fausto had kept that magic quality of making him feel good, as on that long-ago day when he had only to see him to forget the revulsion and the stench that were tormenting him. From that time on, as soon as he exchanged the first word with him he felt relieved, refreshed, light on his feet, as though the heaviest of burdens, physical and moral, had been lifted. That was the way it was now. When he was at death's door, when he felt that his lungs could, with infinite effort, scarcely take in a breath of air, when his heart beat slowly and unwillingly, each throb threatening to be its last, he had only to contemplate the odd figure of that man to feel better, to feel calm and serene. He made up his mind at last, his will stiffened by the proximity of death, to ask his friend something that he had been ever so close to asking for more than thirty years: "Fausto, sit down." His voice was no longer as weak. "I've been wanting to ask you something for a long time, but a sense of discretion that's somewhat puzzling even to me has kept me from doing so. Now, with death waiting just around the corner, that sense of discretion is gone. I have no intention of carrying my question unanswered to the grave . . ."

"Go ahead, ask, Denis."

"Believe me, my friend, I've known many, a great many unusual people in my life . . ."

There came to his mind that amazing monk he had met in Russia. In Catherine's court, there had been a great deal of talk about the miracles of Serge Pugachov (that was the man's name), but he, Denis, of course, did not believe the stories. Like Saint Thomas, he had to see to believe. So they took him to a monastery on the outskirts of Moscow. On a promontory that rose above one bank of the Moscow River, it was a building as ugly as it was imposing, and it seemed older than Christianity. The interior walls were at least three yards thick, and in order to go from one room to another, it was necessary to travel through passageways in the shape of a semicircular arch, so low that one had to make one's way along them practically on all fours. "It's to protect us from the cold," one of the monks accompanying him explained. Finally, after crossing many identical rooms, bare and gloomy, dimly lit by crude tallow candles and decorated by a few icons whose frames, owing to the governing darkness, appeared to be made of antique bronze rather than gold, they reached a room much larger than the others. This one, by contrast, was very brightly lit, with countless tapers and oil lamps. The floor was covered with gorgeous Persian carpets, and the most beautiful icons in Diderot's experience hung from the walls. In the middle, sitting on a very roughhewn chair, was Pugachov; alongside him was a small table that held a giant samovar and a set of earthenware mugs. The man, dressed wholly in black, with a heavy cross from Caravaca on his breast, was praying with his eyes closed. His great, long beard, very gray, ended in a point that was resting in his lap. He appeared not to notice the presence of those who had just arrived. He sat like that for a long time, deep in prayer. Suddenly, he lifted his face and looked straight ahead. Actually, he wasn't looking at anything: the irises of his eyes, a deep black, seemed to be turned upon what was going on inside his head. Forcefully, he stretched out his right arm, raised it high with the palm open, and snapped his fingers. A monk, who was attentive to the slightest movement on the part of his master, filled one of the mugs with boiling-hot tea and handed it to the man, who, in a mechanical, almost military, motion, raised the mug to his lips and drank the scalding liquid down in a single swallow. Diderot could almost feel the fire in his throat. But it did not seem to affect the holy man in the least. He remained as he was for some time more, with his eyes staring into space, until he raised his arm again, this time violently flinging the mug aside. They served him another. The scene was repeated until the eight mugs that had been on the table lay in shards on the hearth in one corner of the room. After draining the last swallow and flinging the last mug away, the man had closed his eyes tight. He opened them again at once, but now the irises had disappeared, as if to get a better look at the inside of the man's head. From the outside, the only thing visible was his dead-white eyeballs. His face, a yellowish color until then, slowly turned red; it went from a rosy pink to crimson in a short time and then turned a dark purple in an instant. As it changed color, the face swelled to the point that Diderot instinctively raised his arm to protect himself from what looked to be an impending explosion. Diderot could scarcely believe what he was seeing: the monk's face as round as a melon, a deep purple from his exertion, and his eyeballs as white as snow, to all appearances about to leap out of their sockets. He was so deeply absorbed in the sight of the monk that he didn't notice that everyone accompanying him had thrown himself facedown on the floor, to pray there like Bedouins in the desert. It was when he lowered his eyes, however, that he saw the real miracle: the huge man—who must have weighed a good two hundred pounds—was, chair and all, several hands' breadths above the floor. Just as they had told him, the man was floating in the air like a soap bubble. Diderot saw it; now he could believe it. The monk remained floating like that for a time that seemed forever to the philosopher, until a heavy vapor began to come out of his ears, nose, and mouth, as from a boiler about to explode.

By then he was more than two yards above the floor and his head was at risk of hitting the ceiling. Finally, as though the invisible thread holding him aloft was cut, he fell down full length. The chair was reduced to splinters—Denis understood then why it was rough-hewn—and the man hit the floor with a terrible thud. Had it not been for the carpets, he would have broken at least a few bones. His companions helped him to his feet. Diderot had to go to the man to congratulate him. "It's incredible!" he said to him enthusiastically, "a real miracle . . ."

"It's not a miracle at all," the great hulk of a man replied apathetically, in perfect French though in a high-pitched, screeching voice that didn't seem to go at all with his imposing anatomy. "It's the work of God; for God, nothing is impossible."

"Aren't you afraid of dying when you do that? Your veins looked as though they were about to burst . . ."

"No one should fear the the work of God!" the saint screeched, offended and wanting no more to do with the Frenchman. A little while later in St. Petersburg, Diderot learned many arresting things about the man. Among them, he discovered why he had such a high-pitched voice: the holy man had castrated himself with his own two hands . . .

". . . I've known many unusual people, but none like you, Fausto, really and truly. From the day you came to my house in the rue St-Victor, I've been conscious that you're hiding something. A secret, a gift . . . how should I know? All I'm certain of is that there's something hidden within you. What is it, Fausto? Don't leave this dying man in suspense, because it's plain that even on my deathbed my curiosity hasn't deserted me. What is it, Fausto?"

Actually, that question had been hanging before you, too, for a long time. Diderot's gaze had posed it every time you were with him. In fact, you'd decided how you'd handle such a contingency: if he ever screwed up the courage to question you, you'd tell him the truth. Now, finally, you had the chance to do that.

"I see the future, Denis."

Curiously enough, Diderot, the old materialist, did not seem at all surprised by what you said.

"And how far away is this future you see?"

"It will be here within two centuries . . ."

Diderot asked no more questions; his eyes simply invited you to tell him your story. You accepted the invitation. As with Mariana before, you told him everything, beginning with that afternoon in autumn in the lap of Angustias, your wet nurse. You told him about the Marquise de Gironella, about orgasm, about your first doubts: "For a long time I thought it was simply a question of hallucinations . . ." Your friend's eyes guided you as you spoke. When he failed to understand something, or wanted you to elaborate on it, his inquisitive expression told you so. ". . . They were fleeting, Denis. How long can an orgasm last?" you answered him. Or else, "No, in the beginning, I didn't have the slightest idea what period it was I was seeing . . ." The pantophile's curiosity didn't make it easy for you, not even now, when death had his bags all packed.

He interrupted you only once, when you were unable to understand what his eyes were asking: "And when you masturbate, do you have visions?"

You couldn't keep the smile from your lips. That man is a real philosopher, you said to yourself.

"No, Denis. At least when I masturbate, I'm normal . . ."

You also told him about the miracle with Mariana: "That nightmare disappeared; with her, I never had a vision . . ." But while you said that to your friend, you were aware that you might be fooling yourself. Maybe what happened with Mariana . . . maybe Mariana herself . . . was only another tremendous vision, you thought, as you already had many times before.

"Do you remember her?" You asked Diderot that question and awaited his reply. It was as if by answering yes with his eyes—as, in fact, he did—he'd help you keep Mariana safe, keep that beloved woman safe from the terrible possibility that she was nothing but a mirage. Relieved by your friend's answer, you went on: "But when she disappeared, the visions came back. And they were more peremptory, so to speak, for they began to assail me even in the absence of orgasm; they came . . . they come at any moment . . ."

You explained to him that the visions were much more prolonged now, "as in dreams, where time seems to flow at a different speed. So it is with my visions: a couple of minutes in our time can mean whole hours there . . ." You spoke to him, finally, of that young man you had seen for the first time scarcely five years ago in the little house in Macharavialla, within two centuries of the present—can all this be explained, for heaven's sake?—and who kept appearing more and more frequently in your visions.

". . . He doesn't just appear to me, Denis. It's very strange." Now the one who smiled was the dying man. "I don't see him from outside, the way I'm looking at you, for instance. Rather, I enter him. I see through his eyes; I feel through his body . . . No, I don't think with his mind," you said in answer to your friend's inquiring gaze. "No, not that, up until now, at any rate. Our minds haven't fused. I say, 'our,' because undoubtedly that man has his own human understanding. Why do I say, 'up until now'? Because something tells me that we'll end up with our two minds becoming one. That would at least clear up a lot of the enigma." Diderot looked at you with his questioning gaze once again. "What is all this? Why does it happen to me? What explanation is there for all the absurd things I've said? I've been asking myself these questions for more than fifty years, my friend. I've considered many answers, though all of them, unfortunately, slithered away from the sphere of reason. Today at least I think I know the answer. There are only two possibilities: either I'm as crazy as a loon—and I believe that that's what's likelier—or else I'm part of the fevered dream of a madman who lives in the future. In the second case, I'll inevitably fuse with the mind of that man, since I'm persuaded that it's from there that all this is coming. I'll eventually end up returning to the place where I was conceived . . ."

"It could be that you've dreamed the madman up out of your own madness."

"That's possible too. Why not?"

You felt deeply relieved after talking all this over with Denis. He too looked serene. What could be going through his head? Perhaps he would think that his friend was delirious—that was what was likeliest—or perhaps he was feeling a profound sadness, even if his face didn't show it, on discovering the extent to which madness had made his beloved Fausto a stranger to him. But upon hearing what he said to you, you realized that he wasn't thinking anything of the sort.

"You know what, Fausto? I think Mariana's in the future . . . and that pleases me. It's odd, but only now am I finding out why I never wanted to ask about your mystery, despite its being so obvious that you had one: if I'd asked you about it earlier, I'd have ended up telling you to your face that you're mad and I might even have fallen into a rage over such a bunch of nonsense. But now, with death at my side, I see things very differently. If all a man has to do is drink a few mugs of boiling-hot tea in order to float in the air like a seagull—and I saw that with my own eyes—why shouldn't you be able to see into the future whenever your senses are aroused? Why aren't we willing to imagine such a thing? Or why shouldn't we even experience it? Why does it seem so strange to us to lose ourselves in time if, as far as the full picture goes, we've been lost in it from the very start? I'm convinced that the universe—whatever that is—has existed for millions, perhaps billions, of years. Alongside that, what are fifty, a hundred, two hundred years? Nothing, or almost nothing: anyway, a far shorter time than a sigh lasts in comparison with a long life. We're compressed into an instant. Not only our era but all eras inhabit one and the same instant. How long has it really been since your much-admired Louis X rode along at a gallop, right here where we are, chasing after a hare or a partridge? How long has it really been since the bygone Celts settled on the Ile de la Cité? Those six hundred, those two thousand, years are really nothing compared with the development of the universe. If we submitted to being measured according to the scale for that, my friend, it would be impossible to discriminate ourselves from the Celts, the Goths, or the men you see in your orgasms. Even Micromegas, that fictional character Voltaire described so humorously, would be an infinitesimal being compared with the spatial and temporal dimensions of the universe. And when human history lasts only as long as a sigh, what's so strange about parts of the sigh mingling together every so often? It's happened to you. To me too, though not in such a striking way, of course: I've often caught myself trying to remember something that hasn't happened yet. And to bring to mind what is going to happen is to peer into the future . . . I like what you've told me, Fausto; it pleases me a great deal. Ah, gypsy! You're fated to be a balm to my existence. You know what? Thinking about all this, I've managed to give my fancied materialism a blow that sends it reeling. Perhaps, I thought as I listened to you, perhaps I'll meet my Sophie again. In the final accounting, the pious aren't as simpleminded as they appear . . ." Again you saw his touching smile. "Tell me one last thing: What's the future like?"

You thought long and hard about how to answer. You didn't want to poison this last pleasant moment that your friend was enjoying. You were on the point of lying, of describing to him an idyllic future in which the customs of humankind had improved at the same rate as its inventiveness, where hunger and war and selfishness and stupidity had no place. But something deep down advised you against that. You knew it wasn't right to deceive your friend on his deathbed.

However well intentioned your lie might be, it wasn't the proper medicine for that man, who had loved truth above and beyond anything else in his life.

"Frightful, Denis," you finally said. "Science, technology, and human ingenuity have reached astonishing levels. They've even gone so far—to capture their achievements in a single example—as to set foot on the moon. But their conduct, their ethics . . . their morals, in short . . . haven't improved a bit. If Plato were to see them, he'd regard them as barbarians. They're like us: cruel, selfish, and terribly aggressive, with the one difference that, in their methods of destruction and annihilation, they've moved far beyond us. I've come to believe that, if they continue on the same path, it won't be long before they exterminate themselves . . ."

Denis looked at you tenderly. My poor friend, he was doubtless thinking. His eyes smiled affectionately.

"I was afraid of that, Fausto, my friend, I was afraid . . ."

With those words he fell sound asleep. They were the last words you heard from the philosophe.

On the night of Tuesday, July 14, 1789, Fausto Rasero was in his laboratory, futilely trying to obtain hydrogen gas from red-hot iron and water, according to a procedure his friend Antoine Lavoisier had explained to him. The sizzling sound produced when the hot metal was plunged into water was suddenly drowned out by the commotion that could be heard in the hallway.

"Uncle Fausto! Uncle Fausto! Revolution! The Revolution has broken out!" Michel was shouting at the top of his lungs.

He finally made his way to the laboratory, opened the door, and stopped at the threshold. He was dressed completely in white, except for his coffee-colored boots and the dark blue sash around his waist. The front of his shirt and both its sleeves were torn and, like his trousers, badly stained; the dark blackish grease spots on them almost completely hid that they were originally white. His face was very dirty as well, as though he had rubbed soot on it.

"It's fallen, Uncle! The Bastille has fallen! It's fallen!" he repeated like someone possessed.

"Calm down, my boy. Let's go to my study, where we can talk. But just look at you! You're as dirty as a charcoal maker. What kind of a scrape have you got yourself into?"

"The Bastille's fallen, don Fausto! . . ."

Rasero dragged the boy bodily to his study, sat him down in an easy chair, and poured him a generous glassful of brandy. Michel, very excited, drained the drink in one swallow and tried to get to his feet. The Malagan kept him from it, pushing him back down into the chair and pouring him another glass.

"Now, tell me what's happened."

Michel began to speak fervently, stumbling over his words. It was not easy to follow him. "Camille started the whole thing. He was the one, there's no doubt about it. If you had only seen him on Sunday at the Palais Royal! He looked like a Caesar haranguing his troops. That was what started the whole thing, Uncle. Though, of course, the king's stupidity in dismissing Necker had something to do with it, don't you think? Naturally, with Necker at the helm probably all this wouldn't have happened . . . But who knows? The people are fed up now. You should have seen them this morning! They attacked Les Invalides, and no power of earth could have stopped them. There was a regiment of grenadiers, some eight hundred guards, but they didn't dare intervene. They couldn't, and do you know why? Because the soldiers are fed up too; they're no longer about to shoot at the people. We carried off more than thirty thousand rifles and several cannons! But of course there was no ammunition there. The crafty sons of bitches had moved it to the Bastille last week. They've been scared to death ever since then. And they have every reason to be. Do you know how many toll barriers they burned yesterday? Forty! Almost all the gates in that damned wall were shattered to bits. So who wouldn't be afraid?"

(Rasero was, certainly—though not for himself. On hearing about the burning of the barriers, he thought fearfully of his good friend Antoine: That damned wall! Why didn't he listen to me, for heaven's sake?)

"Ah! What happened this afternoon was wonderful. There they were, in front of the hateful fortress—the people who live in Saint-Antoine, in Saint-Marcel, in Les Halles, as well as a few rope makers, of course. You wouldn't believe how well entrenched the defenders were, Uncle. Ever since last week, when we Parisians demanded arms from the town hall, they'd been afraid of this attack; so they equipped themselves very well. They were devilishly clever at choosing the places where they set up their cannons; their field of fire swept from one side to the other, like a fan, and the wretches shot cannonballs of up to eight pounds at us. In all fairness, though, I didn't harbor any hard feelings toward the disabled soldiers who were defending the square: there were more than eighty of them. I'm sure they were fighting against their will. It must be terrible to be forced to fire on your brothers! For those soldiers are like brothers to the people in Saint-Antoine. They've been living there for so many years! The Swiss, though, are something else again. There were more than thirty of them reinforcing the disabled soldiers. The swine! They, for their part, were more than willing to fight; they went at it like lions. I had to see them fight to understand why they're hired everywhere as mercenaries. They couldn't be more courageous, the bastards! One of them lost his life, but at least fifteen of our countrymen paid for it with theirs. He was a wild beast! And believe me, Uncle, I've never seen anybody with as good aim as that man. They could only finish him off when his ammunition gave out. I think if that Swiss had had ten thousand cartridges at hand, the fortress would never have surrendered . . ."

"Did the commander of the fortress surrender?"

"Of course. There was nothing else he could do. The power of the people is extraordinary: when it's unleashed, there's nothing that can stop it . . ."

"Is that your comment or Desmoulins'?"

"Mmm . . . both . . . Where was I? Ah yes . . . of course that wretch surrendered! He pulled the wool over our eyes three times. He agreed to talk the situation over with a committee of rebels and promised them to settle the question of the ammunition, even though we all knew that what he wanted was to gain time. He'd done the same thing at Les Invalides this morning . . . Still, there was going to be a fourth meeting with him, when the louse greeted the committee by shooting at them. That was when he signed his death warrant . . . The guards the bastard was expecting for relief never did arrive. Why should they? The army, as I've said, Uncle, is on our side. The troops, that is. You know very well that the officers are lackeys of the court. But what is an army without troops? They stayed where they were, at the Saint-Antoine gate; they didn't advance one step toward the Bastille. That cretin de Launey, the commander of the fortress, caught on too late. He never should have fired on the people . . . He paid dearly for daring to do that! . . ." Michel didn't want to tell his mentor—he knew he wasn't going to like it at all—of the sinister picture of that artisan from Saint-Antoine waving back and forth, as though swinging a banner, a long pike topped with the head of the luckless de Launey. "It was wonderful, Uncle. I'm certain that after this memorable day, the court will never again presume to oppose the will of the Assembly of the People; thirty thousand well-armed Parisians will see to that. A new France has been born today, Uncle. A free France . . ." He heaved a deep sigh, as though a millstone had been lifted from his chest.

"Come on, Michel, calm down and have another drink . . . Now, let's see if I understand. Frankly, it hasn't been easy to follow you; you've left my head whirling. First off: Last Sunday your friend Desmoulins harangued people at the Palais Royal. Who and why?"

"Anyone who cared to listen. And there were lots who did, believe me. We were in a café at the Palais Royal when we heard about Necker's sacking. On top of that, the rumor spread that foreign troops would begin arriving at the Champ-de-Mars. There was no doubt about it: the court was preparing a coup d'état against the National Assembly. Camille was beside himself with indignation; he began to speak to us, all wrought up. His voice grew louder and louder, so that the people of the neighborhood began to listen to what he was saying. They agreed with him and began to applaud. Inflamed, Camille leaped onto the table, and from there, shouting at the top of his voice—you could hear him as far as the Seine, I swear—he delivered the most terrific speech I've heard in my life. When he'd finished, there were more than five hundred people around him, and they applauded him madly, clapping as one man. His message spread through the outlying neighborhoods of Paris like fire in dry straw. From that point on, demonstrations were springing up all over the city; the people demanded that a militia be formed to defend the Assembly from the foreign troops. More than five thousand people gathered in the Tuileries, and the Germans mounted a charge against them. They killed many of them, but all they accomplished was to increase the fury of the crowd."

"And then they attacked the barriers . . . ?"

"And stormed the Royal Repository," Michel interrupted.

"Les Invalides and then, finally, the Bastille . . . And there was quite a brawl there. How many prisoners were there inside?"

"Five patriots, I believe . . ."

Michel noted a sly smile on his uncle's face.

"And that militia that's been formed—is it made up of bourgeois or of commoners?"

"How should I know? As far as I've been told, it was originally bourgeois, but I don't doubt that after the Bastille the commoners will form one. How does that matter?"

"It matters, it matters very much, Michel . . . ," Rasero replied thoughtfully. "Well, then, my boy. What you must do now is take a bath and get some rest. You're worn-out, and the way I see things, you're going to be in action for quite a while . . ."

Later, in bed, Rasero tried to concentrate on the Book of Revelation. He couldn't. Michel's words kept buzzing in his head: "A new France has been born, Uncle . . ." Could that be true? Everything seemed to indicate that it was. The old structures of the French kingdom, whose foundations lay hidden in the depths of time, were finally about to be blown to pieces. "For good or for ill, my dear Fausto?" he imagined his old friend Diderot asking him. For good, of course. At least that's what reason held. How could it be a bad thing to do away with absurd privileges that let a few men and women lead an idle, useless life, a life of sheer futility but great riches? Wasn't it right for the good people of Paris—the industrious, happy, and tireless people you came to know on your outings with Mariana—to free themselves once and for all from the burdens that were crushing them, from the notorious injustice that forced them to carry on their shoulders the deadweight of a minority so indolent and extravagant as to defy credulity? Wouldn't your beloved Voltaire and Diderot, and even that misanthrope Rousseau, dance for joy if they could see the multitudes in the streets, weapons in hand, shouting for freedom and equality? That couldn't be bad; it was bound to lead to a better future . . . *A better future.* That was where the problem lay. Would the future be better? Surely not. You were all too aware of that. Yet what would the future be like if nothing were happening now, if the parasites' privileges were maintained forever, if the atrophied descendants of Henry IV went on ruling the destiny of France without anyone's raising a voice in protest, if the poor continued to be mercilessly exploited, if they were doomed till the end of time to lead the wretched lives they did now, full of dire want, of sicknesses, ignorance, and killing work, especially work, so that the wealth they created sustained forever the well-being of the leeches dependent on them? Would that future be better? Where the devil was the answer? Was it to be found? Was there even one hope left? . . . He saw the carved nymph bathing in the pool at the foot of his bed. Her pretty smile set her wooden face alight. A sparrow swooped toward the palm of her hand to drink the water she was offering it. He envied the girl's calm, her indifference . . . "And there was given me a reed like unto a rod," he read wearily, and fell asleep.

You awoke in the future. There too you were lying in a bed, although this one had no carvings. From the ceiling—which rested on beams of dark wood—hung a yellow bulb that illuminated the bedroom. Lying at your side was the thin man. He had his eyes fixed on one of those artifacts that look like a wooden box with one of its sides made of glass. It was on a little table, to one side of the foot of the bed. Colored pictures could be seen in the box. You tried to make out what they represented, and you succeeded. We were seeing, Rasero, nothing less than the parade commemorating the Second Centenary of the French Revolution. Affected, you recognized the Champs-Elysées. You especially liked the bands, in which young musicians, very neatly uniformed, were playing pleasant military marches. You saw a sea of joyful faces. The people on both sides of the line of march were applauding happily and waving little tricolor flags. At times you could see the night sky lit up by marvelous fireworks. Not even at that masked ball at Versailles, when they celebrated the dauphin's engagement, did I ever see a spectacle like this, you said to yourself. Rasero, my friend, you were all agog. You turned your face and looked at me. I smiled. He's happy too, you thought. What nonsense! I was making fun of you, Rasero, that's why I was laughing. You were not yet able to fuse your mind with mine. That was a shame, since you would have avoided many confusions. Alas, things might have turned out better had you been able to read what was going through my mind at that moment. I'll tell you now what I was thinking: The poor French, how low they've sunk. Look at that tasteless parade they're mounting. Good grief, it's as if it's the Parade of the Roses in Pasadena! The only thing missing is Mickey Mouse sporting a tricolor cockade on one of his big ears . . . Those were more or less my thoughts, Rasero. Perhaps, as I was saying, if you had been aware of my reaction, you wouldn't have thrown yourself into that absurd adventure which in the end cost your beloved Michel his head . . . But never mind. Things like that are bound to happen, and that was what happened. You must forgive me. Strictly speaking, I couldn't do a thing about it. I didn't yet know that you were at my side, also watching television, though, in a manner of speaking, I noticed your presence. No, not your presence. That's what I think now, but at that moment I didn't; at that moment what I saw just as the fat black lady who so impressed you began to sing—what I saw was your bedroom. I saw the nymphs in the pool very clearly; I saw the swallows flying there in the bed's wood. I saw them, Rasero. But like you, I didn't understand a thing; I may even have been a little scared. Okay, I was very scared, though it was something I'd been anticipating for ten years. But your vision pleased you a great deal, Rasero, particularly when you saw that black woman, imposing, robust, as nice and plump as anyone could wish, enveloped in that gigantic tricolor flag which was defiantly unfurling, flapping gaily in the wind, many steps behind her. The woman was singing, singing a very beautiful song, as beautiful as her voice, which was like that of an authentic siren. You saw in all that—or tried to see—a happy omen, a clear answer to the question that had been gnawing at you before you fell asleep. The future will indeed be better, you now said to yourself. There won't be any racism (isn't that black woman great?); the people, healthy, happy, united in brotherly love, will each year celebrate the heroic fight of the residents of Saint-Antoine to throw off the chains of feudalism. Perhaps—why not?—perhaps that frightful future you'd been witnessing was only the hypothetical projection of the unjust order in existence up till now. And if that order changed, you thought with lamentable logic, it wouldn't be at all strange if the future were different too . . . You had finally found the nail on which to hang up your despair. The image you had in your head of the enormous black woman succeeded in dispelling your doubts, and even your certainties, certainties like the one you arrived at—why did you no longer remember it?—six years before, when you saw, along with half of Paris, a gigantic balloon of cloth and paper inflated with hot air rise up from the Champ-de-Mars. In the basket that was suspended from its base, Jean-François Pilâtre de Rozier and the Marquis d'Arlandes smiled with satisfaction and waved to the crowd, which they could see growing by the minute, until it turned into an army of ants. Everyone was elated over the Montgolfier brothers' invention except you, Rasero. You were the only one there who remained dour and rueful. We've begun already . . . we've begun already . . . , you admitted to yourself in horror as you saw the two men rise in the air . . .

Beginning on the day when Rasero had the vision of the Second Centenary of the French Revolution, his attitude toward what was happening in France changed radically. After many years, he came out of his voluntary confinement. He left the laboratory and his experiments, and set his manuscript on Gothic France aside. I'll have time to return to that in a little while, he said to himself and went out into the streets of Paris, which in those days were bustling with greater activity than ever. He strolled into the outskirts of the city; he often went to the town hall to observe the lively meetings that succeeded one another, day after day, like beads of a necklace. He went to the cafés of the Palais Royal, where he listened to many heated exchanges: it seemed as if every young politician had in his back pocket the plan that could resolve all the problems threatening to destroy the kingdom. He visited the clubs, the rope makers' in the Convent of Saint Francis—very near home—as well as the Jacobins' (in the Convent of Saint James, and even the Feuillants' in a palace behind the Tuileries. He read every gazette and pamphlet that fell into his hands—a great many came his way—and he searched for his old acquaintance Count Mirabeau, for he realized that that curious character was the key to everything that was happening.

It wasn't easy to track him down. The count appeared to be the busiest man in France. When he wasn't in the Assembly addressing its members in his matchless style, he was shut up at home writing his speeches, or in some salon electrifying the guests, or in the Jacobins' club leading the debates, or—since this was almost always where he greeted the dawn—in a brothel making two and even three whores writhe with pleasure at the same time.

"My friend, I'm very afraid that this is the work of the queen's clique and the royal princes . . ."

They were talking together in a tavern in the rue St-Honoré. The tribune was relating the most recent events and subjecting them to relentless scrutiny. As he listened to him, Rasero congratulated himself on his perseverance in searching out the man. The effort had been worth it, great as it had been. For at least two weeks he had been hot on his trail. Mirabeau, besides knowing every detail about each of the multitude of events so rapidly occurring in those days, had reached sound assessments: nobody else had so carefully weighed the events' importance or so adequately understood their real meaning. For that very reason, Mirabeau was less susceptible than many to the general euphoria the first successes of the Revolution gave rise to—among them the king's compliance, shortly after the storming of the Bastille, with the decisions of the Assembly (he sent the foreign troops out of Paris and restored Necker to his post), the abdication of royal power in the face of the sovereignty of the people (Louis, in the Tuileries, adorned his own tricorn with a tricolor cockade and drank straight from the bottle with the fierce sansculottes), the abolition of the feudal privileges of the nobility, the clergy, and the court, on the fourth of August, and the memorable ceremony in which the Constituent Assembly read to the citizens of France and to the entire world, for the first time, the Declaration of the Rights of Man, on that bright morning of August 26.

". . . Things are happening too fast, and that can't be good. It's like erecting a building without waiting for the cement of the foundation to harden. For evidence of this, recall the great fear that swept through the kingdom during the summer. If things are going so well, why was there that fear then? The fear was palpable, my friend. Even people in the most isolated and wretched little villages were dying of fear, awaiting God only knows what calamity. Maybe this stemmed from the perverse feeling of guilt that priests have been drumming into the heads of country people for hundreds of years. That must have been part of it, there's no doubt about it. But the fear gripped the entire kingdom. However spontaneous it may appear to have been, that collective fear was orchestrated from above. It's the work of the queen's clique and of the royal princes," he insisted. "It's impossible to be more dim-witted than that bunch of scoundrels. All they're going to do is place the king in a desperate situation. If they manage to turn him against the Revolution, it's going to be pandemonium, you needn't doubt that, my friend. And in the end they're the ones who are going to be hurt the most, since even if the fear inculcated in the people by religion is enormous, the hatred that's built up against the nobility is even greater, and if that explodes, there won't be any power at all that's capable of stopping it. The storming of the Bastille will seem like child's play, you'll see. Once the sewer of power is unplugged, filth pours out in torrents, and there won't be anyone who'll escape getting spattered, marquis . . ."

During the following five years, Rasero remembered often the words of the great tribune. He remembered them on the fourteenth of July of '90, when he went, along with half of Paris, to the Champ-de-Mars to commemorate the first anniversary of the storming of the Bastille. The king, dubious, silent, had receded into the background. The outstanding figure of the day was the Marquis de Lafayette, the undeniable head of the revolutionary movement and of the brand-new National Guard—a militia of bourgeois who applauded him madly. Lafayette, elegant, arrogant, and vain—"like an Indonesian peacock," Diderot would have said—directed the secular ceremony in his capacity as high priest. At his side, the bishop of Autun—a man whose extraordinary cynicism was surpassed only by his intelligence—made no effort to suppress a sardonic smile. Don't forget, dear friend, that all this is a masquerade, his eyes seemed to say to the revolutionary leader. Later at the commemoration, he went back to his religious duties, for he who only a few days before had from the rostrum of the Constituent Assembly sought the abolition of the privileges of the clergy, the confiscation of their wealth, and their subordination to the civil Assembly, he who was the first French curate to swear loyalty to the new order and unrepentantly scorned his superiors (the archbishop of Paris and, especially, the pope), he, the future Prince Talleyrand, had been chosen to celebrate the solemn mass. Queen Marie Antoinette looked at him with hatred in her eyes. Her brothers-in-law—the brothers of the king—would have done the same had they been present, but they had left the kingdom some time before. In neighboring Belgium, living the grand life, they stole a little time from their idle pleasure to hatch conspiracies the aim of which was to put an end to the Revolution and perhaps—with a little luck—to finish off their fool of a brother as well, in order to return in triumph, with a crown awaiting them. Mirabeau was delighted to head the members of the triumphant Constituent Assembly. All the actors in the drama were present, like a united and happy family, including the king, the axis—even if very much to his regret—around which everything revolved, shouldering the responsibility for the legendary indecision of the Bourbons with resignation, and the queen, beautiful and unbending, in her little Hapsburg head denying what was happening, pursing her lips, hoping that the whole nightmare would end soon and the centuries-old order that was God's will for the sovereigns of Europe would be reinstituted. As all this was going on, she looked out the corner of her eye at the Swedish ambassador, her beloved Fersen: Ah, if only I weren't queen, if I had had the good fortune to be a mere marquise, I'd be in your arms, my dearest Hans, far away from all this filth—in a garden in flower, surrounded by great oak trees, with gentle little streams where fat cows and darling sheep drink. There your shepherdess would be, my love . . .

The courtiers were there, greedy, corrupt, and cowardly, hating with all the might their miserable spirits could muster the traitor

Lafayette for having turned his back on his blood brothers to place himself at the head of those wretched bourgeois, who were unable to tell the difference between an andante and an adagio: Presto! That's the only tempo that bunch of thieves knows; they're out to rob, presto, out to cheat, presto, to take away from us, presto, the rights that it was God's will to give us for more than a thousand years.

The bourgeois were there, happy—they were the winners for the moment—in their blue uniforms or their black frock coats and trousers, staring defiantly at their ancestral enemies: We've taken Paris over from those scoundrels! Wealth will finally belong to those who make use of it. We're done with supporting those idlers. They behaved as though they weren't themselves idlers, as though it were real work looking over their ledgers to add up their receipts and subtract their expenses and thus calculate how much a wretched worker could produce in fourteen hours of hard labor. The bourgeois looked affectionately at the commoners, the people, their natural allies, whom they protected with all the attention and deference they would a madman: Poor things, they're so noble!

The people, so noble, so content, were happily cheering their betters. Bread was cheaper now. The price had peaked just a year before. It was indeed high priced then, if it could be come by at all, because the little there was had been stashed away by the accursed hoarders—the same ones who, in their uniforms as national guards, were now looking at them beatifically—and what was available could hardly be called bread: it was black and foul-smelling rocks that had to be hacked at with an axhammer. There was bread now, however, and it was cheaper. Those despicable tollgates in the wall were gone. The king had sworn submission to the people's deputies, and even that Austrian woman had resigned herself to her fate . . . So that day the good people of Paris even applauded Queen Marie Antoinette: they were so happy that, prodigal and generous, they wanted to share a little of their pleasure with the king's wife . . .

Mirabeau found himself face-to-face with the queen and gave her a broad smile from the depths of his ugly face. Marie Antoinette, almost imperceptibly (*almost,* since many people managed to see it), greeted the deputy with a very slight nod of her head. If they can reach the point of understanding each other, this may work, Rasero said to himself, persuaded that Count Mirabeau was the only person capable of balancing the vastly disparate forces that were so plain to see on that summer morning on the Champ-de-Mars.

A year later, when the second anniversary of the revolutionary epic was celebrated, the situation of the kingdom was very different. The big family had quickly fallen apart: the ties that held it together—hypocrisy, self-interest, and ambition—could not withstand the tensions. The sewer was unplugged, and the struggle for power threatened to be fierce. Almost all the nobles and courtiers had fled. From exile, they egged foreign sovereigns on to venture to restore the old order. Meanwhile, their numerous agents inside the country were involved in financial speculation when they weren't spreading rumors—a specialty of the house—or trying to buy consciences among the ranks of the bourgeoisie. The king, closeted in the Tuileries, finally yielded to his wife's pressure and decided to attempt an escape from France. Ferson, the Swedish ambassador, mapped out an ingenious plan for fleeing the country. It failed only because of minor mishaps. The adventure ended in the house of an apothecary in Varennes, a remote little village in the north of France. The king returned to Paris and was looked upon as a scoundrel; the good people never forgave him for the offense of trying to abandon them and fly into the arms of the traitors in exile. To top it all off, one morning in April of that same year, '91, Mirabeau was found, soused and tumid, in bed between two whores who were screaming hysterically. The great tribune had died in the middle of one of his epic amorous feats, leaving without a sponsor the one possibility of a concerted way out of the great crisis about to swoop down on France. On the death of that man, there also died the chance of bringing into balance powers that were becoming more diametrically opposed by the day. It then became a matter of everything or nothing: restoring the absolute monarchy or removing the king from the throne and setting up a republic. Mirabeau took to the grave with him the mediating plan of a constitutional monarchy. The result was a confrontation between the two allies in the revolutionary cause: the bourgeois, headed by the Marquis de Lafayette, who were satisfied with what had been accomplished and tried against all odds to uphold the throne and the constitution, and the people, especially the people of Paris. The Commune had gone far along a path of its own: it no longer accepted the monarch, much less his harpy of a wife who tirelessly plotted to restore the old order. The people wanted a republic, to do away, right then and forever, with all privileges. The people wanted, finally, to count in history. Three days after the date commemorating the storming of the Bastille, Lafayette's National Guard massacred the sansculottes on the Champ-de-Mars. From that moment, there was no turning back: it was the people against the privileged, whether aristocrats or bourgeois.

"We must do away with the monarchy once and for all! Believe me, Uncle, if we don't, everything will go to hell . . ."

From the beginning, Michel had embraced the people's cause, and as events took their course, he had become more and more radical. Some time had passed since he abandoned his studies to devote himself body and soul to the cause, along with his friend Camille Desmoulins, whose secretary, confidant, and inseparable companion he became. After the king's failed attempt to flee the country, he repeated his pet refrain against the monarchy more and more regularly: "As long as that cretin's in power, he will go to any lengths to wipe us out. You saw what happened, Uncle, on the Champ-de-Mars: the National Guard went over to the king's side, and that swine Lafayette didn't hesitate to fire on the people. If we don't stop them, things are going to go back to being the way they were before. When gangrene sets in in someone's leg, there's only one choice: either the leg gets amputated or the victim dies. And nowadays the king and his courtiers are the gangrene of France, and you can see that, far from rooting it out, the cowards drew up a constitution that lets it make further inroads. 'Sovereignty resides in the people,' its prologue reads. Oh, yeah! What sovereignty can the people have if the king is given the right to veto any decision that comes from the Assembly? if he's the one who appoints the minister and plans the kingdom's economy? He's being given enormous power. It's a power that that traitor in no way deserves, and that he will not hesitate to use, as I've already said, to wipe out the Revolution . . ."

Rasero listened thoughtfully to the young man. Every so often he stroked Nostradamus' back as he lay comfortably on his lap. He felt on the back of his hand the dry, rasping little tongue of the animal licking away contentedly. He agreed with what Michel was saying. The bourgeoisie, in fact, was now satisfied with the changes that had taken place—changes that, of course, benefited it—and didn't want to go any farther. A king who would put into effect the decisions they had made seemed the ideal solution. That was why they were so pleased with their brand-new constitution. But the expectations they themselves had had a hand in arousing in the people were very far from being fulfilled, and Rasero did not have the slightest doubt that the bourgeois would be as firm as, or even firmer than, the aristocrats in repressing the common people if they insisted on asking for more than what those in control were prepared to give. On the other side, though, he was not completely convinced that the solution lay in a republic. He remembered very well what Count Mirabeau had said to him: "It is essential that the king remain on his throne. The executive power, my friend, must belong to a man by right of blood. Otherwise, it's like throwing a piece of meat to a pack of famished hounds; they'll tear each other to pieces for power, you needn't have the slightest doubt on that score. With a republican regime, France would turn into a perpetual battlefield, or in the best of cases, into the booty of an astute and ambitious dictator. Believe me, Monsieur Rasero, I know my countrymen very well . . ."

"A republic entails many dangers, Michel. In any event, I don't believe that Barnave or Duport will prove to be better rulers than Louis . . ."

"Of course not! But, obviously, they wouldn't be the rulers of the republic. The best of its men would be elected democratically by the people and very closely watched by its representatives. This is nothing new, don Fausto. It worked marvelously well in ancient Greece." (Athenian democracy killed Socrates, Rasero thought, although he didn't say as much to the young man. After all, we all have the right to dream of our utopia.) "Take the republic of the Americans, for example. You won't deny that what they've accomplished in ten years is impressive. Or if you regard that republic as being too young to know its true potential, I'll cite you the Swiss cantons: they've been without a king for more than five hundred years, and I don't think anybody doubts that they've succeeded in creating a great country. Or Venice, which you'll agree reached its greatest splendor when it was an independent republic . . ."

It's plain to see that you've all been giving the subject thought, Rasero reflected. Ah, that Desmoulins is tireless . . . He found that man very congenial. He had met him a few days before the fall of the Bastille, when, galvanized by what he had seen in the future, he finally gave in to Michel's pleas and agreed to meet with his revolutionary friends. In any case, he was eager to meet the man who had made himself into almost a legend by delivering that memorable philippic to the Parisians from atop a table in a café at the Palais Royal on that already historic Sunday in July of '89. He was a thin, nervous young man. His eyes were constantly alert, as though expecting a prize or a punishment. Quick to become impassioned, enthusiastic and vehement, he was a formidable orator when he was inspired, but he was also susceptible to doubts and depression whenever an obstacle, no matter how trivial, blocked his path. Michel found more to worry about in his friend's depressions than in the intrigues of the courtiers. And indeed Camille was insufferable when melancholy or fear assailed him. He'd abandon everything—meetings, publications, conversations—and seemed even to scorn his beloved wife. He would then lie in bed, staring at the canopy above. He could spend entire days like that. "It's all shit . . . ," he'd repeat until he was worn out, until, as suddenly as discouragement had overcome him, his enthusiasm returned and, leaping out of bed, he once again took up, with even more vigor than earlier, his revolutionary burden. Desmoulins' character, stormy and contradictory, reminded Rasero of that of his beloved Voltaire. Often, as he listened to Camille, he thought that as a young man Voltaire must have been very much like him: thin, intelligent, impassioned, a bit inclined toward exaggeration and melodrama. Curiously, Voltaire was the acquaintance of Rasero's who most interested Desmoulins. His credo, of course, was derived from Rousseau, but his curiosity and even his admiration inclined him toward the old Parisian philosopher. "Was he really a homosexual?" he asked Rasero. "Not as far as I know, no," the Malagan replied. Or, "Did he write sitting down or standing up, as they say that d'Alembert did?" Or, "Is it true that he wrote more than ten thousand letters?" Or, "Was he really ill, or was he a hypochondriac . . . ?"

Rasero satisfied the young man's curiosity as best he could. "He was the most intelligent man I've known in my life, and behind a mask of false vanity, he was tenderer than a newly hatched chick. I've known few persons whom intolerance and injustice made as indignant as they made him . . ." Rasero contemplated with satisfaction the big smile that came over Desmoulins' face when he heard those words. He's Voltaire reborn, he said to himself, but now it's not with his pen, with ideas, that he's fighting the old order but with direct face-to-face confrontation against all that the patriarch of Ferney so detested. François would be very proud of himself if he could see this youngster . . . And proud of so many of the others. For in those times when ideas had turned into action, the young men who fought generously against the Old Regime were many. Rasero knew almost all of them—from the most moderate, who gathered in the salon of Necker's daughter, to the most radical, Michel's friends. He was inclined toward the radicals. Ever since that memorable vision, he was convinced that they were the ones destined to change the world . . . and the future. At the age of seventy-five he threw himself into the fight with the enthusiasm of a man of twenty. He contributed the only thing he could: his ideas, his memories, the vast experience of the fifty years he'd lived in a world he wanted to see disappear forever. He kept his distance from the moderates—except for Lavoisier, to whom he was bound by ties much solider than politics—and clung to the arms of the Cordeliers and the most radical Jacobins.

It was, in fact, through Desmoulins that Rasero met Jean-Paul Marat, the fearsome "friend of the people." He did not find that person, so ugly and unsociable, very appealing. Moreover, it was easy for him to discover that in Marat, behind a violent love for the dispossessed, there lay hidden a profound resentment against a society that had been contemptuous of him. He talked with him a few times. Marat was interested in Rousseau, no one else, and brought the discussion around to him in each of the conversations with Rasero, who always felt uncomfortable when it came to that man. The Malagan searched his memory for the few pleasant memories he had of the Swiss philosopher. "He was prodigiously intelligent," he said to Marat cautiously. "There was no one like him to point out to us where we'd end up if we didn't humanize ourselves . . ."

"True, quite true . . . ," the friend of the people agreed.

The last time Rasero saw him was in July of '91. Rasero remembered it very well: Marat was lying submerged in a tub, like Diderot forty years before, fighting a skin disease that was tormenting him. On his face was a bitter, annoyed expression. "Citizen Rasero! What a pleasant surprise! Please sit down and tell me what I can do for you . . ."

Leave Antoine in peace. What are you planning to do, have him lynched? Rasero thought, though of course he didn't say that. Instead he improvised a rather muddled speech, in which, amid quotations from Rousseau, criticisms of the king and the moderates, and praise for the sansculottes, he spoke of the importance of science and its development in the society of the future: ". . . Rousseau himself said as much, and there was nobody like him to warn us of the dangers that science holds, but he was familiar too with its enormous promise . . ." And so, as though Fausto were doing so reluctantly, he paid tribute to the greatness of French chemistry, "the best in the world, and in large part thanks to Antoine Lavoisier. He's a tax collector, I know that very well, but he's also the most respected scientist in Europe."

When Marat caught on to Rasero's game, he flew into a rage and let loose a terrifying diatribe against Lavoisier and against him. "Monsieur Rasero, I see to my great regret that your blood is beginning to speak for you. Only from an aristocrat would I expect to hear such blather." Rasero didn't remember what else he said, although he was certain that if the man had had a knife at hand at that moment, he wouldn't have hesitated to slit his belly with it. It happened that when the man began his angry speech, Rasero was in the grip of a vision. In the last two years the future had oppressed him only a couple of times, and to tell the truth, on that occasion it didn't oppress him but, rather, saved him from the fury of that man who was shouting like someone possessed as he looked, first of all in surprise, and then frankly taken aback, at Rasero's undisturbed expression, his blank stare and his broad, satisfied smile: that blessed time, Fausto had seen his Mariana again . . .

Georges-Jacques Danton was very different. Rasero had taken a liking to him from the day they first met. It was at the end of '89, during a meeting of the Cordeliers' Club in the Convent of Saint Francis. When Rasero arrived, the committee meeting was nearly over. Danton, already on his feet, was giving last-minute instructions: "Not one step backward, comrades, or they'll squash us like toads: either they give us those weapons or we won't leave the town hall. Agreed?"

"Agreed!" all those gathered there shouted, breaking into applause.

"Now, one last piece of advice . . ."

During this, Rasero took a good look at the leader: he was a big, imposing man, even taller than Mirabeau, though much less ugly looking. In fact, he would even have been good-looking had it not been for the cruel marks of smallpox scattered across his face. How many men and women that terrible disease has condemned to be ugly! Rasero thought, remembering Voltaire pacing back and forth in his library. And all out of fear of a needle prick. Danton's voice was deep and very powerful—it seemed as though he were speaking through a Greek theatrical mask—and he knew how to pitch it and modulate it astonishingly well: it could be seductive and flattering just as effectively as it could be threatening and terrible. He could go from one tone to the other even in the same speech, like a snake that, crawling along the ground, enters the water without varying its movements in the slightest.

When they'd finished, Michel took Rasero over to his leader to introduce his mentor to him. There was no need: the moment Danton saw the elderly bald man, he recognized him: Desmoulins and Michel himself had spoken to him about Rasero a good many times.

"Monsieur Rasero! What a great honor to meet you!"

Danton approached the Malagan and gave him a hearty embrace. Rasero felt that his bones were being dislocated one by one. This man's a bear, he said to himself.

"The honor is mine, Citizen Danton."

The giant of a man was pleased by the title the bald man used to greet him: in those days very few people used the honorific *Citizen*, which a few years later was to become detestably obligatory.

"Ah, my friend! Allow me to call you that. I know very well that you were a great friend of Diderot's, and anyone who was a friend of Diderot's is my friend as well."

"Nothing would give me more pleasure than enjoying your friendship . . ."

"Did you hear, Michel? Learn from your uncle; those are the manners of a gentleman," Danton said with a smile. "Well then, my friends, let's celebrate this treasure we've found. What do you say to a good supper with an even better wine?"

"A great idea."

The supper lasted till daylight. They spoke of a thousand things, Rasero above all, who found himself subjected to one question after another without a letup. Danton riddled him with questions. The curiosity of that man went with his temperament: it was indefatigable, as eager as a woman in heat, and utterly disorganized. The conversation went from the political situation of the kingdom to the bonhomie of Benjamin Franklin, to the genius of Mozart and the nymphomania of Catherine of Russia.

"Tell me, did you know the Marquise de Pompadour?"

Rasero answered enthusiastically. Danton listened a little skeptically to the fervent praise that the Spaniard showered on the lady. The subject didn't interest him, and he abruptly cut him off: "And do you know Du Barry?"

"No. I haven't been at the court in more than twenty years."

"Well, they say that that woman was a great piece of ass, that she screwed better than Aphrodite herself. Do you know what? I'd like to have fucked that brazen hussy. I've heard that she was so expert that after you put your flute up her, she got it ready for you to play a concert on," Danton said, and exploded in a loud guffaw that must have carried to Versailles.

During the evening, Rasero had a chance to observe closely that altogether unusual man. What most impressed him about Danton—and that is saying a lot—was his tremendous vitality. He had never known anyone who lived every moment so intensely. He ate with gusto and pleasure, as though it were the last dish he'd taste in his life, and one that had been exquisitely seasoned. The same thing was true of the wine: the swallows he downed were enormous, every one as though it was the last before they removed the wine from the table in the middle of dessert, but at the same time he enjoyed what he was drinking so much that watching him made one inevitably want to join him in a glass. Also, it had little effect on him. Except for the gleam in his eyes that grew noticeably brighter, and the redness of his big nose, it seemed as if the wine were like water for that man. After draining four bottles, he seemed as fresh and clearheaded as when they arrived at the tavern.

"And Diderot—how did he have the time to do so many things?"

As he talked to him about his cherished friend, Rasero realized that, in a certain way, Danton was very much like Denis. As he had seen Voltaire in Desmoulins, he now saw many characteristics of the Encyclopedist in Danton. Like Denis, this man was restless, avid, a seducer, and terribly sharp-witted; like him, Danton too was wrapped up in activity, movement, the tireless work that allows no rest. Diderot, however, had operated in the realm of ideas, in the world of knowledge; Danton, on the other hand, moved in the world of direct, concrete action. It was not *knowledge* that concerned him most, it was *doing*—to which he devoted himself with the same vigor and enthusiasm, with the same surprising energy, that Rasero's beloved Denis had shown for accumulating knowledge. Both were like busy bees, but whereas one worked amid the flowers of theory, of history, of science, and of art, the other did so amid the fruits of everyday life; one was attracted by books, the other by persons; one was a guide for men of intelligence, the other a leader of combatants. In a word, whereas one sowed, the other reaped. Rasero was pleased with the metaphor. It could not be otherwise. There was a way in which the existence of men like Michel, Desmoulins, and Danton completely justified the efforts of his own generation. Yes, this world definitely promises to be better, Rasero thought as he went on talking about his old friend. This world is going to be better . . . and the future too.

Rasero had few opportunities to share Danton's company after that. The man was caught up in the whirlwind of one event after another in those years, and he ended up becoming one of the era's protagonists. It was not easy to find him, since his frantic activity took him from one end of Paris to the other as he attended marathon meetings that never ended before daybreak. Even so, the few occasions on which Rasero was with him were as enjoyable as the first time, and they only increased the admiration he felt for the young head of the revolutionary movement. He soon had to add to his feeling of admiration that of gratitude—or reproach?—for the Malagan reached the point of owing his life to Georges-Jacques Danton . . .

It was in October of '92. The Revolution of the tenth of August had sealed the fate of the Crown. Louis XVI, the victim of his indecision, of his wife's stupidity, of his brothers' treachery, and of the ambition of his European counterparts, looked on helplessly as the thousand-year-old throne of Saint Louis collapsed. Louis was forced to leave the palace of the Tuileries for a prison in the Temple, and to exchange his ruler's staff for shackles. The monarchy had died, and on top of its ashes, the Republic was born, on September 24. Terrible threats hung over the head of the newborn creature: allied foreign armies had already invaded French territory and appeared to be about to attack Paris. In the interior, counterrevolutionary forces were making intelligent moves that almost always met with success and brought about a string of peasant revolts. For many, it was a question of days, months at most, before the newborn Republic would succumb to the formidable offensive of the allied armies. Few, really very few, suspected what enormous energy the French people had amassed. They had become a force that would soon manifest itself in an explosion of violence that was badly to shake not only France but the entire world. Danton, the undeniable hero of the revolutionary events that had taken place in August, was part of this force. He had absolute faith in the Revolution and in the new order that it proclaimed to the world. But it was imperative for all the people to watch over it, to protect it, to defend it even with their teeth from the hatred of their enemies. So he organized an elaborate system of defense for which the Committee of Public Safety was eventually to serve as the nucleus. Moreover, weapons were handed out to the people, resulting in a powerful army, not of professional mercenaries now, as had been customary up until then, but of peasants, workers, and craftsmen ready to fight like wild beasts to defend their Revolution. (Europe would soon learn what it was like to fight against an armed people.) In the interior, very drastic measures were taken. Everyone suspected of collaborating with foreigners was arrested, and the revolutionary tribunals could scarcely get their fill of trying and condemning traitors. By September, those arrested numbered in the thousands, and confronted with the imminent arrival of foreign troops in Paris, the masses, infuriated, began to take justice into their own hands. They attacked the prisons and massacred countless aristocrats, collaborators, suspects (many of them innocent), petty thieves, and whores, as well as anyone else unfortunate enough to be in a prison during those bloody days. Rasero, who paid close attention to what was happening as soon as he learned of the killings, searched in alarm for his friend Lavoisier. For good reason, he feared that Antoine had been a victim of the hatred unleashed in Paris. He looked at the Arsenal and didn't find him. Someone there told him that the chemist had been seen in the middle of a squad of militiamen who were taking him to a prison near the town hall. In a panic, the Malagan headed there.

The cells were jammed full. There the democratic spirit, so fashionable in those days, had earned its first great triumph, for behind the bars of a frightful cell—dank and dark, giving off a penetrating stench of urine and excrement that had soaked into the straw and the blankets on the floor—there could be seen nobles with titles going back four centuries beside prostitutes from the outlying neighborhood of Saint-Antoine, venerable abbots beside fierce bandits, wealthy bankers beside cruel murderers. The place reduced the differences to nothing. Fine, elegant clothing had long since lost its splendor and now looked as tattered and filthy as the rags of the poor. Disheveled wigs were even more pitiful looking than big manes of unkempt hair. Pale faces, eyes red from weeping, and an expression of panic were, without exception, common to rich and poor, nobles and plebs. Rasero went from one cellblock to another searching—and in terror of finding—his dear friend amid that sea of figures straight out of Dante. All of a sudden, a guard planted himself in his path and kept him from going any farther. "What do you want?" he asked in a surly voice. The man was plastered to the gills.

Rasero tried to explain why he was there, but the soldier was scarcely listening. Instead, he coolly looked him up and down. Rasero's attire annoyed him, his bald pate displeased him, his presence irritated him. His face showed distaste, and as the Malagan went on talking, he grabbed a big bunch of keys hanging from his waist. Slowly, as he heard the name Lavoisier issuing from the mouth of the bald man, he opened a barred grille and gave Rasero a rough shove. He tried to resist, and even clung to the bars to avoid being forced into the cell, but the guard gave him a brutal kick in the behind, so that he fell headlong onto the stinking straw.

The place was way overcrowded; there were about a hundred people in a space no bigger than a bedroom. Rasero squatted on his heels in one corner, leaning his back against a wall that seemed to be made not so much of bricks and mortar as of water. This dampness comes from the Seine, he thought. He buried his head between his thighs and clasped his knees. About once an hour, two or three guards came to the cell, read aloud a list of ten or fifteen names, and forced those on the list to move up to the door. When they were done, they opened it and took them off at bayonet point. In a little while, the firing of rifles sounded the end of those unfortunates. Rasero was still concerned about Lavoisier. His own situation mattered very little to him; he saw it, rather, as a relief. At last he was going to leave this absurd world. It did not sadden him to die at the hands of a revolution in which he had believed and for which he had fought; what annoyed him and even revolted him was that things had to be that way. In those days there was much talk of equality, liberty, and even fraternity, and it appeared that in order to reach those noble goals it was necessary to kill a great many people. He remembered that Mariana had once said to him that the ancient peoples of Mexico traditionally sacrificed many people, "for they thought that the blood of men was the only thing that satisfied their gods. In exchange for it, their divinities saw to it that they prospered." And we, fatuously, regard those men as savages. We're exactly like them . . . he thought.

When dawn broke, fewer than ten persons were left in the cell. Rasero supposed that the reason they hadn't called him was that the guard locking him up hadn't bothered to ask his name. Perhaps the same thing had happened to the others still in the cell. Rasero didn't want to see them. In fact, from the moment that he sat down in that corner he hadn't seen anyone. He didn't want compassion to disturb the morbid pleasure he felt at the thought of his approaching death.

"Come over to the door, all of you!" the same guard who had arrested him shouted. He looked refreshed now; he had no doubt slept off his hangover. Rasero rose to his feet with difficulty, for his legs, which had remained bent all night long, resisted his command.

"Hurry it up, you old shit!" the guard shouted, hitting him on the back with the butt of his rifle.

Finally, the nine men left the cell.

"That's the way, all in a neat line," the guard said sarcastically. "Now, you cherubs, you're going to eat your fill of lead. Move ahead, you bastards!"

"Monsieur Rasero!" Danton shouted as he approached with long strides. "Halt, sergeant." The guard obeyed and came to respectful attention in front of the enormous man. "What in heaven's name are you doing here?"

"I wish I knew. Maybe you can ask the guard?"

Danton gave the sergeant a furious look. "Well . . . ?"

"I arrested him, citizen."

"And why did you do that?"

"Ah, because it's plain to see that he's a revolting noble, a perfidious traitor, no doubt. We have instructions to do away with people like him. I was only following orders . . ."

"You're going to be locked up! We'll see if prison teaches you to tell an enemy from a friend, you stupid ass."

Danton looked very tired. His pale face and the big dark circles under his eyes showed that the man hadn't slept for days. In recent weeks, besides the brutal work that organizing the defense of the young Republic represented, he had taken the time to go through the prisons at night, trying to keep such atrocities from happening. He had had very little success. The slaughter in those days was terrible, but at least he was able to save a few unfortunates. As he was now, when by luck he'd arrived in time to save Rasero. If they'd shot him, it would certainly have been a great injustice, because, though he was an aristocrat, he had given proof of his loyalty to the cause. Murdering a friend of Diderot's! And on top of that, Michel Gautier's mentor. Somehow there has to be a stop to this, or everything is going to turn to shit . . . , the revolutionary said to himself.

Rasero asked about Lavoisier.

"He's all right, don't worry. He hasn't been arrested. Though I warn you that your friend has to watch his step. I wouldn't bet a single sol on the life of the farmers-general. To tell you the truth, if he and not you had been the man I came across this morning, I wouldn't have ordered the sergeant to halt . . ."

The last time you spoke with Danton was only a couple of months ago. After much trying, you finally got an audience with him.

"Citizen Rasero! What can I do for you?"

His big smile couldn't conceal the worry that showed on his face. He was much thinner and older looking, as though the trip to Champagne, where he had supposedly gone to rest, had taken twenty years off his life. You went straight to the point: "It's Antoine Lavoisier. He's been arrested."

"I know."

"My friend, you must do something. I'm not going to weary you by talking about the talents of that man. You know what they are, though I greatly fear that you don't appreciate them. But for the love of heaven, get it through your head that the Republic can't allow itself the luxury of murdering a man like him . . ."

"If it's for its good, the Republic can do whatever it likes," Danton replied, somewhat annoyed.

"Please, Danton. You're an intelligent man. Don't deliver me little revolutionary sermons. The Catholic church still hasn't recovered from the stupid error it made when it ordered Giordano Bruno to be fried to death. Do all of you want to make the same mistake? The Republic of fraternity, and guillotining its most eminent scion. A fine example for history!"

"But . . ."

"Yes, I tell you. Even though it's painful to all of you to admit it: that odious farmer-general is the greatest man alive in France. A revolution that kills off its intelligentsia is committing suicide, and you know it very well . . ."

"Granted. Enough, Monsieur Rasero, you're making me feel like a child who needs correcting. Of course, I don't want that man killed either—maybe for reasons entirely different from yours, but we agree: Lavoisier shouldn't be killed. Be patient. We've already managed to shut Hébert up, and he was surely the most serious threat to your friend. We must now proceed with great finesse, however. Believe me, the situation couldn't be more delicate . . . even though I'm sure we'll get out of the fix we're in. The threat of foreign armies is only a bad memory now, you see; they instead have to worry about our forces. The waters are receding; I'm persuaded of that. Now all we have to do . . ." He lowered his voice almost to a whisper and told you by a look how dangerous what he was about to confide in you was. "Now all we have to do is keep a tight rein on certain rogues. So long as they're in the provinces cutting off heads as though they're melons and plundering with more abandon than Ali Baba, a sad future awaits the Revolution. They have to be done away with and . . . perhaps along with them, certain people who confuse the cause with a religion and have taken upon themselves the sacrificial duty of being its inquisitors. If we succeed in saving France from that threat, your friend Lavoisier will go free, I guarantee you that. If not . . . his head will roll, along with ours, my dear friend . . ."

"Citizen!" the lieutenant called to him. "Citizen Robespierre will receive you now. Please follow me."

The man rose to his feet with some difficulty and, clearly limping, started down a long corridor. Walking behind him, Rasero could watch the soldier's odd gait. His right leg, as rigid as a ruler, described a broad arc at each step; it resembled the leg of a compass. Perhaps the lieutenant had a feeling that he was under observation, because he stopped for a moment to allow the old man to catch up with him and then said to him, without the slightest sign of taking offense, "It's a souvenir of the tenth of August. Right here, in the Tuileries, you know. I got it from the caress of cannon shot from the Swiss Guard. All I heard was the explosion, boom! and there I was on the ground, wallowing like a pig. The bone splintered just above my knee. How it hurt me! I lay for almost an hour right in the line of fire. That they didn't put a bayonet through my breast shows there must be a God in heaven. In the end, when the fracas was over, they dragged me to a garden, and right there on the grass, good Gouret, with a knife that could scare you half to death just looking at it, removed the splinters of bone. I swear by Christ that I thought I'd die of the pain—even though I'd drunk a whole bottle of brandy. A lot of good it did me! To make a long story short, when I felt the knife scraping the bone, I passed out. When I came to, the first thing I saw was that rascal Gouret, with a big grin on his face, holding the splinter between his fingers. Do you know what caused it? A nail half an inch long! Everybody knows that those dolts didn't have any ammunition left. So I've been lame ever since, but still alive and wagging my tail. I owe that to Gouret, and that's the pure and simple truth. He's my buddy, you know what I mean? I love him like a brother. Oh, bless those hands of his! Nobody handles a knife better than he does."

"Is he a surgeon?" Rasero asked, intrigued. He found it hard to imagine a sawbones among those who attacked the Tuileries.

"Gouret? I should say not! If he'd been a doctor, I'm sure I wouldn't be here telling you all this. A doctor would have killed me, or if I was lucky, he would have cut off my leg. They're asses. Gouret, though, is the best butcher in Les Halles. Well, he used to be, because now he's a captain in the national guard. Who better than him to put you under the knife?"

"Quite true."

At the end of the corridor was a swinging door. On either side, a soldier was standing guard. When the pair of them saw the lieutenant coming, they stood at attention and saluted him. The man knocked on the door, opened it and said in a very loud voice, "Citizen Fausto Rasero is with me."

"Very well, show him in," a voice said from inside.

When Rasero entered the room, he saw Maximilien Robespierre in front of him. He was saying good-bye to a young man standing with him. Robespierre put both hands on the young man's shoulders and brought his face close to his to say something in his ear. When he finished, without taking his hands from his shoulders, he kissed him on both cheeks. Finally, he lowered his arms and took his friend's right hand between his, and then clapped him on the back paternally. He said to him out loud, "Be very careful, Louis-Antoine."

"Don't worry, Maximilien. Everything will turn out all right."

Rasero had recognized Saint-Just. He detested that man. He could never forget his wrathful speech at the Convention, in which the Jacobin, full of hatred and cruelty, demanded the blood of Danton, of Camille Desmoulins, and of his Michel. Saint-Just looked like a Caligula or a priest of Baal. This man isn't going to stop till there's not a single Frenchman still alive, Rasero thought as he listened to him.

"Are we going to let them, citizens—are we going to allow them to destroy our handiwork . . . ?"

"No!" came the answer from the Girondins sitting in the Plain. In fact, the cretins were half-dead with fear. "Well, then, they must be done away with! You must understand, citizens, that nowadays hesitation is treason, tepid reactions are treason, indulgence is treason, pity is treason . . ."

Saint-Just turned toward the door. Rasero avoided his eyes. He felt a profound queasiness in the pit of his stomach. He wondered whether he'd be able to restrain himself, to keep himself from spitting in that swine's face when he passed by him. Luckily for him, Saint-Just went out another door at the far end of the room. Relieved, Rasero felt his queasiness pass, though not altogether, for he had no great liking for Robespierre either—far from it.

"Come on in, marquis. I'm very pleased to see you."

"Good evening, citizen."

"Do sit down," Robespierre said, pointing to some armchairs upholstered in damask that were positioned around a little round table in one corner. "Please forgive me for making you wait so long, but you must understand that matters of state are very time-consuming."

"Yes, I understand."

But that "*you must* understand . . . ," Rasero thought. Every time that man speaks, it's an order. Maybe given in a subtle or even elegant way, but it's still an order . . .

"Will you take some wine? You must try it; it's exquisite."

Without waiting for a reply, he poured out two glasses of white wine. Slowly, he settled himself comfortably in the armchair, took one of the glasses and clinked it gently against his guest's. "To your good health and for old time's sake!" he said. The look in his eyes was almost a smile.

"Well, then, marquis?"

Rasero cleared his throat. He was having trouble working up nerve to begin. It had never been easy for him to talk to that man, and it was even less so now, when the life of his beloved Antoine was at stake . . .

He met Robespierre at the beginning of the year '90. Rasero was in his studio, looking over a speech by Desmoulins that was going to be published in the next issue of his gazette, when Louise came in with a calling card in her hand.

"A gentleman wishes to speak with you," the woman said as she handed him the card.

"Maximilien Robespierre, Attorney," Rasero read. Maximilien Robed-in-Stone. Now there's a name for you! If that gentleman is as ridiculous as his name, we're in for it. Though, to tell the truth, it's the pot calling the kettle black. Fausto Hermenegildo Bare-Stick isn't such an elegant name either, I suppose . . .

But the caller wasn't dressed in stone. He was wearing a dark-colored frock coat, well cut, and knee breeches with very tight hose below them. His wig, clean and powdered, really suited him. He was one of the very few people that absurd headdress didn't make look ridiculous. Impeccably neat, with refined manners, of medium build, with a pale complexion dotted with light freckles, a broad forehead, though slightly receding, and light brown eyes, small but penetrating and alert, the man looked like a porcelain figurine. Rasero remembered seeing him several times at the Assembly and at the Jacobins' club. He had also heard him delivering a speech. It wasn't anything extraordinary. The man was stiff and too fastidious about his selection of words, with the result that every so often it took him unbearably long to find the right one. Meanwhile some of his hearers took to whispering among themselves, and many others were frankly yawning. Robespierre, undaunted, went on with his improvised speech, and despite the obvious lack of interest on the part of his listeners, didn't stop until he had finished every last word of it. That poor attorney has no business on a rostrum from which men like Mirabeau, Danton, Barnave, and Talleyrand frequently speak, Rasero said to himself as he listened. Although from his looks and his demeanor, anyone would have thought he was a moderate, in the Assembly he always sat on the left side and belonged to the group of the most radical Jacobins, according to what Desmoulins said at the time.

Rasero invited him to sit down and offered him a glass of brandy. The man took the merest sip of it, fixed his myopic little eyes on the Malagan's face, and said solemnly, "Monsieur Rasero. First off, allow me to extend to you an expression of the profound satisfaction it gives me to have the honor of meeting you . . ."

Good God, Rasero thought, a bit sarcastically and completely taken aback.

"Thank you very much, sir," he managed to answer. "But tell me, how may I be of service to you?"

Without setting his pompous and affected style aside for even one second, Robespierre explained to the Malagan the reason for the visit. It so happened that, for a long time now, "since my most tender youth came into flower . . . ," the attorney had felt a profound admiration for the works of the Swiss thinker Jean-Jacques Rousseau:

"I can state to you, marquis, that without exaggeration Rousseau has been the most intimate companion that I have had in all the twenty years of my life . . ." And now that the inhabitants of his native Artois "have bestowed upon me the lofty honor of naming me their representative in the Assembly of the States General," he wanted to take advantage of his stay in Paris to "gather together all the information possible concerning the life of that great man, for I have the intention of writing his biography—a biography that must be meticulously factual and truthful without conceding one tittle to emotion or sentimentality . . ." The investigation he was pursuing had led him to the door of Fausto Rasero's house, for he had learned somewhere that the Swiss philosopher had spent several days there. "If you would be so kind as to answer a few questions for me regarding that visit, believe me that you would be doing me an immense favor . . . ," Robespierre said as he took a memorandum book and a lead pencil out of his frock coat.

"With great pleasure. Though I must warn you that my memory is not very good and all that was a long time ago."

Anxiously, the attorney began questioning him: "In what year did Rousseau visit your house?"

"The first time? . . . In '57, I believe."

"You believe?" Robespierre responded very seriously. "Aren't you certain?"

"Yes, it was in the summer of '57."

"Hmm . . . that is correct. I have it right here: it must have been in August of 1757," he said, pleased, after looking through his notes. "And did he come by himself or was someone with him? . . ."

His questions followed one upon the other for more than two hours. Rasero answered as best he could, although he was unable to understand what importance could possibly be attached to the fact that Rousseau salted his food heavily or sparingly, that oysters gave him indigestion, that he always walked on the right side of streets, or that he made sure that the bed he was going to sleep in faced west. This is certainly going to be a minute biography! Rasero said to himself. At this rate, it'll take more years to write than Rousseau lived . . .

Despite the many questions that remained unanswered, the attorney seemed satisfied. "Ah, Monsieur Rasero! You have no idea of how valuable this has been for me. Believe me, everything you've told me is going to be very useful to me. Now, if you will allow me, I'd like to ask one final question: What did you, who had the enormous privilege of being on intimate terms with Jean-Jacques Rousseau, think of him as a human being? What impression did you have of him as a person?"

As he was to do four years later, Rasero cleared his throat and reflected for a good while before answering. He knew that his reply, if it was candid, was not going to please the attorney at all. He found him so enthusiastic, so engrossed in the study of his idol, that he did not wish to introduce a bitter note into the project. Besides, Robespierre surely would not believe anything unfavorable he might say about Rousseau. All he'd do was earn his enmity, for it was evident that this man wasn't ready to accept the slightest criticism of Rousseau, however objective and truthful he wanted his study to be. Rasero thought he had hit on an ingenious way out: he spoke to him at length and with great enthusiasm about the writings of the Swiss thinker. This wasn't hard: Rasero really did admire his work. Robespierre listened to him with satisfaction, concentrating hard. Every so often he nodded his head, having taken a note, so that his informant would go on. But Robespierre was no dummy. As soon as Rasero finished, he pressed on: "And what about the man himself? You've spoken to me at length about his work, but you've said very little about him. Several persons I've interviewed have told me that he was a little difficult to get along with. He himself admits as much in his *Confessions.* Was he really as disagreeable as people say?"

Rasero could contain himself no longer: "*Much more* disagreeable. To be frank, he was unbearable. Nothing ever satisfied him. If a person tried to give a helping hand, he suspected at once that the gesture was motivated by self-interest . . . 'Suspected' is the proper word. That man spent his life suspecting everything and everybody . . ."

Unburdened, Rasero began cataloging the defects of the Swiss philosopher. Robespierre kept looking at him, very serious. Nothing in his facial expression betrayed that he was angry. This man is very good at hiding his emotions, Rasero thought, nettled by his own willingness to put up with the attorney, and thus inclined to intensify his criticism until it became a veritable philippic. Robespierre remained to all appearances unfazed. Only when Rasero mentioned the regrettable matter of Rousseau's children could he see in the attorney's face a symptom of anger that escaped his mastery: a vein in his left temple began to pulse wildly. At this point, Rasero stopped: "But despite everything, he was a great man. Lives disappear and works remain, sir, and Rousseau bequeathed us an immense body of work."

The vein stopped pulsing, and Robespierre counterattacked: "It's a shame someone as intelligent as you was incapable of discovering the person, so tender and so good, hiding behind a mask of unfriendliness and misanthropy. It's enough to read his *Confessions* to understand him . . ."

That's quite a work, all right, Rasero thought, but he didn't have the will to embark upon an argument that, all in all, didn't interest him in the least. Before he bade his guest good-bye, his eyes searched the shelves of the bookcase, and finally he removed a hefty volume he found there. "It's a souvenir of Rousseau that I value highly," he lied, "but I know you'll appreciate it even more than I . . ."

It was a first edition of *The Social Contract.* On the flyleaf, Rousseau had written,

For Marquis Fausto Rasero,
An upright, wise man and a kind host.
Most gratefully,
J.-J. Rousseau

Robespierre's eyes shone with delight on reading that signature, "in his very own hand!" He ventured a smile and with warm feelings took the Malagan's right hand in both his own.

"Sir, I'll never know how to repay you for this. But you can be sure that, from this day on, you may count on having an unconditional friend."

His new and "unconditional" friend visited him fairly often. Although the old man seemed unable to realize Rousseau's grandeur, Robespierre appreciated his experience and wisdom. He always listened well to the interpretations the Malagan put on events, and although he did not always follow them, he took his advice seriously.

During the spring of '92, Robespierre came to the town house in the rue St-Jacques almost every day. Those were very hard times for the former deputy. (When the constitution had been drawn up and made public, in September, 1791, the people's representatives crowned their work by passing, as Robespierre himself had proposed, a law prohibiting the deputies from being reelected for the following legislative term.) Practically all the factions in the new Legislative Assembly—the monarchists, the moderates who belonged to Madame Roland's circle of Girondins, and the radical Montagnards—agreed, although for very different reasons, to launch France upon a war against the European powers. Robespierre was one of the few radicals who stubbornly opposed this. His position ended up leaving him isolated from his group. His speeches at the Jacobins' club commanded less and less interest, and several times he had to interrupt a speech when it was drowned out by jeering. He stopped insisting; he realized that the times were against him. His chance would come. Meanwhile, he applied himself to his study of Rousseau and went on visiting the Spaniard, in whom he found the consolation of knowing that he was understood, for Rasero too was unambiguously against the war. (War again, Rasero. It wasn't seven months since France got its first constitution, and already they were avid to try it out by waging another war. And you had come to believe that this revolution would end wars forever! What nonsense! Man can't measure the value of his ideas if they aren't tempered by a bloodbath. It hadn't been three years since the Bastille, and already your old certainties were regaining ground. What was that Revolution going to accomplish in the end? It was only going to make possible that odious future which had been tormenting you almost since you began to reason. Acts *make* the future, Rasero; they don't change it. Now, with the new tricolor flag, the French armies were going to rip open the bellies of the Austrians in Flanders. Barely a year before, in January of '91, during the next to last vision you had had, you saw a frightful war where men didn't even play a part—it was a battle waged by machines, Rasero—except to be crushed to death like rats.)

Rasero had grown accustomed to Robespierre's evening visits. He almost missed him when he didn't appear in the late afternoon ready to have a coffee and talk for a couple of hours about the Revolution, the war, and Rousseau—in that order. By dint of hearing his caller talk about the Swiss philosopher, Rasero came to see Rousseau in Robespierre. Jean-Jacques had been much better looking, infinitely more manly, but their vehemence, their unparalleled arrogance, the absolute conviction that what they thought was the only right thing, their profound contempt for others made them brothers in spirit. The Malagan once again found himself with an old philosopher replicated in a young revolutionary. He had always thought that Rousseau was much more dangerous than either Voltaire or Diderot; his person and his ideas were more dangerous because, of the three, the Swiss thinker was the only one who'd never bend. His intelligence had not imbibed the generous Cartesian spirit of doubt; rather, it had been molded by the hard, rigid thinking of Luther and Calvin. Rousseau was a great critic certainly, but he never mistrusted his own ideas; unlike the other two, he had a blind faith in them, and that is always dangerous.

The same thing was true of Robespierre. Despite his isolation, despite being ignored, despite finding very few who took his ideas seriously, he did not doubt for one second that he was right. "If everyone in the world were against me, the only thing that would mean was that everyone in the world was mistaken. And you must believe me, there would be nothing strange about that . . . ," Robespierre said to him once. As Rasero listened to him, he could swear that he had heard exactly the same thing from the mouth of Rousseau.

A year later, in that terrible '93, when the Republic had triumphed and the people of Paris saw the head of the last of the Capetians fall at the feet of the proud statue of Liberty—which now occupied the spot where the statue of his grandfather, Louis XV, had stood flanked by the four virtues—the Terror, on the arm of its lover, the towering guillotine, settled over France. Robespierre's chance came then. Of course, he stopped visiting the old man; his advice was no longer relevant to him. The poor old man despised the guillotine as much as he did war, when that fine instrument was nothing but a pair of enormous shears to prune the garden of France, lopping off the diseased branches that threatened to ruin the fruits of the revolutionary tree. Robespierre, a merciless gardener, ended up lopping off healthy branches in his zeal to do away with the malady. Driven out of his mind, perhaps, he was determined to cut down the very tree itself should he reach the point of deciding that the rot in it left no hope for its recovery. In the final analysis, he, the great gardener, along with his helper, his adored Saint-Just, and the good people of France were the only ones who deserved to go on living. All the others, rich and poor, nobles and commoners, all selfish and corrupt, were an accursed disease, a perennial threat to his garden. They had to be pruned away, pruned away . . .

And so, in the name of the people of France, he saw to it that the real people, that is to say, the flesh-and-blood inhabitants of the country, began to be exterminated—many, a great many, of them, faithful revolutionaries, tireless fighters against the ancien régime, veterans of the storming of the Bastille, of the Champ-de-Mars, of the Tuileries, and of the wars against the foreigners on the frontiers and in the ports. The real enemies of the Revolution, the true bad weeds, had fled long before; they were traitorously plotting against the Republic as they danced gay minuets at the courts of Belgium and Germany.

But the revolutionaries, moderates and extremists alike, ended their lives stretched out on a plank, where a sharp-edged steel blade sliced off their heads.

Toward the beginning of '94, there was almost no one left who could stop that man. Death, but above all fear, had wiped out all resistance. Danton was the last of the great revolutionaries to try to put an end to the slaughter. A loyal ally of Robespierre's for a long time, and as convinced as he was that it was necessary to impose the strictest of order to save the Republic, he finally realized that his confederate was not going to stop until not a single Frenchman was left alive. He tried to convince him: the massacre had to end, or everything would go to hell, he told him. Anyhow, they were killing whores and petty thieves but leaving the real swine alive, the ones who, paradoxically, were working the guillotine. But these were also—and Danton knew it very well—Robespierre's most fervent supporters. The hypocrites appeared before him under the aspect of irreproachable, incorruptible revolutionaries like their leader. But as soon as he turned his back, they robbed, killed, and plundered with diabolical skill. "In the end, they'll do us all in," Danton had said to him. But Robespierre wouldn't listen. For a long time now—perhaps from the very start—his ears had refused to hear one word of criticism; only flattery and adulation pleased him. He no longer saw only himself but France in the mirror, and anyone who dared to cloud that image, anyone, even Danton, whom he so dearly loved and respected, was a traitor. What the advice of his friend aroused in Robespierre was suspicion. He started to suspect Danton, as he already suspected all of France. (Ah, he and Rousseau were so much alike!) With deep sorrow, convinced that he was making a sacrifice of the magnitude of the one that Abraham made when his God required it of him, Robespierre decided to close, once and for all, that mouth which, with its impressive booming voice, tormented him and threatened the security of the *patrie.*

Rasero tried in vain to see Robespierre after that fateful morning when the guards of the Convention had ransacked Marcel Gautier's printshop and confiscated nearly a hundred leftover copies of the gazette that Danton's moderation and Desmoulins' boldness and Michel's cooperation had produced, and when the printer and his son had been taken to the prison in the town hall without hindrance by the shouts, threats, screams, weeping, and even blows of Annette. He went to the rue St-Honoré, where the leader lived in lodgings provided by the Duplay family. They told him there that Robespierre was ill and unable to receive anyone. He next wrote his former caller a desperate message. It was futile: he received no reply. He went to that house three days running; he waited for hours. No one would give him the time of day. Meanwhile, in the Revolutionary Tribunal, not even the fiery eloquence of Fouquier-Tinville, the public prosecutor of the Republic, could mask even slightly the brutal infamy that was being perpetrated against Danton and his *indulgents.* The man defended himself like a wounded lion. Even the president of the tribunal had trouble several times controlling his hands when, spontaneously, they moved to applaud the powerful speech the hero of the tenth of August delivered in defense of himself and his comrades. Nonetheless, the trial was a sham: the death sentence was signed long before the verdict was announced. Danton, the leafiest branch of the young tree of the Republic, would die. With this branch gone, what was left was a dead trunk.

No, Rasero, don't remember. Don't remember that horrible morning in March in the Place de la Révolution. Barely three months ago, Rasero: Annette going mad. Danton's hard, defiant face, more beautiful and impressive than you had seen it before. The lamentable state Camille Desmoulins was in. Like your old Voltaire, Desmoulins was unwilling to accept death: he was weeping like a baby and trembling worse than an epileptic, while Michel was averting his eyes, suffering to see his beloved ally reduced to such a state. Pale, scarcely even trembling, the lad behaved like a real man. If he wet his pants when he saw the blade come down on Camille's head, it was because of the pitcher of wine you gave him just before leaving for the square, which he drank in one swallow. But what a good thing it was that he wet his pants! This upset him a great deal, and his distress left no room in him for fear. When they laid him down on the plank, he roundly cursed God, his Son, Robespierre, and Saint-Just. "See you never! you cowards!" was the last thing he shouted, as he saw—he'd refused to be blindfolded—the executioner let the blade loose to fall on his neck. His father, good Marcel Gautier, whose only crime was to own the printshop where a gazette was printed that cast mild doubts on the wisdom of The Incorruptible, was beyond question the one who behaved best in the face of death. Not even Danton looked as serene. Although he made every effort to appear valiant and defiant, the big, robust man couldn't hide the agitation caused him by the thought that he was about to lose his life, he who loved it so. Marcel, however, showed nothing but scorn. Moving calmly and efficiently—and forcefully reminding you of Louis XVI's behavior in the very same situation—he settled himself comfortably on the plank, as though getting ready to take a nap . . . No, don't remember anything more, Rasero. Please. Diderot-Danton and Voltaire-Desmoulins died cruelly, and Rousseau-Robespierre cut a splendid figure by his absence. There was no way you could have got to see him, Rasero. Now, at any rate, he's deigned to receive you. Watch very carefully what you say, or you'll have to watch your dear Antoine lying facedown, awaiting the blade's swift blow.

"Well, marquis?"

"I know you're a very busy man, so I'll try to get straight to the point. Maximilien, sincerely, I believe that it's not a favor to the Republic when its best men are imprisoned and brought before the Tribunal . . ."

"I presume you're referring to Lavoisier." Rasero nodded. "I want you to know, marquis, that that man is under arrest not because he's a man of learning but because he was a farmer-general. You know very well the immense harm tax collectors have done France . . ."

"The only thing I know is that Antoine is an honest man. They've subjected him to two hearings, and not one ill-gotten louis has been unearthed. Nor does the penitential sanbenito of a traitor fit him. When all this began, he could very well have skipped out of France, the way so many others have done. But he didn't. He participated in the revolutionary movement with enthusiasm, as you know very well."

"On the side of the monarchists . . ."

"Of the constitutionalists, it would be more accurate to say, don't you think?"

"They're the same thing, marquis. They're traitors, all of them."

"For the love of God, Maximilien! Do you think everybody in France is a traitor? Lavoisier has never betrayed his country. Indeed, few men have done as much for it as he. Who do you think invented proper streetlighting and had it installed in the center of Paris, preventing God knows how many robberies, attacks, and murders? Who do you think invented the gunpowder our troops use to load the cartridges that have given them their overwhelming superiority over the armies of Europe? Who . . . ?"

"Marquis, who do you believe erected that odious wall which doomed thousands of Parisians to misery?"

"Many people, Lavoisier among them, it's true. But also a couple of brand-new deputies of the Plain, who doze off at Assembly sessions without daring to open their mouths or even yawn. Moreover, was that wall really such an abomination? It wasn't erected against the people of Paris, as you're aware. It was built to put a stop to the unbridled plundering that the bourgeois of the city were engaged in. I know from very reliable sources—and you, of course, must know much more about it than I do—that Monsieur Carnot is thinking very seriously of putting the customs barriers back up in order to control the trafficking and ensure that the government gets the revenue it's owed. Isn't that so?"

"This project is still only something under consideration."

"A project that will doubtless be carried out . . . But to return to our subject. You have to admit that the charges against Lavoisier are very flimsy."

"The charge of treason isn't flimsy."

"Treason again! So where do we stand exactly? Is he being tried as a farmer-general or as a traitor?"

"As both. Every tax collector is a traitor."

"Is that so? And why then are they going to allow three of those traitors to go free? And mind you, those three are true scoundrels. So why are they going to release them?"

Robespierre's eyes were riveted on his questioner. His priestly face showed less emotion than if it were a stone mask. Nonetheless, on hearing this last, the vein in his left temple began to pulse wildly.

"I haven't heard anything about that."

The Incorruptible, Rasero thought. He couldn't keep his contempt from showing in his eyes: "Don't you know, citizen? Well, you should find out; you have every means of doing so. Three malefactors are going to be set free; they won't even appear before the Tribunal. It's an open secret . . . But I didn't come to talk to you about them. Antoine . . ."

"Look, marquis, excuse me for interrupting you, but I don't see any reason for continuing this conversation. I believe you're wasting your time terribly and making me waste mine. Why come to me with all these stories? I can't be of help. I'm just a deputy of the Convention. If for the time being I take care of certain matters within the Committee, that doesn't mean very much. The Convention has arrested your friend and the Revolutionary Tribunal will try him. I have no hand in any of the business. In any case, I don't see why you're so concerned. If Lavoisier is as uncorrupted and honest as you say, they'll no doubt let him off . . . but it's the judge and the jury who'll have to decide. I'm only a bystander. So if you don't have anything else to discuss with me, allow me . . ."

They've decided to put him to death, Rasero thought. Antoine was right; there's no power on earth that can spare him from the guillotine . . . He stared at Robespierre. He saw his dark-colored coat, his shirt frills of white silk, his wig, so well fitting and powdered, his wide-open, arrogant eyes, and his mouth with those thin, delicate lips clamped tightly shut. There, perhaps, one could catch a subtle expression of hatred and contempt. Rasero, even more inexpressive than the deputy, felt his blood boil. Impotence, indignation, anger hit him in the pit of the stomach like a violent blow. Finally, he burst out, "No, I won't allow you anything, citizen. I now see plainly that Lavoisier is going to die on the guillotine. You've already arranged it. Yes, you. Whom are you trying to fool with your hypocrisy? I'm an old man, Robespierre, but I'm not an idiot. Antoine's life is in your hands, as is that of every living soul in France. You know that very well, and I imagine that nothing in the world can please you more. I know they're going to put Antoine to death, but at least you're going to listen to me. What happened, my friend, to your dreams, your ideals? Where in the devil is that French Republic you talked about with such enthusiasm just a couple of years ago? Do you know where it is today? In your imagination. That splendid republic of free and industrious men that you think you see every time you stroll down the Champs-Elysées, puffed up like a peacock and surrounded by your little court of worshipful minions, exists only in your imagination. Those people exist only inside your head. Outside . . . do you even know what's outside? Fear, fear and hatred, nothing else. My friend, you're destroying everything; your republic of free and indomitable men has turned into a reign of cowards and traitors. Those are the real traitors: all those who puff mightily to inflate your extraordinary vanity, all those hypocrites who make you feel like the Pericles of the eighteenth century. The Incorruptible. Bah! Maximilien, I doubt that there is anyone in France, in the whole world, who's more corrupt than you are. Me corrupt?! you think in surprise as you listen to me. I know that's what you think, even though you take refuge behind that impenetrable mask. Me corrupt? I, Maximilien Robespierre, who don't have more than two changes of clothes, who don't even have a house and furniture of my own, who haven't touched one single pound in the state treasury when there's nobody to keep me from it if I felt like it? Me corrupt, when I haven't deviated one inch from the thought of Jean-Jacques Rousseau, the greatest man who ever trod this earth? Me corrupt? Well, yes, my friend, you're a man who's completely corrupt. You haven't been corrupted by money, it's true, you're too worthy a man to be a venal one. Power, however, has corrupted you. No one has yet been born who, reaching power, is not corrupted, and you, my friend, are very far from being the exception. Indeed, you prove the rule better than others. You've acquired absolute power, a power that allows you to cut off lives, the way one snips wild flowers in the countryside. And that power has corrupted you absolutely—so absolutely that everything I'm saying to you is perfectly useless. The crazy old man, he's a traitor, you must be thinking. You can't be thinking anything else, since even your brains are corrupted. Your ears are no longer able to hear anything but praise. That's how corrupted you are! Though it's useless to ask you, think, think just a little. Was Danton really a traitor, or Brissot, or Madame Roland? Do you truly believe that they wanted to restore the old order? Do you truly believe that Lavoisier is a danger to the Republic? Ah, my friend! The only danger confronting the Republic is you yourself. And so I greatly fear that your own head is soon going to roll. And I say, 'I greatly fear,' because those who are going to do the deed are much worse than you are. It will be those Fouchés, those Barrases, those Talienses, that bunch of scoundrels that you yourself have armed so that they'd go out and sow terror and plunder without restraint the remotest corner of France. Those pigs will finish you off. And that is sad, very sad . . . but there won't be any way out, because nobody else is left; you've sent all the men who were worth anything off to the guillotine. Yes, all those who are now living in grand style in Belgium, in England, in Italy, and in Germany are going to come back—what doubt can there be of that? Perhaps one of the princes of the blood will see his dream of inheriting his unfortunate brother's crown fulfilled. I greatly fear that that is what's going to happen. And it can't be otherwise: they're the only ones still alive. There, I've come to the end of what I wanted to say. I'm going to leave you in peace now so that you can go on planning your executions, among which I hope there's room for me. I offer my head with the greatest of pleasure; believe me when

I say I want to spare myself from seeing the spectacle of yours falling. I advise you to send me to the guillotine, because I for my part am determined to do everything I can—although what an old man can do who has been left more to himself than Robinson Crusoe on his island is very little—to rescue this Revolution, if there's still anything to rescue. And you, of course, don't fit in with my plans . . ."

Robespierre listened to him without turning a hair. Had it not been for the pulsing of that vein in his temple, anyone might have thought that he was listening, with great concentration, to the complicated disquisition of a scientist.

"You have no idea, don Fausto, how much I regret that we have a very different view of things. It grieves me deeply to note that you've been the victim of those deadly ideas that are infecting France. It's a real shame; you could have been very useful to the Revolution . . . Even so, allow me to voice my respect for you and my unwavering decision to do everything in my power for you."

"Well, you now know what you must do. Let's see if you are capable of doing it well! . . . Good night, citizen."

"Good night, marquis . . ."

Rasero stayed awake all that night. He was giving careful thought to the steps he would have to take now that he knew his end was imminent. After having said what he had to Robespierre, his life was not worth a sol; he was certain of that. This did not cause him any anxiety whatever; on the contrary, he felt profoundly relieved. In the end, he had found a fairly dignified way of abandoning this filthy world. His head, along with Antoine's and that of so many men he had been fond of, would finally roll to the feet of the statue of Liberty. But before that happened, he wanted to leave Annette and her daughter well protected. He wrote several letters to relatives and acquaintances in Spain (when the devil would they get there?) and went over his will. Though he found everything in order, he feared that, because it had been notarized in the days of the monarchy, the authorities would refuse to recognize it. He therefore decided to rewrite it from beginning to end and take it to a notary of the Republic the following day. Fortunately, he had taken the precaution five years before of sending a copy of the old will to Spain. It must be in the safekeeping of Francisco, the eldest son of his cousin José, whose honesty he did not doubt in the slightest. Even so, Annette's future was a matter of concern to him. The one sure thing he could offer her was a pouchful of louis that he kept in his study. He was willing it to her, but the house risked being seized by the government, along with all the goods inside. And, even though Francisco would doubtless help her, Annette could have many problems when she tried to take over the old mansion in Málaga and the lands and rights that he was also bequeathing her. After giving the matter prolonged consideration, he found a solution that seemed exactly right to him, just as dawn broke. It was as though the rising sun had also shed its light on the inside of his head. He put on his best clothes and carefully tidied himself up. When he was ready, he went upstairs to Annette's. "Annette, dear, get yourself into your best clothes, and tell your daughter to do so too. We're going out."

Annette, who had lost a great deal of weight and had dark circles under her eyes and hair that had turned almost white, seemed to have aged twenty years in the last six months. Her great energy, her liveliness, even her bad temper, had disappeared. The guillotine had snatched them away. She looked like a sick and bored old lady, like a Carmelite who had been cloistered for fifty years. If she went on living, it was doubtless because of Véronique, her daughter; the idea of abandoning her in this hell that France had turned into horrified her.

"Where are we going, don Fausto?"

"To the town hall."

The moment she heard that place referred to, the woman felt a violent shiver run down her back.

"Don't be frightened, Annette. It's not for anything serious."

"Then why are we going there?"

"To get married, Annette."

The woman opened her eyes so wide she almost tore the folds of her eyelids. Can don Fausto have gone mad? she wondered.

"But, don Fausto . . ."

"Come on, hurry. I'll explain to you on the way . . . Ah!" he said as he took a heavy leather pouch out of his frock coat. "Take good care of this money, Annette—as though it were your life. It's all we have left."

They made the trip to the town hall on foot. Rasero had sold his carriage a long time before—it was no time for such luxuries—and at that hour it was no use thinking of hailing a coach for hire. Anyway, as he had told her, he wanted to take advantage of the walk to explain to the good woman his reasons for wanting to marry her.

"Look, Annette, I suspect that very soon they're going to haul me to the guillotine. Yesterday I said certain things to Robespierre that he's not going to forgive till a month with thirty-two days in it comes along . . ." The woman was about to burst into tears. "Stop that, woman. If you're as fond of me as you say you are, you ought to be glad that this is happening. Don't you realize that I'm completely fed up? What pleasure do you think life can be for this miserable old man after what's happened? In two or three days they're going to guillotine the last friend I have left. How glad I'd be not to have to experience the horror of seeing him die! But it's a solace to think that I'll be following him very soon . . . You and Véronique are the only persons I regret leaving behind, my dear, and that's why we must get married. Listen closely: when they come for me, leave Paris at once. Don't try to do anything to save me; it would be completely useless, and with that temper of yours, I greatly fear that you'd end up sharing a prison cell with me. Don't try to do anything, is that clear?" The woman nodded her head. "Promise me that." Annette promised. "Well, as I was saying, once they arrest me, the two of you go to Troyes. With the money I gave you this morning you can get along very well at your brother's. When you're there, wait for things to calm down. It won't be long before Robespierre is overthrown. Then, little by little, the waters will recede. In all likelihood they'll seize everything I possess in France. Don't try to get it back; it'd be useless, and to tell the truth, it doesn't amount to much. What the two of you must do, as soon as things begin to settle, is go off to Spain, by boat or by coach, but as soon as you can. In Madrid, you're to look up my nephew Francisco." He gave her a letter. "Take good care of it. In it are the names and addresses of the people you must see in Spain. They'll help you. What I'm leaving you is sufficient. You can live comfortably; you won't lack for anything . . ."

The woman listened to him with full attention. If she had heard this a year ago, she would doubtless have burst into tears and wept like a Mary Magdalene. But too many things had happened; she even doubted that tears could still come to her eyes. Besides, she understood the old man. He'd suffered enough already; why persist in living? She herself, if it weren't for her daughter, would go spit in the face of the man robed in stone, so that he'd do her the favor of dispatching her to the next world.

The ceremony was simple and quick. Republican austerity at least freed them from the unbearable protocol of a religious wedding. The secretary simply recorded the marriage in the civil register and the judge—a young man who looked like a village lawyer—read three stupid paragraphs and declared them man and wife in the eyes of the laws of the French Republic. Annette and the Malagan put their rings on their fingers—the same rings Rasero had bought thirty years before in the rue St-Honoré and had kept in his little coffer, awaiting the right day to surprise Mariana, a day that never came—kissed each other on both cheeks, and left the judge's chamber as man and wife. The hired witnesses yawned indifferently. Only Véronique seemed touched and happy. With tears in her eyes, she embraced and kissed her mother and her stepfather. They went to a café at the Palais Royal to celebrate the event and from there went to a notary's office, where after waiting for more than three hours, Rasero managed to have his new will officially endorsed. They went back home as dusk was falling. Annette took the time to prepare kidneys in white wine, the favorite dish of her brand-new husband.

The following morning, Rasero went to visit Lavoisier. His trial was imminent, for he had already been transferred to the Conciergerie. Rasero had a long wait before he was able to see him, since many friends and relatives of the accused had arrived before him. When he was finally able to go in, they let him stay barely ten minutes with the chemist. Lavoisier looked serene and resigned. "There's no help for it, Fausto dear; we were able to get the better of the phlogiston theory, but not of the Committee of Public Safety. Politicians have much harder heads than our colleagues, and that's saying a lot," he remarked to Rasero, doing his best to smile.

"Don't give up hope, Antoine. There's still the trial. If those fools have even a pinch of common sense, you'll get to go free. You'll see."

"Ah, Fausto! Asking those men to use their common sense is like asking a cow to fly. I'm grateful for your good intentions in trying to keep up my morale, but believe me, I've no need for that. The die is already cast, and I'm resigned to my fate. It's not that I'm a brave man or that my life doesn't matter to me. It's just that I, at least, have a little common sense. If there isn't any way of saving my life—and there isn't—I don't see the point of collapsing, of spending the few hours of life I have left lamenting my fate. You know what? Just last night I was thinking about you. I remembered Seton the Cosmopolite, and I couldn't help being amused by the thought that I'm going to end my days in much the same way as he. That pleased me, for I've always had a great liking for that character . . . Who knows? Maybe he really did discover the philosopher's stone, eh?"

Rasero found himself unable to answer him. He had always admired the chemist, but never as much as that day. Lavoisier took advantage of their short time together to ask his friend to do him several favors. He handed him a list of names of colleagues, both in France and in England, and asked him to write them in order to pass on certain information related to science which he hadn't had the opportunity of sending them himself. "I've also asked my wife to do this, but I greatly fear that those wretches are capable of sending her to prison . . ." And so the ten minutes went by like a sigh. What with the names of chemists and substances, formulas, recipes, and methods, there was scarcely time left to bid each other farewell, much less to grow sad. ". . . Explain to them, please, why I regard that nomenclature as being more precise. It's very important that the names of the elements and compounds be simple for all of us, no matter what language we speak. That's why I believe that the use of Latin roots is best . . . ," Lavoisier was saying when the guard interrupted them. Rasero was ordered to leave.

"Farewell, my friend," Rasero said. "I promise you I'll send the letters. I don't ask you to have courage, because I see that you have more than enough."

They gave each other a strong embrace and would have remained in each other's arms for a long time if the guard hadn't brusquely drawn the Malagan away.

In the passageway, Rasero met Auger de Villes, a cousin of Lavoisier's. The man was sitting on a bench and looked much more downcast than his relative. Rasero had spoken with him on a number of occasions. He was a young man of refined manners and a pleasant disposition; Lavoisier was very fond of him. Rasero greeted him and sat down alongside him.

"Have you seen him? How is he?" the young man asked anxiously.

"He's fine. Very calm. Your cousin, sir, is a great man."

"He certainly is! Ah, Monsieur Rasero! How can they possibly commit an act of such barbarity? The world has gone mad . . ."

"I greatly fear that it's always been mad."

"Look, read this. It's a letter Antoine sent me last night. Read it, and tell me if it's right to kill a man like that."

He held the paper out to him and could control himself no longer: he collapsed into tears. Rasero read the letter. It was truly moving; one had only to read it to realize what sort of man the revolution was preparing to devour:

> I have had a rather long career, above all a happy one, and I believe that regret over my death and perhaps a certain fame will accompany the memory of me. What more could I have wished for? The events in which I find myself involved may spare me from old age. I shall die in the prime of my life; that is another of the advantages I must add to the ones I have enjoyed. If I am experiencing certain painful feelings, it is because I have not been able to look after my family—it is owing to the fact that I have been stripped of everything and am unable to give either her or you any token of my affection and gratitude. It is hence true that the practice of all the social virtues, the services given to the country, and a career usefully devoted to furthering the progress of the arts and human knowledge are not enough to preserve one from a sinister end and to keep one from dying like a person who has been judged guilty! I am writing to you today, because perhaps tomorrow they will not allow me to do so, and because in these last moments it is a sweet consolation to turn my thoughts to you and to the persons whom I love. Don't forget me when you meet those who are concerned about me; may this letter be for them too. It is surely the last one I shall be writing to you . . .

Rasero made a great effort not to burst into tears too. He consoled Auger as best he could—more than his cousin, it was he who looked like the one sentenced to the guillotine—and left the Conciergerie feeling revulsion. Why are we such monsters? he wondered as he walked aimlessly about the back streets of Paris. The most intelligent species in creation is also the most pitiless and bloodthirsty. "Do you know why we kill our neighbors?" he remembered Voltaire asking him once. "Because we're the only animal that has an awareness of death. We know, therefore, that life is the most precious thing we have. So then, what better punishment can we inflict on our enemies than to take their life from them? We are human enough to be conscious of death, and beastly enough to bring it about without regard for our brothers . . ." We are, we have been . . . and we will be . . . much more animal than human. And precisely because we're intelligent, we're the worst monsters in creation: we're conscious of what we're doing, and yet that doesn't stop us. In the final analysis, Rousseau was right; as we have gone on honing our intelligence, the only thing we've accomplished is to make our savagery more sophisticated. The only thing that distinguishes us from primitive peoples is our ability to hate and to kill, which is infinitely superior to theirs. Murderers . . . we never have been, nor will we ever be, anything else . . .

After roaming about for a couple of hours, Rasero went to the studio of the painter Jacques-Louis David. The studio was bustling; David, with his apprentices, was in the habit of working on five or more works at the same time.

"Monsieur Rasero, how pleased I am to see you!" the painter said as he embraced him warmly. "Look, allow me to show you something. Just this minute . . ."

"Pardon me," Rasero interrupted him. "But I'm very short of time . . ."

He explained to him in a few words the reason for his visit: he had decided to give the artist all the paintings, sculptures, and engravings he possessed. (He had decided this the night before. He was certain they were going to confiscate his possessions; he wanted to keep his paintings at least out of the hands of those louts. It was then that he thought of David. Of all the people he knew, he was doubtless the one who would most appreciate those works and take the best care of them.)

"All of them?" David asked, unable to believe his ears. In his mind he saw, in all its splendor, the superb portrait by Velázquez that he had seen at the Spaniard's house several times and had never tired of praising.

"All of them. This document," he answered him as he held it out to him, "makes the transfer to you legal. Everything is in order. I beg you to send someone to get them immediately. I greatly fear that the government is going to confiscate everything I possess; if the authorities arrive before you do, you won't get any of them."

"Confiscate your possessions? . . . Why, Monsieur Rasero?"

"There isn't any time left for explanations. The only thing I can tell you is that I'm certain that the Convention is going to detach my head from my body any minute now. So for the love of heaven, hurry up. I've time to ask only one favor of you. Promise that when they take me away to prison, you'll do everything possible to protect the two women who live in my house. They're my wife and daughter."

"Set your mind at rest, don Fausto. I'll do anything in my power on their behalf. But . . ."

Rasero didn't give the artist time to finish what he was saying; he embraced him and left the studio. He went on walking through the city for some time, watching dusk fall as he nursed his rancors. He reached his town house after dark. There were two guards at the door. They've already come, he thought with relief, although the next minute he began to worry. Can David have sent for the art works in time? . . .

The men were waiting inside the house. They explained to him that they were delegates from the Convention. Rasero offered them a glass of brandy. He couldn't hide his smile on seeing the bare walls.

"Citizen," the one who looked like the person in charge said. He was an ill-shaved man of about fifty, with no more than four teeth in his mouth. "The Convention has entrusted me with the task of delivering this document to you. Please sign here. It's your attestation that you've received the notification."

Rasero signed. The men drained their glasses and looked eagerly at the Malagan. He offered them another drink. They happily held out their glasses. Not another word was spoken. Once the bottle was empty, the men bade him good-bye.

"What? Aren't you taking me with you?"

"Kindly read the notification, citizen. Good night."

Rasero read the document. Heaven only knows what thoughts must have gone through Robespierre's tortuous mind, but he had decided to spare the Malagan's life: the Convention, concerned about the suspicious behavior of citizen Fausto H. Rasero, and in view of his foreign origins, had decided that, before the aforementioned citizen could cause the Republic any problems, he was to leave the country. He was given forty-eight hours to leave the city and a month to leave France. In the event that these orders were not obeyed, the suspect would be arrested wherever he was found and brought before the Revolutionary Tribunal. His possessions were temporarily confiscated; all he could take with him from Paris were his personal effects, in no more than two trunks. He could, in addition, be accompanied by up to two persons. Enclosed was a safe-conduct, signed in Robespierre's own hand, so that he could pass without hindrance through the tollgates, customs booths, and barriers in the regions where fighting was going on.

Rasero was extremely annoyed. "The worst thing that can happen when a person wants to die," he remembered having read once, "is to desire death. Being treacherous by nature, it never obeys the wishes of one who summons it . . ." How true that is, damn it all! For a moment he thought of disobeying the orders of the Convention and remaining in Paris so that it would carry out its threat, but then he thought of Annette and Véronique, and it didn't seem right to abandon them when he had a chance to look after them. With resignation, he began making preparations to leave.

Two days later, shortly before dawn, Fausto Rasero and the two women climbed into the carriage. It had been fifty-four years—a whole lifetime—since he had arrived in this city. Young, almost a child, happy, full of illusions, he intended to conquer the most beautiful city in the world . . . Now he was leaving it, and his life, incredible as it seemed, wasn't yet over. It was cruel to make him go on living. Perhaps God was taking his revenge because he had always refused to believe in him; perhaps that skinny man still hadn't tired of dreaming of Rasero, or perhaps Rasero's madness made him believe that he was still alive when he'd never even existed. Be that as it may, he was now leaving this old city, where there was nothing left but bitter memories. He was beginning the journey back to the old mansion in the calle Miaja. There, Rasero would be able to be at peace; there death awaited him. There, finally, he'd forget and be forgotten . . .

The carriage was leaving the last suburbs of the great city behind, when the sun, red and radiant, appeared in the east. Rasero looked at the enormous red platter, his attention held by it. His friend Lavoisier, lying face downward on the guillotine, was also watching it. It has the color of chromate, they both thought. A great live-oak tree hid the sun from the Malagan for an instant, the same instant at which the steel blade prevented the greatest chemist born in France from continuing to gaze at it . . .

IX
Goya

Málaga, July, 1812

That morning, as she had been doing for a long time now, Annette entered her husband's bedroom and drew back the heavy dark flannel curtains so as to allow the bright sunlight to enter. She opened the window, and a fresh breeze, suffused with the subtle aroma of seawater, invaded the room. As always, Fausto Rasero was already awake. Sitting in his old rocking chair, he allowed the fresh air to enter his lungs. Leaning on the windowsill, the woman felt the sun's warm caress on her face as she listened to the joyous trilling of the birds, which now and again mingled with the sounds of the peddlers who were beginning to appear on the streets: the hoarse voice of the old-clothes dealer, the cheery call of the fish vendor offering his sardines for sale, and the high-pitched whistle of the knife grinder.

"Ah! it's going to be a splendid day, don Fausto. What would you say to a little stroll along the Alameda late this afternoon? A fine outing, don't you think? We'll go after your nap, I promise you. I'd better get a move on, though, and tidy up the house. It's a mess! Véronique is going to come by with her husband and children. I'm dying to see those little rascals! It's almost a month now since they've been here. To me, it's been like a century."

Annette spoke without taking her eyes off the street, so that the sound that reached Rasero's ears was barely a murmur. The man took a long look at his wife. Although she was now close to seventy, she was still a good-looking woman; in fact, if she had been just a bit more coquettish, he could have claimed she was just over fifty and nobody would have doubted it, she was so well preserved. Her robust flesh still looked firm and solid, and the pretty rosy color of it gave her a very lively look. What could he have been thinking as he watched his wife? Perhaps on seeing that ruddy flesh and that white hair pulled back in a neat chignon, there came to mind the cherished image of his beloved Angustias, who, in his memory, was becoming something like a darker Annette with olive skin and pitch-black hair, a sort of gypsy Annette. No, Annette was, rather, his Angustias with a lighter, rosier complexion; she was his French Angustias. Or perhaps on contemplating his wife's round, ample, still-firm buttocks, Rasero remembered the first time he saw that woman—when, walking with her short, quick little footsteps, gracefully waggling those same buttocks, she headed for the kitchen of the inn in Troyes to bring him a bottle of almond liqueur.

God only knows what he must be thinking, Annette said to herself, as she had done so many other times when—as now—she saw her husband settled comfortably in his rocking chair, dressed in his red velvet bathrobe, and more silent than a dead man. He was very thin and looked small and frail; his body had shrunk, and his skin had taken on the texture of a nutshell. In his withered face, of a yellowish cast, his features had given way to wrinkles: the only thing that could be seen in it were deep folds, like the scars of innumerable knife thrusts. Only his eyes gave a sign that someone was alive behind that parchment mask. Very dark and bright, they looked like two lumps of coal rubbed with oil. Although imposing, the look in them was not intimidating, for he seemed not to see, or to be precise, it seemed as though he were looking inward, as when we fix our eyes on an object as we try to lay hold of an idea that escapes our grasp. Concentrating hard, we don't see the object; we look inward, searching for that idea. That was what Rasero's gaze was like, an absorbed gaze, pondering heaven only knows what thoughts.

"Shall I pour your tea?" Rasero nodded. "Be careful; it's very hot. That's the way; sip it slowly, for goodness' sake. I can't understand how it is you don't burn yourself. Your tongue must be made of leather. Do you want a little more?" Rasero shook his head. "All right . . . Now let's get you dressed." She was about to bring him a pair of trousers, when Rasero took her by the wrist and an odd expression came over his face. "Do you want to wash up first?" He nodded again. "But I gave you a good wash yesterday; how could you have got dirty sitting down all day?" The woman looked again into her husband's face. "The heat . . . you've sweat a lot? I understand. All right, I'm going to bring you some water; meanwhile take off your bathrobe and your underwear. Do you want me to bring you some cologne?"

She did not wait for his reply and left the bedroom. It had been a long time, in fact, since Annette had waited for her husband to answer her questions: Rasero hadn't uttered a word for nearly eight years. So much time had gone by that it was hard for the woman to remember don Fausto when he still spoke. By nature he was never very talkative; you always had to get words out of him with a crowbar. But after they left Paris, don Fausto became more and more silent and taciturn. Whole weeks went by when he said scarcely more than a few words. So when he fell completely silent, it came as no great surprise to anyone. Annette didn't remember when her husband had spoken for the last time. It was Véronique, their daughter, who was sure she remembered. "It was at my wedding, Mama," she explained to her countless times. " 'God bless you,' he said to Adolfo and me. It's as if I could see him this minute! Since then, he hasn't said another word, I'm sure of it . . ." Annette didn't answer. She didn't remember his saying that, but neither did she remember having heard him speak since the wedding. The poor thing! she said to herself. It's bitterness that's robbed him of his voice. Ever since the day that little Spanish woman disappeared, he's the saddest man I've known in my life . . .

When he was tidied up and dressed, Rasero left his room. He began his daily routine, from which he hadn't deviated at all in the last eight years: he spent all morning sitting in a comfortable armchair in the gallery on the second floor. Alongside him, on a little table, Annette had left a big plateful of bread that had been sliced, along with cheese and some fresh fruit. He washed the repast down with a glass of anisette diluted with water. At two o'clock he had lunch with Annette in the kitchen. Afterward, he went back to his bedroom, where he took a siesta for a couple of hours. Two or three afternoons a week—if the weather permitted—the couple went out onto the streets of the city. Generally they walked down the Alameda de Hércules till they came to the cathedral. They sat there, in front of it, for a time, while Annette threw bread crumbs to the pigeons that crowded around as soon as they saw the two of them sit down. When they returned home, Rasero shut himself up in his bedroom and settled down in the rocking chair. At ten in the evening, his wife entered the room and lit a lamp: Annette had discovered long since that it made not the least difference to her husband whether it was dark in the room at night or whether there was a lamp lit. She gave him a big cupful of broth and a piece of bread. Then she helped him get undressed and put his nightshirt on. At eleven on the dot, he climbed into bed.

That morning, as he had done so many other times, Rasero settled himself comfortably in the armchair in the gallery to receive the greeting of the sun's rays on his old skin. Every so often he raised a grape or a bit of cheese to his mouth. He chewed them very slowly, and once he had swallowed them, he sipped a little of the diluted anisette. He then returned to his well-nigh eternal immobility. The joyous song of the little birds was accompanied by the continuous, restful sound of the water gushing from the quarry stone fountain down below, in the middle of the patio . . .

But you didn't listen to those sounds, Rasero. You hadn't heard anything for a long time. Nor did you see the little colored tiles of the floor of the gallery, nor the forged iron railing, nor the wall of Moorish mosaic tiles that reached from the floor to almost the height of a man's chest, showing its intricate cream-colored designs standing out against the cobalt blue background. Nor did you see the four huge paintings that your father commissioned to decorate each side of the gallery. You were unable to see the gypsies who have always been there, in the left wing of the gallery, gathered around a campfire playing their guitars and singing their plaintive songs, as the little gypsy girl gracefully bends one leg, affording a glimpse of her pretty calf. Nor could you see the fearsome brigands, with their hair held back in nets beneath their cloth caps and their enormous muskets dangling from their shoulders. There the three of them are, crouching behind an oak tree. One of them has his hand cupped around his ear so as to hear the clatter of the coach drawn by two strong Percherons that is approaching in the distance. It is close now: ah, there it is, rounding the cliff. Its poor passengers—whose two little faces in profile can just barely be made out inside the vehicle—haven't the least suspicion of the terrible events that await them. In the coach box, the driver and his young assistant are merrily chatting together. Perhaps, you thought many times as you looked at this picture when you were a little boy, they're in cahoots with the bandits. No, you couldn't now see that eternal ambush hanging in the right wing. Nor could you see the virgin who's there opposite on her cloud, as though she's about to take off. Her eyes have already done so; they are looking toward heaven with relief. The long-suffering face of the woman is a fair imitation of those splendid virgins, olive-skinned and melodramatic, painted by Murillo, the Sevillian. At her feet, or at the sides of the cloud, the cherubs have their cheeks puffed out—as florid as if they were the sons of Germans—for they are blowing. ("Why are they blowing?" you asked many times when you were a little boy. "It's so that the blessed lady can ascend to heaven," your uncle Luis said to you with a smile one day.) You were even less able to see the painting behind you, just above your head; you would have had to turn your head around to see it, but you couldn't. And what a good thing you couldn't, because that painting had horrified you since you were a youngster, do you remember, Rasero? Only to your father would it have occurred to commission such a monstrosity. "For the love of God, don Enrique! What a frightful thing!" good friar Silvestre had said to your father as he crossed himself. "It rends the soul just to look at it."

"I shit on God! Has anybody ever been born who understands priests? When it was you yourself, Fray Silvestre, who advised me to commission a painting on a biblical subject for the gallery."

"Well, I admit that's true, sir. But since there are so many beautiful passages in the Holy Bible, why did you choose that horror?"

"I didn't choose it. I let God make the decision. Since I didn't know what passage had a particular appeal for me, I proceeded in the same way the fathers of the church did: I let the Bible fall from a table, I picked it up, and with my eyes closed, I put my index finger on one of the pages it had fallen open at. And then I read, and I remember it well, '. . . and the dragon stood before the woman which was ready to be delivered, for to devour her child as soon as it was born . . .' You can't deny, don Silvestre, that the artist produced a magnificent painting . . ."

He had indeed: the woman, heavy with child and sad faced, with her eyes swollen from weeping, had fallen to the ground and lay there with her legs spread apart. She was trying to get to her feet, for she was leaning one hand on the ground and the muscles standing out in her forearm proved the effort she was making as she tried to raise her body. Her strong legs were visible beneath her skirt rolled up to her hips. On her left side, a torrent of blood was gushing out, from her crotch to her knee. At her side, standing, the Evil One, with his bull's horns, his goat's beard, and his repellent body covered with greenish scales, had opened his disgusting mouth—in which only his incisors could be seen and from which a forked tongue hung down past the tip of his chin—and was about to devour his prey, a newborn baby boy, as rosy and plump as a piglet, whose little body, hanging suspended by the ankles from one of the beast's claws, was writhing in anguish. The painting was very dark and gloomy. Amid the ochers and grays, the red of the blood, the baby's pink skin, and the devil's greenish color stood out. It was really frightening; not even Boucher, with his sepia ink and his skillful hand, had achieved the effect that the Malagan artist had. Alongside this imposing work, the illustration that your friend had made of the same scene seemed naïve, almost sentimental. No, you couldn't see that painting, Rasero. And what a good thing that was, because if you could have seen it, there would inevitably have come to mind that despicable thought it prompted in you every time you saw it: No, it is not the church, nor its Son, nor the devil that is depicted there. It's the earth, nature, and man . . . Man, the insatiable beast . . . You did not understand that thought when it came to your mind for the first time, eighty years ago. Seventy years had to go by so that, when you returned to this house, you would understand it. Although . . . what was happening to you, Rasero? Why were you looking at the glass in your hand that way? Were you really seeing it? Did you see the milky liquid trickling down its sides? Could you smell that sweet and penetrating aroma? Rasero, Rasero . . .

That morning something extraordinary happened. After gazing for some time at the glass he was holding, Rasero left it on the little table, turned his head, and looked with concentration at the impressive painting hanging behind him. Annette, as always, was coming and going along the gallery mumbling to herself and scolding the servants at the top of her lungs, when she saw her husband staring at the painting. How strange, she thought.

"Ah, don Fausto! When are you going to let me take that frightful painting away from there?"

"Never," Rasero replied.

"What?!" the woman said, taken aback.

"Never, I said . . . Annette, dear, tell me: do you know where my little ebony coffer is?"

"What's that? . . . What? . . . Your little coffer? . . . Don Fausto, you're talking!" the woman cried and overjoyed went to her husband to give him a hug and a kiss. "It's a miracle, don Fausto!"

Annette had never looked so much like his beloved Angustias as she did that day. All Rasero had to do was close his eyes to see and hear the gypsy woman, joyfully thanking all the angels in heaven, but above all her tortured Cachorro, for such a miracle.

"Don Fausto is talking!" the two of them repeated, filled with happiness—Annette now, Angustias ("my Faustillo is talking") eighty-two years before.

"My little ebony coffer, Annette. Do you know where it is? . . ."

About my great-uncle, don José Adolfo de Gálvez, I knew very little. He was the only brother of doña Juana, my paternal grandmother. As my grandmother used to explain to anybody who would listen, her brother Adolfo, despite being five years younger than she, was a male and therefore the legitimate heir of the marquisate of Sonora, a title borne proudly by his father, my great-grandfather, don Francisco de Gálvez, the admiral of the Royal Spanish Armada and harbor master for many years in the Philippines, where both his children first saw the light of day. I still remember with pleasure those afternoons I spent at my aunt Ana's listening to my grandmother talking about her illustrious family. Sitting in her rocking chair with the broad back, looking down from the height of the sixth floor on the little roundabout in front of the building—with that strange monument rising up in the center, which, when I was small, looked to me like a big stone barrel-organ cactus, though when I was older, it looked to me more like a gigantic phallus—she summoned to mind memories that she spoke of in a very low voice, with her elegant accent of a refined Andalusian lady.

My grandmother must have been a very beautiful woman when she was young. She always dressed in black, with her gray hair pulled very tightly back from her broad forehead and caught up in a bun atop her head. Her eyes, small and very slanted, seemed Asian. (My grandmother's eyes, along with my aunt Ana's and my sister Mercedes', were the butt of an old family joke: "Maybe," we used to say, "the distinguished chief harbor master of the Royal Admiralty in the Philippines counted on the collaboration of a native of those islands to father his heiress.") Her nose was small, thin, and very straight; it looked like the handiwork of a delicate craftsman. That was also true of her mouth, with its fine, well-delineated lips, beneath which was hidden a gleaming white, perfect set of teeth. Her firm, slightly prominent chin was the mark of her energetic temperament. Her cheeks, full and generous, framed a face that must have been an impeccable oval at one time, although now, of course, they drooped more than a little.

And so, with her eyes fixed on the stone column, doña Juana spoke for hours at a time of her childhood and her early youth, which had apparently been the best years of her life. "My father presented us at court during the fiestas that were held to commemorate the beginning of the new century. Ah, my boy, what splendor! There was no woman more refined and dignified than the queen mother . . . And her son, Alfonso XIII, as good-looking as a sun . . ." I listened to her enthralled. I don't believe that if she had told me tales of fairies, witches, and dragons, as grandmothers are said to do, she would have captivated me the way she did by relating those memories of hers, so stately and strange. What I liked most to hear, and asked my grandmother time and again to tell me, was the story of her great-great-grandfather, the attorney don José de Gálvez, the first Marquis de la Sonora. Don José, who was also the count of Macharavialla, came to New Spain for the first time in 1761, having been sent there by the Council of the Indies. Some time later, he was appointed inspector general and was the official primarily responsible for putting the modernizing reforms drawn up at the court of the Spanish Bourbons into effect in the colony. Don José's name was closely tied to those energetic measures that succeeded in giving the most precious jewel in the Crown one last shining splendor. An indefatigable man, he also took steps to change the fiscal organization of the colony and transform its administration by creating districts supervised by an intendant to replace the old kingdoms. He furthered the development of mining techniques for extracting silver, and helped put down the uprisings attendant on the expulsion of the Jesuits in 1767, and was also behind the taking-up of arms to go off to Sonora to pacify the Yaqui Indians. The inspector general came to be more powerful and more feared in New Spain than the viceroys themselves, whom he dealt with as he pleased, going so far as to get the Crown to appoint as viceroy his eldest brother, don Matías de Gálvez, and when the brother died, his son (the son of don Matías, that is), don Bernardo Gálvez, who fought fiercely against the Apaches in Texas and the Seminoles in Florida, as well as against the English in Louisiana. Unfortunately, don Bernardo died at an early age, when he had been in power for barely two years. Even so, he had time to finish the project that his father had started: the building of Chapultepec Castle. My grandmother talked so much about it that I have always felt a little as though that castle were mine. Perhaps that was the reason I was so fond of going to visit it. As I went through its main rooms, I tried to imagine don José de Gálvez sitting at a big table, whispering into the ear of his nephew Bernardo advice as to what he should say in the State Cabinet meeting. It was hard to imagine it, though: the castle is pervaded by the presence of Maximilian of Hapsburg and his wife; the asphyxiating weight of the nineteenth century leaves little space for the preceding reign. There remain, at least, the portraits of my forebears.

Don Matías appears in a half-length portrait, in three-quarter profile. He looks very serious and severe, in a close-fitting, austere wig with just one curl in it. A big nose and a firm chin, average-sized eyes, but with a sharp and piercing gaze; perhaps they look like that because of the furrow that his eyebrows form over his nose. What makes this portrait memorable, however, and what as a child never ceased to intrigue and even terrify me, are those eyebrows. Thick and coal black, the tips of them, as though they were combed and waxed, rise up toward his forehead, giving an unmistakably demoniacal look to his face.

In a large-sized oil painting, don Bernardo is shown full length, mounted on a horse that is rearing. A large tricorn hides his head; the only thing that can be seen is one of the two curls in his wig. His full oval face is quite pleasant, for his eyes are set far apart and appear intelligent, although he has an aquiline nose longer than a wait in the rain. Together with that nose, his small mouth and his somewhat prognathous jaw make his face more or less resemble a caricature. This painting has one oddity that impressed me tremendously ever since the first time I saw it. The tricorn, the face, the jabot, and the starched ruff that peek out from his coat are painted in the same manner as in any painting: their volumes are rendered in heavy brush strokes with contrasting colors—the black tricorn, the pink face, and the white frills. This, of course, has nothing special about it, but the rest of the figure and the entire horse are rendered in a curious curvilinear line on a black background: their bodies are depicted in thin white lines intertwined in a whimsical filigree design. The effect is striking; at first glance it looks as though it were iron grillwork, but after contemplating it for a while, the viewer finds that the forms and volumes of the bodies seem to be clearly discernible and even have a certain solidity. In the lower part of the work are the words "Finished on the twentieth day of October of 96, Fr. Pablo de Jesús, by F. San Gerónimo."

Don José, like his brother, is also shown from the waist up, but full face, looking toward the painter. His face is very good-looking. Almost rectangular in shape, the lower part of it ends in an energetic and gracefully outthrust chin. His eyes, very far apart and good sized, suggest kindliness and a keen mind. His nose, thin and straight, seems to be cast in the mold from which the noses of my grandmother, my father, and me also came. His mouth, with thin, discreet lips, appears to hide a smile. He is in formal dress, wearing a satin coat with lovingly embroidered lapels. Standing out conspicuously on his chest is a large medallion in the form of a cross with an oval in the middle, inside which the portrait in miniature of a woman can be seen—an important decoration, doubtless, as is the blue sash edged in gold that slants downward across his chest from his right shoulder. In his left hand—slightly extended, as though showing them to anyone who wishes to see them—he is holding several sheets of parchment folded lightly in two. It is not possible to read what is meant to look like a text written on them, except for his name, but it must be the royal letters patent whereby don Carlos III, king of Spain, rewarded this brave gentleman with the title of marquis de la Sonora in recognition of the innumerable services he had lent the Crown under Alfonso the Wise.

My father was greatly annoyed by my grandmother's discourses. I was never able to learn anything from him about his ancestors. "It's all nonsense," he said to me. "What the devil do I care about the Marquis de la Sonora or his four generations of noble forebears? Nobility, my son, only interests idiots . . ." Thanks to my father, however, I was able to find out other things that also greatly intrigued me, such as, for instance, Why did the great-great-granddaughter of the Marquis de la Sonora, count of Macharavialla and universal minister of the Indies beginning in 1775, spend her last days in a modest apartment in the Colonia del Valle of Mexico City, contemplating from the utter boredom of her rocking chair an absurd stone column? It seemed that in my great-grandfather, the admiral, the blood of his illustrious forebear was already extremely diluted. He was a lazy sort, frivolous, and a notorious philanderer. With the same zeal his ancestors had shown in chasing down Yaquis in Sonora and Seminoles in

Florida, don Francisco spent his life chasing married women, unmarried women, waitresses, whores, and all other females who might be hiding good legs under their skirts. He did the same thing equally in his native Málaga and in the Philippines, Cuba, Puerto Rico, the Canary Islands, and all the other places to which his assignments took him. Hence, the admiral began the new century without a cent in his pockets and with a virulent strain of syphilis in his blood. There was nothing he could do, then, save to allow his daughter to marry a doctor in Málaga, a member of a respectable family in the city that, although lacking ancestors of noble lineage, had at least amassed a fair fortune. Nor was don Francisco able to prevent his son José Adolfo from abandoning his military career, thus breaking with a four-generation tradition, to devote himself to the study, first, of philosophy and, then, of bohemia. Don Francisco died in the second decade of this century. His son Adolfo inherited his estate, which, except for the resounding titles, amounted to very little. Nonetheless, it appears that don Adolfo administered the estate wisely, for he managed to live all his long life on the proceeds from it, and it allowed him, besides, to finance his activities as an anarchist, activities in which he had been seriously involved for a number of years, up until the dictatorship of Primo de Rivera, when, disappointed by his comrades, he shut himself up in his old mansion in Macharavialla, never again to leave it. Not even the Spanish Civil War could force him out of his retreat; fortunately Macharavialla was far removed from all that, and don Adolfo didn't care at all whether the Nationalists or the Republicans won the war. ". . . They're all the same: ravens, vultures eager for power," my father told me that his uncle had written to him in one of his letters. Doña Juana, on the other hand, plunged into the adventure of the Republic with great enthusiasm. Paradoxically, she was very much in favor of Alfonso XIII's abdication, and from the beginning sided with the most radical group of Republicans, the Communists. She joined the Party and forced her husband and her children to do the same. Later on came the Civil War and a story of departures that I do not wish to recount here: from Málaga, from Valencia, from Barcelona, and from France, finally landing her in old Mexico City, of which her glorious forebear had been lord and master for such a long time.

All I knew about my great-uncle Adolfo was that he spent more than forty years in a village in Andalusia, painting at times, writing at others, or playing his old violin. He never married nor, as far as anyone knows, lived with anyone at any time. His only contact with the world was my father, to whom he wrote four or five letters a year. I could never learn what he wrote about, for my father, once he'd finished reading them, burned them, following—as he explained to me—his uncle's instructions.

My father died in 1966, and since then I had learned nothing more about Uncle Adolfo—until the spring of 1978, when I received a letter from his executor in Madrid informing me that don José Adolfo de Gálvez y Rodríguez de Arias, who had recently died, had named me his sole heir . . .

"It's in the bedroom, don't worry, don Fausto. I swear to you that I haven't touched it in all this time," the woman finally answered. Her eyes were wet with happy tears.

"What day is today?"

"Wednesday, the twenty-fourth of July."

"Of what year?"

"Of 1812, don Fausto . . ."

Eight years! . . . , Rasero thought.

"Yes, you haven't said one word for almost eight years," his wife said, as if she had read his thought.

"I see you're now talking like a real Andalusian, Annette."

"What do you expect? We've been here close to twenty years now. Tell me, don Fausto, don't you remember anything?"

"Not one thing. The last thing I remember is Véronique's wedding. To me, it's as though it had taken place yesterday. By the way, how are they?"

"Very well, thank God. Although, believe me, Adolfo has had his little problems . . . What with this war, who hasn't? But little by little they're getting over them, don Fausto, they're getting over them. Ah, they also have two very pretty children. Don't you remember them?"

"No."

"Well, take my word for it, you've seen them! Francisco José will be seven in October, and Juana Inés was five in February. They're very likable, lively little rascals and—thanks be to God!—they're healthy and as sturdy as oak trees. That's what counts: all I ask is for them to be healthy . . . They're going to be here tonight. Would you like to see them?"

"Of course, woman. I'll be delighted to meet them."

"It's odd, all the times you've seen them, and yet you talk now of meeting them . . . I swear that all this is really strange! Don Fausto, do you have any idea what happened to you?"

"No, Annette," he lied. "My mind simply went blank. Perhaps it's because my brain is too old, and on seeing that I wasn't about to die, it decided to take a rest on its own, don't you think?"

"Who can tell! Even though one of the doctors who saw you told me something very similar: that the veins in your brain had hardened and that kept you from thinking. Another one told me that you were just plain crazy, that he'd seen many cases like yours, even in persons much younger, and there was nothing that could be done. 'He'll never regain complete consciousness,' the stupid idiot told me. And still another one—he was the worst of all of them!—diagnosed you as having the eggs of some worm encysted in your head. 'When they hatch,' the fool told me, 'he'll suffer from terrible headaches and will die in just a few days.' You see how much use doctors are. I'll tell you this, and I'm not reproaching you for it—after all, everything I possess is yours—you wouldn't believe how much money they got out of me with their famous consultations. If that's how much they charge just for a diagnosis, I said to myself, I don't even want to think of what it's going to cost if they manage to cure him. They would have left you cured, all right, but out on the street . . ."

"You spoke of a war . . ."

"Aye, don Fausto! What bad years we lived through. Even if they're my compatriots, those French are scoundrels. Not content with devouring half of Europe—good Christ, the whole of Europe!—they had to invade Spain. The Corsican could think of nothing better than to make his drunkard brother Joseph king of the country. That was four years ago. And, the Virgin is my witness, what an uproar that caused! The Spaniards have fought like cats pinned on their backs. Pepe the Toper has had to leave Madrid twice, running away like a hare. Adolfo will explain this whole mess to you tonight better than I can; he's involved up to his neck in politics. What my Véronique hasn't suffered! It's been frightful, don Fausto. They're getting killed not only on the battlefields now but wherever they get caught. Saragossa is destroyed, and so are many other cities. And they deal with each other with such hatred! There's not a day that dawns without a couple of Spaniards hanged in front of the Church of the Trinity and three or four Frogs with their bellies ripped open lying on some dung heap. I swear to God, they never tire of killing each other! . . . Sault's troops invaded this very city a year ago. What savages! I swear to you, don Fausto, they didn't leave one virgin, even as an example. Thank God you lost your memory! Why, those ruffians even set foot in this house! It was a company of Gascons. The numskulls! They didn't even know how to speak French. Luckily there were the wine cellars. The swine quieted down once they discovered them. They drank up three grape harvests, I'm not exaggerating, don Fausto. We had them down there for a whole week. You should have seen what a state they left the cellars in! If they'd been a herd of mules, the place wouldn't have been such a wreck or so filthy . . . But let's not talk about sad things. The important thing is that you're here . . . How funny, when you've always been here, for heaven's sake! Well, you know what I mean."

"Of course I do, woman."

"I'm going to bring your little coffer to your room right this minute, and then I'm going to go on with the housework. Ah, don Fausto, I'm so happy to hear you speak!" Annette kissed her husband's forehead and went off toward the kitchen.

That night, Rasero ate dinner with his family. He looked at Véronique and Adolfo with curiosity. It wasn't that they'd grown old; they were still young, but they had matured quite a bit. Adolfo had two big bald patches above his forehead, and little wrinkles had formed at the outer edges of his eyes. Véronique had mellowed; perhaps she was prettier now. Her honey-colored eyes were even more beautiful that Rasero remembered, for they had a more serene and more intelligent look about them. The first gray hairs could be seen mingled in her black hair. The Malagan found it difficult to accept that he had gone almost eight years without seeing his grandson and granddaughter. It was even stranger seeing them. Paquito was a thin boy with fine features. His straight little nose, his eyes, wide open and alert, and his small mouth with thin lips reminded Rasero of his cousin José de Gálvez, the boy's great-grandfather. But his cheerful, restless, and mischievous disposition couldn't have been more like that of his uncle Michel when he was that age.

"Hey, Grandpa, why didn't you talk?"

"I couldn't, my boy."

"And now you can?"

"You can see that I can . . ."

"And you're not going to go silent again?"

"I hope not."

"That's good!"

"Why do you say that?"

"I didn't like seeing you that way. It made me a little scared. You seemed like a madman."

"Paco!" his mother reprimanded him.

"Leave him alone, woman. Don't scold him; when all is said and done, he's right. It must not be very pleasant to see an old man like me as mute as a stone. And didn't it frighten you, my darling?"

"No, Grandpa. Just a wee little bit," his granddaughter, Juana Inés, answered, a pretty, very serious little girl. She looked a lot like her mother and even more like her grandfather Marcel, the printer. Such a good man . . . , Rasero thought.

The one who didn't stop talking during the whole meal was Adolfo. He was in high spirits. Only a few days before, the Anglo-Spanish forces had overwhelmingly defeated the French at Arpiles. "They're making ready now to leave Madrid again, though this time they won't be back, you'll see. They don't have the strength to counterattack. The Corsican took more than half a million men to Russia with him; they don't have any reserve troops left . . ."

"And how has the Frenchman governed this country?" Rasero asked.

"I regret to admit it, but he's done fairly well. He appointed Luis Urquiza prime minister; although he's gone over to the French, there's no denying that he's an honest and intelligent man. In fact, he's taken certain measures by decree that are identical to the ones the deputies in Cádiz who are loyal to Spain have been demanding."

"Such as?"

"The Inquisition has been abolished!"

"Stupendous!"

"And that's not all. He's abolished feudal privileges and done away with domestic customs duties. He's also proposed adapting for Spain Napoleon's civil code, which, I needn't tell you, is a masterpiece. In all truth, it's a pity that Joseph Bonaparte is French and has been forced on us in such a bad way, because I believe in all sincerity that he would have been a good king."

"Better than that cretin Ferdinand, that's certain. Is that man still as arrogant and stupid as ever?"

"He's just the same, perhaps worse, but he's the king that God chose for Spain and we're obliged to defend his crown like lions. Besides, he's always sworn his loyalty to the Cortes. When he occupies the throne once again, he'll respect the constitution that the deputies in Cádiz drew up. Absolutism in Spain is over forever, Uncle, you may be certain of that."

"Well, I wouldn't put too much stock in that. An oath sworn by Ferdinand is about as trustworthy as one by a courtesan swearing that she's a virgin. You must all be very careful . . ."

"We will be, Uncle, don't worry. We're never going to allow the blood of so many Spaniards to have been shed in vain. In this war many leaders of the people have suddenly appeared, such as the ones known as The Stubborn and Moreno and Espoz y Mina, who, just as they have fought against the Frogs, would fight against Ferdinand if he dared go back on his promise . . ."

"So Napoleon has attacked Russia?"

"Yes. I think that man has finally made a great mistake. If he hasn't been able to get the better of us, just imagine what awaits him there! Deep inside that enormous country, fighting against the Cossacks, who, according to what people say, are the fiercest and most savage army in the world. And just wait till winter comes! The Corsican is going to meet his end there: in the snows of the steppes . . ."

"They're going to find him on an island, within ten years . . ."

"And how do you know that, don Fausto?"

"I really don't know; it was just a conjecture . . . But tell me, when are you thinking of leaving?"

"Tomorrow, as a matter of fact." Véronique looked sadly at her mother. "It's not going to be easy to get to Lisbon, but once I'm there, I won't be in any danger."

"Adolfo, my son, must you really go?" Annette asked anxiously.

"Of course, madam. I'm a captain in the Spanish Royal Army. My obligation is to be at the front fighting against the invaders. And even if I weren't an army officer, I'd gladly do the same thing. Every healthy Spaniard must fight till the French leave the kingdom. But don't worry, doña Ana, I'm going to take very good care of myself; I don't intend to die before I see my Paquito made a lieutenant, isn't that right, my boy?"

"A ship's captain, Papa. That's what I'm going to be."

"Better still. Well, then, I promise all of you that I won't die before seeing Paquito in command of a frigate," he said as he gave a happy smile and kissed the cheek of his wife, who was unable to hide her sadness. "You don't know how pleased I am to see that you've recovered, Uncle. I'm going off with my mind much more at ease knowing that Véronique and the children will be in your care."

"I don't think an old man like me, with one foot in the grave, will be of much help, but I promise you, Adolfo, that I'll do everything in my power to watch over the safety of everyone. By the way, Annette, I've been thinking that now that my nephew is leaving, it would be better if we all went to Macharavialla; by going there we'll be far away from the fracas."

"But, don Fausto . . ."

"Don't worry, woman, I can make the journey; I feel quite strong enough. Macharavialla is close by; I'll stand traveling that short way very well. You can put your mind at rest. Anyhow, I think it will do me a great deal of good to spend a season in the country."

"It seems like a good idea to me, Uncle," Adolfo put in. "You'll all be safer there."

"Well, then, we needn't discuss it any more . . . Adolfo, my son, take good care of yourself . . ."

Rasero embraced the husband of Annette's daughter with tears in his eyes and went off to his bedroom.

Three days later, Fausto Rasero, the women, and the children arrived in Macharavialla. Rasero insisted on moving into the house of the former administrator of the estate, since no one was living there. No matter how much Annette and her daughter pleaded with him to stay in one bedroom or another of the manor house, Rasero was unyielding. "I'll have more peace and quiet there," he explained to them. "I must write quite a few things, and I don't believe I have much time left to do that . . ."

Rasero found the main bedroom of the house very pleasant. It was on the second floor and was quite large. A big window facing south kept the room well lit practically all day. A large bed, with its enormous canopy, stood in front of the window. To one side was an ordinary-sized table, against a wall. Rasero set his little ebony coffer down on it. His old rocking chair was the only piece of furniture he added to the bedroom. When he had finished moving in, he sat down in it to contemplate the dark mountain peaks of the Sierra Nevada.

The old overseer must have been a real believer, Rasero said to himself when he saw the decorations. On the walls were two large oil paintings and eight engravings, all of them of religious subjects: a holy family, a Saint Sebastian, young Jesus in the temple, the Virgin of Remedies, Lord Jesus before Pilate, a Sacred Heart, Judith with the head of Holofernes, the Master with the two thieves crucified on

Mount Calvary, and Saint John the Baptist preaching in the desert. There were, furthermore, four vaulted niches: one pair in each of the walls flanking the one where the window was. They were identical in size, rectangular and topped with a semicircular arch. They contained statuary, quite well executed, of the Virgin of Macarena, of the Virgin of Dew, of the Virgin of Remedies, and of the Virgin of Victory.

When you saw the place, you smiled at the thought that this was where you were going to write what you had had in mind for some time. I couldn't find a less suitable atmosphere, you said to yourself. When dusk fell, you ate the fruit and cheese that Annette had brought you, poured yourself a glass of wine, lit a pair of lamps, and sat down at the table. You carefully prepared a couple of goose-quill pens and filled the inkwell. Then you opened the lower drawer of the black coffer and took out your book of notations and the manuscript of the Book of Revelation. You opened the biblical text: "I. The Revelation of Jesus Christ, which God gave unto him, to shew unto his servants things which must shortly come to pass; and he sent and signified it by his angel unto his servant John . . ."

You read. Finally, you took out of the same drawer the packets of Angoulême paper that had been left over when you transcribed the work of Saint John sixty-five years before. Having been inside the drawer all that time, they had lost their whiteness and brightness: they looked yellowed and opaque. You took a sheet of the paper and placed it in front of you. You wet the pen in the sepia-colored ink, and without a great deal of thought, you wrote in big letters on the upper part of it, "Why I Despise You . . ."

As might be supposed, the news made me tremendously excited. An inheritance! That was something I hadn't ever even dreamed of. Up until them, I was convinced that things like that happen only in films or in cheap novels. Sole heir of don José Adolfo de Gálvez, I said to myself aloud and filled my imagination with foolish notions. I saw myself in an enormous castle, waited on by an impeccable butler, the owner of a great fortune, the lord and master of my time. I could say to hell with everything and finally devote myself to my old plan: I would have all the time in the world to write my novel. My wife could leave the theater company and organize one of her own—why not? There wouldn't be any more uncertainties: I would take on the responsibility of financing the best stage sets ever seen in Mexico. We'll be rich and free . . . , I said to myself.

"We'll be rich and free, woman," I said to my wife. I still had the Spanish lawyer's letter in my hand. Then she asked me a question that caused all the smoke inside my head to disappear in an instant.

"Was your uncle very rich?"

"He must have been; if not, why would he make me his heir?" I answered without conviction. Now doubt took the place of euphoria. As far as I knew, my great-uncle hadn't been a rich man. According to what my father had explained to me, my great-grandfather, the admiral, was the last rich Gálvez, and he squandered his fortune. As for don Adolfo having amassed another fortune, it sounded frankly absurd. What kind of fortune could have been made by a man who was half mad and who spent almost fifty years of his life isolated in a little village in Andalusia? Maybe he won the lottery . . . or a soccer pool. Prizes like that are worth a lot of money in Spain, I said to myself, or maybe he himself inherited money from a relative . . . And what if it was debts that he bequeathed me? It wouldn't be unusual. I'd heard of many cases where the inheritance consists of mortgages and promissory notes. It's absurd; I don't believe my uncle would be so mean as to bequeath his debts to a nephew he didn't even know. If only my father hadn't burned don Adolfo's letters . . . !

Needless to say, I didn't sleep that night. As soon as I laid my head on the pillow, I sat up again as though the pillow were of stone. I then lit a cigarette and returned to my reflections, or to be precise, my uncertainty. I managed to persuade myself that I had inherited a large fortune and gave my imagination free rein: Where will we live, in Málaga or in Mexico? The best thing to do would be to spend half the year here and the other half there. From April to September in Spain, and from October to March in Jiutepec . . . When I realized the rattle-brained fantasies I was getting caught up in, I put on the brakes, so to speak, and my reflections inclined toward the dark side. And what if my uncle owed a lot of money? Can they put someone in jail if he refuses to pay a relative's debts? . . . I saw myself behind the bars of a jail in the port of Málaga. This thought was so absurd that I definitely rejected it so as to return to the sunny side, full of money and pleasures. At times a certain clear-mindedness came over me, and I managed to get out of this vicious circle: Why not telephone the executor in Madrid and have him tell me what I inherited? Don't be silly, I answered myself, in the letter he tells you very clearly,

"You will have to come to Madrid in person so that the notary can read the will in your presence . . ." And how the devil are we going to go to Madrid if we're practically in the poorhouse? We can sell the car. And what about school? It's still four months until vacation! No, I can't bear four months like this. And what about the theater? They're giving the first performance in two weeks . . . Screw them! My wife's coming with me . . . And what if I write to the executor telling him that I'm not interested in the inheritance, that I prefer to give it to a charitable institution? . . . And what if it's a fortune? . . . And what if there are debts to pay? . . . At least there's the house where my uncle lived . . . And what if it's been rented, or there's a mortgage on it? Moreover, what can a house in a little town like that be worth? . . . Incidentally, where the hell is Macharavialla? . . . I knew it was in the province of Málaga, but that was all. It was odd; as many times as I'd heard the name of that town on my grandfather's and my father's lips, it never occurred to me to ask them exactly where it was. I leaped out of bed and searched in my geography books and in several encyclopedias. Nothing. Macharavialla didn't turn up anywhere. Maybe it doesn't even exist . . . Then I remembered that a friend had an old UTEJA encyclopedia. If it isn't in there, it's because it really doesn't exist, I said to myself. Even though it was almost 3 A.M., I could contain myself no longer and phoned Elena. She was a good friend all right! Half asleep, and more surprised than annoyed, she looked in the encyclopedia. "Yes, Paco, it's here: 'Macharavialla. A municipality in the province of Málaga and administrative headquarters of three villages. It is situated within the district of Vélez-Málaga and has 861 inhabitants.' " Damn! It was even smaller than I had imagined. At least I knew where it was: near Vélez. I then looked at a map again. It was easy to locate Vélez-Málaga; it was very near the capital and seemed like an important city. Of Macharavialla, not a trace. As for the location of Vélez, it might just as easily be on the coast as in the mountains. For no particular reason, I imagined it in mountain country. Can a person be very rich and live there? I wondered. Of course not. I would write for sure to the executor tomorrow to tell him that the inheritance didn't interest me.

In the morning, I had made up my mind. My curiosity was stronger than my fear: we would sell the car, we would give up our jobs and leave for Madrid as soon as possible.

If instead of being a matter of a notary about to read a will aloud, it had concerned a doctor about to read me the results of my electrocardiogram, I don't think I'd have been more nervous. The notary, a young man with refined manners, could not have done his work more calmly. As though he were concealing a profound envy, he took pleasure in serenely studying my anxious face. He smiled, cleared his throat, adjusted his eyeglasses, mulled something over in his mind as he nibbled on his pen, called the secretary over the intercom, and took off his glasses. The woman came in; the executor, a man who seemed a hundred years old, looked lustfully at the young woman's legs as she placed a document on her boss's desk and left the room. The notary put his glasses on again, looked the new document over, raised his head, pushed his glasses up onto his forehead, looked at me thoughtfully for a time. "We'll begin right away," he said. He adjusted his glasses once again, nibbled on the pen, cleared his throat, and . . . called the secretary on the intercom. He did so at least three times. I thought I'd go crazy. I squeezed my wife's hand so hard that one time, just as that idiot was about to begin reading, my wife gave a sharp cry of pain. It took us a long while to explain to that man that nothing had happened, everything was fine. He didn't calm down till he'd taken a careful look at my wife's hand. At that point, I'd almost passed out, and didn't even have the strength to spit in the wretch's face.

Finally he began reading the will aloud. As he went on, I felt reality descend, like an enormous heavy gray theater curtain, weighed down with all its mediocrity. No, it wasn't debts that I had inherited, but certainly not a large fortune either. Uncle José Adolfo had left me his little house in Macharavialla, a few acres of land, a small principal on long-term deposit at the state bank which brought in about twenty thousand pesetas a month. That was all. No, that's not quite true: he also bequeathed me, if I was of a mind to claim it, the title of marquis de la Sonora. My great-uncle had never done so, but he had kept the documentation that validated the title, which the notary now placed in my hands.

"Congratulations, marquis," he said to me sarcastically, the son of a bitch . . .

As I had imagined, Macharavialla was in the mountains. Actually it was very close to Vélez-Málaga, although it took us an hour and a half to get there, since the old royal way that joins the two towns winds laboriously up the mountains and continually detours for several miles so as to connect the countless small towns and villages that are scattered all through the region. The road is very pleasant. As it goes higher and higher, the multiple gifts that nature has bestowed on that isolated region of Spain become evident. The smell of the sea is still in the air when vast stretches planted in sugarcane and bananas appear. A little higher up, there are the vineyards and the olive groves that cover the valleys and the hollows between the mountains. Finally the cultivated fields disappear, but not the greenery: dense groves of pine and live oak cover the mountainsides. The little villages, gleaming with whitewash, glow like pearls in the countryside. Shortly before arriving in Macharavialla, the road descends sharply, for the little town is in the middle of a hollow, surrounded by olive groves, vineyards, and fields of sunflowers. "The town certainly is small," my wife said to me as we looked down at it from above. The bell tower of the old church and a large three-story building, very white, looming across from it, could be seen. The rest of the town consisted of little whitewashed private houses one or two stories high with two-sloped roofs of fired clay tiles. It took us some time still before we reached the town, since the small road that leads to it—a branch of the royal way—is very narrow, badly paved, and very winding. We stopped the car that we had rented in Málaga in front of the church, on a little square with a quarrystone fountain in the middle surrounded by fifteen or twenty chestnut trees, under which it was possible to take one's ease on stone benches as white as snow.

We sat there for quite some time, recovering from the tiring trip. We enjoyed ourselves looking at the pleasant little square, the chestnut trees, the church, the tall building across from it, the well-paved streets, and the few people out on them at that hour. The men, almost all of them short, were wearing dark-colored pants and white shirts with the sleeves rolled up. Their complexions, deeply tanned, testified to their occupation: they were men who worked in the fields. The women, most of them dressed in black, had slightly paler skin. Many of them had pretty eyes, very large and light colored, green ones in particular. They cast sidelong glances at us, as though we were odd sorts, although those who passed nearby wished us "good afternoon" in loud and resonant voices. One had only to raise one's eyes to feel the mute but imposing presence of the mountains all around. It's a charming town, I thought.

"Do you know what, darling? I think it was worthwhile coming here."

"I should say so. It's a darling town. Which house did you inherit,

I wonder?" she asked me as she looked toward the end of the narrow little main street. The small two-story houses with crude iron grilles over the windows were very pretty. Any one of them would have satisfied me. I had only to see them to erase from my mind the idea of the town that we had had before coming.

"Mariana, I've been thinking . . . I wouldn't like to sell the house. We could come live here a couple of months a year. What do you think of the idea?"

"Splendid! I was thinking the same thing."

On second thought, I said to myself, the inheritance I received wasn't that small after all. A little house in this wonderful place and twenty thousand pesetas a month . . . If we go back to work in Mexico, we can easily put aside fifteen thousand pesetas a month; with that much money, we'd have more than enough to spend a couple of months a year here, very comfortably . . .

"Who can tell us about the house?" Mariana asked.

"The mayor, I suppose. Listen!" I called out to a youngster who was dabbling in the water in the fountain. I had already learned in Málaga to say, "Listen!" whenever I wanted to talk to someone. Before, my "I beg your pardon" or my "Please excuse me" brought nothing but expressions of surprise or doubt: "What am I supposed to pardon you for?" Andalusians invariably answer you.

"What is it, zeñó? . . ."

If it isn't easy in Málaga to understand people because of their strong accent, in which all the *s*s and *c*s turn into very long *z*s, and eight out of ten final syllables of words in a sentence are omitted, in Macharavialla it was even worse: the accent of its inhabitants is so difficult to understand that they seem to be expressing themselves in a language that has practically nothing to do with standard Spanish.

"Where is the town hall?"

The boy stared at us. He seemed lost in thought. He began mumbling, very fast, a string of words of which we didn't understand a single one. Fortunately he stretched his arm out toward the building opposite.

"Zat door . . ."

"Thank you very much."

"Don' menzun it."

The town hall is located—along with the jail and the cellars for storing the oil, the barrels of wine, and the various cereals the town produces, as well as a fair number of private apartments—in the only big building in the town. It is four stories high, over sixty yards long and forty wide; it is made of stone covered with whitewashed stucco. It is very old; it dates from the seventeenth century, according to what I was told, and despite having undergone many changes over the years and losing a large part of the quarrystone blocks that at one time framed its big doors and windows, it still has a certain grandeur about it. The main door, in the middle of the facade, is made up of two heavy swinging panels of pinewood nicely carved with rustic subjects. The door still has most of its iron decorations: twenty pretty ornamental studs with fluting running from the center to the edges and six huge gracefully forged hinges. It is framed by superb pink stonework, typical of the eighteenth century. There is a pilaster on each side with columns in the form of inverted pyramids, in the Solomonic style. The pilasters support capitals, above which is a frieze in the form of a semicircular arch. In the middle is a large rectangular niche, also rounded off at the top in an arch. Inside it is a curious statue of Saint Gabriel. He is dressed like a Roman centurion with his sword unsheathed, brandishing it threateningly above his head. His black eyes seem to watch whoever passes through the doorway, for his head, with long wavy hair, is turned slightly downward. Inside the doorway is a broad vestibule that leads to a large patio and its peristyle. In the middle is the inevitable quarrystone fountain. On the right-hand side are the offices of the town council.

The mayor, don Prudencio Gálvez—after being in Macharavialla for only a short time, we discovered that more than half the town had Gálvez as either a first or a last name—was a short man of about fifty with a healthy complexion, a big round head, and coarse hair with gray strands in it, though it still had a fair share of its original copper color. He had big brown eyes, a fine-drawn straight nose, a small mouth surrounded by a very heavy beard that, although closely shaved, left the lower half of his face very noticeably gray. Like all the important people in the town, he was not deeply tanned, and he was wearing a black suit, with a very white shirt buttoned to the collar but without a tie. A red handkerchief, exquisitely folded to a point, peeked out of his breast pocket.

"You don't say: don Franzisco!" he answered when I introduced myself. "We'vebeewait for you for some time . . ."

And he embraced me heartily, as though I were a prodigal son. Mariana looked at me puzzled as she listened to the man address her, gallantly kissing her hand at the same time. Of course she didn't understand one word. "He said to you, 'My lady, I am at your feet,' " I said in her ear, taking advantage of a moment in which the man left us to go get a handful of keys from the drawer of his desk.

Don Prudencio was a very congenial man and as good as fresh-baked bread. He insisted on accompanying us personally to the "house of the marquis." When I told him not to bother, he answered: "Whythell not, my gooman. It's just a step away. How could I fail to do don Adolfo's nephew that favor?" or something of the sort. When we left the building, seeing the church reminded me of an old anecdote my grandmother told many times. It seems that the inspector general, don José de Gálvez, was seriously wounded in the course of one of his expeditions against the Yaquis. His leg had been hit in the calf by a poisoned arrow. "He was in very bad shape," my grandmother told me. "Nobody believed his life could be saved. Then, on the verge of death, don José made a promise to Saint Gabriel, the patron saint of his family . . ." He promised the archangel that if he succeeded in saving his life, he would pave with gold doubloons the floor below the altar of God's warrior in the church of Macharavialla, the town where don José had been born. The archangel heeded his prayer, and don José, once he'd recovered of course kept his promise: he sent to Spain, in the Veracruz flotilla, a heavy trunkful of gold coins, accompanied by the necessary instructions. But when the time came to carry them out, they came upon a problem that, probably because of the fevers he had had, the illustrious inspector general had not foreseen. "When the administrator of the affairs of the Gálvez family got ready to comply with the instructions of his employer and ordered the mason to place the first coin in the fresh cement, the man discovered to his horror that the face of his beloved sovereign, don Carlos III, on the coin, risked being stepped on by the parishioners. He then ordered the mason to turn each coin over, but it also seemed to him a sacrilege to expose the royal shield of Spain to the shoe soles of the townspeople. The administrator thought the matter over for a long time, praying in his heart to the archangel on the altar to help him find the solution to such a thorny problem. Saint Gabriel, perhaps a little dissatisfied that the promise made him had not yet been fulfilled, immediately planted an inspiration in the mind of the administrator. In complete happiness, he saw the solution: 'Place them on edge,' he said to the mason. And that is what was done, although of course the doubloons don José had sent from New Spain were not nearly enough to pave the whole floor in that way; just a quarter of the area was covered in gold, some two hundred square yards . . ."

When I asked don Prudencio whether he knew that story, he replied solemnly, "Zey're still righ'there. Would you like to zeezem?"

And we headed for the church . . .

Then you wrote the first prayer or verse:

WHY I DESPISE YOU

1. When you read this manuscript again for the first time, within 166 years, you will not yet know that I was the one who wrote it . . .

You read aloud what you had just written. In your mind, that absurd phrase had an impeccable logic. You gave a satisfied smile and went on writing. You didn't stop again until you had finished the first chapter, just twenty verses farther on.

Twenty-two days later, you had finished. Like Saint John's, your Book of Revelation consisted of twenty-two chapters and 495 verses, and like your manuscript of the Book of Revelation, it had twenty-two blank spaces awaiting a skillful hand to illustrate them. You knew perfectly to whom that hand belonged, and you knew where to find him. Shortly before returning to your own time, you reread a passage in Francisco Goya's biography and fixed it firmly in your memory: "August, 1812. He is ordered to replace the portrait of Joseph Bonaparte by the word "Constitution" in the *Allegory of Madrid* . . ."

So he is in Madrid, then. You don't know his address, but if you write him at the Academy, he will surely receive the letter. The poor man! He has to be terribly downcast. It has been only a couple of months since his wife, Pepita Bayeu, died, his faithful and self-sacrificing companion of many years. In addition, his deafness has been growing more and more severe; although he has refused to acknowledge it, he is becoming deafer than a post. And the war, above all the war . . . It must have left the man prostrated. You have known few, very few, human beings with the talent and sensitivity of Goya. His spirit is like an open wound; human stupidity falls into it like lemon juice. It torments him; it makes him writhe, suffer, despair. But he doesn't give up; far from giving up, he answers proudly, he answers with his *Caprichos,* with his *Disasters of War,* with his monsters, with his enormous works that are insolent slaps in the face of the human race, reminding it of, portraying, its obscene behavior, its tireless eagerness to show what cruel, heartless, carrion beasts they are. He is a great man, Rasero, a ferocious man . . . Do you remember when we met him . . . ?

In the summer of 1796, don Francisco José de Gálvez, Rasero's eldest nephew, showed up in the old mansion in the calle Miaja, accompanied by a man of around forty, almost as bald as the Malagan, short in stature, chubby, and with a luminous smile.

"Uncle, allow me to present Agustín Esteva. He's a great artist. Do you remember the portraits of my father, my uncle Matías, and my cousin Bernardo that I showed you in Macharavialla? . . . Well, they were done by this man's hand."

"I congratulate you, sir. They strike me as really splendid."

"Thank you very much, marquis," the painter answered, his face flushed and a smile from ear to ear.

"Agustín has just finished a portrait of my family that's something to see. When you come to Macharavialla, I'll show it to you. It's extraordinary. Especially my son Adolfo. Agustín, you made him look as though he's about to step out of the painting."

"Please, don Francisco . . ."

"But it's true. Ah, and his miniatures, Uncle, they're unique. I don't believe there's a better miniaturist in Spain than he is. Why didn't I think of bringing along the ones he's made from our portraits, for you to see! Where could my head have been? But anyway, you'll have a chance to see them, Uncle. And now, before I forget, let me get to the point of my visit: inasmuch as Agustín has become a sort of official painter of the family—he looked at the artist and smiled—I thought he ought to make a big portrait of you, Uncle. We don't have a single one of you in the house. So our descendants won't have any way of knowing you."

"And why would they want to know me? Look, Francisco, I don't feel like . . ."

"I won't let you say no. Agustín is going to paint you, and that's all there is to it. I'll take care of his honorarium."

"That's not the reason. It just happens that . . ."

"I want to make a gift of it to you, Uncle. And don't offer any more objections, because the portrait is going to be painted, isn't it, Agustín?"

"With the permission of the marquis."

"It doesn't seem as if there's going to be any way out of it . . ."

"You can commit yourself to posing for it, don Fausto," his nephew broke in, smiling.

"All right, then, I agree. But I'm going to ask you, maestro, to paint me sitting down. My legs tire easily."

"Whatever you wish, marquis."

"I scarcely envy you, Agustín. Having to paint this ugly mug . . . But please remember that it's Francisco's fault."

"Don't say that, don Fausto. To tell you the truth, I was observing your face as we were talking. Believe me, it's a very interesting one. Please don't be offended by my outspokenness when I say that you have the oddest eyes I've ever seen in my life. They seem like mirrors!—as though a person were seeing himself in them. It's going to be a challenge to capture them on canvas."

That same day the artist installed himself in the house. The following morning, very early, Agustín Esteva was ready to begin work. He placed Rasero's old rocking chair in the south wing of the gallery, very close to the wall. He had chosen the tile wainscoting there as the background for the portrait. He placed his easel almost in front of the rocking chair, perhaps a couple of feet to the right, and five paces away, so that he was very close to the railing.

"Everything is ready, marquis. Please sit down. Hold your head up, and look steadily at this cross," he said as he pointed with the end of his paintbrush to a green cross that he had painted on the back of the canvas, near the upper corner at the side closer to the model. "That's it! That's fine," Agustín said as he moved as far away as possible from the man he intended to paint. He looked at him with his right eye—he kept the other one closed—past his thumb sticking up from his fist, at the end of his outstretched arm. There wasn't much space behind him, so he found it necessary to lean his body over the railing.

"Be careful. Don't fall," Rasero said.

"Don't worry, marquis . . . Now, now I've got it," Agustín said, and going over the canvas, he began to sketch a silhouette with energetic, quick strokes.

Besides being a magnificent painter, Agustín Esteva was a very likable man. Good Valencian that he was, he was cheerful and talkative by nature. Luckily for him, the craft he practiced required only the use of his hands, so that his mouth was free to chatter on and on. This man must have been a barber, the Malagan said to himself many times as Agustín painted him. The minute he began his work for the day, the painter also began his interminable monologues:

anecdotes, almost all of them spicy, jokes, popular sayings, and recollections came forth from his prodigious tongue at a dizzying rate. Rasero pretended to listen to him. Looking steadily at the green cross that the artist had shown him, he used the time to reflect on his memories. When he heard a loud guffaw from the painter, he smiled as though what he had said was very amusing. That satisfied the Valencian. He attributed don Fausto's almost uniform failure to answer the questions he asked him more to the deafness the old man doubtless suffered from than to any lack of interest in what he told him.

On one of those mornings, Rasero, lulled by the artist's endless flow of talk, was remembering the wonderful conversations with his friend Denis Diderot when Diderot had held forth on the subject of painting. Nobody knew that art the way he did, he was thinking. I'm going to reread his *Salons.* All of a sudden he heard a word that brought him out of his daydreaming. "Did you say Goya?"

"That's right, Francisco Goya," the painter answered, raising the volume of his voice, as though he were speaking to a deaf man. "As I was telling you, he's the best painter in Spain today. And it's a good thing I can say, 'is,' because two years ago he was very ill, he almost died on us, don Fausto. But thanks be to God, he managed to get over it, though it left him with a handicap, a very bad one." Rasero looked at him questioningly. "He's been deaf ever since then; he can hear practically nothing," he said, almost shouting.

"By the way, Agustín, I for my part hear quite well. You don't have to scream at me."

Well, then, he simply didn't pay attention to what I was saying, the painter said to himself, a little annoyed.

"And do you know that man?" Rasero asked.

"Of course, marquis. He was my teacher, and I can pride myself on having had his friendship for many years. He's a great man, a bit testy, especially after his illness, but at heart he's a man as good as gold . . ."

Rasero had heard the name of Francisco Goya for the first time two years before, when, during the trip back from Paris, they had stopped for a few days in Saragossa. There he visited the Church of the Virgen del Pilar and had been able to see the magnificent frescoes decorating the cupola. He found out that they, along with some other good paintings he saw in various public places in the city, were the work of a painter who had been born there although he now lived in Madrid. He was told that Francisco Goya was one of the most highly esteemed court painters. In the capital, Rasero was able to see several more of the artist's works. He especially liked the tapestries he saw in the Royal Manufactory and several portraits that hung in the Academy of Saint Ferdinand, but even more a magnificent Christ that decorated the grand staircase of this venerable building. The style of painting of the Aragonese held a strange fascination for Rasero. He didn't know why yet, but he was convinced that that man, and above all his art, would play a fundamental role in his life. He wanted to meet him then, but it proved to be impossible: Goya had fallen very ill and was in Andalusia recovering. The opportunity will come one day, Rasero said to himself at the time. Now, as he listened to Agustín Esteva, he realized that the opportunity had come.

"I'd like very much to meet that man. Do you think he'd receive me in Madrid?"

"You don't have to go that far, marquis. Goya is now at Sanlúcar de Barrameda, in the country palace of the dukes of Alba. And he's thinking of staying there for several months; he told me so in a letter I received barely a week ago."

"And do you think he'd receive me?"

"I'm sure of it . . . If you like, I can write to him. In any case, I've heard that your nephew, don Francisco, is a good friend of the Duchess of Alba's. I'm certain that if he puts in a word in your behalf, the lady will receive you with pleasure."

"Receive *us,* Agustín. Wouldn't you like to accompany me to Cádiz?"

"It will be an honor, marquis."

Doña María Teresa Cayetana de Silva, the thirteenth duchess of Alba, kindly received them at her pretty country palace of Sanlúcar de Barrameda. She was a mature woman, just past thirty. Her face was far from attractive. Beneath very thick eyebrows that nearly met, her black eyes were good sized but bulging. Her nose, long and not at all comely, stood out above a mouth that was pinched and small, especially by comparison with the width of her face, with its very full cheeks and a double chin that was beginning to form, which gave a roundness to what should have been oval shaped. But if nature had been stingy in bestowing gifts on her face, it was extraordinarily generous, on the other hand, when it came to her hair. Rasero had seldom seen such a lovely mane. Abundant, deep black, curly, and very long—it really made one want to sink into it. The same was true of her body: her breasts, irrepressible and proud, couldn't have been more appealing; beneath them, her waist, very narrow and svelte, prefigured adorable hips. Her legs were hidden under her dress, but it was enough to see her arms, long, slender, with smooth, very white skin, to surmise that her lower limbs must be long, firm, and strong, as suggested by her pretty ankles peeking out from beneath the folds of her skirt. That imposing body, along with the grace and charm with which the woman expressed herself—she was in the habit of smiling in such a way that her eyes became smaller and her mouth as large as possible, so that her ugliness turned into prettiness—made her extremely attractive. As he contemplated her, Rasero remembered with nostalgia the old days when pleasure made his senses explode and led him to his fantastic visions.

After they had installed themselves in their rooms and tidied themselves up, they were led to the garden of the palace by a servant. On a terrace, protected from the burning-hot Andalusian sun by a canvas awning, sitting in a comfortable armchair, with his hands busy drawing rapidly in a notebook, was Francisco Goya. He was making quick sketches of doña Cayetana, who was in the middle of the garden, with her eyes blindfolded, playing blindman's buff with a merry group of young people.

"Maestro, what a pleasure to see you!" Agustín Esteva said in a loud voice.

"Well, if it isn't Agustín! And to what do I owe this miracle?" the artist answered, rising to his feet to embrace his colleague.

The Valencian came out with a long, confused explanation of the visit—an explanation that, Rasero was certain, the Aragonese didn't understand a word of, for he merely smiled impassively at Agustín Esteva's jubilant cries.

Agustín finally said, "Allow me to introduce the Marquis de Rasero; he has been extremely eager to meet you."

"What was that again?" Goya asked.

Rasero then took a calling card out of his frock coat and placed it in his hands.

"Marquis Fausto de Rasero. Ah! Delighted to meet you, marquis. It's a great honor. Please do sit down . . . So you're Francisco Gálvez' uncle?" Rasero nodded. "His father, don José, was a great man . . . You must be his cousin, no?" Rasero nodded again. "He was a real gentleman. An indefatigable man, my friend, indefatigable . . ."

The two men took to each other immediately. They spent the entire afternoon sitting on that terrace, drinking chilled wine and eating cold meats, cheese, and fresh fruit, as they kept up a delightful conversation. Goya, aware that he was almost totally deaf, had developed a very ingenious form of conversation: he led the exchange, into which from time to time he interjected very specific questions, for which a yes, a no, or a "Who knows?" were enough of an answer. He was thus freed from having to interrupt the conversation continually with repetitions of the deaf man's question "What was that again?" which he so detested. Rasero caught on to his system at once and confined himself to nodding or shaking his head or, at times, raising his eyes heavenward as if asking for the answer. Meanwhile, he took great pleasure in listening to the sharp-witted reflections of the Aragonese. Goya, an inquisitive and well-informed man, found in Rasero, practically a new arrival from the now much discussed France, a source of invaluable news. The Malagan found himself once again bombarded with questions, like a student standing before his professors. He could not help remembering Madame Denis, Camille Desmoulins, and Danton when, as Goya was now doing, they delved relentlessly into his memory.

"So you knew Denis Diderot? An extraordinary man, I'll wager. Please believe me, marquis, that it was my reading of his *Salons* that showed me the path I should follow. Those marvelous critiques! To me, they were like giving eyes to a blind man . . ."

His questions ranged from painting to politics and from there to history, flitting like bees from one flower to another. Rasero, while offering his yeses, noes, and who-knowses, was surprising himself with the abundant information stored in his memory. Every so often, they were interrupted by doña Cayetana, who came over to them with a smile to ask if they were being properly taken care of. "Never has a lady's gallant servant been as well served . . . ," Rasero replied good-humoredly.

"Well then, go on enjoying each other's company, gentlemen, for we're going off to town to look for a group of gypsies who are making merry . . ."

Goya looked at the woman mistrustfully. Even before that, Rasero had noted the profound influence that the duchess exerted over the artist. Goya interrupted their conversation several times to contemplate doña Cayetana with eyes full of jealousy and rancor as she unconcernedly allowed herself to be fondled by a roguish lad during their ridiculous children's game.

"Would you like to go with them?" Rasero said to Goya in his ear. (He had now found the distance and the tone necessary to make himself heard.)

"Certainly not. Go on and have a very good time, madam," he said to the duchess without hiding his displeasure. That man couldn't be more in love, Rasero thought.

The following day, doña Cayetana, accompanied by her friends, left for Seville. She was obliged, as she explained to them, to take certain steps with regard to the estate of her late husband—the duke had died, before his time, barely two months before—and, above all, to make the necessary arrangements for the solemn memorial mass for the duke that was to be celebrated the following month in Madrid. Agustín Esteva seized the chance to join the company, since he too needed to attend to certain matters in Seville. This pleased Rasero a great deal, since it gave him the opportunity to enjoy the painter's company without interference by the magnetic and disturbing presence of the duchess or the endless chatter of the Valencian. Thus the new friends spent several altogether pleasant days, if not sitting on the terrace talking about the political situation of the kingdom, then strolling at leisure about the beautiful Andalusian countryside or drinking together in one tavern or another in Cádiz. They spent a great deal of time in the taverns, observing the customers, letting time go by, without saying a word to each other, giving their minds free rein to relax, each with his own ideas and memories.

"Do you know what, marquis? Sometimes I think that my deafness is a blessing from God—and that's when my stubborn old head leaves me in peace. I then enjoy a calm, a delightful serenity, and am freed from having to listen to so many stupid comments. But when that stubborn old head of mine starts churning—which happens very often, alas—my deafness becomes a real torment, since nothing coming from outside can distract me from my thoughts. I'm forced, stripped bare, to confront everything that resounds in my mind, those frightful screams, those terrible images . . ."

He talked to you about it one afternoon as you were returning from the city, after looking at the magnificent canvases he had painted in the Holy Cave in Cádiz. He talked to you about his illness, of the terrible fevers that had attacked him: "At times, I found myself in the ninth circle of hell . . . Dear God! If it hadn't happened to me, I'd never believe that a man can stand that much. I saw death, don Fausto, I saw it within reach of me. You can't imagine how sweet it seemed compared with the torment my life had become. But it didn't come . . ." What came were visions, "hair-raising visions, marquis: monsters, chimeras, furies, all the devils of all the religions filed past my mind. And they howled, they howled horribly. I think that that was what made me deaf: the infernal din that broke loose inside my head. My eardrums blew out, I'm sure of it . . ." You were deeply touched as you listened to him. You had found a twin soul, another pathetic victim of his own mind. "And they're still here, don Fausto," he said to you as he pointed to his head with his index finger, stubby and unrefined like all the rest of his body, for he looked like an ungainly peasant from the north of Spain. "They're encysted in it like larvae in a piece of fruit. When I least expect it, they appear, dragging me off to madness. It's terrible, marquis, terrible . . ."

When they reached the mansion, Goya showed the Malagan a sketch book. "It's what I've done these last two months. If I go on working like this, I'm going to die of hunger," he said with a smile.

On seeing those magnificent sketches, almost all of them of the Duchess of Alba—he had made sketches of her in every possible position, from combing her hair to dressing to dancing, even to making the sign of the cross—you recognized the hand of the master who had done that marvelous illustration you glimpsed for just a moment during the vision, almost twenty years before, which took you to the little house in Macharavialla, where you saw for the first time, moreover, the thin man. You now understood the fascination that the works of that man held for your mind; the strange omen you had seen in the painting entitled *Shipwreck* when you studied it in Madrid now made sense. Its desperate men fighting against the rough sea, and the woman, the only person who is shown standing, with her arms uplifted to heaven, pleading for the Lord's attention—when you saw that painting, you felt the woman was calling you so that you would drown with them. Now you understood . . .

"Maestro, I want to show you something," you said when you had finished looking through the notebook.

You went to your bedroom and returned with the manuscript of the Book of Revelation underneath your arm. You began to leaf through it as you stood before the painter. As you turned the pages, you saw how your friend's face became more and more serious, almost somber. Goya murmured something that you didn't understand and snatched the book out of your hands. Then he put it on a little table, beneath a lamp so that it would be well lit, sat down, and began to look closely at the first illustration. "Marvelous," he exclaimed in a low voice. "Marvelous," he repeated. He was so absorbed in contemplating the work that he didn't even notice when you left the drawing room to go off to your bedroom for the night.

The following day, you encountered the artist in the very place you had left him the night before. On the table were several candle stubs and countless sheets of paper filled with charcoal drawings. "Ah, my friend!" the chubby man said happily. "This is a jewel. A real jewel. I would never have suspected that Boucher was capable of such a miracle . . ."

Goya kept the manuscript till the day you left. When he gave it back, you could sense the deep pain it gave him to do so; it seemed as though he were handing over a son to you. You were on the point of making a gift of it to him, but something inside, very deep down, kept you from it. The chubby man embraced you warmly. "Thank you, marquis!" he said to you, and went off with his eyes glistening with tears.

You never saw each other again, although you both kept up your correspondence for a long time, until trapped in the future, you were no longer able to answer your friend's letters.

When was that? . . . In 1799, I believe. Yes, the century was coming to an end, I remember it well now. It was then that he sent you that letter. Look for it, look for it . . . It has to be here somewhere. Here it is, here it is! March, 1799. Didn't I tell you so?

Dear marquis,

I am pleased to learn from your letter than you are enjoying the blessing of good health, both you and yours. Unfortunately, I am unable to say the same for myself. The fevers have not ceased to torment me. As punctually as if they were governed by the stars, they come every six months to remind me of my misfortune. But never mind, it could be worse. My dear ones, thanks be to God, are all well.

I have been working very hard. Ah, how I miss those delightful days of idleness in Sanlúcar! I miss your conversation even more, dear marquis. God willing, may there come a chance to meet again, for I pray you to believe me, I treasure our last meeting among my fondest memories. I enclose with this letter a sketchbook with my *Caprichos,* a collection of engravings that has cost me my life's blood, but I believe that it was worth it. Please tell me sincerely what you think of them. I for my part believe—and I hope you agree—that I have found a very rich lode that will allow me to give free rein to all those little concerns that you already know about . . .

Lastly, I want to tell you that this work, in my heart of hearts, is dedicated to you: to you and to that great French artist whose treasure—which you have in your custody (and you don't know how much I envy you that, marquis)—is in large part responsible for the lode I mentioned to you above. Ah, don Fausto! I am in your grace's everlasting debt. May God give me the chance to repay you some day. Yours,

Francisco Goya

Well, that day has come, don Francisco. Come on, Rasero, write him now. For the love of God! stop writing poems now. Write this minute, for you have very little time.

Macharavialla, August 20, 1812

Dearest maestro,

First of all, a strong embrace: I have learned of Pepita's death. God must surely have her with him in his glory; a woman like her cannot be anywhere else. Next, my apologies for not having written to you for such a long time, but I have a splendid excuse: I lost my reason eight years ago. I was still alive, though I had no soul. I was more like a plant than a human being. The doctors, as usual, have a good number of explanations about what happened, but none that are convincing. Much less can they explain why, after eight years, I recovered my reason. All in all, it really interests me very little. At my age, my friend, one's only wish is to die. Fortunately, I believe that I will not have to wait much longer. To be frank with you, though, I wouldn't like death to overtake me before I have fulfilled a certain desire—or a caprice, rather (though not one of genius, as yours are). And no one in the world except you, don Francisco, can satisfy it.

I am placing in your hands a few bits of nonsense that I wrote a little while ago, after I recovered from my illness. Who knows what strange ideas came to my mind while I was away, but there is no denying that they inspired me to write these stupid things . . . In any event, maestro, I place the manuscript in your hands, and in your heart the plea that you will deign to illustrate it with your marvelous hand. Believe me that, if you do so, you will make this old man infinitely happy!

Knowing your kindness, which I am certain will keep you from declining to do as I have asked, I take the liberty of sending you ten thousand reales as an honorarium for your work. If you deem that this sum is not sufficient, please let me know, and I will gladly send you however much you say. In addition, abusing your patience, allow me to ask one last favor of you: when you have finished the work, I will be much obliged if, before returning it to me, you send it to a workshop to be bound. I would like it to be in cherry-colored calfskin.

With boundless gratitude, receive an embrace, in his arms and his heart, from your friend,

Fausto Rasero

There! Now, to wait. A couple of months, three at most. Enjoy the countryside. Breathe the fresh air from the mountains. Let the sun caress your face. Play with the children. Chat with the miners, the peasants, the town doctor. Read the newspapers, and find out more about the beating they're giving the Corsican there in Holy Russia. And most of all, forget the last eight years. Try to be, if only for the few days of life you still have left, a normal person, Rasero . . .

The church in Macharavialla is an old stone building covered with whitewashed stucco. It has its slender bell tower and an impressive main door, framed in splendidly carved pink quarrystone blocks. It reminded me a great deal of those common in towns in Mexico, but in the church in Macharavialla the stonework, though very skillfully done, is much more sober and austere than that in Mexican churches. When we went past the entrance, the inside dimensions surprised me, for from the outside the interior looked much smaller. The main aisle is more than thirty yards wide, and just in front of the main altar, beneath an attractive cupola, the two lateral aisles, each of them a bit over ten yards wide, meet.

The man smiled in satisfaction and explained to us that, more than two hundred fifty years before, when a large silver mine was discovered, Macharavialla became a very important and very rich town. "In its best moments it had almost ten thousand inhabitants. They came from all over to work here, even from as far away as Extremadura." But at the beginning of the last century the seam was exhausted and many people left. The only ones remaining were a few peasants who looked after their vineyards and olive groves and raised sheep and goats. Nonetheless, in recent years the town has been experiencing a sort of renaissance, "thanks to your uncle Adolfo, and may God keep him in his holy glory . . .": some fifteen years ago, don Adolfo introduced Indian sunflowers into the region as a commercial crop. "The plant grows very well in our fields, and there is more and more demand for sunflower oil. So, little by little, we're making progress. We already have more than two thousand residents . . ."

The inside of the church looks very run-down, though it still preserves traces of an earlier opulence. On the main altar there is a magnificent life-sized Christ crucified. "It's the work of Francisco Hurtado, a great Andalusian artist. It's three hundred years old," don Prudencio explained to us. In the right aisle there is a small altar dedicated to the Virgin of Victory. Alongside it is the door that leads to the sacristy. In the left aisle is the altar dedicated to Saint Gabriel. On seeing the beautiful image of the soldier of god in exquisitely adorned wood, dressed in fine blue, purple, and white silks full of embroidery and lace, with jewels on his hands and about his neck, crowned with a heavy diadem of pure gold with several precious stones mounted in the frontal section of it, and lit by many candles, one realizes immediately that this is the most venerated image in the town. Mariana and I were looking at the votive offerings surrounding the archangel when don Prudencio said to us, as he pointed to the floor to the left of the altar, "Look. Here it is."

The floor directly below the corner of the altar did in fact have a square slab set upon it, measuring approximately a yard and a half on a side and four inches in thickness, made of gray cement. It was dense with grooves, almost all of them holding coins. When we went closer, we could see that the coins were of different sizes and colors; there were silver, copper, and black ones, although it was obvious that all of them were more or less modern.

"But . . ."

"Let me explain," don Prudencio interrupted. "The gold doubloons disappeared long, long ago. There are only two of them left. Look here." Just at the far corner, there were two gold pieces, both of them more than halfway embedded in the cement. "Nobody has dared dig out those two . . ."

"And what about the others?"

"It's a very old custom in the town; it's been one since my grandfather's day, at least: every time someone says a prayer to Saint Gabriel, he or she leaves a coin in a groove. And there it stays until somebody who feels a need for it picks it out. It's a sort of contingency fund for the town, if you know what I mean," the mayor said with a smile. "Suppose you'd like a little drink in the tavern and don't have one red cent in your pocket. Well, you go to Saint Gabriel's altar, recite an Ave Maria, and ask him for a small loan. The saint is very patient, and he's never asked anybody for interest," he concluded, laughing heartily.

"If we're going to live in the town, I think we ought to cooperate, don't you?" Mariana said, and placed a couple of five-peso Mexican coins in each of several vacant grooves.

"Well, you're already residents of Macharavialla. And God grant that you stay for many years . . ."

We left the church and got into the car. We didn't go directly to the house. Don Prudencio wanted to take advantage of our having a car to take us around to see the outskirts of the town. We saw the olive groves, the little vineyards, and the vast fields of Indian sunflowers, the pride of the town. We followed the old path that leads to the former mine. The stone shell of what used to be the building where they processed the ore can still be seen. Then don Prudencio took us to see Macharavialla's "river." It's actually a little brook whose waters feed into a branch of the Guadalhorque. "In winter the water level rises a lot; the overflow reaches almost to there . . .", the mayor told us as he pointed to some rocks that were some fifteen yards from the brook. How Andalusians do exaggerate, I thought.

Mariana and I were charmed. The more we became acquainted with it, the more we liked the countryside around the town. Finally, as dusk fell, when the goatherds could be seen coming down from the mountains with their lively flocks, we went to our new house. It was on the outskirts of town, a few miles from the church. The building—also made of stone with a smooth facing of stucco and whitewashed, and two stories high, with a two-sloped roof with tiles of fired clay and an almost square layout—was in the middle of a plot of land covered with sunflowers. A couple of old ash trees kept its southern-oriented cool. In the distance, the house looked quite large.

"Was this the residence of the Marquis de la Sonora?"

"I should say not! The Gálvez mansion was the building you were in this morning. Don Francisco Gálvez, our Adolfo's father, sold the mansion to the town at the end of the last century. This other house belonged to the Gálvez family, of course, but it was only the residence of the administrator of his affairs."

Close up, the house wasn't as large as it had seemed from a distance. It was very run-down; moss had turned the walls green for at least a foot and a half up. The stone blocks of the windowsills and those framing the windows had almost completely disappeared, and only one of the four windows in the facade still had its original iron grille. Nonetheless, the building had a certain appeal. It seemed splendid to me, and to Mariana too.

The main door was a sort of miniature replica of the one we had seen at the town hall: the two panels of carved pine, the Solomonic pilasters framing it, a little niche above the capital and underneath a semicircular arch. But in this vaulted niche, Saint Gabriel was no longer to be seen: only his feet, ankles, and part of his legs attested that at one time a complete statue of him must have stood there. Before entering, don Prudencio took us around to the back of the house to show us where the master switch was (he turned it on), as well as the water pump and other utilities. When he had explained everything completely, we headed for the front door. The mayor opened the heavy door and said to us solemnly, "Madam, don Francisco. I leave you in your house. May God grant that your life here will be a happy one."

He did not accept the drink or the coffee we offered him. He was in rather a hurry, he explained to us, since there was a meeting of the town council at seven on the dot. Nor did he want us to take him back to town in the car. "For heaven's sake, don Paco, it's just a short walk. What you two must do is settle in and get some rest. You've already done enough rushing around for today . . . Ah!"—he stopped on the threshold—"I'll send you Pascuala right away tomorrow."

I remember very well the strange impression the house made on us when we saw it for the first time. I can still smell the odor it had: a little sour, a mixture of dampness, old wood, dust, books, and oil paintings. The house was permeated, besides, by the presence of my uncle Adolfo. After living fifty years between its walls, he could not but become part of it. We felt a bit intimidated, as though we were in a venerable place in which there was no room for us. When Mariana turned on the dining-room light and we could see the downstairs clearly, our faltering gave way, little by little to curiosity. We went through the whole building the way a person visits an exotic museum. Perhaps *exotic* isn't the word that best expresses the impression the place gave us, but I can't come up with a better one.

This main room was quite large, although at first glance it didn't seem so: the enormous dining section devoured almost the entire space. We had never seen one so sizable: the table was easily more than five yards long by a yard and a half wide. It was in the nineteenth-century

Spanish style and made of walnut; there were six big chairs on each side and another one at each end, though the chairs at the ends had arms. The china closet that matched the table was also enormous, so big that it overlapped the frame of the kitchen door by at least eight inches. It must have been along the opposite wall, I said to myself, and it disheartened me just to think of the effort it would take to move it back there. It contained a set of dishes and a number of decorative pieces in porcelain that, together with little plastic figurines in the worst taste, made an absurd collection.

Above the middle of the table hung a chandelier with eight light bulbs, five of which were burned out; in addition, it had lost most of the glass prisms that had once hung from its arms. Across from the china closet was a large sideboard decorated with a silver tea set, though it looked more like iron, it was so tarnished. Above it, hanging on the wall, were two large paintings—portraits in oil. One of them showed my great-grandfather, don Francisco de Gálvez, the admiral. He was visible from the waist up, in three-quarter profile, and was dressed in a fancy navy blue uniform with the chest full of medals and decorations. In the crook of his left arm he held a big Napoleonic-style hat with bright ostrich plumes jutting out. His broad forehead, with big receding bald spots in his chestnut hair, very fine and plastered to his skull, as well as his green, haughty eyes, his slender, straight nose, and his good-looking mouth, beneath which was a ridiculous goatee, reminded me very much of my father's features. The mystery of genes . . . , I thought. He looks exactly like my father. I said as much to Mariana.

"And what about her: whom does she look like?" she answered me as she pointed to the portrait alongside that of the admiral.

It was obviously doña María Pastora Rodríguez de Arias, my great-grandmother. She was in precisely the same position as her husband, dressed in a sumptuous white dress trimmed with quantities of lace, tulle, and brocade. On her head she was wearing a curious headdress of the same color. Peeking out from underneath it were thick pitch-black curls. This portrait reminded me a lot of those I had seen of the Empress Carlota. Doña María Pastora did not look particularly pretty, though, still, she had a winning face. Perhaps this was because of her eyes, which were small and very slanted but intelligent and mischievous at the same time.

"She looks like my grandmother Juana and my sister Mercedes," I answered my wife. "If my family had had a chance to see this portrait, they wouldn't have made up that joke about the Filipino who cuckolded the admiral. Just look at those eyes. She seems Chinese, doesn't she?"

"That's right. Actually, they're exactly like your sister's eyes and your nephew Diego's . . ."

The mystery of genes, I thought again.

The dining section barely left space in one corner of the main room for a tiny Victorian-style parlor area with incredibly threadbare rugs. What pleased us most about this corner were a pretty Art Nouveau floor lamp and an old radio receiver on top of a little table. "It goes back to the '30s at least," I commented to Mariana. Accustomed as we were to living in an apartment, the kitchen seemed bigger to us than it actually was. It was painted in a horrid beige-colored oil paint, which covered not only the plasterwork at the top of the walls but also the ceiling, the tile wainscoting that rose a yard and a half above the floor, and the wood stove. Alongside the wood stove, the modern kitchen range and refrigerator looked odd, although the word *modern* is only a manner of speaking, since they were at least thirty years old.

"Who could ever have had the idea of painting over the patterned tiles?!" Mariana exclaimed, as she scratched at one of them with a knife. "When they're Talavera porcelain! Can the paint be removed?"

An old wooden staircase with a pleasing wooden balustrade formed of delicately turned banisters led to the upper floor of the house. The stairs creaked unreassuringly as we went up. "We're going to have to repair this staircase," I said to Mariana. "It's about to collapse . . ." By this point I had already lost count of the expenses that would be entailed in repairing the house. It's going to take another inheritance, I said to myself.

The upper floor consisted of three bedrooms and a very large bathroom. No doubt it was a bedroom that was made into a bathroom, I thought as soon as I saw its ample dimensions. Like the kitchen, it was painted in that frightful beige-colored oil paint, though here from floor to ceiling. The washbasin, the toilet, and the tub were very old. I had seen their like only in gangster movies of the '30s. In one of the bedrooms—the smallest—my uncle had installed his painter's studio. The only furniture in the room was two easels, a little commode with several jars full of paintbrushes on top, an old armchair, and a regular-sized table covered with books on painting and tubes of watercolors and oil paints. The walls were filled with paintings, and on the floor, leaning against the wall, many canvases were piled up. We spent a long time studying my uncle Adolfo's work.

"Don Adolfo was a man of fixed ideas," Mariana said, smiling.

And indeed almost all the paintings had the same configuration: they were of three women seen full face, the one in the center standing erect while her companions on either side leaned their heads on her shoulders. There were women of all sorts: seen full length and half length, blondes, brunettes, redheads, ones with fair complexions and dark, with straight and curly hair, short and long, hanging loose and pulled back, naked and clothed, bejeweled and unadorned. There were even a great variety of pictorial styles: from totally academic to very modern, with simple, energetic brushstrokes reminiscent of certain works by Picasso. The paintings ranged across Impressionist, fragmented Cubist, and colorful Fauvelike styles, and there was even one that might be called Expressionist, with the three women with mouths open in a circle and dark and very deep-set eyes. But always there were three women in an identical pose. Among the paintings, three or four were really good. Once Mariana and I agreed on our choice, we put them aside to hang them later on some of the walls of our new house. Apart from the women, there were several drawings of nude women's bodies, almost all done in charcoal or oil paint of a single color. There was a grayish blue one, showing a naked woman sitting on the floor with her legs slightly parted, that struck us as splendid. We added it to our original selection.

The next room was a sort of combination study and library. There was a big wooden rolltop desk that fascinated us. On the floor was quite an old hi-fi set. Modern objects age much more quickly than old-fashioned ones: as I repeated this cliché to myself, I inspected the RCA turntable. Alongside it, on a little table, were a few records. They were very old. Some were 78 rpm. Some were of classical music, the most modern of them conducted by Toscanini; others were of flamenco. I can hardly say how pleased I was to see those old records. The legendary names of great *cantaores* I had only heard of, especially when as a little boy I listened to my father go on and on about flamenco singing with his friends, were now before my eyes, printed on the labels of the heavy acetate records: el Cojo de Málaga, Tomás Pavón, Juanito Breva, Pepe de la Matrona, la Piriñaca de Jerez, Manuel Torre, don Antonio Chacón, la Niña de los Peines, Aurelio Selle, and el Pericón de Cádiz. There were also a few names that were unknown to me. "The inheritance would have been worth it just for this," I said, deeply touched, to my wife. I put a record by Tomás Pavón on the turntable and was happy to find that, though the sound was a little distorted, it was a reasonably good recording.

As I heard the fervent *soleares* of the Sevillian, I began to inspect the books that covered a whole wall of the room. A strange man, my great-uncle Adolfo! It would be practically impossible to deduce anything about his character from what he read: there were a number of the volumes of Freud's complete works in French; in addition, the works of Sue, Hugo, Dumas *père* and *fils,* Stendhal, Balzac, Maupassant, Gide, Flaubert, Rimbaud, Mallarmé, Valéry, Baudelaire, Zola, and others, all in their original language, gave proof that don Adolfo had been a fancier of Gallic letters. But there was also a respectably large collection—almost all in Spanish—of the classics of anarchism. Bakunin, Malatesta, the Reclus, Kropotkin, Salvochea, and many others were stored in the old bookcase, keeping subversion alive in its heart. Down below was the complete collection of Miguel Zévaco's *Los Pardaian,* also in Spanish, and next to it were various volumes on the history and geography of Spain and a SOPENA encyclopedic dictionary. Finally, on the remaining shelves, and occupying a large part of the bookcase, there were any number of cowboy novels. I would never have guessed that Marcial Lafuente Estefanía had written so many. As my uncle's bookcase attested, this author easily outdid Balzac: more than half the novels of this genre were by him—some fifty, according to my estimate. In one corner of the bookcase I came across some very old pornographic magazines, dating back to the '30s and '40s probably. The women, brazen and smiling, were lifting their satin skirts to show their thighs confined within black silk stockings, where, underneath dark curly hair, those other mouths, hungry and lascivious, offered incomparable delights. How many times can don Adolfo have looked at these women? How many times can he have masturbated as he contemplated all that luxuriant flesh? I closed the magazines and hid them in a far corner. For a moment I felt as though I had violated my great-uncle's privacy.

Finally, there was the bedroom. It was the largest upstairs room and faced south. The big window—the only one that still had its iron grille—was just above the big front door of the house. The furniture in it consisted of a brass double bed, with a thin old mattress rolled up at the head of it; a fine-looking desk lacquered in black; a big walnut wardrobe with two doors, each with its mirror, and five drawers; a bureau; three chairs; and an Austrian-style rocking chair. The bed was alongside the door and across the room from the window. Underneath the window were the desk and a chair. The wardrobe covered almost the whole wall on the right, with a rectangular niche topped by a semicircular arch at each side of it. The niches held busts, of bronze-painted plaster, of Bach and Beethoven. In the opposing wall there was just one niche, which held a bust of the divine Mozart. The remainder of this wall was covered with paintings by my uncle: four triads of women, executed in four different styles. Alongside the women, there was a strange oil painting. Obviously it was very old. Somewhat more than a yard and a half high and a yard wide, it was a portrait of an old man seated in an armchair. The background consisted of Moorish tiles with cream-colored geometrical filigree designs against a cobalt blue background. The man, very rigid, with his arms crossed in his lap, was dressed entirely in black except a jabot down his chest, and the ruffles at his cuffs, which were gleaming white. He was a very old man; his face was extremely wrinkled, and there wasn't a single hair on his head. His features were fine and even delicate, particularly his rather pointed chin. But his eyes, which stared back at whoever was looking at them, were the center of interest in the painting. The artist had cleverly placed those splendid eyes—very far apart, deep black, wide open, and remarkably bright—in the golden rectangle of the painting. Mariana and I stood a good while contemplating that strange figure.

"He reminds me of Picasso when he was old," she commented.

I barely heard her, for that man's gaze had oddly perturbed me. At times, I felt that the depths of my soul were being examined, not by that man but by myself—as though those eyes were something like mirrors in which I saw myself, or to be more precise, in which I saw my soul and found it confused, anxious, forsaken.

"I feel something very strange when I see that man. Don't you, Paco?"

I nodded and returned to looking at those eyes for a good while longer, until a sudden and almost uncontrollable impulse to burst into tears compelled me to lower my eyes. Only then did I see the bronze-colored medallion painted in the lower right-hand corner of the painting. The letters, simulating ones engraved in metal, said,

Don Fausto H. de Oquendo, marquis del Razero
P. by Agustín Esteba
MDCCXCVII

"Seventeen hundred ninety-seven," Mariana read. "It seems incredible. How can a person who lived almost two hundred years ago seem so familiar to me? . . ."

And there she was, weeping away. I unrolled the mattress and made her sit down on the bed.

"Come on, woman, what's the matter?" I said to her as I kissed her cheeks, lapping at the tears streaming down.

"I don't know . . . I don't know. It's very strange. I don't feel sad, believe me, Paco; it's a very odd feeling . . ."

She cried for some time. Her weeping little by little became gentler and slower, until it finally stopped.

"Those tears did me good," she said happily. (Ah, her marvelous mouth!) "I'm going downstairs to get a little ham and cheese. I'm dying of hunger! In the meantime, why don't you make up the bed? There must be sheets and blankets in the wardrobe."

"All right, but bring a bottle of wine too."

When I finished making the bed, I sat down and lit a little lamp on the bureau. Above it, my great-uncle had hung a fair number of family photographs. In one of them, I recognized my grandmother when she was young. She was dressed in the Andalusian style, with a tortoiseshell comb and a mantilla. She looked very pretty, but her strong chin and her broad, haughty forehead were signs of her energetic disposition. In among many people I was unable to identify, I came across my great-uncle José Adolfo. It was the first time I had seen my benefactor. In what was a studio portrait, Uncle Adolfo, slightly bent over, with limp and rebellious hair falling over his forehead, looked serene and forthcoming. He looks like an intellectual, I thought. Perhaps that impression was due to his pensive look and the English pipe he was holding in his left hand. He looked mature though still young, around forty. He didn't look like my grandmother: his eyes weren't slanted, and although large, they seemed to me to be slightly bulging and myopic, and his lips were too thick for what the Gálvez family had led us to expect. No doubt my grandmother was much better looking than her brother, I said to myself, although there is also no denying that don Adolfo must have had a much better disposition than his sister. The haughty and pitiless expression of doña Juana was not evident in his face; he instead looked like a gentle and even-tempered man. The portrait was autographed at the bottom in a large, steady hand:

For my darling Mari Pepa
from her Adolfo, 19 VII 1932

Who can Mari Pepa have been? Why is the photograph here if he dedicated it to her? I wondered. A curious sort, don Adolfo: an aristocrat come down in the world, who fought with the anarchists and ended his life as a hermit . . . He could be a fine subject for a novel.

Alongside this photograph, I saw another one that attracted my attention even more. "Look at this, Mariana," I said to my wife, who had just come back into the bedroom. She had brought a tray with cold cuts, bread, an uncorked bottle of wine, and two glasses. In the photograph, my father (very young), my sister Mercedes, and I—she and I both still children—appeared. We were walking down the avenida de San Juan de Letrán, and my father was holding us each by the hand. He was looking straight ahead, my sister at the ground, and I at the camera.

"Your father was certainly handsome!"

With his well-tailored suit over an athletic body, his fine hair plastered down flat over his skull, his light-colored eyes, his small, straight nose, and his elegant mustache above an attractive mouth, he was in fact a very good-looking man. He looked very much like his grandfather, the admiral, whose portrait I had just seen in the dining room. It was all very strange: seeing myself as a child, along with my sister and my father, on the wall of that house located in an isolated little town in the mountains in the south of Andalusia, and finding so many things belonging to the family in such a remote place, family keepsakes that until just a few hours before we didn't even imagine existed. The photograph, the painting, genes, and time . . . what a devilish game they can play in our minds . . .

The wine was delicious. We emptied the bottle in no time, as we did the next two. We didn't begin on a fourth because, in the state in which we found ourselves, it was physically impossible to venture down the old staircase. So, very tipsy and happy, our minds saturated with images and reflections, we initiated Uncle Adolfo's bed into our lovemaking; it creaked noisily, perhaps because it had forgotten the undulating motions of pleasure.

"To your good health, don Fausto!" Mariana said, raising her glass to the old man in the portrait, as I became drunk, much more than on the wine, on the exquisite aroma emanating from her neck . . .

Rasero, sitting in the shadow of an olive tree, amused himself watching his grandchildren playing.

"He's getting away, Paco, he's getting away from you!" his sister screamed to the boy as she pointed with her little hand to the hole down which the lizard was slithering. "He got away from you, you dummy."

"Look, son, come here. You're never going to catch him by throwing stones at him. You have to make yourself a good sharp-pointed pole from a tree branch. That way you'll catch a lot of them, you'll see."

"And how do you know that, Grandfather?"

"Ah, son. I was a great lizard hunter in my day, though I wasn't as good as your great-grandfather José. He was terrific!"

"Don't pay any attention to your grandfather," Juana Inés broke in. "Go on chasing them with stones."

"Why do you say that, Juanita?"

"Because he won't kill them with stones. I don't care if he scares them, but I don't want the poor things to die . . ."

Don Alonso, the administrator of the Gálvez family's affairs, coming in great, long strides down the path from the town, approached the house.

"Doña Verónica! News from the marquis," he shouted.

In an instant, Véronique and her mother were standing in front of the man.

"It's his handwriting, thanks be to God!" Annette exclaimed in relief. "Let me have it right now. Ah, don Alonso! You're going to drive me mad. And what's that package?"

"It's for don Fausto, madam."

With the package underneath his arm, Rasero wearily climbed the staircase leading to his bedroom. On reaching his desk, he put his glasses on, and before opening the package, read the accompanying letter:

Dear marquis,

After the enormous sorrow caused by the death of my dear Josefa, the Lord, perhaps in compensation, has brought me two great joys. The first is learning that you have recovered from your terrible illness—of which don Adolfo, your nephew, has sent me news throughout its duration—and the second is being allowed the opportunity to be useful to you through the work of my clumsy hands. I accompany this letter with your manuscript, duly illustrated and bound. Believe me, don Fausto, it was no simple matter to meet your request! It cost me a great deal of effort to understand the document. In all truth, I don't believe that I will ever altogether understand it. Nonetheless, as far as my poor intelligence could see, I realized that it was something very beautiful and very terrifying. May God grant that the sketches I made in it match your intention!

As for the honorarium that you kindly sent me, my first thought was to return it at once. I would never presume to charge a fee of a person like you, a person to whom I owe so much. But then I thought better of it and decided to donate the money to the fund that is being collected to help the victims of this despicable war. (There are so many victims, my friend.) I am certain that you will approve of my decision. As I was studying your manuscript, I thought a great deal about this war, and about all wars . . . Ah, don Fausto! May God take pity on us. Yours,

Francisco Goya

Open it right now, Rasero! Calm yourself; you're very nervous. If you stay that way, it's going to be longer still . . . There, that's the way. What a beautiful calfskin your friend chose! The gold letters gleam:

WHY I DESPISE YOU
By Fausto H. Rasero
Illustrated by Francisco Goya

It's clear that the man remembers your manuscript of the Book of Revelation perfectly; the two volumes resemble each other like peas in a pod. Come on, open it now . . .

We had been living for two weeks in our new house and doing very nicely. Mariana had hit it off with the parish priest and the schoolmaster, whom she turned into eager collaborators in her plan: for Christmas she wanted to put on a comedy by Vital Aza, with some of the town's schoolchildren as the actors. She took her work very seriously. Since practically all the kids wanted to take part in the play, she had to organize auditions in order to see what talents each of them had. "I need twelve actors, and there are more than forty trying out," she told me.

"Maybe it would be better to put on Lope de Vega's *Fuenteovejuna.* It has more than twenty characters, and all the extras you care to put onstage."

"No, Paco, that's a very hard play for them. We'll see how Vital Aza turns out first."

She spent her mornings holding auditions and preparing for rehearsals, and her afternoons going over the text and typing out copies. I for my part was pursuing the idea of writing a novel based on the life of my great-uncle Adolfo. I took advantage of my morning strolls to chat with the townspeople about the "marquis," as they called him. At night, after the obligatory drink or two in the tavern, I began to make my notes. The calm, the peacefulness, of the place had taken possession of us. We had never before been so serene. Never before had we felt time go by at such a leisurely pace; the days seemed to us to last forever.

One morning—it was July 2, 1978, a Saturday (how could I forget it?)—after having taken a walk out past the old mine, I came back home, put a record on the RCA, fixed myself a glass of anisette diluted with water, and stretched out on the bed to listen to the music as I mulled over my literary project. The chords came to my ears from a distance—it was Beethoven's Fifth Symphony, conducted by Toscanini—and they mingled in my mind with the problem I was stewing over: In what year must I put the birth of don Adolfo for him to be a contemporary of Emile Henri's? The day before, I had awakened at daybreak with the brainstorm of having Adolfo spend his youth in France, at the end of the last century. There he could meet the French anarchist Emile Henri, who became notorious after setting off a powerful bomb in a Parisian tearoom crowded with elegant ladies, many of them accompanied by their children. The self-defense by the young anarchist before a tribunal of the republic at his trial made his name even better known. The address he offered in his own defense was so impressive that, according to the accounts of several authors, he came close to being acquitted. In the morning, though, as I stretched out on the bed, the thought that had come to me no longer seemed such a good one: if don Adolfo lived in that era, he would have to be quite old at the time of the Civil War, and that didn't fit with the story of his love for Mari Pepa that I'd been working on. This was the point I had reached when the fourth movement of the symphony began. Every time I've listened to it—and that's been hundreds of times—its chords have acted on me like a sort of electrical discharge. Whenever I hear it, my thoughts vanish as a matter of course and I leave my mind and spirit completely open to receive the music, which I consider among the greatest ever composed. So I forgot my uncle, Mari Pepa, and Emile Henri, and left the magic of Beethoven free to do as it pleased in my consciousness. When it reached its final end—and I say, "final end," because this marvelous movement is ending from the very moment it begins—I turned my face to the right, toward the niche with the bust of the German musician. I looked at it for a long time. In my heart I thanked him for his genius. Beethoven, very solemn, seemed to see me but not to hear what I was saying to him. Alongside him, in another niche, was Bach. He looked irritated; perhaps he felt a jealousy because of my fervor for his countryman. Across from him, Mozart, with his beautiful face, smiled indifferently; he, the darling of the gods, was not capable of feeling jealousy toward anyone. My eyes continued traveling along the wall and stopped at the portrait of the old man. It was then that I realized that there was a niche lacking on that side of the room. I looked again at the one in which Bach was placed. Yes, just across from it was Mozart's niche. I looked again at Beethoven; across from his niche there hung the portrait of the bald man. There must have been a niche there, my mind kept insisting, and beginning to get excited, I climbed out of bed, took the portrait down, cleaned off the cobwebs that had formed between it and the wall, and hammered with my fist, first at a spot alongside where the painting had been, where the wall was unquestionably solid, and then just where the painting had been. The second spot sounded slightly hollow. I hammered harder. It sounded hollow, there was no doubt about it! And the hollow I felt in the pit of my stomach was even bigger. I left the bedroom like a shot to get a hammer that was in the kitchen. I don't believe it took more than three minutes to get it, but by the time I returned, a prodigious number of conjectures had paraded through my head, involving stories of buried treasures in the colonial mansions of Mexico City, messages from beyond the grave, and tales of Edgar Allan Poe. Even the image of the Count of Monte Cristo, with his long beard and his face of a madman, had time to reach my mind.

Once I was in front of the wall again, I began to hammer in earnest. As great pieces of plaster and cement came loose, a thick panel of wood was gradually exposed. This panel was much harder to remove, for it was very firmly attached to the frame of the niche.

At this point, I had no doubts left: this had been a niche whose proportions were identical to those of the other three. When I managed to loosen the upper corner of one of the boards that formed the panel, I used the handle of the hammer as a crowbar and peeked through the opening that I'd made. What goes on in a person's head is very odd: I can swear that at that moment there came to my mind the image of Lord Carnarvon seeing the tomb of Tutankhamen through a little orifice. I didn't see anything of course; it was very dark. In desperation, I struggled against the boards till I could pull one of them out completely. Then I saw the back of a black object with gleaming white decorations.

When the all the boards had given way, the treasure was revealed to my sight: it was an ebony coffer with mother-of-pearl insets forming pretty geometrical designs. It was resting on one side and filled almost the entire space. It's very heavy, I said to myself, highly excited, as I lifted it into my arms. I placed it on the bed and tenderly dusted it off. It had six drawers in the front, each one with its ivory pull in the form of a pear: three drawers in the upper part, two, a little larger, in the middle, and only one in the lower part, although it was as long as the two in the middle together. With the greatest care, I carried it to the desk, like someone who is carrying the relics of a saint, and set it down there on its four little feet—of ivory also. I spent a long time looking at the coffer without daring to open the drawers. I was even more nervous than on the day the notary in Madrid read us Uncle Adolfo's will. I reached out toward the coffer and then drew my hand back; I felt afraid—as though I were profaning a grave. I finally screwed up my courage and pulled out the little drawer in the upper right corner. It was empty, which, far from making me feel disappointed, calmed me down. Feeling more serene, I pulled out the one alongside it. It too was empty; as was the third one in the upper part. Who could have had the idea of hiding an empty coffer in a wall? I asked myself as I confidently opened one of the drawers in the middle part. This one wasn't empty: it contained a pair of eyeglasses with a gold frame. The lenses were small and had great magnifying power. They're for weak eyes, I thought, as I put them on and saw the coffer in a blur. Along with the eyeglasses, there was an exquisite ivory paper knife. The handle was decorated with tiny birds, beautifully carved. On passing my fingertips over the blade, I discovered that it had an unexpectedly sharp edge for the material it was made of. In the drawer alongside, there was an attractive silver locket with a long silver chain. It was pear shaped and the size of a walnut. It was made of silver wire in whimsical filigree. It's Moorish, I'm certain, I was saying to myself when I discovered a sort of little door in the locket. When I opened it, I could see a lovely yellow pearl inside. In the same drawer I found a miniature, done in oil. The medallion, framed in fine gold filigree, showed the face of a young woman. She was quite pretty, with her big black eyes, a delicate nose and mouth, slightly prominent cheekbones, and a somewhat pointed chin. Her brown hair was abundant, though her hairline was very far up on her broad forehead. On the back of the portrait was written, "Doña Inés de Oquendo."

Finally, I opened the large drawer in the lower part. I found three notebooks covered in leather, one black and the other two wine red. When I took the first one out of the drawer, a sheet of paper with writing on it fell out from among its pages. It was a poem:

> In a single day
> two miracles.
> In the same instant,
> him and her.
> He, a magical child;
> she, a fine mare.
> Tiny, pale,
> he was almost nothing
> —but he was everything.
> Pretty, smiling,
> she was almost everything
> —but she was not nothing.
> Blessed child, enlightened,
> bright as suns . . .
> and then a Mason.
> A Creole woman, young and fresh,
> wise because so innocent . . .
> and then the future . . .

I read it several times. The poem disconcerted me at first, and finally disappointed me. It's too modern, I said to myself; it did not have the same air of belonging to the past as the objects I had found. Until that moment, I had harbored the hope that the coffer had remained in that niche for more than a hundred years, but on reading the poem, I realized that that was impossible. Perhaps this is the work of Uncle Adolfo. They say he was an eccentric. With this idea in mind, and without as much excitement now, I began to leaf through the black notebook. It did not have a title. The pages were very yellow and the writing on them, done in sepia ink, had almost completely faded, so that it was practically illegible. I barely managed to make out a few dates and a few fragments that didn't make any sense to me at all: ". . . March 2, 1757. Style of dress: they do not wear jabots. Very slender colored ties knotted at the neck . . . "; "November 8, 1750. The man had lost his leg; he was howling with pain; again that light, absolute, total, terrifying . . ." A strange man, don Adolfo . . . , I said to myself.

Then I took out the first red book. It was a slender volume, the size of a sheet of letter paper. On the cover, engraved on the calfskin in gold letters, it said,

THE BOOK OF REVELATION
By Saint John
Illustrated by François Boucher

I began to leaf through it. It was a manuscript in a clear and elegant hand. The countless spelling mistakes and the use of that strange symbol that was once used to represent certain *ſ*s were proof that the text was written in the eighteenth century at the latest. I deduced this later, though, because from the moment that I began to read the notebook I paid practically no attention to the written text: my interest was almost completely held by the marvelous illustrations in sepia aquatint. Twenty-two very beautiful plates illustrated the terrible visions of the apostle. Contemplating those images, terrifying and moving at the same time, filled me with such anxiety that I felt close to fainting. I abruptly closed the book and also closed my eyes; the formidable vivid images had embedded themselves in my head. I could not keep back the big tears that ran down my cheeks, nor the immense fear that had settled in the pit of my stomach. Never in my life had the mere contemplation of a collection of illustrations had such an effect on me. Not even Goya's *Caprichos* or his *Disasters of War,* which we had seen in the Prado shortly before coming to Macharavialla—Boucher's etchings reminded me a great deal of Goya's—and which up until then I had considered the most terrifying illustrations that an artist's hands had executed, had aroused in me an anxiety as great as those of the Book of Revelation. I tried to calm down. Boucher . . . Boucher . . . , I thought, trying to retrieve that name in my memory. It was useless; that artist was completely unknown to me. I then looked in the SOPENA dictionary: "Boucher, François (1703–1770). French painter. As an artist and as a decorator, he firmly established the rococo style . . ." Then this manuscript is more than two hundred years old . . . How did it get here? Why did my uncle hide it in that niche? . . . What the devil is going on? . . . I tried to think it all through so as to drive away the fear that had overtaken me. Far from succeeding, the more I forced myself to make sense of what was happening to me, the more frightened I became.

No, of course, all this doesn't make sense; there's no rational explanation . . . But everything must have a reason, I contended with myself, it's simply a question of finding it and then everything will be clear. But why hide this coffer? Why hide from the world those marvelous plates? . . . Good God, I can't find the reason! . . . (That's precisely how, Rasero, I began to lose my reason.) I saw out of the corner of my eye the second red book that was still in the drawer. Perhaps I'll find the answer in this one, I said to myself, and prepared to take it out. Then I restrained myself. And what if there's something even stranger in it . . . ? Fear—an irrational fear, as I was perfectly aware, but as absolute as death—paralyzed my hand. Paco, please, you're acting like an idiot, I said to myself to work up my courage. Take a look at this book once and for all; you'll see how it clears up everything . . . My mind finally made up, I took the book out of the drawer. It was a notebook of the same size, thickness, and color as the one that contained the Book of Revelation. In its lower right-hand corner was written, also in gold letters,

WHY I DESPISE YOU
By Fausto H. Rasero
Illustrated by Francisco Goya

On reading those two names, I felt as though I'd been struck by lightning. The bald man in the rocking chair and Goya, the painter . . . No, in heaven's name, what did all this mean? If the fear that I had felt up to then seemed insurmountable, the terror that assailed me now infinitely surpassed it. Wall up that coffer again! Burn all this! my intuition told me, as in league with my immense fear it fought tooth and nail against my curiosity. My curiosity proved more powerful: I stood up with the book in my hands and opened it at random. Two repulsive monsters, drawn with supreme mastery, looked at me contemptuously. Terrified—that's the right word—I raised my hand to my head. The terror swelled, or worse still, began to turn into madness at that point: I felt as if I didn't have a single hair on my head. The palm of my hand, as I rubbed it back and forth again and again, felt only a smooth round surface, like a large eggshell.

It was then, Rasero, that I felt for the first time in my life, that I wasn't who I was . . .

He's the greatest painter there is, you thought as you contemplated his marvelous work. There it all was, Rasero, right there: Denis Diderot in his tub; the execution by firing squad of the Asturian anarchists; Maria Pastora, the woman bandit, with her scarlet wasps; the siege of Madrid; the concentration camps; the atomic bombs; Damiens about to be quartered; Gagarin in space . . . and wars. They were all there, Rasero: World War II, the Korean War, the Algerian War, the butchery of Vietnam, that of the Middle East; the surgical bombarding of the old Mesopotamia, the killings in postmodern Europe, the invasion of Cuba; the extermination in South Africa . . . all, all, Rasero. There were also those terrible eight years that you lived—ah, I hadn't yet—in the future. There was—splendidly illustrated—the Empire of Selfishness and Stupidity, the gods of the twenty-first century, Rasero. You were forced to tolerate this empire during those horrible eight years: famines in the Third World, the turning of the planet into a desert; the inundation of low-lying land, and the epidemics, Rasero—the plague, cholera, AIDS, smallpox, and so many other diseases, some of them forgotten for centuries, others new, recently invented, but all of them with their incredible train of fatalities, a death toll in the millions, a death toll brought about deliberately, as you knew very well, Rasero, a death toll caused by the powerful. Since the end of the '70's, they had incubated in their laboratories the germs that were finishing off the world.

When this became known, at the birth of the new millennium, it was too late: the sinister weapon ended up turning back against them; nobody could now control the epidemics. How well Goya illustrated it, Rasero! They all ended up rotting away, like Louis XV on his deathbed; they all carried that stench which prostrated your beloved Diderot so many times. Rottenness and death, Rasero, how well the hand drew them! They all fell into the nets of the germs: rich and poor, whites and blacks, good and bad, the brave and the cowardly . . . You're right, Fausto Rasero: they're despicable. It's curious: you were born in the century of the Enlightenment and you died in that of progress, but your orgasms took you to the century of horror . . .

All done. The mason has finished now. He's a good man; look at his anxious face. Give him a couple of doubloons; he deserves them. Yes, everything's all taken care of now. Go to bed . . . Annette brings you your tea. She is still so beautiful and so good! Too bad you don't believe in God; you could have thanked him for the privilege of not having seen any of the three persons you loved most in your life die.

"Rest well, don Fausto," he says to you.

Yes, you'll rest now; you already feel how life is departing from your old body. Are you afraid? No, who needs to fear death at the age of eighty-eight, especially when you aren't even sure you existed? Yes, you existed, Rasero; although now you're about to cease to exist. What are you hearing? It's a piano . . . it's the piano of the magical child, brilliant as suns; it's those eternal, lilting, marvelous notes. How gently they suffuse your death! Look, look how they linger in your Mariana's eyebrows. Now they're running down her neck; they're fluttering in her ears; they're caressing her cheeks. They've stopped at her mouth, ah, that mouth, Rasero! They're tinkling, their movement like that of busy bees . . . Now, now they're going away, Rasero. There goes the last one; it's taking your last sigh with it . . .

Thirteen years have gone by since I discovered your manuscript, Rasero. No, I don't want to remember the rest. Why speak of my madness, or of *your* madness? No, I'm not going to begin again. I've already written quite enough. Everything's been said, don't you think? Yes, I haven't spoken any more about Mariana. I don't want to. Why remember her anguish, the terrible years she lived seeing her man ebb away little by little until, for a year now, he hasn't been able even to answer her? It breaks my heart to see her like that: looking at me anxiously, waiting for a gesture, a slight movement that is proof that I'm still there. But it's useless; I don't answer. Sitting on the terrace, with my eyes fixed on the mango tree in the middle of the garden, I'm as still, as mute, as a statue. No, I don't want to remember the way Mariana looked in despair at the doctor's gesture of helplessness when he was examining the irises of my eyes and saw that my pupils didn't respond to the light be beamed into them with his little flashlight. Because I am already you, and I am here, there, in the century of the Enlightenment, doing chemistry experiments and suffering from the absence of our Mariana. I am already here,

Rasero; there, it'll be a long time before I can return. Another thirteen years. Thirteen years that will be terrible because I can no longer even write. My poor Mariana. Look at her, look at her, here she comes; she's bringing us anisette. Look at her eyes, Rasero; there's not a trace of her happiness left. Look at her mouth, ah, that marvelous mouth! What's the matter, Rasero, why are you weeping? Of course, I understand: it's been almost thirty years since you saw her, hasn't it? My poor Mariana! If I could even move one finger! Yes, yes, I can, because I'm writing . . . No, don't be silly, Paco; you wrote this two years ago, remember? It was shortly after the second centenary of the Revolution, in July of '89, don't you remember, Paco? . . . Of course, of course, I remember . . . Ah, how naïve we were then, Paco! To believe that the world was going to get better . . . I swear to God, Rasero, never, never has the world been worse. What's that again? Ah, of course you're right: it's going to be much worse in thirteen years . . . Yes, frightful, Paco, frightful. What a good thing Denis died in '83! I don't believe that I'd have dared describe to him the world of 2004. I would have ended lying to him. Ah, and to think that we must see it yet again . . . No, not me; I haven't seen it yet, Rasero . . . That's true, excuse me, Paco; but I've seen it so many times that it's easy for me to get everything all confused. I feel as though I were between two mirrors: I go and come, come and go. It's the future that arrives to become the past, which again becomes the future. Good God! When is all this going to end? . . . It's going to be some time yet, Rasero. To be exact, Paco, it's going to be twenty-one years from now. Then, only then, in 2012, when it's been two years since your death, are we going to live in peace . . . In 2012, all human beings are going to be at peace, Paco . . . Are you sure, Rasero? That's not clear in your manuscript, you see . . . How could I have stated this exactly if I returned to my time just before the hecatomb? We were already very close, though. It could be five, ten, a hundred years more, but the end is inevitable. Ah, Paco! Not even you who have been with me for all this time, not even you who delve into my mind, not even you who are almost my mind, are able to suspect to what lengths human selfishness and stupidity can go. But, drop the subject, Rasero. You'll see; we'll see. Jean-Paul Marat is going to receive us now—yes, this very day, July 26, 1791. Don't lose your temper; be careful what you say to this man. He's a beast. We must do everything possible to persuade him to stop hounding Lavoisier . . . No, don't take it into your head to tell me what's going to happen to Antoine.

Even though I fear the worst, Paco, I don't want you to tell me. Let me go on acting for a while as my free will tells me to; don't deprive me of the uncertainty of the future . . . Look who's talking! And didn't you write that manuscript, didn't you hide it in the coffer, to drive me mad, to make me certain of the future? If I know more than you yourself do, it's your fault, my friend . . . Let's not start, Paco, let's not start. I'm tired of explaining to you . . . Be still a minute! They're summoning us. No, Marat doesn't look anything like the magnificent portrait that David made of him. He looks as though they had just murdered him in that very bathtub . . . So he's going to be murdered? I've asked you not to talk to me about the future, Paco . . . I'm sorry. But now that I've said it, let me go on: he looked splendid, generous, with his head wrapped in a towel, the fatal wound underneath his right shoulder blade, his body dissolving in the bathtub like thick honey, his long, naked, wiry arm dangling out of the water holding the goose quill with which he had just written one of his memorable articles for the *Friend of the People,* which he was still holding in his left hand. His face looked serene, almost smiling, as though he were already enjoying the delights of Eden. How different from reality, Rasero! Marat is an ugly, unpleasant sort. Look at his skin; he resembles a slaughtered ox . . .

"Citizen Rasero, what a pleasant surprise! Do sit down and tell me what I can do for you," he says to us. He doesn't even offer apologies for receiving us in a bathtub; he's an oaf. How different from Denis Diderot, when we met him, inside a bathtub too, more than forty years ago! On that occasion, curiously, he was trying to imagine this man; he was wondering if the stench might assail the Jacobin. That was what Denis was thinking, or what we thought he was thinking, do you remember, Rasero?